Critical acclaim for [illegible]lacci's novels

'Al[illegible] among the w[illegible]
Baldacci hardly needs to prove himself [illegible] he's
created one of the most intriguing, complex
anti-heroes ... Impossible to put down,
especially because of Decker, who
weaves a powerful spell'
Daily Mail

'A typically twisty plot never flags, and benefits
from having the likeably offbeat sleuth
(whose gifts include synaesthesia and
photographic memory) as its pivot'
Sunday Times

'Alternately chilling, poignant, and always
heart-poundingly suspenseful'
Scott Turow, *New York Times* bestselling author

'A mile-a-minute read that proves once again
why David Baldacci has readers the world
over flocking for more'
Jane Harper, *New York Times* bestselling
author of *The Dry*

'As ever, Baldacci keeps things moving at
express-train speed ... this one will whet
appetites for the next appearance
of his agent hero'
Daily Express

The Amos Decker thrillers by David Baldacci

Memory Man

Amos Decker's photographic memory means he forgets nothing and sees what others miss. Struggling with his own traumatic past, his life is changed forever when he's pulled into a tragedy at a local high school.

The Last Mile

Newly appointed FBI special agent Amos Decker's infallible memory is put to the test to prove the innocence of a man who awaits his sentence on death row.

The Fix

Amos Decker – the FBI's most unique special agent – witnesses a cold-blooded murder outside the world's biggest crime fighting agency in Washington D. C. It proves to be the catalyst for an investigation which exposes a plot to blow apart the nation's security.

The Fallen

What was supposed to be a relaxing vacation for special agent Amos Decker and his FBI partner, Alex Jamison, turns into a murder investigation in Baronville.

Redemption

FBI consultant Amos Decker discovers that he may have made a fatal mistake when he was a rookie homicide detective. Back in his home town, he's now compelled to discover the truth . . .

Redemption

David Baldacci is one of the world's bestselling and favourite thriller writers. With over 130 million worldwide sales, his books are published in over 80 territories and 45 languages, and have been adapted for both feature film and television. David is also the co-founder, along with his wife, of the Wish You Well Foundation®, a non-profit organization dedicated to supporting literacy efforts across the US. Still a resident of his native Virginia, he invites you to visit him at DavidBaldacci.com and his foundation at WishYouWellFoundation.org.

Trust him to take you to the action.

Also by David Baldacci

The Camel Club Series

(An eccentric group of social outcasts who seek to unearth corruption at the heart of the US government)

The Camel Club • The Collectors • Stone Cold
Divine Justice • Hell's Corner

King and Maxwell series

(Two disgraced Secret Service agents turn their skills to private investigation)

Split Second • Hour Game • Simple Genius
First Family • The Sixth Man • King and Maxwell

Shaw series

(A mysterious operative hunting down the world's most notorious criminals)

The Whole Truth • Deliver Us From Evil

John Puller series

(A gifted investigator with an unstoppable drive to find out the truth)

Zero Day • The Forgotten • The Escape
No Man's Land

Will Robie series featuring Jessica Reel

(A highly trained CIA assassin and his deadly fellow agent)

The Innocent • The Hit • The Target
The Guilty • End Game

Amos Decker series

(A damaged but brilliant special agent who possesses an extraordinary set of skills)

Memory Man • The Last Mile • The Fix
The Fallen • Redemption

Atlee Pine series

(A tenacious female FBI special agent assigned to the wilds of the western US)

Long Road to Mercy

Vega Jane series

(The bestselling young adult adventures series)

The Finisher • The Keeper • The Width of the World
The Stars Below

Other novels

True Blue • Absolute Power • Total Control
The Winner • The Simple Truth • Saving Faith
Wish You Well • Last Man Standing
The Christmas Train • One Summer
One Good Deed

Short Stories

No Time Left • Bullseye

DAVID BALDACCI

Redemption

PAN BOOKS

First published 2019 by Grand Central Publishing, USA

First published in the UK 2019 by Macmillan

This edition published 2019 by Pan Books
an imprint of Pan Macmillan
20 New Wharf Road, London N1 9RR
Associated companies throughout the world
www.panmacmillan.com

ISBN 978-1-5098-7441-5

1 3 5 7 9 8 6 4 2

A CIP catalogue record for this book is available from the British Library.

Typeset in Bembo by Jouve (UK), Milton Keynes
Printed and bound by CPI Group (UK) Ltd, Croydon, CR0 4YY

To Lindsey Rose,
who made all the trains run on time
and handled so much with grace and efficiency.
Congrats on the new gig!

CONFIDENTIAL

DEPARTMENT OF JUSTICE · FEDERAL BUREAU OF INVESTIGATION · FIDELITY · BRAVERY · INTEGRITY

FBI Agent Profile

Name: Amos Decker

Date of Birth: Early forties, looks at least ten years older but feels at least a century older than that.

Place of Birth: Burlington, Ohio

Marital Status: Widowed - his wife and daughter were brutally murdered.

Physical characteristics: A big man, six-five, and about halfway between three and four hundred pounds – the exact number depends on how much he eats at a particular meal. He was a college football player with a truncated stint in the NFL, where a vicious blindside hit altered his mind and gave him pretty much a perfect memory.

Relatives: Cassandra Decker (wife), Molly Decker (daughter), Johnny Sacks (brother-in-law) - Amos discovered all three murdered in his family home.

Career: College football star, then NFL with Cleveland Browns, where he met his wife Cassie. Destined to be a professional football player, his career was cut short following a devastating injury that

CONFIDENTIAL

permanently damaged his brain. Used to be a cop and then a detective and now works as an FBI Special Agent.

Notable Abilities: His football injury gave him one of the most exceptional brains in the world. His cognitive sensory pathways got melded from the hit resulting in an infallible, photographic memory also known as hyperthymesia. Also has synesthesia, the ability to see colours where others don't. In numbers, in places and objects. Extraordinary strength and speed for such a big man. Possesses a turbocharged brain that has somehow unlocked what we all have but never use.

Favourite film: *The Usual Suspects*. With his prodigious memory he would have caught Keyser Söze in the first act.

Favourite song: 'I Will Remember You', by Sarah McLachlan. A close second would be 'Thanks for the Memory' by Frank Sinatra.

Dislikes: Doesn't like being touched. Jokes; they don't really register with him anymore. People who waste his time, which seems to be most people he runs in to. Exercise. Head injuries.

Likes: The truth. Large portions of food. Substantial legroom in a moving vehicle.

Redemption

1

On a refreshingly brisk, beautifully clear fall evening, Amos Decker was surrounded by dead bodies. Yet he wasn't experiencing the electric blue light sensation that he usually did when confronted by the departed.

There was a perfectly good reason for this: None of these were *recent* deaths.

He was back in his hometown of Burlington, Ohio, an old factory city that had seen better days. He had recently been in another Rust Belt town, Baronville, Pennsylvania, where he had narrowly escaped death. If he had his druthers, he would have avoided such minefields for the foreseeable future, maybe the rest of his life.

Only right now he didn't have a choice.

Decker was in Burlington because today was his daughter Molly's fourteenth birthday. Under normal circumstances, this would have been a happy occasion, a cause for joy. But Molly had been murdered, along with his wife, Cassie, and his brother-in-law, Johnny Sacks. This devastating event had happened shortly before her tenth birthday, when Decker found them all dead in their home.

Gone forever. Taken from life in the most outrageous manner possible by a deranged mind hell-bent on violence. Their killer was no longer among the living, but that was of absolutely no solace to Decker, though he'd been instrumental in ending that life.

That was why his birthday visit was at a cemetery. No cake, and no presents. Just fresh flowers on a grave to replace ones long dead from a previous visit.

He figured he would be here for every one of Molly's birthdays until he joined his family six feet under. That was his long-term plan. He had never contemplated any other.

He shifted his weight on the wood and wrought-iron bench next to the twin graves, for daughter lay next to mother. The bench had been gifted by the Burlington Police Department where Decker had once toiled, first as a beat cop and later as a homicide detective. On it, tarnished by weather, was a brass plaque that read: *In memory of Cassie and Molly Decker.*

There was no one else in the small cemetery other than Decker's partner at the FBI, Alex Jamison. More than a dozen years younger than the mid-fortyish Decker, Jamison stood a respectful distance away, allowing her partner to visit his family in solitude.

Once a journalist, Jamison was now a fully fledged, duly sworn-in FBI special agent, having graduated from the Bureau's Training Academy in Quantico,

Virginia. Under a prior arrangement, she had been sent immediately back to the task force where she and Decker were members, along with two other veteran agents, Ross Bogart and Todd Milligan.

Sitting next to the graves, Decker cursed his condition of hyperthymesia. The perfect recall had been initiated by a wicked blindside hit on an NFL playing field that triggered a traumatic brain injury. Decker awoke from a coma with the ability to remember everything and the inability to forget anything. It seemed like a wonderful attribute, but there was a distinct downside to the condition.

For him, the passage of time would never deaden the details of painful memories. Like the one he was confronted with presently. For the overwhelmingly intense manner in which he recalled their deaths, Cassie and Molly might as well have been laid to rest today instead of four years ago.

He read the names and inscriptions on the tombstones, though he knew by heart what they said. He had come here with many things he wanted to say to his family, but now he inexplicably suffered from a complete failure to articulate any of them.

Well, maybe not so inexplicably. The brain injury that had given him perfect recall had also changed his personality. His social skills had gone from high to quite low. He had trouble voicing his emotions and difficulty dealing with people.

In his mind's eye he conjured first the image of his

daughter. It was sharply in focus—the curly hair, the smile, the cheeks that rode so high. Then the image of his wife, Cassie, appeared—the anchor of their family, the one who had kept Decker from succumbing to his condition, forcing him to interact with others, compelling him to come as close as possible to the man he used to be.

He winced in pain because it actually physically hurt to be so close to them, because they were dead and he was not. There were many days, perhaps most, when he simply could not accept that state of affairs.

He glanced in the direction of Jamison, who was leaning against a broad oak about a hundred feet away. She was a good friend, an excellent colleague, but absolutely powerless to help him through what he was facing now.

He turned back to the graves, knelt, and placed the bundles of flowers he had brought on each of the sunken plots.

"Amos Decker?"

Decker looked up to see an older man walking slowly toward him. He had materialized out of the dusk of elongating shadows. As he drew closer, the man almost seemed a ghost himself, so very painfully thin, his features deeply jaundiced.

Jamison had seen the man coming before Decker did, and had started striding toward them. It could simply be someone from the town whom Decker knew. Or it might be something else. Jamison knew that crazy things tended to happen around Amos Decker. Her hand went to the butt of the pistol riding in a holster on her right hip. Just in case.

Decker eyed the man. Aside from his unhealthy appearance, the fellow was shuffling along in a way that Decker had seen before. It wasn't solely due to age or infirmity. It was the walk of someone accustomed to wearing shackles when moving from point A to point B.

He's a former prisoner, speculated Decker.

And there was another thing. As he sometimes did, Decker was seeing a color associated with the man. This was due to his also having synesthesia, which caused him to pair colors with unusual things, like death and numbers.

The color tag for this gent was burgundy. That was a new one for Decker.

What the hell does burgundy mean?

"Who are you?" he asked, rising to his feet and brushing the dirt from his knees.

"Not surprised you don't recognize me. Prison takes it outta you. Guess I have you to thank for that."

So he was *incarcerated.*

Jamison also heard this and picked up her pace. She actually half drew her pistol, afraid that the old man was there to exact some sort of revenge on Decker. Her partner had put many people behind bars in his career. And this fellow was apparently one of them.

Decker looked the man up and down as he came to a stop about five feet away. Decker was a mountain of a man, standing six-five and tipping the scale at just about three hundred pounds. With Jamison's encouragement and help in getting him to exercise and eat a healthier diet, he had lost over a hundred pounds in the last two years. This was about as "lean" as he was ever going to be.

The old man was about six feet tall, but Decker figured he barely weighed a hundred and forty pounds. His torso was about as wide as one of Decker's thighs. Up close, his skin looked brittle, like aged parchment about to disintegrate.

Hacking up some phlegm, the man turned to the side and spit it into the consecrated ground. "You sure you don't recognize me? Don't you got some kind of weird-ass memory thing?"

Decker said, "Who told you that?"

"Your old partner."

"Mary Lancaster?"

The man nodded. "She was the one who told me you might be here."

"Why would she do that?"

"My name's Meryl Hawkins," said the man, in a way that seemed also to carry an explanation as to why he was here.

Decker's jaw fell slightly.

Hawkins smiled at this reaction, but it didn't reach

his eyes. They were pale and still, with perhaps just a bit of life left inside them.

"Now you remember me, right?"

"Why are you out of prison? You got life, no parole."

Jamison reached them and put herself between Decker and Hawkins.

Hawkins nodded at her. "You're his new partner, Alex Jamison. Lancaster told me about you too." He glanced back at Decker. "To answer your question, I'm no longer in prison 'cause I'm terminal with cancer. One of the worst. Pancreatic. Survival rate past five years is for shit, they tell me, and that's with chemo and radiation and all that crap, none of which I can afford." He touched his face. "Jaundice. You get this, it's way too late to kick it. And it's metastasized. Big word, means the cancer's eating me up everywhere. Brain too now. It's the last inning for me. No doubt about it, I'm done. Hell, maybe a week at best."

"Why is that a reason to release you?" asked Jamison.

Hawkins shrugged. "They call it *compassionate release*. Inmate usually has to file for it, but they came to my cell with the paperwork. I filled it out, they got doctors to okay it, and there you go. See, the state didn't want to foot the bill for my treatments. I was in one of those private prisons. They mark the bill up to the state, but it doesn't all get reimbursed. Gets expensive. Hurts their bottom line. They figure I'm harmless now. I went into prison when I was fifty-eight. Now I'm seventy. Look like I'm a hundred, I know. I'm all jacked up with drugs just to walk and talk. After I leave here, I'm going to be throwing up for a few hours and then take enough pills to sleep a bit."

Jamison said, "If you're on prescription painkillers, somebody's helping you."

"Didn't say they were *prescription*, did I? As a matter of fact, they're not. But it's what I need. Not like they're putting me back in prison because I'm buying street drugs. I cost too much." He chuckled. "If I'd known that, I woulda got sick years ago."

"Do you mean they don't provide any help for you on the outside?" asked Jamison incredulously.

"They said a hospice place would take me, but I got no way to get there. And I don't want to go there. I want to be here." Hawkins stared at Decker.

"What do you want from me?" asked Decker.

Hawkins pointed his finger at him. "You put me in prison. But you were wrong. I'm innocent."

"Don't they all say that?" noted Jamison skeptically.

Hawkins shrugged again. "I don't know about anybody else but me." He glanced back at Decker. "Lancaster thinks I'm innocent."

"I don't believe that," said Decker.

"Ask her. It's why she told me where you were." He paused and looked at the dark sky. "You got another chance to get it right. Maybe you can do it while I'm still alive and kicking. If not, that's okay, so long as you get there. It'll be my legacy," he added with a weak grin.

"He's with the FBI now," interjected Jamison. "Burlington and your case are no longer his jurisdiction."

Hawkins looked nonplussed. "Heard you cared about the truth, Decker. Did I hear wrong? Come a long way for nothing if that's so."

When Decker didn't answer, Hawkins pulled out a slip of paper. "I'll be in town the next couple of nights. Here's the address. Maybe I'll see you, maybe I won't. But if you don't come, well, fuck you from the hereafter."

Decker took the paper but still said nothing.

Hawkins glanced at the twin graves. "Lancaster told me about your family. Glad you found out who killed 'em. But I suppose you still felt guilt, though you were innocent. I can damn well relate."

Hawkins turned and walked slowly back between the graves until the darkness swallowed him whole.

Jamison turned to Decker. "Okay, I know nothing about this, but it's still nuts. He's just taunting you, making you feel guilty. And I can't believe the guy would come here and butt in while you're trying to . . . trying to spend time with your family."

Decker looked down at the slip of paper. It was

clear from his features that something akin to doubt had just now crept into his mind.

Jamison watched him, resignation spreading over her features. "You're going to see him, aren't you?"

"Not until I see someone else first."

2

Decker stood alone on the porch. He had asked Jamison to not accompany him here. He preferred to conduct this visit alone, for a number of reasons.

He remembered every inch of the more than four-decades-old split-level ranch. This was not simply due to his perfect recall, but also because this house was nearly an exact copy of the one in which he and his family had once lived.

Mary Lancaster and her husband, Earl, and their daughter, Sandy, had resided here for as long as Lancaster had been on the Burlington police force, which matched Decker's tenure there as well. Earl was a general contractor who worked sporadically owing to the fact that Sandy was a special needs child who would always require a great deal of time and attention. Mary had been the family's primary breadwinner for a long time.

Decker stepped up to the door. He was about to knock when it opened.

Mary stood there dressed in faded jeans, a blood-red sweatshirt, and dark blue sneakers. Her hair had once been a pasty blonde. It was now full of gray and hung limply to her shoulders. A cigarette was perched in one hand, its coil of smoke drifting up her slender thigh. Her face was as lined as a thumbprint. Lancaster was the same age as Decker yet looked about ten years older.

"Thought I might see you tonight," she said in a smoker's gravelly voice. "Come on in."

He checked for the tremor that used to be in her left hand, her gun grip hand. He didn't see it.

Okay, that's a good thing.

She turned, and he followed the far shorter woman into the house, shutting the door behind him, a tugboat guiding a cargo ship safely into port. Or maybe onto the rocks, he didn't know which. Yet.

Decker also noted that Lancaster, always thin to begin with, was even more gaunt. Her bones seemed to jut out at odd angles within her loose clothing, as though she had left multiple hangers in them.

"Did the gum stop working?" he asked, glancing at her lit cigarette.

They sat in the living room, a small space littered with toys, stacks of newspapers, open cardboard boxes, and a layer of chaos that was palpable. Her home had always been like this, he knew. They'd started using a maid service before Decker left town, but that had come with its own set of problems. They'd probably decided terminally junky was preferable.

She took a drag on her Camel and let the smoke trail out her nostrils.

"I allow myself one a day, about this time, and only when Earl and Sandy are out. Then I Febreze the hell out of the place."

Decker took a whiff and coughed. "Then use more Febreze."

"Meryl Hawkins found you, I take it?"

Decker nodded. "He said you told him where I was."

"I did."

"That was taking a liberty. You knew why I was in town. I gave you a heads-up."

She sat back and scraped away at a spot on her skin with her fingernail. "Well, I sure as hell didn't do it lightly. But I thought you'd want to know."

"Hawkins also said you believed him."

"Then he went too far. I told him I could see his point."

"Which is what, exactly?"

"Why would he come back here, dying, to ask us to clear his name if he's not innocent?"

"I can think of one reason, benefiting him."

She took another puff and shook her head. "I don't see it that way. You get to the end of the line, you start to think differently. Not a moment to waste."

Decker looked at the open cardboard boxes. "You guys moving?"

"Maybe."

"Maybe? How can you not be sure?"

Lancaster shrugged. "What about life is guaranteed?"

"How're things in Burlington?"

"Town's hanging in there."

"Unemployment's down around the country."

"Yeah, we have lots of ten-dollar-an-hour jobs. If you can live on twenty grand a year, even in Burlington, more power to you."

"Where are Earl and Sandy?"

"School function. Earl handles those more than me. Work's been a bitch lately. Bad times make for bad crimes. Lots of drug-related stuff."

"Yeah, I've seen that. Why did Hawkins come to see you?"

"We worked that case together, Decker. It was our first homicide investigation."

"When did he get out? And is he really terminal? He definitely looks it."

"He wandered into the station two days ago. Shocked the hell out of me. At first I thought he'd escaped or something. I didn't accept his story but straight away checked with the prison. He's telling the truth about his cancer. And his release."

"So they can just kick out terminally ill prisoners to die on their own?"

"Apparently some see it as a good cost-cutting tactic."

"He told me he's staying in town a couple more days. He's at the Residence Inn."

"Where you used to live."

"He could use some fattening up with the buffet, but I doubt he has much appetite. He says he gets by on street drugs, basically."

"Sad state of affairs."

"He wants to meet with me again."

She took another puff. "I'm sure."

"He came to see me at the *cemetery*."

Lancaster took one more luxurious drag on her smoke and then crushed it out in an ashtray set on a table next to her chair. She eyed the remnants with longing.

"I'm sorry about that. I didn't tell him exactly *why* you were in town when he came back to the station earlier today and asked, though I did tell him about your family. And I didn't actually tell him to go to the cemetery." She studied Decker, her pale eyes finally focusing on his. "I presume you've gone over the case in immaculate detail in your head?"

"I have. And I don't see any issues with what we did. We went over the crime scene, collected evidence. That evidence pointed like a laser to Hawkins. He was arrested and put on trial. We testified. Hawkins's lawyer put on a defense and cross-examined the crap out of us both. And the jury convicted him. He got life without parole when he could have gotten the death penalty. It all made sense to me."

Lancaster sat back in her chair.

Decker ran his gaze over her. “You don’t look so good, Mary.”

“I haven’t looked good for at least ten years, Amos. You above all should know that.”

“But still.”

“You’ve lost a lot of weight since you left here, Amos.”

“Jamison’s doing, mostly. She’s got me working out and watching my diet. She cooks a lot of the meals. All salads and vegetables, and *tofu*. And she got her FBI badge and creds. Worked hard for them. Really proud of her.”

“So you two are living together, then?” said Lancaster with hiked eyebrows.

“We are in the sense that we’re residing in the same condo in D.C.”

“Okay, then are you two more than work partners?”

“Mary, I’m a lot older than she is.”

“You didn’t answer my question. And, news flash, lots of older men date much younger women.”

“No, we’re *not* more than work partners.”

“Okay.” She sat forward. “So, Hawkins?”

“Why are you having doubts? It was a clear-cut case.”

“Maybe too clear-cut.”

“That doesn’t make sense. And what’s your evidence?”

"I don't have any. And I don't know if he's telling the truth or not. But I just think since the guy's dying and he came back here to clear his name, maybe it's worth a second look."

Decker did not look convinced but said, "Okay, how about now?"

"What?" she said, looking startled.

"Let's go over to where the murders took place. I'm sure no one's moved in there after all this time, not after what happened." He paused. "Just like my old home."

"Well, you're wrong there. Someone *did* move into your old place."

Decker's jaw slackened. "Who?"

"A young couple with a little girl. The Hendersons."

"You know them?"

"Not really. But I know they moved in about six months ago."

"And the other place? Is there someone there too?"

"Somebody moved in there about five years ago. But they left about a year ago when the plastics manufacturing facility closed down and went overseas to join all the other factories that used to be in the Midwest. It's been abandoned since then."

Decker rose. "Okay, you coming? It'll be like old times."

"I'm not sure I need any more 'old times.'" But Lancaster rose too and grabbed a coat that was hanging on a wall peg. "And what if it turns out Hawkins was telling the truth?" she asked as they headed to the door.

"Then we need to find out who really did it. But we're not there yet. In fact, we're not even close."

"You don't work here anymore, Decker. Finding a murderer here after all this time isn't your job."

"Finding killers is my *only* job. Wherever they might be."

3

The Richardses' home. The scene of the crime thirteen years ago.

It was down a rutted crushed-gravel road. Two houses on the left and two on the right, with the Richardses' now-dilapidated dwelling smack at the end of the cul-de-sac on an acre lot of dead grass crammed with fat, overgrown bushes.

It had been lonely and creepy back then, and it was more so over a decade later.

They pulled to a stop in front of the house and climbed out of Decker's car. Lancaster shivered slightly, and it was not entirely due to the coolness of the night.

"Hasn't changed all that much," said Decker.

"Well, the family that was living here fixed it up some before they left. It needed it. Mostly on the interior. Paint and carpet, things like that. The place had been abandoned for a long time. Nobody wanted to live here after what happened."

"You'd think a banker would have lived in something nicer."

"He was a loan officer. They make squat, especially in a town like this. And this house is a lot bigger than mine, Decker, with a lot more land."

They walked up to the front porch of the home. Decker tried the door.

"Locked."

"Well, why don't you unlock it?" said Lancaster.

"Are you giving me permission to break and enter?"

"Wouldn't be the first time. And it's not like we're screwing up a crime scene."

Decker broke the side glass, reached through, and unlocked the door. He switched on his Maglite and led her inside.

"Do you remember?" said Lancaster. "That's a rhetorical question, of course."

Decker didn't appear to be listening. In his mind's eye, he was a recently minted homicide investigator after riding a beat for ten years and then working robbery, burglary, and drugs for several years as a detective. He and Lancaster had been called to the Richardses' house after the report of a disturbance and the discovery of bodies inside by the first responders. This being their maiden homicide investigation, neither wanted to screw it up.

As a rookie uniformed cop, Lancaster had worn no makeup, as though to make herself less conspicuously female. She was the only woman on the entire force who didn't sit behind a desk and type or go make coffee for the guys. The only one authorized to carry a gun, arrest people, and read them their rights. And to take their lives if it was absolutely necessary.

She hadn't taken up her smoking habit yet. That would come when she began working as a detective with Decker, and spent more and more of her time with dead bodies and trying to catch the killers who had violently snatched away those lives. She was also heavier back then. But it was a healthy weight. Lancaster had gained the rep of a calm, methodical cop who went into every situation with three or four different plans on how to manage it. Nothing rattled her. As a beat cop she'd earned numerous commendations for how she handled herself. And everyone had come out of those situations alive. She'd conducted herself the same way while working as a detective.

Decker, on the other hand, had a reputation as the quirkiest son of a bitch who'd ever worn the Burlington police uniform. Yet no one could deny his vast potential in law enforcement. And that potential had been fully realized when he became a detective and partnered with Mary Lancaster. They'd never failed to solve a case to which they'd been assigned. It was a record of which any other police department, large or small, would have been envious.

They had known each other previously, having come up in the same rookie class, but hadn't had much interaction professionally until they exchanged their uniforms for the civilian clothes of a detective.

Now Decker went step by step in his memory from that night as Lancaster watched him from a corner of the living room.

"Cops were radioed in about a disturbance here. Call came in at nine-thirty-five. Two squad cars arrived in five minutes. They entered the house a minute later after checking the perimeter. The front door was unlocked."

He moved over to another part of the room.

"Vic number one, David Katz, was found here," he said, pointing to a spot at the doorway into the kitchen. "Age thirty-five. Two taps. First gunshot to the left temple. Second to the back of the head. Instant death with either shot." He pointed to another spot right next to the door. "Beer bottle found here. His prints on it. Didn't break, but the beer was all over the floor."

"Katz owned a local restaurant, the American Grill," added Lancaster. "He was over here visiting."

"And no evidence that he could have been the target," stated Decker.

"None," confirmed Lancaster. "Wrong place, wrong time. Like Ron Goldman in the O. J. Simpson case. Really shitty luck on his part."

They moved into the kitchen. It was all dirty linoleum, scarred cabinets, and a rust-stained sink.

"Victim number two, Donald Richards—everyone

called him Don. Forty-four. Bank loan officer. Single GSW through the heart and fell here. Again, dead when he dropped."

Lancaster nodded. "He knew Katz because the bank had previously approved a loan to Katz for the American Grill project."

Decker walked back out into the living room and eyed the stairs leading up to the second floor.

"Now the last two vics."

They climbed the stairs until they reached the second-floor landing.

"These two bedrooms." He indicated two doors across from each other. He pushed open the door on the left side and went in. Lancaster followed.

"Victim number three," said Decker. "Abigail 'Abby' Richards. Age twelve."

"She was strangled. Found on the bed. Ligature marks showed that some sort of rope was used. Killer took it with him."

"Her death wasn't instantaneous," Decker pointed out.

"No. But she fought hard."

"And got Meryl Hawkins's DNA under her fingernails," Decker said pointedly. "So, in a way, she beat him."

Decker moved past her out of the room, across the hall and into the bedroom there. Lancaster followed.

Decker paced over to a point against the wall and

said, "Victim number four. Frankie Richards. Age fourteen. Just started at Burlington High School. Found on the floor right here. Single GSW to the heart."

"We found some drug paraphernalia and enough cash hidden in his room to suggest that he wasn't just a user but a dealer. But we could never tie any of that to the murders. We tracked down the man supplying him, it was Karl Stevens. He was a small fry. There was no way that was the motivation to kill four people. And Stevens had an ironclad alibi."

Decker nodded. "Okay, we were called in at ten-twenty-one. We came by car and arrived here fourteen minutes later."

He leaned against the wall and glanced out the window that overlooked the street. "Four neighboring homes. Two were occupied that night. No one in those houses saw or heard anything. Killer came and left unseen, unheard."

"But then you found something when we went through the house that changed all that."

Decker led her back down the stairs and into the living room. "A thumbprint on *that* wall switch plate along with a blood trace from Katz."

"And the perp's skin, blood, and resultant DNA under Abby's fingernails. In the struggle with her attacker."

"He's strangling her with a ligature and she grips his arms to make him stop and the material gets transferred. Anybody who's ever watched an episode of *CSI* knows that."

Lancaster's hand flicked to her pocket and she pulled out her pack of smokes.

Decker eyed this movement as she lit up. "You cashing in on tomorrow's allotment?"

"It's getting close enough to midnight. And I'm stressed. So excuse the hell out of me." She flicked ash on the floor. "Hawkins's prints were in the database because the company he had worked for previously did some defense contracting. They fingerprinted and ran a background check on everyone who worked there. When the print matched Hawkins in the database, we executed the search warrant on his house."

Decker took up the story. "Based on the print, he was arrested and brought to the station, where a cheek swab was taken. The DNA on it matched the DNA found under Abby's fingernails. And he had no alibi for that entire night. And during the search of his home they found a forty-five-caliber pistol hidden in a box behind a wall in his closet. The ballistics match was spot on, so it was without a doubt the murder weapon. He said it wasn't his and he didn't know how it got there. He said he didn't even know about that secret space. We traced the pistol. It had been stolen from a gun shop about two years before. Serial numbers filed off. Probably used in a string of crimes since that time. And then it ended up in Hawkins's closet." He glanced at his old partner. "Which raises the question of why you think we might have gotten it wrong. Looks rock solid to me."

Lancaster rolled the lit cigarette between her fingers. "I keep coming back to a dying guy taking the time to come here to clear his name. He has to know the odds are stacked against him. Why waste what little time he has left?"

"Well, what else does he have to do?" countered Decker. "I'm not saying he came to this house to murder four people. Hawkins probably picked this house to commit a lesser crime of burglary and it snowballed from there. You know that happens, Mary. Criminals lose it when they're under stress."

"But you know his motive for the crime," said Lancaster. "That came out in the trial. Without really admitting his guilt, the defense tried to score some sympathetic points on that. It might have been why he didn't get the death penalty."

Decker nodded. "His wife was terminal. He needed money for her pain meds. He'd been laid off from his job and lost his insurance. His grown daughter had a drug problem and he was trying to get her into rehab. Again. So he stole credit cards, jewelry, a laptop computer, a DVD player, a small TV, some watches, and other miscellaneous things from this house and the vics. It all fits. His motivation might have been pure, but how he went about it sure as hell wasn't."

"But none of those items ever turned up. Not at his house. Not in some pawnshop. So he never realized any money from it."

Decker said, "But he had money in his pocket when he was arrested. We could never prove it was from fencing the stolen goods, and he might well have been scared to try to move it after the murders. That's what the prosecutor postulated at trial, although, reading the jury, it seemed to me that they thought the money he had was from selling the stuff. It's just a cleaner conclusion."

"But none of the neighbors saw a car drive up or leave other than David Katz's," retorted Lancaster.

"You know it was storming like hell that night, Mary. Raining buckets. You could barely see anything. And if Hawkins didn't have his car lights on, maybe no one would have noticed it."

"But no one *heard* it?" said Lancaster.

"Again, the noise of the storm. But I see you really have doubts about the case now."

"I wouldn't go that far. I'm just saying that I believe it deserves a second look."

"I don't see it that way."

"Despite your words, I can tell that you're at least intrigued." She paused and took another puff of her smoke. "And then there's the matter of Susan Richards."

"The wife. Left around five that day, ran some errands, attended a PTA meeting, and then had drinks and dinner with a couple of friends. All verified. She got home at eleven. When she found us here and learned what had happened, she became hysterical."

"You had to hold her down or I think she would have tried to hurt herself."

"Not exactly the actions of a guilty person. And there was only a fifty-thousand-dollar life insurance policy on Don Richards, from his job at the bank."

"I've known people who have killed for a lot less. And so do you."

Decker said, "So let's go."

"Where?"

"Where else? To see Meryl Hawkins."

As they pulled to a stop in front of the Residence Inn, Decker had a moment of déjà vu. He had lived here for a while after being evicted from the home where he found his family murdered. The place hadn't changed much. It had been crappy to begin with. Now it was just crappier still. He was surprised it was still standing.

They walked inside, and Decker looked to his left, where the small dining area was located. He had used that as his unofficial office when meeting potential clients who wanted to hire him as a private detective. He had come a long way in a relatively short period of time. Yet it could have easily gone the other way. He could have eaten himself into a stroke and died inside a cardboard box in a Walmart parking lot, which had briefly been his home before he'd moved to the "fancier" Residence Inn.

When she stepped out into the lobby Decker didn't look surprised.

Jamison nodded at Lancaster and said to Decker after reading his features, "I guess you expected me to turn up here?"

"I didn't *not* expect it," he replied. "I showed you the paper with this address on it."

"I looked up the basic facts of the murder online," she said. "Seemed pretty ironclad."

"We were just discussing that," said Lancaster. "But maybe the iron is rusty." She eyed the badge riding on Jamison's hip. "Hear you're the real deal FBI agent now. Congratulations."

"Thanks. Seemed the logical next step, if only to manage Decker a little better."

"Good luck on that. I was never able to, despite *my* badge."

"He's in room fourteen," interjected Decker. "Up the stairs."

They trudged single file up to the second floor and halfway down the hall to the door. Decker knocked. And knocked again.

"Mr. Hawkins? It's Amos Decker."

No sound came from inside the room.

"Maybe he went out," said Jamison.

"Where would he go?" asked Decker.

"Let me check something," said Lancaster. She hurried back down the stairs. A minute later she was back.

"The front desk clerk said he came in about two hours ago and hasn't left."

Decker knocked harder. "Mr. Hawkins? You okay?" He looked at the other two. "Maybe he's in distress."

"Maybe he died," said Lancaster. "The guy's terminal."

"He might have just passed out," suggested Jamison. "Or overdosed. He told us he was taking street drugs for the pain. They can be unpredictable."

Decker tried the door. It was locked. He put his shoulder to the door and pushed once, then again. It bent under his considerable weight and then popped open.

They entered the room and looked around.

Sitting up in a chair across from the bed was Hawkins.

He was clearly dead.

But the cancer hadn't taken him.

The bullet wound in the center of the man's forehead had done the trick quite effectively.

4

So anyway, a dead guy gets murdered.

It sounded like the opening line of an abysmally poor joke. A man terminal with cancer, who would probably be dead within a few days or weeks, gets hurried along to the end by a bullet.

Decker thought this as he leaned against the wall of Meryl Hawkins's room while the two-person forensic team carried out its professional tasks.

The EMTs had already come and pronounced death. The medical examiner had then made his way over and told them the obvious: death by a single GSW to the brain. There was no exit wound. Small-caliber probably, but no less lethal than a big-ass Magnum with that relatively soft target lined up in its iron sights.

Death was instantaneous, the ME had said. And painless.

But how does anyone really know that? thought Decker. It wasn't like they could go back and debrief the victim.

Excuse me, did it hurt when someone blew your brains out?

What was significant were the burn marks around the forehead. The muzzle of the gun had to either have been in contact with or within inches of the skin to make that imprint. It was like touching a hot iron. It left a mark that would be impossible if the iron was six feet away. Here, the gun's released gases would have done the work when the trigger was pulled.

Decker eyed Lancaster, who was overseeing the forensic team. Two uniformed officers were posted outside the door looking bored and tired. Jamison, leaning against another wall, watched the proceedings with interest.

Lancaster finally came over to Decker, and Jamison quickly joined them.

"We've taken statements. No one heard anything, and no one saw anything."

"Just like when Hawkins went to the Richardses' home and murdered them," said Decker.

"The rooms on either side of this one are unoccupied. And if the perp used a suppressor can on the gun?"

"When I lived here there was a rear door that never properly locked," said Decker. "The killer could have come and gone that way and the front-desk person wouldn't have seen them."

"I'll have that checked out. Hawkins's door was locked until you popped it."

"Presumably he let in the person who killed him," said Jamison. "And these doors automatically lock on the way out. Time of death?"

"ME's prelim is between eleven and midnight."

Decker checked his watch. "Which means we didn't miss them by much. If we had come here first instead of the Richardses' place?"

"Hindsight is absolutely perfect," noted Lancaster.

"Decker?"

He turned to look down at the woman in blue scrubs and booties. She was one of the crime scene techs. She was in her midthirties, red-haired and lanky, with sprinkles of freckles over the bridge of her nose.

"Kelly Fairweather," he said.

She smiled. "Hey, you remembered me."

"That's pretty much a given," said Decker, without a trace of irony.

Fairweather looked over at the dead man. "Well, I remember *him*," she said.

Lancaster joined them. "That's right, you worked the Richards crime scene."

"My first year doing this. Four homicides and two of them kids. It was quite an introduction to the job. So, what are you doing here, Decker?"

"Just trying to figure things out."

"Good luck with that. But I always thought

Hawkins should've gotten the needle for what he did. I know that doesn't excuse what happened here."

"No, it doesn't," said Lancaster firmly.

Fairweather took that as a not-so-subtle nudge to move on. "Well, good seeing you, Decker."

As she moved away, Decker walked over to stand directly in front of the dead man, who still sat there like a statue. Lancaster and Jamison joined him.

Decker said, "So the shooter walks up to Hawkins, who's sitting in this chair, presses the gun against his forehead, and pulls the trigger." He looked around. "And no sign of a struggle?"

"Maybe he was asleep," suggested Lancaster.

"After letting the person in, the guy sits down in a chair and dozes off?" said Jamison.

Decker said, "He told us he was taking drugs. Did you find any?"

Lancaster shook her head. "Nothing in here or the bathroom. No discarded wrappers or empty pill bottles. Just a small duffel of clothes, a few bucks in his wallet. The post will show if he had anything in his system."

Decker looked around the room again, taking in every detail and imprinting it on his memory. He had already done this, but decided to do it again. His memory had been having a few hiccups of late and he didn't want to take a chance that he had missed something. It was like printing out a second copy of a photo.

Hawkins's yellowing skin had given way to a translucent paleness. Death did that to you, what with the stoppage of blood flow. At least the cancer was no longer a factor for the man. With death it had immediately stopped eating away at Hawkins's innards. Decker figured a fast bullet was preferable to a slow, painful death. But it was still murder.

"So, motives and possible suspects?" said Lancaster.

"Not to state the obvious, but does Susan Richards still live in the area?" asked Decker.

"Yes, she does."

"That would be my starting point," said Decker.

Lancaster checked her watch. "I'll have her picked up and taken to the station. We can interview her there."

"So, you want us involved?" said a surprised Jamison.

"In for a dime," replied Lancaster.

"The thing is, we have a day job," said Jamison. "Which often extends into nights."

"I can call Bogart," said Decker. Ross Bogart was the veteran FBI agent who headed up the task force of which Decker and Jamison were members.

"So, you really want to stay and dive into this?" asked Jamison warily.

"Do I have a choice?" asked Decker.

"You always have a choice," said Lancaster, gazing knowingly at Decker. "But I think I know what that choice will be."

Jamison said, "Decker, have you really thought this through?"

He indicated the corpse and said forcefully, "*This* is significant. The guy comes to town saying he's innocent and approaches me and Lancaster to prove him right. Now somebody just killed him."

"Well, like you just suggested, it might be Susan Richards, the widow of the man Hawkins was convicted of murdering."

"It might, and it might not."

Decker turned and walked out.

Lancaster looked at Jamison. "Well, some things never change. Like him."

"Tell me about it," replied Jamison wearily.

5

Ross Bogart said, "This is unacceptable, Decker. And I mean totally unacceptable."

Decker was on his phone, heading to the Burlington police station.

"I understand how you could think that, Ross."

"There's no understanding anything. I let you go rogue once before with the Melvin Mars case. And then when you wanted to stay back in Baronville and work the case there because it was connected to Alex's family. But I can't let you go off willy-nilly whenever you feel like it."

"This is different," said Decker.

"You say that every time," barked Bogart. "You've not only blown up the exception to the rule, you've blown up the rule. The bottom line is you work for the FBI."

"I'm sorry, Ross. This is my hometown. I can't turn my back on it."

"You've made your choice, then?"

"Yes."

"Then you force me to make mine."

"This is all me. Alex has nothing to do with it."

"I'll deal with Special Agent Jamison separately."

The line went dead.

Decker slowly put the phone away. It seemed that his days at the FBI were numbered.

He looked over at Lancaster, who was in the car with him.

"Problems?" she said.

"There are always problems."

They drove on.

Susan Richards was not pleased. "You're shitting me, right? You think I killed that son of a bitch? I wish I had."

Decker and Lancaster had just walked into the interrogation room at police headquarters. Jamison had gone back to her hotel because Decker had not received authorization from Bogart to work on the case. And that permission obviously would not be forthcoming. Bogart had probably already contacted her.

They had had to wait for a few hours while the paperwork was drawn up to bring Richards in after she angrily refused to voluntarily comply with their request. And the fuming woman had apparently taken her time getting ready while the uniforms impatiently waited.

Thus it was now nearly five in the morning.

Lancaster looked ready to fall asleep.

Decker looked ready to question the woman for the next ten years.

The interrogation room's cinderblock walls were still painted mustard yellow. Decker had never known why, other than maybe that was the color of some old paint the custodians had found somewhere in the basement. Leaving the cinder blocks their original gray would have been nicer, he thought. But maybe no one wanted "nicer" in an interrogation room.

Richards had been forty-two when her family was wiped out. She was in her midfifties now. She had aged remarkably well, Decker thought. He remembered her as tall, but plump and mousy-looking, her light brown hair hanging limply around her face.

Now she was much thinner, and her hair was cut in a chic manner, with the tresses grazing her shoulder. She had colored her hair and blonde highlights predominated. Her mousy personality had been replaced by an assertive manner that had made itself known with her outburst the moment the two detectives walked into the room.

Richards looked from Lancaster to Decker as they sat down across from her. "Wait a minute, you're the two from that night. I recognize you now. You know what he did." She sat forward, her sharp elbows pressed against the tabletop. Her face full of fury, she snapped, "You *know* what that bastard did."

Lancaster said calmly, "Which is why, when he was found dead, we thought we needed to talk to you.

So that you could tell us where you were between around eleven and midnight."

"Where in the hell do you think I was at that hour? I was in my bed asleep."

"Can anyone verify that?" asked Decker.

"I live alone. I never remarried. That's what having your family wiped out will do to you!" she added fiercely.

"What time did you get home last night?" asked Decker.

Richards took a moment to compose herself and sat back. "I got off work at six. Three days a week, I volunteer at the homeless shelter on Dawson Square. I was there until around eight last night. There are people who can vouch for me."

"And after that?" said Lancaster.

Richards sat back and spread her hands. "I drove home, cooked some dinner."

"What'd you have?" asked Lancaster.

"Oh, the usual. Smoked salmon on crusty bread with cream cheese and capers to warm up my appetite, then a Waldorf salad, some linguine with fresh clams, and a nice little tiramisu for dessert. And I paired that with a wonderful glass of my favorite chilled Prosecco."

"Seriously?" said Lancaster.

Richards made a face. "Of course not. I made a tuna sandwich with a pickle and some corn chips. And I skipped the Prosecco and had iced tea instead."

"Then what did you do?"

"I ordered something from Bed, Bath & Beyond online. You can probably check that. Then I watched some TV."

"What program?" asked Decker.

"I was streaming. *Outlander.* I'm really getting into it. Season two. Jamie and Claire in France."

"What was the episode about?"

"Lots of political skullduggery. And some pretty intense sex." She added sarcastically, "Want me to describe it in graphic detail for you?"

"And then?" said Decker.

"I finished watching that. Then I took a shower and called it a night. I woke up when the police knocked on my door. *Pounded*, more precisely," she added, frowning.

"You drive a dark green Honda Civic?" said Lancaster.

"Yes. It's the only car I have."

"And you live on Primrose, on the north side?"

"Yes. I have for about five years now."

"You have neighbors?"

"On both sides of me and across the street." She sat up. "One of them might be able to tell you that I was home last night. Or at least that I didn't leave once I got there."

"We'll check that out," said Lancaster. "Did you know Meryl Hawkins was back in town?"

"I had no idea. What, do you think he'd knock on

my door and ask for a handout? I thought he was in prison for life. And I still don't know why he wasn't."

"He was terminal with cancer, so they cut him loose."

"Well, that seems shitty," said Richards. "Don't get me wrong, I hated the asshole. But they just kicked him to the curb because he was dying?"

"Apparently so. And he never tried to contact you?"

"Never. If he had, I *might* have tried to kill him. But he didn't and so I didn't."

Decker said, "You opened a florist shop, didn't you? With the proceeds from your husband's insurance policy? I remember seeing it. Over on Ash Place?"

She eyed him warily. "I buried my *family* with a chunk of the insurance money. And then I went on living. I'm not sure how."

"And the florist shop?" persisted Decker.

"There wasn't that much left after the funeral expenses. But, yes, I opened a florist shop. I've always loved gardening and flowers. It did okay. Provided a decent living. Even did some holiday events for the police department. I sold it a few years back. Now I run the place for the new owners. When my Social Security kicks in, I'm going to retire and just work on my own garden."

Lancaster looked at Decker. "Anything else?"

He shook his head.

"How was he killed?" asked Richards.

"We're holding that back for now," said Lancaster.

"Am I free to go?"

"Yes."

She rose and looked at the pair. "I didn't kill him," she said quietly. "Years ago, I probably would have, no problem. But I guess time does help to heal you."

She walked out.

Lancaster looked at him. "You believe her?"

"I don't disbelieve her."

"There were no usable prints or other trace in Hawkins's room."

"I didn't expect there would be."

"So what now?"

"We do what we always did. We keep digging."

Lancaster checked her watch. "Well, right now I've got to get home and get some sleep or I'm going to keel over. I'll give you a call later. You should get some sleep too."

He rose and followed her out of the room.

Outside, Lancaster said, "I can drop you off where you're staying."

"I'd rather walk, thanks. It's not that far."

She smiled. "Nice to be working with you again."

"You might not think that much longer."

"I've gotten used to your ways."

"So you say."

He turned and walked off into the breaking dawn.

6

A gentle rain kicked in as Decker trudged along the pavement.

It felt very odd to once more be investigating a crime in his hometown. The last time had involved the murder of his family. This one was different, but it still affected Decker personally.

If I was part of convicting an innocent man?

He looked around as he walked. He had decided not to come back for Cassie's birthday, or their wedding anniversary. That simply would have been too much for him to handle. Yet he would keep returning for their daughter's birthday. He had to be here for that milestone, though each visit was emotionally crippling for him.

His long feet carried him past where he was staying, and after a few miles he reached the long-established neighborhood. It was light now. He stopped walking and stood on the corner staring up at the place he used to call home.

The last time he'd been here was two years ago. It looked remarkably unchanged, as though time had stood still since his last visit. Although there were two unfamiliar cars in the driveway, a Ford pickup and a Nissan Sentra.

As he stood there, a man in his early thirties and a girl around seven came out of the side door. The girl was carrying a school backpack and the man was dressed in khakis and a white collared shirt with a windbreaker over it. He carried a slim briefcase in one hand. The girl yawned and rubbed her eyes.

They climbed into the pickup truck and backed out of the driveway. That's when the man spotted Decker standing there watching the house.

He rolled down his window. "Can I help you, buddy?"

Decker studied him more closely. "You must be Henderson."

The man eyed him suspiciously. "How do you know that?"

"A friend told me." He pointed at the house. "I used to live there a few years ago."

Henderson ran his gaze over Decker. "Okay. Did you leave something behind?"

"No, I, uh ..." Decker's voice trailed off, and he looked confused.

Henderson said, "Look, don't get me wrong, but it's a little odd that you're standing out here this early in the morning watching my house."

Decker pulled his FBI creds out of his pocket and

showed them to Henderson. "My friend on the police force told me you'd bought the house."

"Wait a minute," said Henderson, staring at the ID card. "Amos Decker?"

"Yeah."

Henderson nodded and looked anxious. "I heard about—" He snatched a glance at his daughter, who was paying close attention to this exchange.

"Right. Anyway, have a good day. Hope you enjoy the house and the neighborhood. Nice place to raise a family."

Decker turned and walked off as Henderson drove away.

It had been stupid coming back here. He'd rattled the guy unnecessarily. And for what? He didn't need to come here for a walk down memory lane. It was all in his head. Pristine. Forever.

And painfully so.

He retraced his steps and got to the hotel where he and Jamison were staying in time to see her exit the elevator and walk into the lobby.

"Christ, Decker, are you just getting in?" she said, eyeing his grungy, wet clothes.

"Good morning to you too. Would you like to get some breakfast?"

She followed him into the dining area off the lobby. They sat, ordered some food, and sipped their coffees.

"So?" said Jamison. "Was Susan Richards any help?"

"She didn't cop to the murder if that's what you're asking. She doesn't have a solid alibi. She was home asleep, she says."

"Well, considering the hour, that makes sense."

"We may be able to tighten the parameters on that by talking to her neighbors. But I don't think she's good for it. She says she didn't even know he was back in town. And that seems perfectly logical."

"Unless she saw him on the street."

"*I* saw him and didn't recognize him," said Decker. "And I spent a lot of time with the guy all those years ago."

"Have you called Bogart and gotten his permission to work on this?"

He said quietly, "We've, uh, talked. I'm surprised he hasn't called you."

"No, he didn't. So what did he say?"

At that moment their food arrived.

Decker said, "I'll fill you in later."

"Thank you for ordering a veggie omelet, by the way," said Jamison. "And avoiding the bacon."

"You must be growing on me."

"Well, I'm just happy that you're not *growing* anymore. You look good, Decker."

"That's a stretch, but thanks."

He put his knife and fork down and finished his coffee.

"What are you thinking?" asked Jamison.

"I'm thinking that there's a killer walking around town this morning thinking he or she got away with murder, and it's really pissing me off."

"Is that all?"

He looked at her curiously. "Isn't that enough?"

"I mean, do you feel guilty about what happened to Meryl Hawkins?"

"I didn't pull the trigger on the guy. I didn't ask him to come here and ignite this case again."

"But you think that the fact that someone killed him is evidence that he might have been innocent? I mean, you basically said that earlier."

"Meaning that I made a mistake?" said Decker slowly.

"I wouldn't look at it that way. You investigated the case and all the evidence pointed to that guy. I would have seen it the same way."

"Regardless, if he *was* innocent, I have to make it right."

Jamison hiked her eyebrows. "Because the weight of the world's problems always falls on your admittedly broad shoulders?"

"Not the weight of the world. The weight of one case that I handled. Responsibility comes with the territory. My actions took a guy's freedom away."

"No, I'd say *his* actions took his freedom away."

"Only if he did it," countered Decker. "If he didn't commit the crimes, it's a whole other ball game."

Jamison fingered her coffee cup. "If he was set up, whoever did it knew what they were doing. Who would have a beef against the guy that badly?"

Decker nodded. "Good point. And I have no idea. Hawkins was a skilled machinist but lost his job when the factory he worked at had layoffs. Then he went on the odd-job road. Doing what he could to make ends meet."

"Sounds like a lot of people these days."

He eyed the FBI badge that was clipped to her lapel. "How does it feel?"

She looked down at the badge and smiled. "Pretty damn good, actually. Did you ever think of taking the plunge?"

"I'm too old now. Age thirty-seven is the cutoff and I'm not a military veteran, so I can't seek that waiver. And even if I could still apply, I doubt I'd pass the physical."

"Don't underestimate yourself. And since you know the requirements, I take it you looked into it?"

Decker shrugged. "I can do my job without the federal badge. I'm still a sworn police officer. I can arrest people." He paused and added, "And you always have my back."

"Yes, I do."

"I went by my old house early this morning."

She looked startled by this admission. "Why?"

"I don't know. My feet pointed that way and suddenly I was there. Met the dad who lives there and saw his little girl. Lancaster had told me about them. I spooked them a little showing up like that, but the dad had heard about what had happened . . . there. It turned out okay."

Jamison leaned forward. "I know that you don't want to hear this, Decker, but I'm going to say it anyway." She paused, seeming to choose her words with great care. "At some point, you're going to have to let this go. I mean, I get coming back here to visit their graves and all. But you have your life left to live. That means you have to move forward and stop dwelling in the past so much. Cassie and Molly wouldn't want you to do that, you know that."

"Do I?" said Decker abruptly.

She sat back, looking saddened by this comment.

"They shouldn't be dead, Alex. If anyone should be dead, it should be me."

"But you're not. You're alive and you have to spend every day living for them and yourself. Otherwise, it's all wasted."

Decker rose. "I'm going to take a shower and change my clothes. And then we're going to go catch a killer. I'll meet you back down here in half an hour."

"Decker, you need to get some sleep!"

"No, that would just be *wasting* time, wouldn't it?"

As he walked off, Jamison just stared after him, the look on her face one of heartbreak.

7

Decker let the hot water run off his head for a full minute before soaping up. The next moment he had a brief panic attack because he couldn't recall Cassie's favorite color. Then his memory righted itself and the proper shade kicked out of his brain.

He rested his head against the shower tile. *Shit, more hiccups. No, more* malfunctions *because I'm a machine, after all. Right?*

Was his memory going to keep misfiring? Right when he needed it to work precisely? Or would there be a time when it simply stopped functioning altogether? Then a dreaded thought sprouted up: Was he developing complications from his brain injury all those years ago? Like CTE?

He finished in the shower, dried off, and put on fresh clothes. Mentally he still felt like crap, and physically he was tired, but at least he was clean.

Jamison was waiting for him in the lobby. They got into the car and from the driver's seat Jamison said, "Where to?"

"Our only viable suspect right now, Susan Richards."

On the way he phoned Lancaster and told her what they were going to do. He had to leave a message because the call went to voicemail. She was probably still sleeping, surmised Decker.

Richards's home on Primrose Avenue was a small single-story brick bungalow with old-fashioned green-and-white-striped metal awnings over the windows. The patch of yard was neatly laid out, with mature trees and well-shaped bushes and planting beds. An abundance of colorful fall flowers was displayed in pots on the covered front stoop.

"Nice landscaping," commented Jamison.

"She was a florist for years," explained Decker. "Into gardening. Runs the floral shop she sold to new owners a while back."

"Do you actually think she could have murdered Hawkins last night?"

"She could have. But I don't know if she did. That's what we have to find out."

They got out, but Decker didn't head up to the front door. He instead walked over to the house across the street.

"Verifying alibis?" said Jamison as she caught up to him.

He nodded and knocked on the door of the bungalow that was a twin of Richards's home, only with a screened-in porch on one end.

Answering the door was a tiny elderly woman with white hair so thin they could see her reddened scalp underneath.

"Yes?" she said, staring at them from behind thick glasses.

Jamison held out her FBI badge, which the woman scrutinized.

"FBI?" she said. "Have I done something wrong?"

"No," said Jamison hastily. "We were checking on a neighbor of yours, Ms . . . ?"

"Agatha Bates." She looked up at the towering Decker. "Are you FBI? You didn't show me a badge." She ran her gaze over him. "You look too big to be FBI. I watch a lot of TV. No FBI agent is as big as you."

Jamison said hastily, "He works as a consultant for us."

Bates slowly drew her gaze from Decker and settled it on Jamison. "Which neighbor?"

"Susan Richards."

"Oh, Susan, sure. Nice lady. Lived here a while. Not nearly so long as me. I've been here fifty-seven years." She looked at Decker again. "Don't I know you?"

"I worked here on the police force for twenty years."

"Oh, well, I don't have much contact with the police. I pay my taxes and I've never robbed anybody."

"I'm sure," said Jamison. "We were wondering if you could tell us when you last saw Ms. Richards."

"Well, I saw her this morning when the police came to get her. We don't usually have the police around here."

"That was pretty early," noted Jamison.

"Well, I get up pretty early. Only sleep maybe four hours a night. You get old, you don't sleep. I'll be sleeping all the time pretty soon."

"Excuse me?" said Jamison.

"When I *die*, honey. I'm ninety-three, how much longer do you expect me to be around?" She paused and adjusted her glasses. "So why did the police take her in the first place?"

"For some questions. Did you see her yesterday, in the evening, maybe?"

"I saw her come home. It was around quarter past eight."

"How can you be so certain?" asked Decker. "And have you spoken to her this morning?"

"No, I haven't talked to her. If she's home now she hasn't come out of her house, least that I saw. Usually takes a walk in the morning. I have my coffee on the screen porch. I wave, she waves back. I guess the police coming messed that up."

"So you didn't see her come back from the police station this morning?" asked Decker.

"No. I was probably in the kitchen making breakfast, or out in the backyard puttering. I like to putter.

People my age, we putter, and we do it slow. I don't need a broken hip."

"So last night?" prompted Jamison.

"Quarter past eight," she said again, staring at Decker. "She volunteers at the homeless shelter. She always gets in around that time. And I know the time because *Jeopardy!* had been over about fifteen minutes. I got the Final Jeopardy question. The answer was Harry Truman. I remember Truman. Hell, I *voted* for him. All three of the contestants got it wrong. Not a single one was over thirty. What do they know about Harry Truman? I would have won enough to take a vacation somewhere."

"So, you saw her come home last night? Did she leave again? Would you have seen her if she did?"

"She didn't drive in her car if she did," said Bates. "That car of hers sounds like a bomb going off when she starts it up. It's an old Honda. Darn muffler's shot. Told her to get it fixed. Almost makes me wet my pants every time I hear it. My hearing's still good. I can hear pretty much everything and especially that damn car."

"But she could have left another way. Walked or called a cab?"

"Well, I was out on the screen porch doing the crosswords and reading until about ten-thirty or so. I would have seen her leave. After that, I went inside. Hit the hay about eleven or so."

"Okay, to be clear, at least until ten-thirty or so

she hadn't left her house?" said Decker. "And you never heard the car start up, at least until you went to bed around eleven?"

"I thought I just said that. Are you *slow*?"

"That's great," said Jamison quickly. "Mrs. Bates, you've been very helpful."

"Okay, glad to do my civic duty." She jerked her thumb at Decker and said in a low voice to Jamison, "I think the FBI needs better consultants. But you keep doing what you're doing, honey. Nice to see a gal agent."

"Thanks," said Jamison, trying hard to suppress a smile.

They left Bates and headed back to the street.

Decker said, "If Richards walked, she could have gotten to the Residence Inn in time to kill Hawkins. And she clearly could have if she took a cab."

"If she took a cab, we'll be able to find any record of it. I suppose they don't have Uber here?"

"No, I don't think so."

They tried the other two homes, but no one answered their knocks.

"Bottom line is we haven't eliminated Richards as a suspect for Hawkins's murder," noted Decker.

"But do you really think she might have done it?"

"She has the most direct motive, but there are a lot of obstacles in the way. How she would know he was back in town being foremost among them."

"You don't think he would have gone to see her?"

"How would Hawkins even know where she lived? Lancaster didn't tell him, I know that. And if he was innocent of the murders he wouldn't have gone there to apologize."

"You can Google someone's address easily enough," said Jamison.

"He just got out of prison and was terminally ill. I'm not sure I see the guy walking around with a computer and an Internet connection. Or finding one all that easily."

"But he might have gone to get some info from her, especially if he thought *she* did it."

Decker shook his head. "No, Hawkins knew from the trial that she had a firm alibi." He paused and added thoughtfully, "Theoretically, she could have hired someone to do it for her, though there was absolutely no evidence of that. But we still arrive back at the problem with motive. With her husband around, she could stay home and raise the kids. She never got remarried, there was no boyfriend waiting in the wings. She didn't get rich off her family's murders. I just don't see it. And no way she was going to kill her own kids."

"I agree," admitted Jamison.

"There's one guy we can talk to who might be able to tell us more."

"Who's that?"

"Ken Finger."

"Ken Finger? How does he figure into this?"

"He was Hawkins's public defender."

"Is he still around?"

"Let's go find out."

8

Ken Finger was indeed still around.

Decker had finally reached Lancaster, and she arranged to meet them at Finger's office, which was located a block over from the downtown courthouse.

His secretary, Christine Burlin, a woman in her midforties, met their request with a stern look. "Mr. Finger is very busy at present," she said when confronted with Decker, Jamison, and Lancaster.

Lancaster took out her badge. "I think Ken can make some time for this."

Burlin stared at the badge far longer than was needed.

"Come on, Christine," said an exasperated Lancaster. "It's not like you don't know who I am. Some of your kids go to the same school as Sandy. And you know Decker as well from working with Ken."

"Well, I try to maintain a professional atmosphere at work, Detective Lancaster."

"I'm all for professional," said Decker. "So where's Ken?"

Burlin looked up at him. "I heard you were back in town for a few days," she said. "You still working for the FBI?" Decker nodded and she looked at Jamison. "I remember you too. I take it you're still consulting with the Bureau?"

"I'm actually a special agent now," said Jamison.

"That's a strange career change, from journalist to FBI agent."

"Not that strange," replied Jamison.

"Why?"

"An FBI agent looks to find the truth and make sure the right people are punished. A journalist digs to find the truth and makes sure the public knows about it, and that sometimes leads to bad people being punished."

"Hmmm," said Burlin, looking skeptical of this. "I guess that could be."

"Where's Ken?" said Decker impatiently. "We're wasting crucial time here."

Burlin frowned. "I see that *you* haven't changed one bit." She picked up her desk phone and made the call.

A few moments later she escorted them into Finger's office. It was large with ample windows. His desk was constructed of dark wood with a leather top. It was strewn with books, legal pads, files, and stapled pleadings. A large bookshelf held old law books and red file folders, neatly labeled. There were chairs set around a coffee table. A credenza against one wall was set up as a bar, and also held two large glass jars of M&M's. Ken Finger sat behind his desk.

Finger had only been about thirty when he had defended Hawkins against a capital murder charge. There apparently had been no other takers who wanted to defend in court the man charged with brutally murdering two men and two kids.

He was now in his forties and worked as a defense attorney for those who needed it. And in Burlington, like most towns, there were a great many who needed his services. His tidy brown hair was turning gray, as was his trim beard. His pleated trousers were held up by bright red braces and his white shirt had French cuffs. His striped bow tie was undone and hung limply around his wattled neck. His belly stuck out from between the braces.

He rose and greeted them, motioning them over to the seating area around the coffee table.

"I guess I know why you're here," he said, after Burlin closed the door behind her.

"Guess you do," replied Lancaster.

"How the hell are you, Decker?" Finger said.

"Okay," said Decker as he sat down. "So you've heard?"

"How could I not? Burlington's not that big. And although it's not like the attack on the high school when you lived here, it's still newsworthy when a convicted murderer comes back to town and then gets murdered."

Lancaster said, "Had he come to see you?"

Finger shook his head. "Hadn't seen hide nor hair of him since he went to prison."

"You never visited him there?" asked Jamison.

"Well, I take that back. I *did* go visit him there because we filed an appeal, but it was turned down flat. I mean, we didn't really have any grounds for an appeal. If anything, the judge went out of his way to accommodate us. And the jury could have returned a death sentence, but they didn't. I actually told Meryl that his escaping the death penalty was the best he could expect. Why make waves?"

"Were you convinced of his guilt?" asked Lancaster.

Finger shrugged. "It didn't matter to me one way or another. My job is to defend. It's the state's job to prove guilt. I live in the creases of reasonable doubt. All defense lawyers do."

"But did you *think* he was guilty?" persisted Decker.

Finger sat back and steepled his hands. "You know that the attorney-client privilege survives the death of a client."

"I'm not asking for you to reveal any privileged communications," Decker pointed out. "I'm just asking your opinion on the matter. That's not privileged and can in no way injure your client. He was already convicted and now he's dead."

Finger grinned. "You would've made a good lawyer,

Decker. Okay, yeah, I thought he'd done it. I think he went over there just to steal some stuff and ran into a whole lot of trouble that he couldn't handle. It wasn't like the guy was a career criminal. Hell, he hadn't had so much as a parking ticket. I think that was one reason he didn't get the death penalty. I think he lost it and started shooting and strangling, and before he knew it, he had four dead bodies. Then he just got the hell out of there."

"And no one saw him drive up, enter the place and then leave, or hear the shots?" said Decker.

Finger shrugged. "Who knows? People said they heard nothing. One house was playing loud music. In the other the folks said they were watching TV or sleeping. The third house the people weren't home that night, and the fourth house was abandoned. And the houses weren't that close. And then there was the noise from the storm." He gave Decker a funny look. "Hell, Amos, you and Mary are the ones that made the case against him. Prints. DNA. Motive. Opportunity. And the murder weapon found hidden in his home. I mean, as a defense lawyer, I had nothing really to work with. I considered it a miracle he only got life without parole."

"And the stolen goods?" said Lancaster.

"Hawkins didn't have an explanation for that because he said he didn't commit the crime. But if you want my opinion, I think he chucked it all when he knew he couldn't fence them without it tying him to four homicides."

Decker shook his head. "He had five hundred dollars in his wallet the night he was picked up."

"And the prosecution suggested that was the proceeds from his fencing the stolen goods. But the stuff that he was supposed to have stolen would have fetched more money than that, I think."

"And you postulated a theory that Hawkins was planning to use the five hundred bucks to purchase painkillers for his wife, Lisa, off the street. Did he tell you that, or did you just come up with it?"

"Hey, I don't just 'come up' with stuff, Decker," Finger said firmly. "That's what he told me."

"So where'd he get the money?" asked Lancaster.

"He never said."

"I wonder why," said Decker. "I mean if he could have come up with a viable explanation that would have taken a big chunk out of the prosecution's case."

"Believe me, I tried. But he wouldn't say."

Lancaster said, "He'd gotten laid off from his job a while back. They had no money."

"I'm just telling you what he told me about it, which was zip. And I wouldn't let him take the stand, so the prosecution was able to bring out the money during the trial. I tried to poke holes at it and brought up him wanting to buy drugs for his terminally ill wife to get some sympathy in the courtroom, but I could tell the jury wasn't buying it. They were connecting the dots on the money and the stolen goods. There was no way around that. And for all I know the five hundred bucks did come from that. Who's to say what a fence will pay for hot goods connected to a string of murders? And there was no way a fence would have come forward and gotten involved in the case. So there was no avenue for me to investigate unless Meryl opened up about it, which he never did."

Lancaster said, "But more to the point, why would he go to a house that early in the evening and that was full of people?"

Decker interjected, "There were no cars out front. David Katz's car was parked in the back of the house. And Hawkins wouldn't have been able to see that if he approached from the front, which he had to. The Richardses only had one car at the time and the wife had taken it. The other car was in for repairs."

"But there were lights on when the first responders got there," countered Lancaster. "Pretty stupid burglar to hit a house all lit up."

Finger spread his hands. "What can I tell you? That's what happened. Like I said, the guy wasn't an experienced criminal. And he had no alibi. You know that."

Decker said, "And Hawkins might have thought the lights were on just because of the storm. With no cars out front, and the house didn't have a garage, he might have thought it was empty."

Finger added, "And if he didn't do it, someone went to a lot of trouble to frame him. Why would they? He was a nobody. Blue-collar guy his whole life. I'm not saying that's bad. Hell, I admired him for that. My old man was a mechanic, could do stuff I never could. I'm just saying Meryl was a regular guy with a regular life. Not worth the trouble."

"And yet somebody went to the *trouble* of killing him," said Decker. "And his life wasn't exactly regular. His wife was dying and his daughter was a drug addict."

"That's true. Hey, did you check with Susan? She's still around."

"Gee, why didn't we think of that?" said Lancaster.

"So you don't think she's good for it?" said Finger.

"What I think about an active police investigation is none of your business, Ken."

Finger smiled. "Come on, Mary, I thought we were friends."

"We're also professional adversaries because I have to testify in court to put away your guilty clients, and you do your best to discredit my *truthful* testimony."

"Hey, it's called cross-examination. We don't have many arrows in our quiver, but that's one of the prime ones. And the state has all the resources. I'm just one guy."

"Keep telling yourself that. It's a good day when the Internet works at the police station. My computer's about fifteen years old. And I haven't had a raise in eight years."

He smiled impishly. "You can always come over to our side. Be an expert witness. Pays pretty well."

She returned the look. "Thanks, but no thanks. I have a hard enough time sleeping as it is."

"I sleep like a baby," retorted Finger, grinning.

Decker looked over at the bookshelf where a bunch of files were stacked. "We need to see your records on the case."

"Why?"

"Because there might be a clue in there as to who killed Hawkins."

"The privilege still applies, Decker."

Decker looked at the man. "Hawkins came to me and asked me to prove his innocence. He did the same to Mary."

Finger glanced sharply at Lancaster, who nodded. "That was the only reason he was back in town. To tell me and Decker that we got it wrong and he wanted us to make it right. We went to the Residence Inn to meet with him to go over that. That's when we found him dead."

Decker said, "So it seems to me that by his words and actions, Hawkins has waived his privilege, because how else can we prove his innocence if we can't look at your files?"

Finger sighed. "Well, you make a compelling argument, I'll give you that. And I guess it couldn't hurt at this point. But it's been a long time. You think I still have that stuff?"

"Most attorneys I know never throw anything away," replied Decker firmly.

"So you're thinking he's innocent now, after all this time?"

"Some people here thought I'd killed my family," said Decker.

"I wasn't one of them," said Finger quickly.

Decker rose. "So let's go get those files."

"What, you mean now? They're in storage probably."

"Yeah, now."

"But I've got to be in court in twenty minutes."

"Then I'm sure your secretary can help us. Now."

"What's your rush?"

"After all these years, I'm not waiting on the truth one second longer than I have to," replied Decker.

9

"It's over here."

They were in a climate-controlled storage unit. After consulting the iPad she was holding, Christine Burlin pointed to a shelf in the far back of the space.

"You seem very well organized," said Lancaster appreciatively.

"Well, of course I am. Mr. Finger is not the best in that regard, so I have to make up for it. And I can assure you that I do."

Lancaster whispered to Jamison, "She has four kids, the oldest is in eighth grade, and I think she still dresses them in Garanimals."

There were only two boxes dealing with the case, Burlin told them. She made Lancaster sign an electronic receipt before she would allow them to take the containers. They trudged back to their cars with Decker schlepping both boxes.

Lancaster said, "You can take them back to the station. Captain Miller has arranged a room for you to use."

"How is Captain Miller?" said Decker.

"Ready to retire," said Lancaster. "But aren't we all. I'll meet you back there later."

"Wait a minute, where are you going?" asked Decker.

"I have other cases to work," she said incredulously. "And this one is not officially on my plate or even a case for the department."

"But Hawkins's murder is."

"And we don't know if it's connected to what's in those files. So, you go through them and let me know what you find out, if anything. And let me go about trying to solve some *new* crimes, like Hawkins's murder."

She got into her car and drove off. When Decker didn't climb into their rental, Jamison paused, her hand on the car door. "What's up?"

"That's what I want to know: What's up with Mary?"

"What do you mean?"

"I've known her a long time. She's not telling me something."

"Well, she has that right, Decker. But she might come around. And it's nice that you're worried about your old partner," she added.

They drove to the police station and were directed to the room reserved for their use. As they were heading down the hall a man in his early sixties stepped out of an office.

Captain MacKenzie Miller was still short, wide,

and puffy, with an unhealthy tint to his skin. But his smile was broad and infectious. "Look what they let in the door," he said.

He put out his hand for Decker to shake. He nodded at Jamison and shook her hand too, then pointed to the badge on her jacket. "I heard. Congrats, Alex, I know that wasn't easy."

"Thanks, Mac."

Decker eyed the man who had been his superior his entire time on the police force. Miller was a good cop, tough, fair, and he didn't bullshit. He had actually stopped Decker from putting a bullet in his brain once. It would be impossible to dislike the man after that.

"Well, you've been establishing quite a rep for yourself at the Bureau. Ross Bogart keeps me updated."

"Didn't know that," said Decker, the boxes pressed against his wide chest.

"Nice to know there are some things you *don't* know," said Miller. He eyed the boxes. "Lawyer's files? Hawkins?"

"Yes," responded Jamison.

"Well, I'll let you get to it, then. It's good to see you both. Let's grab a beer later if you're able."

Decker said, "Can I ask a question?"

"Would it matter if I said no?"

"What's going on with Mary?"

Miller folded his short arms over his thick chest. "Why do you think anything's going on with her, Amos?"

"We know each other. Something's off."

"You *knew* each other. It's been a couple of years. People change."

"People don't change that much," replied Decker.

"Then ask her." Miller wagged a finger at him. "Just be prepared for whatever answer she has. You up for that?"

Decker didn't answer, and Miller didn't look like he had expected a response.

"I appreciate your letting us work on the case."

"Well, I want to get to the bottom of it as much as you do. If we messed up, we have to make it right. You have my full backing."

"Thanks, Mac," said Jamison.

"I'll leave you to it, then." He disappeared back inside his office.

They proceeded to the room and Decker put the twin boxes down on the metal conference table. He took off his coat and slung it over a chair back.

Taking the top off one box, he said to Jamison, "I'll take this one. You go through the other." He slid it over to her.

"What exactly are we looking for?" she asked, opening the box.

"Hopefully you'll know it when you see it."

She sighed, sat down, and lifted out the first few files.

Four hours later they had each gone through both boxes.

"Not a whole lot here," noted Jamison.

"This is the defense's side of things. I've asked Mary to have someone pull the department's files."

"They keep things that long?"

"Probably only because nobody had the time to throw them out."

"Ken Finger didn't seem to have much evidence to go on."

"That's why the jury convicted his client after only two hours of deliberation. And an hour of that was spent at lunch."

"He was pretty tough on you on cross-examination," said Jamison, holding up a transcript of Decker's time in the witness box.

"That was his job."

"But you were quite firm in your statements."

"Because I believed them to be true."

"Meaning you no longer do?"

Decker looked at her over a piece of paper he was holding. "Meaning back then I didn't necessarily see the forest for the trees."

"Meaning?"

"Meaning I might have been so eager to get a conviction on my first homicide investigation that it didn't strike me as odd that a guy would burgle a house that early in the evening when it might be full of people."

"Well, maybe he wasn't that smart. As has been pointed out, he wasn't an experienced criminal. Maybe he didn't know how to properly case a target."

"Hawkins wasn't dumb. And the thing is, he had never been in any sort of trouble with the law before. That didn't mean much to me back then because the forensics were overwhelming. But to go from never having a parking ticket to four homicides is like going from hopping over a rain puddle to leaping across the Grand Canyon. It should have set off warning bells."

"But like everyone's been saying, he probably didn't go in there thinking he was going to kill anyone. Then it just went sideways."

"Granted, he was desperate. His wife needed pain medicine. His daughter was a drug addict he was trying to help. He might have felt he was up against a wall. He went there just to steal and, like you said, everything might have gone to hell after that."

"And he had the cash in his pocket."

"So if he had the money, why was he still wandering around when he was picked up by the cops?"

"Maybe he was trying to score the drugs to help his wife."

"Maybe," said Decker. "But the thing is, there was

a house next to the Richardses' that *was* empty that night. I'm not talking about the uninhabited one. I mean the Ballmers. They were out of town visiting relatives. Why not go there instead and break in and steal stuff, and avoid having to murder four people? And why did he pick that neighborhood of all places? It was a long way from where he lived."

"It was also isolated."

"I don't think that's a good enough reason."

"The guy who lived there was a banker. Maybe in Hawkins's mind that meant there would be valuable stuff to steal."

"I think that's a stretch. By no means was that the rich part of town. If you're a burglar, you don't go to skid row to do your business. You go where the money is."

"Well, rich people have security systems and extra locks and gates and sometimes private guards too. An area like where the Richardses lived might be more vulnerable."

He shook his head. "It doesn't make sense, Alex. Something is off."

"So despite your previous skepticism, now you're saying that you believe Hawkins to be innocent?"

"No, I'm just trying to get to the truth." He rose. "I'm going to check on the police files. You want some vending machine coffee? It sucks, but it's hot."

"Sure."

Decker walked out and down the hall. Two cops

and one detective he'd worked with greeted him as he passed by. They didn't look happy to see him here, and he could understand why. Word had gotten around. If Hawkins had been wrongly convicted, it would be a slap in the face to the whole department.

It'll be a punch in the gut to me. My first real homicide. Did I want it too bad? And did I screw over Meryl Hawkins to get there?

He was so preoccupied with his thoughts that he almost bumped into her.

Sally Brimmer hadn't changed very much. Early thirties, pretty, efficient-looking. And as he had thought before, the woman's slacks were still a little too tight and too many buttons on her blouse were undone, exhibiting enough cleavage to be intentionally suggestive. She was in public affairs at the police department. Decker had scammed her once, pretending to be an attorney to get a look-see at a prisoner being held here. That had placed her in a bad light with Captain Miller, among others. Decker had taken full responsibility for what he'd done and tried to make sure she was held blameless. However, by the put-out look on her face at seeing him, his actions had not been enough to soothe her harsh feelings for him.

"Ms. Brimmer," said Decker amiably.

Her hands were on her slim hips and a pouty look was perched on her lips. "I heard you were back. I hoped it was just a rumor that would turn out not to be true."

"Uh, okay. Nice to see you too."

"What are you doing here?"

"Working a case. And I need some department files. I thought I'd have them by now."

"You don't even work here anymore."

"I'm working with Mary Lancaster on a case. Captain Miller authorized it."

"You're not bullshitting me again," she said defiantly.

"Actually, it's the truth."

"Right. Fool me once . . ."

"Agent Decker, do you want these in the small conference room?"

They looked over to see a young uniformed officer wheeling a hand truck down the hall on which were stacked four large storage boxes.

"Yeah, thanks. My partner's in there now. I'm just on a coffee run."

Brimmer watched incredulously as the man headed down the hall to the conference room.

"So you *weren't* bullshitting me. Which case?"

"Meryl Hawkins."

"Don't remember it."

"Way before your time."

"Wait a minute. Wasn't that the guy who was just murdered?"

"Yep."

"But that's a current case."

"It is. The reason he was murdered probably goes back to four homicides that took place about thirteen years ago."

"How do you know that?"

"Because I was the one who investigated it."

"Four homicides? Who was the killer?"

"Well, that's the question, isn't it?"

He walked on in search of coffee and found it in the break room. Instead of vending machines, however, they had a Keurig. Times did change, and incremental progress was made. Decker prepared two coffees and was about to head back when his attention was caught by something on the TV that was bolted to the wall of the break room.

It was a local station and the weather report was just now coming on. The forecast was for late afternoon storms.

As soon as Decker heard that, something clicked in his head.

Rain.

10

"What are we doing here, Decker?" asked Jamison. "You never said." She added under her breath, "As usual."

Decker didn't appear to have heard her. He was staring at various spots in the living room of the Richardses' old home, particularly the floor. In his mind he dialed back to that night and laid what was there on top of what he was seeing right now.

And they tallied pretty much exactly.

"Rain."

"What?" said Jamison, looking confused.

"It rained the night of the murders at the Richardses' home. Bucketed down. Started at around six-fifteen and continued until after Lancaster and I got there. It was a whopper of a storm. Lots of thunder and lightning."

"Yeah, his lawyer mentioned that. So what?"

Decker pointed to the floor. "There were no wet footprints inside the house other than those of the first responders. No traces of mud or gravel. And Mary and I and the techs put on booties."

"So how could the killer, who clearly came after the rain was pouring down, have not left any wet marks on the floor or carpet?" She paused. "Wait a minute, you didn't think of this until now?"

Decker's eyes kept roaming the room.

"Decker, I asked you . . ."

"I *know* what you asked, Alex," he said heatedly.

She stiffened at his harsh words.

Not meeting her gaze, Decker said, "I found the print and the blood trace on the wall switch in the living room. It's where someone would put their hand if they were going to hit the light. We had the tech lift it. We ran the print through the databases and Hawkins's name got kicked out."

"Why was he in the system? Finger's files didn't say. You said he'd never been in trouble with the law before."

"His old job was with a company connected to a defense contractor. He'd had to pass a background check and have his prints on file because of his employment there."

"So from that point on?"

"Hawkins was our prime—well, really only—suspect."

"How long did all that take?"

"We got the ID on the print around one in the morning. We immediately went looking for Hawkins after getting his address. He wasn't home when we got there. But his wife and daughter were. They had no idea where he was."

"Where did you find him?"

"We put out a BOLO and a patrol car spotted him a couple hours later walking down a street over on the east side of town. They arrested him and brought him in to the station on suspicion of murder. Lancaster and I met him there."

"Walking? Didn't he have a car?"

"An old clunker. It was parked on the street in front of his house when we got there looking for him. We confirmed later it was the only car they owned. With the rain and cold temperatures, when we arrived, we couldn't tell if it had been driven recently or not. Although by the time we got there, it would have been hours after the murders were committed. The engine wouldn't have been warm anyway. But we later checked with neighbors and they told us the car had been there all day and night. Even so, we did check the car's exterior and tires for any trace from the Richardses' house, but if he had driven it back there after the murders the heavy rain would have washed anything like that away. We didn't have a warrant, so the interior of their house was going to have to wait to be searched."

"So what was Hawkins's story?"

In Decker's mind, he and Lancaster walked into the same interrogation room where they had interviewed Susan Richards. Same mustard yellow walls.

Same sort of person sitting in that chair. The accused. A hunted animal looking for a way out.

"He knew his rights. He wanted a lawyer. We told him one was on the way, but that if he wanted to answer some questions, it would help us eliminate him as a suspect. But if he didn't, that was okay too. We needed to legally cover our butts."

"Did you tell him you had his print at the crime scene?"

"We were holding that back as a trap. We'd gotten search warrants by then, so another team was tearing his house and car apart looking for any trace, and the gun used in the murder. As you know, they later found it behind a wall in his closet."

"Meaning he had to go back home and hide it. And his wife and daughter didn't know about this how?"

"Lisa Hawkins was really sick, of course, and slept in another bedroom. The daughter, Mitzi, answered the door basically in her underwear. She looked like crap. High as a kite on something. She could tell us nothing. We had to go to Mrs. Hawkins's bedroom to see her. She couldn't even get out of bed. She was basically in in-home hospice."

"Damn," said Jamison. "Last thing she needed was for this to drop in her lap."

"She was really upset. Wanted to know what was going on. But she was making no sense, and I'm not sure she could even process what we were telling her.

And her stoned daughter couldn't either. Between the two of them, Hawkins could have driven his car through the front of the house and I don't think they'd have noticed."

"Did Hawkins answer any questions?"

"The uniforms told him what he was charged with when they arrested him. But no other details. I told him basically what had gone down."

"What was his reaction?"

Now Decker's mind fully engaged with the memory. He was no longer in the Richardses' old home. He was in the interrogation room with the younger Lancaster sitting next to him and the still living Hawkins across from him. The man was tall and lean, but strongly built, before the cancer came to tear him down. His face was ruggedly handsome, and Decker remembered his hands being strong-looking and heavily callused. They could have easily strangled the life out of a young girl.

"Mr. Hawkins, while we're waiting for your PD to be assigned, can you clear up a few points for us?" said Decker. "It would be a big help, but you have the right to refuse to answer, just to be clear."

Hawkins settled his arms over his chest and said, "Like what?"

"Like where were you tonight between seven and nine-thirty or so?"

Hawkins scratched his cheek. "Taking a walk. Been

walking all night. Was doing that when your boys picked me up. No law against walking."

"In the pouring rain?"

Hawkins touched his wet clothes. "And here's the proof. When they picked me up, that's what I was doing. Honest to God."

"Where were you walking?"

"All over. Had to think."

"What about?"

"None of your beeswax." He paused. "And, hold on, they never told me who was killed."

Lancaster told him who and where.

"Hell, I don't know those people."

Decker said casually, "So you've never been to that house?"

"Never. No reason to."

"You see anybody on your walk who can corroborate your story?"

"Nope. It was raining. Nobody was dumb enough to be outside, except me."

"You ever been to the American Grill on Franklin Street?" asked Lancaster.

"I don't eat out much. Can't afford it."

"You ever run into the owner?"

"And who's that?"

"David Katz."

"Never hearda him."

Lancaster described him.

"Nope, doesn't ring a bell with me."

A far slimmer Ken Finger, Hawkins's court-appointed attorney, arrived just then, and Hawkins was compelled to open his mouth and provide a court-ordered cheek swab of his DNA.

Hawkins asked Decker what he was going to do with that sample.

"None of your beeswax," Decker replied.

Decker looked at Jamison after describing this back-and-forth to her. "And later that morning, the search team found the gun hidden behind a loose section of wall in Hawkins's closet. Ballistics matched the bullets taken out at the postmortem."

"And the DNA from the cheek swab?"

"It took a while to get the results back, but they matched the trace under Abigail Richards's fingernails.

"Case closed at that point."

"Apparently."

Decker looked at the floor again. "Except for no traces from the rain."

"He could have had another pair of shoes and socks with him. He could have taken off his shoes and left them outside. And changed into the dry shoes."

Decker shook his head. "No."

"Why not?"

"Look at the porch."

Jamison stepped to the window and looked at the small-roofed porch with open sides.

Decker said, "Mary and I got soaked going in, and

that porch offered almost no protection. And I don't see Hawkins having the foresight to bring an extra pair of shoes and socks. And how could he take the time to stop and change out of his shoes before breaking into a house with a bunch of people in it? Anybody could have looked out the front door or window and seen him. And hell, he'd have to have brought another set of clothes and a hair dryer before he set foot inside. Otherwise, there would have been traces."

"Is there another way into the house that he could have used?"

"None that wouldn't leave us with the same problem as now."

"He could have cleaned up his wet traces on his way out."

"After murdering four people he's going to take the time to do that? And from all the different places he had to be in the house to kill them all? And there's carpet too, so he's going to what, get out a steam cleaner and fire it up and get rid of every single bit of mud, wet gravel, soaked blades of grass?"

"But, Decker, you know the alternative if that is the case."

Decker glanced over at her. "Yeah, that Hawkins was right, and I was wrong. He was innocent. And I put him away in prison. And now he's dead."

"That wasn't your fault."

"The hell it isn't," said Decker.

11

There was no place on earth colder than a morgue.

At least Decker was thinking that as he looked down at the body of Meryl Hawkins on the metal table. The ME had drawn back the sheet so that Hawkins's emaciated body was completely exposed. On one side of Decker stood Jamison. On the other was Lancaster.

The ME said, "As I noted, the cause of death was a small-caliber soft-nosed or dumdum bullet. It deformed after cleaving through the skull and then cartwheeled through the soft tissue, breaking up more as it did so, just as it's designed to do." He pointed to the man's brain that was sitting on another table. "You can see that it did considerable damage. Hawkins would have died instantly. Round was still in the soft tissue. In fragments. That's why I can't give you a more exact answer as to caliber."

"And no way to do a ballistics comparison if we do find a gun to test?" said Lancaster.

"Afraid not. As I said, it's just metal slivers and chunks dispersed over a wide area of the brain. Like a bomb exploded. Really no spiral lands or grooves from the gun barrel left to match it to, unfortunately." He added, "There were also traces of polyurethane foam and microbeads embedded in the wound and brain tissue."

"What?" said Jamison, looking puzzled.

Decker said, "The killer used a pillow to muffle the shot."

"Cheap version of a muzzle suppressor," added Lancaster. "The burn marks on his forehead would have been even more pronounced if the killer hadn't used the pillow. It was pretty close to a contact wound."

"They must've cleaned up the trace and taken the pillow with them," said Decker. "There was no sign of it in the room."

Decker pointed to the man's forearms. "They're healed now, of course, but that's where the scratches were, presumably from Abigail Richards trying to fight him off."

Lancaster added, "After he was arrested and jailed, we noted the wounds on his arms. Hawkins said he'd fallen down and scraped both arms. He'd cleaned them up and bandaged them before he was arrested. If any of Abigail Richards's DNA was on him, that probably would've removed it. In fact, we found none. But we did find his DNA on her."

Jamison said, "And that seems to be rock-solid

evidence of his guilt. I mean, he was there. She tried to fight him off. He was good for the murders."

"Yeah," said Decker. "And all we have against that is a guy who said he was innocent and now he's dead."

Lancaster said, "Do you think it could be that Hawkins *did* commit the murders but wasn't alone? He had an accomplice and now that accomplice killed him before he could reveal his identity?"

"He's had thirteen years to do that," pointed out Decker. "And you'd think Hawkins would have fingered an accomplice at his trial, if for no other reason than to cut a deal. And there's something else." He told Lancaster about his rain theory. He added, "Rain residue and other trace from the storm should have been found at the crime scene but wasn't."

Lancaster seemed taken aback by this. "I . . . I never focused on that."

"Neither did I, until now."

"Crap, Decker."

"Yeah."

"What's that on his forearm?" asked Jamison.

The ME, a short, balding man in his fifties, pulled an overhead lamp on a long flex arm closer and turned it on, hitting that spot.

"Yes, I noted that," he said. "Let's take a closer look."

The marks on Hawkins's arm were black and dark green and brown. A casual observer might have concluded that they were bruises. Only they weren't. Closer inspection under the intense light revealed clearly what they were.

"It's a tattoo," said Decker. "Or several tattoos."

"That's what I concluded too," said the ME. "But poorly done ones. I mean, my daughter has one and it's far nicer than these."

Decker opined, "That's because these were done in prison with very crude instruments and whatever they could find to use as ink."

"How do you know it wasn't done before he went to prison?" asked Jamison.

"Because I saw his forearms thirteen years ago. Several times. No tats." Decker leaned down and looked at the marks from a few inches away. "Looks like they used paper clips or maybe staples. That tat looks like they used soot mixed with shampoo for the ink. The other two seem to be Styrofoam that's been melted. Those are pretty popular choices for inmate tats."

"Didn't know you were such an expert on prison tattoos," said Jamison.

"Decker and I have visited our share of prisons over the years," noted Lancaster. "Seen a lot of convict skin with body art. Some cool, some hideous."

Decker was still looking at the tat. "It's a spiderweb."

"Trapped," said Lancaster.

"What?" asked Jamison.

"Symbolizes being trapped in prison," explained Decker. "It's referring to their prison sentence."

"That looks like a teardrop," observed Jamison, pointing to the mark near the crook of the elbow.

Decker nodded. "Right, it is."

"What does that mean?"

Lancaster and Decker exchanged a glance. He said in a subdued tone, "Sometimes, it denotes that the person has been raped in prison. Usually it's inked on the face; where everyone can see it."

"Damn," said Jamison.

Decker closed his eyes and felt sick to his stomach.

And I helped put you there because maybe I didn't do a thorough enough investigation.

Jamison was watching Decker and put a hand on his arm. His eyes popped open and he abruptly moved away from her. He didn't notice her hurt look at his reaction.

Lancaster examined the last mark that was to the right of the teardrop. "I've never seen one like that before, though," she said.

"Looks like a star with an arrow going through it," said Jamison. She looked at Decker. "Any ideas?"

"Not yet," he replied. He looked at the ME. "How far along was his cancer?"

The ME shuddered. "Advanced. If the bullet didn't get him, my guess is he had a few weeks left. Actually, I'm surprised he was still able to function."

"He said he was on street meds," said Jamison.

"The tox screens will show what was in his system. He had nothing in his stomach, no food or anything, I mean. I would imagine his appetite would have been negligible at that point. But he must have been a strong man to keep going with that level of cancer in him."

Decker said, "Well, maybe wanting to prove his innocence gave him that strength."

"Anything else of interest?" asked Lancaster.

"We've got his clothes over there in those evidence bags."

Lancaster looked at Decker. "He also had a small duffel. We've got it at the station. Nothing much in it, but you'll probably want to go through it."

Decker nodded as he continued to stare down at the body.

Three tats. The spiderweb looked to be the oldest. That made sense. When Hawkins had first got to prison, he was probably pissed beyond belief, if he was indeed innocent. The web tat would have been one of his few ways to vocalize that anger. The teardrop tat probably came soon thereafter. Fresh meat in prisons did not remain fresh for long.

Then there was the unidentified one. Star with an arrow through it. He would have to find out what that one meant. Because that one looked to be the most recent. Decker could tell because Hawkins had recently lost weight, probably because of his illness.

The other two tats showed signs of his shrinking weight, and the corresponding change in the width of his forearm. The star, though, evinced no signs of this. And the markings looked fresher too. He might have had it done right before he left prison, in fact.

And if he'd had this tat put on close to when he was released it might have held some significance for him at that time.

And since Decker had missed there being no muddy footprints in the house, he was determined to not miss anything else on this case.

Homicide detectives rarely got do-overs. He wasn't going to screw this one up.

Again.

12

It wasn't much.

Decker was at police headquarters staring at it. The duffel held a few items of clothing. A bus ticket for Hawkins's ride from prison. A wallet with some cash. Some paperwork from the prison that Hawkins had drawn graffiti over.

There was a dog-eared paperback book by a writer Decker had never heard of. It had a garish cover of a man holding a knife against a scantily clad woman's throat. It was straight out of a Mickey Spillane yarn from the 1950s, he thought.

There was also a photo in the wallet of Hawkins's daughter, Mitzi.

Her last name was now Gardiner, Lancaster had found out. She lived in Trammel, Ohio, about a two-hour car ride from Burlington. She'd been in her late twenties when her father went to prison. Lancaster had also learned that she was now married and the mother of a six-year-old boy.

The picture of Mitzi was from when she'd been in elementary school. Decker knew it was her because Hawkins had written his daughter's name and age on the back of the photo. And Hawkins had written there, "Daddy's Little Star." That might be the reason Hawkins had the star tat on his arm. The photo obviously represented far happier times for the Hawkins family. Mitzi looked bright and innocent, all cheeks and smiles, as kids did at that age.

And then the dream had shattered. She had grown up to be a drug addict and petty criminal to finance her habit. She'd done short stints in jail, and longer ones in rehab. The little girl with the limitless future was no more.

Yet apparently she had finally gotten her life together.

Good for you, thought Decker. But he also knew that he would have to talk to her. Her father might have gotten in touch with her after being released from prison.

Lancaster walked in and looked at the pile of items on the table.

"Nothing?"

Decker shook his head. "Got a question."

"Okay."

Lancaster sat down and popped a stick of gum into her mouth.

"Stick to the gum and quit the smokes," advised Decker.

Her lips pursed. "Thanks *Dr.* Decker. So what's your question?"

"Who called it in?"

"What?"

"Who called in the disturbance at the Richardses' house that night?"

"You know we never found out the answer to that."

"Well, I think we need to find it out now."

"How?" she said incredulously. "It's been too long."

"At the time, I read the transcript of the call and listened to the recording as well. The caller was a female. She said she'd heard a disturbance at the house. The cops were sent out and arrived shortly thereafter. Then so did we once the homicides were confirmed."

"That we know."

"But how did the caller know there was a disturbance? The call didn't come from the landlines at the neighboring homes. It didn't come from any traceable cell phone. So where?"

"I guess we weren't too focused on that. We just thought it was a Good Samaritan passing by."

"A *convenient* Samaritan, anyway. And one who is passing by in a monsoon down a dead-end road? Why go down there unless you lived there?"

Lancaster thought about this for a few moments. "And then once we got there all signs pointed to Hawkins once you found the print."

Decker nodded because he knew this was true. And it was grating on him beyond belief.

"Okay," he said. "We need to go over this case from square one. No predisposition that Hawkins was good for it. Fresh eyes, wide open."

"Decker, it's been over thirteen years."

"I don't care if it's been thirteen hundred years, Mary," he snapped. "We need to make this right."

She studied him for a long moment. "You're never going to get over it, are you?"

"Don't know what you're talking about."

"Yes you do."

Decker stared at her moodily. "I need you one hundred percent on this."

"Okay, Decker, but please keep in mind that I've got a slew of other cases to work on, not just Hawkins's murder."

Decker scowled. "This has to be your priority, Mary. If the guy really didn't do it, we screwed his life up, sent him to prison where it looks like he was raped, and then let somebody murder him."

"We didn't *let* anyone murder him," she retorted.

"We might as well have," Decker shot back.

"Problem?"

They both looked over at Jamison standing in the doorway.

Lancaster finally drew her gaze from Decker. "Just two former partners having a discussion." She turned back to Decker. "I'm sorry, Amos. I will work this case as much as I can with you. But my plate is pretty damn full."

"What about your saying it was good working together, like old times?"

"We don't live in old times. We live in the present." She paused and added, "At least I do, because I don't have a choice."

Decker gazed at her stonily.

Jamison said, "Decker, have you heard back from Bogart?"

"He still hasn't called you?"

"No. But he's good with us staying here and working on the case?"

"No, he's not. So you better pack up and head back to D.C."

"When did you hear that?"

Decker didn't answer.

"Decker?"

"A while back."

"And you didn't think to mention it?"

"I'm mentioning it now. I'll see you back in D.C. at some point."

"But you mean you're staying? Decker, you can't."

"Watch me."

He stalked out.

Jamison looked down at Lancaster, who sat in the chair still slowly chewing her gum.

"What the hell is going on with him?" Jamison said. "If he disobeys orders he's going to blow up his career at the Bureau."

Lancaster stood. "Amos Decker has always had

priorities. But his 'career' has never been one of them."

"I know, he just wants to find the truth. He always says that."

Lancaster glanced toward the door. "I actually think he just wants to find some peace. And all of this"—she paused and looked around the room—"all this is just how he survives with more guilt on his shoulders than any person has a right to bear. And what happened to Meryl Hawkins just added a shitload more, because he obviously blames himself for what happened. It's just how he's wired. God, I wish I'd never told Hawkins where Decker was." She touched Jamison on the shoulder. "It was good to see you, Alex."

Lancaster followed Decker out, leaving Jamison alone.

13

Decker sat on a red park bench in the town of his birth.

Burlington, Ohio, warts and all.

It had been crushed when most of the factories closed up decades before. Then it had made a comeback of sorts. Then the recession had come and knocked it down again.

Now it was slowly coming back.

He wondered when the next knockdown would come. It always seemed to.

Jamison had sent him a half dozen texts after she'd left town, and he'd ignored them all. Part of him felt bad about this. None of this was about Jamison. This was all about Amos Decker, he knew.

You're never going to get over it, are you?

Lancaster's words had ripped into him like that round into Hawkins's brain.

You never are going to get over their deaths, are you, Amos? How can you? It was your fault.

He had sat on this bench before, just as now, when fall was speedily giving over to winter in the Ohio

Valley. Back then he'd been making a feeble living as a private investigator. He'd been sitting here awaiting a man and a woman who were headed toward a cocktail lounge that was no longer in business. He had been paid by the woman's wealthy father to convince the con artist creep who had won her heart to leave town. He had been successful. It wasn't that hard, since the man thought himself far smarter and slicker than he actually was. He never counted on running into Amos Decker, who finished him off in a few easy moves of chess play.

While waiting for the couple he had observed those moving around him, making deductions and grafting them onto his memory. He used to refer to his memory as his personal, wired-in DVR. Now he had updated the term to fit modern times.

I have a personal cloud in my head where all my data is kept safe and secure until I want to pull it out.

Two young men walked past arguing about something. Decker noted the clenched hand of the one on the left, in which years ago there would have been five-dollar bags of crack. Now he suspected the dude had some opioid pills that he was trying to sell. The dude on the right was arguing price, no doubt. In his hand was a fistful of Jacksons, in his back pocket a snort bottle of Narcan. In the event of overdose, which was pretty much inevitable, users were bringing their "back to life" medication with them so that a passerby could stick it up their nose and give it a squirt. Thus they would live another day to die once more.

Such was life in the twenty-first century.

He floated this image up to his personal cloud and went in search of others.

He found it in a woman pulling into a parking space on the street in front of what used to be a service station and was now a CrossFit facility. She climbed out dressed in tight workout clothes and slung a bag over her shoulder, her face glued to her smartphone screen and with ear buds in. He looked over her car. The parking permit on her front bumper identified where she lived, for any potential bad guy to see and follow.

He wanted to tell her to find another way to do the parking thing, and not to be so oblivious about her surroundings while she eagerly examined her critically important social media happenings. But he figured she'd just call the cops on him for harassing her.

This scene was dutifully uploaded to his cloud for no apparent reason other than it always went there.

Last shot. An elderly couple walked by, hand in hand. He looked a bit younger than she, perhaps in his early eighties. Her hand was trembling, and she had a tremor along one side of her face. The other side drooped. Either Bell's palsy or she'd previously suffered a stroke. The man had hearing aids in both ears and what looked to be a melanoma growing on his nose. And yet they shuffled slowly along together. Growing old, nearing the end, and still in love. That was the way it was supposed to work.

Decker tried but failed to *not* upload that to his cloud. But he did try to stick it in a particularly remote part of his memory.

So, with Jamison gone, he was alone again. In some ways, he preferred it. He had been on his own after his family had been taken from him. And he had survived.

Maybe it was for the best. Maybe he was destined for a solitary existence. It just felt more comfortable.

He shifted his sole focus to the problem at hand.

Meryl Hawkins. Decker had approximately one million questions and not nearly that many answers. In fact, he had none at all. But he was not parked on this bench merely for his health, or for the sake of nostalgia.

He had spoken to one widow, Susan Richards. Now he was awaiting another.

Rachel Katz walked down the pavement a few minutes later. She and David Katz had never had any children. She lived alone in a condo downtown. It was a luxury loft in an old factory building. Decker had learned that she still worked as a CPA and had her own practice. And she still owned the American Grill. Her office was a five-minute walk from her loft.

Several years younger than her late husband, she

was now forty-four. A striking-looking woman when Decker had first met her all those years ago, she had aged exceptionally well. Her blonde hair was still long and skimmed her shoulders. She was tall and fit, with a swagger to her walk. She moved like she owned the world—or at least Burlington, Ohio.

She was dressed in a black jacket with a white cuffed shirt underneath and a long skirt. Her choice of lipstick was flaming red, her fingernails the same shade. The briefcase she carried lightly smacked against her thigh as she walked.

A couple of construction workers catcalled out to her as she passed by. Katz ignored them.

Decker heaved himself off the bench and went to work.

Just like old times.

14

She looked up at him, recognition flitting across her features as he stopped her on the sidewalk.

"I remember you."

"Amos Decker. I investigated the death of your husband when I worked on the Burlington police force."

"That's right." She frowned. "And I heard on the news that the man who killed him came back to town. And that he was found murdered."

"That's right. Meryl Hawkins."

She shuddered. "Well, I can't say that I was sorry. But I thought he was in prison for life. What was he doing here? The news didn't say."

"They let him out because he was terminally ill with cancer."

She had no reaction to this. "And what are you doing here?" she asked.

"I just have some questions for you."

"Do you still work for the police? I thought I heard that you left town."

"I work for the FBI now. But I'm still a sworn

officer in Ohio." He showed her his official credentials.

"And what exactly are you investigating?"

"Hawkins's murder. And that of your husband and the other victims at the Richardses' that night."

She shook her head, looking confused. "We *know* who killed my husband and the Richards family. Meryl Hawkins."

"We're taking another look at it."

"Why?"

"There are some anomalies we need to sort out."

"What sort of anomalies?"

"Do you want to go somewhere to discuss this rather than out on the street? Or we can go down to the police station."

She looked around at several passersby staring at them. "My condo is right over here."

He followed her into the building, which had a concierge, and they rode up in an elevator to her floor.

"Didn't know they had places like this in Burlington," noted Decker as they walked down the plush corridor. "At least they didn't when I lived here."

"We just completed this a year ago. I'm actually involved with the development company that renovated this building. We're working on two others. And I'm also working with another group in several new projects around town and a slew of businesses, including some restaurants. We have big plans for Burlington."

"Economy finally turning around?"

"Seems to be. We hope to get several large companies to come here. We're really rolling out the red carpet. Two Fortune 1000s have already started building regional headquarters in the area. And a high-tech start-up just opened its headquarters downtown, which brought in a lot of young, affluent people. It's a lot cheaper to live here than in, say, Chicago. And we enticed a hospital system to build a new facility. And we're well along to getting a parts supplier to the Big Three in Detroit to build a new factory on the north side of town. Those people have to live, shop, and eat out somewhere. New restaurants and places to live downtown are already popping up, in addition to what I'm working on. So, yes, things *are* looking up."

"Great."

They entered her condo, which had an open floor plan and lots of twenty-foot windows. Decker watched as Katz used a remote to open the shades to let in the fading light.

"Beautiful place," he observed, looking at all the expensive architectural details, like exposed beams and repointed brick walls, slate floors, high-dollar appliances in the kitchen, and oil and acrylic paintings on the wall. The furniture was big enough not to be overwhelmed by the large footprint, with several comfortable seating areas laid out.

"It was featured in *Luxe*," she said. "That's a design magazine," she added when Decker looked blankly at her. "Targeted to the very affluent." She paused. "Sorry if that sounded snooty."

"No problem. I'm just not very knowledgeable about that stuff. And I've never been affluent."

"Well, I wasn't born with a silver spoon. And being a CPA, I work about a hundred hours a week."

"You must have gotten off early today, then. It's not yet five. I was expecting to be waiting longer before I saw you coming home."

"This is just a little break for me. I head back to the office in a couple hours for a client meeting. And then I have an event later tonight. I was hoping to catch up on a few domestic chores right now, so if we could get down to what you wanted?"

She sat down on a couch and motioned for Decker to sit in a chair opposite.

"So what anomalies were you referring to?"

"I can't get into specifics because it's an ongoing investigation. I can tell you that Meryl Hawkins came back to town to ask the police to reopen the investigation."

"Reopen it. Why?"

"Because he said he was innocent."

Katz's features turned ugly. "So you're taking the

word of a murderer to reopen the investigation? Are you kidding me?"

"No, not just that. There are the anomalies I mentioned."

"And that you won't specify. So what do you want with me?" she said abruptly.

"Can you tell me why your husband was there that night?"

"Good God, I already testified to this."

"It would just take a minute. And you might remember something you hadn't before."

Katz let out a long, annoyed sigh and crossed her arms and legs. "It was a long time ago."

"Just whatever you can remember," prompted Decker.

"Don Richards was the loan officer at the bank, so David knew him. He'd been instrumental in getting the loan for the American Grill construction. My husband was very ambitious. That was one trait that drew me to him. He wanted to make a lot of money and also do things to help bolster the community. I appreciated that."

"When did you two meet?"

"Shortly after the Grill opened." She got a far-off look on her face and smiled. "We were set up on a blind date, of all things. We were both so busy, it was hard to find time to meet people. We hit it off right away and were married six months later."

"And as you said, you still own the American Grill?"

"Yes. It was in both my and David's names. It passed to me after Hawkins *murdered* him."

"Has it been profitable for you?"

"We've had good and bad years. Right now it's doing okay."

"So, as far as you know, your husband was just there that night to shoot the breeze with Don Richards? Or was it about business?"

"I don't know. I told you that before. I didn't even know he was going over there that night. They might have been talking about some business projects, because David had several things going on at that time, and Don was his main contact at the bank. But I don't know why he would have done that at Don's home." She added icily, "As you know, David never came home alive, so he couldn't tell me what they discussed. I thought we'd be together for life. Turned out it was only for a short time."

"Had your husband become friends with Mr. Richards? Did you and his wife hang out with each other?"

"No, nothing like that. They had kids. We didn't. And they were older. And David and I were working all the time. We didn't have time for friends, really."

"And you were *working* that night, correct?"

"I'd just started my own CPA firm. I was burning the proverbial midnight oil." She frowned. "Until I got the call from the police. I couldn't believe it. I thought it was some awful prank." She paused and glanced up at Decker. "I had to identify his body. Have you ever had to do that? ID the body of someone you loved?"

"I'm sure it was very hard," Decker replied quietly.

She suddenly gazed hard at him. "Wait a minute. Oh my God, that happened to you. Your family. I remember now. It was all over the news."

"Doesn't matter," said Decker. "Your husband's wallet and wristwatch were missing. And a gold ring with encrusted diamonds he wore."

She nodded. "I gave that ring to him. For what turned out to be his *last* birthday," she added coldly.

"Anything else you can remember that might help me?"

"I don't want to help you," she said candidly. "Because Meryl Hawkins killed my husband. We were going to have a family. We were going places. We talked about moving to Chicago. I mean, a place like Burlington can only take you so far."

"Then why are you still here?" asked Decker just as bluntly.

"I . . . My husband is buried here."

Decker's features softened. "I can understand that."

She stood. "I really need to get going, so if there's nothing else?"

Decker rose from his chair. "Thank you for your time."

"I'm not going to wish you luck. And I'm glad that Hawkins is dead."

"One more question. Can you tell me where you were between eleven and midnight on the night Meryl Hawkins was murdered?"

She blanched. "Do you really believe I had anything to do with his murder?"

"I don't know. It's why I'm asking. But if you have an alibi, it would be good to get it out there. The police are going to ask you for one."

"Why?"

"Because he was back in town and you believe he killed your husband. If it makes you feel any better, we asked Susan Richards the same thing."

"And did *she* have an alibi?"

Decker didn't answer.

"When was it again?" she asked, evidently upset.

He told her.

She stood there rocking back and forth. "I'll have to check my schedule and see what I can find. I'm so busy I have a hard time remembering what I was doing an hour ago."

As he headed to the door, she called out after him. "Why are you really doing this?"

He turned back, his hand on the doorknob. "There're enough guilty people in the world without us making an innocent person one."

"Do you really think Hawkins was innocent?" she said skeptically.

"That's what I'm going to find out."

"You sound confident. But it's been a long time. Memories fade."

"I don't have that problem," said Decker.

15

He finally answered the phone. He really had no choice. It had now been a while since she'd left town.

"Hello, Alex."

"Well, it's about damn time," she barked.

"I've been busy."

"So have I. The team's leaving to go work on a case in New Hampshire. Plane takes off in an hour."

"Good luck on it."

"Bogart is not happy."

"I'm sure he has every right to be pissed at me."

"You're just placating me. I was calling to see if you wanted to join us in New Hampshire. I checked on flights. There's one you can catch out of Cleveland, with a layover in Newark."

"I can't do that, Alex. I'm working the case here."

"Well, get in good with your old friends at the police force there. I'm not sure you'll have a job at the FBI when you get back."

"I guess I can understand that."

"Nobody wants that, Amos. I hope you know that."

"I do."

"Good luck, with *everything* you're doing up there."

She clicked off and Decker put down his phone and stared at it for a long moment. He was suddenly hungry. And he knew exactly where he wanted to eat.

The place was only about a quarter full when he got there, even though it was the dinner hour. He had noticed some new eateries that had opened up on his walk over here. Maybe they were taking business away from the American Grill.

He was shown to a table and sat down. He glanced at his menu and then scanned the interior.

Waiters and waitresses were making the rounds of the tables. Other wait staff stood against the wall conversing.

His gaze passed one table and then came back to it, his attention suddenly riveted on the couple sitting there. It was Earl Lancaster, Mary's husband. He was there with a woman, only it wasn't his wife. Earl had started out as a construction laborer before becoming a contractor. He had the build of a man who used his muscle for a living. He was about six feet tall, with a Marine buzz cut, thick arms, and a broad chest. He was dressed in an untucked white long-sleeved shirt and dress jeans. A pair of black loafers were on his feet. His companion was in her early forties with a slim build, long, soft brown hair, green eyes, and a pleasant smile as she peered lovingly into Earl's face.

Earl broke off looking at her, gazed around the restaurant, and flinched when he saw Decker staring at him. He said something to the woman, jumped up, and headed over to Decker's table. Decker noted that the woman watched him the whole way.

Earl sat down across from Decker.

"Amos, I heard you were in town. Mary told me."

"Is that right?" said Decker, letting his gaze linger for a moment longer on the woman before looking at Earl.

The man seemed embarrassed. He put his hands together on the tabletop and stared down at them.

"Guess you're wondering what's going on."

"I am, but it's also none of my business."

"Fact is, Mary and I are splitting up."

"Really?" said Decker. "I'm sorry to hear that. And who's your friend over there?"

Earl glanced up. "I know what you're thinking."

"I doubt it."

"Mary initiated this whole thing, Amos. It wasn't my idea. But I have a life to live."

"What about Sandy?"

"We're splitting custody, but I'll have her more. Mary's schedule is too crazy."

"And she's okay with that?"

"She suggested it."

"What's going on with her? Why the divorce? Why letting you get Sandy? This isn't making sense."

Earl looked uncomfortable. "She's a cop. She's got . . . It's a lot of pressure."

"Do you want to get divorced, Earl?"

"I don't have a choice, do I? It's not like I can stop her."

Decker glanced at the woman again. She smiled, but when he didn't return it, she abruptly looked away.

"Well, regardless, I think *you've* already made your choice."

Earl's features turned angry. "I don't need to be judged by you, okay?"

"I'm not judging anybody. I'm simply making an observation. If I'm wrong, tell me so and I'll say I'm sorry."

Earl's anger dissipated. "Look, it's true, Nancy and I are seeing each other. But Mary and I stopped . . . well, we stopped living really as husband and wife a while back. If you know what I mean. And I didn't start seeing her until Mary told me our marriage was over. I swear to God."

"I believe you. And how is Sandy taking it?"

"She doesn't really understand."

"I think she probably understands more than you think."

"We'll get by. We have to."

"No argument there. Hope everything works out for you. All of you," he added.

"I know why you're in town. Mary told me. The Hawkins case. You know one of the victims, David Katz, owned this place?"

Decker nodded. "And now his widow does. You know Rachel Katz?"

"Yeah, I know her. She's involved in lots of projects around town."

"She apparently has big plans for Burlington."

"Well, the town needs a shot of energy. Glad she's doing what she's doing."

"Okay," said Decker.

"I, uh, better be getting back. Good to see you, Amos."

"Yeah."

Earl retreated to his table, where Decker watched him and the woman named Nancy talking and snatching glances at him. He picked up his menu and waved the waitress over after he'd made his decision. She was in her thirties, tall and skinny. A young man was behind her. She introduced him as Daniel, a trainee. He looked to be in his twenties, with dark hair and sharply defined features. He smiled shyly and then watched the waitress, his order pad held out like hers.

When Decker ordered, she smiled and wrote it down. "That's a lot of food."

"Well, I'm a lot of guy," replied Decker.

Daniel laughed along with the waitress.

When his meal came, he ate it methodically, all the while looking around the restaurant. When Earl and his friend left, they did not look in his direction, for which Decker was glad. He was not adept at these moments. Things he could say before his brain injury were impossible to get out now, even if the underlying emotions were inside him. Or else he would blurt out the wrong thing and make everyone uncomfortable.

Mary divorcing. So that was the explanation for her odd behavior. He felt sorry for both Earl and her. Yet he felt sorriest of all for Sandy. He would like to talk to Mary about it but was afraid he would just botch it.

He finished his meal and ordered a cup of coffee. Whenever the door opened, a chilly wind leaked into the space. He would have to get a heavier coat if he was going to stay here much longer. He wasn't that far removed from the days when the only clothes he had were the ones he was wearing.

As he was drinking his coffee, a voice said, "Why do I think you're not really here for the food?"

Decker looked up to see Captain Miller standing next to his table. He was dressed in a suit, but his necktie was loosened. He might have just come from work.

He sat down across from Decker.

Decker said, "I saw Earl. And his lady friend, Nancy."

Miller slowly nodded. "Okay. Then you know."

"I know they're getting divorced. And I heard his side of things. Not Mary's."

"Then you need to ask Mary for her take, if you want to. I suggested that to you back at the police station. So, any startling revelations come to you about this restaurant since you were here last?"

"The coffee still sucks."

"Anything else?"

Decker looked around the mostly empty space.

"Why does Rachel Katz still own it?"

16

Cocoon, thought Decker.

At their meeting Rachel Katz had crossed her arms and legs before settling in to answer his more serious questions. People often cocooned like that when they were getting ready to lie, or at least be evasive. It was as though they were wrapping themselves in themselves, to keep everyone else out. It was an instinctual physical reaction with people, and even though it wasn't a foolproof indicator of someone lying, Decker had found it pretty accurate.

So, what was she lying or being evasive about?

He filed that query away since he had no way to answer it yet.

He was presently standing in front of the Richardses' old house. But he was looking at another house that was two homes over from the Richardses'. This was the only house that was still occupied by the people who had lived here when the murders occurred. Back then Decker had interviewed them and the other neighbors. Out of that he had gotten a big fat zero's worth of help. He hoped the second time was the charm, because Decker seriously doubted he would get a third bite at the apple.

"Mr. DeAngelo, do you remember me?"

Decker stared down at the short, balding, rotund man in his sixties who had opened the door at his knock. Though it was chilly outside he was dressed in a stained undershirt that emphasized his potbelly, and khaki pants with the zipper partially open. He had a cloth napkin in his hand and was wiping his mouth.

He looked quizzically at Decker before recognition breached his features.

"You're that detective. Pecker?"

"Decker. Amos Decker."

"Right, right."

Decker glanced at the napkin. "Looks like I interrupted your dinner."

"No, we were just finishing up. Come on in."

DeAngelo closed the door behind Decker, whose nostrils were immediately assailed with the mingled aromas of garlic and pesto.

"Smells good," he said as he glanced around the tidy interior.

"You want some? Ma made plenty. Always does." He playfully grabbed his belly. "Why I'm so fat."

"No, thanks. I already ate."

"Ma?" called out DeAngelo. "Look who's here."

A petite, gray-haired woman came out from the kitchen drying her hands on a dishtowel. She wore a full apron over her skirt and blouse.

"Mrs. DeAngelo, I'm Amos Decker. I used to work as a detective on the local police force."

"That's right. I remember." She looked him up and down. "Heard you moved."

"I did, but now I'm back. At least for a little while."

"Well, come in and sit, sit," said Mrs. DeAngelo. "Would you like some wine?"

"Sure, that'd be great. Thanks."

She brought the wine and poured out three glasses and they all sat in the small living room that held the exact same furniture as the last time Decker had been here.

"We're retired now," said DeAngelo. "Well, I am. Ma always took care of the kids and the house. Hell, worked harder than I ever did, taking care of them."

"Now I just have to look after you," said his wife with a knowing smile at Decker.

DeAngelo said, "We're thinking of selling the place. Kids are all grown and gone off with their own families. Maybe get a condo down in Florida. I can't take too many more Ohio winters. Gets into your bones."

"I hear you," said Decker.

The couple fell silent and looked at him, apparently waiting for him to explain what he was doing there. Decker felt this curious scrutiny while he sipped his wine.

"I suppose you heard about Meryl Hawkins?" he began.

DeAngelo nodded. "Strangest damn thing. Thought he was in prison for life. Then he's here and then he gets killed. Is that why you're back?"

"Sort of, yes."

"Are you looking for who killed him?" asked Mrs. DeAngelo anxiously.

"Yes, and I'm looking at something else too."

"What's that?" she asked.

"If Meryl Hawkins didn't kill your neighbors all those years ago, who did?"

The DeAngelos had both raised their wineglasses to take a sip. And both of them nearly spilled their drinks.

DeAngelo said, "I don't understand. That Hawkins fellow *did* kill them. That was proven."

"He was convicted of the murders, that's true," said Decker.

"But isn't that the same thing?" asked Mrs. DeAngelo.

"Usually yes," conceded Decker. "But not in all cases. I'm taking a fresh look at the case. You two are the only ones left who lived here when the killings took place."

DeAngelo nodded. "That's right. The Murphys moved to Georgia. And the Ballmers retired to, where was it again, hon?"

"Hilton Head."

"And the other house was empty," noted Decker.

"That's right. Been empty for a while. It's empty

again, though a couple families have come and gone in between. There was a family moved into the Richards house, but they didn't stay all that long."

"Wouldn't catch me moving in there," said Mrs. DeAngelo. "I'd have nightmares all the time. I did anyway after what happened."

"So that night you reported you didn't hear or see anything," said Decker.

"That's right," replied DeAngelo. "Raining like crazy. Thunder and lightning, and the wind. Holy Jesus. I remember it clear as day. We were afraid we'd get a tornado."

"And yet you still managed to fall asleep in front of the TV," his wife reminded him. "We were watching some movie."

"*Blade Runner*," said Decker. "That's what you said."

"That's right," said DeAngelo, looking impressed. "You've got a good memory."

"So nothing you can remember from that night?"

Mrs. DeAngelo said, "Well, I saw that one car come in. Oh, it was before the storm. I was just finishing making dinner. Saw it pass by when I was looking out the window. I told you all that."

"That would be David Katz's car. A four-door Mercedes sedan. Silver."

"Yes, that's right. Beautiful car."

"Probably cost more than our house," commented DeAngelo.

"And you didn't see him get out of the car when he got to the Richardses'?"

"No. Where I was standing in the kitchen, my view is blocked by the house in between ours."

"And it was just you and your husband here that night?"

"Yes, our oldest was in college. Our two younger ones were out with friends."

"So, no other cars? No sounds from the Richardses'? I know you've been asked this before. But if you could think about it again."

"I didn't hear anything from the Richards house, no," said Mrs. DeAngelo.

Decker was about to move on to another question when something in her voice caught his attention. "What about one of the other houses?" he asked.

"Well, it was the empty one. Just to the left of us."

"So the one closest to the Richardses?"

"Yes. It had been abandoned for a long time. Sometimes you had teens over there doing things, drinking and smoking and—"

"Screwing," said DeAngelo.

"Anthony!" exclaimed his wife. "Language."

DeAngelo grinned and settled back in his recliner. "Well, they were."

"So it might have been the same that night?" said Decker. "Some teens over there? What exactly did you see or hear?"

"It was just a glimpse of movement, really." She

rubbed her temples. “Oh, it was so long ago.” She looked at her husband. “But I do think it was a teenager.”

“Male or female?”

“Male. At least I think so. It really was just a glimpse.”

“And do you remember what time that might have been?”

“Well, it was certainly after the storm had started. I was thinking to myself that they were getting soaked.”

“But you don’t have a certain time in mind?”

“No, I’m sorry.”

Decker nodded. “Okay. I appreciate your making the effort.”

He left them there and walked back outside. He didn’t know what he could expect all this time later. Most witnesses couldn’t remember what they saw yesterday, much less thirteen years ago. He walked over to the empty house to which Mrs. DeAngelo had just been referring.

He peered into one of the windows but couldn’t see much. He tried the door. It was locked. He had no idea who even owned the house. Whoever did wasn’t doing much with it.

He headed over to the Richardses’ house and surveyed it.

David Katz had driven his car into the driveway and then past the front of the house and behind it, where he had pulled into a small grassy park-off situated there.

Decker looked back over his shoulder. From here it would have been impossible for DeAngelo to have seen him get out of the car and go into the house. The other neighbors had reported the same thing: They hadn't seen Katz go into the house where he would later die.

And yet it was indisputable that he had.

Decker looked down at the ground here. Katz's car's tires had sunk deeply into the ground, what with all the rain. He had driven in before the storm started, so there weren't really traces of his car tires coming onto the property. As Lancaster had earlier pointed out, the rain would have washed those away. But a car coming in *after* the rain had started should have left some traces. So had the killer walked here? In the driving rain? And left no traces of that inclemency when he had entered the house? It made no sense. But it had to, somehow, because it had happened.

His phone buzzed. It was Lancaster.

"I think we got a runner," she said. "We must've spooked her."

"*Her*? Who is it?"

"Susan Richards."

17

"Hold on, where's the FBI gal? I liked her."

Agatha Bates was staring up at Decker through the lenses of her thick glasses.

Mary Lancaster, who stood next to Decker in Bates's small living room, said, "She's on another assignment out of state. I'm working with Agent Decker now."

Bates nodded. "Well, so long as you got somebody to keep an eye on *him*. He's a strange one," she added, as though Decker couldn't hear her. "I think he's just too big for his own good, if you know what I mean."

Lancaster said to him, "I had gone over to Richards's house to question her again. The car was gone and there was no answer. Mrs. Bates was out in her yard, called me over, and told me what she saw last night."

Decker glanced out the window across the street at Susan Richards's house. "What can you tell us?" he said.

"What I told this lady. It was around nine-thirty last night. I heard that dang car start up."

"You mean Richards's car with the loud muffler?" said Decker.

She frowned up at him. "I thought I just said that."

"Tell him what happened next," said Lancaster quickly.

Bates slowly drew her gaze from Decker and said, "Saw Susan get out of the car while it was running and head into the house. She came out a few minutes later with a big old suitcase. One of them rolling ones. She leaned down and opened the car trunk and heaved it in. Then she slammed the trunk shut and got in the car."

"What was she wearing?" asked Decker.

"Long trench coat and a hat, all I could see."

"And you're sure it was her?" said Decker.

" 'Course I am. I know Susan. Tall, thin, blonde hair and all."

Lancaster nodded. "And then she drove away?"

"That's right. She didn't tell me about taking a trip. But she must be going away for a while. That bag was stuffed."

Lancaster looked over at Decker, who was once more staring out the window. She said, "Richards must have left in a hurry. She didn't stop the newspaper or mail deliveries. I checked."

"So is she on the lam, then?" asked Bates. "What we used to call it when people go on the run. You know, like *The Fugitive*. I loved that show. Don't make 'em like that anymore." Her small face crinkled with pleasure. "And I had the biggest crush on David Janssen. What a hottie he was. He's dead now. Everybody I liked on TV is dead now."

"We're not sure of her reasons for leaving," said Lancaster.

"Well, if Susan killed that man, she probably would try to get away," said Bates. "I know I would."

Decker said, "Did you see anyone else over there last night?"

Bates's gaze swiveled back to him. "No. Woulda told you if I had."

"Nothing out of the ordinary?" he persisted.

Bates thought about this. "Not unless you count somebody going on the lam."

Decker and Lancaster left and walked across the street to Richards's home. A forensic team was inside looking around.

Decker looked to the sky where a storm was coming in.

Lancaster followed his gaze. "Weird weather this time of year. It was warm and humid and not a cloud in the sky last night. Now we're going to get a storm and the temp will drop twenty-five degrees."

Decker nodded absently. "You put out a BOLO, right?" he said.

"Of course. Nothing yet. We also tagged her credit cards and her phone. No charges, and she must have turned her phone off."

"Someone will probably spot the car. Or *hear* it."

"So does this confirm her guilt vis-à-vis Meryl Hawkins?"

"Did you check the rear door of the Residence Inn?"

"Hasn't changed since your time. Still broken. And no CCTV. So, did Richards exact her revenge on Hawkins?"

"I don't know."

"If she's innocent, why run?"

"Same answer."

"So how do we get answers?"

"We need to know more about Hawkins."

"Like what?"

"Everything."

"You mean after he was murdered?"

"No, before."

"How does that help us?"

"If he didn't kill the Richardses and David Katz, there must have been some reason why the real murderer would pick him to place the blame. We might find those reasons by looking at what he was doing *before* the murders."

They walked back to their cars. When they reached them Decker turned to his old partner.

"I saw Earl at the American Grill."

She looked surprised and popped in another piece of gum. "Did you? Was he alone?"

"No."

She nodded. "Did you speak to him?"

"He came over. We . . . talked about things."

"Nuance has never been your strong suit, Decker. And while you're a stone face when it comes to police work, your poker face sucks when it comes to personal matters. He told you about *us*."

Decker looked at her uncomfortably as the wind picked up around them.

"You have time for a drink?" she asked.

Decker nodded.

He followed her to a bar called Suds. Decker had frequented the place so often after the deaths of his family that the owner had used a Sharpie to write his name on the barstool on which he always sat.

The place was three-quarters full as folks drank and ate food from the bar menu. Music played in the background and some pinball machines lined up against one wall kept lighting up and dinging. The smack of pool balls came from another room where patrons could engage in billiards to their hearts' delight, so long as they kept ordering drinks and munchies.

Decker and Lancaster sat at a high table set against one wall. Decker ordered a beer and Lancaster a vodka tonic.

"You okay with your decision to join the Bureau?"

"I'm okay with it," said Decker tersely. "But I didn't think we came here to talk about me."

Lancaster took a sip of her drink and munched on

some nuts from a bowl in front of her. "Life is complicated. At least mine is."

"How does that lead to divorce? I thought you and Earl cared for each other."

"We *do*, Decker. It's not really about that."

"What else is there?"

"What people want out of life, for one."

"What do you want that's different from what Earl wants?"

"I want to keep working in law enforcement."

"And Earl doesn't want that?"

"It's hard on him, Decker. It's hard on Sandy. I get that. But all I've ever wanted to be is a cop. I've worked my entire adult life to get to this point. I can't just chuck it, even if I do care for somebody."

"So it's an either/or?"

"It apparently is for Earl. But I'm not blaming him. You know when those monsters left those mannequins at our home dressed up to look like they'd been murdered two years ago? It scared the shit out of all of us, but Earl especially took it hard. He couldn't stop talking about it. What if it had been for real? Things changed after that between us. And they've never gone back to what they were."

"And what about Sandy? Earl said he's getting more custody than you."

"With my job, how could I have done that? It would be way too hard on Sandy. I'm not going to put her through that."

"She's your daughter."

"And she's Earl's daughter too. And she has special needs. His job is a lot more flexible than mine. I can't suddenly duck out of a homicide investigation or not show up for court so I can pick her up from school because she's having an episode. I know. I tried. It didn't work. You saw that for yourself."

"I did and I'm sorry."

She gave a weak smile. "Apologies? You going soft on me in your middle age?"

"Doubtful." He took a swig of beer. "I'm sorry that my problems intruded into your life. What happened to your family was because of me."

She reached over and gripped his hand. "Every problem in the world is not yours to solve. I know you have very broad shoulders, but no one can take on that sort of responsibility. And it wasn't your fault. It was the fault of a couple of very sick people. You know that's true."

"Do I?" he said. "It doesn't feel that way."

"You can't live this way, Amos. It's not sustainable."

"I never expected to live that long anyway."

She withdrew her hand and said coldly, "No one should wish for a shortened life."

"I'm not wishing for it. I'm just being realistic."

"You've lost weight. You're in a lot better shape than the last time I saw you."

"It's not my weight that concerns me."

She glanced at his head and frowned. "Problems there?"

"Does it matter? I'll just keep going until . . . I don't."

"I guess we can talk in circles all night."

"I'd rather move forward on this case."

"So, you mentioned Hawkins's past. Where do you start?"

"I start with before he allegedly became a murderer."

"You mean?"

"Exactly."

18

Trammel, Ohio.

Decker had never been here, though it was only a two-hour drive southwest of Burlington. It wasn't that far mileage-wise, but the only way there was mostly over state routes and rural back roads.

Trammel's downtown looked just like a photo of his hometown, right down to the dinginess and despair, alleviated by the glimpses of hope in the form of a new business opening and the foundation of a building being dug. And young faces on the sidewalks, and late-model cars on the streets.

Mitzi Gardiner lived in what Decker would call the upscale part of town, made up of large old homes where Trammel's elite had once lived, and where the new money had now congregated. They were large and brick with a past century's small windows, immaculately landscaped lawns with mature trees and bushes, and more modern additions tacked on by recent owners. Most had gated front entrances and luxury cars parked in the curved drives.

After being buzzed in through the gate, he walked

up to the front door, noting the precisely laid-out planting beds, though the flowers had withered or else died out as fall deepened to winter. The house's windows were sparkling clean, the brick veneer seemed to have just been power-washed, and the front double doors looked like a fresh coat of paint had just been applied to them.

Neat, nice, monied. All the things Mitzi Gardiner had never been when Decker first met her. She'd been an unemployed drug addict and petty criminal who would steal and prostitute herself out to anyone to support her habit. He remembered her as tall, scrawny, and pasty, with needle-tracked arms and a deviated septum from all the snorted coke. Her pupils had been dilated, her movements jerky and largely out of her control. A wreck of a human being.

He knocked on the door and immediately heard footsteps approaching. He had phoned ahead. She knew he was coming.

When the door opened, Decker could hardly believe his own eyes. Or, even more incredibly, his infallible memory.

The woman gazing back at him was around forty, tall, shapely, her blonde hair done in such a way as to maximize both its fullness and attractiveness. She wore a pale blue dress that flattered her hips and showed a glimpse of cleavage, a simple necklace with one emerald at the throat, and a large diamond engagement ring and wedding band on her left hand.

Her makeup and complexion were perfect. The once-destroyed septum had been fully repaired. The eyes held not a hint of dilation. The teeth were white and perfect and no doubt veneers, for her drug habit had left her own teeth gray and diseased, he recalled.

She must have registered his surprise. "It's been a long time, Detective Decker," she commented, her full lips curving into a self-satisfied smile at his amazed look.

"Yes, it has. I'm glad to see that you've . . ."

"Turned my life around? Yes, I have. Years of bad choices followed by some far better ones. Would you like to come in?"

She led him inside and then to an old-fashioned conservatory at the back of the house overlooking the pool and manicured rear grounds. A uniformed maid came in with a tray of coffee. Mitzi poured out the coffee after the maid departed.

"I assume you'd heard about your father before I contacted you?" said Decker, his cup cradled in one big hand.

"I saw the news, yes," she said.

"As next of kin you'll probably be called on to make a formal ID. I mean, we know it's him. It's just a formality."

"I would prefer not to. In fact, I would prefer to have nothing to do with it."

"He *is* your father."

"And he also killed four people."

"He has no other family left. And there's the matter of burial."

"They must have protocols for that when someone can't afford to be buried. Can't they just cremate him?"

Decker let his gaze wander around the sumptuous interior of the conservatory. "I guess so, for those who can't pay for it."

"I know you must think I'm a terrible person, Detective Decker. But the fact is I haven't seen my father since he went to prison for murdering those people."

"You never visited him there?"

"Why would I?" She leaned in closer to him. "I have a new life that I worked really hard on. Brad, my husband, doesn't know anything, really, of my past. I moved from Burlington, cleaned up my act, legally changed my last name, finished college, started working in the financial field, and met my husband. We married, and now I'm a full-time mom and loving it."

Decker looked around. "What does your husband do? It must pay well."

"It does. He runs his own high-end job placement platform."

"High-end?"

"Corporate executives, law and finance, manufacturing, Silicon Valley and all its high-tech positions, lobbying, defense industry, even government positions. He's been very successful."

"All that's way out of my league."

Mitzi paused to take a sip of her coffee. "So you see, I have no desire to revisit that part of my life. And I really don't want my family to know about my . . . struggles. In fact, as far as my husband knows, I'm an orphan. And I guess now I am."

"I recall that your mother died before your father even went on trial."

"Thank God. It would have crushed her."

"Did your father try to contact you, either while he was in prison or after he got out?"

"He wrote me letters when he was in prison. But I never wrote back. After I moved, I didn't leave a forwarding address."

"And after he left prison?"

"I had no idea. I thought he was in prison for life."

"So apparently did everyone else. Including him."

"Why was he released? The news didn't say."

"He was terminally ill. The state didn't want to foot the bill, apparently."

She nodded but made no comment.

"And you're sure he didn't try to contact you?"

"He'd have no way of knowing where I was. They said someone killed him? Are you sure it wasn't suicide? You said he was dying."

"No, couldn't be suicide. I can't tell you why, but just trust me on that."

She sat back. "That's so bizarre. Who would want to hurt him? It's been so many years."

"Some people carry long grudges."

"You mean the widows? What were their names again?"

"Susan Richards and Rachel Katz."

"I assume you've checked with them."

"We have."

"And?"

"And we're following up."

"So what do you want with me? On the phone you just said you wanted to talk. I know nothing about the murder of my father."

"I want to talk to you about the murders he was convicted of."

"Why?"

"What if your father didn't commit them?"

Her features sagged. "That's crazy. Of course he did."

"And you know for sure how?"

"Like you just said, he was *convicted* of them. *You* helped convict him. His fingerprints and DNA were found at the house."

"Would it surprise you to learn that he came back to Burlington proclaiming his innocence? That he wanted me to prove it?"

"Would it surprise me? No. But it *would* surprise me if you took it seriously."

"Maybe it would surprise me too. But he comes back saying he's innocent and then somebody kills him, on the same day?"

"Like I said, you have two potential suspects."

"The widows. Did you know they still live in Burlington?"

"Why would I?" she said quickly.

"Well, you said they would be on your list of suspects. They'd sort of have to live in Burlington to make it happen that fast."

"Oh, well, I guess I assumed."

"Can I take you through the case again?"

"Do we really have to? I've worked hard to put this behind me."

"It's really important. And it won't take long."

She looked at her watch. "It *can't* take too long. My husband and I are going out to dinner later. I'd really prefer that you weren't here when he arrives. It would take too much explaining."

"I'll be as expeditious as I can."

She sighed, poured another cup of coffee, and sat back, looking at him expectantly.

"Your father went out that day around three, you said."

"I think that's right. It's been a long time."

"That's what your statement said."

She waved her hand dismissively. "Okay then, whatever."

"They found him very early the next morning walking along a part of town that I would have described back then as being pretty dangerous."

"Okay?"

"Had he ever been to that part of town before?"

"Not that I was aware."

"Had *you* ever been to that part of town?"

She frowned. "What, do you mean when I was looking for drugs to buy? I don't know. Maybe."

"He had the opportunity to give us an alibi but never did. He said he was just walking in the rain. Something no one could corroborate."

She spread her hands but said nothing.

"Before that we came to your house to find him. But he wasn't there. You said he'd gone out."

"That's right."

"And he never told you where he was going?"

"No. We didn't talk much back then."

"Yet you'd come back home to live."

"I had nowhere else to go. Look, I was a total druggie back then. You know that and I know that. My mother was dying and needed looking after and I couldn't even provide that."

"So your father looked after her?"

Gardiner hesitated.

"Your statement didn't really say one way or the other," Decker added helpfully.

"We didn't always see eye to eye, but I have to give credit where credit is due. My dad really cared about Mom. He did what he could. After he lost his job they had almost no money. And her pain was awful." She involuntarily shuddered.

"She was hooked up to a drip line that night," noted Decker. "I remember seeing it."

"Yeah, well, half the time there were no pain meds in that IV bag. They couldn't afford them. *Fucking* insurance companies." She caught herself, put a hand to her mouth, and added, "Sorry, it's still kind of a sore subject with me."

"So your mother *had* insurance?"

"Until my dad got laid off. Then they couldn't afford to stay on the insurance. And cancer was a preexisting condition. So they couldn't get another policy anyway."

"What did he do?"

"He worked every odd job he could and used the money to get what he could from local doctors."

"But then he was arrested and held until trial. What then?"

"She suffered incredibly," said Gardiner, her eyes filling with tears. "My mother was in terrible pain and there was nothing I could do about it."

"Until she passed away?"

"Yes. Fortunately, she died in her sleep soon after." She shook her head. "She worked so hard her whole life."

"What did she do?"

"She was born near Columbus. She was smart but never had a chance to go to college. She worked at OSU. In the cafeteria, when she was in her twenties."

"I actually played football there."

"Really?" She looked him over. "I guess you're plenty big enough. Then she met my dad and they got married. He was working at a manufacturing plant, I think, up near Toledo. They met on a blind date, or so my mom told me. Love at first sight, Meryl and Lisa. Then I came along soon after." She paused. "They had a nice life. Until I grew up and screwed everything up."

"With your drug addiction?"

She nodded. "Look, they tried to get me help, but I kept relapsing. Nothing I did seemed to work. I tried, but it was damn hard."

"It is damn hard, but give yourself some credit. You finally kicked it."

"Yeah, I did."

"Had your father ever mentioned the Richardses? Or David Katz?"

"No, never. I didn't even know he knew them."

"Well, he might not have."

"Well, then why did he go to that house?"

"That's the question, isn't it? Susan Richards and Rachel Katz also testified that neither of them knew him, and weren't aware that their husbands did either."

"So it was a random burglary, then? He just drove around—"

"Walked. He didn't have a car other than the one that was parked in front of your house all that day and well into the night. We confirmed that with witnesses from your old neighborhood."

"He could have stolen a car," she pointed out.

"That's true. But no car was seen approaching the Richardses' house that night except for David Katz's."

"Wasn't it raining like crazy that night? How could anyone say for sure they didn't see a car?"

"Fair point. Talk to me about the discovery of the murder weapon at your parents' home."

"What about it?"

"It was found behind a wall panel in your parents' closet?"

"Okay. So?"

"Did you know about that panel?"

"No. I'd never been in their closet. I never had any reason to."

"And one of the techs found it?"

"I think so."

"You were there?"

"I had to be. I couldn't leave my mother alone."

"So you were there on the day of the murders and then afterwards?"

"Yes. Again, I couldn't leave her alone."

"And you never saw your father after the time of the murders?"

"No. I never left the house. I answered the door when you and your partner showed up that night."

"That's right."

She looked at her watch. "Now, if there's nothing else?"

"There's just one thing."

"Yes?"

"How did the gun get in the closet?"

"What?"

"If your father didn't come home after the murders, how did the gun he used to kill those people end up behind the panel in the closet?"

"I . . . I don't know."

"Maybe you were asleep? Or . . . ?"

"Or maybe I was stoned out of my mind?" she said, a bitter look on her face.

"When we came to interview you later that night, you were sort of out of it."

"Then there's your answer. My father came home, hid the gun, and then left again. And neither my mother nor I saw him."

"Right, that would explain it. And the stuff he stole never turned up."

"I don't know anything about that. You didn't find it in our house."

"No, we didn't. And we looked for it."

"Okay." She made a show of looking at her watch again.

"He had five hundred dollars in his pocket. Any idea where that came from?"

"I assumed from him selling the stuff he stole."

"Right, well, thanks for your time."

She showed him out. At the door Gardiner said, "I'm not really sure why you're putting yourself through this, Detective Decker."

"That thought had crossed my mind."

Decker walked down the drive and the gates automatically opened as he approached them. When he got to his car, he suddenly looked back at the house in time to see a curtain on one of the front windows flutter closed.

He got into the car thinking that people were interesting. Sometimes they just couldn't distinguish the truth from bullshit. Sometimes they didn't want to. It was often easier just to believe a lie.

He drove off with more questions than he'd started the trip with.

And for some reason, that made him happy.

Amos Decker actually smiled as he drove back to Burlington.

He stopped smiling when something rammed into his car on a back road in the middle of nowhere.

19

Decker had seen the headlights coming up on him but figured the person would slow down and back off.

That was not how it played out. Not even close.

The first strike catapulted his big frame straight ahead. His front and side curtain airbags deployed, and he felt his skin tingle and then burn slightly from the released gases powering the safety devices.

Momentarily disoriented by the collision, Decker looked in the rearview mirror and saw the lights coming at him again. The headlights were set higher than his taillights.

Truck. A big one. He thought he could see the huge metal bumper right before . . .

The rear of his car was lifted completely off the road with the next impact.

His airbags having already burst open, Decker felt his chest hit the steering column after colliding with the airbag and crushing it. But the air pocket still prevented serious injury.

He cut the wheel to the right, and then the left.

The truck mirrored those movements. He could smell gasoline.

Great, his tank must've gotten cracked.

He floored it and the car leapt forward.

The truck accelerated to match this burst of speed.

Decker dug in his pocket for his phone. His fingers tapped on the screen.

If he could just call 911 . . .

Then the phone was flung out of his hand when the truck smashed into him again. This sent his car into a sideways spin. He felt like a NASCAR driver who'd had his car's rear tapped by another at high speed. Fishtailing, totally out of control. It was not a great feeling.

But Decker had been in high-speed chases before as a cop. He knew what to do. He didn't fight the wheel but rather steered in the direction of the spin to regain control of the car.

He slid sideways down the asphalt, tires smoking, fuel leaking, and Decker fearful that heat from one would ignite the other.

He came to a stop about fifty feet later. He pushed the deployed airbag out of the way and looked out the window.

The monster truck was heading his way, a T-bone impact definitely in the works.

Well, screw that.

Decker pulled his weapon, rolled down the window, took aim, and unloaded his mag first at the radiator, then down to the tires, and finally up to the windshield. Three fractured circles were imprinted on the glass where his bullets hit.

The truck immediately veered off, ran into the grass shoulder, regained traction, shot back onto the road, and limped off, smoke now coming from its engine.

Decker didn't know if he'd hit the driver or not. He could only hope he had.

He was debating whether to go after the truck, when the smell of gas suddenly strengthened.

He quickly undid his seat belt, bent down and retrieved his phone, kicked open the door, and hustled away from the car. He dialed 911 and told them what had happened, giving his location as best he could. Then he watched with a sickening feeling as a lick of flames emerged at the rear of his ride.

He instantly turned and sprinted away from the car. When the explosion rocked the dark sky, he was flung forward by the concussive blast and drilled face first into the hard shoulder of dirt, grass, and gravel.

And that's where the cops found him when they showed up later.

"You just can't keep out of trouble, can you?"

Decker looked groggily up from his hospital bed at Lancaster hovering over him and furiously chewing her gum.

"Did they find the truck?"

She shook her head.

"I think I might have wounded the driver," said Decker as he touched his forehead and felt the bandage there. "I placed three shots in the windshield right in front of the driver's seat."

"State police are checking it all out. Dollars to donuts we'll be able to find the truck. So who do you think it was?"

Decker sat up a little. "Someone who either followed me to Trammel or picked up the tail after I left Mitzi Gardiner's house."

"And how did that go?"

Decker filled her in on his interview.

"You think she was telling the truth?"

"Almost nobody tells the entire truth. They slant facts to make themselves look better or blameless, or both."

"Sounds like she's really turned her life around, though," said Lancaster, a bit wistfully.

"Which means she has a lot to lose potentially," countered Decker.

"You think she called somebody after you left?"

"I guess you can pull her phone records and check. Although it would be a little obvious if as soon as I leave her somebody tries to kill me. She has to know she'd be on the suspect radar."

"And with her new, chic life, she might not have ready access to hired killers."

"They might have just wanted to warn me off, not kill me."

She looked him over. "I think you need to rethink that. From what I heard, you almost got French-fried in your car."

"It *was* close," conceded Decker. "Any developments on your end?"

"None worth mentioning."

"Well, this attempt on my life tells us one thing," said Decker.

"What's that?"

"It seems that Meryl Hawkins was telling the truth."

20

Talk about coming full circle.

Decker dropped his duffel on the floor of his new digs.

It was the next evening and after a night's stay in the hospital he had moved into the Residence Inn. This was actually his old room when he'd lived there.

He'd gotten a new rental car after spending considerable time on the phone trying to explain to Hertz exactly what had happened to the other one.

"Someone was trying to kill you?" the customer service rep had said skeptically. "I've been doing this a long time and that's a first for me."

"Not for me," Decker had truthfully replied.

He sat in the one chair next to the window and overlooking the street. He popped the cold beer he had brought with him.

That was dinner. Well, really it wasn't, but after nearly getting blown up the night before, he didn't have much of an appetite.

He touched his head where the bandage still was. It was another knock up there to add to all the others. How many more could he endure without something major popping?

And he was tired of getting nearly blown up. He'd almost bought it in a similar way back in Baronville. The only good thing to come out of his almost being killed was the fact that someone was afraid of what he would find out. That meant there was a truth out there that needed to be discovered.

And Decker meant to find it.

One floor down was the room where Meryl Hawkins's life had ended, a bit prematurely.

And violently.

Sipping his beer, Decker walked down to the space. It was still off-limits and stickered with yellow tape, but the officer guarding the door knew Decker and let him pass.

"What happened to you?" the cop asked, eyeing the bandage around the big man's head.

"When I find out, I'll let you know."

Decker closed the door behind him and surveyed the space. Nothing had been touched other than Hawkins's body being removed. He wondered briefly about the man's burial, or cremation. Part of him wanted to haul his daughter down here to take care of her father's remains. Part of him understood why she wanted nothing to do with it.

At the end of the day that was really none of his concern.

He looked at the chair where Hawkins had been

sitting. There were traces of blood on it, not from the exit wound since there hadn't been one. The splatter from the entry wound had been the source.

Pillow, gun, dead guy. No witnesses.

He looked around the rest of the room. It had already been thoroughly searched and nothing else had been found.

They'd gotten the postmortem report on Hawkins but not the tox screen yet. His stomach had been empty. But what was in his bloodstream?

Decker closed his eyes and dialed up his cloud. Hawkins had told him at the cemetery that he was going to take something to help him sleep, after spending a few hours throwing up. There had been no evidence of that in the bathroom, but he might have cleaned it up. But there had also been no sign of meds, either illegal or not.

They'd checked the Dumpster at the rear of the building and found nothing there either. Had whoever killed him taken the meds for some reason? Why would that be? What could they have revealed?

He went back to his room, put his few clothes away, cleaned up, and, suddenly hungry, went in search of dinner.

He chose Suds because it was close and cheap. He sat at the bar and ordered a beer, and a burger and fries with chili. He involuntarily looked over his shoulder once, thinking that Jamison might swoop in and chastise him for the cardiac killer meal plan.

He turned to his right when the person sat down next to him a few minutes later.

Rachel Katz eyed the bandage around his head. "What happened to you?"

"Cut myself shaving," replied Decker as he took a sip of beer.

She looked down at his plate. "Not into organics, I take it."

"What's more organic than meat and potatoes?"

She smiled. "You have a comeback for everything. I didn't see that in you all those years ago."

She ordered a glass of Prosecco.

He glanced sideways at her. "Somehow, I didn't figure you for a Suds patron."

"Oh, I'm full of surprises. But I'll let you in on a little secret." She leaned over next to him. "I'm the majority owner of this bar." She straightened and studied Decker for his reaction to this.

"I'm impressed at the diversity of your holdings. From penthouses to pubs."

She smiled. "Another quip. Good for you. If the detective thing doesn't work out, fall back on stand-up, no pun intended."

Her drink arrived, and she took a sip of it, filling her hand with nuts from a bowl in front of them.

"So, how's the investigation coming?"

"It's coming."

"I thought you would have solved the whole thing by now."

"Investigations don't work that way. They're on their own timetable."

"But you solved my husband's murder really fast."

"Did I?" he shot back.

She munched her almonds and peanuts and looked around the full bar. "It's good to see the town getting back on its feet, isn't it?" she asked.

"So when you finish rebuilding Burlington, what's next?"

She swiveled around and leaned back against the bar. "I'm not sure. There are lots of places like Burlington, but not all have the potential to make a comeback. I don't want to make a ton of money here and blow it on another place that will never make it out of the abyss."

"So how do you calculate that?"

"I won't bore you with the statistics, but a lot of number crunching goes into it. Luckily, as a CPA, my background is all about number crunching. And those numbers can be magic, a road map into the future, if you know how to read them right. All successful people do that."

"All *financially* successful people, you mean."

"Is there any other kind?" She added quickly, "Just kidding. I know we need more Mother Teresas in the world. I'm just not one of them. Not how I'm wired."

"And how are you wired?"

"Me first, I guess. And I'm not ashamed to admit

it. I don't like hypocrites. I know enough people who pretend to care about others while they're stabbing them in the back. I stab people in the chest. They can see it coming from a mile away."

"Thing is, they're still dead," replied Decker.

"Yes, but at least they have a chance to defend themselves," she said sweetly, draining her drink and waving for another one, which was immediately delivered. "I hear Susan Richards has gone missing?"

Decker put down his burger and looked over at her. "And where did you hear that?"

"Oh, come on, I heard it on the town gossip network ages ago. I wonder why she would have disappeared like that?"

Decker said, "Guilt?"

Katz took a sip of her Prosecco. "I didn't say that, but the timing is awfully peculiar."

"Timing in homicide investigations often is."

"You're the expert on that, not me. So, do you think she killed Meryl Hawkins and took off before the cops found proof that she murdered him?"

"Speaking of proof, did you ever come up with an alibi for the time of his death?"

"I was at dinner with a business associate until eleven-thirty or so. Then he drove me home. We got to my place around midnight. I think that lets me off the hook."

"And the name of this business associate?"

She took out a pen and slip of paper from her purse, wrote something down, and handed it to Decker.

He glanced at the paper, his eyes hiking in surprise. "Earl Lancaster?"

"Yes. He's working on some projects for me. He's a first-rate general contractor. Why?"

"He's married to my old partner."

"Not for much longer," said Katz. When Decker again looked surprised, she added, "Small town, Detective." She swallowed the last of her drink. "Well, let me know if you need anything else."

With a whisk of blonde hair, she was gone.

After she left, Decker sat there and wondered one thing.

Why hadn't Earl mentioned that he was working with Katz when they had run into each other at the American Grill?

Because that development royally screwed his wife.

Or soon-to-be ex-wife.

21

"You mean you *knew*?"

Decker looked across at Lancaster. It was the next morning and they were sitting in her car outside the Residence Inn. He'd called her and told her he needed to speak with her but preferred to do it in person.

"I *knew* he was doing some work for Rachel Katz. I didn't know that he was her alibi. Earl didn't tell me that. We don't talk all that much anymore, particularly about his business."

"But why didn't you mention to me that he was working for a possible suspect in a murder we're both investigating?"

"He works with lots of people and I didn't think it was relevant."

"Well, it is. And now that he's her alibi?"

Lancaster said, "I might have to recuse myself from the investigation."

"There's no *might* about it, Mary. You have to."

"Earl wouldn't lie, if that's what you're implying. If he said he was with Katz, he was."

"I'm not implying anything. I just know that you have to get off this case. Any defense lawyer will tear the department a new one if you stay on now."

She popped a stick of gum into her mouth and started chewing furiously.

"And now I need to talk to Earl about this," said Decker.

"I know. And I think I need to talk to him too."

"No, Mary, you can't do that."

"He's still my husband, dammit."

"He's also a potential alibi for someone who had a pretty good motive to kill Meryl Hawkins."

"Shit!" She slapped the steering wheel. "And I didn't think my life could get any worse."

"You're the one asking for the divorce."

"That's what Earl told you."

"Is it not true? You just told me that Earl doesn't lie."

"Does it matter, Decker? Our marriage is over."

"And this woman he's seeing?"

"She's fine. Earl didn't start seeing Nancy until things were over between us."

"Yeah, he told me that. But you're really okay with Earl getting custody of Sandy?"

"We're *sharing* custody. But I told you before, his work is more flexible than mine. It's better and less disruptive for Sandy to have her spend the week with Earl. Her well-being is all I'm concerned about."

"Okay, give up your kid, then."

She looked at him, fury on her features. "What right do you have to tell me that? You don't know jack shit about my situation. It was your choice to leave here and go work for the FBI. So don't come back to *my* town and tell me how to run *my* life." She pointed to the door. "Now get the hell out of my car."

Decker got out, but he poked his head back in.

"The thing with kids, Mary, is that when you turn around for just a second and then look back, sometimes they aren't there anymore."

He shut the door and trudged off.

Later that day, the knock on Decker's door was unexpected.

When he opened it, his surprise instantly turned to exasperation.

"Long time, no see, Decker," said the smiling man on the other side of the doorway.

Blake Natty was a detective with the Burlington Police Department. About six years older than Decker, and more senior at the department, he had been left in the dust by Decker's investigative prowess. And he had not bothered to hide his feelings about it.

He was about five-eight, one-sixty, and dressed in a way that matched his name, complete with pocket kerchief and golden links on his French-cuffed shirt.

"What are you doing here, Natty?" asked Decker.

Natty's smile broadened. "This is just a courtesy call. I'm taking over the investigation on the Hawkins case. Heard Mary got knocked off over some accusation from you. A little surprising considering you two were partners once."

"Well, you got everything about that wrong, which at least shows you're consistent."

Natty's smile vanished. "As I said, a courtesy call. And it's to tell you that we do not require your services in connection with the Meryl Hawkins case."

"Have you talked to Captain Miller about this? Because he was very much okay with me working the case."

"Miller has to answer to the superintendent. And the super has a different opinion."

"Right. Would that still be Peter Childress?"

"It would be. Didn't you call him an ignorant asshole one time?"

"It wasn't just the one time. And he earned it fair and square."

"Well, just do not involve yourself in the investigation. So, with that, I don't see anything keeping you in Burlington. You can just head on out."

"There's the crimes that Meryl Hawkins was convicted of."

"Right. That's also off-limits. It's a Burlington PD investigation, and in case you forgot, you're no longer part of the team."

"No law against me looking into a case if I want to."

"There is a law if you interfere with an active police investigation."

"So you *are* looking into whether Hawkins was innocent?"

"None of your concern. I can have one of my guys run you to the bus station. There's a bus to Pittsburgh that leaves in two hours. And you can catch a flight from there back to your precious D.C."

"Thanks, but I'm staying."

Natty drew closer, nearly chest to stomach, and looked up at the nine-inches-taller Decker. "You don't get a single pass on this, no get-out-of-jail-free card. I catch you in my way, the next room you inhabit is a jail cell. I want to make myself really clear on that."

"You've never had a problem making yourself clear, Blake. Even when you had it a hundred and eighty degrees wrong. Which was most of the time."

"Watch that ego, Decker. Even a guy as big as you won't be able to hold it in."

Decker closed the door in the man's face, went back to his chair, sat down, and turned his thoughts back to the case.

Natty, he was sure, would look for any opportunity to put bite to his threat and plant Decker's butt in jail. Yet Decker had spent much of his life swimming against the current. Natty was an irritant, nothing more. But Decker would have to watch himself.

A text dropped into his phone.

It was from Lancaster.

I'm really pissed at you, but I'm sorry about Natty being assigned to the case. Wouldn't wish that on my worst enemy. Which you're not. At least not yet. M

Decker dropped the phone into his pocket, sighed, and sat back in his chair.

His visit to the old hometown was turning into quite a nightmare.

22

Gentrification sometimes sucked because it made homes unaffordable to those living there before their neighborhood was suddenly hot, and all the money wanted to move into new luxury residences after knocking the old stuff down.

Decker was thinking this as he looked around at the area where Hawkins had been picked up that night on suspicion of a quadruple homicide.

Back then it had been the equivalent of a war zone in Burlington. Drug deals had gone down here, and gangs had fought each other over turf and customers. Cars from the suburbs would line up on the streets, like parishioners to the offering basket, only the money they put in would bring not solace and help for others, but drugs and continued misery in return. Empty homes and businesses were used as needle and coke pipe hangouts or gang headquarters. As a cop and later detective, Decker had spent a lot of time in this part of town. In some years there had been a murder a week. Everybody had guns, and no one had a problem using them.

Now the place was full of upscale apartments and thriving small businesses. Hell, there was even a Starbucks. A park sat where once there had been an empty boarded-up warehouse. Decker had to admit it was a lot better than it had been.

They could film a Hallmark movie here and not change a thing.

He and Lancaster had come here after questioning Hawkins at the police station. In Decker's mind's eye, the area was returned to its miserable state thirteen years prior. The park was gone, the new residences vanished, the streets returned to trash-strewn and crumbling. Addicts staggered down the streets, dealers were lurking down dark alleys hustling their product. Users came in with cash and left with their drugs of choice.

There were hookers too, because they naturally went with the drugs, Decker had found. Almost all of the hookers were addicts too and scored tricks to pay for their daily doses. And the luxurious loft apartment building he was standing in front of once more became an abandoned shirt factory with mattresses strewn inside where the business of sex was negotiated and then consummated.

Through all of this Meryl Hawkins walked with the rain beating down on him, though because of the bad weather, they could find no one out and about to corroborate his story. Yet if he was telling the truth and he had been trudging through this downpour, why? And why wouldn't he tell Decker and Lancaster during their interrogation? Anything he told them could have helped his cause. Silence only hurt him. He could have named a person whom he had met with and they could have followed up on that, and he might have been a free man.

Decker dialed up something in his memory. Something far more recent.

"She was hooked up to a drip line that night. I remember seeing it."

"Yeah, well, half the time there were no pain meds in that IV bag, including that night. They couldn't afford them. Fucking *insurance companies. Sorry, it's still kind of a sore subject with me."*

"So your mother had *insurance?"*

"Until my dad got laid off. Then they couldn't afford to stay on the insurance. And cancer was a preexisting condition. So they couldn't get another policy anyway."

"What did he do?"

"He worked every odd job he could and used the money to get what he could from local doctors."

Had Meryl Hawkins really been out that night scrounging up illegal pain meds for his suffering wife? His lawyer had raised that possibility at the trial. If he had, he could still have committed the murders. There was plenty of time for him to do that and get to that part of town.

Yet if he had gotten the pain meds, none had been found on him. And how could he not have scored some in what was Burlington's premier open-air drug market? But then again, he would have to be careful with what he bought. Half the crap being sold here could kill you, even if you were healthy.

Morphine would have been the presumptive choice, Decker figured. It certainly would be what the hospice folks used with their patients. But Hawkins had to be damn sure of the provenance. He certainly wasn't going to give his wife some half-assed, kitchen-sink-concocted drug, and there had been plenty of those back then.

There were, Decker recalled, some sellers here who had pure stuff. They hadn't made it in kitchen labs; they'd stolen it from pharmacies and hospital supply rooms. They asked premium dollar for it, because of its purity. You got more pop for your dollar and you clearly knew what you were injecting. That meant chances were good that you'd live to be an addict another day.

That, Decker decided, would be the stuff Hawkins would be looking for. If he had learned one thing about the man during the investigation and trial, it was that Meryl Hawkins was completely devoted to his wife. Yet no drugs of any kind had been found on him.

Decker closed his eyes. Five hundred dollars *had* been found on Hawkins. Was it cash he'd gotten for the stolen goods?

But how could the guy have transported all the

stuff he supposedly took when there was no accounting for a car being seen there? It was possible he could have driven a stolen car there and no one had noticed it. Then he could have simply driven away, come here, and tried to barter stolen goods for drugs. He had the cash, so maybe he had been trudging through the rain after fencing the stuff and was looking for the right kind of drugs for his wife when the police had picked him up.

Although given that the man had never even had a parking ticket before that, it seemed implausible that after killing four people Hawkins could calmly go about his task of selling the stolen goods and shop for drugs in the middle of a monsoon. And he had to know the police would be looking for the killer.

Decker opened his eyes.

When they had questioned Hawkins late that night, he had seemed genuinely stunned that he was being accused of murder. Back then Decker and Lancaster had just assumed he was lying like any killer would.

Decker closed his eyes once more and he was back in that interrogation room sitting across from a man accused of four homicides, including two kids.

Decker had slid pictures across of the dead people.

"You recognize these, Mr. Hawkins?"

He hadn't looked at the photos.

"Look at them, Mr. Hawkins."

"I'm not and you can't make me."

But Decker had noticed the man glanced sideways at the photo of Abigail Richards and grimaced, almost looking like he might be sick to his stomach. Back then Decker had taken that as an indication of a guilty conscience.

But now?

"Give us a name, Mr. Hawkins," Lancaster had said. "Of anyone you might have seen or met with tonight. Or who might have seen you. We can follow that up, and if it checks out, you're a free man."

Hawkins had never given a name. And as Decker focused his memory on that exact moment, he recalled seeing something on the man's face that he hadn't necessarily seen before.

Resignation.

"Hey, Decker!"

Decker looked over at the car that had pulled up beside him. The driver had rolled down the window and called out to him.

Decker mouthed a curse under his breath.

It was Blake Natty looking cocksure, as usual.

"I thought I made myself clear, Decker."

"You're going to have to explain that, Natty."

Then he looked past Natty and was surprised to see Sally Brimmer in the passenger seat looking very uncomfortable.

Natty said, "I told you that you cannot investigate these cases."

"No, you told me I couldn't interfere with *your*

investigation." Decker made a show of looking around. "Not seeing any interference. I'm just out for a stroll. How about you, Ms. Brimmer? You see any interference with a police investigation going on here?"

Brimmer looked like she wanted to melt into the car's floorboards. She smiled weakly and said, "I'm not getting in the middle of this, guys."

"Smart gal," said Natty with a slick grin before turning back to Decker. "Maybe you should be that smart. I don't want to have to lock you up."

"I'm sure. I mean why would you want a federal lawsuit landing on the department like a nuclear bomb? Even all the brown-nosing you've done with the superintendent all these years wouldn't be enough to save your butt."

"You better watch yourself, smart-ass."

"I do, Natty, every day of my life."

"And you give me any more lip, your fat ass is going into a cell. Guaranteed."

"Then you get a First Amendment lawsuit on top of the other one. I don't think the department has enough lawyers to cover all that crap, and it would probably hit the national news pipeline." Decker peered past him to look at Brimmer. "You do PR for the police. You care to wade into the middle of *that* one, Ms. Brimmer?"

She held up her hands in mock surrender and looked away.

Decker looked down at Natty's ring hand and then over at Brimmer. "Wait a minute, Natty, aren't you still married?"

Natty barked, "What's it to you?" He glanced quickly at Brimmer. "What the hell are you insinuating? I'm . . . I'm just giving her a ride to . . . her apartment."

Decker glanced at Brimmer again, who was staring out her window now. Then he made a show of checking his watch. It was nearly eight p.m.

"Well, tell Fran I said hello, when you get back from Brimmer's *apartment*."

"Stay out of my damn way, Decker, or you *will* go down."

Natty hit the gas and the car sped off.

Decker stared after it and thought he saw Brimmer looking back at him through the rear glass. Though in the darkness, he couldn't be sure.

Natty and Brimmer. Who saw that coming?

23

The Hawkinses' old home.

It wasn't empty. There was a car parked in the driveway.

It was the next day and Decker trudged up the steps to the front door of the house, as he eyed the kids' toys in the front yard.

He knocked and instantly heard cries from young children, the scraping of animal claws on hardwood, and then the firm tread of grown-up feet coming toward the front door. It opened to reveal a young woman around thirty. Her brown hair was tied up in a ponytail and her face held the weary features of a mother with young children. This was confirmed when three small faces poked out from behind her.

"Yes?" she said, looking Decker up and down. "There's no solicitation in this neighborhood, just so you know."

"I'm not selling anything," he said as he held out his FBI credentials.

She took a step back after looking at his ID.

"You're with the FBI?" she said skeptically. "I thought they wore suits."

"Some do, I'm just not one of them. And I'm kind of a hard size to fit."

She stared up at him and nodded. "I can see that. What can I do for you?"

"How long have you lived here?"

"Two years. What is this about?"

"Over a dozen years ago, a family named Hawkins lived here." He glanced down at the kids. "Can we speak privately?"

She looked back at her children, two twin boys and one girl, all between the ages of three and five. "I'm afraid I don't have any privacy," she said with a resigned smile. "Look, why don't you come in?" She led him inside and the children backed away, staring up at the giant Decker in fear.

"Hey kids," said the woman suddenly. "Cookies in the kitchen. One each only! And I *will* check."

The three took off. They were joined by a wire-haired terrier that shot out from behind a piece of furniture, where apparently he'd been cowering.

"Yeah, some watchdog, that Peaches," said the woman dryly. "Now, what about this other family?"

"I'll get right to the point since I doubt we have much time before your kids come back. A gun that was used in a serious crime years ago was found behind a wall in the master bedroom closet here. I wanted to take a look at that spot."

The woman's features collapsed. "Good Lord. Nobody told us about that when we bought the place. I thought the Realtor had to tell you stuff like that. When did it happen?"

"About thirteen years ago. And no crime was committed here, technically."

"And you still haven't found this person?"

"No, we did. He was in prison. Then he got out. And a few days ago someone murdered him."

"Oh my God," said the woman, putting a hand to her face. "But if he was convicted of the crime involving the gun, why do you need to see the place where it was found?"

"Because I'm not sure if he actually *did* commit those crimes."

Her features took on a look of understanding. "Oh, you mean this is like one of those cold case things? I like those shows. Not that I get a chance to watch much TV anymore."

"Right, exactly. A cold case." Decker heard a rush of footsteps coming their way. "I think the cavalry's returning. So if you could let me see it?"

"Sure, come on back."

She led him to the bedroom. "Excuse the mess. I barely have time to brush my teeth with three rug rats."

"I'm sure."

A crash came from somewhere within the house,

and then the sounds of Peaches barking and someone crying.

"Um," said the woman, looking nervous.

"Go check it out. I won't be long."

"Thanks." She shot out of the room, yelling, "Good grief, what now!"

Decker pushed some hanging clothes out of the way and shone his Maglite over the back wall of the closet. Then he looked to the left, where the panel in question was situated. He rapped against it with his fist. It rang hollow. He rapped against the other two walls and got the same sound. It was just drywall over studs after all.

It had been repaired and painted over and there was nothing really for Decker to see. He thought back to the first time he'd seen this space. The panel had been taken off—it had been cut out and then wedged back into place. Not so very seamlessly, it appeared, which was one reason why it had been discovered so readily.

He remembered that behind the cutout was an open space in between the studs. The gun inside a box had been found there. There had been no prints found on either item. He looked down at the floor. The closet was carpeted, and it looked to be the same carpet as during the Hawkinses' time here. He got down on his knees and hit it with his light.

What are you doing, Decker? After all this time did you

think you were going to find a smoking gun in the frigging carpet?

He straightened and finally admitted to himself that he was grasping at straws. He had not a sliver of a lead on this investigation. Either with the murders all those years ago, or with Meryl Hawkins's more recent one.

He rose and left the bedroom.

And that's where Decker ran right into a wall of police with a grinning Blake Natty bringing up the rear.

24

It was the same cell where Decker—pretending to be a lawyer—had scammed his way in to meet with a prisoner who had confessed to murdering Decker's family.

He didn't know if this cell selection had been made intentionally, but he doubted it was a coincidence. Someone was definitely trying to send a message.

The police waiting for him in Hawkinses' old house had been the first sign. His being read his Miranda rights for interfering with a police investigation had been his second, and more visceral, sign.

But Decker was nothing if not a patient man. He leaned back against the cinderblock wall and waited. They knew where he was. At some point they would have to come to him, because he could not come to them.

An hour later a surprising figure appeared in front of the steel bars.

To her credit, Sally Brimmer didn't look pleased to see him in a jail cell.

He glanced up at her.

"Ms. Brimmer. Having a nice day?"

"Apparently better than the one you're having."

"I wouldn't argue with that."

She drew closer to the bars and spoke in a low voice. "Why did you push it? You know Blake hates you."

"I don't care whether he hates me or not. I have a job to do and I'm going to do it."

"But you're not part of the police force anymore. This isn't your problem."

"It is my problem if I helped send an innocent man to prison."

"Do you really believe he was innocent?"

"Let's just put it this way: I have a lot more doubts about his guilt than I used to."

"Okay, but does it really matter? The guy's dead."

"It matters to me. It matters to his memory. He has a daughter who thinks her father killed four people."

Brimmer's cheeks reddened. "I really hated you for conning me that time."

"I took full responsibility for it. I didn't want you to suffer because of what I did."

"I know that man helped murder your family. I . . . I guess I was surprised you didn't kill him in the cell."

"I wasn't sure he'd done it. In fact, I had doubts."

He paused. "I have to be sure, Ms. Brimmer. It's the way I'm wired."

"I guess I can see that. And I brought that up only because . . ." Her voice trailed off and she looked around nervously. "Because I would have done the same thing if it were me."

He rose and went over to the bars separating them. "Can you do something for me?"

She took a step back looking wary. "What?"

"I need to look at the files from the Richardses' and Katz's murders."

"But I thought you had. I saw the guy taking the boxes to the conference room that day."

"I got involved in running down potential witnesses and didn't get to the files before, well, before I ended up in here."

"But surely you read them all from when it happened." She glanced upward at his forehead. "And I heard you can't forget anything."

Now Decker took a step back and wouldn't meet her eye. "I didn't read them all back then. In particular the pathology report."

"Why not?"

"I didn't have to testify to that. The ME did."

She didn't look convinced.

He finally looked at her and said, "I screwed up, Ms. Brimmer. It was my first case as a homicide detective. I thought Hawkins was good for it pretty much right from the start. So I didn't dot all the i's or cross all the t's."

Surprisingly, she smiled at this.

"What?" he said in reaction to her look.

"That's actually comforting."

"How so?"

"I thought you were infallible, like a machine. Now I know you actually *are* human."

"Depends on who you ask, actually. Can you get me the files?"

"I guess I can make copies. But I can't bring them to you here."

"I won't be here much longer."

Her brow wrinkled. "How do you know that?"

"There *is* something known as a bail hearing. It's sort of required."

"Do you have a lawyer?"

"No, but I'm good on that."

"Are you sure?"

"Pretty sure."

"Blake is not going to make it easy."

"I never thought he would."

"I guess you're wondering why I'm . . . I mean, he and I . . ."

"It's none of my business. And I'm not judging anybody. I don't have the right."

"I appreciate that."

"But I will give you a piece of advice. I had a daughter once."

"I know," she said, looking pained.

"And if she had had a chance to grow up, I would never let her near Blake Natty. Take that for what it's worth. The fact that he's seeing you while he's still married should tell you all you need to know about the guy."

Brimmer looked at him sadly, then turned and hurried off.

25

The judge did a double take when he looked down first at the docket sheet and then up at Amos Decker, who stood behind the counsel table.

At the prosecutor's table stood Elizabeth Bailey, a veteran prosecutor who knew Decker quite well. They had worked numerous cases together while he'd been on the police force.

Behind the waist-high rail where the public could sit, there were only two people: Blake Natty and Superintendent Peter Childress, a tall portly man in his late fifties with gray hair cut short and a puffy, pockmarked face. He had on a dark suit, crisply starched white dress shirt, a blue-and-white-striped tie, and a white pocket square.

"Decker?" said the judge, a diminutive man in his late sixties with a reedy neck and an abundance of silvery hair that contrasted starkly with his dark robe. He peered at Decker through thick black-framed glasses. "Amos Decker?"

"Yes, Judge Dickerson. It's me."

"Obstruction of justice charge?" said Dickerson,

glancing at the charging document. "Interfering with a police investigation? I thought you were *with* the police."

"I left to join the FBI a couple of years ago, but I'm still a sworn officer here in Burlington."

Dickerson moved his lips as he read something off the papers lying in front of him. Then he slid off his glasses, set them down, steepled his hands, and looked at the prosecutor.

She stood there looking quite anxious.

"Ms. Bailey, can you explain to me what in the world is going on here?" said Dickerson.

Bailey was in her forties, her frame big-boned. The woman's blonde hair had dark roots. She wore a beige suit and white blouse along with a small chain necklace. Bailey took a moment to deliver a quick scowl at Natty. She cleared her throat as she looked back at the judge.

"Mr. Decker is being charged with obstruction of justice and interfering with a police investigation."

For a moment it looked like she might continue, but Bailey set her lips in a firm line and said nothing more.

Dickerson looked perplexed. "Well, I *know* that. That's what I just read off the document. What I mean is, I would like more of an explanation."

"Mr. Decker was approached by a man named Meryl Hawkins."

"Meryl Hawkins? *The* Meryl Hawkins?"

"Yes, Your Honor. He was released from prison early because, well, because of medical issues. He met with Detective Mary Lancaster and Mr. Decker, proclaimed his innocence for the murders, and asked them to clear his name."

"And he was subsequently murdered?" said Dickerson.

"Yes."

"And how does that bring Mr. Decker here today?"

"Mr. Decker was asked by Captain Miller to look into the murder of Mr. Hawkins and also to reexamine the previous case against Mr. Hawkins."

Dickerson tapped his finger against the top of his bench and said patiently, "That in no way answers my question about why Mr. Decker is here today. Indeed, it only deepens my confusion, Ms. Bailey."

"Yes, Your Honor. I can understand that. But—"

Childress gripped the railing and abruptly stood. "Judge, please, if I may? I think I can clear this up."

Dickerson slid his gaze over to Childress, and Decker thought he could see a shadow pass over the jurist's features at the sight of Burlington's top cop.

Decker had not been the only one to think the superintendent of police was an arrogant, incompetent jerk who crossed the line when it suited him. There were many who had been stunned to see Childress leapfrog over the more senior Captain Miller for the superintendent job. But rumor was that Miller had declined the position because he wanted to remain closer to the people on the police force. And though he habitually treated underlings badly, Childress was polite and deferential to those above him in the pecking order. And he could make the biggest bunch of bullshit sound totally legit. Decker thought he might be about to get a sampling of that talent right now.

Dickerson said, "Superintendent Childress, I didn't see you over there. Can you explain what exactly is going on? If Captain Miller authorized Decker to—"

"That is absolutely true, Your Honor. However, after we looked at this matter again, we came to conclude that Mr. Decker, who is no longer a member of this department, could bring untold legal liability to the city of Burlington if he did something outside legal parameters while ostensibly acting on the department's behalf. Indeed, he was found searching the residence of Mr. Hawkins's old home without benefit of a search warrant."

"I didn't need a search warrant since I had the permission of the homeowner," interjected Decker.

Childress carried on smoothly, "Be that as it may, we can't run around behind Mr. Decker to make sure he follows the law. Indeed, he was formally told by this department not to involve himself in this investigation, and yet he disobeyed that request. We had no alternative but to take him into custody, and that's why we're here today."

Dickerson seemed to be wavering. "As I recall, didn't Detective Decker solve the case behind the terrible shootings at Burlington High School a couple of years ago?"

"Indeed, he did," said Childress. "In fact, the department awarded Mr. Decker a commendation for his work on the case, and I was there applauding as loud as anyone. This is clearly nothing personal, as I'm a big fan of Mr. Decker's. But we have a department to run and I can't sit by and see him do damage to it."

"All right, I see your point."

Bailey said, "Your Honor, this is simply a bail hearing and a chance for Mr. Decker to enter his plea."

"Not guilty," said Decker immediately.

"Are you represented by counsel, Mr. Decker?" asked the judge.

"Not yet, sir. I'm working on it, if it comes to that." He glanced over at Childress and saw the man staring at him with a grim expression.

Bailey quickly said, "Because of Mr. Decker's previous relationship with the department and his current work with the FBI, we're fine with him being released on his own recognizance."

Childress stepped forward. "I think Ms. Bailey's facts need to be somewhat updated, Your Honor. Mr. Decker no longer has ties to this community. He moved away over two years ago. And he obviously no longer works for the department, which is one of the reasons we're here today. And I have it on good authority that he may not even work for the FBI, so the points made by Ms. Bailey for his being released on his own recognizance fall away."

"Do you really consider Mr. Decker a flight risk?" asked Dickerson.

Childress spread his hands and said in a very sincere voice, "Again, when he was on the force, he had no bigger cheerleader than me, Judge. But he's been gone a long time now. I can't say that I know the man anymore. And, quite frankly, him going rogue like that after he was warned off the case, well, it does not inspire confidence, I have to say."

Dickerson looked over at Decker. "Is all that true?"

"I still work for the FBI. And I *do* have ties to the community."

Childress jumped in. "I'm afraid that's simply not true. He has no home here, or other property. Or job. Or—"

"My family is buried here," said Decker quietly, looking not at Childress, but staring directly at Dickerson. "That's why I came back to town. To visit the graves of my wife and my daughter. It would have been her fourteenth birthday." He paused. "So my ties to this community run very deep. About as deep as they can, in fact."

Natty clucked his tongue and rolled his eyes at this.

Childress looked visibly put out by the statement. However, Bailey's eyes watered and she looked down at her hands.

Dickerson nodded. "Mr. Decker, I accept your not-guilty plea, and you are released without bond on your own recognizance. A trial date will be set. I just ask that if you are planning to leave the area that you let the court know."

"I'm not going anywhere, Your Honor, until *all* of this is settled."

Dickerson disappeared into his chambers. As soon as the door was closed, Childress stepped directly in front of Decker and looked him up and down. Now that the judge was no longer around, the man's entire demeanor had changed from professional and genuine to cocksure and mean.

"I can't tell you how thrilled I am that you're back in town, Decker. Because your ass is going down for this." He looked over at Natty. "What are the sentencing guidelines for this again, Natty?"

"One to three. Double that for aggravated circumstances."

Childress stared gleefully at Decker. "Here's hoping for aggravated circumstances, then."

Decker looked him over. "You must not want to solve Hawkins's murder."

"Why do you say that?" said Childress, the grin still planted on his face.

"You assigned Natty to it. He can't even solve the mystery of why you're a dick."

Bailey coughed and looked away, rubbing at her eye.

"You think you're so much smarter than everybody else, don't you?" barked Childress.

"No. But I know I screwed up the Richards and Katz murders. And I'm here to fix that."

"The only thing you should be working on are your obstruction and interference charges."

"I think that'll play itself out okay."

"Oh, you do, do you?" said Childress, his grin deepening as he shot a glance at Natty before looking back at Decker. "And why the hell is that?"

"I don't want to waste my time telling you, because you wouldn't understand."

Childress jammed a finger in Decker's chest. "I'm smart enough to be the superintendent of this fucking police department."

"No, you're really not. That's all due to you benefiting enormously from a principle."

"You're damn right I have principles."

"No, I said *principle*. Singular."

Childress looked at him strangely. "What the hell are you getting at?"

"It's actually named for you, Childress."

"What is?"

"The *Peter* Principle." Decker turned to Bailey.

"I guess my lawyer, whenever I find one, will be in touch, Beth."

She nodded. "Thanks, Amos. I can give you some recommendations."

Decker looked over at Natty. "When I find Hawkins's and the Richardses' and Katz's murderers, I'll let you know."

"You're not to go anywhere near that," said Natty angrily.

"Somebody tried to kill me," said Decker. "I don't take kindly to that."

"We're working on that," said Natty.

"Any leads?" asked Decker.

"We're working on it," repeated Natty. "I don't like you, Decker. You know that. But I like even less people trying to take out a cop. I'm gonna get whoever did that."

Childress appeared to still be focused on what Decker had said to him.

"There's no law against an FBI agent investigating a crime," said Decker.

"I know you're not working this case for the FBI," said Natty.

"Based on what?" said Decker.

"Based on . . . based on . . . based on I damn well said so."

Bailey gave this comment a well-deserved eye roll, picked up her briefcase, and said in an incredulous tone to the still confused-looking Childress, "The

Peter Principle?" When Childress still looked perplexed, she added, "For God's sake, just Google it."

She walked out.

Decker followed her.

"Where the hell do you think you're going?" snapped Childress.

Decker kept right on walking.

26

Decker had just settled into his bed.

His arrest and the bail hearing had shaken him more than he cared to show. With someone like Childress breathing down his neck, solving this case was going to be even harder. And it was difficult enough as it was.

He rolled over and punched his pillow, shaping it to be more comfortable.

Decker's memory—his albatross and gold mine all in one. It allowed him incredible tools to successfully do what he did, but also imprisoned him within an indestructible cell of recollections any other human being could simply allow time to extinguish.

He was actually glad Lancaster had had to recuse herself and Jamison had gone back to the FBI. Better to suffer this alone. After this case, he might just chuck the FBI and move off somewhere by himself. Well, he might not have a choice about that, actually. He knew Bogart was growing weary of his constantly going off on his own cases. The FBI was many things, and a bureaucracy with rules and ways of doing things was one of the main ones. Decker couldn't keep bucking that bureaucracy and those rules without suffering the consequences.

So it might just be me going it alone after this.

This admittedly self-pitying analysis came to an abrupt halt when the knock came at his door.

Groaning, he looked at his watch.

It was nearly eleven o'clock.

He turned over and closed his eyes.

Knock, knock.

He ignored it.

Then pounding followed.

He jumped out of bed, slid on his pants, padded across the small room to the door, and flung it open, ready to read the riot act to whoever was there. And if it was Natty, to perhaps do more than that.

It was not Natty.

Instead, there stood Melvin Mars—all nearly six-foot-three, two hundred and forty chiseled pounds of him.

Decker was so taken aback that he blinked and then closed his eyes for a full second. When he re-opened them, Mars was still there.

Mars chuckled at this. "No, I'm not a dream, Decker, or a nightmare."

The pair, rivals from their college football days, had run into each other again when Mars, a Heisman Trophy finalist and lock to be a first-round NFL pick as a running back from Texas, had been sitting on death row for murder when another man had come forward claiming to have committed the crimes. This revelation had come on the very eve of Mars's execution.

Decker had helped to prove Mars's innocence, and Mars was given a full pardon and a huge monetary reward from both the federal government and the state of Texas as compensation for the erroneous guilty verdict as well as the racist and brutal treatment Mars had received at the hands of his prison guards. He owned the apartment building in D.C. where Decker and Jamison lived, leasing apartments out to those hardworking folks who otherwise could not afford rental prices in the capital with its high cost of living. He had been dating a woman whom they all had encountered during a previous investigation. Harper Brown worked for military intelligence. Unlike Mars, she came from money, but the two of them hit it off immediately. The last Decker had heard they were vacationing somewhere in the Mediterranean.

"What the hell are you doing here?" said Decker.

"Just happened to find myself in the area."

Decker looked at him skeptically. "Alex called you and told you to come here and watch over me, didn't she? Because she couldn't."

"If I lied and said no, would it matter?"

"Come on in." He closed the door behind Mars, who took a look around.

"Man, the FBI must have a pretty hefty per diem to let you stay in a luxury place like this. Couple levels above the Ritz."

"This actually used to be my home."

"I get that, Decker. My prison cell in Texas was a lot smaller and it didn't have a window."

"Do you have a place to stay? This only has the one bed."

"I'm actually staying here too. Just checked in. Exit date to be determined."

"You can afford to stay at the fanciest place in town."

"I've never needed fancy."

"I wish Alex hadn't done this."

"She cares about you. That's what friends do."

"Did she fill you in on what's been going on here?"

Mars sat down in the only chair in the room and nodded, as Decker perched on the edge of the bed. "She did. Sounds pretty messed up. What's happened since you two parted company?"

Decker started to explain. When he got to the part about being arrested, Mars put up his hand. "Whoa, whoa, wait a minute, your butt was in jail? I would've paid to see that."

"Depending on how things turn out, you might get to see it for free. On visitors' day."

"You're kidding, right?"

"I made some enemies in this town."

Mars's grin widened. "Not you, Decker. You're such a teddy bear. Never rub anyone the wrong way."

"You don't have to be here, Melvin."

"I don't go anywhere I don't want to. I spent twenty years going nowhere, and I had no choice in the matter. Lots of catching up to do on that score. I'm here because I want to be, make no mistake."

"Where's Harper?"

"Back at work."

"How was the Mediterranean?"

"Magical. Never seen that much water in my whole life. West Texas is pretty damn dry."

"You two getting serious?"

"We're having fun, Amos. That's the gear we want to be in right now. No more, no less." He sat back and looked around. "So how do we do this? Looks like you got two mysteries. One from a long time ago. And one from right now."

"But they're connected. They have to be."

"So Meryl Hawkins gets out of prison, comes here, and tells you he's innocent. He wants you and your old partner to prove him right and clear his name. But that same night he gets killed."

"And the widow of one of his alleged victims has disappeared."

"So you think this Susan Richards shot him and now she's on the run?"

"I don't know, but it looks that way. They still

haven't found her car or her. Which is pretty weird in this day and age."

"Well, it's a pretty big country too. Somebody can disappear if they want to. Look at my old man."

"Your father was a little more experienced with stuff like that than I suspect Susan Richards is. And he disappeared before there were smartphones with camera and video capabilities, and social media was nonexistent."

Mars shrugged. "Proof's in the pudding. Lady hasn't surfaced. And you still haven't answered my question. How do we attack this sucker?"

"Other things being equal, I think we need to solve the crime in the past to have any shot at figuring out who killed Meryl Hawkins."

"Well, you solved my cold case, and that one went back even further. So my money's on you."

"I'm not sure I'd take that bet."

"Going back in time. You know how you did it with me. So now?"

"I've spoken to the people involved back then. The widows. The daughter. The only remaining neighbors."

"How about the first responders? The ME?"

"The cops are no longer working. They've moved out of the area. The ME passed away three years ago."

"But you still got the records, though." Mars tapped his forehead. "Up here."

"Not all of them, because . . . because I didn't read

everything. In particular the forensic file, at least not thoroughly."

Mars raised his eyebrows at this.

Decker did not miss this reaction. "I'd been a homicide detective all of five days when the call came in. That's not an excuse. But the print and DNA were slam dunks, or at least I thought they were. I wasn't as diligent about the rest of the stuff. And it might have cost Hawkins his freedom and then his life."

"Only thing that makes you, Decker, is human. And let me tell you I had my doubts about that." He tacked on a grin with this.

"I'm not supposed to make mistakes, at least not like that."

"And here you are trying to make up for it. Doing the best you can. That's all you can do."

When Decker didn't respond to this, Mars said, "What's wrong, Amos? This isn't the guy I know. Something is eating at you. And it's not just that you might have screwed up. So lay it out there, dude. Can't help if I can't follow."

"Some people are meant to be alone, work alone, just . . . alone."

"And you think you're one of them?"

"I *know* I am, Melvin."

"I was alone for twenty years, Amos. Just me and steel bars and concrete walls. And maybe a lethal needle waiting on my ass."

"Now I'm not following."

"Then let me lay it out clean for you. I was convinced I was a loner too. That that was just how life was going to be. But I made a mistake."

"How so?"

"I let circumstances beyond my control define me. That's not good. That's worse than lying to yourself. It's like you're lying to your soul."

"And you think that's where I am?"

"Alex told me why you two were here in the first place. Visiting your family at the cemetery."

Decker looked away.

"You feel tied to this place, and I get that. But see, you're not. You moved from here. Joined the FBI. And if you hadn't done that, I'd be rotting in a prison in Texas, or more likely dead. But this is not about me, it's about you."

"Maybe it was a mistake to move," said Decker.

"Maybe it was and maybe it wasn't. But the point is, you made that choice. You got the world's greatest memory, Amos. There's nothing you can't remember. Now I know that's a blessing and a curse. And with your family and what happened to them it's the worst of all possible things. But all the good stuff? All the happy times? You remember those too like they just happened. Hell, I can barely remember how my mom looked. I can't really remember her touch or her smile. I can't remember any of my birthdays when I was little. I just have to imagine how it was. But you *can* remember that stuff. So, you could move to Siberia and be out in a blizzard and you just got to close your eyes and you're right back here having dinner with your wife. Holding her hand. Getting Molly ready for school. Reading a book to her. It's all there, dude. It's *all* there."

Decker finally looked at him. "And that's what's so hard, Melvin." His voice slightly shook. "I will always very clearly know, like it was yesterday, how damn much I lost."

Mars rose, sat down next to his friend, and put his big arm around Decker's wide shoulders. "And that's what they call life, my friend. The good, the bad, and the ugly. But don't let the last two diminish the first one, 'cause the first one's the important one. You keep that one alive, man, you can face down anything. That is the gospel truth."

The men sat there in silence, but still communicating exactly what they were feeling, as the best of friends often do.

27

"Don't think Alex would approve of this," said Mars.

He and Decker were standing in front of the breakfast bar in the lobby of the Residence Inn the next morning. It was laden with food constituting every cardiologist's nightmare.

"I used to love this part of the day," replied Decker, looking longingly at plates of bacon and plump sausages and scrambled eggs, and then over at stacks of pancakes, waffles, and jars of syrup.

"Well, it didn't love you back."

"Amos!"

They both looked over at the tiny, withered woman who was hurrying toward them carrying a plate of flaky biscuits. She was in her eighties, with sparkling white hair crammed under a hair net.

"Heard you were back in town." She held up the plate. "You want to just take this plate to your table, like you used to? Made 'em myself."

"Hello, June." He looked at the biscuits for a long moment, until Mars poked him in the side.

Decker started and said, "I think I'll pass, but

thanks. I think I'll just get some, um, orange juice and a bowl of the oatmeal."

June eyed him suspiciously. "You've lost weight. I mean, you're almost skinny. You sick?"

"No, I'm actually healthier than I've been in a long time."

Her look said that she highly doubted this was true. "Well, if you change your mind, just give me the high sign." She glanced at Mars. "Your friend could use some fattening up too."

Mars cracked a smile. "Yes ma'am. I'll get right on that, *tomorrow*."

"Well, all right then." She scampered off.

Mars eyed all the food at the buffet and shook his head. "Man, how did you end up not stroking at your table when you lived here?"

They had just finished their meal when Decker's phone buzzed. It was Sally Brimmer.

"I copied all the files to a flash drive," she said, her voice barely above a whisper. "I don't want to email it to you because that could be traced, and I like my job."

"I can meet you somewhere and you can give me the flash."

"I get off work at six. You know McArthur Park on the east side of town?"

"Yeah."

"I can meet you at the little pond there, say six-thirty?"

"I'll be there. And I really appreciate this, Ms. Brimmer."

"Just make it Sally. Co-conspirators should be able to use first names, *Amos*."

The line went dead.

Mars eyed him. "Good news?"

"I think so, yeah."

His phone buzzed again. He thought it might be Brimmer calling back, but it was another number. One that Decker recognized.

"Captain Miller?"

"Amos, first I want to say that I'm sorry."

"For what?"

"For what happened to you. The arrest, and the bail hearing, where I heard from Beth that Natty and Childress made it crystal clear that they're unmitigated assholes."

"I already knew that. And none of this was your fault."

"No, it was, because I let Childress get the upper hand. He outmaneuvered me. But I played another hand last night. I went straight to the commissioner. And then he went to his boss. The result is that right now you are allowed to observe on the case."

"What does that mean exactly?"

"Pretty much like it sounds. Natty and Childress

can't stop you from being there. You can look at clues, you can even talk to witnesses, and run down potential leads. You can't bring suspects in for questioning, though, but you will be privy to forensic testing and other results of the investigation."

"And Natty will still be working it?"

"Unfortunately, yes. I wish to God that Mary hadn't had to recuse herself."

"You're not alone on that. But I appreciate all that you did, Captain Miller. And at least I can be part of the case again." He glanced at Mars. "I do have a new assistant working with me. I assume he can tag along."

"You can try, Amos. Natty will probably blow a gasket, but I'll leave it to you to figure out a way. Now, there's one more thing."

"What's that?"

"They found Susan Richards's car."

"Where?"

Miller gave him the details.

"But no trace of her?" said Decker.

"None. I'm sure Natty is already up there checking it out. Tread carefully. I wish I could offer more, but the bureaucracy keeps getting in the way."

Again, the line went dead.

Decker quickly explained to Mars what had just happened.

"So they found her ride, but not her? What does that tell you?"

"Not much," replied Decker.

"So we head there now?"

"Yes, we do."

June was walking past and Decker grabbed a couple biscuits off the platter without the tiny woman even noticing. He flipped one to Mars before taking a bite out of his. "Don't say I never gave you anything."

Mars looked down at his biscuit before biting into it as well. "Yeah, like a heart attack."

Decker pulled his rental to a stop right on the other side of the police tape flapping in a stiff breeze. Cop cars were everywhere, along with state trooper vehicles.

The car was about two hours outside of Burlington. It had been discovered behind an abandoned motel that had closed its doors about forty years before. It was on a local road that had been shunned by travelers once a nearby interstate opened.

Decker and Mars climbed out of the car and looked around. An officer immediately came up to them. Decker pulled out his creds and held them up.

"FBI?" said the officer. "What are you doing here?"

"Same thing you are. Trying to find Susan Richards."

"Hey!"

Decker had expected this, and still his blood pressure started to rise.

Natty walked over to them. "I guess you talked to Miller."

"*Captain* Miller. Your superior."

Natty pointed a finger in Decker's face. "You *observe*, that's all. You step out of line, your ass is right back in the slammer again."

The cop looked between them and said, "You put an FBI agent in jail?"

"He's not a real FBI agent."

"Really?" said Mars sharply. "This dude saved the life of the president of the United States. Has a direct line to the man in the White House. Had his picture taken with him, got a medal and a letter of commendation." Mars crossed two of his fingers. "Dudes are like this."

The officer looked up at Decker in awe.

Natty bristled and gazed up at Mars. "Who the hell are you?"

"He's my assistant," said Decker.

"I thought you worked with Jamison."

"She's on another mission."

"Is he an FBI agent?"

"He operates under the auspices of my creds."

"What exactly does that mean?" said Natty.

"It means I go to the commissioner if you try to block me from observing, Natty."

"You are so full of shit."

"Who found the car?" asked Decker.

Natty looked like he might not answer.

"Look, Natty, I was being straight with you before. If I can find out who did this, the collar is yours."

"Like I need your help to do that."

"Okay, then I observe without your help. But if I make the collar, the FBI gets all the credit. But I don't see how Childress would want that. And he may be backing you right now, but that wasn't always the case, Natty. He'll throw you under the bus in a second if he thinks it'll make him look good. Remember the Hargrove case?"

At the mention of this name, Natty noticeably stiffened, and though his look was still sullen, he flipped open his notebook.

"Guy Dumpster diving found the car at around four o'clock this morning. Called in the locals. They pulled up our BOLO and notified us."

"Can we take a look at the vehicle?"

"The trace team's already been over it."

"Just observing."

Natty licked his lips, made a grunting sound, turned, and walked off. Decker and Mars followed.

Mars whispered, "Don't see why you thought this guy was an A-hole, Decker. He's a real pussycat."

"Minus the cat," replied Decker.

"So this Childress guy is even worse?"

"He's worse because, unlike Natty, he can slickly pretend to be what he's not, to the *right* people. And that's what makes him so dangerous."

28

The small old Honda with the bad muffler was wedged next to a huge rusted construction Dumpster, like an enormous barnacle on a ship's metal hull.

Decker and Mars stood a few feet away. Decker's gaze swept over the car and the environs, before alighting on the blue-scrubbed tech collecting evidence.

"Hey again, Decker," said Kelly Fairweather. "Who's your friend?"

"Melvin Mars," said Mars, stepping forward and putting out his hand. "I'm, uh, assisting Agent Decker in this investigation."

"Cool," said Fairweather.

"What do you have so far?" asked Decker, keeping one eye on Natty, who was consulting with another tech on the other side of the Honda.

"Well, for starters, no prints other than Susan Richards's. Inside or out."

"Makes sense, it *is* her car," said Mars.

"Her luggage gone from the back?" asked Decker.

"Yep. Nothing there."

"Keys?"

"No keys."

"No meaningful trace?"

"No blood, semen, body parts, human tissue, or other significant biological remains."

"No sign of another person being in the car?"

"Nope. Just her."

"Mind if I take a look?" asked Decker.

"Go ahead. Use these."

He moved toward the car after slapping on the pair of latex gloves Fairweather had handed him. Mars followed behind him.

Natty looked up as Decker approached, but then returned to his conversation with the other tech.

All four doors of the Honda were open, and so was the trunk liftgate. Decker pointed to the Dumpster. "I'm assuming someone checked for a body in there."

Fairweather nodded and made a face. "We did. Nothing but trash. I'll need a tetanus booster."

"No evidence from her or the car in it?"

"Not that we could find."

Decker ran his eye over all of this and then poked his head inside the front driver's-side door and checked the seats there. He did the same for the rear seats as Mars hovered by his shoulder.

"Kelly, have you logged the positions for all prints you found, interior and exterior?"

She nodded and pulled out an electronic pad. "All

on here. Lot easier than the way we used to do it years ago, right?"

"Right," said Decker absently as he looked over the different digital screens.

Fairweather said, "All the usual places. Steering wheel, cupholder, console, glove compartment, gear-shift, control knobs, rearview mirror, dashboard, inside of the door and window."

"And outside?" asked Decker as he moved to that digital page.

"Door handle, driver's front side, and rear doors. And exterior driver's-side window. Again, the usual."

"And we've had no meaningful rain since she disappeared."

"Correct."

"So no recent prints would have been damaged or even washed off by a heavy rain."

"Right."

"How long do prints last on something?" asked Mars.

"Depends on the surface involved, what sub-stance might have been on the fingers, the timing, the weather conditions, a whole host of factors," said Fairweather.

Decker handed her back the pad. "What else?"

"Not a lot. We don't know how far the car's been driven because we didn't know the odometer reading before she left. She did have an oil change sticker on her windshield. The car's been driven about four hundred miles since then, but the oil change happened over three weeks ago. Not much we can deduce from that."

"Insect debris on the front and the windshield?"

"Not too much. But she could have gotten it washed after she left town."

Decker nodded because he too had thought of this.

"So, Decker, have you solved it?" Natty had walked around the side of the car and was looking up at him.

"Just observing," said Decker.

Natty smirked. "Always knew you were overrated."

"Yeah, dude's been here ten seconds," said Mars. "How long you been here?"

Natty looked over at him. "Who the hell are you, really?"

"Decker's *assistant*. You might want to follow my lead on that, you know? *Assist* the man."

"You got a real comedian here, Decker," said Natty irritably.

"One thing I would draw your attention to," said Decker.

"What's that?"

"There's no print on the rear liftgate."

"So what? Richards got in the front seat."

"After she put a really heavy piece of luggage in the rear compartment."

"She used her key fob to open the trunk."

Decker shook his head. "Agatha Bates, her neighbor, said Richards started up the car and then went back inside and brought out a large piece of luggage that she put in the rear cargo hold. And she struggled to do so before slamming the liftgate shut." Decker paused and looked from Fairweather back to Natty.

"There were no prints anywhere on the liftgate," said Fairweather. "I went inch by inch."

"Pretty weird," said Mars.

"No, it's not," said Natty. "She used the button on her key fob to open it, like I just said."

"She couldn't," said Decker.

"Why?"

"The keys were in the ignition. This car is old enough, so you have to put the key *in* the ignition, not just have it with you to start the car. So the key and the fob already would have been in the vehicle." He eyed Natty. "Check out the ignition if you don't believe me."

"Okay, if that's the case, where's the print?" said Natty, looking confused.

"Good question."

"What does its absence tell us?" asked Natty.

"Another good question," said Decker. "And here's one more. Why did she start the car first and then go back into the house and bring the luggage out? Why not bring the luggage out, start the car, and drive off? The way she did it, the lady had to make two trips instead of one."

Natty's brow furrowed. "Okay, I give. Why would she—?"

But Decker had already turned and walked off.

"Damn it, I hate when the sonofabitch does that," exclaimed Natty.

Mars said, "Yeah, I get that. But second piece of advice, man?"

Natty eyed him. "Why should I listen to you? I don't even know you."

"Yeah, but I know Decker. You want to solve this sucker and get your next promotion, give the dude some room to work."

"I'm running this case!"

"But what you don't want to do is run it into the ground. Just my two cents."

Mars turned and followed Decker.

Natty looked at Fairweather, who was staring at him. "What?" he barked.

"I don't know that guy, but to me, he makes a lot of sense."

"Why does everybody think Amos Decker walks on water!" barked Natty.

"Hey, the guy's got his issues. We all know that. But when it comes to catching bad guys, do you know *anybody* who does it better?"

She went back to work, leaving Natty staring down at his shoes.

29

On the drive back to town, Decker said nothing.

Mars would look over at him occasionally, and several times appeared ready to ask something, but then he'd glance away and remain silent.

"You have something to say?" Decker finally asked.

Mars grinned. "Was I that obvious?"

"Apparently."

"That Natty guy has it in for you. What's that about?"

"He didn't like the fact that Lancaster and I solved most of the homicides in Burlington. Well, more than most. Basically all. He was the rising star in the department before I got bumped to detective. He got relegated to investigating lesser crimes, and I think he blames me. Then he made a big mistake on the Hargrove case. Missing person turned homicide. That sidetracked his career. Since I left I guess he's been attempting a comeback. And he kisses Pete Childress's ass, even though the guy hung him out to dry when the fallout came on the Hargrove matter."

"Is he any good at being a detective?"

"He's *competent*. But he always goes for the easiest solution. And he makes mistakes. Gets sloppy at times. Assumes things he shouldn't."

"Like you did with the murders all those years ago?"

Decker glanced over at him. "I deserved that."

"Come on, I was just pulling your chain. I'm telling you, you keep yourself under all that pressure, you're gonna pop one day."

"I think my popping days are over."

"What's on the agenda now?"

Decker looked at the clock on the dashboard.

"We've got some time before we meet Sally Brimmer and pick up the flash drive."

"So where?"

"Susan Richards's house."

Decker pulled his car into the driveway about two hours later and they got out. Decker glanced over at Agatha Bates's home and thought he could see the old woman on her screen porch reading a book.

Mars looked the house over. "You think Richards is dead?"

"No signs of violence in the car. Or outside it. No one's found a body. But still, she could be dead."

"How are we going to get in?"

"I've got a key. My old partner, Mary Lancaster, gave it to me while we were working Susan Richards's disappearance." Decker put the key in the lock and began to turn it.

"Wait a minute, Decker. Will this get you in trouble? Aren't you just supposed to be observing?"

"Well, when I go into the house, I'll just be *observing*."

Decker led Mars into the front part of the house.

"So, Richards packs a big bag and hightails it out of here after you bring her in for questioning on the Hawkins murder."

"And we couldn't confirm her alibi. The other neighbors weren't home during the time in question. And the old lady across the street, the one who saw Richards leaving, can't completely account for Richards's movements when Hawkins was killed."

"Which may explain why she ran for it. She killed the guy."

"But how would she even know he was back in town?" Decker wondered.

"Maybe she ran into him. Or saw him and followed him back to the Residence Inn. That's possible."

"It is *possible*, but not probable."

"Then what are we doing here?"

Decker led the way upstairs and into the woman's bedroom. He went straight for the closet. It had been reconfigured and enlarged, he figured, because the house was old enough not to have originally had such a spacious closet. It was packed with clothes on hangers, sweaters and shoes on shelves, and purses and handbags on hooks. He stood in the middle of the space and looked around.

Mars said, "Harper has a closet about four times the size of this one. And it's packed to the gills. Didn't know one person could need all that stuff."

"Society demands that women care more about their appearance than men."

"Wow, that's very enlightened of you."

"It's not me. My wife would always say that."

"Well, looks like Susan Richards took that to heart."

Decker noted several empty hangers, a space on a shelf where it looked like two pairs of shoes had been removed, and a hook without a corresponding bag.

He left the closet and went over to a chest of drawers. He went through each one. Then he walked into the bathroom and examined every inch of the space, including the bins under the sink.

He got up and opened the medicine cabinet and looked at the line of prescription bottles. He picked them up and examined each one in turn, holding one bottle for a beat longer before replacing it.

"Lady is on a lot of meds," said Mars.

"*America* is on a lot of meds," replied Decker.

They walked back down to the first floor and Decker headed over to the fireplace mantel. He looked over each of the photos lined up there.

"Her family?" asked Mars.

Decker nodded. "Husband and two kids. In an ideal world Susan Richards might be a grandmother by now."

Mars shook his head. "There's nothing ideal about this world."

Decker looked around the room, his eyes taking in everything and then processing it.

"What are you seeing, Decker?" asked Mars as he too stared around the space. "Is anything missing?'

"Not really. And that's the problem, Melvin."

30

It was dusk now and with the dropping of the sun, the temperature had lowered to a level where one could see one's breath.

Decker had left Mars in the car parked at the curb. His rationale was that Sally Brimmer would not appreciate another person being in the loop of her possibly illegal action in giving Decker the records he needed. He strode through the small park to the pond that lay near its rear, which one reached by traversing a winding brick path. There was no one else there that he could see.

When he turned the last corner and the pond came into view, so did Brimmer. She had on a long trench coat, a hat, and gloves. She looked over at Decker and hurried past the pond, which had an aerator in its middle, throwing off streams of water and affording a pleasing sound. That was also good, Decker thought, because it would be difficult for anyone to eavesdrop on them.

She reached him, her hand in her pocket. Brimmer suddenly shivered.

"Winter's definitely coming," noted Decker.

"It's not the weather," she said, a trace of bitterness in her tone. "I'm nervous. What I'm doing could cost me my job."

"No one will find out from me. And if it makes you feel any better, I'm only going to use the files to try to find the truth."

"I know that," she said, her voice now contrite. She looked around and pulled her hand out of her pocket. In her palm was a flash drive.

"How did you manage to scan all the files without anyone knowing?"

"I've been after the department to convert paper files to digital ones. I've actually been doing some of it myself, although it's not technically my responsibility. But I had the time, and it wasn't like some of the older people at the department had any interest, or would even know how to do it. I just included the files you wanted in a stack I was already doing." She handed him the flash drive.

"Ingenious," said Decker.

"High praise coming from you."

"Captain Miller managed to get a meeting with the commissioner, with the result that I'm officially back on the case, as an observer."

"Well, that's something."

"It's better than nothing," agreed Decker. "They found Susan Richards's car and I was able to go over it."

"What about Blake?"

"He was there but voiced no objections. He might be seeing that I could be useful, especially if he gets the credit if I do figure this out."

"He'll turn on you if he gets the chance," said Brimmer warningly.

"I'm under no illusions when it comes to Natty." He cocked his head. "How about you?"

"How about me what?" she said defensively.

"You've got a lot going for you, Sally. You could do a lot better than Natty. Someone your own age who's actually single, for instance. I guess I just don't see the attraction on your end."

"Why do you care? I always thought you were just this . . . machine." She suddenly looked chastened. "I'm sorry, that was really out of line. I didn't mean it."

"You're not the first to say that, and you won't be the last. As to you, I was a father with a daughter, like I said. I . . . I don't want you to be hurt or get in a situation you can't get out of."

Brimmer looked down at the brick pavers under her feet. "I work long hours. All I know are cops. I don't have any family here, and few friends. Blake . . . he took an interest. He even used that old line that his wife just doesn't get him or his work." She laughed hollowly. "And I fell for it, I guess. Just like a million other women. But he did make me feel special."

"*Did*?"

She smiled resignedly. "I've broken it off with him, Amos. It wasn't just what you said, although I needed to hear that too. He *is* married. And I wouldn't want that to happen to me if I were married. It's not fair. And it does speak to a person's character if they're willing to cheat like that, as you said."

"I'm glad you reached that decision."

"You never cheated on your wife, did you?"

"Never even thought about it. I had everything, Sally. A wife who I loved beyond anything I'd ever felt before. And a daughter who I would have sacrificed anything for. Now I don't have either one."

"But you have memories. Good ones."

"Yeah, I do. But it's not the same. Even for someone with a memory like mine. Memories don't keep you warm at night. And they don't make you laugh, not really." He paused. "But they can make you cry."

She put a hand on his arm and squeezed. "And to think, I used to believe that you were this gigantic jerk."

"I can be. As you well know."

"And you can be someone else too, Amos. Someone I would like to call a friend."

"We *are* friends, Sally. I know what it took for you to help me. Even if my memory sucked, I'd never forget that."

They grew silent until Brimmer said, "I better get going."

"I'll walk you out. It's pretty dark in here and there're a lot of places for creeps to hide."

"Never stop being a cop?"

"It's just how I'm wired."

They reached the street a couple of minutes later.

"Thank you again," said Decker.

"No, thank *you*, Amos." She spontaneously went over and hugged him. Decker bent down to hug her back.

Right as the shot hit.

31

Decker felt the woman go limp in his arms at the same time as he felt something wet hit his face. He slumped to the pavement holding Brimmer, as he heard shouts and feet running. He looked up to see Mars sprinting toward him.

"Get down, Melvin!" he called out.

"Over there, Decker!" said Mars, pointing to his left, across the street.

Decker checked Brimmer. The bullet had entered the left side of her head and exited out the other side, in the direction of the park. Her glassy eyes were staring lifelessly up at him.

He knew she was dead, but he still checked her pulse. With no blood pumping through her body, the woman was already growing cold.

"Shit," Decker said, looking dazed and in disbelief. He touched his face where her blood had landed.

He looked over at Mars, and then across the street from where the shot had come. He pulled his gun, got up, and raced across the street, with Mars right behind him.

Decker pulled out his phone, dialed 911, identified himself, and told the dispatcher what had happened and the exact location. "We're in pursuit of the shooter. Get some cop cars out here now and we can box the sonofabitch in." He put the phone in his pocket and picked up his pace.

Mars took a slight lead because he had seen where the shot had come from. As they ran along, Decker said, "Did you see the person?"

Mars shook his head. "Just a silhouette, at the opening of that alley. I had no time to warn you. I just happened to glance that way right as he fired."

They reached the alley and peered down it. Decker checked the building. It was being rehabbed. Construction materials were all over the place, along with scaffolding.

"Think the asshole's still down there?" said Mars.

"Don't know. If he is, we'll get him."

As soon as Decker said this, they could hear the sirens.

"Cavalry's on the way," he noted.

"But if I'm the shooter, I'm getting the hell out of here," said Mars.

"Which is why we're not waiting. Stay behind me."

"You don't have to be my human shield, Decker."

"You're a running back, Melvin. I'm a blocker. But if he takes me out, do not let me die in vain."

They moved down the alley, intently listening for

any sound of footsteps, breathing, or, more ominously, a trigger being cocked.

Decker held up a hand. He had heard something.

"What?" hissed Mars.

Decker put a finger to his lips.

Now Mars could hear it too. Heavy breathing, like someone had been running but had stopped.

As the sirens drew closer, Decker started to pick up his pace. Mars stayed right with him. They reached a spot about midway down the alley when Decker halted once more. The spot was brightly lit by overhead lights. The sound of breathing had grown stronger.

Decker pointed his gun straight ahead and then hustled forward.

The man was lying on the asphalt, his head on top of what looked to be a rolled-up bunch of rags. Next to him was a bag full of items. He was dressed in filthy clothing. The heavy breathing that they had heard was his snoring, apparently.

"Decker," whispered Mars. "Is that a gun?"

Lying on the ground next to the man and within reach of his outstretched hand was a rifle with a scope. Decker stepped forward and used his foot to slowly move the gun away from the man.

The next moment he was slammed against the brick wall. His face hit the rough brick and he felt several cuts opening on his face. His pistol smashed into the brick and he felt something snap. The collision had been so sudden that he felt sick to his stomach.

He turned, eyed the man still lying on the ground, dead asleep. The attack had not come from there.

"Decker!"

Decker regained his equilibrium, cleared his head, and looked back.

Mars was dodging out of the way of a knife strike, as the man who had clocked Decker moved in for the kill. He was small but wiry, and his movements were laser quick and precise.

Decker hurtled forward, and when the man turned the knife on him, he pointed his gun and fired at his leg.

Absolutely nothing happened. The impact with the wall must have damaged the weapon.

The next instant the man kicked the gun out of Decker's hand, then drove his fist into Decker's gut, doubling him over.

Decker staggered back at the same moment that Mars hit the man from behind so hard that he was lifted off his feet, flew forward, and slammed into the wall. He was up in an instant, though, and whirled around, the blade in his hand.

He charged after Mars and slashed him on the arm. Mars fell back and the man was about to cut him again when Decker launched forward and wrapped his big arms around the assailant, pinning his arms and the knife to his sides. Under the illumination of the lights attached to the buildings, he could see that, despite the cold, the man's muscled forearms were exposed, and covered in tats—words and symbols.

A few seconds of struggle later, the man slammed the back of his head against Decker's face. Blood flew out of Decker's nose and mouth. Then the man was able to point the knife downward and jam it into Decker's thigh. Decker cried out and released the man, who hit the ground running and soon disappeared from sight as the sirens grew closer. Decker put a hand over his leg wound.

Mars ran forward, took off his windbreaker, and wrapped it around Decker's thigh.

Decker said, "Are you okay?"

"He didn't get me bad. Who the hell was that guy?"

"He's the one who shot Sally Brimmer."

"You have any idea why?"

"The only idea I have is that he was trying to shoot me. And she just got in the way."

32

The morgue again.

Decker had been in far too many of them.

And the electric blue light sensation was bombarding him almost like the night he had found his family. It was as if a strobe was attached to the ceiling of the room and was blasting the unsettling light into every pore of the place.

He touched his leg where underneath his pants a large butterfly bandage had been applied. The emergency room doctor had told him he'd been lucky. Another couple inches to the left and his femoral artery would have been nicked. And he might have bled out right there in that alley.

He next touched his face, which was covered in Band-Aids and bandages. He was stiff and sore and felt like he'd just played in an NFL game. Mars was next to him, his injured arm in a sling. But at least they were still alive. Lying in front of them was Sally Brimmer's pale body with a sheet pulled up to her neck.

The homeless man in the alley had turned out to

be what he looked like—homeless. And strung out on so much crap that it had taken the EMTs an hour to wake him up. The gun had no usable prints, and Decker knew why. The shooter had been wearing gloves. He had probably flung the murder weapon next to the homeless man to simply get rid of it. He had attacked Decker and Mars because they had gotten to him before he reached the other end of the alley. Lying in wait, he had tried to add two more lives to the one he'd already taken. Unfortunately, he had managed to elude the police and get away.

The ME was in the room, washing a few of his instruments in the sink. There was only one overhead fluorescent light on, throwing the room into shadows and making an already disconcerting sensation worse.

A moment later the door clanged open and there was Blake Natty, his face white, his features screwed up in agony. He lurched over to Brimmer's sheet-draped body and looked down at it. He put a hand to his mouth, and Decker heard the man start to quietly sob.

No one said anything until Natty had composed himself and rubbed his eyes dry on his coat sleeve. He looked over at Decker and Mars. Next, he ran his gaze over their wounds. "Heard he almost got you both too."

"Almost," said Decker. "The guy was a lot smaller than we were."

"Small but lethal," said Mars. "I've seen guys with

shivs, hardened cons, who couldn't wield a blade anything like that dude."

"Guys with shivs? Hardened cons?" said Natty. "Were you a prison guard or something?"

"Or something," said Mars quietly.

Decker rubbed his stomach. "And he had fists like bricks. And some crazy arm tats."

Natty said, "What were you and Sally even doing there?"

Decker knew this question was coming and had prepared several answers. One came tumbling out. It happened to be the truth.

"I arranged to meet Sally at McArthur Park. We were coming out to the street when the guy opened fire."

"Why did you want to meet with her?"

"Because I wanted to get her help on the case. I won't be able to help you solve it by merely *observing*, Blake. You know that, and I know that."

Decker had been prepared for Natty to explode at this comment, but to his surprise the detective merely nodded. He rubbed his nose and said, "I guess I can see that. Do you . . . do you think Sally was the target?"

"No. I was. Someone already tried to kill me once. We were standing so close together that the shooter hit Sally and not me." He paused and looked at the disconsolate Natty. "I'm sorry, Blake. I really am. Sally was just trying to do the right thing."

Mars said, "Why is someone so desperate to kill you?"

"Someone doesn't want Decker to figure out the truth," replied Natty. "I mean, you worked on that case all those years ago. Hawkins came to you and Mary to clear his name. And now they're going to try to stop you. Mary got recused, but you're still on the trail."

"So are you," pointed out Decker. "I think we all have to watch our backs."

"So you think someone hired the guy to do this?" said Natty.

"I do. Which means that Hawkins was innocent. And that means the forensic evidence tying him to the scene was somehow forged."

Natty glanced at him incredulously. "Prints and DNA at a crime scene. Forged?"

"It can be done," responded Decker.

"It would be hard as hell," retorted Natty.

"But not impossible."

"Who would want to frame Meryl Hawkins?" asked Natty.

"Wrong way to look at it."

"What's the right way, then?"

"Someone wanted to get away with murder. Hawkins was the patsy they chose to hold the bag. It could have been anybody, but for some reason they chose him. *That's* how we have to look at it."

"But, Decker, that turns this whole case upside down," said Natty.

"No, the case has always been right side up. We've just been looking at it from the wrong angle."

"You mean we have to start from square one?" said Natty.

Decker pulled the flash drive out of his pocket and held it up. "Commencing with this." He looked over at Brimmer's body. "Because the dead deserve answers," he said. "Sometimes more than the living."

33

Mars was sound asleep on the bed in Decker's room. It was past two in the morning and yet Decker was wide awake sitting in a chair and studying his laptop. He was scrolling through all the information that had been on the thumb drive Brimmer had given him.

He had taken off his belt holster with his new pistol to replace the old one damaged in the fight in the alley and laid it on the nightstand. He was still upset that he had let the shooter get away.

He and Mars had been at this for hours, until Mars had grown exhausted and collapsed on Decker's bed instead of going to his own room. The rain was pouring outside, and Decker could hear the drops ramming his window like thrown handfuls of gravel. It was one of those Ohio Valley storms that sprang up out of nowhere and pounded the entire state for a while.

But right now, he had tuned out the storm and homed in on the critical facts of his case from over thirteen years ago.

The 911 call had come in at 9:35 about a disturbance at the Richardses' house. That should have been a red flag for him, as should many things, in retrospect.

Who made the call? And what was the disturbance?

Not even the neighbors had noticed anything unusual that night. And there were no tracks of any other car coming to the house that night, just David Katz's. With the rain and mud, there would have been fresh tire tracks. So no other car had been there.

And here was the kicker. Decker was looking at the times of death provided by the medical examiner who had done the posts on the four bodies. The ME had said that all four victims had been killed close to eight-thirty. The records showed that he had based his conclusion on several indicators, one being the temperature of the bodies when they were discovered. Although Decker knew that was very tricky and could be affected by numerous factors. But a one-and-a-half-degree Fahrenheit drop in body temperature per hour after death was the standard rule.

But principally the ME had based his conclusion on the contents of the Richards family's stomachs. Susan Richards had testified that she had made dinner for the family and then left it in the oven before she went out. She said the family usually ate dinner at around six. The autopsies of the Richardses had revealed that if they had indeed eaten around six, the state of digestion of their food demonstrated that around two and a half hours had passed between their eating the food and being killed. It was not an exact time, the ME had been careful to stress, but he felt confident. And he could not possibly have been off by a full hour, he said.

Katz had shown up around six-thirty, according to Mrs. DeAngelo's testimony. The meal presumably had been finished and the kitchen had been cleaned up by then. Decker had even checked the dishwasher and seen the three empty plates and accompanying glasses and utensils inside. That probably confirmed that the Richardses had indeed eaten at around six. If they had still been eating when Katz had shown up, they might have invited him to join them, but the contents of the dishwasher demonstrated this had not been the case. He had probably arrived when they were cleaning up after finishing dinner.

Richards had offered him a beer and the kids had gone upstairs. And then someone had come and killed them all.

But that's when things got weird.

Because that meant that four people lay dead in the house for a little over an hour before someone called 911, citing a disturbance. And they had called from a phone that no one had been able to trace.

Now that Decker was looking at all of this with a detached, objective eye, the holes in the story seemed obvious. He actually groaned at his ineptitude.

Okay, time of death does not jibe with the 911 call

citing a disturbance. Four dead bodies could hardly cause a disturbance an hour after they died.

An alternative theory occurred to him suddenly. Had someone entered the house and stumbled upon the four bodies an hour later and that person had been the one to call 911? And had that person been Meryl Hawkins? That might explain how his fingerprints had been found on a light switch. But that could not explain his DNA ending up under Abigail Richards's fingernails. And how could Hawkins possess a phone that couldn't be traced?

Decker put those difficulties aside and focused on another. They really didn't know the order in which the victims had died. They had just assumed that the bodies on the first floor had been dealt with before the killer had gone upstairs to dispatch the two children.

That was problematic, Decker knew. And he had thought so all those years ago too, though he had finally discounted the significance of it. You shoot two people on the first floor, there's going to be some noise, and not just the gunshots. There will be people shouting, presumably, or a scuffle. The house was not that large. Those sounds would surely have carried upstairs.

There was one landline phone upstairs, in the parents' bedroom, and they had determined that neither of the Richards kids had cell phones. But still, they could have tried to reach the phone in the bedroom and call the police, then hide, or escape out a window. But they hadn't.

He could imagine the older Frankie Richards being a little more able to react to something like that than his younger sister. The kid was a drug user and also a small-time dealer, and was thus used to being around potentially bad actors and some level of risk. He kept cash and product at his house, they had found. He had to know that someone might come and try to take either one or both. Back in those days, you didn't have to have thousands of dollars or bricks of coke to warrant a theft like that. People would kill you for fifty bucks and a bag of weed.

Had the sounds of the storm covered the two deaths downstairs? And had the children not known what was happening until it was too late?

Decker passed on to his next question as the rain continued to pound outside. Why had Abigail been strangled when all the other victims had been shot? Decker thought he knew the answer to that one.

But as his eyes hovered over the screen, his mind suddenly filled up with so many blinding images that he almost felt like he would vomit.

In his mind's eye he was at his house the night he'd found his family dead. Electric blue sensations were pounding him from all corners. He had always been able to push, or at least diminish, this memory by banishing it to a far recess of his mind. But now, stunningly enough, he was unable to do so. It was as if he was no longer in control of his own mind. It was like a spontaneous, uncontrolled data dump from a computer.

He stood on shaky legs and wondered whether he could make it to the bathroom before he threw up. But then his stomach cleared, yet his mind did not.

He glanced over at Mars, who was still sound asleep on the bed.

Part of Decker wanted to wake his friend, explain what was happening to him, and ask for help. But what sort of help could Mars possibly give him? And Decker would feel embarrassed even asking.

Instead, he stumbled out of the room, down the hall, and then down the stairs. He used the rear exit door that he had told Lancaster about. He lurched outside where the trash and recycling Dumpsters were located. The rain was still pouring, and in just a few seconds Decker was soaked to the skin.

He finally hunched down under a metal roof that covered part of the rear of the inn. Over and over in his mind he saw himself going through his old house, the one now occupied by the Hendersons. Step by step.

His brother-in-law in the kitchen.

His wife on the floor by the side of their bed, only her foot visible when he entered the room.

And finally, Molly tied to the toilet in the bathroom with the sash from her robe. She'd been strangled to death, just like Abigail Richards.

And they had all died because of—

Me.

Decker put his hands over his head and sat there on the cold asphalt as the rain pounded down on the metal roof above.

He thought he had hit rock bottom when he'd lost his family, his job, his home. He had nothing.

But this, he thought to himself as the images unspooled over and over in his head, beginning with his brother-in-law and ending with his daughter.

This . . . this is rock bottom.

34

"You okay?"

It was the next morning and Mars was staring at Decker from across the table in the Residence Inn's dining area.

"Fine, why?"

"Because when I woke up you were in the bathroom, sounding like you were throwing up."

"Must've imagined it. My stomach was a little rocky, but that's it."

"I knocked on the door, don't you remember that? Asking if you were okay?"

"Don't *you* remember? I told you I was good and then I guess you went to your room. But before that you'd fallen asleep on my bed. You were probably mentally out of it when you checked on me."

Mars studied him for a moment but then shrugged. "You were up late. I ran out of gas."

"I was going over stuff, trying to make sense of things that don't seem to make sense."

"Like what?"

Decker outlined for him what he had thought about last night.

"Okay, they probably died around eight-thirty. And the call comes in an hour later," said Mars. "Well, I know from experience that an hour means a lot in a criminal investigation."

"Actually, it's an hour and *five* minutes, because the 911 call came in at nine-thirty-five. But the ME couldn't nail the TOD to the minute, so it's at least an hour discrepancy."

"What exactly did the 911 call say?"

"That they heard suspicious noises from inside the Richardses' house. People screaming and then a gunshot."

"But that's impossible. They weren't killed at nine-thirty-five."

"We don't know if the person really heard a shot or something else. And we don't know if they heard a shot that killed someone or just a shot."

"Well, dead people don't scream."

"True, but who's to say someone else wasn't in the house screaming at that time and that's what the caller heard?"

"Who would that person be?"

"I have no idea. I have no idea if such a person exists. But I do have a thought about something else."

"What?"

"Abigail Richards was strangled, not shot. Why?"

"You mean why wasn't she shot like the others because it was easier than strangling somebody?"

"Right."

Mars thought about this for a few moments. "I give."

"When you shoot someone, you don't transfer your DNA to under their fingernails. When you strangle someone, that opportunity presents itself."

"Wait a minute, are you saying somebody somehow got some of Hawkins's DNA from his skin and placed that under the girl's nails?"

"Yes."

"So that can be done?"

"Sure. And Hawkins *had* scratches on his arms. So something happened to him. I think that's when his DNA was harvested to incriminate him."

"But if somebody else had scratched him, let's say, and then took that skin and, I guess, blood and hair and put it under Abigail's nails, wouldn't some of that person's DNA also end up under her nails?"

"Possibly but not necessarily. Depends on how it was done. In any event, the DNA screen done at the time confirmed it was Hawkins's DNA under her nails."

"And the fingerprint? Could that have been placed there too?"

"It could be. It's extraordinarily rare to find a forged print. It's far more likely to find a fabricated one at a crime scene."

"What's the difference?" asked Mars, looking curious.

"Cop finds a glass with a suspect's prints on it outside of the crime scene and then places the glass *at* the crime scene and swears he found it there. Or a third party could do the same thing. Person wasn't at the scene but the glass with his print was because it was intentionally placed there. That's a fabrication. A forgery is where you actually take someone's prints from one surface and transfer them to another surface at a crime scene."

"Is that hard to do?"

"Well, you certainly have to know what you're doing. You lift a print with tape, you're going to disturb ridge lines. And prints interact differently with different surfaces. You lift a print from a metal surface and transfer it to a wooden surface, chances are you're going to interject some anomalies into the picture that'll throw up a red flag."

"Then an expert would catch it every time?"

"No, unfortunately. I remember they did a test once to check that very thing. About half the time the forensics folks thought a forgery was a real print and a real print was a forgery. I don't like those odds."

"Gee, that's a little unsettling, particularly for someone like me who got wrongly convicted. Was there anything dicey about Hawkins's print at the crime scene?"

Decker shook his head. "And I checked it very

closely. And we had another expert who I trusted come in at the time and do the same thing. He could find nothing that would lead him to believe it was forged."

"Then Hawkins *had* to be there."

"It seems so. But if he was, how could he be innocent? And if he was there and didn't kill them, he would know who did, presumably. Why didn't he finger that person after he was arrested?"

"I give," said Mars.

"He could have come upon the bodies *after* they were dead. He could have been the one to call 911 at nine-thirty-five and then gotten the hell out of Dodge, although that leaves open the question of why we couldn't trace the call."

"So how did the murder weapon turn up at his house behind the wall?"

"Someone planted it there to frame him."

"Okay."

Decker shook his head. "No, it's not okay. If he happened upon the bodies *after* the real killer had left, how did the killer know to frame Hawkins?"

"Maybe he knew Hawkins was going to break into the house that night. Maybe that's why he killed them that night, because he knew Hawkins was planning to be there later. So he planted the DNA on the girl and then Hawkins hit that light switch himself, adding even more evidence against him."

After he finished speaking, Mars smiled. "How's that theory?"

"You make some good points, Melvin. It doesn't explain everything, but it's still an interesting theory we have to explore."

"And it would explain the time discrepancy too," noted Mars as he sipped his coffee. "And Hawkins would have to describe something weird going on to get the cops to come out. He knew the people had been shot and had probably screamed when they were, so that's what he told the police dispatcher he heard, even though he couldn't have."

Decker nodded and forked some eggs into his mouth. The memories of his discovering his murdered family had finally stopped unspooling in his head at around four in the morning. He had come back to the room and gone right to the bathroom and stripped off his soaked clothes. That's when Mars had heard him retching in there, but he'd lied and told him he was fine.

But will it happen again?

He said, "So how did Hawkins get those scratches on his arms? He had to realize that the DNA taken from his arms was planted under Abigail's nails. Yet he never raised that as a defense. He never said a person had scratched him and presumably gotten his DNA that way. He maintained that he had slipped and injured himself. Even though naming the person might have raised reasonable doubt in the jury's minds."

"You think he was protecting somebody?"

"Possibly."

"You have anybody in mind?"

"Yes, I do."

35

She did not look remotely pleased to see him again.

"I'm going out now," Mitzi Gardiner said from the partially open front door of her beautiful home.

She was dressed immaculately in a pleated skirt, nylons, and low-heeled pumps. Her white blouse had an open collar. Around her neck was a string of small pearls. She had a dark, short-waisted jacket on over the blouse. Her hair had not a strand out of place. Her makeup and lipstick looked professionally applied. She could be presiding over a board meeting at a Fortune 500 company.

"We can wait then or come back another time," said Decker, who was once more struck by her transformation from an emaciated and perpetually strung-out drug addict. "But it won't take long if you can make the time now."

She eyed him and then Mars, who smiled pleasantly back at her.

She frowned and looked at her watch. "I can give you five minutes."

She led them through the house and into a book-lined library. She closed the doors behind them and indicated seats. They quickly sat down on a small couch.

She sat down across from them.

"Well?" she said, staring at him.

He said, "Thanks for agreeing to see us now."

"Five minutes," she said. "Then I have a meeting I need to get to. An important one."

Decker cleared his throat. The questioning would have to be delicate. It was hard because his preferred approach was to figuratively grab a suspect by the neck with a line of queries.

"We're running down some leads and it occurred to us that your father might have been framed."

Gardiner sat back and looked coolly at him. "So you intimated on your last visit. And I told you that you were barking up the wrong tree, if you remember."

"By the way, when I left here to drive back to Burlington after speaking with you before, someone tried to kill me."

She sat up, looking genuinely shocked. "I hope you don't think I had anything to do with that."

"No, not at all. I just wanted you to know because you may want to be on your guard."

"Thank you for your warning. But I carry a gun with me when I'm out."

"Really, why is that?"

"Because I'm wealthy, Agent Decker. And people

who aren't want to take things away from you. I know that better than most, having once been on the other side of the glass looking in."

"Have you had problems with that in the past?"

"I don't think that has anything to do with your investigation." She tapped her watch. "And the clock is running on your time to question me."

Decker plunged in. "There is a substantial time discrepancy in what happened thirteen years ago. That has changed my understanding of the case."

"What time discrepancy? And why didn't someone see it back then?"

"It was just overlooked. But the time of the victims' deaths and the 911 call to police? It doesn't make sense."

She sat back. "All right. I guess I'll take your word for that. But why would that cause you to come to see me?"

"Your father had scratches on his arms. The police concluded that those scratches were caused by Abigail Richards fighting for her life while your father strangled her."

"Do we really have to go through this?" she said irritably.

"When your father was arrested, he was wearing a long-sleeved shirt and a jacket over it."

"So what?"

"If he was wearing that while attacking Abigail some hours earlier, how could she have scratched his arms and gotten his DNA under her skin? Her nails wouldn't have penetrated his clothing, even if she did manage to somehow break the skin. There would have been no transfer of DNA."

"I'm not a detective, so I don't know. Maybe he changed clothes between the time of the attack and when he was picked up."

"But he hadn't been home."

"That I know of. I told you before, I was probably high."

"It was rainy and chilly that night. I doubt he would have been wearing a short-sleeved shirt."

Gardiner was looking at her watch. "Okay, but isn't that beside the point? His DNA *was* found under her nails. That came out at the trial."

"Which leads me to this question. Can you think of anyone who would want to frame your father?"

"Frame him? How? By killing four people that he didn't even know? By putting his fingerprints and DNA at the crime scene? My father wasn't that important, Agent Decker. Why would anyone waste time incriminating him?"

"I take that as a no?"

She didn't bother to answer.

"Your father said the scrapes on his arms were from when he fell down, not from Abigail's fingernails."

"But again, his DNA was found under her nails. Isn't that conclusive?"

"We were also thinking that if your father *was* innocent, he could have raised any number of defenses, implicated other people. For instance, he could have said that another person had scratched his arms. And that that person had used the DNA from under *their* nails to plant under Abigail's fingernails."

Decker sat back slightly. This was the moment of truth. Gardiner was sharp enough, he knew, to realize the implications of his question.

But she surprised him. "After my father lost his job, he started hanging around a bad lot, Agent Decker."

"That never came out at the trial."

"Well, he did. He was desperate for money. For all I know, he started committing crimes but was never caught until the murders. As I told you before, he did whatever he could to get money for my mother's pain medications. So maybe he was in a fight and got the injuries that way. He probably wouldn't tell anyone that, because he was afraid it might incriminate him, or the person might do him harm if he did tell the authorities."

Mars said incredulously, "He was on trial for murder. How much more danger could he be in?"

Gardiner didn't even deign to look at him. She kept her gaze on Decker. "He might have been trying to protect my mother and me. If he talked, his 'associates' might harm us."

It was at that moment that Decker realized he had seriously underestimated Mitzi Gardiner.

"That's an interesting theory," he said.

"Really?" she said. "I would think it was the *only* theory that would adequately answer your question." She looked at her watch again. "Well, time's up."

"And if we have any more questions?" said Decker.

"You can ask someone else for answers."

She walked out of the room, leaving them there.

A few moments later they heard a door open and close. After that, a garage door cranked up and a car drove out. From the window, they watched her drive down to the gate in a silver Porsche SUV. The gate opened, and a few moments later she was gone.

"Gentlemen?"

They turned to see a woman in a maid's uniform. "Mrs. Gardiner asked me to show you out."

As they left the house Mars said, "We just got our asses handed to us, didn't we?"

"Yes, we did."

36

It was six-thirty exactly when Decker and Mars pulled down the drive into the Richardses' old home. Decker drove into the parking area behind the house and they got out. It wasn't raining yet, but it was scheduled to start soon, and the dark clouds confirmed that prediction.

Mars looked up at the old house. "So this is where it all happened? And where you started your career as a homicide detective?"

"Apparently an inauspicious start," commented Decker moodily.

"Hey, it was your first time. You think the first time I ran the ball at Texas I was as good as the last time I ran it? You learn from your mistakes, Decker, you know that."

"Well, I made enough of them on this case to last a lifetime."

He led Mars to the side door. This presumably was where David Katz had gone into the house. Decker had a key that had been given him by Natty. He unlocked the door and stepped into a utility room. Up a short set of steps was the kitchen.

"So we're here to sort of walk through the crime scene?" said Mars.

Decker didn't answer right away. He gazed around at the small room. The HVAC equipment was in here, as well as hookups for a washer and dryer.

"Why would Katz have pulled around here to come into the house?" He was really saying this to himself more than Mars.

"Well, maybe this was the way he always came in."

"There's no record that he was ever here before."

Mars looked around the room. "Well, then I guess that is strange. Why come in here instead of through the front door?"

They walked up the stairs and into the kitchen.

"You think maybe Richards told him to come in that way?"

"I have no way of knowing that," replied Decker. "I don't know who arranged the meeting or why. Or even if it was a meeting or just a shoot-the-breeze sort of thing."

They arrived at the spot where David Katz had been shot.

"He fell here and the beer he was drinking hit the floor but didn't break."

"Okay. And then Don Richards was shot—"

Decker put up a hand. He had just downloaded

something from his "cloud" that was not making sense.

"What?" said Mars, who had seen this expression before.

"Two things. The beer bottle was nearly empty when it hit the floor."

"How do you know that?"

"The spill pattern and volume of beer on the floor."

"Wouldn't some of it have dried?"

"We took that into account."

"Okay, so he drank the rest."

Decker shook his head. "He had almost no beer in his stomach when they did the autopsy."

"That doesn't make any sense. And the second point?"

Decker closed his eyes and brought two images up in his head.

"Katz was right-handed. The print of his we found on the beer bottle was from his left hand."

"Well, that's weird. You didn't see that before?"

"No, actually I did. But I didn't place any great importance on it because sometimes you hold a drink in your other hand. We've all done it."

"But now?"

"But now I'm looking at everything that doesn't seem to fit."

"And what does that tell you, looking at it that way?"

"That someone could have pressed his hand on the beer after he was dead, but used the wrong hand."

"To make it look like he was drinking beer? Why would that matter?"

"I don't know."

Mars looked at Decker nervously. "And if there was almost no beer in his stomach, that wasn't a red flag?"

"Should have been," admitted Decker. He looked down at the floor. "But if Katz didn't drink the beer, who did?" He eyed the kitchen sink. "Maybe it went down there."

"To make it look like he'd drunk most of what was in the bottle?"

"If that was their plan, they didn't know how post-mortems work. Not that it made a difference since I completely missed that because I didn't fully read the PM report." He slammed his fist against the wall and then rubbed the cut the blow had produced. "The fact is, everything changed when we found the fingerprint, Melvin. I was really eager to get the person who'd done this. And that print led directly to Meryl Hawkins. Nothing else mattered at that point."

"I get that, Decker. And I know you want to beat yourself up over this, and maybe you're right to do it. But you got another chance to get it right, so clear your head, get rid of the guilt, and focus. I know you can do this, bro."

Decker took a couple of deep, calming breaths.

"Okay, the problem has always been, how did the killer or killers get here? They had to come down that one road and pass the other houses. No one saw them. There was no trace of another car, and there would have been."

"Maybe they came on foot."

"They had to have come to the house *after* the rain started. Yet there was not a single trace of that in the house. They might have been meticulous in cleaning up, but to not leave a single mark?" Decker shook his head in disbelief. "Not going to happen."

"Well, what if the killers were in the house *before* the rain started. Then they ambushed Katz when he came in. And killed everybody else."

Decker thought about this. "That means they would have come to the house in broad daylight with no rain to give them cover. Someone would have seen them coming down the road."

"Maybe they came from behind the house and not down the road."

"And waited hours to kill everyone? Why?"

"I don't know," admitted Mars. "Maybe they were trying to get some information from them before they murdered them."

"That's a possibility, Melvin. And an intriguing one."

"So the only car found here was Katz's?"

"That's right. Susan Richards had one car and the other was in the shop for—"

Decker froze as another image dropped from his cloud to rest atop another.

"What is it, Decker?" asked Mars.

Decker came out of his reverie and said slowly, "Don Richards and his son, Frankie, were shot once in the chest, both through the heart. Nonsurvivable. But Katz was different. He was shot in the head, *twice*. Temple and the rear of the skull." He looked over at Mars. "Why would that be? Why change the scenario for Katz?"

"Maybe he struggled with them or he ran off, and they had to shoot him in the head. Got him in the back and then in the temple."

"The order of the wounds was actually the reverse of that. Temple first, then the back of the head. The temple shot undoubtedly would have been fatal. He would have fallen to the floor. Why shoot him again in the head when they knew he was already dead?"

Mars shook his head. "Doesn't make sense."

"Abigail was strangled, I believe, because that was the most plausible way to get Hawkins's DNA under her fingernails. If they were that purpose-driven in the way they killed her, maybe there was a similar purpose behind shooting Katz twice in the head."

"But what would that purpose be?"

Decker pantomimed a gun with his hand and held it to his temple. "Bang. The guy drops. They bend over him and, bang, shot to the back of the head."

"Right, but why?"

Decker straightened and looked at his hand. "Because they wanted to cover something up that the temple shot didn't accomplish."

"What would that be?"

"Maybe a contusion on the back of his head."

"From what?"

"From when he was knocked out. *Before* he was brought here to die."

37

A puzzled Mars looked at Decker. "Wait a minute, are you saying that he *didn't* drive his car here?"

"His *car* was driven here, certainly, but who's to say he was the one driving? We just assumed all along that it was him. I think it's possible he was in the trunk or the backseat unconscious, and the killer or killers drove him here. The neighbors only saw the car, not the driver. They didn't know Katz from Adam, so they couldn't have identified him even if they had seen him."

Mars said, "And that would explain why they parked the car in the back and came in that way."

"Right, they couldn't exactly carry an unconscious Katz in through the front door. And that would also explain his left-hand print on the beer. They just pressed his hand against it. They might not have known whether he was right- or left-handed. They just wanted it to look like he had come here of his own free will and was enjoying a beer when someone shot him."

"But you said there was *some* beer in his stomach."

"They could have revived him and made him drink some, or else they poured some down his throat while he was unconscious. And it would explain the absence of any marks by another car, and the lack of rain traces brought in by the killers. They were in the house *before* the rain started, not because they were here before Katz came as you speculated, but because they came *with* him. They left the house after the rain started and therefore wouldn't have left any traces of it inside."

"And if they left out the back on foot, the rain would have covered all those tracks."

Decker nodded. "And I missed all that because of this."

He led Mars back into the living room and pointed at the light switch on the wall. "That's where we found the fingerprint. My attention was drawn to it because there was a smear of blood on the light switch plate. No print associated with it. Like someone had rubbed their arm or hand against it or something. But right after I saw the blood, I checked for a print, and there it was. And it matched Hawkins perfectly. Far more than you need to hold up in court. This was a home run. And he said he'd never been here, so how else could it have gotten here unless he'd been here that night? It showed he was lying, and that pretty much sealed his fate. That and the DNA under Abigail's nails."

"And you said it would be hard to forge a print."

"Yes. But to do it really well, you need some knowledge of forensics and you need some special equipment deployed in a multistep process, and even with all that there are a lot of things that can go wrong."

"Damn, didn't know it was that complicated."

"You obviously never watched *CSI*."

"I was in prison for most of that time, Decker. And for obvious reasons, *CSI* wasn't a real popular show for the inmates."

"Bottom line is I have confidence in the expert who said he believed Hawkins's print was genuine."

"Then Hawkins had to be here, no way around it."

Decker wasn't listening. He was staring transfixed at the switch plate. Then he ran back into the kitchen and looked at the light switch there. Moments later he hustled into another room and did the same. Mars followed him into each new space with a bewildered look on his face.

"Decker, you okay?"

Decker returned to the living room, dug into his pocket, and pulled out a Swiss Army knife. He deployed the screwdriver.

"Dollars to donuts this is the same light switch plate that was on the wall that night."

"Okay, so what?"

"It's different from the switch plates in the other rooms."

Decker unscrewed the plate and removed it from

the wall. Underneath was revealed the imprint of a smaller rectangle.

"Do you see that, Melvin?"

Mars looked at him. "Yeah, but what does that mean?"

"The original switch plate was *smaller*. That's the outline there between the painted area and what was underneath the plate. You can see where the paint faded because it was exposed to light all those years. They needed the same size or a bigger plate there to cover it."

"Wait a second, you're saying somebody got Hawkins's print on that plate and brought it here and replaced the other plate with this one?"

"Yes."

"Damn."

"That way his *real* print is on the *original* surface. That's why my expert swore it wasn't a forgery." He paused. "Instead it was a *fabrication*. They brought the print to the crime scene, but in a way that was beyond suspicion. A glass or other object introduced to a crime scene can easily be placed there. A light switch plate? It seems like part of the house. Immovable. But it's not. Just two screws, in fact. Like I just took out."

"Somebody went to a lot of effort to frame the guy."

"Which means the motivation was pretty significant. But this is not about Meryl Hawkins. He was a pawn. It could have been anybody. But they picked him for a variety of reasons. And this shows the murders weren't the result of a random burglary gone bad. The focus now should be the victims. Who would want them dead?"

"Well, there were four of them. I guess we can discount the kids. I don't see some middle schooler who got his feelings hurt doing this."

Decker nodded. "So David Katz and Don Richards. Either or both."

"You said they had done business together. Katz was the businessman and Richards was the banker."

"Right."

"Had they become friends?"

"Not that we could find. Rachel Katz said no. The Richardses were older and had kids, and they didn't. And they were both too busy with work to form friendships like that, at least that's what she told me."

"And did either of the wives say why Katz was coming over that night?"

"Neither of them knew that he was. Again, that's what they said. It doesn't make it true."

"Did Katz just pop in, then?"

"There *was* a phone call placed the day before from Katz's cell phone to Richards's cell phone. It might have been then that they arranged to meet."

"If Katz called Richards, maybe he initiated the meeting?"

"That could be, yes," agreed Decker. "But even

though Katz called Richards, that doesn't mean he asked for the meeting. He might have just called out of the blue and then Richards asked him to come by."

"When he knew his wife would be out—is that significant?" asked Mars.

"It could be very significant, especially considering that Susan Richards has vanished."

Mars said, "Well, Richards worked at the bank. Maybe something fishy was going on there and he wanted Katz's advice."

"And then someone came here and killed them. And killed the kids too because they would be witnesses. But that would be risky. Why not kill whoever was the target while they were alone, not in a house filled with people?"

"Maybe they were running out of time and were afraid that someone was going to blow the whistle on what they were doing."

Decker was staring miserably at the switch plate. "It's only a small difference, but I should have noticed it before."

"They manipulated you and everybody else."

"Rookie mistake. I assumed things I shouldn't have."

"But now you figured it out and you get a second chance to get it right. Like you did with me. You gave me a second chance."

"You're cutting me a lot of slack."

"Well, sometimes friends have to do that. But then

sometimes they have to kick you in the ass too. And trust me, if it comes to it, I will."

"I would expect nothing less, Melvin."

Decker's phone rang. He answered, and Captain Miller started speaking.

"They found Susan Richards."

"Where?"

"Two towns over."

"You bringing her in?"

"We are. In a meat wagon. She killed herself, Amos."

38

Decker was in the morgue looking at yet another body.

She looked like she was asleep, not dead.

"Bodies really piling up," said the ME as he laid the sheet back down on top of Susan Richards.

"Cause of death?"

"My best guess right now, drug overdose. Women usually go the overdose route when committing suicide. Guys like to blow their heads off with guns."

Richards had been found in an abandoned building by a construction worker working nearby who had noticed an odd smell.

"Time of death?" asked Decker.

"Rigor has resolved so she's been dead a while. I'll have a better time later."

"Could the time of her death be close to when she disappeared?"

The man looked over the body and rubbed his chin. "Yes, actually, it could."

Decker had already been told that the suitcase she

had been seen putting in her car had not been found with the body.

"Any pill bottles found with her? Or a suicide note?"

The ME shook his head. "No, on both counts."

The door opened and Blake Natty walked in, looking shriveled and depressed. He eyed the body of Susan Richards with little interest. "So she killed herself?" he said.

"Unknown as yet," said Decker.

Natty said, "Well, if she did kill herself, we know why: She murdered Hawkins."

"If she did kill him, she got the wrong guy," said Decker.

Natty waved this off. "That's your theory."

"It's more than a theory now," replied Decker. He explained about the light switch plate at the Richardses' old house. "And they placed a smudge of Katz's blood on the plate to draw our attention to it and thus the print."

"Where do you think the print and the switch plate came from?"

"The easiest source would have been Hawkins's home. I think they didn't put Katz's blood on the print because that would have messed up the ridge lines."

"And the DNA under the girl's nails?" asked Natty.

"They picked her because she was physically smaller and weaker than the others. And they needed a plausible scenario to get the DNA under her nails. And a struggle during a strangulation plausibly fit that bill."

"But Decker," said the ME, "I pulled out those reports and went over them after I knew you were looking into the case again. If someone else had scratched Hawkins and then transferred what was under that person's nails to under Abigail Richards's nails, you would expect to find the other person's DNA as well."

"If the other person were a family member, would that make a difference?" asked Decker, who already knew the answer.

"Well, of course it would. All humans' DNA is ninety-nine point nine percent the same. But that one-tenth is dramatically different for all, except if you're a monozygotic or identical twin. But the testing that was done on Abigail's nails would not have picked up on a third party's DNA if the person were a family member of Hawkins. They would have had to do additional steps. Actually, they would have had to do extra steps to check for any third-party corruption, family or not."

Natty eyed Decker. "What family member are you talking about?"

"There really can only be one: his daughter, Mitzi."

"Why would she have set up her old man?" asked Natty.

"I don't know." He looked at the ME. "Is the DNA sample still available to do additional testing, to see if Mitzi's DNA or a third party's had corrupted it? I asked you to check earlier."

The ME nodded his head. "I did check. And there is some left. I'm having an expert in Cincinnati where they have much better equipment and protocols do sophisticated testing on it. They'll be able to differentiate between a father's and daughter's DNA, and also the presence of any third party. But it will take a little time."

"Let me know as soon as you have something."

"You really think his daughter was involved?" said Natty.

"If she were it would explain how the murder weapon came to be found in a panel behind the wall of his closet. I just reread the report of the search team that went over Hawkins's house. They wrote that Mitzi had drawn their attention to some unevenness of the wall. They didn't ask her why she knew about it."

"Are *you* going to ask her about it?" said Natty.

"I think if I go back to that well again, she's going to lawyer up. Probably already has. Right now, she's home free, or thinks she is."

Decker looked back at Susan Richards's body. He closed his eyes and thought back to something that a witness had told him. He put layer after layer of facts on top of that one, pulling them down from his cloud with ease. Until something did not make sense. It stood out, in fact, like a blinking red light.

Natty said, “So, you don’t think she killed herself?”

Decker opened his eyes. “I’m almost sure she didn’t.”

“How?”

“Because I think she was already dead when she left her house.”

39

It was the next day and Decker and Mars were standing in front of the late Susan Richards's house. Across the road, Decker could once more see Agatha Bates sitting on her screened porch.

"You're saying that Richards was in the rolling suitcase already dead?" said Mars.

Decker absently nodded.

"So that means another woman was impersonating her."

"Agatha Bates saw the person from a distance. And it was dark, and judging by the thickness of Bates's eyeglass lenses, her sight is far from perfect. And the person had on a long coat and a hat. That was one thing that made no sense to me. It was warm that night with not a cloud in the sky. So it was a disguise, because they wanted to take no chance that Bates might be able to see it *wasn't* her neighbor."

"But why do you think it wasn't Richards in the first place?"

"Richards's car muffler was really loud. That was

why the person came out and started the car and then went *back* inside to get the suitcase."

"I'm not following."

In answer, Decker pointed across the street. "Think of it this way: This was all a show for Bates. The person wanted her to hear the car start up, knowing that she would look out the window and see who she thought was Susan Richards come out with the suitcase. If she had come out and put the bag in the car and then got in the car and started it, Bates would not have seen what she did. Bates said the person had trouble getting the suitcase in the car. That was probably because of Richards's weight." He paused. "And in addition to that, she barely took any clothes or shoes or other things. So why the big suitcase? And she was on a bunch of meds. I saw them in the medicine cabinet. Most weren't too critical, but one she left behind was: high blood pressure medication. She had to take that every day."

"So someone killed Richards because . . . ?"

Decker said, "To place blame for Hawkins's murder on her. Then she's found, ostensibly having taken her own life out of guilt. Case closed. At least with respect to Hawkins's murder."

Mars nodded thoughtfully. "Gotta admit, it all hangs together."

"But it leaves a lot of questions unanswered and creates a lot of new ones. And it doesn't tell us who committed those murders thirteen years ago, or who really killed Meryl Hawkins."

"Well, you think his daughter is involved somehow."

"But I have no way to prove it. At least not yet."

"So you think it's all connected, then? What happened back then and now?"

"Well, we have one factor unaccounted for."

Mars thought for a moment. "The dude who took a shot at you."

"Right. Who is he? Was he hired to take a shot at me by someone? Was he the one who earlier tried to kill me by ramming his truck into my car?"

Mars rubbed his arm where the guy had slashed him. "Dude could fight, I'll give him that."

"And I have other questions."

"Like what?"

"Why would someone drive Katz over there and kill him, Don Richards, and his kids?"

"Because they knew something incriminating, something that could hurt whoever killed them."

"Right. But if Katz knew something, why drive him over there and kill the others?"

"Because Don Richards knew something too. They had to take them both out. And instead of doing it separately, they did it all at once."

"Right. But the thing is, Susan Richards wasn't there. If her husband knew something that could hurt somebody, you'd think she might know too."

Mars snapped his fingers. "Maybe she *did* know, because she was involved in whatever it was. And that may be the reason she wasn't there that night."

"I've covered that ground before. While I can see Susan letting her husband die, I just don't see her allowing her kids to die too."

"So maybe she was just lucky she wasn't there."

"But she's dead now, because she was a scapegoat for Hawkins's murder, because she had a motive to kill him."

"But what would David Katz or Don Richards know that would get them killed?"

"Rachel Katz has a lot of projects going on around town, with money behind her. She's obviously very ambitious. And she wasn't there that night either, which meant she got to live."

"That doesn't make her a murderer, Decker. In fact, it might make her a target now if people are tying up loose ends from thirteen years ago."

"Well, nine times out of ten, when a spouse dies, it's the other spouse doing the killing. I don't think that was the case with Susan Richards, but it could very well be the case with Rachel Katz."

"Good enough reason never to get married," quipped Mars.

"Don't tell Harper that."

"Like I said, we're just having fun. Don't need a marriage license to do that."

"Well, I think I need to have another talk with Rachel Katz."

"You want me to come along?"

Decker studied his friend. "Yeah, I do. It might really help."

"How?"

"You're a lot cooler than I am and far better-looking. And you're rich on top of it. So I think Rachel Katz will be thrilled to meet you."

40

"Wine?"

Rachel Katz was dressed in black slacks, a white blouse, and high heels. Her hair was done up in an elaborate French braid. It was nearly nine o'clock. She had arranged to meet them after work in her loft apartment. She held up an opened bottle of Cabernet.

Decker declined, but Mars accepted the offer. She poured out a glass and handed it to him. She turned back to the table and picked up her own wineglass.

"So you and Decker work together?"

"No, I'm just in town visiting him," said Mars, taking a sip of the wine and sitting down next to her on the couch, while Decker sat across from them.

She sat back, crossed her legs, took a drink of her wine, and said, "Well, I'm sorry that your visit coincided with murder. Now, what can I do for you?"

"You look like you're ready to go out somewhere," said Decker. "I hope we're not keeping you."

"I am going out, but not until a little later." She glanced at Mars. "It's a new nightclub I'm part owner of. Going to check out the groove. That's important. You do much clubbing?"

"Oh yeah. There's a nice scene in D.C. And I've been dabbling in real estate up there." He glanced at Decker and added, "Even thinking about opening a bar up there with a dance floor."

"Well, then you're welcome to join me tonight. This isn't D.C., but we've put a lot of thought into the business model and the layout of the place. You might see something that might help you in your venture."

"Thanks, I might just do that," said Mars with another quick glance at Decker.

"I guess you've heard about Susan Richards," said Decker. "I know it was on the news this morning."

Katz frowned, uncrossed her legs, and sat forward. "That was truly awful. Taking her own life like that. It's just hard to fathom. But I guess if she did kill Meryl Hawkins . . . ?"

"So you think that she did?" asked Decker.

"I have no way of knowing for sure, do I? But it seems rather obvious."

"And you were with Earl Lancaster at the time Hawkins was killed?"

"As I told you before, and I'm sure he confirmed."

"His wife had to actually recuse herself from the investigation because of that," said Decker. He paused, waiting for her reaction to this.

"I guess I could see that," she said. "It's like an episode of *Law and Order* or something."

"Or something," said Decker. "The night your husband was killed, you said you had no idea why he would be meeting with Don Richards? Or that he was even meeting with him?"

"That's right."

"Did you normally know your husband's schedule?"

"Mostly. But not always. Especially if this was last-minute. He had an office and a secretary. She would have kept his schedule."

"We talked to her back then. But I was hoping you might remember something."

"Well, I can't help you there. And I don't know why you're continuing to bother with this. Hawkins committed the murders. That was clearly established at trial. Now, I have no proof of who killed him, but other things being equal it might be the woman who disappeared and then turned up dead from a suicide." She took another sip of wine. "I admire her, actually. At least she had the courage to finish the guy. I didn't."

"Well, we don't know that she did."

Katz made a careless wave with her hand. "Whatever. You have your job to do. Anything else?"

"Do you happen to know Mitzi Gardiner?"

Katz looked puzzled. "Mitzi Gardiner?"

"You might have known her as Mitzi Hawkins."

"God, do you mean his daughter?"

"Yes."

"No, I didn't know her. Why the hell would I?"

"You might have seen her at the trial. She had to testify."

"No, I don't recall that. But I remember her being mentioned by some of the other witnesses, including you. I'm not sure what she even looks like."

"Well, her looks have changed a lot since then. For the better. She's turned her life around."

"Well, good for her. Couldn't have been easy having a murderer for a father."

"So you never talked to her? Interacted with her?"

"Never."

"She lives in Trammel. Very nice place. Wealthy. She has a young child."

"Good for her. I wanted kids too."

Mars said, "You're still young. Not too late."

Katz smiled at him. "You're sweet, but I think that ship has sailed." She turned back to Decker. "Anything else?"

"Did you talk to your husband on the day of his death?"

"I'm sure I did. We did sleep together and get up together. Probably had coffee before we both left the house that morning."

"I mean after that. During the day?"

"I really can't recall. It's been a long time."

"But no mention of his going to meet with Richards?"

"No. I told you that before."

"Just verifying."

"Why do I feel like you're trying to trap me?" she said darkly. "That would not be very nice, particularly since I have nothing to hide."

"I'm just trying to figure out what happened."

Katz finished her wine in one long drink and set the empty glass on the table. "Well, let me help you out with that. Hawkins murdered my husband and three other people. And then Susan Richards killed him and then killed herself. Case closed. There, that wasn't hard."

She stood and looked down at Mars. "How about we grab a drink before we head over to the club? I know a place."

Mars stood. "Sounds good."

"Melvin, we have something to do first, and then you can meet her there," said Decker.

Mars eyed Katz. "You cool with that?"

"Absolutely." She wrote down an address on a slip of paper and handed it to Mars. "I think you'll have fun tonight, Mr. Mars."

"Make it Melvin."

"Just keep it professional," said Decker in a joking manner.

"I'm always professional," said Katz. "As your friend will find out tonight."

As they walked back to their car, Mars said, "What do we have to do?"

"We're going to wire you up for tonight."

"And where will you be?"

"Right outside listening."

"You sure you're doing this for the case, or to keep me from doing something dumb with that woman?"

"Maybe both, Melvin. Maybe both."

41

Decker was in the front seat of his rental car parked outside of a place called 10th and Main. That was also its literal location. It was the club Rachel Katz had referred to and of which she was a co-owner.

It seemed to be pretty popular, Decker noted. There was a bouncer out front who nearly equaled him in heft, and he had been vetting a long line of mostly younger and seemingly well-heeled men and women vying to get in.

Maybe his hometown *was* on the way back, he thought. Although he didn't know if what amounted to an overpriced bar for well-off millennials was actually a good barometer of an improving economy for the average person.

He reworked his earpiece, and the noise from inside the club, communicated to him by the wire that Mars was wearing, came through loud and clear.

He settled in for a long evening.

Inside 10th and Main, Mars and Katz were seated in a roped-off section of the club, apparently reserved for

VIPs. The music was loud, the bar crammed, and the dance floor full of swaying, already partially drunk people.

"So what do you think so far?" said Katz.

"Good vibe, lots of energy, and I can see your cash flow skyrocketing at the bar right now."

"We put the bar there to maximize access to it from the tables and the dance floor."

"Right. That way you get a continuous flow of business. And dancing makes people hungry and thirsty. And your table-to-patron ratio is good too. Pack 'em in, but without seeming to."

"You sound like you know business."

"Like I said, I dabble. Got some properties here and there. I like to work with low-income folks for the most part, give them a shot. Don't make as much profit, but I don't need the money."

She sipped her cocktail and moved her head rhythmically to the music. "That's very generous of you. I have a slightly different business model."

"What's that?"

"To get as rich as I possibly can." She laughed and rattled the ice in her glass.

"Different strokes," said Mars, grinning.

"How long have you worked with Decker?"

"Well, like I told you before, I don't work with him. I'm not with the FBI or anything. But he and I are buds. We played college football against each other. I was a Texas Longhorn; he was an Ohio State Buckeye. I ran the ball and he tried to tackle me."

"Did he?"

"He did as well as anybody did back then. Which wasn't all that good."

She laughed. "I respect a man who has confidence in himself."

"I was up for the Heisman my senior year but lost out to a quarterback."

Her eyes widened. "Wow. The Heisman? Did you play in the NFL?"

"I would have. But my career took a detour."

"How so?"

"Death row in a Texas prison."

Katz gaped until Mars grinned. She pointed at him. "Good one. I almost believed you for a second."

Mars looked around. "This is an expensive build-out. Did you finance it, or do you have your own cash?"

"I have partners with their own cash. They bring the money, I bring the local know-how. I put the deals together and execute on the plan. My background as a CPA really comes in handy. This is our eighth project together in just the last three years. And we're going to be expanding this same club concept to other cities in other states."

"Long-range strategy. That's a good thing. If you can streamline supply chains and consolidate your backroom and marketing operations, you can gain some economies of scale as you grow the business."

She looked at him with a new level of respect. "Exactly. So, you're here as Decker's friend, but are you helping him with the investigation?"

"I guess I'm a sounding board for the guy. He's Sherlock Holmes and I'm his Dr. Watson."

"Is he really that good?"

"The FBI thinks so. And I've seen him do some incredible things. And somebody tried to kill the guy, twice. So there must be something to hide, right?"

"God, I didn't know that."

Mars flexed his injured arm. "Dude cut me up too before he got away."

"Oh my God, you poor thing."

"Nothing too bad. I'm good to go."

"Any idea who the man is?"

"Not yet. But they'll keep looking till they find him."

"You want another drink? On the house."

"You don't have to do that."

"Yes I do, Melvin."

He grinned. "Okay, thanks. Same, straight up."

She rose and walked over to the bar.

Mars sat there, his head swaying to the music, seemingly not having a care in the world. He moved his mouth as though singing the lyrics of the song being played. "You hear everything okay, Decker?"

"Loud and clear. She seems to really like you."

"She's a beautiful, sexy lady, but she's not my type."

"What's your type?"

"She just seems a little too ruthless for my tastes. Money is her thing. But it's not mine."

"Easy to say since you have so much of it."

"Okay, you got me there. She's coming back now. Over and out."

Katz put the fresh drinks down and sat next to him, this time closer than before.

Mars said, "You ever think about coming to the D.C. area? Maybe you and me can do some business together."

"Now that would be wonderful," she said, flashing him a smile.

"You can use your original partners too, I'm not looking to cut anybody out. If you want me to meet with them, you know, vet me and all. I'm cool with that."

"Yeah, let me think about that." She cradled her drink. "You know Decker keeps coming back to ask me questions. I think he might believe I had something to do with all this. And I didn't. I swear."

"Don't worry about that. He's just dotting his i's and crossing his t's."

"Does he suspect anybody yet?"

"Well, he thought Susan Richards might be good for the Hawkins murder, but now I don't know."

"He doesn't confide in you?"

"Not everything. You know Holmes kept stuff back from Watson too," he added with a grin.

She didn't return the look. "It was awful losing my husband like that."

Mars touched her arm and his features grew solemn. "Hey, sure it was. Nobody should have to go through that. Nobody."

She squeezed his arm. "Thanks."

Mars looked around. "So you got this place and you got the American Grill. Decker told me about the place. Now that's some broad bandwidth." He chuckled.

She smiled. "It was David's first project. I've kept the place to, I don't know, honor his memory, I guess. It's not like the restaurant makes a lot of money. In fact, based on tonight, I'll probably make more in one month here than that place does in six months."

Mars held up his cocktail. "Just start selling some of these fifteen-dollar highballs at the American Grill and you'll see your profit margins soar."

"I'm not sure how big that would go over with the Grill's clientele. They're more into pitchers of beer for five bucks."

"Not to change the subject, but did your husband have any business associates?"

She crossed her arms and her cheery disposition faded. "Why?"

"I'm back to playing Watson, see?"

"I guess I see. To answer your question, no, he was

a solo operation. He got his financing from traditional sources."

"Like the local bank? Don Richards?"

"That's right."

"Anybody else in his past who might have had something against him?"

"Why are you asking these questions? Meryl Hawkins killed him."

"But if he didn't?"

"Why, because he said he was innocent?" she said skeptically. "His prints and DNA were found at the crime scene."

"You can fabricate that stuff."

Katz looked taken aback by this. "I didn't know that. Is that what Decker thinks?"

"Maybe. So, did your husband have enemies?"

"No, nobody I could think of. He was a nice guy," she added quietly. "He treated people well. He treated me well. He wasn't the type to screw people over and make them hate him or hold a grudge."

"So maybe they were targeting Don Richards."

"They?"

"In the event Hawkins is not the guy, there's a murderer out there."

"Do you have evidence that the fingerprints and such *were* fabricated?"

"This is where I pull out my official handbook and tell you that it's an ongoing police investigation."

"But you said you weren't with the FBI."

"Doesn't matter, still can't divulge anything, but you're smart enough to read between the lines, right?"

She nervously drank her cocktail and didn't answer right away. "If Hawkins didn't do it, the real killer might still be out there? Any idea who he is?"

"He, or she?"

She gave him a withering look. "I have an alibi for when it happened."

"Not my meaning. Lots of other 'shes' out there."

"Wait a minute, what about Mitzi, what was her last name?"

"Mitzi *Gardiner*."

"Did she have alibis for the murders?"

"Not sure."

"Well, don't you think you should check that?"

"I'm sure Decker is all over that."

"I remember from some of the testimony at the trial that she was an addict back then."

"I think she had problems in that area, yeah."

"So maybe she needed money for drugs and tried to rob them."

"And Susan Richards?"

"Seems obvious. She killed herself because she killed Meryl Hawkins."

He looked at her doubtfully.

"You don't think so?" she said.

"From how Decker described her to me, Mitzi was a skinny drug addict mostly stoned out of her mind. No way she killed four people, including two grown men. Besides, her DNA and prints weren't found at the scene."

"But you said that could be fabricated."

"It's easier to add stuff to a crime scene than it is to take stuff away, especially prints and DNA. Taking stuff away, you miss one little thing, you're screwed. Trust me, I speak from experience."

"So where does that leave us?"

"Investigating a series of murders."

"Do you think you'll find out who did it, after all this time?"

"I bet once against Amos Decker. And I lost that bet."

"Bad for you, then."

"No, actually he saved my life."

"Seriously?"

"As serious as it gets." He rose. "Thanks for showing me the place. You got a real winner here."

"Wait, do you have time for a nightcap? We could go back to my place."

"Thanks, but it's been a long day. Take a rain check?"

"Sure, okay," Katz said, the disappointment clear on her features. "And it was great meeting you."

"Same here. You gave me a lot to think about, and maybe I did the same for you."

Her expression changed, becoming somber and detached. She recovered from this a moment later, stood, and held out her hand with a forced smile. "Until next time, Melvin."

They shook hands and Mars said, "Look forward to it, Rachel."

He left her there gazing at all the partiers, but perhaps not really seeing a single one.

42

"So what do you think?" asked Mars. He and Decker were driving together back to the Residence Inn.

"I think you'd make a great interrogator."

"I didn't want Katz to think I was drilling down on her."

"That's not what I meant. The really good questioners don't seem like they're prying at all. That's what you did. You did a good job of gaining her confidence and not trying too hard."

Mars fist-bumped Decker. "Thanks. So what else? You think she's in on whatever this is?"

"She's hiding something, I just don't know what. And so is Mitzi Gardiner. And maybe so was Susan Richards, for that matter."

"Lot of people hiding shit in this town."

"Nothing new there," grumbled Decker. "Happens in every town."

Mars checked his watch. "It's midnight. How about some sleep? We're not as young as we used to be, you know."

"Sure," said Decker, although sleep was the last thing on his mind.

After Mars went to his room at the Residence Inn, Decker came back down to the parking lot, climbed into his car, and set off. He drove out of the downtown area and, his mind on autopilot, made his way to the neighborhood and house that he had called home for over a decade.

He pulled to the curb, rolled down the driver's-side window, and cut his engine and lights. He looked out the window at his old house, which was dark, the only illumination a single streetlight and the moon.

He had no real understanding of why he was here. It was punishing to see the place. Memories flooded back to him as easily as drawing breath. He closed his eyes as the images suddenly careened out of control just like last time; they were coming at him like flocks of hurtling birds or fired bullets. He couldn't make them stop. He felt his heart flutter, his gut lurch.

The sweat started to pool on his forehead, his skin grew clammy, and his armpits were suddenly soaked with sweat, the sudden stink assailing his nostrils.

His heart was now racing, and he thought he might be having a coronary. But slowly, ever so slowly, as he gripped the steering wheel as though that might allow some semblance of control over what was happening to him, things settled down in his mind. He finally lay back against his seat, exhausted without having moved at all. He hung his head out the window and sucked in the crisp air as the moisture evaporated off his skin.

This is getting old. And so am I.

He waggled his head, spit some stomach bile out the window, and kept taking deep breaths. He remembered when he'd come out of the coma at the hospital after getting crunched on the football field on opening day. A bunch of people he didn't know were hovering over him, asking him questions. He had IV and monitoring lines running all over him. He felt like Gulliver just awoken as a prisoner of the Lilliputians.

He had come to learn that he had died on the field, twice, only to be resuscitated each time by the team trainer. He'd been hit so hard his helmet had flown off and was lying in the grass far away from his body. The crowd had been cheering the blindside hit until they realized he was not getting up. When the trainer started pounding on his chest, the crowd of seventy thousand people quieted. The network had cut away to another game. It was not good for the NFL brand to show dead football players lying on the turf.

He learned he'd suffered a traumatic brain injury. Later, he discovered his brain had rewired itself around the damaged areas, accessing domains that had never been triggered before. This had left him with the twin conditions of hyperthymesia and synesthesia.

But he didn't know he had them until later. It wasn't like an X-ray could reveal this. The first time he had seen a color burst into his head, associated with something as incongruous as a number, Decker had seriously thought he was going insane.

Then, when he was able to recall things he never had been able to before, the doctors had started testing his cognitive abilities. He had looked at sheets of numbers and words and was able to regurgitate them all, because he could see them in his head, just as they had lain on the page. Then off he had gone to a special cognitive institute in Chicago that dealt exclusively with people like him.

Decker didn't know what was more amazing—his newfound abilities, or the realization that he was far from the only one who possessed them.

Now he snatched one more glimpse at his old home, briefly imagining that it was five years ago and Molly and Cassie were still alive, waiting for him to come home from being a cop. He would play with Molly, kiss Cassie, and . . . be a family.

He held on to that image for another few seconds and then let it go, a phantom that had to be released into the ether where it would simply vanish, because it was no longer real.

You can live in the past, or you can live in the present, but you really can't live in both, Amos.

He started the car, rolled the window back up, put his rental in gear, and drove off.

He was a loner, had always been a loner after he'd died on the field. Cassie, though, had been the one to make sure he did not shrivel up inside his cocoon and keep everyone away. After she died, there had been no one to do that.

Then Alex Jamison had come into his life and somewhat filled Cassie's role.

Decker didn't know where his thirst for justice, for right over wrong, had come from. He did know that he had possessed it long before his family was taken from him.

Maybe because that hit on the field stole me from me. And I've been looking for something to fill that hole all these years. And catching killers seems to be the only thing that cuts it. Because they steal the most precious thing of all: somebody's life.

He had no idea if that was the whole story or not. He just knew that right now, that's all he had to hold on to.

As he drove, he focused on the problem at hand. What he desperately wanted to know was, if David Katz had arranged to meet with Don Richards, and that had been communicated by a phone call that had involved only the two men, how had their killers known the men were going to be meeting that night?

He couldn't believe that Susan Richards had been

party to it, because that would necessitate Decker's believing that she would sacrifice both her kids as well. Decker had seen the woman that night. As Lancaster had said, Susan had been hysterical, utterly out of her mind with disbelief and rage. She was a woman who had been truly shocked to learn that she had gone out for the evening and come home to find out she had no family left.

Decker slowed the car down as he thought back over all these points.

He settled on the phone call between Katz and Richards.

There was actually no way to know that it was Katz who had called Richards. It was just Katz's phone. Anyone could have made that call. And there was no guarantee that it was Richards who had answered, for the same reason.

The possibility was obvious: There could have been no scheduled meeting between the men. Decker had just assumed there was. The killer could have orchestrated all that to make it look like there was a meeting, or just Katz coming over for a beer. The fact that Decker believed that the killer or killers had driven an unconscious Katz over there made sense under that scenario. They could have gone in, held the Richardses hostage, brought in Katz, methodically killed them, laid their evidence casting guilt on Meryl Hawkins, departed the house through the back, and an hour later called in a disturbance.

So now the question was, who was really meant to be killed? Richards or Katz? The banker or the borrower?

And why?

And why did their killers pick that night to do it?

Decker knew if he could find an answer to any or all of those three questions, he might be able to blow this sucker wide open.

But he wasn't there yet. Maybe not even close.

He drove to a very familiar place: Burlington High School, where a little over two years before, a horrific mass shooting had stunned the town.

Decker parked his car and made his way to the dilapidated football field. Burlington no longer fielded a football team—they didn't have enough guys interested in playing the game. He climbed up into the bleachers as a light drizzle began to fall.

He took a seat and stared down at the field where he had been a superstar many years before. The only player in Burlington High history to go on to play in the NFL, if only for one play. He wrapped himself in his coat and stared moodily out.

As his gaze drifted to the right, he flinched as he saw her coming toward him. Mary Lancaster slowly made her way up the metal steps and sat down next to him.

"Didn't we do this before?" she said.

He nodded. "In the rain. After the school shootings. How'd you know I was here?"

"I didn't. You know my house backs up to the school. I take walks late at night. I saw you."

He nodded again. "But it's after one in the morning. It's not really safe for you to be out alone."

"And it is for you?"

"Well," he said. "I'm a lot bigger than you."

She opened her coat and he saw her pistol riding in its holster. "Someone wants to try to mug me, they'll be eating a round."

"I can see that. So, how's it going?"

"It's going. I hear you're making progress on the case."

"From who do you hear that?"

"Of all people, Natty. He seems to have had a change of heart about you after Sally was killed."

Decker said, "Did you know they were seeing each other?"

Lancaster looked stunned. "What? No, I didn't. Natty's married."

"Sally had ended it with him. She knew it wasn't right."

Lancaster shook her head. "I never saw that coming. And I still can't believe she's dead."

He glanced at her as the rain picked up. She had on a long trench coat and a ball cap. Her gray hair flowed out from underneath it. She looked to Decker like she was carrying an enormous weight on her slender shoulders.

"Are you ill, Mary? I mean really ill?"

She didn't look at him, but kept her gaze on the field. "Why do you ask that?"

"Because you're not the same. You've changed. And I don't think it's just because of what's happening with you and Earl."

She clenched her hands and then flexed them straight. "I'm not terminal, if that's what you want to know. I don't have cancer, despite my smoking."

"What, then?"

She didn't answer right away. When Lancaster did respond, her voice held a resigned tone. "Ever heard of early onset dementia?"

Decker gaped. "Dementia? You're still young, same age as me."

She gave him a sad smile. "That's why they call it 'early,' Amos."

"Are they sure? When were you diagnosed?"

"About six months ago. And they are sure. Brain scans, more MRIs than I can remember, blood work, biopsies, everything. I'm on meds, treatment."

"Then they can turn it around?" he said, with a small measure of relief in his voice.

She shook her head. "No, there is no cure. It's just holding the progression back as long as possible."

"What's the prognosis, then?" he said quietly.

"Hard to say. It's not like there are a million cases like me. And everyone's reaction is apparently different."

"Can they give you an estimate?"

She drew a long breath and her face quivered with emotion. "In a year I might not be able to recognize myself or anyone else. Or it could be five years. But not much beyond that. I won't even be fifty."

A long moment of silence passed, as tears slid down her cheeks.

"I'm so sorry, Mary."

She wiped her eyes and waved this off. "I don't need sympathy, Decker, least of all from you. I know it's not your thing." She patted his shoulder and added in a kinder tone, "But I appreciate the effort."

"How did you know something was wrong?"

"When I woke up one morning and couldn't remember Sandy's name for about a minute. I blew that off, chalked it up to overwork. But little things like that started to happen with more frequency. That's when I went to the doctor."

Decker sat back and thought about his momentary inability to remember Cassie's favorite color. "Is that the reason for you and Earl splitting up?"

"Earl is a good guy, couldn't ask for a better one. But he has enough to do taking care of Sandy. I do not need to add to his burden."

"A good guy would not see it as a burden."

She looked at him. "Cassie never saw you as a burden, I hope you know that."

Decker looked away, his gaze drifting over the field where he had run like the wind, opposing players bouncing off him like pebbles flung against a mighty oak, people cheering him on, a normal kid with abnormal, even freakish athletic talent. Those had been some of the happiest times of his life, only to be dwarfed on the happiness scale by his time as a husband and father.

"I know that," he said quietly. "But I don't think you should give up on Earl that easily. The words *are* 'in sickness and in health.'"

"'Till death do us part.' Those vows are easy to make when you're young, healthy and happy and in love, your whole life ahead of you."

"Are you still in love with Earl?"

She looked at him, startled. "What?"

"I'm still in love with Cassie. I'll always love her. I don't care if she's dead. But Earl isn't dead. Earl is right here. I would give anything for Cassie to be here. And nothing, not early onset dementia or anything else, would keep me from her. Any second without her would be a waste of my life."

Decker rose and walked down the steps as the rain picked up.

Mary Lancaster watched him every step of the way.

43

"You look tired. Didn't you sleep okay?"

Mars asked this as he and Decker sat in the dining area of the Residence Inn the next morning having coffee.

"Slept like a baby," lied Decker. He sat back and fiddled with his paper napkin. "Planning went into this. They had to get the print, the DNA, and come up with the light switch plate. They had to kidnap David Katz. They had to commit the murders, leave the evidence, and flee the crime scene. This was clearly premeditated."

"I agree."

"So why did they pick that night, then? To do it? Was it just a coincidence that it was around the time of the only known phone call between the two men for a long while?"

"Maybe they found out about the phone call another way. What time did it happen?"

"Twelve-ten p.m."

"And Richards got the call at work?"

"It was his cell phone, but because of the time

presumably it was—" Decker sat up straighter, his eyes wide.

"What?" said Mars, looking a bit alarmed.

"It was on a Monday in October."

"Okay."

"It was actually also Columbus Day."

"A holiday, then."

"Yes, and that meant two things. There was no school and the bank was closed."

"So where was Richards when he got the call, if not at the bank?"

"He could very well have been at home," said Decker.

"With his kids. And his wife. Do you think one of them might have overheard something, and then told someone?"

"That's certainly possible. But regardless, they would have had to act fast. Get the print on the switch plate and take it with them to the Richardses'. Then someone scratches Hawkins's arms and collects his DNA that way."

"And you think it was his daughter, Mitzi."

"It would explain why he kept quiet. He would obviously know who scratched him."

Mars said thoughtfully, "I see what you mean. His wife was dying, and he didn't want their daughter to get into trouble, even if it cost him his freedom."

Decker nodded. "When they finish testing the DNA sample, I bet it will show that Mitzi's DNA is also mixed up in what we found under Abigail's nails."

Mars said, "But why would she frame her own father?"

"She was a drug addict. Out of her mind half the time. She could have been easily persuaded to do it."

"But what would be the motive of somebody doing all that to kill Katz and Richards? And how does that tie into David Katz going over to Don Richards's house? Wait, do you think those guys were into drugs too?"

"Not that we know—" Decker stopped. "But Richards's son, Frankie, was. And we found out he was also dealing."

"But again, what's the connection?"

Decker closed his eyes and dialed up his cloud. After a few seconds he shook his head. "It's not in the case file."

"What's not?"

"The name of Mitzi's drug dealer."

44

Natty was sitting sulkily behind his desk in the open room of the homicide department. Four other detectives were there working away, including Mary Lancaster.

A moment later Decker and Mars burst into the space. Decker glanced at Lancaster, who had a questioning look on her face, before marching over to stand in front of Natty.

"Karl Stevens," he said.

"Who?"

"He was the dealer who'd sold some stuff to Frankie Richards."

Lancaster had risen from her chair and approached. "We know that, but he had an alibi for the time of the murders. We checked that back then."

"Not the point," said Decker brusquely.

"So, what *is* the point?" snapped Natty.

"Did he also deal to Mitzi Hawkins?"

Lancaster and Natty exchanged a look. Natty said, "I don't know. It's been a long time. Does it matter?"

"It could."

Natty sighed. "I can check. No guarantees that it's in the records anywhere. And Karl Stevens sold to a lot of people."

Mars said, "Where is he now?"

Lancaster answered. "I can tell you that. He's at Travis Correctional Center. It's a private prison now. Stevens is serving ten to twenty on a second-degree murder conviction. He killed a guy over a heroin transaction. He's five years into his term. I was the one who busted him."

Decker said, "Travis Correctional? Isn't that where Meryl Hawkins ended up serving his time?"

Natty got on his computer and tapped some more keys. When he reached the page, his jaw fell. He looked up.

"You're right."

"Were they both in gen pop?" asked Decker, referring to the prison's general population.

"I don't know. But that's usually the case. They don't have the space to segregate prisoners. They're way beyond capacity as it is."

Lancaster said, "They could have interacted at the prison, then." She looked at Decker. "What are you thinking?"

"If they did interact, Stevens could have told him something that led Hawkins to come back here asking us to prove his innocence. I wondered about the timing of all this. I mean, did Hawkins just learn something that made him believe we could prove his innocence? He wanted to meet with me. Maybe it was then that he was going to tell me what he knew."

Lancaster said, "He must have learned it recently, otherwise why wouldn't he have raised it while he was still in prison?"

"What could Stevens have told him?" asked Natty.

"For one thing, that he was Mitzi's dealer," replied Decker.

"So what?"

"That could mean a connection between Frankie Richards and Mitzi."

"What kind of connection?" persisted Natty. "You're not making sense."

"Can you get us permission to visit Stevens?" asked Decker, ignoring the question. "Today?"

"I can try. But what could he possibly tell you?"

"I won't know that until I ask him." He paused. "You, um, you want to come along, Natty?"

The man didn't answer right away. He glanced at Lancaster and then said in a low voice, "I'm . . . I'm actually taking my wife out to lunch today."

Decker gazed at him for a few moments. "I think that's a better use of your time. I'll fill you in when we get back." He pointed at the phone on Natty's desk. "Make the call and tell them it'll be two of us."

"Make that three," said Lancaster.

"Mary, you're recused from—"

"Screw recusal, Amos. This doesn't have to do

with Meryl Hawkins's murder where Earl is providing an alibi."

Decker glanced at Natty, who shrugged. "I have no problem with that."

Lancaster said, "Let's go." She walked out of the room without another word.

"Hey, Decker," said Mars, grinning. "She just did a really good impression of you."

It was a two-hour drive, and Mars dozed in the backseat. Decker had introduced Mars to Lancaster as they headed out.

Lancaster checked the backseat and then glanced at Decker. "At the football field?" she said quietly.

Decker kept his eyes on the road. "Yeah?"

"What you said made a lot of sense."

Decker just kept staring at the road and the approaching storm.

"I talked to Earl this morning."

Now Decker glanced at her, his expression prompting.

"I think we're going to . . . give it another shot."

"And his lady friend?" asked Decker.

"I don't think it would be an untruth to say that I pushed him into that relationship. Don't get me wrong. Nancy's nice and Earl likes her. Hell, I like her."

"But it's not what Earl wants?"

"No. He made that clear this morning. What he wants . . ."

"Is you."

Lancaster touched her wrinkled face and ran a hand down her stringy hair. "Can't really understand why. I look like shit. Nancy, on the other hand, is a real babe."

"Who's being shallow now?"

Lancaster looked embarrassed and dropped her hands in her lap. "I have to say I was surprised that you thought enough about my situation to tell me what I needed to hear."

"Meaning that I only look inward?"

"Meaning that I know those situations are very difficult for you with your special—"

"Maybe I'm growing out of it," interrupted Decker.

Lancaster absently touched her temple. "What did it feel like, when your . . . when your brain changed?"

He glanced over to see Lancaster staring at him with such intensity that he instantly felt anxious in trying to answer her query. He could sense that she was counting on him to tell her it would be somehow okay, or at least not terrible.

"I didn't have much time to make the transition, Mary. I woke up in a hospital and I was different. My mind was doing things it had never done before."

"I, um, I guess you were scared."

He glanced at her again to see the woman now staring at her hands.

"I won't lie to you, Mary. It was *unsettling*. But I got professional help and I was able to adapt. I won't tell you that it gets any easier. I will tell you that I was able to manage it. To live my life."

"It will be a bit different for me, I imagine."

"There's no cure for what you and I have, though they are very different things. But every day they make progress. In five years, who's to say they won't have beat what you have?"

She nodded but her look of anxiety remained. "If I live that long."

Decker reached over and gripped her shoulder.

She looked startled by this personal touch. It was not something that Amos Decker normally would ever do. She knew he didn't like being touched by others.

"You have Earl and Sandy and me to help you through this, Mary."

"You don't live here anymore."

"I'm here right now. And you know I'm going to keep coming back to Burlington."

"Because of your family."

"And now, also because of you."

This declaration caught Lancaster off guard. A small sob escaped from her lips and she suddenly seized his hand with both of hers and squeezed, as the tears, like released water over a dam, broke free and slid down her cheeks.

"You're a good friend, Amos. Sometimes I have trouble remembering that."

"You put up with me for a lot of years, Mary. Longer than anyone else other than Cassie. You probably deserve a medal for that. But all I can offer you is my friendship."

"I'll take that over any medal."

They drove the rest of the way in silence.

45

With its concrete walls, concertina wire, attack dogs, and guards with sniper rifles on towers, Travis Correctional Center rose out of the Ohio soil looking every bit the max prison that it was.

Decker drove up to the entrance and they cleared security, right as the heavens opened up and the rain poured down, forcing them to sprint for cover. Natty had secured an interview with Karl Stevens, and they were escorted to the visitors' room.

All three, Decker, Lancaster, and Mars, were well acquainted with prisons, for starkly different reasons. Catcalls, screams, the smells of over two thousand men kept in close proximity to each other in a facility designed for half that number, together with the comingled aromas of dozens of types of illicit contraband.

They sat at a table and awaited the arrival of Karl Stevens. He was brought in a few minutes later. Decker remembered him as tall and thin with long, dirty hair tied back in a ponytail, and a scruffy beard. The man appearing before them in his orange prison jumpsuit and shackles was thickened with dumbbell-driven muscle. His head was shaved, his facial hair gone. His knotted forearms were bedecked with tats that continued on his neck and up the back of his bald head.

He smiled at the trio as he was seated in front of them and his shackles locked into an eyebolt on the floor.

The guards stepped away but kept a watchful eye from across the room.

Stevens looked at Decker. "I remember you. Decker, right?"

Decker nodded.

Then the inmate turned to Lancaster. "Sure as hell remember you. You're the reason I'm here."

"No, let's keep to the facts, Karl. The reason you're here is because you killed a guy."

"Details, details," said Stevens with a smirk. He glanced at Mars and his expression soured. "Don't know you."

"No, you don't," said Mars.

"You a cop too?"

"He's helping us on a case," said Decker.

Stevens kept his gaze on Mars. "You got the look of somebody who's done time."

"You ever been locked up in Texas?" said Mars.

"No, why?"

"I wouldn't recommend it."

Stevens looked at Decker. "What do you want? I

was going to work out, then I got the word you wanted to see me."

Decker said dryly, "Sorry to interrupt your exercise. We wanted to know if you were Mitzi Hawkins's dealer."

"Who's Mitzi Hawkins?"

"Meryl Hawkins's daughter."

Stevens shrugged. "That doesn't mean shit to me. I dealt to a lot of people." He laughed. "I didn't ask for fuckin' ID."

Decker described Mitzi to him.

Stevens chuckled. "You got to be shitting me. You just described every whacked-out bitch I ever sold to."

"How about Frankie Richards? You remember him? He was only fourteen. He died at his home along with his father and sister and a man named David Katz. They were murdered."

"Nah, can't say that I do. Anything else?"

Decker was looking at the tats on the man's forearms. Words and symbols.

When Stevens noticed this, he lowered his arms to below the tabletop, his shackles rattling as he did so.

"Which gangs do you belong to in here, Karl?" asked Decker.

Stevens grinned. "Hell, I'm Switzerland, man. Neutral. Most guys in here are Hispanic, or they got his skin color." He pointed at Mars. "*They* belong to the gangs, not the white guys. We're in the minority."

"You're not the only white guy in here," pointed out Lancaster. "Not by a long shot."

"Well, most days it seems like I'm in the minority. We got to do something about that." He grinned. "Take back our country."

"How? Lock up more white guys?" said Mars.

Stevens's lips curled back. "No. Just keep your kind out."

"I was born here."

"Ways around that," said Stevens, with another smirk. "We done here?"

Lancaster said, "If you're straight with us, Karl, we might be able to help you out."

He glanced up at her, all attention now. "Help me out, how?"

"Your sentence? It has some flexibility."

"I've done five on a ten to twenty. What can you do about that?"

"That depends on what you can do for us."

He rolled his eyes. "It's always the same old shit with you people. I got to tell what I know, if anything, and then you tell me the deal, take it or leave it. What other businesses negotiate that way?"

Decker said, "This isn't a business. This is you marking fewer years in here than you otherwise would."

Stevens said, "I can lie and tell you anything you

want. Then you cut me a sweetheart deal. How about that?"

"Lies don't cut it. We need the truth, corroborated."

"It happened a long time ago. How do you expect me to remember anything?" As soon as Stevens said this, his features tightened.

Decker said, "*What* happened a long time ago?" When Stevens didn't answer, he added, "I thought you didn't remember anything about Frankie Richards or Meryl Hawkins."

"Just making conversation," said Stevens uncomfortably, his swagger now gone.

Lancaster interjected, "You want to deal or not? We can leave right now, but we'll be sure to note in the record how uncooperative you were. That way you go to the max twenty."

Stevens lunged forward and might have leapt across the table but for his restraints. The look on his face was that of a snarling wild animal. "You screw me like that, bitch, and you're gonna regret it. I didn't ask for you to come here."

"Is that right, Karl?" said Lancaster. "You got friends on the outside?"

"I got friends all over."

"So where were your friends when your ass ended up in here?" She paused. "Some friends. Why do you think you owe them?"

"Who said anything about owing anybody?" he barked.

The guards made a move to step forward, but Decker waved them off. He said, "Because guys like you are a dime a dozen, and Mary and I have seen it all a hundred times. You got stupid and you got caught and your 'friends' ran away from you as fast as they could. The result: You're in here and they're not."

"You got no idea who you're dealing with."

"Then tell us," replied Decker. "I always like to know who's on the opposing team."

Stevens waved this off with a rattle of his shackles. "I'm just spouting, man. Just bullshit."

"Getting back to Richards and Hawkins: You dealt for them both, I'm betting. Maybe you heard something from one of them that might tie into what happened?"

Lancaster added, "And maybe you saw Meryl Hawkins here and you two talked. About stuff? And then he got released."

"That was bullshit. I'm sick too. I got a liver thing."

"So, you *knew* he was released because of his cancer being terminal?" said Decker.

When the inmate once more looked chagrined at his own words, Decker said, "That's the second time you've screwed up talking with us, Karl. I think you need to tell us what you know, and we'll work a deal for you. You'll be out of here sooner than you otherwise would."

"You think it's that easy?"

"I don't know. Why don't you try us?"

"I gotta think about it."

Lancaster said, "What's to think about? You help us, we help you."

Stevens shook his head.

"Tell us this, did you talk to Hawkins?" asked Decker.

"I might have seen him around."

"And might you have discussed the murders with him?"

"Why don't you ask him?"

Lancaster said, "We would, but somebody killed him."

Stevens turned pale and looked like he might be sick. "I gotta go." He looked at the guards. "Hey, I'm done here."

Decker said, "It doesn't have to be this way, Karl."

"Yeah, it does. Now leave me the hell alone."

As he was being led away, Lancaster said to Decker, "I screwed up. I shouldn't have told him what happened to Hawkins."

"I don't think it would have mattered, Mary, but we did get one lead."

"What?"

"The tats on Stevens's arms were very close to the tats I saw on the shooter who killed Sally Brimmer."

"What? Are you sure?"

"Yes, I'm sure."

When they got back to Burlington, Natty met them in the detectives' room. "What the hell happened up there?"

"What do you mean?" asked Lancaster.

"They just found Karl Stevens with a shiv in his neck. He's dead."

46

Decker, Lancaster, and Mars were holding a powwow in the empty dining area of the Residence Inn as the rain beat down outside in the darkness.

"Well, that tells us your theory was right, Amos," said Lancaster. "Stevens was involved in this somehow."

"And by talking to us, he got the death penalty," added Mars bitterly. "I know the guy was scum, but nobody deserves that crap."

Decker sat there, his hands in his lap, his gaze centered on a spot on the ceiling. "The shooter who killed Sally Brimmer had the same tats. There's apparently a connection between him and Stevens."

"Are you really sure they're the same?" asked Lancaster.

"I got a clear look at them in the alley, and at Stevens's back at the prison. I think Stevens knew that, because when he caught me looking, he put his arms under the table so I couldn't see the tats anymore."

"Membership in the same gang," said Lancaster. "That's certainly possible."

"They moved quickly," said Decker. "He was dead within two hours of our meeting him."

"How could they possibly have acted that quickly?" asked Lancaster. "Unless it was unrelated to our visit. Inmates do kill other inmates, all the time."

"That would have to be the biggest coincidence in the world."

"And you don't believe in even small coincidences," said Mars.

"And you saw how Stevens clammed up when he found out Meryl Hawkins had been murdered. He was afraid for his safety. He tried to shut it down, but it was too late."

"With him gone, how do we get to the truth?" asked Lancaster. "Our leads keep dying. And, hell, we don't even know how whoever killed the Richards family and David Katz got there or left."

"No, I think we do know that," said Decker.

He explained to her his theory on Katz being kidnapped and driven to the Richardses' home in his car. And also about the light switch plate change-out and the DNA possibly coming from Mitzi. "I told Natty about it all too."

"So that's why you wanted to talk to Stevens," said Lancaster.

Decker nodded. "I think Frankie Richards overheard the conversation between his father and Katz, and told Stevens about it when he saw him, or maybe he phoned him. The call came in on a holiday and both father and son were presumably home. Whatever Frankie told Stevens about that phone call, Stevens then told others. And they arranged things and the very next night they came and killed them all. That's how they picked that night and also the location, since Richards was probably expecting Katz to come over anyway. That seems to be what the phone call between the two was about."

Mars said, "And maybe they picked that night because they knew Susan Richards *wouldn't* be home. It might be that she knew nothing about what they were planning to discuss."

Lancaster said, "So we figure out what they were planning to discuss, this whole thing unravels."

"They only had one known connection. The American Grill restaurant."

"Which Rachel Katz still owns and operates," said Mars. "And that's puzzling, since she told me she'll probably make more in a month at her nightclub than the American Grill does in six months."

"And she's got all these other projects going, so it's a wonder she wants to keep the place," said Decker.

Mars said, "She told me it was because it was her husband's first deal. But the lady didn't strike me as being all that nostalgic."

"And she also told you she brings the local know-how and her partners bring the cash," noted Decker.

"You think her money partners are involved in all this?" asked Lancaster.

"I don't know. But if they are, they would have had to have been around thirteen years ago. It might be worthwhile digging into who they are."

"Whoever it is, they must have some serious connections inside Travis Correctional," commented Lancaster.

"How do you want to go about doing this with Rachel?" asked Decker. "They already know we're snooping around from our meeting with Stevens. I don't want to spook them even more."

Mars said, "What about me?"

"What about you what?" asked Lancaster.

"Lady clearly likes me."

"The lady also knows you work with us," said Decker.

"She told me a lot last night. Maybe she'll tell me some more."

"I don't like it," said Lancaster.

"I don't like it either," said Decker. "But it might be our best shot. And at the same time, we can find out who her partners are. There has to be paperwork filed with all of her projects."

"Okay, I'll get rolling on that," said Lancaster. She pointed her finger at Mars. "This is not fun and games. These people are killers."

"Yeah," said Mars. "Which is why we're going after them."

"You think you know a lot about killers?"

"Well, I was on death row all those years."

Lancaster looked at Decker. "Will you tell him to be serious?"

"He *is* being serious, Mary."

Lancaster whirled back around to stare suspiciously at Mars.

"Don't worry," he said. "Turns out I was innocent. Only cost me twenty years of my life and ruined any shot I had at playing in the NFL."

"Damn," said Lancaster. "That sucks."

"Oh, it more than sucks, trust me."

"How are you going to approach it with Katz?" asked Decker.

"Look, she probably thinks she can work on me and get details about the investigation. She tried doing that last night. I didn't give her much, but I did give her a taste here and there. I can let her think she's making inroads. And I'll do the same with her." He paused. "And there's something off with her."

"What do you mean?" asked Lancaster.

"I'm not sure. She's attractive, she's got money, education. But she feels like a loner to me. How come she never remarried? And why is she always so guarded about everything? When I asked about meeting her business partners, she didn't look comfortable with that at all."

"You could be right," remarked Lancaster.

"And if we end up in a place where I can snoop around, I will."

"Whoa, now you think you're some kind of, what, spy?" said Lancaster.

"Well, my girlfriend *is* a spy."

"Now you're bullshitting me, right?"

Mars held up his right hand. "God's honest truth."

She looked at Decker, who nodded. "Military intelligence."

"Sonofabitch," exclaimed Lancaster. "You have a whole new class of friends, Amos."

"Hey, if you don't grow, you wither, right?" said Mars.

Decker put a hand on his shoulder. "All that aside, this *is* dangerous, Melvin. You're not going into this clean. They know what side you're on. Things can go sideways fast. If you sense any of that happening, you need to get out, pronto."

"I've always been fast, Decker, you know that from our college football days."

Lancaster said, "Wait a minute, you two played football against each other?"

"Longhorn versus Buckeye," said Mars. "And guess who won?"

"You did," said Decker. "And I hope you win again. Because unlike our college football matchup, I'm rooting for you."

Mars smiled, but when he saw the look Decker was giving him he gripped his shoulder and said, "Look, I know this isn't a game. But people have been killed. For no reason other than some assholes decided they didn't get to live anymore, and that included kids. If I can help you take them down, then I will."

Lancaster exchanged a glance with Decker. "You have seriously upgraded your friends, Amos."

"I know," he said. "And I want to keep them."

47

"What the hell is he doing here?"

Decker, Mars, and Lancaster were walking into the police station the next morning when Childress stormed across the front lobby to confront them.

Decker eyed the police superintendent, who was attempting to stare him down. "I'm observing," he replied. "Like I was told I could. Natty's on board with it."

"I don't give a damn if Natty's on board with it." Childress put a finger in Decker's face. "And I know damn well that you're hardly just 'observing.' You're working this case, I know you are, because I know you."

"Then you know that I want to get to the truth."

In a scoffing tone, Childress said, "You think you can just waltz back in here and try to do our work for us? We're perfectly capable of investigating this case ourselves. We don't need you or the FBI to help us." He glanced at Mars. "Are you FBI?"

"No, just your friendly neighborhood vigilante."

"Nothing wrong with cooperation," interjected

Decker. "Happens all the time." He glanced at Lancaster but was not surprised to see her remain silent. This was her job, this was how she supported her family. And with her health issues, Childress could make her life miserable.

Now Childress got right in Decker's face. "Just remember that we are still pressing charges against you. And you still have a court date to keep. Hired that lawyer yet? Because you're going to need one."

"Well, I won't be hiring Ken Finger."

Childress drew back. "Why not? He's got a good reputation."

"Yeah, he did such a bang-up job for Meryl Hawkins."

"Hell! The world's greatest lawyer couldn't have gotten Hawkins off. The forensic case was overwhelming."

"You think so?"

"You built that damn case, Decker," snapped Childress.

"Only I built it *wrong*."

Childress was about to say something but seemed to swallow his words. "What are you talking about?"

"We were all had, that's what I'm talking about."

"You're nuts. Forensics don't lie."

"No, they don't. But people do. All the time."

"You're making no damn sense at all." Childress glared at Lancaster. "How the hell can you work with this guy, Mary?"

"He gets results. You know that as well as I do."

Childress turned back to Decker. "One step out of line. One. And your ass is mine."

"Well, that's quite tempting," replied Decker.

Childress looked like he was about to throw a punch, but he somehow marshaled his anger and marched off.

"Is he always that mellow?" asked Mars.

"He's actually gotten better," said Lancaster. "He went from Satan to just being an asshole."

"You're really being prosecuted, Decker?" asked Mars. "I thought it was just a joke."

"For now, I am. I doubt it will ever get to an actual trial."

"Don't believe that, if Childress has anything to do with it," said Lancaster.

"He'll keep. And we need to 'keep' our focus on the case."

"What's the next move?" asked Lancaster.

"Someone impersonated Susan Richards on the day she disappeared."

"That's still not been proven," pointed out Lancaster. "It's just speculation."

"Fine, but speculation or not, we have to follow the theory up."

Mars said, "Why don't you two run that down? I'm going to try to connect with Rachel. She left me her cell phone number."

"We want to be around when you do," said Decker.

"Okay, but you can't be hovering over me. I'll let you know what I set up."

"We can wire you up again."

Mars shook his head. "No, I don't want to chance her finding a wire on me. That will blow everything."

"Okay," said Decker reluctantly. "But be careful."

Mars gave him a thumbs-up as he left them.

Lancaster watched him go. "Don't worry, Decker. He looks like he can take care of himself."

"I'd worry less if he were going into a bar fight with five big guys. Melvin would win that battle for sure."

"Then what are you worried about? He's not going into a fight with five guys. He's meeting up with *one* woman."

"*That's* what I'm worried about."

"So, what are we going to do next?"

"Something you can't help me with."

"Why not?"

"Like I said, it has to do with Susan Richards. And what I want to check also involves Rachel Katz. You can't work that part of the case because of Earl."

"Earl was Rachel Katz's alibi for Meryl Hawkins's murder. *Not* for what happened to Richards."

"But do you think Childress will see it that way?"

"Who gives a shit?" In a bit of gallows humor, she added, "Next year I might not even remember who he is."

"Okay, if you're sure."

"I am. But how is Katz involved in Richards's disappearance and murder?"

"Someone impersonated Richards so Agatha Bates could ID her. And both Rachel Katz and Mitzi Gardiner are the right height and build. From a distance and with a long coat and hat on, they could be mistaken for Susan Richards. Especially by someone whose eyesight isn't the best, like Bates."

"You really think that one of them killed Richards and took her place after sticking the woman in that suitcase?"

"Either we prove it is true or we don't."

"Who's first? Katz or Gardiner?"

"We'll leave Katz for Melvin right now. Let's go talk to Gardiner."

"She's not obligated to tell us anything."

"Then let's hear that from her."

"Are you going to just point-blank accuse the woman?"

"You've never appreciated the subtle side of my personality, Mary."

Lancaster looked surprised. "That may be because I've never seen it, Amos."

"Well, hang on, because you're about to."

48

"Okay, this is harassment, damn it."

Decker and Lancaster were standing on the front porch of Mitzi Gardiner's home, while the woman stared angrily across at them over the width of the doorway.

"I can understand your feeling that way, Ms. Gardiner. But the fact is, we're doing our best to solve multiple homicides connected to your father, and, like it or not, you're one of the best resources we have. We just have some questions for you, and we'll make them as painless as possible. I promise."

Lancaster looked incredulously at Decker, having obviously never seen him talk this way to any suspect or person of interest.

Gardiner eyed Lancaster. "I remember you. You two worked the case together."

"We did, yes. And I have to say I doubt I would have recognized you." Lancaster ran her eye over Gardiner's long, healthy frame, her elegant clothes, her perfectly coiffed hair, and her blemish-free complexion.

"I know that I've changed quite a bit from when you last saw me."

"You look great."

"Thank you."

"And I have to say I never thought we'd end up revisiting this case. But then your father came back to town proclaiming his innocence."

Gardiner pointed at Decker. "I already told him that was crap. My father just wanted to mess with you. Make you doubt his guilt."

"We still haven't found out who killed him," said Decker.

"You said you were checking with the two widows."

"Right. Well, one of them was murdered."

Gardiner gaped and Decker saw her fingers on the door tremble. "Murdered? Which one?"

"Susan Richards. We believe she was abducted from her home and then killed."

When Gardiner didn't respond, Decker added, "Can we come in?"

She led them down the hall to the conservatory. She motioned for them to sit while she stood there clasping and unclasping her hands.

"You look pretty surprised," said Decker.

"Of course I'm surprised. First my father and now Susan Richards." She abruptly sat down across from them and stared at her lap.

Lancaster looked around the graceful lines of the room. "You have a lovely home."

Gardiner nodded absently, but still wouldn't meet their eyes.

Decker took something from his pocket and held it out to her. "I thought you might want to have this."

Gardiner looked up but did not reach for the photo.

"It's you as a little girl. We found it in your dad's wallet. There wasn't much else in there. I know you said you never visited him in prison, but he evidently kept this photo all these years."

Gardiner shook her head. "I . . . I don't want it."

Decker put the photo down on the table, face up.

"What are your questions?" said Gardiner, glancing at the photo and then quickly looking away.

"Well, and don't be offended by this, because we're asking everyone connected to this case. We need to know where you were when Susan Richards was last seen."

"You can't possibly believe I had anything to do with her death?"

"Look, I don't want to believe that anyone is capable of murder. However, some people clearly are. But I'm not accusing you of anything. I'm just eliminating suspects right now, and we can do that with you if you can tell us where you were."

"What time are we talking about?"

Decker told her the day and the time in the evening.

Gardiner sat back and closed her eyes. Then she reached into her pocket and pulled out her phone. She brought up her calendar and ran through some screens. Then she seemed to breathe a sigh of relief. "I was at a dinner with my husband. A business dinner. There were six other people with us. It's here in Trammel. At a restaurant. From seven o'clock until well after midnight."

"And your husband can verify that?" said Lancaster.

"Do you have to talk to him?" Gardiner said worriedly. "He knows nothing about any of this ... of my past life."

"Well, if you give us the names of some of the other people there?"

"That's as good as telling him," she snapped. "He's built up a great reputation in this area and people trust him. Something like this could ruin him."

"Well, can you think of someone else who can corroborate your whereabouts?" asked Lancaster.

Gardiner suddenly looked animated. "Wait, I know the owner of the restaurant. She could verify it. We had a private room and we paid with a credit card. You can check the receipt."

"That works."

Lancaster pulled out a notebook and took this information down.

"Is that all?" asked Gardiner, still clearly distracted.

"You need to tell us where you were when your father was killed."

"My father? Now you're accusing me of murdering my own father?"

"Again, I'm not accusing you of anything. I'm eliminating suspects, like we did for you just now with Susan Richards's death."

She looked at her calendar after Decker told her the time parameters. "I was home with my family. In fact, I was probably asleep at that hour. Like most people," she added.

"And your husband can corroborate that?"

"If necessary," she said between clenched teeth. "Is that all?"

"There's another discrepancy," said Decker. "But I'm sure you can clear it up."

Gardiner looked wearily at him. "I remember that you never seemed to stop asking questions all those years ago."

"And I'm afraid I haven't changed. It just comes with the territory."

"What discrepancy?"

"You said you'd never been in your father's closet."

Gardiner seemed instantly on the defensive. "Who told you that?"

"Actually, you did. The first time I was here to question you."

"Oh, okay. But I don't understand the discrepancy."

"The police report indicates that you were the one to show the forensic techs the panel in the closet."

Gardiner frowned. "I don't remember doing that."

"It was in the report."

"Then the report is wrong. It can be, can't it?"

Decker said, "So you're saying you didn't show them the panel?"

"I'm telling you I don't *remember* doing that."

"Okay. So they might have been searching and found it on their own."

"I guess."

"But why would they say that you told them about it?" asked Lancaster.

Gardiner was very pale now. "I . . . I don't know. Maybe I did. I might have been helping them look or something. It's possible. It was a long time ago. And I was not in a good frame of mind. I didn't remember things very well."

Decker said, "Understood. Well, thanks for your time."

He stood. Lancaster quickly did as well, looking surprised that Decker was already done.

"That's . . . that's it?" said Gardiner, looking as surprised as Lancaster.

"For now, yes." Decker slid the photo of her as a child toward her.

"I told you I didn't want it."

"I know. But sometimes people change their minds, don't they?"

Gardiner made no move to pick up the photo.

Decker said, "We'll find our own way out."

As they got into their car Lancaster said, "Okay, I approve of your new 'subtle' nature, Decker. But you really closed out the interview fast. I thought it was just getting good."

"It *was* just getting good. But you can also push someone too far."

"She's scared."

"She *is* scared. Because she knows more than she's telling us. And she's very concerned that someone else will realize that too."

"Are you saying she might be in danger?"

"Everyone connected with this case might be in danger, including you and me."

"We're cops, we signed up for that. Mitzi Gardiner didn't."

"Didn't she?" said Decker as he put the car in drive.

49

Posh.

That was the word that occurred to Mars as he pulled to a stop in the parking lot of the Silver Oak Grill. He didn't know what it used to be, but its old bones had been given new life. He looked around at the other cars parked there and saw a sprinkling of late-model expensive rides. There was even a Maserati convertible parked near the awninged entrance.

He walked in and looked around. The buildout here had definitely been expensive. Mars had learned about construction costs from investing in real estate in the D.C. market. Old beams, pricey stone flooring, an elaborately carved bar, expensive wallpaper, coexisting with contemporary seating.

The place was nearly full with folks having lunch, and there were three people ahead of Mars waiting to be seated.

"Melvin?"

He looked to his right and saw Rachel Katz waving to him from a table in the corner. He walked over and joined her.

She stood and had to rise up on her toes to give him a hug and a peck on the cheek. Then she took a moment to appraise his attire. Gray jacket, black turtleneck, charcoal slacks, and black loafers.

"Terrific outfit."

"Thank you. You're looking quite sharp yourself," he said, noting her slacks, blouse, jacket, and flats.

"Well, I came straight from work."

As they sat, he saw that she had nearly finished her cocktail.

"Drink?" she said.

He eyed the almost empty glass. "What are you having?"

"Dewar's and water. I'm ready for a refill."

"Hitting the hard stuff in the afternoon, are we?"

"We are."

He grinned. "Sounds good to me."

They ordered their drinks and sat back.

"When you called, I was surprised you wanted to see me again," she said.

"Why's that?"

"Well, we left things a little, I don't know, flat."

"I'm into long-range forecasting. Date to date doesn't mean much."

"I'm flattered you referred to it as a date."

Their drinks arrived, and they tapped glasses.

Katz took a sip and said, "And I guess I'm also surprised that Decker is letting you see me. I mean, he is investigating, and despite all the facts to the contrary, I guess I remain a person of interest or something like that."

"You know the lingo," he said, grinning.

"I watch crime shows, what can I say?"

"Surprised you have the time what with work and all your other projects."

She leaned forward. "What would you say if I told you that most nights, I go home, change into my PJs, eat a peanut butter and jelly sandwich with chips on top, and watch old movies?"

He studied her. "I *would* believe that." He quickly added, "Not because you don't have options. I imagine you could have your pick of guys around here."

She made a face. "Thing is, I don't want the guys around here."

"Which raises the question of why you don't just move somewhere else. Chicago's not that far away."

"David and I were thinking of moving there. And then he died."

"So you feel tied to this place?"

"In a way, I guess. He's buried here. What he started to build is here."

"Right."

"You don't believe me?" she said, her mouth creasing into a frown.

"No, I *do* believe you. Look at Decker. He doesn't live here anymore, but he's still tied to the place. Comes back to visit his family's graves. Different people have different motivations. You want to stay here, you stay here. It's your decision, no one else's."

She was about to say something but then took a quick sip of her drink instead. "You want to order? The salmon is really good, but I'm going for the tuna tartare."

He glanced at the menu. "How's the wagyu?"

"It's great. We get it fresh every day."

"We?"

She smiled. "I guess I didn't tell you. I have an interest in this place too."

"A lady with lots of interests. Makes the world go round."

They ordered, and Mars looked around the place before resettling his gaze on Katz. "Lot of money in the parking lot and at these tables. Even saw a Maserati out there."

"The Maserati belongs to that gentleman." She pointed to a shortish man in his late sixties with thick gray hair. He wore a three-piece suit with no tie, crocodile skin loafers, and, despite the chilly weather, no socks. At his table were six other people. Four men and two women.

"Money man?"

"Yes. Duncan Marks."

"Is he one of your partners?"

"No, not really. But he does a lot of projects around town. And we *have* done a couple deals together. But I'm a small fry compared to him."

"Well, you're a big fry where I'm concerned."

She smiled at his statement. "How's the investigation coming?"

"Decker's interviewing Mitzi right about now. Checking alibis and stuff like that."

"You mean for Susan Richards's murder?"

"Yeah, among other things."

"Getting back to my earlier thought. How come Decker is letting you hang out with me? Is he hoping you'll learn some stuff so he can arrest me?" She said this last part in a cavalier way, but Mars could detect an undertone of apprehension.

"Like I said, I'm not law enforcement. I'm his friend. I don't tell him what to do and he doesn't tell me."

"But you still want to help him."

"Sure I do." He spread his arms wide. "And if there's anything you can tell me that will help, let me have it."

She laughed. "You're an interesting man. There aren't that many around this town, at least that I can find."

"You lost one when Decker moved away, that's a fact."

Their food came a few minutes later. Mars tasted his steak and his eyes widened. "Okay, that right there should be illegal, it's so damn good. I don't smoke, but I might just make an exception after eating this."

"We were lucky to get our chef. He's from Indianapolis. Trained under one of those master chefs you see on TV."

"Well, the dude can cook."

"Yes, he can. So, do you think Mitzi Hawkins will have an alibi for Susan's murder?" asked Katz abruptly.

Mars looked up from his plate. "I don't know. Decker must have it by now. If she had one. Then he'll need to check it out."

"Like he will mine."

"That's right." He put down his fork and knife. "You look concerned."

"Are you waiting for my confession?"

"No, because while I don't know you well, you don't strike me as the murdering type. I have a pretty good nose for that. But still, there may be something else weighing on your mind."

"No, I'm good. Just tired, I guess. Been burning the midnight oil lately." She rubbed her temples. "After you left the club, I did a little business. It wasn't nearly as much fun as I had with you."

"You flatter me."

"Not to beat around the bush, Melvin, but I do find you very attractive."

"Hey, you're beautiful, smart, ambitious, sensitive, the whole package."

"Why do I sense a 'but' coming?"

"I'm seeing someone right now."

"Lucky girl."

"I hope she thinks that. And I hope I didn't lead you on."

"No, you made things pretty clear, actually. But a lady can always dream."

Mars sat forward. "Look, Rachel, I like you. I really do. And while I'm not officially working with Decker, I am helping him any way I can, like I said."

Katz leaned back and picked up her drink. "Okay."

"The undeniable fact is there are a lot of people dying around here. You had four people thirteen years ago, including your husband. Then Meryl Hawkins. Then Sally Brimmer, although Decker was the target there. And then Susan Richards."

"And your point?"

"If you know anything, anything at all, you need to tell us. Last thing I want is for something to happen to you."

Katz's spine seemed to stiffen. "Thanks for your concern, Melvin. But I can take care of myself. And I don't know anything, so I have nothing to worry about."

Mars nodded slowly. "Okay, if you're sure about that."

"Very sure."

"Because there's been another murder you might not have heard of."

Katz had picked up her fork. She slowly put it down as she absorbed this news. "What? Who?"

"Man named Karl Stevens. He dealt drugs here. He sold stuff to Mitzi and to Frankie Richards. Decker thinks he might be involved."

"And he's dead?"

"He was in prison. We went to see him. He said he knew nothing either. By the time we got back to Burlington the man had a knife in his neck." Mars picked up his Dewar's and took a sip. "So, apparently, some people don't care if folks know anything or not. They just kill them."

"But how could ... I mean, he was in prison. People get killed in prison all the time."

"You're right about that. But the thing is, the tats that Stevens had on his arms?"

"What about them?" Katz said in a trembling voice.

"They matched the tats on the guy who shot Sally Brimmer. Decker was really sure about that, and nobody's memory beats his."

"And you don't think that might be a coincidence?"

"Do you?"

Katz sat back and composed herself. "Well, I'm sorry about this Mr. Stevens, but that has nothing to do with me."

"Okay, if you're sure."

"I *am* sure."

"Then let's just get back to this lovely meal."

Mars finished all of his steak. Katz barely touched her food. She finished her second Dewar's, though.

As they were leaving, they passed Marks's table. Duncan Marks put out a hand and gripped Katz's arm. "Rachel, I thought that was you over there."

"Hello, Duncan."

"The place is doing fabulous. Another home run for you."

"Thanks."

Marks looked at Mars. "And I don't believe I know your friend."

Mars put out a hand. "Melvin Mars. Nice to meet you, sir."

They shook hands as the other people at the table stared dully at them.

"Rachel said that was your Maserati out there. Beautiful car."

"Yes, it is. German engineering and Italian design, a match made in heaven."

They all laughed.

They walked out of the restaurant and Katz turned to Mars.

He said, "Seems like a nice guy."

"Yeah, look, um, I know we just had lunch, but can we have dinner tonight?"

"Okay, sure. Where?"

She hesitated. "My place. I can actually cook."

When he looked uncomfortable, she gripped his arm. "I promise, it won't be like that. I . . . I just need to have a home-cooked meal and someone to talk to. And I'd like that someone to be you."

Mars squeezed her hand and nodded. "Sure, sounds good."

"Seven okay?"

"I'll be there. Anything I can bring?"

"Just yourself, Melvin, that will be enough."

50

Decker and Lancaster were sitting in the detectives' room when the door opened. It was the ME. He had taken off his white lab coat and was now dressed in a suit. He held up some paperwork.

"Got some results for you," he said. He joined them at Lancaster's desk and thumbed through the pages. "First up, Meryl Hawkins had some painkillers in his system. Oxycodone."

"Would that have incapacitated him?" asked Decker. "Could he have been unconscious when he was shot?"

"He could very well have been," replied the ME. "And Susan Richards. She died of an overdose of fentanyl. Doesn't take much with that drug. Nasty, powerful stuff."

"Any sign during the post that she was a regular drug user?"

"No, nothing like that at all. She was in good shape, actually. Would have lived a lot longer."

"And time of death?" asked Decker.

"She'd been dead a while, Amos."

"I asked you this before. Could she have been dead from the moment she allegedly left her house that night?"

"Well, I can tell you that her probable time of death would coincide with your theory." He paused. "So you think she was murdered at her house?"

"Something like that."

The ME shook his head. "This case grows more complex by the minute. Glad it's not my job to figure it out."

After the ME left, Lancaster said, "Well, if you're right, then someone killed her and took her body out in that suitcase and then dumped it. That means the person that Agatha Bates saw leaving that night was not Susan Richards."

"Tall, lean, and blonde," said Decker.

"Mitzi Gardiner or Rachel Katz, like you said before. But I checked Mitzi's alibi for the time Richards was allegedly abducted. The restaurant verified that she was there all evening, long after Richards went missing."

"So Rachel Katz, then?"

"Speaking of, any word from your buddy on her?"

"He emailed. They finished lunch. Said Katz was acting weird. Wants to have dinner at her place tonight. He said he thinks she's going to open up to him. He also said he told her about Karl Stevens being killed, and though she tried to hide it, she got really freaked out." Decker added, "Duncan Marks was also at the restaurant. Melvin talked to him. And Katz said he was involved with some of her projects."

"I didn't know that. But you remember Marks, surely."

"I actually did some work for him when his daughter, Jenny, got involved with a con artist. Marks came into Burlington way back and started buying up stuff. Took a little hit with the recession, but then came roaring back, acquiring properties on the cheap. He's made a lot of money. Had the biggest home in the area when I lived here."

"Still does," said Lancaster. "On that hill outside of town. It's like the guy is looking down on the rest of us."

"Reminds me of another guy with a big house on the hill in Pennsylvania. But he was broke, and wasn't looking down on anyone, actually."

"Well, Marks isn't broke. He's got money coming out of every pore of his skin. I heard he actually made a lot of money before coming to Burlington. Investments or some such. IPOs and other crap I'll never understand and never make a dime off."

"Why'd he pick Burlington? I never knew."

"I heard that his father was from here. Worked in the old shoe factory before moving away, I believe. Marks bought that and turned it into luxury condos."

"That's also where Rachel Katz lives."

Lancaster snapped her fingers. "That's right."

"So according to Melvin, Katz was freaked out by the news of Stevens's murder. And now she might want to talk to him. And he's having dinner with her tonight."

"Hawkins wanted to talk to you too, and he's dead now. And who knows, maybe the same for Susan Richards."

They looked at each other.

"Maybe we need to keep an eye on your buddy tonight."

"That's exactly what I was thinking."

51

When Rachel Katz opened the door, Mars filled the doorway of her condo.

He was dressed in light gray slacks and an open-collared white shirt with a dark blue jacket over it. He had a bottle of red in one hand and a bouquet of flowers in the other.

Katz was dressed casually in jeans and a long-sleeved shirt, and she was barefoot.

"I feel overdressed," commented a smiling Mars as he walked in.

"You look great. I just felt like a jeans-and-no-shoes night."

She thanked him for the flowers and wine and gave him a kiss on the cheek. "You didn't have to do that," she said as she got out a vase and filled it with water, then set the flowers in it after snipping off the ends of the stalks.

"My mom taught me it was always polite and respectful to bring something."

"Well, your mother taught you right. Do you see her much?"

"No, she and my father both passed away."

"Oh, I'm sorry."

He shrugged. "It happens. You want me to get this wine going?"

"Yes, please. My Dewar's seems ages ago. The opener's in that drawer."

He poured out two glasses and handed one to her as he sniffed the air. "Something smells good. What's for dinner?"

"Caprese to start, chicken parm with my own secret sauce for the main, and cannoli to finish. Call it my Italian extravaganza."

"You did that after working all day?"

"I like to cook. But I admit the cannoli is store-bought."

"Still, damn impressive. You need any help?"

"You did your job by opening the wine and bringing the flowers."

"Guys always get cut slack."

"You are a wise man, Mr. Mars."

They ate about a half hour later. After they were finished, Mars insisted on clearing and cleaning. "You cooked and now it's my turn," he said firmly.

As she watched him collect the dishes, she stroked the stem of her wineglass and said, "I hope the woman you're seeing appreciates what she has."

"I think she does. But in a relationship, you gotta keep working it, from both sides."

"David used to say the same thing."

Mars rinsed the plates, glasses, and utensils and put them in the dishwasher. "Sounds like you two had a great relationship."

"We did. Only it was cut short."

Mars finished up and joined her in the living area, sitting next to her on the couch. She drew her legs up under her, holding out her glass as he refreshed her wine.

"Right. That was beyond tragic."

"But at least I thought it was over. And now Decker is back opening the whole thing up because he's convinced Meryl Hawkins didn't do it. But if he didn't, who did?"

"Did your husband have any enemies?"

"No, nothing like that. I told Decker the same thing."

"Maybe Don Richards had enemies. Or your husband was in the wrong place at the wrong time."

"That's what I *thought* had happened, but I also thought that Hawkins had committed the murders. And it *was* a robbery or a burglary. Things *were* taken."

"That could have just been a cover."

She nodded slowly but hardly seemed convinced of this.

Mars said, "When you invited me here tonight, it seemed that you had something on your mind. You said you wanted to talk."

Katz set her glass down and looked over at him. "I'm afraid."

"Of what?"

"Like you said at lunch, people are dying, Melvin. Hawkins. Susan Richards. That woman from the police department."

"I know, Rachel. It *is* scary."

"And someone murdered my husband. And ... everything from the past just seems to be coming back. It's like I'm being haunted by ghosts I thought were long buried." She put a hand to her face and wiped at her suddenly teary eyes.

He put an arm around her shoulders. "Let me tell you something. Not that long ago, I was in a world of trouble. I mean bad, bad stuff. Then Decker came along. And he got to the truth and the man changed my life. After twenty years of people believing that a lie was the truth. But not him. Not Decker. He just keeps digging. Dude never stops."

Katz shivered a bit. "He sounds like a man to be reckoned with."

"Oh, he is. And people have tried. And he just keeps rolling."

"Does ... does he understand that there can be different shades of truth?"

He drew a bit away from her, watching the woman closely. "Such as?"

"I mean, there are times when you can tell the truth, but people may not see it as the truth, not the same way that the person telling it does. And . . . and sometimes people feel they have to do things for, you know, reasons that might seem . . ."

"Seem what?"

"Wrong, I guess. But not to the person having to do the things. They might think it's the only thing they can do."

Mars looked confused by all this. "You've lost me."

"I . . . look, never mind. I know I'm not making much sense."

"Take your time. I've got nowhere to go."

She changed the subject. "So, Decker really believes that Hawkins was innocent?"

Mars looked at her for a long moment, clearly disappointed in the change in direction of the conversation. "Let's put it this way. Hawkins didn't try to kill Decker twice, because the man was already dead when those events occurred."

"You mean someone doesn't want the truth to come out? They're trying to stop Decker. And they silenced Hawkins because he might know something?"

"That's the way we see it, yeah." He paused. "So, do *you* know something that could help us?"

"If I did, I would've told you. I would've told people thirteen years ago."

"But there are shades of truth, that's what you just said."

She moved slightly away from him, as though symbolically distancing herself from this conversation. "It's amazing what a few drinks will do to loosen someone up," she said, tacking on a brief smile.

"I'm just trying to get to the truth, Rachel. That's all."

"But sometimes the truth doesn't set us free, does it? Sometimes it traps us."

"Is the truth trapping you?"

"No, of course not. I was just . . . speculating. Talking off the top of my head."

He took her hand. "I want to help you, Rachel."

"But you work with Decker."

"That shouldn't matter. I already told you I don't think you killed anybody."

"But . . ." she said quickly, and then stopped.

"But what?"

She abruptly rose. "I'm really tired all of a sudden. I think I'm going to call it a night."

Mars stared up at her, and then his expression changed. He leapt up and tackled her as one of the large glass windows shattered. They both fell heavily to the floor, as the shot fired through the window hit its intended target.

52

"Son of a bitch!" cried out Decker.

He and Lancaster leapt out of his car, which was parked down the street and across from Katz's building. They drew their guns and hunkered down next to the vehicle.

"There," said Lancaster, pointing to the opposite building. "The shot came from there. I saw the muzzle flash."

"Call in reinforcements," bellowed Decker as he punched in Mars's number.

It rang and rang, with no answer.

"Shit."

"Do you think the shooter's still there?" said Lancaster, putting away her phone after making the call. "If we go to check on Mars and Katz?"

"Right, he'll pick us off." He glanced at Lancaster. "It could be the same guy who killed Brimmer. You wait here for the cops to show. Keep trying to call Melvin." He texted the number to her phone.

"What are you going to do?"

"I'm going after the shooter."

"Amos—"

But he was already running down the street, keeping right next to the building where the shot came from, to make it difficult for whoever was in there to draw a bead on him.

He reached the front entrance of the building and looked it over. Plywood on the lower windows. The place looked abandoned. But it had a perfect sightline into Katz's apartment from the upper floors.

He raced up the steps to the front entrance and noted that the large double doors were chained shut. He heaved his bulk against them, but not even his size and strength could budge them.

He hustled on down the street, turned left at the next intersection, and raced down it. He was listening at the same time for a car starting up or footsteps running away. The night air was brisk and the sky clear for once.

He could hear nothing except his own breathing.

He reached the next corner and peered down it.

Nothing. No one and no car waiting to take the shooter away.

He forced himself not to think about Mars's fate. He had said a simple prayer that his friend was okay. And if he wasn't, Decker was going to risk his life to avenge him.

He raced over to the rear entrance, and that was where his luck turned. The door was open. And Decker well knew why.

The shooter had entered this way.

He eased the door open and stepped through. He knew he was a big target, and he squatted down to make himself less of one.

He took stock of the situation. The shooter might have already fled, out the door, and either driven off or used his own two feet to get away.

Only Decker had heard nothing that would indicate either had happened. And he doubted enough time had elapsed for the shooter to make his exit.

That would leave the person still inside an empty building, probably with a long-range, high-powered rifle, while Decker only had his new pistol, which he had never once fired, and would not be that accurate over any meaningful distance. The shooter could nail him from a lot farther away than Decker could the shooter.

He saw a bank of elevators but knew there probably was no power turned on in the building. That left the stairs. He used his Maglite to show the way and reached the door to the stairwell.

Like Lancaster, he'd seen the muzzle flash and downloaded the image in his head, counting up the floors.

Sixth.

He cautiously opened the door and made his way up, slowly. He might meet the shooter coming down. Or the person could be up there waiting for him.

He counted the floors until he reached number

six, understanding that the shooter could have gone to a lower floor, let him pass by, and then made his escape out the rear.

A moment later, he heard the sirens. Okay, the good guys were on their way. And an ambulance too, depending on what had happened in Katz's apartment.

He opened the door to the sixth floor and peered inside.

He hesitated to use his Maglite because it would just make him a target. There was enough light from the windows to allow his eyes to adjust rapidly. The floor plan was open, which was good and bad. It cut down on the places Decker would have to look, but it also allowed him no cover while he did so.

He closed the door quietly behind him and skittered over to behind an old metal desk.

Take your time, focus, and listen.

All he heard were the sirens coming closer.

That could be drowning out any sound of movement up here. He redoubled his efforts to hear any noise the gunman might be making.

His position had been chosen wisely. If the shooter wanted to escape, he would have to leave through the door Decker had come through.

He decided to try to move the needle.

"Police. You're surrounded. Put down your weapon and come out into the open where we can see you. Hands over your head, fingers interlocked. Do it now!"

He fell silent and waited.

The sirens outside had stopped. Any moment he expected to hear the front door being knocked open, followed by feet pounding into the building.

All he had to do was hold his position.

Come on, come on, show yourself.

If it was the same shooter, Decker didn't fancy getting into another hand-to-hand battle with the guy. If it was the same man, he probably outweighed him by well over a hundred pounds. Yet he had grave doubts that he would win such an encounter.

That's when he saw it.

The red dot swooping over the space, looking for him.

The guy had a laser scope.

That gave him the advantage over Decker, at least in some respects. But as Decker watched the dot flit around, the dust in the abandoned building was doing something quite remarkable. It was gathering around the light beam emanating from the scope, as though someone had clapped chalk erasers around it.

Decker quietly slid to his left, moving out into the open briefly before taking cover behind some crates. He peered over the top of the crates, but didn't see the red dot anywhere.

He ducked back down as the shot came his way,

smacking the wall behind him. The dot had apparently been on his head.

He kept moving, keeping behind the limited cover until he had worked his way to the far side of the room. He lay on his side and peered around the leg of a desk. He could see the red beam again.

This time he followed the thing to its source.

He lined up his shot. A large wooden box.

He fired five times, four through the wood, and when those shots flushed the guy, he unloaded his fifth shot at the exposed flesh.

He heard a grunt of pain.

Okay, he'd hit the guy. But it wasn't over yet.

He looked for more red dots, but saw none. He slid forward on his belly until he had halved the distance between them.

He heard footsteps coming up the stairs.

He was sure the other guy could too. That might draw him out, make him desperate.

It did, only not in the way Decker was expecting.

A blur came out of nowhere, leaping through the air and landing on top of him before he had a chance to fire.

The pair rolled around on the floor, struggling for the upper hand. Decker collapsed on top of the guy, trying to use his far heavier weight to crush him. He felt something on his face and realized it was the other man's blood.

Then a wedge of elbow slammed into the side of his face, stunning him.

He gripped the man's chin with his hand and forced it back, trying to take the neck to a place necks were not designed to go.

He had not accounted for the man's other hand, though. The fist hit him once and then twice, both pummeling shots. Decker's grip was broken and he was forced to roll off the guy.

He saw the flash of blade and put up an arm to protect himself.

Two shots rang out.

He saw the man above him flinch once, and then a second time.

He dropped the knife. And then he fell to the floor with a thud.

Decker sat up to see Lancaster slowly lower her gun.

53

It was morgue time again.

Decker still felt slightly queasy from his fight.

He stared over at the body on the gurney. *I'd be on this slab instead of him but for Mary.*

Decker had been tremendously relieved to learn that Mars was unharmed, though Rachel Katz had been shot and was still in surgery.

He lifted the sheet to stare down at the man. The tats on his arms *were* nearly identical to the ones Karl Stevens had. Decker had had the prison take pictures of Stevens's tats for comparison just to be sure.

He looked at them more closely and was once more struck by the unusual variety of images inked there. But they all had something in common: They were symbols of hate groups. He looked over them, starting with the right forearm and going over to the left arm. Decker knew many of these symbols from his work with the police and later with the FBI. The folks represented by these tats were not exactly law-abiding.

The number 88. That was the numerical equivalent

(the eighth letter of the alphabet being H) of "Heil Hitler."

Then the shamrock and the swastika, taken together, was often the mark of the Aryan Brotherhood.

The Blood Drop Cross, which was the primary insignia of the KKK and known by the acronym MIOAK, meaning "mystic insignia of a Klansman."

And the initials KI, which might refer to another hate group, though Decker didn't recognize them.

Still, there were some Decker had had to Google. The Aryan Terror Brigade symbol, and *Weiss Macht*, which was German for "white power." The sonnenrad, which was an ancient Indo-European sun-wheel and had been co-opted by the Nazis, who had placed the swastika dead center.

Then there were the SS bolts, another Nazi symbol, and the triangular Klan symbol, which looked like three triangles within a triangle, but upon closer inspection would show itself to be three letter k's in the triangle facing inward.

All in all, it was quite the smorgasbord of ink. Decker had no idea why the man had all this on him, but he had obviously been one seriously demented man.

The guy looked tough, even in death. A man with no scruples about ending someone else's life. As Decker's eyes traveled over the body, he saw scars and old wounds and other indicia of a violent life.

He thought about Mitzi Gardiner. She'd had a rough life growing up. And then she'd turned it around. She'd once more become her father's little star, of sorts. Like on the back of the photo he'd found in Hawkins's wallet. Her star had fallen. And then she had been reborn. Or had she?

Decker glanced over at the wall of slide-out cabinets where the corpses were kept. He strode over to the last one on the left. He opened the door and slid the rack out. He lifted the sheet and looked down at the body of Meryl Hawkins. He reached down and lifted up the man's arm.

The tattoo with the arrow piercing the star.

Symbolic of what? Then it clicked.

He phoned Lancaster. She was still at the office filling out forms.

"Hawkins told us the prison initiated his compassionate care release."

"I know he did," said Lancaster.

"I think he was lying."

"Why?"

"His daughter was his star. He drew stars on the back of his photo of her that he carried around. The latest tat he got was the arrow through the star. I think he ran into Karl Stevens and Stevens told him the reason why his daughter framed him. And then Hawkins applied for a compassionate care release, got his tat, and got out of prison to come back here."

"But he said the prison people came to him," countered Lancaster.

"I think when we check into that, we'll find out that's not how the system works. The inmate files for it, not the prison authorities."

"Okay, but you believed that he suspected that his daughter helped set him up from the get-go. And he did nothing back then."

"Only then he didn't know the real reason. The people behind it. Maybe he just thought she was stoned and had screwed up somehow. It could have been some of her drug addict friends looking to do a robbery and he didn't want to implicate her. Then he found out the truth."

"You mean you think he found that out from Stevens?"

Decker said, "That's right. And maybe Stevens knew somehow that Mitzi was now living high on the hog. At that point Hawkins didn't care about his daughter. She'd cashed in big-time by framing him. Before he died, he wanted his name cleared. He put an arrow through his little 'star,' got out of prison, and came to us."

"If his daughter knew that, she would be a prime suspect in killing him."

"She didn't have an alibi for his murder, so we're going to have to dig deeper on that." He paused. "Oh, and Mary?"

"Yeah."

"Thanks for saving my butt tonight."

After Decker clicked off, he looked back down at Hawkins's shriveled body. The man had gone to prison for a crime he hadn't committed. Then he'd found out that he had been set up and he wanted the truth to come out, as his last act before dying.

Well, Decker was going to carry the ball forward now.

"I'm sorry, Meryl. You deserved better. From me and everybody else."

He rolled Hawkins's remains back into the cabinet and closed the door.

It was too late to see Mitzi Gardiner now, but he had somewhere else he needed to go.

54

He drove over to the spot where he'd nearly lost his life tonight. But he didn't go back into the abandoned building. He ventured inside Rachel Katz's condo building and took the elevator up after flashing his creds at the officer guarding the crime scene's perimeter.

The forensic team was still processing the area. Decker nodded at Kelly Fairweather, who was doing a bloodstain pattern analysis by the couch. In another corner of the apartment, Natty was talking with a second tech. He saw Decker and quickly headed over.

"Boy, close call for you tonight," said Natty.

Decker nodded. "Mary really saved my butt."

"And she nailed the bastard who killed Sally," said Natty with a grim smile.

"Any word on Rachel Katz?"

"Still in surgery. Last I heard, she's going to make it. Close, though, bullet nearly hit an artery. Your friend saved her life."

"I know. Melvin's over at the hospital now with her, probably adding another layer of protection."

"Guy had a fancy sniper rifle with a sophisticated scope."

"That laser scope gave me a bit of an advantage."

"Yeah, well, the guy could have made that shot from triple the distance away and still nailed his target, easy. Or so my firearms guy tells me."

"Any luck on identifying him?"

"We're running his prints through the system."

"He had pretty much the same tats as Karl Stevens had."

"Yeah, Mary texted me and told me. You think there's a connection, obviously."

"We talk to Stevens and he's dead. The shooter kills Sally and then tries to kill Katz. Yeah, I think we can definitely say there's a connection. But the tats may help us narrow this down to a gang. They look to be some oddball collection of neo-Nazis and Klansmen."

"Great combo," said Natty sarcastically. "But the thing is, Decker, would that sort of gang have been operating here thirteen years ago? I mean, I don't remember anything like that going on in Burlington then."

"Neither do I. But keep in mind they could be muscle brought in now by the folks who *were* doing all this crap thirteen years ago."

"Right."

Decker eyed him. "How did your lunch go with your wife?"

At first, Natty looked like he might erupt in anger, but when he focused on Decker's sincere expression, he said, "It went okay."

"Did she know . . . anything?"

"No. I don't think so. She might have suspected. But look, Decker. Sally and me, we never, you know. We were just friends. Okay, maybe more than friends." He let out an exasperated breath. "It's this damn job. It gets to you. I'm not trying to make excuses."

Decker thought of Lancaster and her marriage. "The job gets to a lot of people, Natty."

"So, what are we supposed to do? How do we handle it?"

"If I knew the answer to that, I'd be a consultant to cops. A rich one. But spending time with your wife is a good first step. You mind if I look around?"

"Help yourself. Just don't keep your 'observations' to yourself."

Decker nodded and went exploring.

He entered the bedroom and gazed around the space. He wasn't exactly sure what he was looking for. He doubted Katz would have left a box with the word *Secret* engraved on it for him to find, revealing all.

But Katz was an accountant with a precise turn of mind. She was organized, paid attention to the details. You just had to look around her home to tell that. So there might be something she had that she felt she needed to keep. If only for protection from someone.

He went through all of her drawers and then did the same methodical examination of her closet. She had a lot of clothes and shoes, like Susan Richards, but even Decker could tell that the stuff Katz owned was far more expensive than the items in Richards's closet.

He dug back in the very rear of the closet and went through boxes and bags, but came away a half hour later with nothing to show for his efforts.

He went into the bathroom and searched. When he got to the medicine cabinet, he found that Rachel Katz was on prescription anti-anxiety medication. That was not unusual. Lots of people were on meds like these. But still. He wondered what exactly she was so anxious about.

Well, the fact that someone tried to kill her demonstrated that she was certainly right to be anxious.

He picked up her purse, which was on the nightstand. Inside were her wallet, a set of keys, and a building security access card. He pocketed those items and walked back into the main area to find that Natty had left to go back to the police station. The forensic team was finishing up and Kelly Fairweather was packing up her kit.

"Find anything of interest?" asked Decker.

"Just blood. And the bullet. It went into the

couch." She held up a small plastic container with a lid on top.

Decker took it and looked at the bullet, which was in pristine condition.

"Seven point six two," observed Decker of the round's caliber.

She nodded. "Right. It's called the NATO round. Lots of military forces use it, including ours. If that had hit her in the head instead of the shoulder, she'd be in the morgue, not the hospital."

Decker looked at her strangely.

"You okay?" she asked.

"I'll be okay once we solve this case."

He left and hit the street. He had another place left to check where Katz might have kept something of value. Her office. It was only a few blocks from her apartment, so Decker was just going to walk.

When he got there, he found the door to the building locked. He took out the key card, held it over the card reader pad, and the door clicked open. He checked the lobby marquee for Katz's office number and rode the elevator up. He strode quickly down the hall to her office door. All the other offices he'd passed had standard metal doors. Katz's office had a far more expensive solid wood door with matching trim. Knowing how she liked things just so, he wasn't surprised.

He tried several keys he had taken from her purse until one worked. He unlocked the door and went in. He decided to use his Maglite instead of turning on the office lights. There was a front reception desk, and a short hall off to the left. Two offices were off this hall and then a kitchen/workroom with a door that opened back into the reception area. The security pad was hung on the wall next to this door, its light glowing green.

He went back to the first office and opened the door. This was clearly Katz's office. It was larger than the other one and outfitted with custom shelves, a seating area with plush chairs, and a handsome partners desk. The shelves were lined with business memorabilia, photos of Katz with various city officials and others he assumed were her business partners. There were also photos of what looked to be her various properties and commercial projects. In each photo, Katz was smiling broadly, looking triumphant and happy.

And yet as Decker peered more closely, it appeared to him that the looks were hollow, that an underlying melancholy was present in each image. Maybe that was just him imposing what he knew now onto the woman's photos. Or maybe not.

Then he noticed the power cord lying on top of the desk. It was for a laptop, but there was no computer there. And there hadn't been one at Katz's home either. He opened some file drawers and his suspicions were heightened.

Someone had done a very good job of searching

the office without seeming to have done so. He closed the drawer and looked at the shelving system built into the wall. He recognized it, since Katz had an exact duplicate in her condo.

But not exactly exact.

He stepped closer and noted a panel set between two open shelves. This same type of panel had been in her condo as well. But there was a difference. The one in her condo had a knob on it. Decker had presumed that was because the panel was actually a door and there was storage behind it. He had found this actually to be the case because he had looked inside it.

Yet there was no knob on this panel. He stepped back and looked at the unit again. He took the template from his memory of the one in Katz's condo and laid it over what he was seeing now. The absence of the knob was the only difference.

He strode forward and felt around the perimeter of the panel, probing with his fingers. Then he pressed down on the lower left-hand side of the wood and the door popped open. Behind it was a space filled with documents and files.

He pulled them out and set them on the desk. He was about to go over them when he stopped, rose, left the office, and walked into the kitchen area. On the wall was the security pad.

Why had it been turned off?

Decker hadn't done it. He didn't have the code.

He had known of the possibility that Katz would have her own independent security system for her office. The exterior of the building had security. The front door to her office had been locked. But the security system had not been engaged.

An oversight, or . . . ?

The whooshing sound of something igniting and the resulting smell of smoke that reached him a few moments later definitively answered the question for Decker.

55

Okay, that's a problem.

The reception area was on fire, which meant the only way out was blocked.

Decker called 911 and reported the fire and calmly asked for the fire department to get there before he was burned to nothing.

He peered around the edge of the hall to see the reception area filling up with smoke. Next, he looked to the ceiling. There were sprinkler heads mounted there. So why the hell weren't they going off?

He coughed and fell back from the flames.

Well, this told him that he'd been right. There was something here that someone didn't want discovered. They had searched the place, but out of an abundance of caution, they'd decided to then burn it down and somehow had disengaged the sprinkler system.

He retreated to Katz's office and looked desperately around. He was on the fifth floor, so breaking the window and going out that way was not going to cut it.

He put all the items he'd found behind the panel

in a cardboard box, ran into the workroom with it, grabbed bubble wrap off the shelf, and taped it all around the box. He rushed back into Katz's office, ran to the window, and looked out, to make sure no one was walking down below on the sidewalk. He picked up her chair, carried it over to the window, and pounded it against the glass until the window shattered and fell away. He used the chair to scrape the rest of the glass away.

He looked down to make sure it was still clear and dropped the box. It fell to the sidewalk. He could hear the bubble wrap air pouches collectively pop when it hit the pavement. He hadn't been concerned about anything in the box shattering on impact. Paper didn't break. But it was very windy outside and if the box had burst open, he would have been running around the city trying to find the contents.

The problem was, his opening the window had let the wind and, with it, enormous amounts of oxygen into the space from the outside.

He turned and saw the flames right at the door of the office.

Okay, this was getting damn tight.

He heard sirens and the screech of brakes from below and saw two fire engines pull up. He leaned out of the window and cried out, "The fire's coming into this space. I need to get out. Now!"

The fireman signaled to him and four of them rushed to one of the trucks and pulled out an inflatable jump cushion, which they quickly pumped up and positioned under the window.

Decker looked down at it. From up here it seemed about the size of a twin bed.

Shit!

"Jump!" yelled one of the firemen.

"I'm a big guy. Will that hold me, or do you have a larger size?" Decker called back.

"This will hold you, don't worry," the fireman yelled back. "Just jump away from the building. Back to the ground. We'll reposition if need be."

Reposition if need be. Well that's comforting.

He wondered when these guys had done their last refresher course on catching huge guys falling from great heights. He hoped it was this morning.

Decker turned to look at the flames.

Do I take my chances there?

Suddenly an explosion racked the office space and a gust of hot air blew embers over him.

Here goes nothing.

He climbed up on the windowsill, looked down to make sure he was lined up as best he could be with the cushion, said a silent prayer, and jumped.

He was looking up at the sky, which was better than looking at where he was going. Were they repositioning right now? Or were they freaking out because they'd totally screwed up? Was he about to slam into the pavement?

Unsettling thoughts, but he needed something to

pass the time because it felt like he was falling for about five miles, instead of five floors.

When he hit the cushion instead of the pavement, all the air was still knocked out of him. Hands grabbed at him and hoisted him quickly to his feet.

"You okay?" asked one of the firemen.

"I am now."

"Anybody else in there?"

"Not in the office I was in now. I don't know about the rest of the building."

"Any idea how it started?"

"Yeah, which is why I'm calling in the arson squad." Decker showed the stunned firemen his creds. "Someone turned off the sprinkler system in the building," he said.

Another fireman came up with the box Decker had dropped. "We found this on the street."

Decker took the box from him. "Right where I dropped it. Thanks."

As the men were fighting the fire, Decker sat on the opposite curb and called up Burlington's arson squad and filled them in. Then he called Lancaster and did the same.

"You *jumped* out of a building?" she said.

"Well, not by choice. It was either that or be quick fried. I wouldn't recommend either, actually."

"What the hell is going on, Decker?" she said. "It feels like the whole town is under siege."

"That's because I think it is."

"I'm still filling out forms. I'm starting to regret shooting the guy."

"I'm heading back with a box of stuff I collected from Katz's office. I'll meet you at the station."

Decker hefted the box and looked at the ladders and hoses and men combatting the fire. He set off down the street, climbed into his car, and drove to the police station.

Decker met Lancaster inside. He followed her into the same small conference room, set the box on the table, cut away the bubble wrap, and opened it. He handed Lancaster a stack of stuff and put another stack in front of himself.

"Her laptop wasn't there. I think whoever searched her office took it. Or maybe she has it somewhere else. When she comes out of surgery and regains consciousness, we can ask her."

Lancaster looked at him doubtfully. "You think she's going to cooperate?"

"Considering somebody just tried to kill her, what choice does she have?"

"You might be surprised."

"Well, life is just full of surprises. That's why we play the game."

He turned his attention to the stack in front of him. Financial documents, construction plans, Excel spreadsheets.

"She had a lot of business going on," commented Lancaster as she started going over her set of files.

"Did you have any luck running down any of her backers?"

"Not really. But we did find out that they were shell companies for the most part with locations in countries where they believe transparency is a bad word."

"I wonder why that is."

"It would seem that her financial backers don't want to be publicly known. But they might still be legit."

"And I *might* be short and skinny," said Decker. "Is there any way we can find out who's behind those companies?"

"How about your people at the FBI?"

"I'm not sure they're *my* people anymore."

"Then you're stuck with the resources of a small-town police force."

"Great."

Lancaster glanced up. "I heard you shoot when I was coming up the stairs. How'd you get a sightline on the guy?"

"His laser worked against him in that environment. I followed it back to its source thanks to a bunch of dust in the air. Katz was lucky that Melvin knocked her down when he did. I saw the guy's scope. Sucker was super sophisticated. He could have made that shot from a mile away—"

Lancaster looked up from what she was doing. "What is it? You okay?"

"I'll be right back," said Decker, who was not even looking at her. He got up and hustled out of the room.

He hurried down the hall to the evidence room and checked in with the officer manning it. He told the man what he wanted and was let into the cage, where the officer took him over to a shelf against the wall. The officer held up the rifle with the scope still attached. It was in a large plastic evidence bag with the department tag.

Decker looked at the rifle and scope. Then he thought back to the moment it had been used.

He rushed back to the room where Lancaster was.

"What is going on with you?" said Lancaster.

"*I* wasn't the target, Mary, that night outside McArthur Park."

"What are you talking about?"

"Sally Brimmer was."

56

"Eric Tyson. Former military. Washed out of Ranger School and then out of the Army."

Lancaster looked up from her report the next morning. Decker sat across from her at her desk.

"We just got this back from the Army. We ran his prints through all the criminal databases and got a hit. Tyson was arrested on an assault charge about ten years ago, while he was in the military. It was off base against a civilian. That's why we were able to access his prints. We checked in with the Army, told them what had happened, and they sent us this file."

"Special skills?"

"Trained as a sniper. So you were right. The shot he took that killed Sally wasn't meant for you. He could have shot her from a mile away. Tyson was barely fifty yards from his target."

"How'd he wash out of the Army?" asked Decker.

"Got in with some bad company, apparently. Earned him a DD."

"So he leaves with a dishonorable discharge. What's he been doing since his military days?"

Lancaster shrugged. "Not sure. We're looking into it. Hope to have something soon. We can't find anything that shows he's been in prison."

"Well, considering all his tats, it was not anything good that he was up to, despite never having been in prison."

Lancaster sat back in her chair. "Okay, but why kill Sally Brimmer? You never said last night."

"I don't know. But I'm a huge target. He could hardly miss me. Sally was going to give me a hug when the shot came. But I'm nine inches taller than she was. And a lot wider. Doesn't matter how close she was to me, he couldn't have missed, if I'd been the target." He slapped the top of the desk with his palm. "I should have seen that a long time ago."

"Same goes for me. But that doesn't tell us why she was the target."

"She had gotten me the files I'd asked for, after you got knocked off the case."

"How'd you even connect with her?"

"She came by to see me when my butt was sitting in jail. I asked her to do that for me and she agreed. We met in the park. As we were leaving, that's when she got shot."

"If they knew she was passing you information, why not shoot the both of you and take that information?"

"I don't think that was the reason," said Decker.

"Why?"

"Because if they knew she was giving me information, they probably knew what it was: police files. Big deal. Why would that be a death warrant for her? I could have gotten those any number of ways. Killing her wasn't going to stop that."

"So you're saying she was, what, complicit in something?"

"Or she knew something that was dangerous to other people."

Lancaster glanced up at him. "What people?"

Decker looked around the confines of the empty room. "She worked here."

Lancaster's voice sank to a whisper. "Decker, do you know what you're saying?"

"There are bad people everywhere, Mary. Cops are not immune, you know that."

She shook her head. "Granted, but none of this makes sense."

"It *does* make sense. We just haven't figured out how yet. Any word yet on the fire at Rachel Katz's office?"

"We got a prelim from the arson squad. They found an incendiary device attached to a timer. They must have placed it there after they searched her office. You just picked the wrong time to make your visit."

He rose.

"Where are you going?"

"To the hospital to check on Katz and Melvin."

"Is that all?"

"Then I'm going to see Mitzi Gardiner."

"You want me to tag along?"

"Aren't you deskbound after the shooting?"

"Well . . ."

"I'll talk to you when I get back."

"They think she's going to be okay," said Mars.

He and Decker were sitting in the visitors' room outside the critical care unit at the hospital.

"They *think?*"

"Well, she's stable, *critically* stable, but at least she's stable."

"Okay."

Mars rubbed his eyes.

"You look beat, Melvin. Why don't you go get some rest?"

"No, I'm good. I napped on the couch." He stretched his long arms. "They got cops outside her room."

"Yeah, I know."

Mars shook his head. "Why do I feel like it's my fault she's lying in that hospital bed?"

"Your fault? How do you figure?"

Mars said, "The people who shot her? They knew she was talking to me. They were afraid she might open up. So they decided to kill her. I don't push it, she's okay."

"That's pretty convoluted, Melvin. And wrong. You saved her life. She'd be on a slab but for you."

"I saw this red dot hovering over her face. Man, it scared the crap out of me. Then I just grabbed her and down we went right as I heard the glass break. I thought she was okay. You know? Then . . . then I had her blood all over me."

"What did she tell you, before she was shot?" asked Decker.

"She was really nervous. Afraid for her life."

"Well, she turned out to be right about that. What else?"

"I think she wanted to talk. But couldn't bring herself to do it. She said something about there being 'shades of truth.'"

"Shades of truth? What does that mean?"

"I don't know."

"Maybe a guilty conscience?"

Mars looked pained by this possibility. "Maybe. And she said that sometimes people have to do things that might look wrong to other people, but just seem like the only way to go for the person. And also that the truth could trap you."

Decker took all this in and said, "You know she might have been the one to impersonate Susan Richards. Mitzi Gardiner was the other possibility, but she has an alibi."

"If she did, then Rachel knew about her murder. That would qualify as a guilty conscience."

"Yes, it would. We'll need to talk to her when she's able."

"Now maybe she'll tell us the truth."

"Well, almost getting killed should be a great motivator," replied Decker. "And they burned her office down after searching it. So, they mean business."

Mars stared goggle-eyed at him. "Burned her office down?"

"While I happened to be in it. I had to jump out the window."

Mars gaped. "You jumped out a window?"

"From five flights up. Point is, I don't think Katz has an option now."

"And if she is guilty of something?"

"We'll work a deal. She who talks first gets the best one."

Decker stood to leave. "You need anything?"

"A little less excitement in my life would be nice."

"Then you're going to have to stay away from me, apparently."

57

When Decker pulled up to the Gardiners' home, the gate was open, so he pulled through. This time a man answered the door. He was in his forties, tall, broad-shouldered, and good-looking, and dressed in a suit that might have cost more than Decker's entire wardrobe. No, there was no *might* about it.

"Yes?" said the man.

"I'm here to speak to Mitzi Gardiner."

"What about?" the man asked suspiciously. "This is a no-solicitation area," he added warningly. "How did you even get inside the gate?"

"It was open." Decker took out his creds. "But I'm not selling anything. She'll know about this. I've been by before."

The man looked puzzled. "Here? You've been here?"

"Yes. Are you her husband?"

"I'm Brad Gardiner."

"Is she in?"

"She's not up yet. In fact, she's not feeling well."

"I can wait."

"No, that doesn't work. She . . . she's ill."

"Mr. Gardiner, I can understand that, but the fact is, this is a murder investigation. So time is of the essence."

"Murder! What the hell are you talking about?"

"It's okay, Brad."

Decker looked past Gardiner to see his wife standing there in a bathrobe and slippers. She scowled at Decker. "I can handle this. Why don't you get to work? You have that meeting."

"But, Mitzi."

She kissed him on the cheek. "It's okay, sweetie, I've got this. Trust me."

"If you're sure."

"I am very sure."

After her husband left, Gardiner looked at Decker. "You just won't leave it alone, will you?"

"I'm just trying to do my job."

"Isn't that what all cops say?"

"I don't know. I'm just one cop."

She led him back to the conservatory, where they sat down across from each other.

"What?" she said expectantly.

"Some recent developments I thought you might want to be made aware of."

"Such as?"

"Someone tried to kill Rachel Katz. Took a shot at her through her condo window."

To her credit, Gardiner didn't visibly react to this. "Is she all right?"

"She was shot with a sniper round. She's out of surgery and is critically stable. Another inch to the right and they'd be making funeral arrangements."

"Well, I'm glad they're not."

"The man who tried to kill her was then killed by police."

"Do they know who he is?"

"Yes." But Decker would go no further.

"What does any of that have to do with me?"

"You have the picture I left you?"

She appeared startled by this and sat up. "Um, no, I think I threw it away. Why?"

"Good thing I took a picture of it." Decker took out his phone and held it up.

She looked at the screen. "But that's the wrong side. That's the *back* of the picture."

"Well, for my purposes, *this* is the relevant side." He pointed at the writing. "Daddy's little star. He was a very proud papa."

Gardiner looked up at him from under hooded eyes. "That was a long time ago."

"Yes, it was. Things change. People change. I have another picture to show you." He flipped through the screens. "This is a picture of your father's forearm taken during the autopsy."

"Oh, please, God, I am not looking at that," she said in disgust.

"There's nothing gruesome about it, Ms. Gardiner. I just want you to look at the tattoos on the forearm."

"My father did not have tattoos."

"He got these after he went to prison."

She became subdued. "After?"

"Yeah. Here's the first one. A spiderweb." He explained the symbolism.

"I'm sure lots of prisoners get that one because even though they're guilty they can't accept what they did," she said defiantly.

"Here's the second one." He showed her the teardrop and looked at her expectantly.

"What does that one mean?" she asked dully.

"Travis Correctional is an all-male facility. And some of the men there get . . . lonely. And they take out that loneliness on other men, like your father."

She blinked rapidly as she processed this. "You . . . you mean?"

"Yes. I do. Now, here's the third one. And this is the one I really want you to focus on." He brought up the screen with the arrow through the star. "I've seen a lot of prison tats. I've never seen that one before." He looked at her for a reaction.

For a moment it looked like the woman had stopped breathing. Then she licked her lips, dabbed at her eyes, and looked away.

"Any idea what that might mean?" he asked.

"I know what you're getting at."

"What's that?"

"The photo! The writing on the back." She waved her shaky hand at the photo of the tattoo on his phone screen. "And . . . that."

He sat back and studied her.

She dabbed at her eyes again with her sleeve. Finally, she looked up at him. "What exactly do you want from me?"

"The truth would be fine."

"I've told you everything."

"No you haven't."

"This happened a long time ago. What the hell does it matter? Everyone has moved on with their lives. I know I have."

"Tell that to Susan Richards and Rachel Katz . . . And your father."

She shook her head and looked down.

"I'm not here to send you on a guilt trip, Ms. Gardiner."

She barked, "Oh, just call me Mitzi. That's all I'll ever be. Ditzy Mitzi. An addict who was always a disappointment to her father." She looked up at him and said coldly, "You put lipstick on a pig, it's still a fucking pig."

"Turning your life around could not have been easy."

She waved this off. "Doesn't matter now."

"I'm also here to make something as clear as possible."

"What?"

"People connected to this case are dying or in the hospital fighting for their life. By my count, you're the only one left."

"I told you before I could take care of myself."

"I'm sure the others thought the same. But the guy who shot Katz was a real pro. Ex-Army turned bad guy white supremacist type. Trained sniper. Hired to do the hit. He's dead, but who's to say another one won't replace him? And maybe you go out armed, but a pistol isn't going to save you from a long-range rifle shot you won't ever hear or see coming before it kills you."

"You're just trying to scare me," she said offhandedly, though her voice shook.

"I *am* trying to scare you. For your own good."

"I don't see how I can possibly help you."

"Can't or won't?"

"As far as I know, my father killed those people."

"How did your father feel about your drug use?"

"He hated it. Why?"

"I understand he was trying to get you into rehab."

"He'd done it before, but I could never make it stick. He kept trying."

"So he never did drugs himself?"

"Are you crazy? He was as straight as they came on that. He attacked a guy who came to our house trying to sell me some stupid weed."

"Okay. Your dad was picked up in a bad area of town. At his trial the defense laid out the possibility that he was there trying to get drugs for your mother's pain."

"We've already been over this. He might have. I mean, I told you before that he did his best to take care of her." She unexpectedly smiled. "He could build anything, really. Make anything work. He built a little scooter for me when I was ten, for my birthday. I mean, he made it out of scrap parts. It had a little battery and a motor. He made those too. Only went about five miles an hour but I rode it everywhere." Her smile faded. "But he couldn't build anything to help Mom. That was beyond him."

"How did he know to go to that area to get drugs?" asked Decker.

He saw Gardiner flinch slightly.

"What?"

"You just told me that your father didn't do drugs. Hated them. So how'd he know where to go? Or who to talk to, to buy the stuff? And where did he get the five hundred bucks he had in his pocket when the police picked him up?"

"I . . . I don't know where he got the money. And it was pretty easy to tell back then where the bad areas were if you wanted to score drugs. I already told you that. And you know that too from being a cop here back then."

"Well, Mitzi, the thing is, he didn't want just *any*

drugs for your mother. He wanted something like pure morphine. Stuff that had been stolen from a hospital or pharmacy, not off-the-street crap. And having worked the narcotics detail as a cop here, I know that there were very few people in that particular market. And you really had to know your shit to get to them."

Mitzi looked extremely apprehensive in the face of all this. "I . . . I don't know what to tell you."

"And on top of that, your old man was still walking around quite a few hours after allegedly killing four people. You'd think the guy would have been running for the hills."

She licked her lips nervously. "Maybe . . . maybe he was confused or shocked at what he'd done. Or he was just trying to lie low. And hope that the police would conclude what you just did."

"But if he *had* committed the murders, he would know his DNA was likely to be under a dead girl's fingernails. It was just a matter of time before we came knocking on his door."

She let out a quick breath. "I can't explain it. It's just what happened."

Decker rose. "I'm sorry."

She glanced up at him, trepidation on her features. "Sorry about what?"

"Your life must have truly been in the gutter for you to have done this to your father."

"I don't know what—"

He put up his hand. “Don’t bother. I don’t have the patience or time for more bullshit from you.” He lowered his hand. “I think you gave him the five hundred bucks after someone gave it to you. Then you managed to scratch the shit out of him at some point and passed his DNA off to whoever paid you. Maybe your father just chalked it up to you being in a drug-induced fit. He’d probably seen that many times before. And then you told your old man where to go to get the stolen hospital drugs. Only the person wasn’t there because there was no person. You probably told him to keep trying, to go to lots of different places, where there was nobody either. But it was for his wife, after all. And so he did. That way he’d have no alibi for the murders, and we’d end up finding him in a bad part of town with a chunk of money in his pocket. And when we showed up that night, you pretended to be whacked out. You’d probably already been given the gun and stashed it behind the closet wall.”

The whole time Decker was talking Gardiner’s eyes kept widening and her jaw kept falling.

Decker continued, “I can only imagine the look on your old man’s face in prison when he ran into that scumbag Karl Stevens. And Stevens tells him what his ‘little star’ did to her own father.” He took a moment to gaze around at the beautiful room.

“I hope it was worth it, Mitzi. But I can’t possibly see how it could be.”

58

The house.

The rain.

Decker sat in his car and watched his old home from across the street.

The gloom of the night was actually brighter than what he was feeling.

He had told himself that he could live in either the past or the present, but he couldn't do both.

Which do I choose? It should be an easy decision. So why isn't it?

His case was at a dead end, in more than one way. Gardiner was the key and it didn't look as though she was going to cooperate. Unless Rachel Katz regained consciousness with a willingness to help them, Decker wasn't sure they would ever get to the truth.

So he had come here. Back to where many things had begun for him.

He saw the lights on in the front room. Someone would pass back and forth every so often. The little girl he'd seen. Then her parents.

The Henderson family. Really just starting out in

life, like Decker and his family had once done. Building dreams and burnishing memories that would last a lifetime for all of them.

His last Christmas with his family had been a memorable one. Decker had gotten a couple days off, and thankfully no one had decided to murder someone else that close to the holiday.

They had gone to see Molly perform in her school play. It had been a Christmas version of *Peter Pan*. Molly had played Wendy. She had worked on her lines for two weeks, reciting them to whichever parent was around to listen to her, barging in on Decker when he'd been shaving, or even dressing.

She had carried it off without a hitch, helping others to perform their roles too because she'd apparently memorized everyone else's lines as well.

Great memory.

She didn't get that from her dad. Before his injury Decker had been pretty normal with his recall. And he couldn't imagine he could pass on the elements of a traumatic brain injury to his kid.

He sat next to Cassie in the audience that night watching their little girl act her heart out, surprising him with little things, tiny nuances that she seemed to instinctively add to her performance. She might have grown up to be a great actress.

Now no one would ever know.

Yes, it had been a great Christmas. They'd gone out

to dinner after the play and celebrated Molly's performance. They'd toasted her with vanilla sundaes.

Decker had relished every moment but had of course believed there would be many, many more just like them. Enough to fill a lifetime of memories, even for someone like him. She would grow up, marry, have kids, and he would become the doting grandfather, or as close to that as someone like him could be.

He glanced over at the window again as he saw the little girl sit on the sofa next to her mom. A book was opened. A story was commenced.

Decker started up the car and drove off.

He could barely see the road for the tears.

He should never have come back here. It was literally tearing him apart, when he could least afford it.

It's always about the next case, though, right? Even when Cassie and Molly were alive. He had never dwelled much on all the time he had missed with them because there was always some bad person he had to track down. All the nights getting home long after they both had gone to bed. And then getting up and leaving before they awoke.

I just thought I'd have more time. Just . . . more time.

But then again, another sunrise was guaranteed to no one. Certainly not to his family.

And by association, not to him.

Thankfully, the farther away he drove, the faster these thoughts left him. For now.

He drove downtown and stopped in front of the building where he'd almost died. Across the street was where Rachel Katz had nearly perished, lending a macabre symmetry.

He checked in with the officer guarding her apartment and started to look around. He glanced across at the broken window, the blood on the couch and carpet. That told a story he already knew.

Katz had mysterious backers, offshore shell companies funneling the money for her myriad projects in little old Burlington, Ohio. What was the attraction?

It did make one wonder.

And then there was the American Grill. There were thousands of places just like it all over the country. Thick piled-high burgers, mammoth mounds of fries, chicken wings, pitchers of beer, large-screen TVs for sports. There would always be a clientele for that, but no one was getting rich off it, like Katz had told Mars.

He had done another search of her apartment and came away not knowing any more than he had on entering the place.

They would just have to wait until she woke up.

This was a frustrating case because he could not seem to make traction on any lead. He could not make Mitzi Gardiner talk. And he had nothing to charge her with. There was absolutely not enough evidence. He knew that she had worked to frame her father, but he couldn't prove it. She had been amply rewarded, with a new life. And yet as he'd left her home, he'd also left behind a woman who was clearly racked by guilt.

But that meant nothing in building a case. He would have to find a road to the legal truth somewhere else. It would not apparently go through Mitzi Gardiner.

He sat down on a chair in the kitchen and studied his possibilities. There weren't many, so they didn't take him long. He quickly settled on one.

Sally Brimmer.

She'd been killed for a reason. He had to find out what that reason was.

And he could start in one of two places.

He picked one, called Lancaster to meet him there, and set off.

59

Lancaster met Decker outside of Sally Brimmer's apartment building on the west side of town. It was a nondescript six-story structure wrapped in dull brick.

"How's Katz?" Lancaster asked as she walked up to him.

"Still not conscious, but apparently out of danger."

"Well, that's good."

"Yeah, and it'll turn into *great* if she wakes up and tells us everything."

They walked into the building and rode the elevator up to the fourth floor. Lancaster had a key to Brimmer's apartment.

"It's already been gone over, and nothing was found. But I'm not sure how thoroughly it was done. After all, we thought *you* were the target."

"I did too until I stopped thinking I was."

They entered the apartment and looked around. Brimmer's job had not paid all that much, they both knew, but her apartment was well laid out and nicely furnished, with pillows and curtains and sturdy furniture and lovely oriental rugs over the hardwood floors.

Decker looked at Lancaster. She said, "Her parents have money. I was over here once for a holiday party and met them. Very nice people. They helped her out financially, I came to understand."

"Okay."

"They were devastated, obviously. They came to get her remains. The family's from the East Coast."

"How'd Brimmer end up here?"

"She went to college up the road from Burlington. Had a couple of PR jobs out of school. Her brother's a cop in Boston. I guess she got interested in that field from him. The department had an opening. She moved here and was doing some really good work. I doubt she would have stayed here long-term, though. She had a lot of potential. And she was still so young."

"We all have a lot of potential, until we don't," noted Decker grimly.

"So what are we looking for?"

"Anything that seems to be relevant."

"Great, thanks for the hint."

They went methodically from room to room, ending up in Brimmer's bedroom. Decker checked the attached bathroom while Lancaster went into the closet.

After a few minutes, Lancaster called out, "Hey, Decker?"

He walked into the large closet to see Lancaster holding something up.

"What?" he asked.

She held the item up higher. It was a short-haired wig.

Blonde.

Decker lifted his gaze to Lancaster's. "You think *Sally* impersonated Susan Richards?" he said.

"I think she might have. It wasn't Gardiner. And if it wasn't Katz, who else fits the description?"

"Sally was the right height and build," conceded Decker.

Lancaster fingered the wig. "And this is nearly the cut and style of Susan Richards's hairdo. And from a distance, with her back turned and an old woman looking out into the darkness? She could have been fooled."

Decker took the wig in his hand and looked it over. The memory came back to him effortlessly. Sally at the park. She had on a trench coat, gloves, and a hat. Exactly what the person leaving Richards's house was seen wearing.

"So if she participated in that, did she know Richards might be in that suitcase, either already dead or drugged?" he said.

"I can't believe she didn't know," replied Lancaster. "But then the question becomes why would she do it?"

"She was acting funny," said Decker. "When she

interacted with me. Before and after Richards went missing."

"Funny how?"

"Guilty, maybe. But then I just associated that with her having a fling with Natty."

"Guilt, then, but of a different nature." Lancaster shook her head. "Brimmer was such a straight arrow in my book. Why in the hell would she have become involved in something like this?"

"Well, we don't know for sure that she was. We found a wig that looks like Richards's hair, but that could be a coincidence. Women do have wigs in their closets."

"That's true. And even if we find evidence of Sally's hair inside this wig, it'll prove nothing. If she's not involved, she presumably bought the wig to wear it."

"We have to find other proof. If she was paid off, we might be able to find a record of that in her financial accounts."

"And if she wasn't paid off?"

"Then someone might have coerced her into doing this."

"How?"

"Maybe someone who knew about her relationship with Natty?"

"Well, that could be. They kept it pretty secret. Hell, I didn't know."

Lancaster took back the wig and placed it into an

evidence bag she drew from her coat pocket. "And you still think the motivation to kill Richards was to place blame for Hawkins's murder on her?"

"They had to cut that investigation off, Mary. The police start looking into Hawkins's claims, things could get dicey for whoever's behind all this. Her seeming to commit suicide was a good way to do that."

"Only it didn't work."

"They couldn't know that. They had to try. And Richards was their best bet for that."

"Why not Rachel Katz? She had a motive to kill Hawkins too."

"That's right, she did. But I don't think they could afford to kill Katz."

"Why not? Someone ended up trying to kill her."

"That was later."

"So how'd they choose between the two women?"

"Look at it this way: Katz has prospered since the death of her husband. Richards hasn't."

"So you think Katz was involved with the murders thirteen years ago?"

"I'm not going to go that far, Mary. But I think Katz ended up being useful. Richards didn't. So she was dispensable."

"What in the world is going on here, Decker?"

"Well, whatever it is, it's been going on for at least thirteen years."

"Dating back to the murders?"

"Actually sometime before them, probably."

Lancaster looked at the bagged evidence. "I'm going to have to tell Natty about this. He's in charge of the investigation now."

"I don't think he's going to take us suspecting Sally of being an accomplice in Richards's murder very well."

"That's an understatement. Unless he's involved as well," she added with a sudden thought. "Do you think he might be?"

"I think everybody's a suspect until they're not."

60

"How's it going down there?" Alex Jamison asked.

It was the next evening and Decker was in his room at the Residence Inn, on his phone.

"It's going. How about you?"

"Long road ahead, I'm afraid. Not making much headway. Bogart is missing your horsepower."

"Did he say that?"

"I can tell."

"He laid down the law to me when we last spoke. I'm not sure I'll have a place on the task force when I'm done here." He said this in part to get it off his chest, but also to get Jamison's reaction.

"I'm not sure about that either, Decker."

His spirits plunged. It had occurred to him that he did want to go back to the FBI after this was over. Now that might not be possible.

"I guess I can see that," he said.

"Look, if it were up to Bogart, I think you'd be okay. But he's got bosses too. And they know you're still in Burlington despite orders to the contrary. And they're not happy about it. Bogart went out on a limb for you, Decker, on a number of occasions. He shielded you from heat from the higher-ups. Now, we all know what you've done for the Bureau, and the number of lives you've saved in the past. But that will not always save you, I guess is what I'm saying."

"Thanks for your candor, Alex. I appreciate it."

"I'd expect the same from you if our positions were reversed."

"Not to change the subject, but if I send you a list of companies, could you find time to check them out?"

"Decker! Are you kidding me?"

"I know, Alex. I know. But it's really important."

"And what I'm currently doing isn't?"

"No, I didn't mean it that way. Only we don't have the resources that the FBI does."

There was such a pregnant pause that he thought she might have hung up on him. Then, finally, "Email them to me and I'll see what I can do."

"Thanks, Alex, I appreciate it."

He sent her the names of the companies and then lay down on his bed. The wind was picking up outside, which probably meant another storm was coming. Since it was getting colder, they might get some sleet or a dusting of snow with it.

Decker wrapped himself more tightly in his coat because the Residence Inn didn't have the best heating system in the world. It was like it only had the capacity to push heat a certain distance into the hotel before giving up and letting the majority of the unfortunate guests fend for themselves.

He didn't miss the Ohio winters. The East Coast had its share of cold weather, for sure. But there was nothing to stop the wind here; it beat relentlessly across the land.

But still, this was his hometown, his home state. He had played for the mighty Buckeyes and then, albeit briefly, the Cleveland Browns. He was a product of the Midwest. He never got too high and never got too low. He looked at the world realistically. He was a jeans and beer kind of guy. He could never fit inside a Ferrari, not that he would ever want to. He always tried to do the right thing. He helped others when they needed it.

And he tracked down killers nonstop.

And that was pretty much the sum total of Amos Decker.

He lifted his hands from his pockets and rubbed his temples. He scrunched his eyes closed. Something was funny up there. He felt a pang of anxiety start up from deep within him. He lurched up and went into the bathroom and drank handfuls of water in an effort to calm himself down.

He tried to push back visions of volcanic masses of memory loops cascading down on him, but he was powerless to stop his own mind from tormenting him.

He lay back on the bed, shuddered once as though

he might be sick, and then drew a long, deep breath. With that one physical machination, the anxiety left him.

Maybe I should take up yoga. A downward dog every morning might do the trick.

He glanced out the window and decided that he was hungry. And he only had one place in mind to go.

He drove to the American Grill.

He had never answered the question of why Rachel Katz still owned it. And he didn't believe it was because it was her husband's first business venture.

He walked in, got a table, and sat and perused the menu. The place was about three-quarters full at seven o'clock. Most of the clientele seemed to be blue collar, some with spouses, some with kids. There were a few teens wolfing down burgers and wings. On the big-screen TV was an ESPN show where the panel was talking about the upcoming Sunday of football.

Decker looked out the window at the building across the street. It was a bank. The one where Don Richards had worked. On the other side of the Grill was an apartment building. Decker knew this because he had briefly lived there when he returned to Burlington after his football career ended.

He eyed the interior of the Grill. Large model prop planes and ships and cars suspended from the ceiling. Pictures of old movie stars framed on the walls. Humorous signs dotted in between them. Dusty fake plants standing in corners. A buffet bar set up in the middle of the place. The wait staff wore white shirts and black pants.

The kitchen was through a set of double swing doors. Restrooms on the right for men and the left for women. Greeter station right at the front door. Computer stands at the back where the wait staff logged in their orders. Full bar at the very back of the restaurant where multiple TV screens were bolted to the wall. The carpet underneath was a dull green, designed not to show dirt or stains. The tables were a heavy wood. There were four-topper tables set up along the perimeter. He could smell an alchemy of fried foods, cheap beer, and sweet desserts.

It was Americana at its monotone finest.

It wasn't all that profitable. And yet it was still in business when Katz had far more glamorous projects on which to spend her time.

Decker ordered his food, a Reuben and fries, and a Michelob to top it off. He once more almost looked around guiltily for Jamison to suddenly pop up and reprimand him.

The sandwich was good, juicy enough without being all over the place. The fries were warm and crisp. The beer tasted fine going down.

He eyed the table where he'd seen Earl Lancaster with his "friend." He hadn't expected his talk with

Mary at the football field to have carried the day, but he was happy that they were giving it another shot.

This happy thought receded when he dwelled for a few moments on what the next few years of his former partner's life might be like.

The brain was the most unique organ humans possessed. Decker knew that better than most. When it failed you, it was unlike any other breakdown in your body. If your heart went, so did you, six feet under. Gone but remembered, hopefully fondly, for who you had been.

But if your brain went, you were also gone, though your body lingered and became dependent on someone else to take care of it. And that would be your loved ones' last impression of you, even though it wasn't really you, at least not anymore.

Decker came out of these musings in time to glance up. Through the window of the door going into the kitchen, he caught a man watching him. It was just a quick look, and then the man was gone. The only thing Decker could really observe was dark hair and a pair of penetrating eyes.

Decker, the cop, was instantly intrigued. He had spent almost his entire adult life as a policeman. Reading people's faces, separating the bad from the good, the scared from those trying to hide something. It was not a skill he could teach someone else. It really had become almost instinctual over time. It was a million little things processed together to spit out something close to a useful deduction.

And his antennae were quivering.

He slowly eased his phone out of his pocket, turned the flash off, and, while ostensibly checking his phone screen, snapped a series of pictures of the wait staff flitting around the restaurant. He recognized the waitress from the last time he was here. And trailing behind her was the young man named Daniel, who was learning the craft of being a waiter.

When he put the phone away, he glanced over at the kitchen double doors and thought he had seen someone at the window there.

Had it been the same guy watching him?

Decker motioned to the young woman who had been serving him. Daniel had gone into the kitchen.

She came over. "You want anything else?"

"No, the food was great."

"I'll get your bill."

"Looks like you're hustling tonight."

"Yeah, it gets a little crazy sometimes."

"Been working here long?"

"About a year."

"Last time I was in, you had a trainee following you around."

"Oh, right, yeah, well, that's how we learn the job."

"So, you did that too?"

"No, I already had several years of waitressing

experience. Only reason I got the job. But it's kind of silly, if you ask me."

"What is?"

"Training all these people. They never stay. Two or three months on the job and then they're gone. I guess some people don't respect hard work or the time and money it takes to train somebody."

"Yeah, you're right. That doesn't make much sense."

"I won't be working here much longer, so it doesn't matter to me. I got another job offer and I'm taking it. Better pay, and benefits."

"Great."

"My mother used to work here, oh, about ten years ago. She was the one who told me to apply. Pay's not great, not that any wait job's is, but the tips aren't bad, especially on the weekends when the guys get drunk and open their wallets. Makes up a little for all the stupid stuff they say, but if they get handsy, and a lot of them do, I bring the hammer down."

"Good for you. Did your mother work here long?"

"No. I mean, she wanted to. But after about a year they let her go."

"Why's that?"

"They never told her. Then later, a friend of hers was hired to be a waitress here. About a year after that, they let her go too. No reason."

"That is really odd."

"Well, it's not my problem. I'll be out of here. Come to think of it, I've been here about a year. I guess if I wasn't leaving, they might fire me too."

"Maybe the management has changed since your mom's time."

"No, it hasn't."

"Come again."

"Bill Peyton is the manager now. And he was the manager when my mom was here. She didn't like him. He was always watching everything so closely."

"I guess that's what managers get paid to do."

"I guess. And the kitchen staff, they haven't changed either all that time."

"How do you know that?"

"Because they're the same people when my mom was here. I told her some of their names when I first started working, and she recognized them all. They were here from when the place opened, for all I know."

"You mean the cooks and busboys and all that?"

"Right."

"What are they like?"

"What do you mean?"

"Old, young, men, women, Ohio farm stock?"

"All guys. And, no, I don't think any of them are from Ohio. To tell the truth, I'm not sure where they're from. They don't interact with us much. Age-wise, they're probably in their fifties."

"Long time to be a short order cook or a busboy."

"I guess they're content with what they have. You get in a rut, you know? That's why I'm getting out. And I'm taking coding classes too. I don't want to be a waitress my whole life."

"Hey, well, good luck with your new gig."

"Thanks. I'll bring your check."

He gave her a nice tip and left.

On the way out, he looked at the plaque next to the door. It read: *Manager: Bill Peyton.*

He looked back into the restaurant.

He had never been a regular here. But he'd been here a few times before his life had fallen apart. He had never considered it anything special until now.

And now something that he had found at Katz's office took on a heightened importance.

61

"What are you doing, Decker?"

It wasn't Lancaster asking him this question as he looked up from the document he was studying in the small conference room at the police station.

It was Blake Natty, looking disheveled and exhausted.

"Just the nuts and bolts of detective work. Nothing personal, Natty, but you look like shit."

Natty wiped his stubbly chin, ran a hand through his unkempt hair, and attempted to tighten the knot on his tie before giving up. He sat down across from Decker and clasped his hands in front of him.

"Fran threw me out."

Decker sat back and slowly took this in. "What happened?"

"She found out."

"About you and Brimmer?"

Natty nodded.

"How?"

"Some bastard emailed her pictures of us together in my car."

"You could have just been driving somewhere."

"We weren't . . . driving."

"Right. But she has to know what happened to Sally."

"She does. But I don't think it mattered. You see . . ." He stopped, looking nervous.

"Was Sally not the first time?" asked Decker.

"No. I screwed up . . . before. Fran took me back. But I don't think she's going to do it this time."

"I heard Sally's family came to take her remains."

Natty nodded. "I wanted to go to her funeral. But I didn't think it would be appropriate."

"You're probably right about that." Decker shifted in his seat. "I'm sorry about all this, Natty."

Natty said nothing. He just stared down at the table.

"Look, had Sally been acting, I don't know, weird lately?"

Natty glanced up. "Weird? What do you mean by weird?"

"Like she had something on her mind?"

"We were having a fling, Decker. She probably had *that* on her mind."

"I don't mean just that. The thing is, when she agreed to help me, I could tell there was something on her mind. And it wasn't her relationship with you. I already knew about that."

"What else could it be?"

"I just thought she might have mentioned something to you."

Decker would have much preferred to come straight out and ask the guy, but he couldn't. Right now, he didn't know who was involved in what, and he didn't want to give any of his suspicions away unnecessarily.

Natty rubbed the back of his neck and seemed to mull over the question. "She seemed a little jumpy lately. I just thought it was because you saw us together that day."

"Well, you made it pretty easy for me. You just drove up and started yelling at me while she was in the car."

At first Decker thought Natty might snap back at this comment, but he didn't. Maybe Brimmer's death and his wife's kicking him out had changed the man.

"I was the big dog here, Decker, before you came along. I made detective grade before you, and great things were expected of me."

"You did your job, Natty. You worked your cases, caught bad guys. Just like I did."

"Come on. There was no comparison. You were born for this."

"I'm not sure I was born for it, but right now it's the only thing I have in my life."

Natty looked pained by this simple, straightforward admission. "When your family got killed, I couldn't believe it. I really couldn't. Nothing like that had ever happened here. And then, and I'm ashamed to admit it, I relished watching you hit rock bottom. Every day you went lower and lower. And more to the point, you were no longer competition for me in the department."

Decker said nothing to this. *He* could have erupted over this baldly cynical statement, but he chose not to.

"And then a funny thing happened. We weren't closing nearly the number of cases we used to. And then the shooting at the high school happened. And we couldn't make a dent in finding out who did it. And then you came and solved the whole thing."

"I didn't have much choice, Natty. Seeing as how I was directly connected to the 'whole thing.'"

"But then you got the gig with the FBI and you were gone again. I did some cases with Mary and things were going okay. Maybe I'd get promoted up the ladder." He paused and chewed on his tongue for a moment. "And then this thing with Sally started. It was stupid. We both knew it was, but we couldn't stop." He glanced up at Decker. "We only had sex a couple of times. I wanted to do it more. But Sally, well, she was funny about that."

"You don't owe me an explanation on any of this, Natty."

"And then you came back to town and this whole shit with Hawkins started up again. When I saw you back, I just freaked. To be honest, I thought I was rid of you forever. And then there you were."

"I came back to visit my family's graves. I didn't ask for Hawkins to walk up to me and say he was innocent. But for that, I'd be long gone from here, for at least another year."

Natty cleared his throat and sat back. "I've been a cop longer than I haven't been a cop. It's become my whole life. I'm good at it, I think. But I'm not you."

"No one ever said you were," replied Decker. "And you wouldn't want to be me."

"Well, now Sally's dead and my wife is gone. Luckily, the kids are pretty much grown. So, all I got is . . . this," he added, looking around the room.

"When this case is done, Natty, I'll be gone. You can have it all to yourself."

Natty grunted and gave a hollow chuckle. "I'm finding out that my problems run a lot deeper than my jealousy of you, Decker."

"Then face them and try to work through them. You've seen a lot of shit in your life. So have I. Life is never perfect. You make the most of what you have. You can sink into self-pity or you can rise above it. Why don't you choose to rise above it, starting right now? And really think about my question about Sally. Was anything bothering her?"

Natty looked at him suspiciously. "Why do you keep asking that? Did you find something that . . . ?"

"Sally had reddish hair."

"I know that," said Natty, looking confused.

"She ever wear a wig?"

"A wig? What, are you being funny?"

"No. A blonde wig, cut short."

"No, why? Why would she wear a wig? Do women even wear wigs anymore?"

"I don't know. Maybe some do."

"Well, not Sally. At least not that I ever saw. She had really nice hair. Why are you asking me that? Did you find a wig?"

"In her closet."

"What were you doing in her closet?"

"Lancaster actually found it. We were searching her place looking for a motive for murder."

"But you were the target, not her!"

Decker shook his head. "The guy who shot Katz was the same guy who shot Brimmer. We recently found out he was a trained sniper. He had a laser scope that could have nailed me from a thousand yards away. No way the guy misses a shot from a twentieth that distance. Look at me, Natty. I'm the size of a barn. *You* could've made that shot with your damn pistol."

Natty slumped back in his chair. "But why in the hell would anyone want to kill Sally? She was . . . she was a good person. She had no enemies."

"That you know of."

Natty glanced sharply up at him. "And what does the wig have to do with this?"

"The wig pretty much exactly matches Susan Richards's hairdo."

It took a few moments for this to connect with Natty. "Wait a minute. Are you saying that—"

"That Brimmer put on a wig to impersonate Richards? Yeah, I am. I think Richards's body was in that suitcase. It was all a show for Richards's neighbor. To make us think she'd done a runner. And then committed suicide."

"You're saying that Sally killed Richards? No fucking way. I've run into a lot of murderers, Decker. So have you. Sally couldn't have hurt a fly."

"I don't think she killed Richards. She might not have even known what was in the suitcase. It might have been locked. But I think she was forced to impersonate Richards and leave in her car with the suitcase. At some point others took the suitcase and then left the body where we found it."

"Why would Sally be part of something like that?"

"Maybe somebody was blackmailing her."

"About what?"

"One guess, Natty."

Realization spread over his features. "Our … fling?"

"Someone tells her they'll spill the truth to your wife unless Sally puts on the wig. Otherwise, she'd be ruined professionally. They didn't have to tell her that Richards was dead, or in the suitcase. She just had to drive it away in the car." Decker paused. "So, that's why I want to know if Brimmer was acting funny."

"But Sally was killed *before* they found Richards."

"But Sally could have already known she was dead."

Natty took a few moments to process all this. Then the detective in him seemed to win out and he sat forward.

"I thought it was just her being nervous about our relationship. But we were having a drink at her place one night, this was shortly after Richards disappeared."

Decker sat forward. "And?"

"And she wanted to know what I thought about Richards's disappearance. I told her maybe she'd killed Hawkins and had gone on the run."

"What was her reaction to that?"

"She didn't seem to buy it, if you want the truth. I actually picked up on that and asked her if she had any theories."

"Did she?"

"She . . . she said that sometimes people looked at things from the wrong way round. Almost like looking in a mirror. She even gave an example. In a mirror you lift up your right hand, but in the reflection, your mind tricks you into thinking—"

"That it's your left," finished Decker.

Natty nodded. "What do you think she meant by that?"

Decker didn't answer.

Though he had an idea of exactly what the dead woman might have meant.

62

On his bed at the Residence Inn, Decker laid out all the construction plans for the American Grill that David Katz had built about fifteen years ago. The plans seemed pretty normal for such a restaurant buildout, but he didn't recognize the name of the architect set forth on the plans. In fact, the address of the business showed that it was from out of state.

He called Lancaster. She was at home. He asked her to put Earl on.

"What's up, Amos?" said the man when he got on the phone.

"Got some construction-related questions for you."

Earl seemed relieved that the questions were not of a more personal nature. "Okay, shoot."

"You remember the American Grill project?"

"The Katzes' restaurant?"

"Right."

"Yeah. I mean, I didn't work on it, but I remember it going up."

"Did you try to work on it?"

"I didn't have my GC license back then, but I had my finish carpentry business. I put in a bid to do some of the interior work. Didn't get it."

"Do you know who the GC was?"

"Funny thing you mention that. I didn't know the GC. Nobody did, because Katz used a company from out of town. Hell, out of state, I think."

"What, you mean the workers too?"

"Yeah. Nobody local that I know worked on that project."

"Why would he have done it that way? Wouldn't it have been more costly?"

"Well, you'd think so. Bringing guys in like that, they have to live and eat somewhere. Guys who live here, we just go home at night. So, yeah, you'd have to pay more."

"Was there no capacity back then? Did he *have* to go out of state?"

"Hell no. That was one of the slackest periods I can remember. Everyone was looking for work. When they rejected my proposal, I even went around to Katz's office to see if there was anything else I could do. Mary and I hadn't been married all that long and we wanted to have a family. I was trying to build up my business. And Katz had blown into town with a lot of money and ambition and I was anxious to get on that train."

"And what happened when you met with him?"

"I didn't actually meet with him. I met with one

of his people. Forget the name. He told me in not such polite terms that Mr. Katz had his own crew. Well, that pissed me off a little bit. I mean, why ask for proposals from local people if you're going to use your own crew?"

"What did that guy say?"

"I gotta tell you, Decker, I'm no wallflower. I'm a big, strong guy, but this guy scared the bejesus out of me just the way he was looking at me."

"Can you describe him? I know it's been a long time."

"No, I can. That's the sort of impression he made on me. He was about my height and weight. Dark hair, dark eyes, and, I don't mean this to sound un-PC or anything, but, well, he just didn't seem to be American. At least not in my mind."

"Did he have an accent?"

"Not that I could tell, but I'm not real good about picking up on things like that."

"So you left it there?"

"What else could I do? I couldn't force the guy to use me."

"So all the work was done with nonlocal people?"

"Far as I know. Well, I take that back. The excavation work was done by Fred Palmer, he's local."

"Excavation?"

"Yeah, for the foundation and everything. That can involve some heavy equipment. Katz may not have wanted to truck that in."

"Palmer still around?"

"Oh yeah, I got his number. I use him on projects. He's a good guy. Does first-rate work." Earl gave him the contact info.

"Thanks. Do you remember the construction work going on for the Grill?"

"Yeah, I'd drive by it every once in a while."

"Anything strike you as unusual about it?"

"Well, they had a high fence and security around the place."

"That's not unusual at a construction site, is it? I mean it's to keep people out and stop theft of equipment and materials."

"Yeah, but they had it there from day one. Before they had any materials on site. And you can't really steal a ten-ton piece of equipment and drive it off down the street." He paused. "And they tarped everything."

"What do you mean?"

"They covered everything up."

"You mean so no one could see in?"

"Right. I thought that was strange."

At that moment, apparently Mary Lancaster snatched the phone from her husband. "Why all this interest in the American Grill?"

"Just a theory."

"What's your theory?"

"I'm still forming it. But I think we made a mistake."

"What mistake?"

"By commencing our investigation at the point of the murders."

"Where else should we have started it?"

"Why did David Katz choose to come to Burlington, Ohio? Or did someone else make that decision for him?"

63

Fred Palmer was in his seventies, overweight and bald, with a cheerful face and ruddy complexion. His office had one window, one desk with a chair, and two chairs fronting the desk. There were no pictures on the wall. No carpet underfoot.

He was leisurely turning the pages of a file on his desk while Decker and Lancaster sat impatiently across from him.

"Been in business nearly forty-five years," he said.

"Right, you told us that. Have you found what you're looking for?" asked Lancaster.

"Okay, here it is. Thought so. The American Grill. Don't eat there myself. I've got acid reflux. Everything they serve gives me reflux."

"And the construction? My husband said you worked on it."

"Earl, now there's a nice guy. Nice guy. You're lucky, ma'am, to have him."

"Yes, very. The file? You said you had it?"

Palmer planted a thick thumb down in the middle of the page. "Heavy equipment rental."

"*Rental*?" said Decker. "Did you not do the work?"

"No, that's what *rental* means." Palmer laughed and gave Lancaster a funny look. "Can tell he doesn't know shit about construction."

"What sort of equipment?" asked Decker.

"Excavator, dump truck, front loader, bulldozer. It's all there." He tapped the file.

"How long did they rent it?"

Palmer looked over the page. "Says here two weeks."

"Did you normally rent out equipment like that, or did you also typically do the work?"

Palmer sat back and closed the file. "We like to do the work, of course. But that was an odd project."

"Why do you say that?" asked Decker.

"This Katz guy. Darren?"

"David," corrected Decker.

"Right, David Katz. He later got murdered, you know."

"Do tell," said Lancaster, nearly rolling her eyes.

"Oh, yeah. Killed. Him and some others. Anyways, he came into town and got this loan and wanted to build this restaurant. Okay, fine. Lots of people here could have done that for him."

"But he got a company from outside the area to do it," said Decker. "We know that."

"And he tarped things off and had really tight security around the construction area," added Lancaster.

"That *was* odd. I tried to get the work, but we got

turned down. We were the biggest outfit back then. Still one of the biggest today. Surprised me, but it was his money."

"Was that the only thing odd about it that you found?" asked Lancaster.

"Well, no." He tapped the file. "That was."

Lancaster looked confused. "You've lost me."

"What I mean is, what do you need all that heavy equipment for, if you're just digging a foundation for a restaurant? I mean, how much excavation is there to do? Most projects like that, there's none. You just grade the property, lay your foundation, and build up from there. Hell, what they rented from me, they could've dug down to China, nearly." He laughed. "China, get it?"

"And did you ever ask them why they'd rented so much equipment like that?" asked Decker.

Palmer gaped at him. "What, are you serious? 'Course not. It was more money to me. None of my business what he does, so long as he pays. And he did. I will tell you that the construction took longer than it should have. And they had to pay some additional fees to me because of it. I remember driving by some days and wondering when the hell they were going to finish up."

"Why do you think it took extra time?" asked Lancaster.

"Not sure. But it did, that's all I know." He laughed. "I do remember one thing."

"What?"

"When we got the equipment back, they'd washed it all. Clean as a whistle. Now, I can never remember that happening before. Most times it comes back all crapped up and we have to clean it up. But not that time. I could've eaten my lunch off the stuff." He laughed heartily. "Eaten my lunch. Get it?"

"Yeah," said Decker. "I get it."

After leaving Palmer's office Lancaster looked up at Decker. "So what did we just learn?"

"That David Katz undertook, apparently, the strangest construction project in the history of Burlington."

"And what does that tell us?"

"That it's time for us to find out who the hell David Katz really was."

They were walking down the street when a car drove past and then stopped. The window came down.

"Amos Decker?"

Decker glanced over at the expensive car. Duncan Marks was sitting in the driver's seat.

"Mr. Marks, how are you?"

"Well, I'm fine, but you look great. Lot different from the last time I saw you."

"Yeah, things have looked up for me."

"Heard you were back in town."

"Yeah, for a bit."

"Never forgot what you did for my daughter."

"Hope she's doing okay."

"She is, actually. I think Jenny finally figured it out."

"Good to know."

"God, I heard what happened to Rachel Katz. That was awful. Is she going to be okay?"

"We hope so," said Lancaster.

"We've done some projects together. She's quite a businessperson. Very smart."

Decker slowly nodded. "Would it be okay if we asked you a few questions about Katz? We're trying to dig into who attempted to murder her, and you might be helpful."

"Sure. Absolutely. Hey, come to dinner tonight at my house." He looked at Lancaster. "Bring your friend here too."

"You don't have to do that," said Decker.

"No, I insist. Least I could do after your help with Jenny. Say around seven?"

Decker nodded, and Marks drove off.

Lancaster looked over at him. "Might be an interesting dinner."

"Let's hope it's something more than interesting."

64

Decker and Mars looked down at the woman. She was so covered in tubes and monitoring lines that it was almost difficult to discern the living person under this medical canopy.

But it was Rachel Katz. Still alive. And still critically stable.

"What do the doctors say?" asked Decker.

"That she'll wake up at some point. They just don't know when."

"You've been in here most of the time. Has she come to at all? Made any sounds? Talked in her sleep?"

"No, nothing like that."

"You need to take a break from here, Melvin. She's got great care. And she's well protected."

"I don't know, Decker," he said doubtfully.

"I *do* know. And I've got some place I want you to go with me tonight."

"Where?"

"Duncan Marks's house. He invited me and Lancaster to dinner. I don't think he'll mind you tagging along. He was asking about Rachel today."

"Okay, but why are you having dinner with the guy?"

"Because he did some business with her. And I need to know more about the history there."

"Okay, if you think it will help."

"At this point, Melvin, anything will help."

They drove in Decker's car up the long, winding road to Marks's home, or, more aptly, his estate. They pulled in front of the mansion and parked in a stone-paved motor court.

Decker looked in the direction of Burlington and saw the lights of the town winking down below. Marks certainly had a fine view from up here.

When they got out, Lancaster tugged self-consciously at her dress and then prodded a few stray hairs back into place. "I didn't really have anything in my closet for something like this," she said, staring up at the enormous stone and stucco house, which looked like it belonged in the French or Italian countryside. "And I had no time to get my hair done."

Decker said, "You look fine."

"It's different for guys, Decker," she said in an annoyed tone.

"Just so long as you have your gun," he said.

"I hope you're joking," she said, grinning.

He didn't smile back.

Decker wore a corduroy jacket that looked like it had been new about thirty years ago, and khaki pants. And the cleanest shirt he had left.

Mars looked resplendent in a tailored wool jacket, white button-down shirt, slacks, and a pocket square.

"You, on the other hand, look like you could be in *GQ*," Lancaster said to Mars.

"Thanks. For twenty years I wore the same clothes, white prison jumpsuit, so this is a nice change."

They walked up to the massive double front doors and Decker rang the bell. A few moments later it was opened by a man in butler's livery, who escorted them through to the library, where he said Marks and the rest of his party had gathered for cocktails before dinner.

It was a long wood-paneled room with few books but a roaring fire in the fireplace and clusters of seating areas full of plush furniture that looked custom made and probably was.

Marks was standing near the fire with a drink in hand, with two other men and three women clustered around him. Decker recognized his daughter, Jenny. She was in her twenties, tall and blonde and vapid, at least in his estimation. She'd already done more falling in love than most people did in a lifetime. Her only problem had been that all these men had loved her father's money far more than they'd loved her.

She looked at Decker with unfriendly eyes, he

thought. She was probably pissed that he knew more about her and her failed relationships than she wanted him to. Jenny was the product of Duncan Marks's second marriage to a younger woman who had called it quits and left after Jenny was only three years old. To his credit, Marks had raised her. But he'd given her more than he should have, was Decker's opinion. And with that, he had taken away any ambition she might have had.

"Decker," called out Marks, waving them over.

"This is my friend, Melvin Mars," said Decker. "I think you've met. I didn't think you'd mind if he came too."

"Right, right. You were with Rachel." Marks shook his head sadly. "That was so tragic. I hope she's going to be okay."

"She's hanging tough," replied Mars. "I've been with her at the hospital and things are looking up."

"Good, good." He waved to the others in his group. "Decker, I think you know Jenny, my daughter."

Jenny Marks gave Decker a small nod.

"And these are some of my business associates."

Decker ran his eye over the small group of men and women. They all looked intense, well-heeled, and unimpressed by him and his appearance. The women were elegantly slender and dressed expensively with earring-draped ears and necklace-draped necks, and they looked condescendingly at the plain

Lancaster. One of them leaned into her friend and said something to make the other woman smile.

Decker saw Lancaster clutch her jacket more closely around her.

They were served drinks and gathered closer by the fire. They could hear the wind whistling down the chimney.

"God, Ohio winters, here we go again." Marks laughed. "Gets right into my bones."

"Dad, you spend winters either in Palm Beach or Palm Springs," his daughter pointed out.

"Well, I spent enough of them *here* in the past," he retorted with a smile. "You ever been to Palm Beach, Decker?" he asked.

"No, I never have."

"It's beautiful there."

"If you have a lot of money," said Jenny.

Her father said, "No, it's beautiful even without money. The scenery and weather are free. But the money makes it a lot more fun, I'll grant you that." Marks turned back to Decker. "Now, do you have any leads on what happened to Rachel? I mean, what sick bastard would have done something like this?"

"We *have* the sick bastard who did it." Decker pointed to Lancaster. "Thanks to my partner here, who shot him dead before he could kill me, at great personal risk to herself."

Now the other women looked at Lancaster quite differently. The one who had made the joke, probably at Lancaster's expense, paled and took a step back, staring at the detective with far more respect.

"Now *that's* impressive," said Marks. "The only *killing* I've ever made is in the real estate business," he added, without a trace of humor. He raised his glass to her. "Thank you for your bravery, Detective Lancaster."

The others followed suit. She smiled, blushed, and took a quick sip of her gin and tonic.

Decker continued, "We believe it was a murder for hire."

Marks snapped, "A murder for hire! Who in the hell would want Rachel dead?"

"I don't know." He looked around at the group. "You did business with her. Did she have any enemies?" He looked at each of them as they slowly shook their heads.

"I'm really the one who had the business relationship with her, Decker," said Marks. "Although we don't do much together anymore. She has her financial backers and really doesn't need someone like me. I can't say that I knew everything about the woman. But it never occurred to me that she had enemies. I mean, I know what happened to her husband, but that was a long time ago. And he was just in the wrong place at the wrong time, if I remember correctly."

The butler came in and announced dinner.

Marks grinned at Decker as they filed into the

dining room. "I know, it's quite British, the butler thing, I guess. And silly. But what the hell. I like it."

In the long dining room, Marks placed Decker next to him, while he put Mars in between the other two women and Lancaster between the other two men. Jenny Marks sat across from Decker, while her father took his place at the head of the table.

As they were eating, Decker asked, "So what did you know about David Katz?"

"David?" Marks rubbed his mouth with his napkin. "Well, he came to town years ago, young and smart and ambitious as hell."

"I understand he had already made money doing something."

"That's right. I heard that too."

Marks chewed on a bit of steak.

"Do you know exactly what he made his money in?" asked Decker.

"Not really. I thought it was the stock market, or the bond market, but I can't tell you definitively."

Meanwhile, the women next to Mars were asking him about himself.

"You look like an athlete," said the brunette on his left. "Were you in the pros?"

"Played some college ball. Wanted to play in the NFL, but never made it."

"You look like you could still play right now."

"Don't know about that. Those boys are a lot bigger and faster than when I played."

The woman on his right, indicating Decker, said, “How do you know that guy?”

“Dude saved my life once.”

“Isn’t he a detective or something?” said the woman.

“One of the best.”

“He doesn’t look like a detective.”

“What are they supposed to look like?”

“I don’t know. Like on TV, I guess.”

“I’d take Decker over all those guys.”

The man on Lancaster’s left nibbled at his bread while watching her out of the corner of his eye. She sensed this and turned to him. “You been working with Mr. Marks for a long time?”

“Does it matter?” asked the man. He changed expressions when the guy on the other side of Lancaster made a face. “I mean, yeah, about fifteen years now. He’s a good boss.”

“What do you do for him?”

“Basically, whatever he wants me to do for him.” The man gave what he probably thought was a disarming smile.

Lancaster didn’t return it. She focused on her meal and asked the attendant for a top-off on her wine.

“Why all the interest in David Katz?” Marks asked Decker.

“You ever been to the American Grill?”

Marks laughed. “Not my sort of place. I can’t eat

burgers and fries anymore. And I'm more into wine than beer."

Jenny was sitting across from Decker. "You said you think someone hired a person to kill Rachel?"

Decker nodded and focused on her, as her father sat up straighter in his chair. "That's right."

"But why would anyone do that? Rachel has never hurt anyone."

"You know her well?"

"I would consider us friends. She's actually taught me a lot about handling myself. I've started to work with Dad, and she's been in the business world for a long time. I consider her a mentor."

"And you've been doing a good job too," said Marks proudly.

Decker's surprise must have shown on his face, because Jenny smiled sardonically and said, "I've grown a little since you last knew me, Detective Decker. Even earned my MBA."

"Glad to hear it, Ms. Marks."

"Oh, just make it Jenny. You saved me from that low-life jerk over two years ago. You deserve a first-name relationship."

"Okay, Jenny. When was the last time you talked to Katz?"

"Oh, probably about a week or so ago. We had lunch, just a catch-up sort of thing."

"She seem okay?"

"Yes, nothing out of the ordinary."

Marks said, "What do you think is going on, Decker?"

"I'm not sure. Someone wanted her dead. And her husband was murdered too."

"But that was a long time ago. And they caught the guy who did it."

"No, we didn't. A man was convicted, but he didn't kill David Katz and the others. He ended up coming back to town and being murdered too."

Marks said, "Wait a minute, that's right. I remember hearing about that. What was his name again?"

"Meryl Hawkins."

"That's right. It was all over the news. Those murders all those years ago cast a long shadow on this town, I can tell you that. And now you say he's innocent?"

Decker noticed that Jenny Marks had flinched at her father's remark. "What is it?" he asked her.

"Just something that Rachel said."

"When?"

"The last time I talked to her. We were discussing business and that's when she said it."

"What?"

"It was really weird." She paused to recall it. "Something about sins and *long shadows*."

"*Old* sins cast long shadows?" said Lancaster, who had been raptly listening to this exchange.

Jenny pointed at her. "Yes, exactly. Old sins cast long shadows."

Lancaster said, "Sounds like something out of a British detective novel."

Decker caught Mars's eye. He said, "Shades of truth."

"What?" asked Marks.

"Just something else that Rachel told someone. Do you know anything else about David Katz's background?"

"Well, I had him checked out when we were talking about doing some deals together. They never came to fruition because he was killed. Everything seemed to check out okay."

"How far back did your check go?"

"Um, I'm not sure. George?" He looked at the man on the right of Lancaster. He was small and slightly built, with thinning dark hair and a bony face.

George said, "We usually do a financial dig on the person. Go back about five years. I didn't do the one on this Mr. Katz, but that's generally the drill."

"Five years," said Decker, really to himself.

"Do you think that's far enough?" asked Marks.

"Apparently not," replied Decker.

65

It was seven a.m. and Decker sat on his bed at the Residence Inn, once more going over the construction plans for the American Grill. He had sent off texts to Jamison asking her for help on a variety of questions. He hadn't gotten responses yet on those, or the research he had asked her to do about the shell companies backing Rachel Katz's projects. He didn't know if he ever would.

He was slowly turning the pages of the construction drawings when he stopped and peered more closely at a particular page. Then he flipped back a few pages and studied the information there. Next, he grabbed another handful of documents and went down the list of line items. Finally, he picked up his phone and made a call.

Lancaster answered. "I'm just about to step into the shower, Decker, can I call you back? And I had too much to drink last night. My head is splitting."

"It's actually Earl I want to talk to."

"Hang on."

A few moments later Earl's voice came on the line. "What's up, Amos?"

"Got another construction question for you."

"Okay. Shoot."

"I'm looking at the construction plans for the American Grill and invoices for construction materials."

"All right."

"You know the size of the place, right?"

"Generally. It's a typical footprint for a retail restaurant operation."

"Talk some more about that."

"Well, I mean a four-exterior-wall, one-story basic rectangle. Cinderblock construction with brick veneer and a flat tarred and pebble-topped roof where the outside HVAC units are housed."

"What sort of square footage are we talking?"

"For a sit-down restaurant as opposed to a fast-food place, about sixty percent of the space goes to the dining and bar area and forty percent to the kitchen, prep areas, and storage. The Grill, I would estimate, is about five thousand square feet, so about three thousand of that would be the dining and bar and the rest for kitchen, prep, and storage. Then you have your enclosed Dumpster area out back. The interior layout allows about fifteen square feet of space per patron seat. That's the general rule of thumb in the industry. That way, the Grill could comfortably accommodate a couple hundred diners at a time.

Which I think is around its fire code limit of customers at any one time."

"Okay, how much concrete are we talking about for a place that size?"

"You'd pour your footers. That's not all that much. Then you'd lay your block walls." He gave Decker an estimate of the concrete, and the blocks required.

Decker looked at the line item on the page he was looking at. "The cinderblock count is pretty much spot on. But what if I told you the concrete outlay was way over quadruple what you just said?"

"That's impossible."

"Tell me a way that it wouldn't be impossible."

Earl was silent for a few moments. "Well, the only way to justify that much concrete is if they built a full basement, so their pour obviously would be a lot more. But why would a restaurant want a full basement instead of just footers and foundation you build on? You couldn't possibly need that much storage."

"Good question," said Decker. "Hope I find the answer."

He thanked Earl, told him to have his wife call back when she was done, clicked off, and looked down at the plans.

The American Grill was turning out to be far more special than he had previously thought.

A full basement for what?

And maybe whatever *that* was would explain why

David Katz had built it, and why Rachel Katz had kept it all these years.

He went on his laptop and loaded in the name William Peyton and added the qualifier "the American Grill." Nothing remotely relevant came up in connection with the longtime manager of the restaurant.

He took out his phone and pulled up the photos he'd taken of the trainees including the one named Daniel. The trainees who never stayed very long. Then his memories shifted to the guy who'd been staring at him from the kitchen. There clearly had been suspicion in that look.

He glanced back at the construction plans and then focused on Earl Lancaster's words:

The only way to justify that much concrete is if they built a full basement.

But as he'd also pointed out, why would David Katz have gone to the additional time, trouble, and expense for more storage area than he could possibly ever need? And if there was an underground room, it would have to be accessible somehow. There would have to be a door down there. And steps. And what would be down there?

Mary Lancaster called him back twenty minutes later.

"Long shower," he grumbled.

"I had to dress and dry my hair too, and do it all with a friggin' hangover," she snapped. "Earl told me about your questions. Where are you headed with this?"

"I think there's another room under the American Grill."

"Why would that be?"

"I have no idea. But Earl couldn't think of another reason why so much concrete would have been used. And maybe that's why Rachel Katz hid the documents I found. That's where the additional concrete was listed."

"Meaning she knew about a possible underground room?"

"Katz told me that she and her husband met on a blind date. And six months later they were married. This was *after* the American Grill opened."

"So maybe she didn't know about the underground room, then?"

"At least not at that point. And that might explain why they used tarps over the construction site and used outside contractors and rented equipment. They didn't want anyone to know what they were doing."

"And Fred Palmer told us that the equipment they rented was a lot more horsepower than was needed. But they might need all of that if they were going to remove enough dirt to make way for a full basement."

"Right. Although I guess somewhere in the permitting process, they'd have to tell the folks in government about their plans and get approvals. Code compliance and inspections and all that. But I guess there's also no law against having a basement underneath your restaurant."

"But you would have to have a way to access it," said Lancaster.

"A waitress at the restaurant told me some interesting things." He quickly told her about the trainees and wait staff, the longtime manager, and the seemingly one-year turnover for all except the kitchen staff.

"Okay, this is just getting weirder and weirder," noted Lancaster. "What is going on in this alleged room underneath the restaurant? Do you think it might be a drug operation?"

"If so, it's certainly an odd one."

"And that would mean that instead of an innocent citizen who was murdered for being in the wrong place at the wrong time, Katz was dirty. Maybe that's what led to his getting killed."

"That could certainly be the case if somebody wanted him out of the way."

"But why kill the Richards family too?"

"Don Richards gave him the loan for the Grill. Maybe that ties in somehow." He paused. "I wonder about something."

"What?"

"I'm wondering if the loan was ever paid off," said Decker.

66

"Okay, I've got bad news and bad news, which do you want first?"

Decker was talking to Alex Jamison on his cell phone.

"Well, I guess it doesn't matter, does it?" he said.

"Okay, we struck out on the shell companies you gave us. We can't penetrate them."

"Okay."

"And the tattoos on the two dead guys? I ran them through the relevant databases and came up with zip. I mean, most of the tats taken separately are well known. But the Bureau has never seen them all strung together like that before. It's quite a mix of hate groups. Nazi, Aryan, Klansmen."

"Well, thanks for checking."

"No, you don't understand, Decker. I've got people freaking out here. When the FBI can't find out something, that's news. And they're also afraid that maybe these different hate groups are starting to come together, sharing resources, coordinating terrorist actions, accomplishing more terrible things together than they can separately."

"You mean the shell companies are unusually hardened, and the tats may reflect some new sort of terrorist threat?"

"Bingo. When I told Bogart, he was really concerned."

"Well, I share that concern."

"Anything from Rachel Katz yet?"

"She hasn't regained consciousness. The doctors are getting worried."

"What else can you do?"

"I can find out what's in the basement of the American Grill."

"Haven't you seen the movies? You *never* go down to the basement."

"I did in Baronville."

"My point exactly."

Decker clicked off and went in search of Lancaster, finding her getting some coffee in the break room.

"You want a cup?" she asked.

He shook his head. "We need to go to the bank."

"Why, do you need money?"

"No, answers."

On the drive over to Don Richards's old bank, Decker said, "David Katz owned a late-model Mercedes sedan when he was killed. It's the car I think his murderer drove over in. Katz and his wife were living in a very nice apartment in town. He owned the American Grill after building it with a construction and operating loan. And he might have had other loans."

"So?"

"So how do you get a big loan like that without putting up collateral?"

"Maybe he put up collateral."

"Meaning he had money of his own."

"Well, yeah. He came to town with money. You know that. Duncan Marks mentioned it at dinner."

"Yeah, everybody keeps telling me that. But no one can tell me *where* the money came from."

"Well, maybe the bank can help."

"Only reason we're going there. Otherwise I wouldn't set foot in one."

"You don't like banks?"

"Not since they foreclosed on my house here and repossessed my car. And with my shitty credit score, *they* don't like *me* either," replied Decker.

Bart Tinsdale was the bank's vice president. He had been at the institution long enough to have known Don Richards. Tinsdale was tall and lanky but his suit was ill-fitting, the pants and coat sleeves too short for his limbs. His shoes were old and battered, and his socks seemed to have lost their elasticity.

However, he had an alert eye and firm handshake, and quickly guided them back to his small glass-enclosed office area off the main lobby, where they all sat around his desk.

He pointed out the window. "Every time I look out that window and see the Grill, I think about Don and David."

"So you knew them both?" asked Decker.

Tinsdale nodded. "I was just a bank clerk back then."

Lancaster said, "Well, you worked your way up. VP now."

Tinsdale's face crinkled. "I'm a little fish in a little pond. And I'm perfectly happy about that. Good place to raise kids, and I've got five."

"Wow, I've got one and some days it's more than I can handle."

The banker nodded appreciatively. "My wife is a saint. And if the kids turn out well, it's more because of her than me. But I do the coaching bit. Soccer and baseball. And I'm an assistant coach for basketball. I played in high school. Pretty full schedule."

"I can see that."

He sat forward. "But you didn't come about that."

Decker said, "No. We've reopened the investigation into David Katz's and Don Richards's murders. And we're also investigating the attempted murder of Rachel Katz."

Tinsdale involuntarily shuddered. "Been way too many killings around here." He gazed at Decker. "You were here when the shootings happened at the high school. My oldest daughter was a freshman when that happened. Thank God she was okay."

"Yeah, thank God," said Lancaster.

"So what can I do for you?" asked Tinsdale.

"For starters, we'd like to know more about the loan that Richards made to David Katz. Do you have those records?"

"Well, they'd be on the computer. Everything's on the computer. Even the old stuff now." He looked at his keyboard before glancing up. "Do you need to get a warrant for that?"

"Katz is dead. I don't see what harm there is in looking at old bank records."

"I guess that's true." Tinsdale tapped some keys and maneuvered through some screens. "Okay, what exactly do you want to know?"

"How much was the loan for?" asked Decker.

Tinsdale read off the screen. "Two point five million."

Lancaster gaped. "That's a pretty big loan, isn't it?"

"Well, I've done bigger. But it is fairly substantial for a restaurant in Burlington, I'll grant you that, particularly since it was so many years ago. But it was apparently an expensive buildout."

"Have you been to the Grill?" asked Decker.

"I have in fact, yes."

"It seemed like a million other restaurants I've been in. Not particularly high-end."

Tinsdale was nodding before he finished speaking.

"I have to admit that I thought the same thing, actually. But the loan *was* granted."

"Did he have to put up any collateral for the loan?"

"Well, we put a mortgage on the property, of course, and the improvements. That's standard. And, yes, I would imagine he had to put up some money of his own. We don't generally fully fund projects like this. We want the borrower to have some skin in the game, so to speak. He was applying for money for the construction and also operating funds to get the business up and going. It's not like he could start paying down the loan from day one while they're still building the thing. The interest would be wrapped into the principal and payments calculated off that. Let me just check on a few items." He read down several more screens. "Okay, yes, he did put up some money of his own. A little over five hundred thousand. That went into the land purchase. And he also personally guaranteed the loan."

"Is that typical?" asked Lancaster.

Tinsdale gave her a knowing look. "Oh, yes. Especially with a restaurant. Failure rates on those are really high. And if the customer defaults, the bank doesn't just want to have to look to the collateral. We're not in the business of running a restaurant. And the resale rates on a failed restaurant operation are not very good. Pennies on the dollar. People figure if a location failed, why would a second try succeed?"

"So, if he personally guaranteed the loan, he must have had some wealth," said Lancaster.

"Assuredly yes. We would have done a complete financial due diligence on him. And he would have had to show proof of collateral funds and we would have filed a security interest on those assets. Stocks or bonds or cash accounts or whatever the collateral was, giving the bank a secured interest in those assets in case of default."

"Could you tell us what his net worth was back then?" asked Decker.

Tinsdale hit some more keys. "Let's see. Okay, we took an interest in some CDs that he had that were worth eighty percent of the loan amount. All told, it shows that his net worth back then was about nine million dollars."

"Wow," said Lancaster. "With all that money, why not just fund the construction out of his own pocket?"

Tinsdale smiled knowingly. "First rule of business, when you can, use someone else's money."

"Right."

"What was the main source of his wealth?" asked Decker.

"Seemed to be stocks and bonds mostly. Couple of annuities. It was all liquid."

"But does it show where his wealth initially came from?"

"No, it doesn't. But all the assets were legally in his name."

"And he was the only borrower?"

"Yes, he wasn't married when he did this deal."

"And Don Richards did everything by the book?" asked Lancaster.

"Absolutely. All done in accordance with the bank's loan requirements."

"What was Katz's background? Education? Birthplace? History?"

Tinsdale looked over the screens. "Says here on his loan app that he had a BA and an MBA. He listed his occupation as entrepreneur."

"But again, no source for his wealth other than the net worth figure?"

"Well, it was *his* money. That was verified. He might have inherited it."

"I assumed when he died that the loan rolled over to his widow?"

"No, it didn't."

"Why not?"

"It was a construction loan that was rolled into a five-year loan with a fixed interest rate. But Katz paid the whole thing off about six months after the restaurant opened."

"How did he do that?" asked Decker.

Tinsdale studied the screens once more. "It's not entirely clear, but it seems like he raised some private money from investors and used that to pay off the loan completely."

"And did he take out any more loans with the bank?"

"There were two lines of credit for a million each that he took out around the same time. He fully drew down on both and then paid them off. Then he bought an old factory building for about three million with an eye to turning it into retail and living space. He took out a loan for that too. It was finished after he died."

"Is the loan still outstanding on that one?"

Tinsdale moved through some more screens. "No. Katz paid that one off too."

"When?"

"Let me see. It says here it was paid in full one year after he took it out."

"But you said the building was finished *after* he died," said Decker.

"That's right. They were only about halfway done when he was killed." Tinsdale shrugged. "Apparently he had another round of investment money come in and they took the loan out."

"And did Don Richards work on all these deals?"

"That's right. He was sort of Katz's go-to person."

"Has Rachel Katz applied for any loans from the bank?"

"No. She doesn't even have a personal account with us. I think she has some deep pockets behind her. Doesn't need a commercial lending source anymore. She seems to be rolling in money right now."

"Nice job if you can get it," said Lancaster dryly.

Outside, Decker looked to the sky. "We were led to believe that the only deal Katz and Richards worked on was for the American Grill. But that wasn't the case. There were the lines of credit and the old factory building."

"Okay, but what did we get out of all that except that some people have all the friggin' luck, *and* all the money?" asked Lancaster.

"When somebody keeps paying off big loans unusually early because they got 'investment money' rolling in from shell companies, it tells me one thing." He looked at his partner.

Lancaster nodded. "David Katz was cleaning money."

"Exactly. And I wonder if Rachel Katz took over the *laundry* business when he died."

67

Decker and Lancaster were seated across from Bill Peyton in his small office at the American Grill. Peyton was a big man, about six-two, two-twenty, with thick shoulders and muscular arms. His gray hair was cut in a bristly flattop turning silver at the temples. In his early sixties now, he looked like he could bench-press a truck.

"Thanks for meeting with us," said Lancaster.

"No problem. How is Ms. Katz doing?"

"She hasn't regained consciousness," said Lancaster. "But the doctors are still hopeful."

Decker slid a photo out of a slip of plastic and handed it across to Peyton. "Do you recognize this man?"

Peyton fingered the photo. "No, who is he?"

"The man who attempted to murder your boss. He was killed during the encounter. His name is Eric Tyson. Former military."

"No, never seen him before, certainly not here. I can ask around to the staff and see. But the fact is, Ms. Katz didn't come here much."

"But she still owns the place," pointed out Lancaster.

"She does. But in the grand scheme of her empire here, we're small potatoes." He grinned briefly. "And she trusted me to run the place, just like her husband did."

"You've been here from the get-go," said Decker.

"That's right. David Katz hired me."

"I guess you've run restaurants before?"

"I know my way around the business."

"It can be challenging. Lots of restaurants fail."

"Yes, they can. And we've had some new competition come in. But we're holding our own."

"Were you around when the place was being built?" asked Decker.

"I was, yes. David brought me on early enough, so I could have input in the process."

"How was David Katz to work for?"

"I always found him professional and focused. Later, I found his wife to be the same." He looked at his watch. "Anything else?"

"What will happen to the business if Rachel Katz doesn't recover?" asked Decker.

"I have no idea," said Peyton. "I guess that depends on what's in her will and what her relatives want to do. I hope we don't get to that point."

"Absolutely," said Decker. "Well, thanks for your time." He pulled out another photo of Eric Tyson from his pocket and handed it to Peyton. "And let us know if anyone remembers seeing that guy around."

Peyton took the photo without looking at it. "Will do."

They left and went outside.

"Well?" said Lancaster.

Decker took out the plastic slip with the photo inside. "Looks like a beautiful print on the photo. We'll run it and see if Mr. Peyton is who he says he is."

Decker dropped Lancaster and the photo off at the station and continued on to the hospital, where Mars was once more ensconced in Katz's hospital room.

"Nothing?" said Decker as he sat down next to him.

Mars shook his head.

"Got something to tell you." He filled Mars in on his theory of money laundering.

"So you think she was in on it?" asked Mars as he glanced at Katz.

"I don't know for sure, but it would be a stretch to conclude that she didn't know about it. She's got financial backers that even the FBI can't pierce."

Mars slowly nodded. "Could be the reason for her guilty conscience and all the weird stuff she was saying to me."

"Could be. We met with the guy who manages the American Grill. We got his prints through a bit of sleight of hand, and Mary's running them through the database."

"What could that tell you?"

"I don't think this is just about money laundering, Melvin. I think something else is going on. You don't need to build a basement under a restaurant to run a money laundering business. You just need legitimate businesses to flush bad money through and turn that bad money into other assets and a clean line of cash flow. That's what all of Katz's businesses could allow them to do."

"But you don't think that's all. So what else could there be?"

Decker shrugged. "I don't know. But I believe that David Katz and Don Richards were killed because something went wrong."

"Went wrong. Like what?"

"Something in the business. Someone felt threatened somehow, by one or both of them. They killed them and pinned it on Meryl Hawkins, with his daughter's help."

"And her payoff?"

"She got remade, new life, new everything. From the bottom to the top in a flash."

"Like Audrey Hepburn in *My Fair Lady*. One of my favorite films."

Decker looked at him in a bemused way. "Didn't see you as a *My Fair Lady* kind of guy."

"Hell, I could relate, Decker. I had to remake

myself every second of every day, when I was growing up in West Texas and then when I was in prison. And when I got out of prison."

"Why not just be yourself?"

"Easy for you to say."

Decker sat back. "I guess you're right about that."

"Yeah, I was the high school and college sports star back then. Whole damn state loved me. I was a hero. But God forbid I eat at their table. Or date their daughters."

Decker suddenly glanced at Katz. "Jenny Marks said that Katz had been a real mentor to her. Showing her the ropes of being in business."

"I heard that. So?"

"So, even though Katz said she didn't know her, I wonder if she did the same thing for Mitzi Gardiner?"

"Wait a minute, you think Gardiner was Hepburn?"

"And that means Rachel Katz might have been in the role played by Rex Harrison."

68

"We . . . Look, um, I think there's a problem."

Decker stared at Brad Gardiner, who was standing, pale and shaking, in the doorway of his home. Decker had just knocked on the door and Gardiner had flung it open.

"What sort of problem?" asked Decker.

"Mitzi . . . she's locked herself in our bedroom and she won't come out. And . . . and I think she has a gun. She's threatening to shoot herself, or anyone who comes through that door."

"Have you called the police?"

"I . . . no. I don't know what to do."

"Is anyone in the room with her? Your son?"

"No, he's at school, thank God."

"Anybody else?"

"I had the maid leave when . . . when things got weird."

"Why are you home at this time of day?"

"I forgot some papers. I came back for them. That's when Mitzi screamed at me when I tried to open the bedroom door."

"Okay, is she on something? Has she been drinking?"

Gardiner seemed to be on the verge of tears. "I don't know. What the hell is going on?"

"Show me to the bedroom."

Decker followed him down the hall and they arrived at the door.

"Honey, I have Mr. Decker here."

"Get him the fuck out of my house!" screamed Mitzi.

"Ms. Gardiner?" said Decker.

The next moment they both leapt back because she fired a round right through the wood. The slug missed both men and embedded in the far wall.

"Jesus Christ!" cried out Gardiner as he dropped to the floor shaking.

Decker slid over to him, keeping low. "What kind of gun does she have?"

"It's . . . it's a Sig Sauer. I bought it for her. But she picked it out."

"What model?"

"Um . . ."

"Think!"

"P238."

"What's it look like?"

"Small. She can carry it in her clutch purse."

"P238 Micro Compact chambered in .380 auto?"

"Yes, that's it. Exactly."

"Standard mag with it, or did she do something special?"

"No, standard."

Decker nodded. "Call the police and wait for them by the front door."

"What the hell are you two doing out there?" screamed Mitzi, followed by another shot through the door.

With one backward glance at the door, Gardiner did as Decker requested, sliding down the hall on his hands and knees. Then he rose and sprinted off. Decker straightened and, keeping well away from the bedroom door, said, "Mitzi, it's Amos Decker."

"I said to get out of my house, you bastard."

"We need to talk."

"About what? You've ruined my life. What the hell else is there to talk about, you shit!"

"How exactly did I do that?"

Another round blew through the wood and hit the opposite wall about a foot below the other two bullets.

"You know damn well how. You just . . . you just had to dig all this shit up, didn't you? From all that time ago. You couldn't give a crap how it might affect people. How it might affect me! You asshole!" she shrieked.

Another shot came through the door. Decker flinched with the impact against the wood but held his ground.

"That was not my intent."

"Don't you dare bullshit me. That's *exactly* what you wanted."

She fired another round through the door, ripping a big chunk off it as the wood around the other holes gave way.

"Look, if you stop shooting, we can have a conversation."

"I'm not talking to you. I'm going to kill myself."

"Why would you want to do that?"

"Because my life is over!"

"Your husband doesn't think that. Or your son."

"Don't you dare talk about my son. He's the only good thing I've ever done in my miserable excuse for a life."

"I think we *have* to talk about him if you're planning on leaving him motherless."

Now she started to sob. He could hear the gut-wrenching noises coming through the door.

He took a chance and peeped through one of the holes. She was lying in bed, wearing only a long T-shirt; her uncovered legs were long and pale. The gun was in her right hand.

"Mitzi, I can help you if you let me."

"N-nobody can help me. Not now."

"I don't see it that way."

"I told you to get out."

He ducked down as the shot came through not the door, but the wall. It must have hit a nail in the stud under the drywall, because it careened into the hall at a weird angle, nearly hitting Decker in the face.

He stayed low, breathing heavily and wondering where the hell the cops were.

"I can't leave you like this. I'm afraid you're going to hurt yourself."

"Fuckin' A, Sherlock. I'm going to do more than hurt myself, you idiot!"

"Rachel Katz wouldn't want that, Mitzi. She was the one who helped you to turn your life around. And now she's fighting for her life."

Silence.

A few moments passed.

"What do you know about anything?"

"I know a lot, Mitzi. I'd like to know more."

"You came here and . . . and accused me of framing my own father."

"So tell me that you didn't. Tell me that you're innocent."

"You wouldn't believe me if I did."

"Try me."

In a more subdued tone she said, "Look, it's . . . it's complicated."

"Believe me, I know that. But why do I think that Rachel Katz was blindsided by what happened? And you didn't really know what was going to happen either, Mitzi, did you? I think you were both used. I think you both thought you had no way out."

"I . . . I don't want to talk about it."

"At this point, you're going to have to."

"Screw you, Decker!"

He flattened himself to the hallway floor right as the bullet blasted through the door. The next instant he was up and had smashed into the door, breaking it open.

An astonished Mitzi gaped at him as he charged toward the bed. She aimed her pistol at him and fired.

Click. Click.

Decker wrenched the gun out of her hand and pocketed it. He looked down at her. "P238 Micro Compact has a seven-round standard mag." He looked at the bullet-pocked door and wall. "And you just fired your last bullet."

He turned back to her, as she covered herself with a sheet. "Get out!" she screamed.

"I can't do that. The police are on their way."

She looked confused. "Why?"

"Well, for starters you tried to kill me and your husband."

"No I didn't. I was just trying to make you leave me alone."

"Not sure the court will see it that way. You fire a gun at someone, deadly intent is pretty much implied."

Her lips trembled. "Do you mean I could go to jail? But I'm innocent."

"Like your father? He *was* innocent. And he still went to jail. Then someone put a bullet in his head. They didn't even let him die peacefully."

Decker sat on the edge of the bed and gazed at her.

"This is the moment, Mitzi. The crossroads. Now is the time where you can make the right decision instead of the selfish one. You can correct a lot of wrongs. Will you do it? Do you have the courage to do that?"

"What if I don't?" she said, drawing her legs up and gathering the covers around her.

"Then you go to jail. It's as simple as that."

"I'm going to jail regardless."

"Not necessarily. Or you could hang out here until someone tries to kill you, like they did with Rachel Katz."

He glanced at her nightstand and started when he eyed the half-empty prescription pill bottle. "How many pills did you take?" he snapped.

"Not that many," she said hesitantly.

"How many is that?"

"Four or five."

He snatched up the bottle and read the label. "Christ, Mitzi."

He called 911 and requested an ambulance, pronto, for a possible drug overdose.

She lay back against the headboard and looked around the room. She smiled. "I have a perfect life; did you know that?"

"Tell me about it."

"Can't you see for yourself? Perfect home, perfect husband. Perfect child." She uncovered her bare legs. "Perfect body." She tapped her teeth. "First-rate veneers to hide the shitty, ugly gray." She covered herself back up as her smile faded. "But the shitty, ugly gray is right below the surface. Right underneath. They couldn't take that away. It'll always be with me."

"But you made the change. That was a lot of work. You had to be determined. It wasn't easy kicking what you kicked."

"It . . . it was either do that or end up dead." She looked at him defiantly. "I chose to live."

"I'm glad you did. Now you have a family. A son who's counting on you. So choose to live this time too."

Her lips trembled when he said this. She rubbed at her eyes. "But now, it's . . . a-all effed up. I don't k-know what to . . ."

As Decker listened to this, he saw her eyes becoming droopy, her features more and more listless. He let a few seconds pass and, trying to keep his voice calm, asked, "Do you have any Narcan here?"

She smiled and shook her head. "That's for druggies. I'm not a druggie. Not anymore. I am the princess of the manor. The lady is perfect. Everybody says so."

"Are you sure it was just four or five pills?" he said quickly.

She stretched out like a cat. "Maybe it was more. I don't remember." She lay back and closed her eyes.

"Stay with me, Mitzi. Come on now." He sat down next to her and slapped her face. It was a poor substitute for Narcan, but he had to do something.

"Hey," she said angrily, swatting at him. "Y-you a-assaulted m-me."

"You framed your father. Why?"

She didn't answer.

"Why?" he said, shaking her. "Come on, talk to me."

"I did it for drugs."

"For drugs? You mean for you?"

She waved this comment off. "No, stupid. For Mom. Morphine. For her drip line. Pure stuff. Right from the hospital. Gave it to her t-till she died. And she died p-peacefully. All I could do for her. But it was s-something, right?"

"Right. Who got it for you?"

"They did."

"Who's they?"

She waved her hand around the room. "You know. Them!"

She yawned and closed her eyes.

He slapped her again. This time, she didn't complain. Or open her eyes.

Shit.

He could hear the sirens now.

Decker gripped Mitzi's shoulders to keep her upright as she started to slump sideways. "What did they promise you, Mitzi? A new life? A new everything? Did Rachel Katz help you out? Did she become your mentor?"

Mitzi mumbled, "She's a n-nice person. H-helped me."

"I bet she did. So they killed her husband and Don Richards. And the others. And set up your dad."

"Set him . . . up."

"And how did they approach you?"

"Ka, Kar . . ."

"Karl Stevens. Right. He was the go-between. Who was he working with?"

"He's dead. You tol' me . . . d-dead."

The sirens were growing closer.

"That's right, he's dead. But you're not. You can tell me all about it."

She shook her head. "Too l-late for th-that."

"It's never too late for the truth."

She started to fall sideways. He slapped her again. To no effect. The sirens had been growing louder and louder all this time. Then the sound died. They were in the driveway.

"Karl Stevens is dead, that's right. But who was he working with? Did it have something to do with the American Grill? Bill Peyton? Do you know him? Peyton?"

She opened her eyes.

"Pey-ton."

"Right. The manager at the American Grill. Did he come to you? Did he ask you to help frame Meryl?" He shook her violently. "Did he?"

She closed her eyes again and went limp in his arms.

He could hear footsteps pounding down the hall. The door burst open and three EMTs were there.

Decker called out, "Amos Decker with the FBI. She took pills from that bottle. More than five. I'm starting to lose her. I think she's unconscious."

One of the EMTs grabbed the bottle and looked at the label. "Okay, step back."

Decker moved away from the bed as the EMTs crowded around Mitzi, who had started to shake violently and then suddenly slumped over. One of the EMTs sprayed Narcan into her nostril. She didn't move for a long moment, and then she sat straight up and let out a lungful of air.

"Okay, ma'am, just relax. We're going to take you to the hospital to get checked out."

"W-what?"

Then she went limp again and fell over sideways.

"Shit," said the EMT. He sprayed another shot of Narcan up her other nostril.

She stirred but did not come fully back.

They started a saline drip line and put a blood pressure cuff and pulse monitor on her.

"Her pressure and respiration are really low," said one of the EMTs. "Critically low. I think she took something more than was in that bottle. Let's roll. Now!"

They were loading her onto a gurney when Decker noticed something.

"Wait a minute, where's her husband?"

"Who?" said one of the EMTs.

"Her husband. Tall guy. He let you in."

"Nobody let us in. The front door was open. We just followed the noise to back here."

Decker ran out of the room, down the hall, and out the front door. A late-model Audi 8 had been parked in front when he'd gotten here. It was no longer there.

He looked up and down the road fronting the house.

Brad Gardiner was gone.

And Decker had no clue why.

Am I ever going to get out ahead of this damn case?

69

"I don't like getting played," grumbled Decker.

He was sitting alongside Lancaster and Mars in the visitors' waiting room at the local hospital in Trammel, where Mitzi Gardiner had been admitted into the critical care unit. As with Rachel Katz, they had armed guards stationed 24/7 outside her room.

Though the doctors were hopeful that she would recover, they could not guarantee what her mental state might be when she regained consciousness. One of the doctors had told them, "When abused, the drug she took can have a particularly destructive impact on certain areas of the brain having to do with memory."

"Well, that's great," Decker had replied. "Since we need for her to remember a lot of stuff."

Lancaster now said, "We found Brad Gardiner's car abandoned about two miles from his house. He might have been picked up there and taken somewhere else."

"It never occurred to me that her husband might be a part of all this," said Decker miserably.

“Playing a role all these years?” said Mars. “That’s a commitment and then some.”

“Agreed,” said Lancaster. “I mean, they had a kid together.”

“I’m not saying the guy doesn’t love her or didn’t want to marry her and have a child,” said Decker. “But I can’t think of another reason why he would have vanished like that, unless he was afraid we were going to find out something.”

“This goes way beyond money laundering, Decker,” said Lancaster.

“We need to find out all we can about Brad Gardiner.”

Lancaster said, “I’ve already started digging. He went to college in Illinois. Moved here about fifteen years ago. Worked at a variety of jobs in the financial sector. Now he specializes in an upscale placement market.”

“Mitzi told me a little about that. She called it a high-end job placement platform.”

“That’s right,” said Lancaster. “Apparently he’s not placing people in low-paying jobs. He focuses on finance, law, high tech, manufacturing, energy, those sorts of fields. They pay the big bucks and he gets big commissions.”

“I wonder how he hooked up with Mitzi,” said Decker.

“You really think this was all arranged after the murders thirteen years ago?”

"She didn't marry him thirteen years ago. She had to go through her big makeover. She told me that Katz helped her with that. Then Gardiner steps in and marries Mitzi and they have a kid and a wonderful life."

"And Gardiner came to the area about the same time as David Katz was opening the American Grill," noted Lancaster.

"Right. Mitzi said her husband knew nothing about her past. Now, either she was lying, or she didn't know that her marriage might have been a setup."

"Assuming it was, why would they go to all those lengths to give Mitzi a second shot at life?" wondered Lancaster.

"She helped them by framing her father for four murders. They wanted to keep her in line."

Lancaster shook her head and said, "Okay, but if they were afraid she might talk, why not just kill her? These folks don't seem to mind solving their problems with violence. And it's not like she was a major player in whatever they're doing."

"Maybe they were afraid with another murder so soon after the others that people would get suspicious and start digging. With Meryl fingered as the killer, no one looked anywhere else. I know that better than anyone."

Mars said, "And it worked, apparently, all this time."

Decker looked thoughtful. "But now, with Gar-

They forced open the front door of the restaurant, which immediately set off the alarm. One of the firefighters hastened to turn it off using a special code he inputted into the alarm panel.

"A call will go out to whoever's on the notification list," said Lancaster.

"What I'm hoping for," replied Decker.

The firefighters went in first and gave the all-clear about twenty minutes later.

"Okay," said Decker, turning on the lights. "We need to search this place for possible arson materials. No stone unturned. Let's hit it."

The officers fanned out.

Decker immediately went into the kitchen area, followed by Lancaster and Mars.

The kitchen was spacious, scrupulously clean and organized, and virtually everything in the place looked made of stainless steel. They spent an hour going over every inch of it.

Afterward, Decker leaned against one of the counters and looked around, his thick arms folded over his chest.

"They're not making this easy," said Lancaster.

"Lots of people come in and out of this kitchen, including people who have no connection to any of this. So it can't be apparent. But even so, it has to be somewhat accessible."

Lancaster looked around. "I don't see anything

diner and Katz in the fold, we may be able to find out what's going on."

"Well, Katz hasn't woken up yet, despite what the doctors told us, and Gardiner isn't out of danger yet," said Lancaster. "And you heard the doctor about the state of her memory if she does come out of it. I'm not sure we can rely on either one."

"I agree," replied Decker. "Ground zero for us is the American Grill. We have to find out what's inside there."

"Okay, but we have no probable cause whatsoever to search the place for an underground room," pointed out his old partner.

"We can ask nicely," said Mars.

Decker shook his head. "And this Bill Peyton will be within his rights to say that the only person who can properly grant that request is lying in a hospital bed unconscious. And if we tip him off, and he is in on whatever's going on, that would not be good. The guy struck me as really cagey."

"So what do we do, then?" asked Mars.

Decker looked at Lancaster. "Did you run Peyton's print?"

"We did. And got nothing back. He's not in the system."

"Just because he has no criminal history doesn't mean much. Can we do a deeper dive on him? Try to find out his background? What he was up to prior to coming here?"

"We can. I just don't know how far we'll get. If he's not in the system, it might be hard to build a profile on the guy. I presume that there are a lot of Bill Peytons in this country."

"Yeah, I did a preliminary search online and found squat. But we have to find a way to search for that secret room," said Decker.

"I agree. I just don't know how we can."

"If Katz wakes up, we can get her consent."

"Right, but that might be *never*," retorted Lancaster.

"Then we have to try something else," said Decker.

"I get that, but what?"

"Up to this point, we've been entirely reactive. They've been leading us around by the nose. And I'm getting sick of it."

"Okay, so?"

"So, let's jerk their chain for once."

70

The call came in at one in the morning. Smo coming from the American Grill. A fire, apparentl Two fire companies responded, along with the police.

Decker, Mars, and Lancaster followed on the heels of the arson squad as they approached the smoke-engulfed restaurant. The firefighters reported that it was only smoke and no fire.

That made sense, because the smoke bombs that had been placed earlier on the roof of the Grill and in the Dumpster in the rear could produce no flames.

Decker looked at the arson boss, Chuck Walters "That's very suspicious, Chuck. I think we need t look inside for a point of origin. This might be som sort of feint, with the real fire to come once v leave."

The notion was fairly nonsensical, but Chu nodded and said, "I think that's a good idea. Ne know what might be on the inside."

"Never know," agreed Decker.

But hopefully we're about to find out.

that fits the bill unless we're talking a trapdoor in the floor."

Mars looked down. "It's tiled. With no breaks. A trapdoor would be pretty obvious."

Decker pushed off the counter and went back into the large freezer room. It was about ten feet deep and eight feet across. He shivered slightly as he moved around the space, examining all the shelves and food stacked on them. He came back out and looked at the outside of the freezer compartment.

"Anybody got a tape measure?" he asked.

Neither Lancaster nor Mars did, but one of the cops had a rolling distance tracker in his trunk. He used it to measure distances during traffic accident reconstructions.

Decker took the roller and paced off the depth of the freezer, going in between the shelving at the rear to tap his wheel against the back wall. Then he measured the width.

He checked the measurement and then went outside the freezer and measured the distance from the front of the freezer to the back wall of the kitchen. And then from the side of the freezer to the far wall.

He checked the measurement. "I'm two feet short. This wall is two feet longer on the outside than the depth of the freezer on the inside. And the width is off by over eighteen inches."

"How could that be?" asked Lancaster. "Maybe a load-bearing wall at the back or the side?"

"Why would it just be in the freezer and not out here?" said Mars.

Decker hustled into the freezer, followed by Mars and Lancaster. He went straight to the back.

"Melvin, help me with these shelves."

Together the two big men moved the heavy shelves out of the way with the food still stacked on them. When they were done, they were staring at a seemingly blank wall.

Decker hit every angle and corner of the wall with his light. He got down on his hands and knees and felt along the bottom where the wall met the floor.

Lancaster was shivering. "Can we hurry this up before I get hypothermia?"

Decker stood and faced the wall. "I don't see a button or anything like that. That would be too risky anyway. Someone comes in here, sees it, and pushes it to see what happens. Your secret is out."

"Like the floor, I don't see any break in the wall, Decker," observed Mars. "If there's a door hidden in here I just don't see it."

Decker looked back at the shelves they had moved. "With those shelves in front and food stacked on them, no one would be able to even get close to the wall."

"And what exactly does that mean?"

Decker put his palms against the wall. "It means that maybe the wall *is* the door."

He set his feet and pushed. The entire wall easily rolled back. Revealed off to the left was a door. He opened the door: there was a set of narrow steps going down.

"Open sesame," quipped Mars.

They went single file down the stairs and came out into a darkened space. Decker shone his flashlight around, as did the others.

The space held desks, maps on the wall, computers, telephones, racks of clothing, thick binders, and other pieces of equipment. On one side of the room, a long curtain had been drawn around a space about six by ten feet. The lights suddenly came on and Mars and Decker looked around to see Lancaster standing by a light switch.

"I don't like the dark," she said, turning off her flashlight.

Mars and Decker put away their flashlights and gazed around.

"Holy shit, what is this place?" asked Mars.

Decker strode over to a desk and looked down at the items lying there, next to a piece of machinery.

"They're making IDs here." He picked one up to see a young man staring out from what was a Virginia driver's license. The name on the license was Frank Saunders. Born in 1993 and with an address in McLean, Virginia.

"This guy I saw working at the restaurant as a wait

staff 'trainee.' Only his name, I was told, was Daniel, not Frank."

Mars held up a stack of credit cards in one hand and sets of American passports and birth certificates in the other. "Okay, I'm no expert, but these damn things look genuine."

Lancaster had drawn back the curtain to reveal what looked like a rudimentary operating room and was now standing next to a gurney. She pointed to an array of surgical instruments lined up on a table. Next to that was a portable high-intensity light. And next to that were oxygen tanks and an IV stand with empty bags hanging from it. Lined up against the wall were a variety of medical monitoring instruments.

Lancaster exclaimed, "Okay, this is freaking me out. They're operating on people down here?" She pointed to the large sink set against the wall. "Maybe that's where they scrub up before doing whatever the hell they do."

Mars was looking at the racks of clothes. "They got everything here, for both men and women." He picked up a wig. "Including these."

Computers were set on each desk. Stacks of paper sat next to the computers. Decker picked up the top page of a stack.

"What is that?" asked Lancaster, coming over to him.

"It's a list of forty cities across the country. There's an X next to each city."

He pointed to the maps on the wall. "These documents might correspond to the red and green pins on those maps. Looks like they have pretty much every major metro area covered."

He picked up another piece of paper. "This reads like someone's bio. Birth information, background. Work experience. Marital status."

He looked down at the bottom of the page. He read off, "Gardiner and Associates."

Lancaster said, "Brad Gardiner?"

"Well, he runs a job placement business."

"But that's not illegal," said Mars. He looked around the space. "Now *this* place definitely looks illegal."

"Whether it's illegal or not depends on who you're placing in those jobs," said Decker.

He looked over at the gurney and surgical instruments. "That's obviously to change someone's appearance. The clothes, wigs, fake IDs, credit cards, passports, birth certificates, and fabricated backgrounds all work to complete a new identity. And then Brad Gardiner places them in positions around the country. And he's not placing people as waiters or maids. He's placing them in finance, the high-tech field, lobbying, government, and other sectors. That's what Mitzi said."

"Yeah, but what sorts of people?" asked Lancaster.

Decker looked around the room. "People created here?"

"But they must have experience in those fields," said Mars. "I mean, you can't walk into Goldman Sachs or Google or GE or the U.S. government without knowing what you're doing."

"Oh, I'm sure they know what they're doing," said Decker. "And now we know this place wasn't really just laundering money."

"What do you mean?" asked Lancaster.

"They were laundering people."

71

"What in the hell do you mean, you lost him?" said Lancaster.

She was staring at a pair of plainclothes detectives who she'd assigned to watch Bill Peyton's apartment. They were back at the police station after thoroughly going over the lower-level room at the American Grill.

"He was there, Detective Lancaster," said the larger of the pair. "And then he was gone."

His partner added, "When you called and told us to bring him in, we knocked and knocked on the door. Then, when there was no answer, we forced the door and searched the whole place, top to bottom. There was no sign of him."

"He lives in an apartment building," said Decker. "Did you think to search the building?"

"But we had the front and back entrances covered."

"He could have gone into another apartment when you came into the building, and then left while you were searching his place," pointed out Decker. "If he was watching you watching him."

"Well, I guess he could have," said one of the detectives.

"There's no *guessing* about it," barked Lancaster. "He did."

After the men left them, Lancaster said, "Idiots. We had him, Decker. We had him. And now, poof, he's gone. You knew he was going to be on the security call list. That was supposed to flush him out. And then these morons lose him."

"Vanishing people seems to be a recurring theme with this case," said Decker sardonically.

"So now what?"

"We have a lot of information to process."

"My team is collecting all the evidence from that underground room. It's a ton. But the computers all are password protected. And my tech guy says the hard drives are clean. Which means everything is kept in some cloud somewhere that we can't access."

"But there's other evidence in there. The IDs, the documents, and the rest."

"You said they were laundering people?"

"The 'trainees' at the Grill. I think they came to Burlington to be processed. Given new identities, maybe some had their features changed through plastic surgery, then they were sent out into the world, probably at positions gotten for them by Brad Gardiner."

"But for what purpose?"

"I don't know."

"And why Burlington, Ohio?"

"I think this has been going on for as long as the American Grill has been in business. That underground room would explain the need for the additional concrete and the way they tried to hide it during the construction process."

"So David Katz was involved in this from the get-go?"

"I don't see how he couldn't be. And he paid off his loans early with fresh money."

"And Bill Peyton?"

"He's been there since the inception too. He had to know about the room. That's why he disappeared. I think he's a smart enough guy to see what we were doing. Using a 'fire' to get in and search the place."

"But a smart defense counsel could get all the fruits of our search thrown out as tainted. We didn't have a warrant and the fire explanation may not hold up at trial."

"We'll cross that bridge when we come to it. But I'm less worried about that than I am about stopping what's been going on here, Mary."

"So why was David Katz killed? And the Richardses?"

"Bad guys kill other bad guys when they feel threatened. It could be that Katz wanted more money to do what he was doing. Or maybe he got cold feet and was thinking of going to the cops and telling them what was going on."

"And the Richardses?"

"The banker told us that Don Richards was Katz's go-to person there. Maybe the people behind this were afraid that Katz had told Richards too much. We've already speculated that Karl Stevens learned through his drug deals with Richards's son about some communication between Katz and Richards. Stevens must have told someone and then they struck on the idea of pinning all this on Meryl Hawkins."

"Because Stevens knew Mitzi."

"Right. Hell, Stevens might have been the one to suggest pinning it on Hawkins. He certainly knew about Mitzi's drug addiction and probably also about her mother and her need for pain meds. But Meryl wasn't stupid. He must have figured out that his daughter set him up. But he didn't know why. Maybe he just thought she'd gotten in trouble. He said nothing because he didn't want to add to her grief, and to his wife's."

"But then he runs into Karl Stevens in prison. And Stevens maybe runs his mouth. He lets Hawkins know the truth, or close to it."

"So he gets that tat of the arrow through his little star, symbolically killing his daughter. And comes back here trying to prove his innocence."

"And somebody kills him," said Lancaster. "But how would they have known what he was up to?"

"Stevens might have tipped off someone on the outside about Meryl getting out of prison. When he shows up back here, they decide they need to get rid of him before he can start making waves."

"Fortunately, he reached us before they could kill him," pointed out Lancaster.

"It won't be *fortunate* if we can't figure out the truth," Decker retorted.

"So Gardiner and Peyton are both on the run. You think they're going to hook up at some point?"

"Anything's possible. Gardiner really outsmarted me. But the guy was scared, Mary. And he wasn't scared of his wife, even though she was shooting at both of us."

"He was scared because of the people he's involved with."

"Well, considering what they've done so far, who can blame him?"

His phone buzzed. It was Jamison.

"Hey, Alex, I'm a little busy ri—"

She interrupted, "The team's coming to Burlington."

"What? I thought you were in New Hampshire."

"We were. But another case is suddenly taking precedence."

"What case?"

"Yours."

72

Ross Bogart looked every inch the FBI agent someone would expect to see on TV. Tall, physically fit, good-looking, with sharp features, alert eyes, and a quiet competency. But it was more than looking the part. The man was a gifted investigator and worked exceedingly long hours at his job.

Todd Milligan was nearly a carbon copy of his boss, albeit a bit shorter and about a decade younger. He and Decker had been at cross-purposes early on in their professional relationship but had long since reached common ground. The fact that Decker had saved his life once hadn't hurt either.

The FBI team had flown into the nearest regional airport and driven straight to Burlington, telling Decker that they preferred to meet at his place rather than the police station. Now they were standing in Decker's room at the Residence Inn. Melvin Mars was there as well, as was Mary Lancaster. The male FBI agents were dressed in matching dark suits, starched white shirts, and striped ties, and they sported impassive features. Alex Jamison had on a black pantsuit with a white shirt and low heels. Her expression was equally serious.

"Detective Lancaster, it's been a while, good to see you," said Bogart.

She replied, "Well, looks like we're hunting with Decker again. Like old times."

Decker said, "Why are you here, Ross? You didn't say."

Bogart leaned back against the wall and folded his arms over his chest. "We cracked the wall around two of those shell companies that you sent to Alex."

"Meaning the backers for Rachel Katz?"

"Yes. Although the financial relationships apparently go back farther than that. To the time of David Katz's being in charge of the business."

"And what did you find?" asked Lancaster.

"Both companies were set up by a businessman with known ties to a Russian oligarch. That's why we're here."

Lancaster gaped. "A Russian oligarch is bankrolling a business in Burlington, Ohio? How does that make sense?"

Bogart said, "It's a fact, so somehow it makes sense. We just have to figure out how."

Lancaster looked over at Decker. "I didn't see that one coming."

"The room underneath the American Grill," said Decker. "We speculated that it was laundering people. Giving them new identities, and then sending them off into the American workforce in places of influence through Brad Gardiner's placement business."

"But what they're really doing is spying on us?" said Jamison.

Lancaster nodded. "Exactly. And let's face it, legit businesses don't have ID mills hidden under restaurants. Their intent is clearly nefarious."

Decker had been typing in something on his phone. He looked up and said, "We need to find Gardiner and Peyton. And we need to dig into Gardiner's business."

"We didn't know about Brad Gardiner," said Bogart. "But now that we do, we'll get going on that. You said he's disappeared?"

"Along with Bill Peyton, the manager of the American Grill. Ironic, isn't it?"

"What?" said Bogart.

"That they called it the *American* Grill, since it was apparently financed by a Russian oligarch." He thought of something else. "The tats on the two dead guys, Tyson and Stevens."

"What about them?" said Bogart.

"Aryan Nation, Nazi, and KKK."

"Right."

"But there was one more."

Bogart thought for a moment but then shook his head. "Which one?"

"KI."

"I thought that was something to do with the Klan," said Jamison.

"I did too. And there is actually a Klan symbol close to that." He held up his phone. "But I just did some digging after you told us about the Russian connection."

"And?" said Bogart.

"Back in the forties, KI was sort of a foreign intelligence agency in Russia. KI apparently stands for 'Committee of Information.'"

"Damn," said Jamison, while Bogart looked intensely interested.

"How does an old and presumably now-defunct spy agency figure into this?" he asked.

"I look forward to asking Bill Peyton, or whatever his real name is, for the answer," replied Decker.

"But David Katz built the Grill fifteen years ago," said Lancaster. "Are you telling me that the Russians were involved in this stuff here all that time ago?"

Bogart said, "People think the Russians just started messing with us. It was long before that. They've had spies all over this country ever since the Cold War started."

"But a spy operation in Burlington?" said Lancaster.

"Softer target," said Bogart. "Not as many resources. And for a lot of these people, I imagine they don't end up working in Burlington. I imagine that

Gardiner places them all over the country. This is just the launch pad."

"The map we found in the underground room confirms that," noted Decker. "These tentacles go all over the country, and to the largest metro areas."

"So, Gardiner's a traitor," exclaimed Lancaster. "And so is Peyton."

"If they're even American," pointed out Bogart. "Now we just have to find them and prove it. I'm calling in more assets, but we want to do this on the QT. We have no idea who else might be involved in this. That's why I didn't want to come to the station initially."

Lancaster looked stunned. "Wait a minute. Are you saying . . . ?"

"What he's saying, Mary, is that no one is above suspicion," said Decker. "And I agree with him."

Lancaster looked put out by this but remained silent.

Bogart gazed at Decker. "You've been in the trenches here. And know the territory better. How do you want to do this?"

"BOLOs on both Peyton and Gardiner. Maintain round-the-clock protection on Katz and Mitzi Gardiner. Right now, they're the only witnesses we have." He paused. "We need to get a search warrant for Gardiner's business. Hopefully we'll be able to find out who he's placed and where."

Decker eyed Mars. "And I'm afraid that Rachel Katz would have had to know about all this at some point."

"But she kept quiet and played along," said Mars.

"Looks that way."

"Maybe she had no choice," said Mars defensively.

"People always have the choice to either be a traitor or do the right thing," said Milligan sternly.

"And Mitzi Gardiner?" asked Lancaster.

Decker said, "She was an addict who set up her father. She probably didn't know about the possible spy operation, and she didn't need to know."

"But why have Gardiner marry her?" said Lancaster.

"What better way to make sure she doesn't do anything stupid than by having one of the people involved right there every day? And Mitzi turned out to be a great mom and doting wife. For Brad Gardiner it was probably a win-win. He was playing a role and I'm sure he was well compensated for it. There are worse ways to spend your life than being rich."

Jamison said, "I think I'd rather stay single."

Bogart said, "We'll run those leads down and search Gardiner's business. What else?"

"Bag and tag everything that was in the Grill's underground room."

Bogart said, "You were lucky that an *apparent* fire

broke out, so you could search the place and find that room." He stared pointedly at Decker.

"I'll always take luck when I can get it," replied Decker. "Even if I have to make it myself."

73

"Stripped clean," Bogart said over the phone to Decker. "Gardiner's office didn't have a thing left in it. He must have had an exit plan in place. As soon as you spooked him, he probably had the place wiped. Same thing for Peyton's apartment. Nothing left, if there was anything ever there."

Decker said, "We need to find out all we can about them, Ross. And his house and office have to be full of the guy's prints. Same for Peyton's apartment."

"I already have a team looking for that. Now, these 'trainees' you told me about at the American Grill?"

"Yeah?"

"I doubt any of them will show up for work. Peyton would have given them a heads-up. But I'll have people there just in case they do. And we'll track down where they were staying and search all those places too."

"Let me know if you turn up anything," said Decker.

"What are you going to do?"

"I'm going to take a little trip down memory lane."

Decker sat across from Lancaster at her house. In the background he could hear Earl and Sandy getting ready to go out.

Sandy burst into the room. She was a fireball of energy, always in a good mood, until she dropped into the blackness of despair, something that could occur within seconds. Her coat was half on and a ski cap covered her eyes.

She pulled it up and announced herself. "I know you," she said to Decker. "You're my mommy's partner. You're Amos Decker."

"And you're Sandra Lancaster." This was a little ritual that the pair had always engaged in.

Earl hustled in and grabbed Sandy's hand.

"We'll be back later," he said, glancing first at Decker and then at his wife.

"Right, hon, thanks," said Lancaster.

After the pair left, Decker refocused on his old partner. "Things going okay?" he asked.

"We're taking it day by day, hour by hour. I have to tell you that Earl teared up when I told him what you said to me on those bleachers that night. He's very grateful for your talking some sense into me."

"It was just my opinion, Mary. I can't judge you, because I haven't walked in your shoes."

"Well, I think you stopped me from making a big mistake. When things go bad, you need your family. You don't push them away."

"No disagreement from me."

"Okay, the case?"

"It's starting to make sense, but there are some gaps."

"*Some* gaps?"

"We know that Meryl Hawkins was set up. His daughter helped to frame him for the four murders. We don't know the exact motivation for the killings, but the fact that Katz had some sort of spy ring going on underneath his restaurant gets us close to it. He either had a falling-out or demanded more money, or whoever killed him was feeling threatened by him."

"Okay."

"Fast forward to today. Hawkins learns the truth from Karl Stevens. He gets out of prison and comes back here to enlist our aid to prove his innocence. Someone kills him that same night."

"And we still have no idea who that is."

"Since we've learned that the spy ring or whatever it is was still operating in Burlington, it seems to me that the spy ring's the likeliest culprits. Now we have Rachel Katz. She was the point person for a consortium of shell companies that Bogart has discovered have a Russian connection. Now, Rachel was waffling some. Look at her discussion with Melvin. They might have been afraid that she was going to turn on them. So they tried to kill her. They tried to kill me too. And they *did* kill Sally Brimmer."

"Because she impersonated Susan Richards. But we still don't know how someone got her to do that."

"No, we don't. That's still an open question, but they might have blackmailed her by threatening to tell Natty's wife about their affair. Now Mitzi Gardiner, overcome with guilt, tries to kill herself with pills. I think she was lucky she had a gun."

"Why?"

"Otherwise, her hubby might have saved her the trouble."

"You think he would have killed her?"

"I can't really assume otherwise. We found the underground room and all the evidence there pointing to some sort of spy ring. Peyton has made a run for it, as has Brad Gardiner. Now we've got two women in hospital beds and we're waiting for them to wake up to tell us what they know."

"*If* they wake up. And if they do, we have no guarantee they'll tell us anything."

"We have leverage over them. Mitzi tried to kill me. And there's no way that Rachel can plausibly argue that she had no knowledge of that room under the American Grill. If they talk, they can work a deal. If they won't they go to prison for a long time. But

I don't want to count on them. We have to keep pushing."

"The FBI may find out some stuff that could help us."

"Maybe. But they also might end up with a big fat zero. These people obviously had an exit plan in place, and they executed it pretty damn well."

"So we may be back at square one then, after all this time."

"Maybe not," he said.

"What do you mean?"

"It's occurred to me that this whole thing runs deeper than I previously thought. It seems to me that someone connected to this is hiding in plain sight."

"Okay, how do we find out who that is?"

"We let them do it for us," Decker said cryptically.

74

They had brought Mitzi Gardiner from the hospital in Trammel to the one in Burlington. Both women were in the same room so that their protection could be consolidated. Policemen and state troopers were arrayed around the hospital and outside their room. Across the street, counter-snipers were posted to prevent anyone from taking a long-range shot at the women.

Decker, Lancaster, and Mars were waiting outside the room because they had been told that Rachel Katz seemed to be coming around.

A few moments later, Natty showed up with Pete Childress and Captain Miller. Childress looked chastened and anxious, Miller grim and focused. Childress glanced at Lancaster, but would not look at Decker.

"Natty told me all the work you've done on this, Mary. Good job. In Burlington! I can hardly believe this crap is going on."

Lancaster said firmly, "Decker's done most of it, Superintendent. Without him, we'd be in the dark about everything." Childress seemed to wince a bit at her words.

He finally looked at Decker and nodded curtly. "Right, yes. Well, that's good, Decker. I'm, uh, I'm glad to see that you've been of assistance to the department."

"Maybe you can put a good word in for me with my obstruction case," replied Decker.

This time Childress perceptibly flinched. "Yes, well." He cleared his throat heavily. "I think that won't be a problem."

Miller added, "I'm *sure* it won't be. We're dismissing the charges, Amos."

"Good to know."

"Okay," said Childress. "Is she ready to talk yet?"

"Let's go see," said Decker.

They all trooped into the room. The beds were right next to each other, with Katz on the left and Gardiner on the right.

Gardiner had not regained consciousness. She looked like she was resting peacefully. Decker glanced at Katz. She was moaning slightly and seemed to be moving around a bit, as though she were in pain.

"Well?" said Childress sharply. He was pacing nervously around the room. "Is she going to talk, or did I get called down here for no reason?"

"The doctor's heading in momentarily," said Lancaster.

Childress kept pacing and shaking his head. He

looked up at Decker. "I know the FBI's in town. Have they made any progress on this?"

"Not that I know of," said Decker. "The spy ring got flushed out but had exit plans in place, it seems."

"I understand that Brad Gardiner managed to slip away from you," said Childress, a note of gleeful triumph in his tone.

"He managed to slip away from a lot of people," said Lancaster defensively.

Childress glared at her. "I don't think Decker, of all people, needs anyone to stand up for him, Mary."

"I made a mistake," conceded Decker. "But in my defense, Mitzi Gardiner was shooting at me at the time."

This statement seemed to take all the fire out of Childress. "Yeah, I guess I would have probably lost him too under those circumstances." He looked at Lancaster. "Where's the doctor?"

A moment later a female physician dressed in blue scrubs walked in and greeted them.

Decker said, "How is she?"

"Ms. Katz is stable. And we're weaning her off the pain medication slowly. There was a great amount of internal damage done. More than we thought initially. She had a very close call." She glanced at the monitor next to Katz's bed. "I can't guarantee anything as far as her being communicative. But let me just make clear that her physical well-being is my chief concern.

And if I see any adverse reaction in my patient, I will cut this off instantly. Understood?"

Childress didn't seem pleased by this but nodded and said gruffly, "Understood. Can we push forward, then? Because this is important."

The doctor went over to the machine hooked to the IV and manipulated some of the controls. A minute went by and nothing happened. Then Katz began to stir. Everyone drew closer when her eyes fluttered open, though they nearly instantly closed.

While the doctor was watching her closely, Katz opened her eyes once more and slowly looked around. When her gaze alighted on Mars she smiled tenderly.

"You . . . you saved . . ." Her voice trailed off and her eyes drooped.

Mars gripped her hand and smiled back. "You're getting better every day, Rachel. Doc says you're doing good. Real good."

Decker stepped forward to stand next to Mars. "Rachel, do you feel up to answering some questions?"

She looked up at him, her brow furrowed. "Questions?"

"Yes. Do you know what happened to you?"

Katz reached up and touched her shoulder. "Sh-shot."

"Yes. Someone tried to kill you."

"W-who?"

"We don't believe he has any personal connection to you. We think he was hired to try to kill you."

"I-I don't understand."

Mars gripped her hand again. "You were telling me about shades of truth, Rachel. Remember?"

She nodded slowly.

"Well, in this case I think shades of truth *will* set you free."

Decker said, "We found the room under the American Grill." He wanted to see her reaction to this, muddled as it might be because of the meds she was on.

She swallowed with difficulty and her eyes fluttered.

Natty came to stand next to Decker, with Childress next to him.

Natty said, "Ms. Katz. We know about Bill Peyton and Brad Gardiner. His wife is lying in the bed next to you. She almost died of a drug overdose."

Katz looked up at them one by one and her lips started to tremble. "M-Mitzi."

"Yes," said Childress. "Lots of people are dying around here, and, frankly, we need answers or others could die too."

Tears started to stream down Katz's face and she started to shake. An alarm on her monitor sounded.

The doctor immediately cranked her meds back up and Katz slowly slid back into unconsciousness as the alarm subsided.

"That's all for now."

"But we didn't get anything," protested Childress.

Natty put a hand on his boss's arm. "We'll come back. We'll get what we need. But she needs to rest now. Let her be."

Childress looked strangely at Natty, glanced at Decker with a hike of his eyebrows, and shrugged. "Fine. But we can't let this drag on."

"It won't," said Natty.

Decker looked at Natty for a long moment before glancing at Mars, who was still gripping Katz's hand and staring down at her. He used his finger to wipe the fresh tears away from her cheeks.

"It'll be okay, Melvin," he said quietly.

"You don't know that."

"No, I don't, but we can hope it will."

"Call me when she can talk again," said Childress brusquely. He turned and left.

Natty looked after him. "He's really afraid this is going to reflect badly on him. A spy ring operating right under his nose."

"I could see how that might give him some sleepless nights," remarked Decker.

Lancaster approached him. "So what now?"

He looked between Gardiner and Katz. Then his gaze went to the window and he suddenly turned thoughtful. He looked down at his feet, then back up. "The answer's out there," he said. "We just have to keep looking."

Lancaster said, "Where? We've got everything covered that we can. But you and I know that Peyton and Gardiner and their team of spies could be out of the country by now, especially if they had access to a private jet."

"Doesn't matter. I think we can still find the answers we need."

"How?" asked Natty.

Decker glanced at him. "You just never know when a helpful witness might pop up."

"What witness?" said Natty.

Decker headed to the door. "Let's see if I can show you. But first, we have to take care of something. And take care of it right now."

75

The uniformed man walked up the steps to the top floor of a building across the street from Burlington's main hospital. He carried a sniper rifle and took up a post at a window looking out onto the street. He glanced to his right and then his left. He blended in with the counter-snipers in the area.

He manipulated his scope, and drew his sightline.

He made sure to keep to the shadows as he pointed his weapon at the window opposite his position. In his mind he envisioned the space behind the closed blinds and worked some numbers into his shot calculations.

He recalibrated his scope and then took aim once more. His trajectory calculations complete, his finger slid to the trigger. He would fire three shots, in rapid succession.

He settled down his respiration and with it his heart rate. In truth, the distance was not a problem. However, he was, in some ways, firing blind. Yet he should still be able to hit his target.

His eye and grip as steady as humanly possible, he

squeezed the trigger slowly three times, moving his barrel in a precise pattern as he did so.

Then he dropped his rifle and sprinted to the back of the building. From there, he quickly made his way down the stairs and out the exit. He rushed down the street to where a car was waiting for him.

He jerked open the door and climbed in.

"Hit it," he said.

When the car didn't move, he looked over.

Four guns were pointed at his head.

Special Agent Alex Jamison, who held one of those guns, said, "You're under arrest."

Decker looked at the shards of glass strewn around the hospital room—the empty hospital room, although earlier that day it had housed both Rachel Katz and Mitzi Gardiner. They had been moved to another room well away from here, at Decker's request.

He brushed the floor with his foot where the three shots had hit. They lined up with Katz's bed. The woman, had she still been in the room, would have been dead.

But there had been no shots aimed at Gardiner.

Lancaster stood in the doorway watching Decker. When he glanced over at her, she shook her head, her lips in a straight line. It was as disapproving a look as Decker had ever seen on his old partner.

"Old sins cast long shadows," murmured Decker.

Lancaster nodded as Special Agent Bogart appeared beside her. "It's still a bitter pill to swallow," she said.

"I feel the same," replied Decker. He glanced at Bogart and then returned his gaze to Lancaster. "You ready?"

"I'm ready."

They climbed into Bogart's rental and drove over to the police station. They took the elevator to the homicide detectives' office. Lancaster opened the door and poked her head in. Natty was the only one in there, reading over a file at his desk.

Lancaster said, "Blake, you got a minute?"

He glanced over at her. "Sure, what's up?"

"You'll see. But you need to come with us. Now."

Natty looked puzzled and apprehensive. He slipped on his jacket, which had been hanging on the back of his chair, and walked out into the hall, where he saw Decker and Bogart.

"What's going on?" he said, looking at Lancaster.

"Like I said, you'll see," she replied.

"One thing, Natty," said Decker.

"What?"

"I need your gun."

"What?" said Natty, drawing back and looking stunned.

Decker put out his hand. "Your gun?"

"I'm not—"

"Yes, you are," said Bogart. He had drawn his weapon and was pointing it at Natty.

"What the hell is going on?" barked Natty. "You're breaking the law pointing your weapon at me."

"The price of admission to the party is your gun, Natty," said Decker. "No exceptions."

Natty slowly pulled his Glock from his shoulder holster and handed it, butt first, over to Decker, who kept his gaze on the other man the entire time before pocketing it.

"I don't know what the hell you guys are accusing me of," began Natty.

"Shut up, Blake," snapped Lancaster. "And follow us."

Along the way they picked up Captain Miller, who was also looking as stern as Decker had ever seen him.

"Captain?" began a worried-looking Natty.

But Miller held up his hand. "Not now, Natty."

They walked up one more flight of stairs and headed down the hallway to the end. Decker didn't knock. He just walked in.

Peter Childress looked up from his massive desk. Behind him on the wall were an array of photos of him with local politicians and at public events, together with a shelf full of citations and awards bestowed upon him over the years.

His brow furrowed as the group walked into his office. "What are you all doing here? Is there a development?"

"Yes, there is," said Decker. "Would you please stand up?"

"Excuse me?" said Childress.

"You know the drill, Pete," said Miller. "You have to stand up."

"What the hell for?"

Lancaster came forward and took out a pair of handcuffs. "Peter Childress, stand up. Now!"

"Where the fuck do you get off—"

Lancaster grabbed him by the suspenders and yanked him out of his chair.

"I'll have your badge, Lancaster!" he roared.

"I think you got that backwards," said Decker.

Lancaster roughly cuffed Childress's hands behind his back. "Peter Childress, you're under arrest for conspiracy to commit murder, conspiracy to commit espionage, conspiracy to commit money laundering, and about a hundred other charges, but those will do."

Childress froze.

Natty stood there staring at his boss, his jaw hanging open.

Childress roared, "You all are going to prison over this shit!"

Decker stood a step forward. "We've got the guy who tried to kill Rachel Katz."

"Tried!" said Childress before catching himself. "Wh-what are you talking about?"

"I had them transferred into another room, right

after we met there this morning," said Decker. "They're safe."

"Transferred? Nobody asked for my approval on that."

"Well, there was obviously a good reason for that."

"Look, I don't know what you're getting—"

He stopped when Decker started pacing around the room.

Decker counted his steps as he went. "We're about the same height, you and me, Pete. Same length of stride. Six paces over from the wall to the end of Katz's bed. Then two paces more to reach her chest."

Decker glanced at Natty, who was watching him, spellbound. "You remember him pacing like that this morning, Natty?"

The detective slowly nodded.

"He was measuring the distance from the wall to the bed, so he could feed it to the shooter. Otherwise, he'd have been shooting truly blind into that room."

"Bullshit! Prove it!" roared Childress.

In answer, Decker looked at Bogart.

The FBI agent took out his phone. "We got a warrant to tap your phone." He held up his phone. "You sent this text out thirty minutes after you left the hospital. It gives out the measurements to target the woman."

"And your guy was good," said Decker. "All three shots hit where they were supposed to."

"I don't know what 'guy' you're talking about."

Bogart said, "Well, that's funny, because the *guy* we just arrested for the attempted murders had your text on his phone. He's already talked to us, Childress, and he's already fingered you. Your ass is cooked."

"I . . . I," stammered Childress.

"But why not target Gardiner?" asked Decker. "Why just Katz?"

Childress shook his head and said nothing.

"Okay, did you tell Eric Tyson where Sally would be, Childress?" asked Decker. "When you arranged for *her* to be shot? Or did you just have her followed?"

The blood drained from Childress's face. He stole a glance at a stunned Natty.

"Look, Natty," began Childress. "It's . . . it's not like that. I . . ."

"You fuckin' prick!" screamed Natty. His hand went to his holster, but his gun wasn't there. He launched himself at Childress and managed to land a shot to the man's gut, doubling him over, before Decker, who had been slow to respond to the man's attack for some reason, grabbed him and pulled him away.

"Why?" screamed Natty. "What the hell did Sally ever do to you?"

"He used her, Natty," said Decker. "Like I suggested to you before. He forced her to impersonate Susan Richards, probably by threatening to tell your wife about your relationship. Then he got scared when he found out Sally was helping me. When she came out of the park with me, he had her shot."

Childress slowly straightened up, still gasping for air.

Miller stepped forward. "Not in all my forty years behind a badge have I seen anything like this. You're a disgrace, Childress."

"But you can make amends," said Decker. "By helping us."

Childress slowly shook his head. "This is a lot bigger than you think, Decker."

"All the more reason to stop it."

Childress said to Lancaster, "I want protection inside. I mean it."

"What are you scared of, Childress?" asked Lancaster.

"You all should be scared," said Childress. "Every last one of you."

76

As Childress was led away, Bogart said, "He might be right about that."

"Why?" asked Lancaster.

"We got back a report on those fingerprints you took of Bill Peyton."

"We couldn't find anything on him in the databases we had access to," said Lancaster.

"Well, we have access to a few more. Including some international ones, actually. And not the typical ones. But it was still very difficult for us, and that's what took so long. We actually had to turn to our friends at Mossad to score this information."

"The Israelis?" said Decker. "So I take it his name isn't Bill Peyton?"

"Not even close. His real name is Yuri Egorshin. And the general physical description given by the Israelis matches what you told us about Peyton."

"Let me guess—Russian," said Decker dryly.

"He was actually born in East Germany when the Wall was still up but came to the United States for college under a special program in place at the time. He went to Ohio State, same as you, Decker."

"How does that make sense?" asked Lancaster. "That a guy from that part of the world can just come here like that and go to school?"

"Well, he didn't come in announcing himself as a spy, and maybe then he wasn't technically one. He was a student with all the proper credentials and visas. And it showed him coming in from *West* Germany, not East Germany. Don't know how they managed that, but they did. He graduated and returned home. Sometime after that is when we believe he became associated with the KGB, or at least Mossad believes that."

"No, he was probably recruited by them before he came here for school, just so he could spy on us," said Jamison.

"That may be. Anyway, after the Wall came down, he officially became part of the FSB, the KGB's successor. He apparently worked very closely with a lot of the upper-echelon players there. Then he vanished. So, for the last twenty-odd years, no one knew where he was."

Decker said, "Well, he ended up in Burlington running a restaurant, and has for the last fifteen years. That would tie in with a Russian oligarch bankrolling Rachel Katz."

Lancaster said, "He didn't sound Russian when we

met with him. He seemed pretty American to me. Whatever that means," she added.

"That's the point," said Decker. "They don't all sound like villains from James Bond films. They're supposed to blend in and seem just like everyone else. And his time in the U.S. allowed him to do that. It made him very valuable."

Bogart said, "It's more than that, actually. We dug deeper and found out that Egorshin's mother, interestingly enough, was American. She was a defector after World War II. She sought asylum in Moscow and married a Russian, Anatoly Egorshin. He was an officer in the Russian army during World War II and afterward worked for the Soviet regime in East Germany."

"Like father, like son. And his mother could have taught him American ways and speech then," said Decker. "And that probably helped him adapt when he came here for college, and also when he returned to Burlington to operate the spy ring."

"I'm sure all of that made him even more valuable to the Soviets, and then the Russians," added Bogart.

"Have we made any progress on all the people they've placed over the years?" asked Lancaster.

"It's complicated. There were no records of those people at the Grill, just the ones they were still 'processing.' And they've all vanished, as have the kitchen staff. We'll interview the other wait staff who weren't part of the operation. They may be able to tell us something that will help us track them down. And we do have an opportunity, though, in that Gardiner placed a lot of these people. We're going to reach out to as many places as we can to determine if they hired any of his recruits."

"If they're still there," said Decker. "They may have all made a run for it."

"That could be. If so, at least we're rid of them, which is something. But we'll reverse engineer this thing as best we can. Even if we can't locate these folks, we can at least assess the damage they might have done at their jobs and try to turn that around."

"It's a long shot, but it's all we have right now," conceded Decker.

Natty said to Decker, "Now I know why you took my gun. I would've shot the sonofabitch."

"I know." Decker took out Natty's pistol and handed it back to him.

"Why would Childress have done this?" asked Natty.

"Why else? Money. I think when we dig into his finances, we'll find some secret accounts flush with cash."

"Do you think Childress has been working with them all this time?" asked Lancaster.

"Think back thirteen years ago, Mary."

"Okay, the four murders."

"We were newly minted homicide detectives."

"Right."

"So brand-new detectives were sent out on a four-person murder scene with no seasoned detective to head up the investigation."

She glanced at Natty. "That's right. There were more senior detectives available to investigate the case. Including you, Blake."

Decker said, "I looked back through the records from that night. You want to guess who assigned us to that case?"

Miller said disgustedly, "Childress, when he was heading up the detective division."

"That's right. He wanted inexperienced people on that case who would jump all over the forensic evidence that had been planted and never look anywhere else."

Decker glanced at Natty. "You might have seen what we didn't see back then, Natty."

"Maybe, maybe not. But I wouldn't have figured it out all these years later, I can tell you that. Not like you did."

"Well, hindsight is twenty-twenty. And I didn't figure it out in time to save Meryl Hawkins."

Bogart said, "We'll keep looking for Egorshin and Gardiner and the rest. In the meantime, you all have to be on your top guard. From everything we know so far, you blew up a substantial spy ring operating in this country. The odds are these people will hightail it out of the country to live to fight another day."

Decker said, "But there's always a chance that

they're going to hang back and exact their revenge. That's sort of a very KGB thing to do."

"Exactly," said Bogart. "In fact, there's no reason for you to stay around, Decker."

"No, there's unfinished business I have to take care of."

"Like what?" asked Bogart.

"Meryl Hawkins."

"You can't bring him back to life."

"No, but I can do the next best thing."

77

Both men stirred when her eyes fluttered open.

Decker and Mars were sitting next to Rachel Katz's bed in a hospital room that had no windows, for obvious reasons. Mitzi Gardiner had been moved to another windowless room, which was also heavily protected by both local police and FBI agents. They were taking no chances now.

Mars stood and took her hand. "Hey, how do you feel?" he asked.

She slowly nodded and managed a weak smile. "Better." She glanced at Decker and her expression grew solemn. "How much do you know?" she asked cautiously.

"Well, Bill Peyton is really a Russian named Yuri Egorshin, and Brad Gardiner has been placing Egorshin's spies all over the country for years now from an operation initiated at the American Grill. And we also know about the secret room underneath your restaurant where they create fake identities, backgrounds, and maybe even faces for these folks. Other than that, not much."

Katz put a hand to her face and groaned. She finally withdrew her hand and looked at the lines and tubes running over her body.

"Am I going to recover?"

"Yes, you are," said Mars. "We were just waiting for you to fully wake up."

Her mouth quivered. "I don't know what to say."

"I'll take a *shade* of the truth," said Decker. "Unless you want to tell us the whole thing."

"Can you lift my head a bit?"

Mars hit the bed control to accomplish this.

After she was settled, Katz drew a long breath. "The first thing you have to understand is that when I married David, I knew about none of this. There's still a lot I don't know."

"He'd already opened the Grill before you met," said Decker.

"Yes. And our life was good. We had the restaurant and I had my business. And he was already working on other projects. Everything was aboveboard, at least as far as I knew."

"And then the meeting with Don Richards?"

"And he was dead." Katz started to weep.

Mars handed her a tissue, which she used to dab at her eyes.

"I was devastated. It hit me out of the blue. I couldn't fathom why someone would want to kill him."

"But then?" said Decker expectantly.

"But then I was thinking of selling the Grill. I was tired of Burlington and the memory of what had happened to David. I just wanted to start over fresh."

"And something happened to make you change your mind?"

"It was Bill Peyton or this Yuri person. I had told him I was thinking of selling out. He didn't tell me a lot, but what he did tell me was stunning. He said that David was a criminal. A member of an organization that had done terrible things. And that his death was a result of that membership. He had apparently done something to anger them. They had found out and made the decision to kill him."

"Why kill the Richards family?"

"I don't know. Peyton never told me."

"Why didn't you go to the police?" asked Decker.

"Because Peyton told me that the other members of this organization were still very much around. And that if I wanted to stay alive, I would do exactly as they told me to do. They even threatened to harm my parents in Wisconsin. And my sister in California. They knew where they lived and everything."

"What did they want you to do?"

"Most importantly, I was never to sell the Grill. They wanted to keep it running for some reason."

"As I said, they were operating a spy ring in a secret room under the restaurant," said Decker.

"I didn't know that," said Katz, putting her hands

over her face. "After David died, I never really went there."

"What else?"

"They told me that they would fund other business ventures. They allowed me to pick the projects and they provided the money. I assumed they did something similar for David."

"They were laundering money," said Decker. "Probably dirty oligarch money."

Katz slowly nodded. "I thought it might be something like that."

"Did you meet with anyone other than Bill Peyton on these matters?"

"Yes, there were other men. Very hard-looking men. We never met in Burlington. They flew me to Chicago. We'd meet there."

Mars said, "I wonder why they just didn't buy the Grill from you and keep doing what they were doing. They wouldn't have had to explain anything to you."

"I wondered about that too," said Katz. "But from some of the things they said, they liked, well, legitimate people fronting what they were doing. If you buy a business, there are always questions and inspections and there are ways for things to go wrong. They had set up a relationship with my husband and they wanted to keep it going exactly the same. That was clear from my discussions with them. Only now it was me, not David."

"What about Mitzi Gardiner?"

Katz looked puzzled. "That was the very odd thing. They wanted me to help her. She was a drug addict. But they paid for her rehab, and when she came out of that, they paid for a complete change in her appearance, education, clothes, plastic surgery, everything. They had me become her mentor. Teach her how to conduct herself, work in business, give her contacts. Just help mold her."

Mars looked at Decker. "Why would they do that?"

"She provided the patsy for the murders, her father."

"I get that," said Mars. "But why not just kill her? We talked about this before. And I don't buy the explanation that they were worried about the police digging deeper. Hell, she was a drug addict. They could have just made her OD and no one would have thought that she was murdered."

"That's a good question that I don't have the answer to. Yet."

"I didn't know that Hawkins was innocent," said Katz. "After Peyton met with me, I thought he'd been hired to kill David and the others."

"Didn't you have a problem with helping the daughter of the man who you believed had killed your husband?" asked Decker.

"I did, at first. But she had done nothing wrong. At least that I knew. And she was so, I don't know, fragile. And lost. I guess I just ended up wanting to help her. Making something good come from something so awful." She paused and clutched the sheets with her hand. "I guess I should have gone to the police, but I was just so scared. As time went by, I just convinced myself that it was . . . that it was legitimate somehow. I was just building up my businesses and living a nice life." She paused again. "But that was just me lying to myself. It's another reason I never remarried. How could I ever trust someone after what happened with David?"

"Well, considering that a prominent policeman was involved with Egorshin and his gang, you were probably wise not to go to the police," noted Decker.

"What . . . what will happen to me?" she said fearfully.

"I don't know."

Mars said, "Hey, Decker, like she said, she was terrified. They threatened her. She didn't know that they were spies."

"I get that, Melvin. I really do. But that part is out of my hands." He turned his attention back to Katz. "But your cooperating with the FBI will only act in your favor. You might not spend any time in prison." He paused. "In fact, I think it far more likely that you end up in witness protection. These people have long memories and assets in the most unlikely places. And they have no problem killing anyone in their way.

They tried to kill you again while you were in the hospital."

"Oh my God!" Katz drew a long breath and squeezed Mars's hand. "A part of me, a big part of me, is so glad that all this is finally out in the open. It's actually such a relief. It was tearing me apart."

Mars nodded. "Speaking for someone who's seen a lot of deception in his life, I can understand that. The truth is always better. Even if it really hurts."

She glanced nervously at Decker. "Witness protection?"

"It's better than prison."

"Yeah," agreed Mars. "Just about anything is."

She looked at him curiously. "You sound like you speak from experience."

"What better place is there to speak from?" replied Mars.

78

Decker and the house.

Again.

Where he'd found the bodies of his family. He couldn't seem to stay away, even with everything else going on. It was a magnet and he was a chunk of metal.

His phone dinged. It was from the ME. As he read down the email, he learned that more sophisticated tests had been performed on the DNA found under Abigail's fingernails. The results were shocking. It was confirmed that an additional set of DNA had been found under the nails, meaning a third party *was* involved. But they conclusively ruled out that party being a blood relation to Meryl Hawkins.

So that leaves out Mitzi Gardiner. So who then? Who's left?

As he sat in his car absorbing this, he suddenly pulled his gun and pointed it at the passenger window. At the figure who had appeared there. Then he lowered his weapon and unlocked the door.

Jamison climbed in and looked at him.

"Didn't mean to startle you," she said.

"Sure you did," he groused. "But I could have shot you."

"I have faith in your judgment, at least most times," she replied, drawing a sharp glance from him.

He resettled his gaze on the house, even as his hands played nervously over the steering wheel.

"I guess you're wondering what I'm doing here?" she asked.

"No, I'm just assuming that you thought you'd find me here when you went to the Residence Inn and I wasn't there."

"Well, you'd be wrong."

He glanced at her again.

"I was here *before* you." She pointed down the street. "My car's right over there. I saw you drive in. And I'm not alone."

Another figure appeared at the driver's-side window and tapped on the glass.

An annoyed Decker unlocked the doors once more and Mars climbed into the backseat.

"So you were spying on me?" Decker said angrily.

"How could we be, when we got here first?" said Mars. "I just wanted to see your old home, Decker. It's nice."

Decker gazed out the window. "It *was* nice," he said quietly. "The first and probably only home I'll ever have."

"Don't be too sure about that," said Mars. "Life throws you curveballs, you and I both know that."

Decker glanced in the mirror at him. "And your point?"

"Never say never. You just don't know. My future was death row. You think I ever thought I'd be here, today?"

"You were an unusual case, Melvin."

Jamison snorted. "And you're not?"

Decker fell silent and shifted his gaze to the house again.

It was late, but there was a light on in the upstairs on the left. That had been Molly's bedroom. He supposed it might be the Hendersons' little girl's room now. He didn't know why her light was on at this hour; maybe she was sick and her mother was tending to her.

He closed his eyes when powerful images and lights started to bombard him, like before. Their deaths spilling over him, threatening to bury him. He began to shake.

"Decker, you okay?" said a voice.

He felt something grip his arm and his shoulder. He opened his eyes to see Jamison's hand on his arm, and Mars clenching his shoulder. Jamison was looking at him anxiously. Mars the same.

He blinked rapidly, and, thankfully, the images vanished.

"I've been having . . . some issues."

"What kind?" asked Jamison.

He drew a long breath. "The memories of finding my family dead have started to just empty out of my head, over and over, the colors, the images, the . . ." He rubbed his temples. "I don't know when it will happen, and I can't seem to make it stop."

"But it has stopped now, right?" asked Mars while Jamison looked on with a horrified expression.

Decker glanced at her but then quickly looked away after seeing her tortured features. "For now."

"When has it happened?" asked Jamison quietly.

"Once when I was in my room." He glanced at Mars. "When you fell asleep in my room. I barely made it to the toilet. Then I went outside in the rain. I thought . . . I thought I was really losing it. Then, other times." He thumped the side of his head painfully.

"Had it happened to you before you came back to town this time?" asked Jamison.

"I know what you're going to say, Alex. I know I can't live in the past."

"Knowing is one thing. Doing something about it is another."

Decker didn't respond.

"What makes you come back here, Amos?" asked Mars. "I mean, Burlington, I get. But why come back to the house where it happened?"

In his mind's eye, Decker saw himself climbing, bone-tired, out of his car after an exhausting shift at work. It was nearly midnight. He was supposed to have been home hours before. But he had decided a case he was working on might get a breakthrough if he put some more time into it. He had called Cassie and told her. She hadn't been happy about it, because they were supposed to go to dinner with her brother, who was in town staying with them. But she told him she understood. She told him she knew his casework was very important to him.

My damn casework.

And then she told him that they would just go out to dinner the next night. Her brother was staying over, so they'd have another opportunity.

Another opportunity that never came to be.

Those were the last words that Decker had ever spoken to his wife. He had gone into the house with the intention of slipping into bed without waking her, and then taking her, Molly, and his brother-in-law out to breakfast the next morning. As a surprise, to make up for that night.

And then he had walked into his home and entered a nightmare.

His life had never been the same. Not in any conceivable way.

And the bottom line was clear to him.

I was not there when my family really needed me. I failed them. I failed myself. And I don't know if I can live with that.

"Decker?" prompted Mars.

"I guess I keep coming back here," began Decker. "To imagine how it could have been . . . different."

The light in the upstairs bedroom winked out. For some reason that made Decker withdraw even further into whatever hole he had mentally dug for himself.

His head was throbbing. It was like his brain was melting.

Something tapped on the window.

"Who the hell else did you bring?" snapped Decker.

He glanced at Jamison, who sat rigid in her seat. He eyed Mars in the mirror. He was sitting exactly the same way as Jamison.

Decker slowly turned to his left.

And saw the figure there.

And the gun pointed at his head.

He looked to his right and saw a figure and a gun at the passenger window.

Two others were at the two rear doors.

The driver's-side door was wrenched open and something struck him so hard on the back of the head that it drove his face into the steering wheel.

And that was the last thing he remembered.

79

When Decker came to, he had a vision of something that felt familiar. When he opened his eyes fully and looked around, he understood why.

He was in the Richardses' old home, sitting on the floor.

In the kitchen, where Don Richards and David Katz had died.

He felt the zip ties around his wrists and ankles.

He looked next to him and saw Jamison and Mars similarly bound. They were staring across at the doorway where a man was standing.

Bill Peyton, or more correctly, Yuri Egorshin, did not seem like a happy man.

There were three other men in the room. They all looked tough, hardened, chips of iron with guns in their hands. Decker didn't recognize any of them from the American Grill. To him, they all looked like muscle. Russian muscle, which was pretty damn intimidating.

Egorshin pulled up a chair and sat down opposite the three bound people.

"You have royally messed up my work, Decker," he said quietly. "I hope you realize that."

"Well, it's sort of my job."

"If the optics weren't so bad and other ... conditions not so adverse to me, I could probably beat your bullshit search at the Grill. You found all that stuff without a warrant. None of it would be admissible."

"Yeah, but the whole Russian spy thing? I'm not sure the Fourth Amendment really applies to protect people like you."

"And there we have the limits of the democracy you Americans tout so fiercely."

Decker glanced out the window into the darkness. "I'm surprised that you would bring us here."

"What? You mean witnesses? Are you concerned the DeAngelos might have seen us?" Egorshin stopped and his lips set in a firm line. "You don't have to worry about them. Whatever they might have seen, they will be able to tell no one about."

"You didn't have to do that," said Decker grimly, his features turning angry.

"Do you know what Mr. DeAngelo told me right before I put a bullet in his head?"

Decker said nothing.

"He told me that all he wanted to do was retire down south. I saved him the expense. And I needed ... privacy, to deal with you and your friends."

Decker felt sick to his stomach about the fate of

the DeAngelos. He said, "You've wasted a lot of time hanging around here. You could be gone from the country. Now it's too late. It's death penalty time for you."

"Please don't worry about me. I'm well provided for. I have assets in places you couldn't even imagine."

"I don't know, my imagination is pretty good. And if you're thinking about Peter Childress, you better have other assets."

"This does not concern me in the least."

"Why's that?"

"For the same reasons that the DeAngelos do not concern me."

Jamison blurted out, "You had Childress killed?"

Egorshin looked at his watch. "With confirmation twenty minutes ago. No, the assets of which I speak go far higher than a police superintendent in a nothing place like this."

"What do you want with us?"

"After every intelligence operation there must be a debriefing." Egorshin spread his hands wide. "So this, this is my debriefing."

"We're not going to tell you anything," barked Jamison.

"I cannot tell *you* how many times I have heard that over the course of my career." He held out a hand. One of his men pulled something from his jacket and handed it to Egorshin. It looked like a metal billy club.

Egorshin slid a lever on the side of the club, leaned over, and tapped Mars with the end of it. Mars instantly cried out as volts of electricity shot through him. He slumped over to the side, his breathing ragged.

"Melvin!" screamed Jamison. She tried to reach out to him, but merely fell onto her side. With a nod from Egorshin, she was pulled up and slammed back against the wall.

Decker had never once taken his gaze off the Russian. "What sort of information?"

"How much you know. Your forward-looking plans. Anything at all that would be helpful to me."

"And then you'll what, just let us go?"

"No. I will not lie to you about that, because I would not want someone to make false promises to me in such a situation. What I offer you, in exchange for your information, is this." He slipped a pistol from his jacket pocket and tapped the muzzle. "One bullet to each of your brains. You will feel nothing, I promise."

"Yeah, painless, instant death. I've heard that before. It still doesn't appeal to me."

"The information?" said Egorshin. "Or shall I give your friend another zap?" He held out the electric prod.

Decker said, "We now know pretty much everything. Rachel Katz has given her statement implicating you. We have all the information from the underground room. We've raided Brad Gardiner's office."

"And found nothing since there is nothing there."

"Well, there are other avenues of pursuit. We know you've planted spies all around the country."

Egorshin ominously took out a muzzle suppressor and spun it onto the barrel of his pistol. "What else?"

"Mitzi Gardiner will fill in the rest."

"Doubtful. Where is she?"

"Still at the hospital, under heavy guard."

"You miss my point."

Decker looked at him thoughtfully. "You didn't try to kill her at the hospital. And I wonder why you even kept her alive all these years."

Egorshin looked at one of his men and pointed to the doorway leading into the kitchen. The man left and came back a few moments later with Brad Gardiner. His hands were bound behind him and he looked disheveled and exhausted.

Decker glanced up at him. "You hung around too. Pretty stupid."

"Well, it wasn't his choice," said Egorshin. "It was mine."

"Is his name even Brad Gardiner?" said Jamison. "Or is he Russian, like you?"

Egorshin rose. "No, he's American. Like David Katz. They were in it just for the money. A lot of money. Americans love their money."

Jamison said, "Katz didn't make much money before

being killed. He just owned the American Grill. Hardly an empire."

Egorshin shook his head wearily. "Where do you think he got the money to start his career? This was before he even moved here. His Mercedes and his expensive clothes and his investment portfolio worth millions and the down payment for the Grill and the various lines of credit? And how they were paid off so quickly? Katz was a marginal talent who didn't want to work too hard for his fortune."

"How did you two meet up?" asked Decker.

"Doesn't matter. In much the same way I met up with this one," he said, motioning to Gardiner. "A necessary though distasteful part of my job."

Gardiner wouldn't look at any of them. His gaze remained downcast. He was visibly trembling.

Jamison eyed Gardiner. "So you sold out your country for money. That makes you a traitor."

"And traitors deserve to be executed," said Egorshin.

Before anyone could react, the Russian placed the pistol against Gardiner's temple and pulled the trigger.

The bullet blew through the man's head and the slug plowed into the far wall of the kitchen. Brad Gardiner fell where he had stood a moment before.

80

They all stared at the body lying on the floor of the kitchen.

"Damn," exclaimed Mars, who had recovered from the cattle prod shock and had sat up, his back flat against the wall.

Decker looked up at Egorshin. "Why kill him?"

"It reduces complications for me."

"Okay. Why a restaurant, of all things?"

"What better way to become 'Americanized'? Interacting with the customers, you learn everything: slang, dialect, mannerisms, pop culture, sports. Americans love their sports. French fries! Social media etiquette. Simply becoming Americans. Back in Russia, it would have taken us years to accomplish what I was able to have my operatives do in a few months. It was simple, but most brilliant things have an underlying simplicity."

"And the underground room?"

"Well, we couldn't exactly do up in the restaurant what was required."

"We saw the operating room."

Egorshin waved his hand dismissively. "Some of my superiors still dwelled in the Cold War days. We rarely used it. Instead, we simply recruited from our assets those who already looked westernized."

"It took us a while to figure out where the entrance was."

"May I ask how you did so?"

"Space dimensions were off compared to the area outside the kitchen."

Egorshin wagged his finger at Decker. "One of my men at the restaurant reported that you seemed overly interested in speaking with one of the wait staff. You were clearly a man to watch."

"And to attempt to kill?" said Decker. "On the way back from Mitzi's?"

"Forgive me, it is the usual way in which we deal with difficulties."

"Eric Tyson and Karl Stevens had KI tats on their arms."

"My father was privileged to work for the KI, and so we had some of our recruits get that tattoo. However, we hid it among many hate groups' symbols to throw off detection."

"Recruits?"

Egorshin held up his hand. "That goes beyond what I can say. It is a game, and you do the same to us. But let us never lose sight of the fact that it is a game with very real consequences." He glanced at Gardiner's body.

He sat back down and slipped the gun into his waistband.

Decker said, "One thing I don't get. Mitzi said her husband placed people in high-end jobs, in law, finance, high tech, government."

"And your point?"

"Even with the new identities and such, it would be difficult for your agents to survive a background check. You can create the right docs and all, paper the schools they went to, but the background check will go to where they attended school and lived, talk to old neighbors, relatives, teachers, coworkers, and all the rest."

"That is true. And that is why we approached it in a different way."

"How?"

"First of all, Mitzi had no idea what her husband really did. She only told you what she had been told. As a matter of fact, he did *not* place our people in these so-called high-end jobs. You're right, the scrutiny would have been rather intense."

"So what did you do then?"

Egorshin smiled. "'Low-end' jobs are much better sources for intelligence collection."

"What do you consider 'low-end' jobs?" asked Jamison.

"For example, chefs for wealthy people. Security guards at sensitive corporate facilities. You would be astonished how lacking they are in vetting their security forces. We would never do it that way in Russia. Americans outsource everything. And these companies cut costs. And background checks are expensive and take time. We deploy personal drivers for executives and former government officials. It is amazing how chatty they are in their cars, as though the driver is deaf. Flight attendants on private aircraft. Domestic help, cleaning crews, and nannies with your class of movers and shakers, particularly on both coasts. Personal assistants to these same people. IT personnel who gain access to passwords and clouds and the most sensitive data, and who are on-site listening to everything. Attendants of all ilk at high-end hotels, restaurants, spas, and private retreats. Again, Americans talk as though these peons do not exist. And these peons just soak it up. Indeed, I have been on your Acela train. I simply sit there and listen to people loudly talking on their phones: lawyers and corporate executives, journalists and television news presenters, and even your government officials, giving away the most critical data like it is nothing. In my country they would be shot. I turn my recorder on and sip my drink and it is so easy. That is why we have people who work there and also wherever sensitive information can be captured by seemingly insignificant people. America is one gigantic leaking balloon and it is truly wonderful."

Jamison glanced worriedly at Decker, who kept staring at Egorshin.

"The list of these types of occupations goes on and on. The opportunities for us are endless. My agents are well trained for all that they have to do. Their work credentials are authentic. Then they just have to do their jobs and the information flows nonstop. We will bury your country without firing a shot or launching one missile. We won't have to, because you are simply defeating yourself by your own stupid carelessness. And we will be there to step in as the victor."

Jamison said, "I thought all of your spying was done in the cyber world now. Hacks and bot armies to sway public opinion."

Egorshin shrugged. "Cyber warfare certainly has its place. And it has worked well for my country against the United States and others. But while bot armies and hacking and message multiplication and the spread of false stories are effective, there is, in my opinion, no substitute for boots on the ground, what you call human intelligence. People gathering information directly from the source. Humans can deceive in infinitely flexible, subtle ways that you cannot duplicate by writing lines of code."

"I guess I can see that," conceded Jamison.

"Now tell me about Mitzi," said Egorshin.

"Why?" asked Decker.

"I have an interest. What will happen to her?"

"No telling yet. Depends on her degree of guilt."

"She may have no guilt at all."

"We believe that she set up her father."

"No, she didn't."

"How can you possibly know that?" asked Jamison.

Decker was staring strangely at Egorshin but remained quiet. He closed his eyes, and in the depths of his memory he reread his most recent email from the medical examiner.

No familial ties to Meryl Hawkins.

Decker opened his eyes and refocused on Egorshin. "I'll give you a little more debriefing. I just found out that the DNA under Abigail Richards's nails was contaminated with a third party's DNA. I thought it was Mitzi Gardiner. But the test showed the third party was unrelated to Meryl Hawkins."

"So the person was not Mitzi," said Jamison.

Decker didn't seem to hear her. He kept his gaze on the Russian. "You know, I always wondered about the name."

"Peyton is a typical American surname."

"No, not your fake name. Mitzi's *real* name."

"Why wonder about that?" said Egorshin, his features tightening a bit.

"I looked it up a while back because it's unusual for an American. Mitzi is a nickname that Germans give daughters who are named Maria. *You* were born in Germany."

Egorshin shook his head. "My father was Russian.

Egorshin is not German. And East Germany was far more like Russia than West Germany."

"Maybe your father was Russian, but you and your family still lived in East Germany. And your mother was American."

"I see you have done your homework. But what is your point? Mitzi Gardiner is not German. She was born here."

"Yes, she was. And you're sixty-two years old. While Mitzi is forty."

"Decker," said Mars. "What are you getting at?"

Decker kept his focus on Egorshin. "Mitzi's mom worked in the cafeteria at Ohio State while you were a student there. At age twenty-two you would have probably been in your senior year. She was a few years older than you."

Egorshin eased back in his seat.

Jamison's jaw lowered. "Wait a minute. Are you saying?"

Decker said, "It *was* Mitzi's DNA under those nails, but it wouldn't show that she was Meryl's daughter, because she wasn't. *You're* her father. You got Lisa pregnant in college. Did she have the baby when you were still there?"

"Damn," muttered Mars.

Egorshin said in a subdued tone, "The day after she was born, I was recalled to my country."

"So you just left, without a word?"

"I loved Lisa. I . . . wanted to be with her. Raise the

child. We named her after my paternal grandmother, Maria. But I told Lisa about the name Mitzi."

"Well, it seems to have stuck around. More than you did."

"I could not stay. It was impossible."

"So, she met Meryl, they got married. He adopted Mitzi. They probably never told her about it, she just thought Meryl was her real father, and they moved eventually to Burlington." Decker paused. "And that's why you chose *this* town for your operation when the time came."

Egorshin looked at his men and then stood and paced. "I wanted . . . to see what had become of her. When I arrived here to do my . . . work, she was . . ."

"A drug addict."

"It was terrible to think that she was that way. And my dear Lisa."

"Had cancer."

"Yes. There was no hope."

"What did you do then?"

"I arranged to meet Mitzi through someone."

"Her dealer, Karl Stevens?"

"Yes. I told her that I had known her mother a long time ago and I wanted to help them. I got her mother medicine and gave it to Mitzi."

"But you also set her father up for murder, with her help."

Egorshin suddenly stopped pacing and roared, "He was not her father! *I* was!"

This outburst didn't faze Decker. "You left, he didn't. He raised her. You didn't. He did his best to help her. You didn't. That's what I call a father."

Egorshin started to pace again, rubbing the back of his head in his anxiety.

Decker watched him. "You needed to get rid of David Katz. Why?"

"He was like this one," said Egorshin, motioning to the dead Gardiner. "Whatever we gave him was not enough."

"But why kill the Richardses?"

"You think we didn't have Donald Richards in our pocket too?"

"He was helping you launder funds through the bank and he wanted more?"

"It became untenable. So we acted."

"How did you get Mitzi to go along?"

He shrugged. "I told her things about Meryl that . . . that made her side with me. I told her I wanted to help her mother. Lisa died peacefully because of me."

"No, she died with the knowledge that her husband was an accused killer. I don't think that qualifies as peaceful."

"I don't care what you think, Decker."

"So everything was great. Until Meryl came back here to prove his innocence." Decker paused again. "And you went to the Residence Inn and you murdered a dying man."

"There was no other way."

"And you set up Susan Richards for the murder and she ends up a supposed suicide apparently from guilt. But you killed her too."

"These matters *had* to be dealt with."

"And I guess we're next."

Egorshin sat back down. "I will tell you this, Decker. There is one way for you to live. And only one. I want Mitzi. I want her to come with me."

Decker shook his head. "I don't see how that's possible. She's still unconscious in the hospital, surrounded by guards."

Egorshin pulled out his gun. "Then perhaps you should think very hard on it, unless you want me to shoot one of your friends. Which one? I'll let you pick."

When Decker said nothing, he pointed at Mars. "You, stand up."

"Wait," said Decker. "I'm the one you want. Take me out."

"No, Mr. Decker, I'm counting on you to solve my dilemma." He pointed at Mars. "Stand up. Now. Or I'll shoot you where you sit."

Mars glanced over at Decker and shook his head. "Man, this has R43 wide gap seal written all over it. I mean, shit."

Egorshin barked, "Get up. Now!"

"Okay, but I need some help. I *am* tied up."

Egorshin looked over at two of his men and

nodded. The men went over to Mars, bent down, and each grabbed an arm.

As they began to lift Mars up and the bottoms of his shoes touched the floor, he exploded off his feet, headbutting the man on the right, cold-cocking him. Mars whirled and caught the other man right underneath the chin with his shoulder, slamming him into the wall. His head bounced off the hard surface, his eyes rolled back in his head, and he fell to the floor.

The moment that Mars launched into action, Decker had catapulted to his feet. Even with his feet bound, he squatted down and then leapt forward, slamming into a distracted Egorshin so hard that the FSB man was knocked completely off his feet. He soared backward, hit the sink, flipped over it, and crashed right through the window, the shattered glass ripping at him as he fell out of sight outside.

The remaining man aimed his gun at Decker and was about to pull the trigger when the sound of a shot pierced the room.

The man looked down at his chest and saw the red spot dead center there.

Decker and Mars stared over at Jamison. She had managed to roll forward, swing her legs between her wrists, grab one of the fallen men's guns, take aim and fire, all within the span of about three seconds.

The last man fell to his knees and then toppled forward.

Jamison searched one of the men, found a clasp

knife, and used it to free herself and then Decker and Mars.

Decker snatched up a gun and raced toward the front door, even as he heard a car start up. He got to the front door in time to fire at the taillights of the car being driven by Egorshin. Within a few seconds, though, it was gone.

Jamison grabbed her phone from her pocket. She called Bogart and filled him in on what had just happened.

She clicked off. "He's sending a team over here. And he's put out a BOLO."

Decker was still staring off into the night. "I'm not sure that will be enough."

Mars gave her a hug. "Damn, Alex, that was some fancy footwork back there. And nice shooting, girl."

"Thanks. But what the hell was that R43 stuff you were talking about?"

Decker turned and looked at her. "R43 wide gap seal. It was the University of Texas's favorite run option when Melvin played for them. The right tackle helps the right guard by chipping the DT, and then he and the tight end seal off the defensive end while the wideout drives the cornerback to the sideline. At the same time, the tight end peels off from the DE and engages the strong safety. That left Melvin to go wide through the gap straight to a one-on-one with the outside linebacker."

"And that would be Mr. Buckeye Decker," said a grinning Mars.

Decker looked chagrined. "He scored three touchdowns in the game on that one play, and all three times he ran right over my butt."

"Hey, man, you did your best. And you guys played us hard. I got stopped quite a few times early on in that game. But when life gives you lemons, you know what you do?"

Jamison made a face and said, "Yeah, you make lemonade. Everybody knows that."

Mars shook his head. "No, Alex, you score *touchdowns*."

Jamison said, "So by calling out that play, you told Decker what you were going to do? Take out two guys. And then Decker figured out what he was going to do?"

"That's right."

"Maybe I should start watching football, just in case that ever comes in handy again with you two."

"Hey, what life tells you is, you just never know," said Mars.

"You just never know," repeated Decker, as he turned back around and stared out into the night.

81

Decker handed her another tissue and then sat back.

Mitzi Gardiner dabbed at her eyes as she sat there in her hospital bed. She had finally regained consciousness and the doctors expected her to make a full recovery.

Decker had told her some, but not all, of what had happened. But he had told her about her husband's death. And also about his participation in Egorshin's spy operation.

"I always wondered why a guy like Brad would have chosen someone like me," she said, sniffling.

"Don't sell yourself short."

"And I can't believe that this Bill Peyton was a Russian spy named, what was it again?"

"Egorshin. And that's sort of the point. To make it not obvious."

He had decided not to tell her that Egorshin was her real father, because Decker considered Meryl Hawkins to have earned that distinction. And he wasn't sure the fragile Mitzi could actually handle the truth.

"I guess." She tossed the tissue into the trash can next to her bed and looked at him. "That's not all, is it?"

"No, it's not."

"You're here for other reasons?"

"Yes."

"What happened to Rachel?"

"She's been charged, but can probably work a deal. Since we still haven't located Egorshin, her life is in danger. She might end up in witness protection once she tells the Feds all she knows."

"But won't he come after me too?"

"Doubtful. He seems to have liked you."

"He *did* help us. I remember he got painkillers for my mom, though I knew him as Bill Peyton. I still can't believe he was a Russian."

"Yeah, but he wasn't so kind to your father."

"He told me things about my dad. Not good things."

"And they were lies. He told me they were. He just wanted to get you on his side, Mitzi. That was all."

"But I believed him. And I helped send my father to prison."

"Did you know that they planned to frame him for murder?"

She shook her head. "Absolutely not. I had no idea. I didn't know what was going on really. I was so strung out back then."

"They probably wanted to keep you in the dark,

because they couldn't count on your not telling someone. But after he was charged? And then convicted?"

"I didn't know what to think. Part of me thought he was guilty."

"I think he figured out, at least partly, your complicity. But he wasn't going to do anything to implicate you in the deaths. So he just kept quiet and went to prison. It was only after he ran into Karl Stevens that his mind changed. He was dying, after all, and what Stevens told him about your involvement and the people behind it probably didn't sit well with him. So he came back here to clear his name."

"I can't say I blame him." She lay back and closed her eyes. "I'm so tired." Then she snapped forward. "Oh my God, my son, where is—"

"He's fine. He's with child services. He knows nothing about any of this, though."

"I . . . I can't believe I just thought of him."

And the woman did look truly stunned at her thoughtlessness, Decker observed.

"Well, you just came out of a drug coma. You can't be thinking too clearly."

"You're being too kind, Decker." She hesitated. "But I get the feeling that's about to change."

He stood and looked down at her. "Do you know how many people go through life without a second chance to get it right?"

"I . . . what do you mean exactly?"

"You messed up, Mitzi. You helped frame your father. He suffered greatly for that. He went to prison, where terrible things happened to him."

"I know all that. I was . . . I was out of my mind on drugs, Decker."

"And now you're not. You're clean and sober and hopefully thinking clearly."

"What do you want me to do?" she said warily.

"How about the right thing."

"And what is that precisely?"

"You go into court and you make a statement, clearing your father, returning him his good name, and accepting responsibility for what you did."

"And then I go to prison? That's what you're asking me to do, isn't it?"

"Well, I think I have the right to ask, considering you did your best to blow my head off back at your house."

"I . . . I can't go to prison. My son will have nobody."

"Maybe you won't have to."

"How?" she said pleadingly.

"This is not a typical case. I might be able to get the authorities to make a deal. You tell us what really happened, your father's reputation is restored, and you go on with your life."

"Do you really think that's possible?"

"Anything is possible. But aside from the obvious

benefits to you, I think there might be something else positive in that scenario for you."

"What?"

"You've been living all these years with guilt, Mitzi. Whether you know it or not. And that does something to you. It changes you. It makes you become someone maybe you don't want to be but can do nothing to stop. Even with all the money in the world. It tears away at you little by little."

She clutched at her sheet and glanced up at him. "You … you sound like that might have happened to you."

"There was no *might* about it. I wasn't there for my family when they needed me. Because of that, they died. I'm never going to see my wife and my daughter again, and I guess I've always accepted that as my penance." Decker drew a long breath. "But that's no way to live, Mitzi. Trust me."

Tears were sliding down the woman's cheeks. She reached out and clutched his hand. Not too long ago, Decker would have flinched from this contact.

Yet when Melvin Mars had put his arm around him when Decker had been at one of his lowest points here, and then Mary Lancaster had gripped his hand in the car, just wanting the comforting embrace of another human when she had felt so scared, something had happened to Amos Decker.

And it was a good thing. Because despite all the unsettling things that his mind had been doing while he was here, the ability to be hugged or have your hand clenched by another without flinching, that simple act, which just about everyone else took for granted, had brought Decker a bit closer to the person he had once been. Before he had died on a football field and woken up as someone else entirely.

So, Decker reached out his other hand and closed it over Mitzi's.

"Will you do that, Mitzi? Will you take that step? Will you right the things you can? And finally free yourself of the guilt?"

An uncomfortably long moment passed until she spoke.

"Yes. I will."

82

Bogart said, "Apparently, in addition to meddling in our democratic process, Moscow is also trying to recruit the more marginalized among us and turn them into foot soldiers on our home turf, in the hopes of breeding even more division and unrest."

He, Mars, Jamison, and Decker were having dinner at Suds.

"So Eric Tyson and Karl Stevens were part of that pack?" asked Jamison.

"Right."

Decker finished his last French fry while sneaking a glance at a disapproving-looking Jamison. Then she suddenly brightened and said, "Okay, you earned your junk food quota for today. But tomorrow is another story."

Bogart said, "They found Childress in his cell, dead. It was his food. Some type of industrial chemical poison. The Russians are really good at that. They must have had more assets in the police department than just Childress. Captain Miller is currently looking into that."

"Any word on Egorshin?" asked Mars.

He shook his head. "We think he made it out of the country the same night he fled from the Richardses. He's probably back in Moscow by now. His two men whom we took into custody aren't saying anything. I'm surprised they didn't have cyanide pills in a tooth filling. We're going to get nothing from them. But we did find other records of the 'trainees' who worked at the Grill. We're using that, together with other information, to trace Egorshin's spies around the country."

"Well, I hope you find every last one of them," said Mars.

"And what will happen to Rachel Katz?" asked Decker.

"Witness protection, most likely. Same for Mitzi Gardiner and her son. Gardiner gave a full allocution in court absolving her father of the murders. His record was expunged. He's now a completely innocent man."

"And also dead," said Decker grimly. "So he'll never know."

Mars said, "Hey, man, you got to keep the faith. And my faith tells me that the man *does* know. He asked you to prove his innocence. And you did."

"Just give me a few minutes," said Decker.

He climbed out of a car that Jamison was driving, with Bogart and Mars riding in the backseat.

Bogart said, "But you are coming back with us, correct? No more detours along the way to investigate another case that pops up?"

Decker nodded. "No. I think I've had my fill of that, at least for now."

"Good, Decker," said Mars. "Because when we land back in D.C., dinner's on me. Harper's going to join us."

Decker nodded and headed off down the street. He looked up to see Mary Lancaster coming from the other direction. They met in front of Decker's old house.

"Thanks for meeting me here, Mary."

"I assumed you wanted to say goodbye." She glanced at the house. "But I'm not sure why here."

"It's complicated."

"I wouldn't have supposed otherwise."

"I'll be coming back to see you."

"You don't have to do that." She looked in the direction of the car where Jamison, Mars, and Bogart were waiting. "You have a new life, Amos. Away from here. And it's a good thing too." She glanced at the house where Decker had suffered so much misery. "You need to be free of this place, once and for all."

"I'm not going to do that, Mary."

"But why?"

"You're my friend."

"And you're my friend too. But—"

"And you're going to be experiencing some

things in the coming years that I may be able to at least help you with, in some small way."

Lancaster looked down, drew out a cigarette from her pack, glanced at the smoke for a long moment, and then tossed it away.

"I'm still scared."

"There's nothing wrong with that. Most people would be. But you have Earl. And you have me."

She looked at him with perplexity. "You've changed, Amos. Since leaving here."

"How's that?"

"You just have. You seem to be . . ." Her voice trailed off, as she seemed at a loss for words.

"More aware of things?" said Decker, a small smile creasing his lips.

"One way of putting it."

Her features grew somber. "I appreciate the offer. And I look forward to seeing you again." She glanced at the house and then looked at him inquiringly. "But why here of all places?"

"You said you didn't know the Hendersons?"

"No, but they seem to be a nice family."

"I'm sure they *are* a nice family. And this is a fine place to raise a family."

"Well, you've surely made it nicer by getting rid of the Russians."

Decker took a step back and peered at his old digs.

"Full of memories," said Lancaster. "Especially for someone with a memory like yours."

"It *is* full of memories. Most wonderful. A few beyond horrible."

"So which ones do you hold on to?"

"In my case I don't have a choice. But I *do* have a choice in how I prioritize them."

"Do you think you can do that?"

"I can try."

Decker thought about the episodes in which the violent scenes of his finding his family murdered kept unspooling in his head.

"I can try harder, at least. I have to, in fact."

"I wish you every success on that. I really do."

Before he left, Decker surprised Lancaster by embracing her in a long hug.

"I didn't expect that," she said, when they each stepped back.

"Maybe neither did I. But . . . it felt good."

"Yes, Amos, it did."

Decker walked back to the car and climbed in. "I wonder what burgundy means," he said.

"What?" asked Jamison, while Bogart and Mars looked on with puzzled expressions.

"When Hawkins walked up to me at the cemetery that day, there was a burgundy color around him. I've never experienced that before."

They were all silent for a few moments, until Jamison said, "Maybe it's your brain's new way of signaling a good person in need of some help."

"If that's the case, I think I might see it a lot more often, then."

As they were sitting there, watching Lancaster head off, Mr. and Mrs. Henderson and their daughter came out of the house and got into the Nissan Sentra. They drove off a few moments later.

Jamison glanced at Decker anxiously as he watched this happening.

In the backseat, Mars said, "They look like a nice family."

"Yes," said Decker. "I expect they are."

Jamison's fingers played nervously over the steering wheel.

Mars said, "It's a happy house, then."

Jamison cast him a sharp glance in the mirror before looking at Decker once more.

"A happy house," said Decker quietly before nodding at Jamison.

She put the car in drive and they headed off.

Away from this place.

For now.

Yet Amos Decker would be back.

For a lot of reasons.

Acknowledgments

To Michelle: Decker is back. If only I had his memory, you wouldn't have to get on me for all the things I forget to do.

To Michael Pietsch, for your excellence.

To Andy Dodds, Nidhi Pugalia, Ben Sevier, Brian McLendon, Karen Kosztolnyik, Beth deGuzman, Albert Tang, Bob Castillo, Kristen Lemire, Anthony Goff, Michele McGonigle, Cheryl Smith, Andrew Duncan, Joseph Benincase, Tiffany Sanchez, Morgan Swift, Matthew Ballast, Jordan Rubinstein, Alison Lazarus, Rachel Hairston, Karen Torres, Christopher Murphy, Ali Cutrone, Tracy Dowd, Martha Bucci, Rena Kornbluh, Jeff Shay, Lukas Fauset, Thomas Louie, Sean Ford, Laura Eisenhard, Mary Urban, Barbara Slavin, Kirsiah McNamara, and everyone at Grand Central Publishing, for always being so supportive.

To Aaron and Arleen Priest, Lucy Childs, Lisa Erbach Vance, Frances Jalet-Miller, John Richmond, and Juliana Nador, for always having my back.

To Mitch Hoffman, for seeing the forest *and* the trees.

To Anthony Forbes Watson, Jeremy Trevathan, Trisha Jackson, Katie James, Alex Saunders, Sara Lloyd, Claire Evans, Sarah Arratoon, Stuart Dwyer, Jonathan Atkins, Anna Bond, Leanne Williams, Natalie Young, Stacey Hamilton, Sarah McLean, Charlotte Williams, and Neil Lang at Pan Macmillan, for being all-around amazing. See you in September!

To Praveen Naidoo and the team at Pan Macmillan in Australia, for taking me to #1!

To Caspian Dennis and Sandy Violette, for being so cool. It was terrific seeing you on this side of the pond!

To Steven Maat and the entire Bruna team in Holland, for your great work.

To Bob Schule, for your wonderful comments and friendship.

To Roland Ottewell, for good copyediting.

To charity auction winners Christine Burlin (Community Coalition for Haiti), Kelly Fairweather (Soundview Preparatory School), Kenneth Finger (Project Kesher), Mitzi Gardiner (Muscular Dystrophy Association), and David Katz (Authors Guild). Whether your characters were good or evil, I hope you enjoyed them. And thanks for your support of such wonderful charities.

And to Kristen White and Michelle Butler, for helping me make the most of every day.

Introducing FBI
Special Agent Atlee Pine.

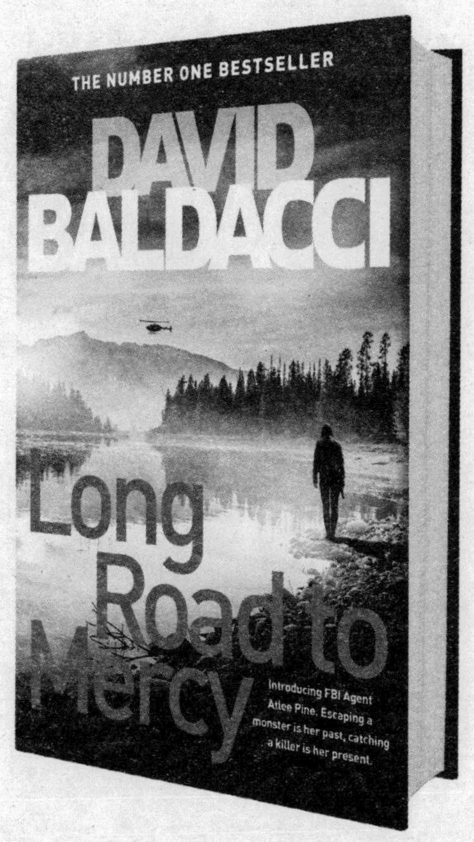

OUT NOW

Read on for an extract . . .

1

Eeny, meeny, miny, moe.

FBI Special Agent Atlee Pine stared up at the grim facade of the prison complex that housed some of the most dangerous human predators on earth.

She had come to see one of them tonight.

ADX Florence, about a hundred miles south of Denver, was the only supermax prison in the federal system. It was one of four separate encampments that made up the Federal Correctional Complex, Florence, each with a different security rating. In total, over nine hundred inmates were incarcerated on this parcel of land.

From the sky, with the prison lights on, Florence might resemble a set of diamonds on black felt. The men here, guards and inmates, were as hardened as precious stone. They had to be. It was not a place for the faint-hearted, or the easily intimidated, though the deeply demented were clearly welcome.

The Florence supermax held, among others, the Unabomber, the Boston Marathon bomber, 9/11 terrorists, serial killers, an Oklahoma City bombing conspirator, spies, and assorted cartel and mafia bosses. Their ages ranged from mid-twenties to nearly eighty. Most of the men currently living here would die in federal prison under the official weight of multiple life sentences.

ADX Florence had opened in 1994. Its creation was largely due to the murders of two prison guards at Marion Prison in Illinois. The main function of Florence was to take violent prisoners from other penitentiaries and tame them, so that they could be eventually transferred back to peacefully serve out their sentences. The average length of time spent here was about three years, though some of the more infamous inmates would be at the supermax until they died.

The prison was in the middle of nowhere. No one had ever escaped, but if they did, there would be no place to hide. The topography around the prison was flat and open. Not a blade of grass grew around the complex. There were no trees or bushes to provide cover.

This was all intentional.

The windows were four inches wide and four feet long, cut in thick concrete, through which only the sky and roof of the facility could be seen. Florence had been designed so that no prisoner could even tell where in the structure they were located, making an inside escape highly improbable. Outside the prison rose twelve-foot-high perimeter walls topped with razor wire and interlaced with pressure pads. These spaces were patrolled 24/7 by armed guards and attack dogs. Any prisoner reaching this spot would almost assuredly be killed either by fangs or bullets. With the worst of the worst, the Bureau of Prisons was not into taking chances. And there would be no one who cared about a serial murderer, terrorist, or spy face-planting in the Colorado dirt for the final time.

The cells were seven-by-twelve and virtually everything in them, other than each inmate, was made from poured concrete. The showers automatically cut off, the toilets could not be stopped up, the walls were insulated so no inmate could communicate with another, the double steel doors slid open and closed on powered hydraulics and meals came through a slot in the metal. Outside communication was forbidden except in the visitor's room. For unruly prisoners, or in the case of a crisis, there was the Z-Unit, also known as the Black Hole. Its cells were in complete darkness and restraints were built into each concrete bed.

Solitary confinement was the rule rather than the exception here. Twenty-three hours in-cell, and one out that did not involve time spent with another human being. If you wanted rec time, you spent it all by yourself. Some marched along in what looked like an empty pool, one foot in front of the other, counting off steps, counting off the seconds left in their lives.

Atlee Pine's truck had been scoped and searched and her name and ID checked against the visitor's list. After that she was escorted to the front entrance and showed the guards stationed there her FBI special agent credentials. She was thirty-five and the last twelve years of her life had been spent with this shiny badge riding on her hip. The gold shield was topped by an open-winged eagle, and below that was Justitia, holding her scales and sword. It was fitting, Pine thought, that it was a female on the badge of the preeminent law enforcement agency in the world.

She had relinquished her standard-issue 9 millimeter Glock 23 chambered in .40-caliber. Pine had left behind, in her truck, the throwaway Beretta Nano that normally rode in a holster on her left ankle. This was the only time she could remember voluntarily handing over her weapon. At the FBI, the only time you gave up your gun was when you were dead. But America's only supermax had its own set of rules by which she had to abide if she wanted to get inside, and she very much did.

After giving up her gun, she walked through a metal detector, which did not ding because she had been careful not to bring anything that would make it do so. She had stripped off her belt, watch, pinky ring, and St. Christopher's necklace and left them in the truck along with her Beretta.

She was tall: over five-eleven in her bare feet. Her height had come from her mother who was an even six feet. Despite her stature, Pine was hardly lithe or willow. She would never grace a runway as a stick-thin model. She was solid and muscular, which had come from pumping iron religiously. Her thighs, calves, and glutes were rocks, her shoulders and delts sculpted, her arms ropy, her core iron.

She also had competed in MMA, kickboxing, and had earned a red/black 7 belt in Brazilian jiu-jitsu, the foundation of which was enabling a smaller person to take on and subdue a larger one.

All of these skills had been learned with one aim in mind: survival.

She knew she toiled in largely a man's world. And physical strength and the toughness and confidence that came with it was a necessity. If she had played on a football team she would have been a middle linebacker – good wheels and she could deliver pain when she got to her destination. She had dark hair that fell to shoulder length and mismatched eyes, right one a pale green, left one a murky blue. It was the only asymmetrical thing about her, she felt. Otherwise, she was ramrod straight.

At least on the outside. She was working on the internal part. Well, maybe not so much.

She had never been to Florence before, and as she was escorted down the hall by two burly guards who hadn't uttered a word to her, the first thing that struck her was the ethereal calm and quiet. As a federal agent, Pine had visited many prisons before. They were normally a cacophony of noise, screams, catcalls, curses, trash talk, insults, threats, with fingers curled around bars, menacing looks coming out of the cells' darkness. If you weren't an animal before you went to prison, you would be one by the time you got out. Or else, you'd be dead.

It was *Lord of the Flies*.

With bars and flush toilets.

But here, it was as if she was in a library. She was impressed. It was no small feat for a facility housing men who, collectively, had slaughtered thousands of their fellow humans using bombs, guns, knives, poisons, or simply their fists. Or in the case of the spies, with their treasonous acts.

Catch a tiger by its toe.

Pine had driven over from St. George, Utah, where she'd previously worked. In doing so she'd motored across the entire state of Utah, and half of Colorado. Her navigation device had told her it would take a little over eleven hours to traverse the six hundred and fifty miles. She had done it in under ten, having the benefit of a lead foot, a big-ass engine in her SUV, and a radar detector to get through the inevitable speed traps.

She'd stopped once to use a restroom and to grab something to eat for the road. Other than that, it had been pedal to the floor mat.

She could have flown into Denver and driven down from there, but she had some time off and she wanted to think about what she would do when she got to her destination. And a long drive through vast and empty stretches of the Land of the Free allowed her to do just that.

Growing up in the east, she'd spent most of her professional life in the open plains of the west. She hoped to spend the rest of it there. There were good reasons for this.

She didn't necessarily enjoy company.

And she definitely did not enjoy tight spaces.

After five years at the Bureau Pine had had her pick of assignments. This had been the case for only one reason: she was willing to go where no other agent wanted to. Most recruits were desperate to be assigned to one of the big shops, one of the FBI's fifty-six field offices. Some liked it hot so they aimed for Miami, Houston, or Phoenix. Some aimed for higher office in the FBI bureaucracy, so they fought to get to New York or D.C. Los Angeles was popular for myriad reasons, Boston the same. Yet Pine had no interest in any of those places. She liked the relative isolation of the RAs in the middle of nothing. And so long as she got results and was willing to pull the duty, people left her alone.

And in the wide open spaces, she was often the only federal law enforcement for hundreds of miles. She liked that too. Some would call her aloof and a control freak. She would call herself a cop with a job to do.

After working at the fairly large Flagstaff RA, Pine had taken a position at the St. George, Utah, RA. It was a two-person outfit and Pine had stayed there for three years. When the opportunity arose, she had transferred to a one-agent office in a tiny town called Shattered Rock. It was a recently established RA due west of Tuba City, about as close to Grand Canyon National Park as it was possible to be, without actually being in the park. She enjoyed the support of one secretary, Carol Blum, who was in her late sixties and had been at the Bureau for nearly four decades. Blum claimed former FBI Director J. Edgar Hoover as her hero, though he'd died long before she joined up.

Pine didn't know whether to believe the woman or not.

Visiting hours were long since over at Florence, but the Bureau of Prisons had accommodated a request from a fellow fed. It was actually midnight on the dot, a fitting time, Pine felt. Because didn't monsters only come out then?

And at Florence, whether it was day or night really made no difference to anyone there. It was not the sort of place that was impacted by the normal contours of life, because there was nothing ordinary about the men who were imprisoned there.

She was escorted into the visitor's room and sat on

a metal stool on one side of a sheet of thick polycarbonate glass. In lieu of a phone, a round metal conduit built into the glass provided the only means to orally communicate. On the other side of the glass was where the inmate would sit on a similar metal stool bolted into the floor. The seat was uncomfortable; it was meant to be.

If he hollers let him go.

She sat awaiting him, her hands clasped and resting on the flat laminated surface in front of her. She had pinned her FBI shield to her lapel because she wanted him to see it. She kept her gaze on the door through which he would be led. He knew she was coming. He had approved her visit, one of the few rights he possessed in here.

Pine tensed slightly when she heard multiple footsteps approaching. The door was buzzed open and the first person she saw was a beefy BOP guard with no neck, and shoulders that nearly spanned the width of the door. Behind him came another guard, and then a third, all equally large and imposing.

She briefly wondered if there was a minimum heft requirement for a guard here. There probably should be. Along with a tetanus shot.

She dropped this thought as quickly as she had acquired it, because behind them appeared Daniel James Tor, all six-foot-four-inch shackled feet of him. He was followed in by a trio of other guards. They effectively filled the small enclosure. The rule of thumb here, Pine had learned, was that no prisoner was moved from one place to another with fewer than three guards.

Apparently, Tor warranted double that number. She could understand why.

Tor had not a hair on his head. His eyes stared blankly forward as they seated him on his stool and locked his chains into a steel ring set into the floor. This was also not typical of the visitor's policy here, Pine knew.

But it was obviously typical for fifty-seven-year-old Tor. He had on a white jumpsuit with black rubber-soled shoes with no laces. Black-framed glasses covered his eyes. They were one piece and made of soft rubber with no metal pins at juncture points. The lenses were flimsy plastic that could not be molded into a jagged edge. It would be difficult to turn either into a weapon.

In prisons, one had to sweat the small details, because inmates had all day to think of ways to do harm to themselves and others.

Under the jumpsuit she knew his entire body was virtually covered in largely self-inked tats. The ones that he hadn't done himself had been inked on by some of his victims, forced into becoming tattoo artists before Tor had dispatched them into the hereafter. It was said that each tat told a story about a victim. Pine didn't know if that was true or not. And, at this precise moment, she didn't really care.

She was only here to talk about one of the man's victims.

Tor weighed about two hundred and eighty pounds and Pine calculated that only about 10 percent of that would qualify as fat. The veins rippled in his forearms and neck. There wasn't much to do in here except work out and sleep, she assumed. But he had been an athlete in high school, a sports star, really, born with a genetically gifted physique. It was unfortunate that the superb body had been paired with a deeply deranged mind.

The guards, satisfied that Tor was securely restrained, left the way they had come. But Pine could hear them right outside the door. She was sure Tor could as well.

She imagined him somehow breaking through the glass. Could she hold her own against him? It was an intriguing hypothetical. And part of her wanted him to try.

His gaze finally fell upon her and held.

Atlee Pine had stared through the narrow width of glass or in between cell bars at many monsters, a number of whom she had brought to justice.

Yet this one was different. Daniel James Tor was different. He was perhaps the most dangerously sadistic and prolific serial murderer of his, or any, generation.

He rested his shackled hands on the laminated surface on his side, tilted his thick neck to the right until a kink popped. Then he resettled his gaze on her after flicking a glance at the badge.

His lips curled momentarily at the symbol for law and order.

"Well?" he asked, his voice low and monotone.

The moment, an eternity in the making, had finally come.

Atlee Pine leaned forward, her lips an inch from the thick glass.

"Where's my sister?"

Eeny, meeny, miny, moe.

2

The dead-eye stare from Tor didn't change in the face of Pine's question. On the other side of the door where the guards lurked, Pine could hear murmurings, the shuffling of feet, perhaps the smack of palm against a metal baton. Just for practice, just in case it needed to be wrapped around Tor's head at a moment's notice.

From Tor's expression, she knew he could hear it too. He apparently missed nothing, though he had eventually been brought down by missing *something*.

Pine leaned slightly back on her stool, folded her arms across her chest, and waited for his answer. He could go nowhere, and she had nowhere to go that was more important than this.

Tor looked her up and down in a way that perhaps he had used in sizing up all his victims. There were thirty-four of them confirmed. *Confirmed*, not total. She was here about an unconfirmed one. She was here about one victim not even in the running to be added to the tally of this man's infinite depravity.

Tor had escaped a death sentence solely due to his

cooperating with authorities, revealing the locations of three victims' remains. This revelation had provided a trio of families some closure. And it had allowed Tor to live. In her mind, she could see him easily, perhaps smugly, striking that bargain, knowing that he had gotten the better end of the deal.

He'd been arrested, convicted, and sentenced in the mid-nineties. He'd killed two guards and another inmate at a prison in 1998 where they did not have the death penalty. That had led to him being transferred to ADX Florence. He was currently serving forty-one consecutive life terms. There was no plan to rehabilitate Tor with the goal of sending him off to another facility to serve his time in peace. Tor and peace were mutually exclusive.

Unless he pulled a Methuselah, he would die in here.

None of this seemed to faze the man.

"Name?" he asked, as though he were a clerk at a counter checking on an order.

"Mercy Pine."

"Place and time?"

He was screwing with her now, but she needed to play along.

"Andersonville, Georgia, June 7, 1989."

He popped his neck once more, this time to the other side. He stretched out his long fingers, cracking the joints. The huge man seemed one enormous jumble of pressure points.

"Andersonville, Georgia," he mused. "Lots of deaths there. Confederate prison during the Civil War. The commandant, Henry Wirz, was executed for war crimes. Did you know that? Executed for doing his job." He smiled. "He was Swiss. Totally neutral. And they hanged him. Some justice."

The smile disappeared as quickly as it had emerged, like a spent match.

She said, "Mercy Pine. Six years old. She disappeared on June 7, 1989. Andersonville, southwestern Macon County, Georgia. Do you need me to describe the house? I heard your memory for your victims was photographic, but maybe you need some help. It's been a while."

"What color was her hair?" asked Tor, his lips parted, revealing wide, straight teeth.

In answer, Pine pointed to her own. "Same as mine. We were twins."

This statement seemed to spark an interest in Tor that had not been present before. She had expected this. She knew everything about this man except for one thing.

That one thing was why she was here tonight.

He sat forward, his shackles clinking in his excitement.

He glanced at her badge once more.

He said eagerly, "Twins. FBI. It's starting to make sense. Go on."

"You were known to be operating in the area in

1989. Atlanta, Columbus, Albany, downtown Macon." Using a tube of ruby red lipstick taken from her pocket, she drew a dot on the glass representing each of the aforementioned localities. Then, she connected these dots roughly, forming a familiar figure.

"You were a math prodigy, even taught briefly. You like geometric shapes." She pointed to what she had drawn. "Here, a diamond shape. Gets you off apparently. That's how they tracked you. And eventually caught you."

This was the *something* Tor had missed. A pattern of his own creation.

His lips pressed together. She knew that no serial murderer would admit a mistake, or having been outsmarted. She did not intend to let him dwell on this. She had said it only to give her a measure of equality with him, to exercise a nuance of control.

The man was clearly a sociopath and a narcissist. While virtually everyone understood the dangers of a sociopathic personality, people often discounted narcissism as relatively harmless. The term sometimes conjured the image of a beautiful and seemingly innocuous man staring longingly at his reflection in a pool of water or a mirror. How could such a person hurt anyone?

However, Pine knew that narcissism was probably the most dangerous trait someone could possess for one critical reason: the narcissist could not feel empathy towards others. Which meant that the lives of others held no value to them. They could kill without remorse, without feeling, without the inhibition and off switches that kept the vast majority of humans from committing such heinous acts. Killing could be like a drug to a narcissist, like a hit of fentanyl: instant euphoria from the domination and destruction of another.

And that was why virtually every serial murderer was a narcissist. And that was why all narcissists were potentially deadly.

She said, "But Andersonville was not part of that pattern. Was it a one-off? Were you freelancing? What made you come to my house?"

"It was a rhombus, not a diamond," replied Tor.

Pine didn't respond to this.

He continued, as though lecturing to a class. "My pattern was a rhombus, a lozenge, if you prefer, a quadrilateral; a four-sided figure with four equal-length sides, and unequal length diagonals. An equilateral parallelogram. For example, a kite is a parallelogram only when it's a rhombus." He gave a patronizing glance at what she had drawn. "A diamond is not a true or precise mathematical term. So, don't make that mistake again. It's embarrassing. And unprofessional. Did you even prepare for this meeting?" With his manacled hands, he gave a dismissive wave and disgusted look to the crude figure she'd drawn on the glass, as though she had written something foul there.

"Thank you, that makes it perfectly clear," said Pine, who could give a shit about parallelograms specifically or math in general. "So why the one-off? You'd never broken a pattern before."

"You presume my pattern was broken. You presume I was in Andersonville on the night of June 7, 1989."

"I never said it was at night."

The smile flickered back. "Doesn't the boogeyman only come out at night?"

Pine reflected for a moment on her earlier thought about monsters only striking at night. To catch these killers, she had to think like them. It was and always had been a disturbing thought to her.

Before she could respond he said, "Six years old? A twin? Where did it take place?"

"In our bedroom. We shared a bed. You came in through the window. You taped our mouths shut so we couldn't call out. You held us down with your hands."

She took out a piece of paper from her pocket and held it up to the glass so he could see the writing on that side.

His gaze drifted down the page, his features unreadable, even to Pine, who had read them all. At least until now.

"A four-line nursery rhyme?" he said, tacking on a yawn. "What next? Will you break into a homily?"

"You thumped our foreheads as you recited it,"

noted Pine, who leaned forward a notch. "Each word, a different forehead. You started with mine and ended on Mercy's. Then you took her and you did this to me."

She swept back her hair to reveal a scar behind her left temple. "Not sure what you used. It was a blur. Maybe just your fist. You cracked my skull." She added, "But you're a big man and I was just a little kid." She paused. "I'm not a little kid anymore."

"No, you're not. What, about five-ten?"

"Add over an inch. My sister was tall too at age six, but skinny. Big guy like you, you could have carried her easily. Where did you take her?"

"Presumption again. As you said, I'd never broken a pattern before. Why would you think that I had then?"

Pine leaned closer to the glass. "Thing is, I remember seeing you." She looked him over. "You're pretty unforgettable."

The lip curled again, like the string on a bow being pulled back. About to let loose an arrow. "You remember seeing me? And you only show up now? Twenty-nine years later?"

"I knew you weren't going anywhere."

"A weak quip, and hardly an answer." He glanced at her badge again. "FBI. Where are you assigned? Somewhere near here perhaps?" he added a bit eagerly.

"Where did you take her? How did my sister die? Where are her remains?"

These practiced queries were fired off rapidly.

Tor, though, was unmoved by this. He simply continued his line of thought. "I assume not a field office. You don't strike me as a main-office type. Your dress is casual and you're here outside visitor's hours, hardly by the Bureau book. And there's only one of you. Your kind likes to travel in pairs if it's official business. Add to that the personal equation."

"What do you mean?" she asked, meeting his gaze.

"You lose a twin, you become a loner, like you lost half of yourself. You can't rely on or trust anyone else once that emotional cord is broken. You're not married," he added, glancing at her ring finger. "So you have no one to interrupt your lifelong sense of loss until one day you kick off, alone, frustrated, unhappy." He paused, looking mildly interested. "Yet something happened to lead you to come here after nearly three decades. Did it take you that long to work up the courage? For an FBI agent? It does give one pause."

"You have no reason not to tell me. They can take off another life sentence, it won't matter. Florence is it for you."

His next response was surprising, but perhaps it shouldn't have been.

"You've tracked down and arrested at least a half-dozen people like me. The least talented among them had killed four, the most talented had disposed of ten."

"Talented? Not the way I would describe it."

"But talent does come into play. It's not an easy business, regardless of what society thinks about it. They weren't in my league, of course, but you have to start somewhere. Now, you seem to have made a specialty of it. Of going toe-to-toe with the likes of me. It's nice to aim high, but one can grow too ambitious, or become overconfident. Flying too close to the sun with the wax betwixt the wings, that sort of thing. Death so often results. It can be a divine look, but not, I think, on you. However, I'd love to try."

Pine shrugged off these lines of free association ending with the threat against her. If he was thinking of killing her, that meant he was interested; she had his attention.

She said, "They were all operating in the West. Here, you have wide open spaces without a policeman on every block. People coming and going, lots of runaways, folks who have lost their way, looking for something new, long strips of isolated highways. A billion places to toss the remains. It encourages . . . *talent* like yours."

He spread his hands as wide as he could with the restraints. "Now see, that's better."

"It would be far better if you answered my question."

"I also understand that you came within one

pound of making the U.S. Olympic team as a weightlifter when you were in college." When she didn't respond right away he said, "Google has even reached Florence, Special Agent Atlee Pine from Andersonville, Georgia. You've even earned your own Wikipedia page. It's not nearly as long as mine, but then again, it's early days for you. But long careers are not guaranteed."

"It was one kilo, not one pound. The snatch did me in, never my best pull. I'm more of a clean-and-jerk girl."

"Kilos, yes. My mistake. So actually, you're a bit weaker than I thought. And, of course, a failure."

"You have no reason not to tell me," she repeated. "None."

"You want *closure*, like the rest of them?" he said in a bored tone.

Pine nodded, but only because she was afraid of the words that might come out of her mouth at that moment. Contrary to Tor's assertions, she had prepared for this meeting. But one could never fully prepare for a confrontation with this man.

"You know what I really, really like?" said Tor.

Pine kept staring at him, but didn't react.

"I really, really like that I have defined your entire life."

Tor suddenly leaned forward. His wide shoulders and massive bald head seemed to fill the glass, like a man coming in through a little girl's bedroom window. For one terrifying moment, Pine was six again and this demon was thumping her forehead with each word of the rhyme, with death to the one last touched.

Mercy. Not her.

MERCY.

Not her.

Then she let out a barely audible breath and involuntarily touched the badge on her jacket.

Her touchstone. Her lodestone. No, her rosary.

The movement did not go unnoticed by Tor. He didn't smile in triumph; his look was not one of anger, but of disappointment. And then, a moment later, disinterest. His eyes hollowed out and his features relaxed as he sat back. He slumped down, his energy and animation gone.

Pine felt every cell in her body start to shut down. She'd totally just screwed this up. He'd tested her and she had not risen to the challenge. The boogeyman had come at midnight and found her lacking. Like he had called her: a failure.

"Guards," he bellowed. "I'm ready. We're done here." As soon as he finished speaking, his lips spread into a malicious grin and Pine knew why.

This was the only time he could order them around.

As they came in, unhooked him from the ring, and began to lead him away, Pine rose.

"You have no reason not to tell me."

He didn't deign to look at her.

"The meek shall never inherit the earth, Atlee Pine of Andersonville, twin of Mercy. Get used to it. But if you want to vent again, you know where to find me. Just bring your A-game. And don't bring the diamond. But now that I'm aware of your existence—" he suddenly looked back at her, a surge of ferocious desire flashing across his features, probably the last thing his victims ever saw— "I will never forget about you."

The metal portal shut and locked behind him. She listened to the march of feet taking Tor back to his seven-by-twelve poured-concrete cage.

Pine stared at the door a moment longer, then wiped the lipstick off the glass, the color of blood transferred to her palm, retraced her footsteps, retrieved her gun, and left ADX Florence, breathing in crisp air at exactly one mile above sea level.

She would not cry. She hadn't since Mercy. She wanted to feel something. But it just wasn't there. She was weightless, like being on the moon, nothing, empty. He had drained whatever she had left right out of her. No, not drained.

Sucked.

And, worst of all, what had happened to her sister was still unknown.

She drove a hundred miles west to Salida and found the cheapest motel she could since this trip was all on her dime.

Right before she fell asleep, she thought back to the question Tor had asked.

And you only show up now? Twenty-nine years later?

There was a good reason for this, at least in Pine's mind. But maybe it was also a flawed one.

She didn't dream about Tor that night. She didn't dream of her sister, gone nearly three decades now. The only visual her subconscious held up was herself at six years old trudging to school for the first time without Mercy's hand inside hers. A bereaved little girl in pigtails who had lost the other half of her, as Tor himself had intimated.

The better half of her, thought Pine, because she had been the one constantly in trouble, while her ten-minute-older "big" sister had habitually stood up for her, or covered for her, in equal measure. Unfailing loyalty and love.

Pine had never felt that again, in her entire life.

Maybe Tor was right about her future.

Maybe.

And then his other jab, the one that had gotten through her defenses, and nailed her right in the gut.

You define me?

When she felt her lips begin to tremble, she rose, walked to the bathroom, and stuck her head under the shower. She left it there until the cold was so unbearable she nearly screamed out in pain. Yet not a single tear mingled with the freezing tap water.

She rose at the crack of dawn, showered, dressed,

and headed home. Halfway there she stopped to get something to eat. As she got back into her SUV the text landed in her phone.

She closed the SUV door, fired up the engine, and floored it.

3

The Grand Canyon was one of the seven natural wonders of the world, visited by five million people from around the globe every year. However, only 1 percent of those folks would ever reach the spot where Atlee Pine was currently: the banks of the Colorado River right on the floor of the canyon.

Those who did make it down here could do so in only one of three ways: in a river raft, by mule ride, or courtesy of their own two feet.

Phantom Ranch, located at the bottom of the canyon, was the most popular under-roof accommodation in the valley itself, because it was the *only* one. There was a heliport there, but not for commercial aircraft. Tour choppers could fly a thousand feet below the canyon's rims, but no lower. That meant none could land in the canyon, unless there was a catastrophic event, as there had been in the past, with wreckage and bodies hurtling into the mile-deep abyss.

Pine had driven to the Grand Canyon National Park Airport, the second busiest in Arizona behind

Phoenix's Sky Harbor. There, she had climbed inside a waiting National Park Service chopper and made a vertical descent of about a mile. After landing, Pine and her companion had immediately set off on foot.

The Grand Canyon could be a nightmare when it came to figuring out who had legal oversight over criminal events happening there. The National Park Service, the Bureau of Indian Affairs, at least three Native American tribes, the Hopi, Hualapai and Navajo and their respective tribal police forces, the Arizona state and local police, and Pine's FBI could all claim some jurisdiction to bad deeds committed within the park.

Yet now, it was just Pine and a National Park Service Ranger named Colson Lambert.

As they walked along, the sun was beginning to set as it usually did here – swiftly, because of the canyon's towering walls.

Lambert, who was in his forties, hiker-fit and medium height with a weighty Adam's apple riding up and down his throat, said, "Thought you would have been here hours ago. Where were you when I texted?"

"Out of town, personal," Pine tersely replied.

She strode along, eating up ground with her long legs, her gaze looking for rattlers and scorpions, the most dangerous of which was the smallest, the bark scorpion. A rattler bite, untreated, could easily kill you, and the bark scorpion was no insignificant matter either.

She had already passed about a half-dozen of the snakes, and had waited on the path twice to let the serpents cross. As hard as it was to believe, they were more afraid of people than people were of them. That was one reason nature had given them a rattle, to make people leave them alone.

Where's my rattle? thought Pine.

"When was it found?" she said over her shoulder.

Lambert scurried after her.

"This morning."

They passed a slight curve in the rock and there it was. A tarp had been erected around it. Pine counted two men there. One dressed as a cowboy that he undoubtedly was. The other, like Lambert, was in the uniform of the National Park Service, gray shirt, light-colored flat brimmed hat with a black band on which were the letters USNPS. Pine knew him, his name was Harry Rice. In physique, he was a carbon copy of Lambert, though a few years younger.

Pine approached, flashed her badge, and asked the cowboy what he was doing there.

He was long and lean and his face had been viciously carved by the outdoor life he led in an unforgiving environment. He was closer to fifty than forty, with thick graying hair that had been shaped by the wide-brimmed hat he held in one hand. "I work at Phantom Ranch," he replied.

"What's your name?"

"Dave Brennan. I'm one of the mule wranglers.

Pack and riders. I bring 'em down and then back up and then do it all over again."

"Did you discover it?"

Brennan nodded. "Before breakfast. Saw the buzzards circling."

"Be more precise."

"Um, seven-thirty."

Pine passed by the strung tarp wall as Lambert and Rice joined her. There was no one nearby to see anything; the floor of the Grand Canyon was hardly Grand Central. But pretty much everyone who came down here brought binoculars. And it was a crime scene after all, even if it didn't involve a human being.

Yet.

Pine squatted down and looked over the carcass.

The mule weighed about a half-ton, she figured, and would stand about sixteen hands high. A mare bred with a donkey produced a mule. They pulled more slowly than horses, but were surer-footed, lived longer, and pound for pound were about as strong as anything on four legs, and possessed enormous endurance.

Pine slapped on a pair of latex gloves she had pulled from her fanny pack. She touched the stiffened foreleg of the beast. The air was rank with the smell of the dead carcass, but Pine was certainly used to that.

"It's in rigor," she said. "Blowflies all over it. Eggs hatched. It's definitely been here a while."

When it came to death, humans and animals weren't all that different. And the insect world treated them exactly the same. Good for the cops, bad for the bad guys.

Lambert nodded, as did Rice.

Pine said, "You found it at seven-thirty. Was it stiff like it is now?"

Brennan shook his head. "Not so I could tell, no. Definitely not the legs all stiff like that. Had to chase some critters away. They were already starting to get into it. You can see that there and there," he added, pointing to various places where flesh had been ripped away by interested carnivores. "There was a rattler right next to it eating a squirrel. They don't usually come out that early, but it never really gets that cool down here at night or in the morning. I just let it be until it was done and moved on."

Pine checked her watch. It was just now six-thirty p.m. So, eleven hours had passed since it had been found. Now she needed to establish a parameter at the other end.

She shifted her position and looked at the belly of the beast.

And the wound that had presumably taken its life.

"Gutted," she noted. "Sharp knife with a short blade. Upward stroke and then a slit along the belly, severing major blood vessels along the way. Bleed out was max."

She looked up at Brennan.

"I take it this is one of yours?"

Brennan nodded and squatted on his haunches. He looked sadly at the dead animal. "Sally Belle. Riding mule. Been with us for six years. Good, strong, dependable. She was a pack mule for three years. Steady as a rock. No problems. Damn shame. I don't know why anybody would've done this."

Pine looked at the dried blood. "It would have taken some time for her to bleed out. And it wouldn't have been painless. No one heard anything? Mules can make a lot of noise."

"It's far enough away from the ranch that maybe no one would have," suggested Rice. "And there's no one else around. And the blood loss would have weakened her pretty quickly," he added.

"There's a park ranger station here," noted Pine.

Rice nodded. "I checked on that this morning. The ranger I talked to didn't hear or see anything. He's a good guy. Reliable."

"Okay, but there had to be people at the Bright Angel Campground?"

Lambert said, "There were. Hikers. And some rafters too. But it's about a half mile from Phantom and over a mile and a half from here. They might not have heard anything."

"Phantom Ranch is that far away from here, but the mule corral is closer than that," noted Pine.

"Well, it is, but it's still a good ways away, and on the other side of Bright Angel Creek. And you know how dark it gets down here because of the steep walls. Even with a sky full of stars."

Pine did not look convinced. The canyon was one big subwoofer, really. Sound bounced off the walls and reverberated everywhere. "More to the point, who has the balls to lean under a thousand-pound mule and start slicing into its belly?" said Pine. She looked up at Brennan. "And maybe in the dark. How plausible do you think that is?"

"Not very. Particularly if the mule didn't know the person. Our mules are well-trained and disciplined, but they can get spooked, just like any animal. And if a mule kicks you in the head, that's it for you. And for what it's worth, in my opinion, you gut a mule and you're going to hear it in the next county."

"Let's file that one away for now." Pine eyed the saddle. "Okay, it's really shitty that someone murdered a mule. But where's the rider?"

She looked up at the three men, all huddled around the dead beast. "When you called you said there was someone missing. You don't call in the FBI for a dead mule."

Lambert shook his head. "You know this area. You've worked with us before. And more importantly, the superintendent knows you and trusts you."

Pine said, "Well, the chief reason the Bureau established the RA in Shattered Rock was because of its proximity to the Grand Canyon. This hole in the ground is an important national asset."

Lambert continued, "Our Visitor and Resource Protection Division will have the lead on this, at least initially, that's why Harry and I are here. But at some point, depending on how this plays out, the Bureau may need to be involved. That's why we thought it smart to bring you in at the beginning. But depending on how this plays out, ISB might get involved."

ISB, Pine knew, stood for the National Park Service Investigative Services Branch, and the special agents who worked there.

"Right. So, the rider?" she said.

"Benjamin Priest," said Rice promptly.

"No sign of him?" asked Pine.

"Not that we can find, no," said Lambert.

Brennan took up the thread. "He came down yesterday. Part of a crew of ten."

"That's your limit, right?" said Pine.

"Yeah. We're pretty much always maxed on that. You have to reserve about a year in advance. Same for a bunk and meals at Phantom. Next year they're going to a lottery. Pretty popular destination."

"So, he rode down here and then what?"

"We stopped overnight at Phantom like we always do. We were going to head out this morning after breakfast. Across the suspension bridge and up the South Kaibab to the Rim. Just like normal."

"Five and a half hours down and an hour less back up?" said a Pine.

"Just about, yeah," agreed Brennan.

Pine surveyed the area. It was over eighty degrees on the canyon floor and twenty degrees cooler on the South Rim and even cooler on the taller north side. She could feel the sweat collecting on her face, armpits, and the small of her back.

"When was it noticed that Priest was missing?"

Rice said, "This morning when folks came to the dining hall for breakfast."

Brennan added, "And one of my guys saw that Sally Belle was gone from the mule corral. That's why I was out looking for her."

"Where was Priest staying?"

Brennan said, "One of the cabins."

"Had to be others with him," noted Pine. "Bunk beds."

Lambert said, "There were. We talked to them. They slept soundly. Pretty much all people coming down here do. Mule riding to the bottom takes it out of you."

"Yeah, I've done it. Last night?"

Brennan said, "They all had dinner in the dining hall. Some folks played cards, wrote postcards. Some sat on boulders and cooled their feet in the water. Typical stuff. Then everyone went off to their sleeping quarters."

"And it was confirmed that Priest went to his cabin?"

"Yes."

"When was the last time anyone saw him?"

Rice answered. “Best as we can tell, around nine last night. One of his bunkmates remembered seeing him then. Out on the porch.”

“But no one actually saw him go into the cabin, get into his bunk, or later leave the cabin?”

“No.”

“The mules would have been in the corral by then,” said Pine. “So how did Sally Belle get here? You said she was missing when someone checked and you went looking for her?”

“Right,” said Brennan. “At first, I just thought she had gotten out, but I couldn’t see how. The corral was all intact. Then I noticed her saddle and bridle were missing. Well, you can see she’s got both on. Someone had to do that. We take off their gear when we put them in the corral. The mules work hard coming down here. They don’t need anything else on their back after carrying a person all that way on rocky terrain.”

“So, it could have been Priest who saddled her and took her out here. The probability lies there unless anyone else is missing.”

“No one else, just Priest,” replied Lambert.

She eyed Brennan. “You saw the mule was missing, and the tack too. What were you thinking at that point?”

Brennan didn’t answer right away; he fidgeted with his hat. “Well, I thought maybe somebody had decided to go off on a joy ride before breakfast.

Wouldn't have been the first time. I've seen some crazy shit by people. They act like they're in a resort down here."

"What's Priest's background?" asked Pine.

Brennan shrugged. "I don't have that info. He just seemed like a regular guy."

"Description?"

"Oh, in his forties. About five-feet-seven. Maybe one-eighty. We have weight limits for mule riders."

"White? Black?"

"White. Dark hair. He was pretty chubby. Probably had a desk job."

"Yeah, I guessed that with his height and weight. Did you ever talk to him?"

"Some, coming down. I wasn't at his table for dinner. He talked to some other people."

"Seem out of sorts? Nervous?"

"No, nothing like that."

She looked at Rice. "What do you have on him?"

Rice took out a notebook and unclipped the cover. "He's from D.C. Works at one of those government contractors around the Beltway."

"Which one?"

"Capricorn Consultants. Never heard of them. But I've never been to D.C. either."

"Family?"

"Not married, no children. Has a brother who lives in Maryland. Parents are deceased."

"So, you've notified him?"

"We let him know that his brother is missing. That's where we got this information. Asked him to let us know if he gets in contact."

"I'll need that info."

"I'll email it to you."

"How did his brother sound?"

"Worried. He knew his brother was doing the Grand Canyon trip. He wanted to know if he should fly out. I told him to sit tight until we knew more. Most people who go missing do turn up okay."

"But some don't," replied Pine. "He couldn't have decided to hike back up on his own?"

"Nobody rides a mule down and hikes back up," said Brennan. "You pay for both ways regardless."

"Besides," added Lambert. "His backpack's still in the cabin."

"ID, phone?"

"None of that was there," replied Lambert. "He must have taken them with him."

"But we had his contact information on file," said Brennan. "They called his cell phone, but there was no answer. He had his brother's contact information on his application for emergency purposes. That's how we were able to phone him."

Rice added, "His brother phoned him too after I talked to him. Also tried his email. He called me back and told me there was nothing. No response."

"Facebook or Twitter activity?"

"I didn't think to ask about that," said Lambert. "I don't use either one. I can follow up."

"How'd he get here? Car? Bus?"

"I heard him say he came via the train," volunteered Brennan.

"Did he come up yesterday?"

"The day before actually," said Lambert. "He did come by train. We checked with them. At least, he had purchased a ticket."

"Where was he staying?"

Rice said, "We checked at El Tovar, Bright Angel, Thunderbird and the rest of the possible places. He wasn't booked at any of them."

"If he came up the day before he took the mule ride down here, he had to stay somewhere."

"It could have been at one of the campgrounds. Some you have to reserve; others are first come, first served," noted Lambert.

Rice added, "Or realistically, he could have slept under a tree nearby. We can't patrol every inch of the space. And at night, it would have been pretty easy to stay under the radar."

"We'll need to check on all that," said Pine. "It seems weird that we can't find out pretty easily where he stayed. If he came from D.C. presumably he flew. That can be checked. If he took the train up, odds are he flew into Sky Harbor from the East Coast. He might have stayed somewhere there until he went to Williams, Arizona. That's where the train leaves from, right?"

Lambert nodded. "And there's a hotel at the train depot there. He might have stayed there before coming here?"

"Okay, we'll need to confirm all that. Have you made a search down here?"

"I had a team of rangers come in. We covered as much ground as we could. We didn't find any tracks or footprints leading from here. Without that, it's hard to know where he might have gone. Now we're losing the light. No good searching at night down here."

Pine took all this in. In the distance came the sharp bark of a coyote followed by a closer rattle of a snake. There might be a standoff going on out there between predators as the lights of nature grew dim, thought Pine. The muscular walls of the canyon held a complex series of fragile ecosystems. It was the human factor that had intruded here. Nature always seemed to get on all right until people showed up.

"We'll need to bring in an organized search team tomorrow, with thermal finders, and go grid by grid," said Pine. "Both ways as far as we can. And we'll need a chopper to do an aerial sweep. What about the other mule riders with Priest? And the campers?"

Lambert said, "They all headed out a long time ago. We had no reason to detain them. And we had more riders and hikers coming down. There wasn't space for them."

"I'll need all their names and contact info," said Pine. "And let's hope if something did happen to Priest that we didn't let whomever did it walk or ride a mule or raft it out of here."

Lambert looked uncomfortable with this and quickly glanced at his fellow ranger.

"There were over a hundred people," said Rice defensively.

"Still need them."

"Okay."

"Anybody keep watch over the mules during the night?" Pine asked.

Brennan shook his head. "Never saw a need to post somebody out by the corral all night. The Ranger Station isn't that far from it. I walked over and checked on them around eleven last night. Everything was fine. We got some coyotes and mountain lions down here, but they're not going after a pack of mules. They'd get the shit stomped out of them."

"Right, like someone would when they gutted her," said Pine pointedly, looking at the dead Sally Belle. "So at least at eleven, Sally Belle was here and alive. The ranger on duty didn't hear anything with the mules either last night or early this morning?"

Lambert said, "He would have told me if he had."

"What's his name?"

"Sam Kettler."

"How long has he been with NPS?"

"Five years. Two here at the Canyon. He's a good guy, like I said. Reliable. And he's got a lot of experience in the Canyon. He's hiked all over it."

"I'll need to talk to him," said Pine, as she mentally catalogued all she had to do on this case.

She rose and took some photos of the dead mule with her camera phone.

Then Pine noted something. "Sally Belle's on her right side. Belly cut obviously pointing to the left. So why is the bleed out I'm seeing on the ground on the opposite side? Above her withers? It should be on the right. It couldn't have flowed underneath her and pooled on the other side, or at least not that much."

All the men looked at each other, puzzled.

She said decisively, "The mule was moved after it was killed. We need to turn Sally Belle on her other side."

Each one gripped a stiff leg and they slowly maneuvered the dead animal onto its left side.

"Shit," exclaimed Brennan.

Down Sally Belle's long neck and leaching onto her torso was a series of strange symbols, like hieroglyphics.

"What the hell is that?" asked Lambert.

What the hell is that? thought Pine.

The UK financial system

The UK financial system

Theory and practice

Fourth edition

Mike Buckle and John Thompson

Manchester University Press
Manchester and New York

distributed exclusively in the USA by Palgrave

First edition published 1992 by Manchester University Press
Second edition published 1995
Third edition published 1998

This edition published 2004 by
Manchester University Press
Oxford Road, Manchester M13 9NR, UK
and Room 400, 175 Fifth Avenue, New York, NY 10010, USA
www.manchesteruniversitypress.co.uk

Distributed exclusively in the USA by
Palgrave, 175 Fifth Avenue, New York,
NY 10010, USA

Distributed exclusively in Canada by
UBC Press, University of British Columbia, 2029 West Mall,
Vancouver, BC, Canada V6T 1Z2

British Library Cataloguing-in-Publication Data
A catalogue record for this book is available from the British Library

Library of Congress Cataloging-in-Publication Data applied for

ISBN 0 7190 6772 3 *paperback*

This edition first published 2004

13 12 11 10 09 08 07 10 9 8 7 6 5 4 3

Typeset by R. J. Footring Ltd, Derby
Printed in Great Britain
by Bell & Bain Limited, Glasgow

To Margaret and Fiona

Contents

Figures

Tables

Boxes

Chapter 1

Introduction to the financial system

1.1 Introduction

We begin our study of the UK financial system with an introduction to the role of a financial system in an economy. We start this introduction with a very simple model of an economy and then extend the analysis throughout the rest of this and the next chapter. A second objective is to establish some of the basic financial concepts which will be drawn upon throughout this book. Finally, we hope to introduce readers to the many sources of data available relating to the UK financial system. In particular we explain the relationships between the various sets of financial statistics.

1.2 The role of the financial system

To help us to understand the role played by a financial system in a mature economy such as that of the UK, we start by constructing a simplified model of an economy. In this model the economy is divided into two distinct groups or sectors. The first is the household sector, which is assumed to be the ultimate owner of all the resources of the economy. In the early stages of development of an economy the household unit would have undertaken production of any goods consumed. As economies have developed, a form of specialisation has generally taken place so that the proximate ownership and control of much of the productive resources of the economy, such as land, buildings and machinery, have been vested in units making up the second sector, which we call the firms sector. We will examine the financial relationships between these two sectors later. In our simple model it is the firms sector which organises the production of goods and services in the economy. In exchange for these goods and services, households hire out their resources of land, labour and so on. At this stage we ignore the role of the government and we assume that the economy is closed, so that

there is no exchange of goods and services with other economies. The real flows in this simple economy are set out in the inner loop of figure 1.1.

In this simple economy it would not be an easy task for households to attempt to satisfy their wants. The greater the number of commodities available in the economy, the greater would be the task. This can be seen by considering the choices open to households. Households can consume the commodities they own, they can exchange these commodities for commodities owned by other households or they can use these commodities as inputs to create new commodities. In the last situation the household would have to hire out the commodities to an existing firm in exchange for the firm's output or alternatively create a new firm. In the case of exchanging commodities with other households there would clearly be many difficulties. For a successful transaction to take place between two parties in such a barter economy, it is necessary for each of the two parties to want simultaneously that which the other party is offering to exchange. This requirement is termed 'double coincidence of wants'. There would be considerable costs involved both in searching for a suitable party with which to trade and also in reaching an agreement over the terms of the trade. Such costs would limit the amount of trade taking place and would eventually lead to pressure for general

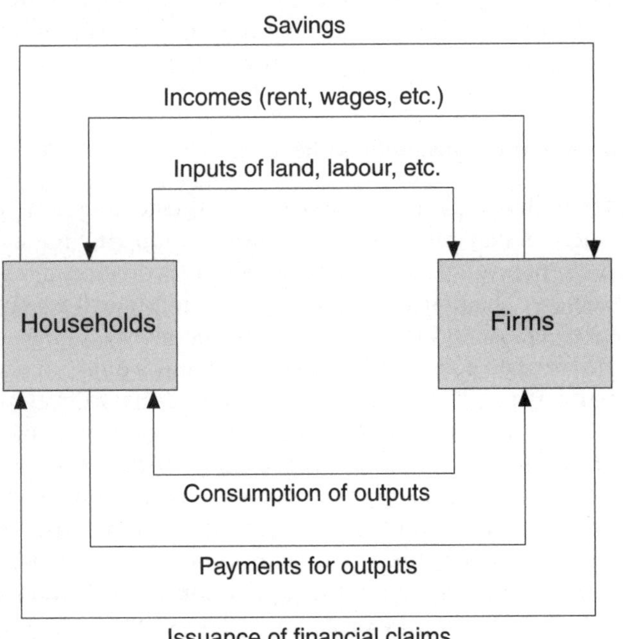

Figure 1.1 The circular flow of income, expenditure and finance.

agreement to use a single commodity as a standard unit of exchange into which all other commodities can be converted. The commodity used as the unit of exchange is known as money and various commodities have been used as money over time, including cowrie shells, cattle, gold, silver and cigarettes. The main criterion for the development of a commodity as money is that it is generally acceptable in exchange for other commodities. With the development of money, the act of sale can be separated from the act of purchase.

We can now introduce money into our simple economy, so that households are paid in money for the resources they hire out to firms and in turn households use that money to purchase the outputs of firms. The middle circuit in figure 1.1 denotes these monetary flows. We should note that by aggregating all firms into one sector we are considering flows taking place only between firms and households and are therefore ignoring the considerable flows which take place between firms. That is to say, we are considering only inter-sector flows and ignoring intra-sector flows.

In this simple economy any expenditure in excess of current income by a household or a firm could occur only if the household or firm had accumulated money balances by not spending all of its income received in past periods. This is clearly a constraint on economic development since firms need to invest, that is, replace, maintain or add to existing real assets such as buildings and machinery. As the economy becomes more sophisticated, investment requires larger amounts of accumulated funds. Various expedients were developed to enable firms to overcome such constraints. For example, partnerships were formed so that accumulated savings could be pooled. The next major stage in the development of financing arrangements came with borrowing. Those households which did not spend all of their current income on consumption, that is, saved some of their income, could lend these funds to firms, which in turn could use these funds to finance investment. In exchange for these funds, firms would issue claims, which are effectively sophisticated IOUs, which promise some benefits to the lender of funds at some date or dates in the future. The nature of financial claims and the various types of claims in existence are discussed in the next section.

The ability to finance investment through borrowing undoubtedly encourages economic development and the existence of financial claims stimulates household saving. The investment and saving flows in our simple economy are represented by the outer loop of figure 1.1. The non-spending of income (or saving) by households can be regarded as a leakage of funds from the circular flow of income and expenditure captured in the middle loop of figure 1.1. This household saving, though, finds its way into firms' investment and firms' investment involves the purchase of capital equipment from other firms, so the leaked funds are injected back into the circuit.

We can now see one of the main roles of a financial system, which is to provide the mechanisms by which funds can be transferred from those with a surplus to those who wish to borrow. In other words, the financial system acts as an intermediary between surplus and deficit units. In terms of figure 1.1, this function is represented by the outer loop. It is clear therefore that the financial system plays an important role in the allocation of funds to their most efficient use amongst competing demands. In a market system such as the UK financial system this allocation is achieved through the price mechanism, with the various prices being set within the relevant financial markets, which are themselves part of the financial system. The existence of financial markets also enables wealth holders to alter the composition of their portfolios. A secondary role for a financial system is to provide the mechanisms for the middle loop of money flows, that is, the payments mechanism. A further function of a financial system is the provision of special financial services such as insurance and pension services.

Before we consider in more detail the lending and borrowing flows (sections 1.7 and 1.8) represented by the outer loop of figure 1.1, we examine in the next sections the nature of the financial claims which underlie these flows.

1.3 Financial claims

A financial claim can be defined as a claim to the payment of a sum of money at some future date or dates. A borrower of funds issues a financial claim in return for the funds. The lender of funds holds the borrower's financial claim and is said to hold a financial asset. The issuer of the claim is said to have a financial liability. By definition therefore the sum of financial assets in existence will exactly equal the sum of liabilities in this closed economy. To take an example, a bank deposit is a sum of money lent by an individual or company to a bank. The deposit is therefore a liability of the borrower of funds, which is the bank. The depositor holds a financial asset, that is, a financial claim on the bank. Another term commonly used to denote a financial claim is a financial instrument.

The existence of a wide variety of financial instruments in a mature financial system, such as the UK system, can be explained by reference to consumer theory. Traditional consumer theory explains the demand for a commodity in terms of utility and a budget constraint, with the implication that a particular good can be identified as separate from other goods. In contrast Lancaster (1966) argues that:

(i) all goods possess objective characteristics, properties or attributes;
(ii) these characteristics form the object of consumer choice.

In the same way, a financial instrument can be considered to be a 'bundle' of different characteristics. Because individual agents place different emphasis on the various characteristics, a wide range of financial instruments is supplied. It is now necessary to examine the different characteristics possessed by financial instruments. The most important of these are risk, liquidity, real value certainty, expected return, term to maturity, currency denomination and divisibility.

1.3.1 *Characteristics of financial claims*

Risk

Risk is a fundamental concept in finance and it is one which we will return to many times throughout the book. What follows is a brief introduction to the nature of financial risk.

When we talk about risk in relation to a financial instrument we are referring to the fact that some future outcome affecting that instrument is not known with certainty. The uncertain outcome may, for example, be changes in the price of the security, or default with respect to repayment of capital or income stream. Although such outcomes are uncertain, an individual may have some view about the likelihood of particular outcomes occurring. Another way of stating this is that the individual will view some outcomes as more likely than others. Such views are likely to be formed on the basis of past experience of such outcomes occurring, although other relevant information may also be used. The next step in assessing the particular risk of the financial instrument is to assign subjective probabilities to the different outcomes that may occur. The resulting probability distribution provides us with the individual's view as to the most likely outcome, that is, the expected value of the distribution. The spread of the distribution indicates the degree to which the outcome could be much greater or much less than expected. The greater the spread, the greater is the risk that an outcome far removed from that expected will occur. The most common measure of risk is in fact the standard deviation of the probability distribution, a measure which increases as the spread widens.

To take an example, a person invests £1,000 in the ordinary shares of a company. The value of the shares in one year's time, that is, the price of those shares plus any income received from them in the form of dividends, is uncertain. The value may have risen or fallen; however, this person will believe some range of values are more likely than others. For example, he or she may believe that there is a 50 per cent chance that the value of the shares in one year's time will be in the range £1,000 to £1,200. Figure 1.2 illustrates one possible distribution of likely values. The expected value of this distribution is £1,090 and the standard deviation, or measure of risk, is £161. A larger spread, that is, a larger standard deviation, would indicate the potential for a larger reward and, conversely, the potential for

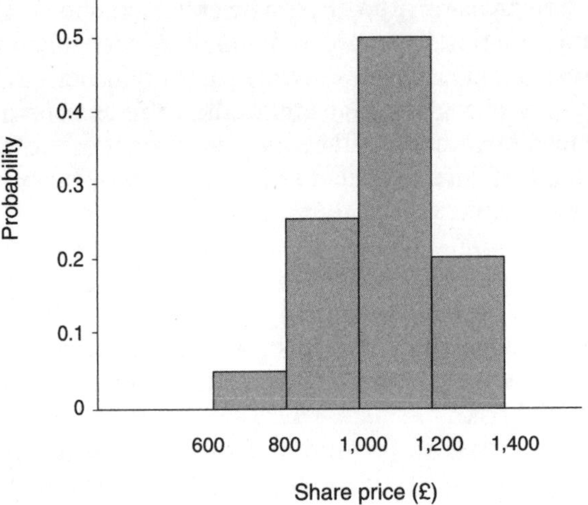

Figure 1.2 Hypothetical probabilities of a share price in one year's time.

a larger loss around a particular expected value; that is, the level of risk is higher.

In these introductory remarks on the nature of risk, two types of risk were mentioned, namely price risk (or market risk, i.e. the risk that the price of the security will change) and the risk of not being repaid the sum lent or any interest promised in the claim, known as default risk. During the course of this book we will consider many other types of financial risk.

Liquidity

Liquidity refers to the ease and speed at which a financial instrument can be turned into cash without loss. This will depend upon on the asset being redeemable or marketable on an organised market. Thus for example a bank sight deposit can be withdrawn or redeemed on demand and is therefore very liquid. In contrast listed shares can be sold on a stock exchange but the precise amount of cash obtained will depend on the market valuation at the time of sale. Hence listed shares are less liquid than sight deposits. As a final example a bank loan is an agreement between two parties, the bank and the borrower, and so there is unlikely to be a third party willing to purchase the loan from the bank before it matures. That is to say, the bank loan is not marketable. (Note that since the 1980s there has been a growing trend towards packaging loan-type assets, such as mortgages, to make them marketable so they can be sold on; this process is part of a larger phenomenon termed securitisation – for further discussion see section 4.3).

The existence of an organised market for an instrument and the ability to deal at short notice therefore enhances the instrument's liquidity. It is possible to devise a spectrum of liquidity along which different financial instruments can be positioned. Such an analysis is crude and subject to a number of exceptions but is still illustrative. At the very liquid end we would find short-term deposits, moving through longer-term deposits, where funds are tied up for longer periods, through bonds and shares, where their marketability provides some degree of liquidity, to long-term loans, life policies and pension rights. Life policies and pension rights are considered to be very illiquid when they are held to maturity, although it has become increasingly easier to turn them into cash at short notice, albeit at considerable financial penalty, the further the date of encashment is from the maturity date.

Real value certainty

A third distinguishing characteristic of financial instruments is real value certainty, which refers to their susceptibility to loss due to a rise in the general level of prices. The maintenance of the real value of an asset is likely to be an important consideration for those who are lending funds over a long time period. An individual acquiring assets to draw upon in retirement will want to ensure that the purchasing power of those assets is at least as great in retirement as when the assets were acquired. Financial instruments whose values are fixed in money terms, for example a bank deposit, will find their real value eroded when the rate of inflation exceeds the rate of interest earned. Over most of the 1970s, inflation exceeded the interest rate earned on bank and building society deposits in the UK and as a consequence the real value of such deposits was eroded. Ordinary shares, if held over the medium term, have shown a trend to increase in value in line with or above the rise in the general price level. This is despite periodic falls in share prices, such as that experienced over 2000–02. The asset which has tended to provide the best protection against erosion in value by inflation is not a financial asset but the physical asset of property. As with shares, this is not to say that there are not times when the real value of property does decrease, and an example of this is the decline in the real value of residential property in the late 1980s and early 1990s. Rather, it is to say that, if held over a number of years, the increase in value of property has tended to exceed inflation. This, as we shall see in chapter 6, explains why the long-term investment institutions are significant holders of property in their portfolios.

Expected return

Most financial instruments offer an explicit cash return to their holders. This return takes the form of a rate of interest or dividend and, for those

instruments subject to changes in their market price, there is an additional element of return in the form of an appreciation in their value. Instruments subject to changes in price are termed capital uncertain and include bonds and equities. For such capital uncertain instruments it will be the expected return (see above section on risk) that is used to determine whether to purchase or hold on to them. *Ceteris paribus*, the higher the expected return the greater will be the demand for the instrument. In practice, however, a high return on an asset may indicate that there is a premium component to the return to compensate the holder for some disadvantage such as illiquidity or high risk.

Term to maturity

Financial instruments vary widely according to the characteristic of term to maturity. Sight deposits at banks have zero term to maturity, as they can be withdrawn on demand. At the other end of the spectrum 'consols' (a type of government bond) and equity have no redemption date and therefore possess an infinite term to maturity. Between these two extremes are many other types of financial instrument. In general, returns on instruments identical except for their term to maturity will reflect both expectations of future interest rate changes and the loss of liquidity in holding long-term as opposed to short-term instruments. This is examined in more detail in chapter 9.

Currency denomination

With the general reduction in restrictions on the movement of capital across national boundaries, the currency denomination of a financial instrument has assumed greater importance. This adds a further component to the return on non-domestic instruments, in the form of the appreciation or depreciation of the relevant exchange rate.

Divisibility

This characteristic reflects the degree to which the instrument can be subdivided into small units for transaction purposes. For example, a sight deposit is fully divisible whereas Treasury bills are sold in minimum denominations and hence are not divisible. The degree of divisibility is therefore an additional determinant of an instrument's liquidity.

The characteristics approach to analysing financial instruments can also provide some indication of why an economic agent, such as an individual or company, will desire to hold more than one type of financial asset. It is likely that economic agents will hold their wealth in different forms so as to meet a number of different financial objectives. For example, an individual may be uncertain about her or his level of income or consumption in the

near future and so can meet this uncertainty by holding wealth in a form which can be drawn on at short notice. That is, some wealth will be held as liquid assets, such as bank deposits. The individual may also have the objective of holding wealth over a long period of time, for the purpose of providing income in retirement, and will want these funds to keep their purchasing power. This may lead to the holding of some funds in the form of ordinary shares. From this analysis we can see that an economic agent is likely to hold a collection, or portfolio, of assets, where the mix of characteristics underlying the assets in the portfolio will satisfy the various objectives of the agent.

We have referred to some specific types of financial instruments in this section, such as a bank deposit and an ordinary share. These are examples of the two general types of claim, namely debt and equity, which dominate the types of financial instruments in existence. We shall finish this section with a look at the characteristics of these two general types of claim.

1.3.2 *Types of financial claim*

Debt

Debt is a financial claim which is normally due to be repaid on a specified future date, with interest being paid at regular intervals until repayment. Examples of debt instruments are deposits, loans, bills and bonds. A deposit is a claim which records the liability of a financial institution to repay a sum of money in the future to the depositor (the lender of funds to the institution). A variety of deposit types exist, differing mainly in the arrangements for repayment; so, for example, a sight deposit with a bank would be repayable on demand whilst a time deposit is repayable after a given period of notice. Deposits are generally considered to be at the liquid end of the spectrum of liquidity, although there are some exceptions to this – for example a deposit may have a repayment date of up to five years from the time of issue. Deposits are susceptible to default risk, albeit such risk is considered to be relatively low, as financial institutions rarely default – although exceptions do occur, as in the case of the Bank of Credit and Commerce International (BCCI) in 1991.[1] Deposits can also be classified according to their size: retail deposits are small and wholesale deposits are large. Financial institutions have also issued certificates of deposit (CDs), which are instruments that acknowledge the existence of a deposit for a fixed period but which can be sold on the money markets (i.e. they possess the characteristic of marketability – see section 10.2.2 for further discussion).

The majority of loans are made by financial institutions and usually have a specified date for repayment. The term to maturity of the loan generally varies according to the purpose for which the finance is required, and may be 30 years or more in the case of a mortgage. Most bank loans, though, have a repayment date of less than ten years from the date they are

issued. Loans are susceptible to default risk; however, as we shall see in the next chapter, financial institutions attempt to minimise such risks through a variety of methods. Loans which are secured, such as a mortgage on property, have a lower default risk than unsecured loans as, in the event of non-repayment, the holder of the claim can sell the security to recover the debt. Loans are generally considered to be illiquid because they are agreements between two parties and therefore not marketable.

Bills of exchange can be considered to be promises to pay a certain sum of money at a fixed date and are analogous to postdated cheques. Commercial bills are used to finance trade and help to reconcile the competing interests of the buyer of the goods, who wishes to delay payment, and the seller, who desires prompt payment. The buyer issues a bill which promises to pay in the future and the seller receives a financial instrument which can be resold in the money markets (i.e. it is negotiable). The price received from the sale is less than the face value of the bill on maturity and so the bill is said to be discounted. For example, if a £1,000 bill due for redemption in three months' time is sold for £950, the rate of discount over three months is 5.3 per cent ((50/950)×100), or approximately 21 per cent per annum. Bills are also issued by central government (Treasury bills) and local authorities.

Deposits and loans are claims which generally pay variable rates of interest. In contrast, a bond is a claim which pays a fixed rate of interest, known as a 'coupon payment', at regular intervals. The bond may have a known repayment date, at which time the bond's par value, which is generally £100, is repaid. Some bonds, though, have no definite repayment date and are known as undated bonds, for example 2.5 per cent consolidated stock (consols) issued by the UK government in 1888. In the UK, central government, local government and companies issue bonds. Bonds issued by the UK government are commonly known as 'gilt edged', as the risk of default on such stocks is as close to zero as is possible on a financial instrument. Bonds issued by companies, known as debentures or loan stocks, do carry some risk of default, as do bonds issued by some foreign governments. Another type of bond traded in London is the eurobond (for a full discussion on which see section 12.2.1).[2] Eurobonds are issued by international companies, governments and government agencies, and are distinguished by not being subject to the tax and other regulations of the country in whose currency they are issued. This freedom from restrictions has led to many innovations in the characteristics of eurobonds and so there exists a wide variety of interest, currency denomination and repayment terms for these bonds (see chapter 12 for further detail on this).

All bonds have the characteristic of marketability, which enhances their liquidity. The yield to maturity on a bond can be defined as the rate of discount, which equates the current market price of the bond with the future

coupon payments and the repayment of the principal. Thus, for example, the yield to maturity on a five-year £100 bond with a coupon of 10 per cent paid once a year can be calculated by solving for *i* (the yield to maturity) in the following formula:

$$\text{Market price of bond} = \frac{10}{(1+i)} + \frac{10}{(1+i)^2} + \frac{10}{(1+i)^3} + \frac{10}{(1+i)^4} + \frac{10}{(1+i)^5} + \frac{100}{(1+i)^5}$$

The price at which bonds trade in a market will change as yields on other financial instruments change. It can be seen from the above formula that there is an inverse relationship between the price of a bond and its yield to maturity. This is more easily understood by examining the behaviour of the price of a non-redeemable bond such as a consol. This is equivalent to a perpetuity (a regular payment received without any time limit, i.e. forever). Thus the price of a consol paying a coupon value of £2.50 will be $2.5/i$, assuming that the coupon is paid once per year. Thus, if the market rate of interest on similar securities (i) is 10 per cent per annum, the price of the consol will be £25. However, if the market rate falls to 5 per cent per annum, the price of the consol will rise to £50. If yields on competing financial instruments change then, given that the coupon is fixed, changes in the market price of a bond keep its yield in line with that of similar financial instruments. Consequently, if a bond is not held to maturity, there is a risk that the price at which the bond is sold will be less than the price at which the bond was bought; that is, bonds are subject to price risk.

A final point about the characteristics of debt instruments is that they are normally susceptible to a reduction in real value due to general price inflation (when the nominal rate of interest is less than the rate of general price inflation). There are some exceptions to this, where debt instruments have been issued with yields that are linked to the retail price index. In the UK two examples of such instruments are index-linked government bonds and index-linked National Savings certificates.

Equity

Equities differ from the types of financial instruments so far described in that they represent a claim to a share in the ownership of a company, rather than evidence of debts. The principal type of equity instrument is the ordinary share issued by limited companies. The main characteristic of ordinary shares is that the income to be received from them is not fixed in any way. This income payment, known as dividends, constitutes a share in the profits earned by the company. The amount of the total profits earned by the company which is distributed to shareholders is determined by the company's management. The factors determining the dividend payment will include the financial performance of the company and the extent to which the company wishes to retain profits to finance investment. In addition

to uncertainty about the income payments on ordinary shares, known as income risk, ordinary shares are also subject to price risk. Ordinary shares are marketable, although it is easier to trade listed shares in the larger, well known companies than it is in small companies. The liquidity of the particular ordinary share will therefore depend on its degree of marketability. In times of panic in share markets, for example October 1987, it may not be possible to sell a share without incurring a significant loss. One characteristic of ordinary shares which is highly valued is their real value certainty – when held over a sufficiently long period of time the value of shares has generally increased at a rate in excess of the rate of inflation.

1.4 Sectoral analysis of the financial system

In the simple circular flow model of the economy introduced in section 1.2 the economy was assumed to be made up of two separate groups of decision makers, or sectors, namely households and firms. To take our analysis of the financial system further we need to consider both a further disaggregation of these two sectors and an extension of the economy to introduce a government and trade with overseas economies. The further disaggregation involves splitting the firms sector into industrial firms and firms whose primary activity is financial. The other changes introduce a public sector and an overseas sector. We have now achieved a sectoral breakdown of the economy which roughly corresponds to that used by National Statistics for the UK economy. National Statistics in fact identifies five main sectors of the UK economy, with a further breakdown of three of these sectors:

(i) households and non-profit institutions serving households (NPISH);
(ii) non-financial corporations –
 (a) private non-financial corporations,
 (b) public non-financial corporations;
(iii) financial corporations –
 (a) monetary financial institutions,
 (b) insurance corporations and pension funds,
 (c) other financial intermediaries and auxiliaries;
(iv) general government –
 (a) central government,
 (b) local government;
(v) rest of the world.

The household and NPISH sector consists mainly of households, along with some other groups such as charities, universities and so on, which the statisticians find difficult to separate out. Ideally we would like data relating solely to households; however, it is not thought that these other groups distort the overall picture of household behaviour to any significant degree.

As described above, the firms sector is split into non-financial and financial corporations. National Statistics then disaggregates each of these groups further in the construction of sector financial accounts. The general government sector represents government institutions and in most analysis by National Statistics this is further split into central government and local government. The public sector is therefore composed of general government and public non-financial corporations. We shall adopt this sector definition for much of the analysis that follows.

1.5 National wealth

We begin our examination of the financial relationships within the UK economy with a look at the extent of national wealth. We will then move on to examine a breakdown of this wealth by sector.

The first assessment of wealth relating to the UK was the Domesday Book, which, just over 900 years ago and using a census approach, set out the value of the land, animals and mills of England. Over the last 30 years government statisticians and academics have adopted statistical techniques to provide an assessment of the nation's wealth.

The tangible wealth of a nation consists of its national resources and its stocks of goods (which include buildings), durable equipment (which provides services to consumers and producers), stocks of finished goods, raw materials and work in progress. In addition, a nation also possesses intangible wealth, which includes the skill, knowledge and character of its people, otherwise described by economists as human capital. The final component of a nation's wealth is its claims on wealth in other countries net of other countries' claims on its own wealth. The complete UK national balance sheet for the end of 2001 is summarised in table 1.1.

Table 1.1 UK national balance sheet for end 2001

	Value (£billion)
Tangible assets	4,211.8
Intangible assets	323.7
Net financial assets/liabilities	–39.9
Net national wealth	4,495.6

From table 1.1 we can note that the net national wealth of the UK at the end of 2001 was approximately £4,500 billion. This is just over four and a half times gross domestic product for the UK for that year. This figure for

net national wealth is of course only an estimate because of the exclusion of certain items and because many of the included items are measured with error.

1.6 Sector balance sheets

The national balance sheet shown in table 1.1 hides most of the financial wealth held by the various groups which make up the UK economy. A person may be wealthy without possessing any of the wealth counted in national wealth. This is because, to take an example, wealth held in the form of a bank deposit by a person (i.e. an asset to that person) will have a corresponding liability held by the bank. So, assuming that the bank deposit is not held outside the UK, aggregation of the net wealth of the personal sector (which contains the person's bank deposit as an asset) with the net wealth of the monetary sector (which contains the bank deposit as a liability) to form national wealth causes the asset and liability to cancel each other out. The financial relationship between the person and the bank is said to be 'netted out'. It therefore follows that the only financial wealth appearing in the national balance sheet is those assets held by UK residents which are claims on the overseas sector (i.e. the corresponding liability is held overseas). These are included in the item 'Net financial assets/liabilities' in table 1.1. As we move down to the sectoral level of the economy, the more financial wealth is revealed. In this connection, balance sheets are now constructed for the domestic sectors of the UK economy identified in the earlier section and it is to these that we now turn our attention.

1.6.1 *Households sector*

The household sector balance sheet showing how its wealth was made up at the end of 2001 is shown in table 1.2. Tangible assets of the personal sector are principally houses. Intangible assets are as defined for table 1.1. The financial assets and liabilities of the personal sector are many and varied and will be examined more closely later in this chapter, when financial accounts are considered (section 1.8).

Table 1.2 Household sector balance sheet for end 2001

	Value (£billion)
Tangible assets	2,261.7
Intangible assets	300.7
Financial assets	2,983.7
Financial liabilities	817.5
Total net wealth	4,728.6

There are a number of important points to note about the household sector's balance sheet. First, its financial assets greatly exceed its financial liabilities; therefore the sector has been a net lender of funds to other sectors of the economy. This is not to say that all members of the personal sector have been net savers but that in aggregate the personal sector has been a net saver. This highlights again the point about aggregation hiding information: a disaggregation of households by, for example, age would reveal more information about the ultimate lenders and ultimate borrowers in the economy. A second point not revealed by the figures in table 1.2 is that over the period 1975 to 1987, when the household's sector net wealth rose by over £2,200 billion, over four-fifths of this increase was due to price changes of its tangible assets (mainly houses) and financial assets (mainly equities, held directly and indirectly). Therefore most of the increase in personal sector wealth was due to positive changes in the value of assets already held rather than increases in the quantity of assets held; this has not been so in more recent years.

The balance sheet shown in table 1.2 can be rewritten in a more conventional format, as in table 1.3, which shows that net wealth, sometimes known as 'net worth', is the item which brings assets and liabilities of the sector into balance. This format of balance sheet is the one we adopt for the rest of this chapter.

Table 1.3 Household sector balance sheet for end 2001: conventional format

Liabilities	£billion	Assets	£billion
Net wealth	4,728.6	Tangible assets	2,261.7
Financial liabilities	817.5	Intangible non-financial assets	300.7
		Financial assets	2,983.7
Total	5,546.1		5,546.1

1.6.2 *Non-financial corporations sector*

The balance sheet for the non-financial corporations (NFC) sector for 2001 is shown in table 1.4. Tangible assets for the NFC sector are mainly the buildings, plant and machinery which provide the means of production, along with any stocks of raw materials, finished goods and work in progress. Financial assets held by this sector are mainly funds held to meet short-term needs, loans to subsidiaries and trade credit provided. On the liabilities side the main item is issued share capital or equities, with the rest made up of loans from banks and trade credit received (this is approximately balanced

Table 1.4 Non-financial corporations sector balance sheet for end 2001: conventional format

Liabilities	£billion	Assets	£billion
Net wealth	–178.1	Tangible assets	1,261.3
Financial liabilities	2,674.6	Financial assets	1,235.2
Total	2,496.5		2,496.5

by trade credit provided). The NFC sector, in contrast to the households sector, has generally been a net borrower, as evidenced by the excess of financial liabilities over financial assets outstanding at the end of 2001. It should be noted that, as equities are a liability of companies, the value of these liabilities will change as the prices of shares change. This leads to the rather curious result, seen over the 1990s as the equity markets enjoyed a long period of boom, that an increase in equity prices can give rise to an increase in the liabilities of companies greater than an increase in their assets, resulting in a reduction in the net wealth of the NFC sector. Indeed, the total net wealth of this sector was negative for 2001.

1.6.3 *Financial corporations sector*

For the purpose of this analysis of sectoral wealth we will take the three financial corporation subsectors together, as they are sufficiently similar in respect of their wealth structure. The balance sheet for this sector is summarised in table 1.5. The striking points about the balance sheet of this sector are the substantial financial assets and liabilities alongside a comparatively low net wealth. This follows from the nature of their activities as financial intermediaries. Their business is to lend and borrow funds, hence their substantial holdings of financial assets and liabilities. The near equality of the financial asset and liability positions again reflects the nature of their business as intermediaries. Unlike companies in the NFC sector,

Table 1.5 Financial corporations sector balance sheet for end 2001: conventional format

Liabilities	£billion	Assets	£billion
Net wealth	–386.6	Tangible assets	109.3
Financial liabilities	6,729.2	Financial assets	6,296.3
Total	6,405.6		6,405.6

Table 1.6 Public sector balance sheet for end 2001: conventional format

Liabilities	£billion	Assets	£billion
Net wealth	258.1	Tangible assets	579.5
Financial liabilities	541.7	Financial assets	220.3
Total	799.8		799.8

they do not need substantial investment in plant, equipment and stocks to undertake this business, hence the relatively low level of tangible assets. These tangible assets are mainly buildings, for example the branch networks of the banks and building societies, and equipment such as computers.

1.6.4 *The public sector*

As with financial corporations, for this analysis we examine the combined public sector balance sheet, shown for 2001 in table 1.6. The public sector's tangible assets rose only slowly in value over the 1980s and hence its share of national wealth declined from 18 per cent in 1980 to under 6 per cent in 2001. This was due in the main to the policies of privatisation (sales of public corporation assets) and sales of council houses (sales of local authority tangible assets) initiated by the Conservative administration of the 1980s. The policy of privatisation has continued, although at a slower pace as the stock of saleable public sector assets is much smaller.

1.7 **Sector financial transactions**

The analysis of sectoral financial relationships has so far examined balance sheets. These show the breakdown of wealth by sector and the financial relationships between sectors at one point in time – the day the balance sheet is constructed. In addition to information on stocks of assets and liabilities, it is also useful to have information on financial transactions in these stocks, recorded over periods of time. By comparing the balance sheets of a sector at two different points in time and noting the changes that have taken place, balance sheet data can be converted from stock to flow form. However, the changes in stocks of assets and liabilities observed from this process could have come about either by transactions in those assets/liabilities or by revaluations of the stocks (i.e. price changes). The sector financial accounts published by National Statistics are not, at present, reconciled with the published sector balance sheets. The financial accounts that are published are part of the national accounting framework which relates sector accounts for income, expenditure, capital and financial transactions. Thus, for a sector we have:

	Income	Income and
+	Inter-sector transfers	expenditure
–	Expenditure	account
=	Saving	
–	Capital transactions	Capital account
=	Financial surplus/deficit	

The income and expenditure accounts describe the economic identity of income, and income less expenditure gives the residual of saving, after an adjustment is made for inter-sector transfers (these are mainly in the form of government benefits and capital grants, which assume positive values, and taxes, which assume negative values). Capital transactions are mainly investments in physical goods. The financial surplus/deficit is then the link between the real transactions of the sector and its financial transactions. If a sector has a financial surplus then it has funds available to add to its financial assets or to reduce its financial liabilities. A financial deficit implies the sector needs to raise funds by selling financial assets or increasing its financial liabilities by borrowing.

To introduce the construction of sector financial transaction accounts we will consider a simple two-sector economy – households and firms – which has two financial instruments available for transactions – trade credit and equity. Trade credit is an asset of firms, that is, it represents funds lent from firms to households. Equity, on the other hand, is an asset of households. At 31 December 2002 our imaginary household sector is described by the balance sheet in table 1.7.

Over 2003 the household sector undertakes the following transactions:

	Income	£500 million
–	Expenditure	£300 million
=	Saving	£200 million
–	Investment	£100 million
=	Financial balance	£100 million

So for 2003 the household sector has a financial surplus of £100 million, which implies that it has funds available to enable it to acquire additional

Table 1.7 Example of a household sector balance sheet at 31 December 2002

Liabilities	£million	Assets	£million
Net wealth	1,400	Tangible assets	800
Financial liabilities	200	Financial assets	800
Total	1,600		1,600

Table 1.8 Example of a household sector balance sheet at 31 December 2003

Liabilities	£million	Assets	£million
Net wealth	1,600	Tangible assets	900
Financial liabilities	300	Financial assets	1,000
Total	1,900		1,900

financial assets or reduce existing liabilities, or both. For this example we take the situation where households acquire £200 million of company-issued equities as well as increasing their liabilities by £100 by borrowing from companies through the medium of trade credit. Any other collection of financial transactions is possible as long as the net transactions are consistent with the financial surplus. As a result of these transactions the household sector balance sheet for the end of 2003 will be as shown in table 1.8.

The increase in tangible assets is the result of investment over the period. The value of financial assets and liabilities has increased by the value of the transactions over the period. The change in the value of net wealth comes about to bring the balance sheet of households back into balance. Another way to see the increase in net wealth is that it is equal to the value of saving over the period. Saving, which is the value of funds coming into the sector which are not consumed, is one way in which the size of the balance sheet of the sector can increase. The other way is for the value of assets already held to increase. In the case of households, the value of housing may increase as a result of an increase in house prices. So it is possible for the net wealth of a sector to increase without it saving any funds out of its income. However, changes in the value of assets are not captured within financial accounts.

If we now consider the firms sector in our imaginary economy, its balance sheet for the end of 2002 is given in table 1.9.

Table 1.9 Example of a firms sector balance sheet at 31 December 2002

Liabilities	£million	Assets	£million
Net wealth	300	Tangible assets	500
Financial liabilities	400	Financial assets	200
Total	700		700

The firms sector flows over 2003 are given below:

Income	£200 million
Consumption	–
Saving	£200 million
Investment	£300 million
Financial balance	£–100 million

The firms sector has retained earnings of £200 million over 2003 but invests £300 million, leaving it with a financial deficit of £100 million. This implies that firms must sell existing assets or borrow new funds to finance the deficit. The financial decisions of the firms sector are implied by the household sector flows described earlier. This is because in a two-sector economy, as one sector increases its asset holdings the other sector must be increasing its liabilities by the same amount, for the reasons explained in section 1.3. The financial decisions of firms are therefore to borrow funds through the issue of £200 million of equities and at the same time to increase holdings of financial assets by £100 million. The resulting balance sheet for the firms sector for the end of 2003 is given in table 1.10.

Table 1.10 Example of a firms sector balance sheet at 31 December 2003

Liabilities	£million	Assets	£million
Net wealth	500	Tangible assets	800
Financial liabilities	600	Financial assets	300
Total	1,100		1,100

The financial transactions for the two sectors can be brought together in a financial account, as shown in table 1.11.

Table 1.11 Financial account for the two-sector economy (£million)

	Households	Firms	Total
Saving	200	200	400
Investment	100	300	400
Financial balance	100	–100	
Trade credit	–100	100	
Equities	200	–200	
Net financial transactions	100	–100	

The convention of financial accounts is:

(i) a positive value implies an increase in financial assets or a decrease in financial liabilities
(ii) a negative sign implies an increase in financial liabilities or a decrease in financial assets.

So in the financial account in table 1.11, a negative sign on trade credit transactions for the households sector implies that this sector is increasing its liabilities, that is, it is borrowing more from companies through the medium of trade credit. It should be clear from this example that in order to interpret a particular figure in the financial transactions account we need to know not only the convention stated above also but whether the instrument transacted is an asset or liability of that sector.

From this simple financial account we can discern the accounting rules which underlie its construction and the construction of all financial accounts. First, the sum of the financial surpluses and deficits is zero, which reflects the fact that the financial assets of one sector are by definition the financial liabilities of another. Second, the net financial transactions of a sector will equal its financial balance. Third, the sum of transactions in a particular financial instrument will equal zero. This again follows from the fact that increased holdings of an asset of one sector will be balanced by increased liabilities of another. Finally, the sum of saving across sectors, that is, for the economy, will equal the sum of investment across sectors. In other words, all saving will find its way into investment.

We now turn to examine the financial accounts for the complete UK economy.

1.8 Financial accounts for the UK economy

National Statistics publishes financial accounts for the UK on a quarterly basis in *Financial Statistics* and annually in *The UK National Accounts* (*The Blue Book*).

The financial account for 2000 is presented in table 1.12. This account is fully disaggregated into the sectors/subsectors described earlier. The total number of financial instruments is 33. The matrix in table 1.12 is clearly larger and more disaggregated than the matrix for our imaginary economy in table 1.11. Its structure is also slightly different in that each sector's transaction in an instrument is split into either net acquisition of financial assets or financial liabilities. Where the financial transaction is shown as positive in the section for net acquisition of financial assets then the sector is increasing assets. Similarly, where the financial transaction is shown as positive in the section for net acquisition of financial liabilities it implies the sector is increasing its liabilities.

There are problems with the data used to construct both national income and financial accounts. The figures making up these accounts are recorded with varying degrees of error. A sector's overall financial position, after calculating all income, expenditure and capital flows, is shown in its financial balance. If these flows were accurately recorded and if the sector's financial transactions were likewise identified in full, then the net lending/borrowing from the financial account (sum of financial transactions, shown in line B.9f of table 1.12, should equal net lending/borrowing from the capital account (the financial balance – shown as line B.9). The effects of the errors and omissions in the flows lead to a difference between the financial balance and the sum of financial transactions. This difference is recorded in the summary accounts as the statistical discrepancy (in line dB.9f). For the public sector and financial institutions, where most transactions have to be accurately recorded for policy or supervisory purposes, the statistical discrepancy tends to be small. For the other sectors, where there is less direct collection of statistics, the balancing items are often quite large. For the household sector this item was approximately £8.5 billion in 2000.

However, despite this drawback there are still many interesting points that can be drawn from a study of a financial account. One fundamental thing that the accounts show is that those people who save in an economy are not the same as those people who invest in physical assets. The financial account thus demonstrates one of the reasons for the existence of financial institutions, which is to channel funds from savers to investors, and it shows the various routes by which the funds flow. This will be considered in more detail in the next chapter. The financial account, by setting the flows for each sector together in a consistent framework, also allows us to obtain a more complete picture of financial relationships when compared with looking at each sector's flows individually. For example, if we examine row F.221 in the account in table 1.12, we can see each sector's transactions in deposits with monetary financial institutions (banks and building societies). Here we see that all sectors were acquiring bank deposit assets

(i.e. a positive sign in the section showing net acquisition of financial assets). This is reflected in an acquisition of financial liabilities by monetary financial institutions (i.e. a positive sign in the section net acquisition of financial liabilities). By looking down the column for insurance corporations and pension funds in the section for net acquisition of financial assets we can see that the principal investment by these institutions in 2000 was medium- and long-term bonds issued by UK residents (corporate bonds). We can also observe that insurance corporations and pension funds were selling holdings of UK government bonds and overseas shares (hence the negative signs for transactions in these instruments in the section net acquisition of financial assets).

This discussion of some of the features of the 2000 financial accounts is intended to show that, bearing in mind the caveat on data deficiencies, some interesting insights into changing financial relationships can be obtained from a study of such accounts.

1.9 **Conclusion**

In this chapter we have started our examination of the role of a financial system in an economy, established some fundamental concepts of finance, have introduced data on wealth and financial transactions in the UK and shown the relationship between these. In the next chapter we build on this and examine further the role of a financial system in mediating between savers and investors, before we look at how financial systems evolve.

Notes

1 Note also that deposits are insured against default to a limited extent – see chapter 17 for further details.
2 When used as a prefix, as in 'eurobond' or 'eurocurrency', 'euro' does not refer to the single currency of the European Union, but rather indicates that a bond or sum of money is denominated in a currency which is different from that of the country where it is issued or held.

Table 1.12

The following eight pages reproduce table 1.7.8, 'Main aggregates and summary accounts: UK summary accounts 2000' from Richard Clegg, ed. *National Statistics. United Kingdom National Accounts. The Blue Book 2002.* London: The Stationery Office. Crown copyright 2002. The first two parts of the table present the assets held by the private and public sectors, respectively; the second two parts the liabilities of these respective sectors. The following abbreviations are used: SDRs, special drawing rights; MFI, monetary financial institution; ROW, rest of the world.

Table 1.12 UK summary accounts for 2000: III.2 Financial account (£million)

		UK total economy	Non-financial corporations	Financial corporations	Monetary financial institutions	Other financial intermediaries and auxiliaries	Insurance corporations and pension funds
		S.1	S.11	S.12	S.121+S.122	S.123+S.124	S.125
F.A	**Net acquisition of financial assets**						
F.1	Monetary gold and special drawing rights (SDRs)	–956					
F.2	Currency and deposits						
F.21	Currency	602	308	–1,413	–1,413	–	
F.22	Transferable deposits						
F.221	Deposits with UK MFIs	143,612	13,455	83,630	39,114	38,606	5,910
F.229	Deposits with ROW MFIs	209,468	25,403	181,316	133,461	47,047	808
F.29	Other deposits	5,726	320	2,685	–6	2,691	–
F.2	Total currency and deposits	359,408	39,486	266,218	171,156	88,344	6,718
F.3	Securities other than shares						
F.331	Short-term: money market instruments						
F.3311	Issued by UK central government	–1,402	–78	–1,113	–1,222	–60	169
F.3312	Issued by UK local authorities	–	–	–	–	–	
F.3315	Issued by UK MFIs	–14,324	–83	–15,673	–19,114	2,091	1,350
F.3316	Issued by other UK residents	–1,330	–2,788	1,399	847	486	66
F.3319	Issued by ROW	–2,508	1,110	–3,862	331	–4,144	–49
F.332	Medium- (1–5-year) and long-term (over 5-year) bonds						
F.3321	Issued by UK central government	–12,038	230	–10,737	–7,675	8,365	–11,427
F.3322	Issued by UK local authorities	–12	–	61	–	28	33
F.3325	Medium-term bonds issued by UK MFIs	2,045	–237	2,282	3,976	–422	–1,272
F.3326	Other medium- and long-term bonds issued by UK residents	65,371	1,148	64,044	18,503	15,580	29,961
F.3329	Long-term bonds issued by ROW	54,868	1,792	47,402	36,532	–902	11,772
F.34	Financial derivatives	–1,616	21	–1,553	–1,553	–	–
F.3	Total securities other than shares	89,054	1,115	82,250	30,625	21,022	30,603

F.4	Loans						
F.41	Short-term loans						
F.411	Loans by UK MFIs, excluding loans secured on dwellings and financial leasing	154,795		154,795	154,795		
F.419	Loans by ROW MFIs						
F.42	Long-term loans						
F.421	Direct investment	22,579	22,050	529	–222	105	646
F.422	Loans secured on dwellings	42,405	–	42,196	28,420	13,608	168
F.423	Finance leasing	–291		–291	–40	–251	
F.424	Other long-term loans	24,856	13,204	6,985	–1,478	5	8,458
F.429	Other long-term loans by ROW						
F.4	Total loans	244,344	35,254	204,214	181,475	13,467	9,272
F.5	Shares and other equity						
F.51	Shares and other equity, excluding mutual funds' shares						
F.514	Quoted UK shares	105,581	87,591	34,649	619	11,328	22,702
F.515	Unquoted UK shares	–19,796	–27,786	14,172	8,931	9,764	–4,523
F.516	Other UK equity (including direct investment in property)	–24					
F.519	Shares and other equity issued by ROW	205,730	179,470	27,031	10,513	32,120	–15,602
F.52	Mutual funds' shares						
F.521	UK mutual funds' shares	13,969	14	7,175	43	118	7,014
F.529	ROW mutual funds' shares	–					
F.5	Total shares and other equity	305,460	239,289	83,027	20,106	53,330	9,591
F.6	Insurance technical reserves						
F.61	Net equity of households in life assurance and pension funds' reserves	43,681					
F.62	Prepayments of insurance premiums and reserves for outstanding claims	412	268	41	–	18	23
F.6	Total insurance technical reserves	44,093	268	41	–		23
F.7	Other accounts receivable	33,435	26,627	–2,452	42	657	–3,151
F.A	**Total net acquisition of financial assets**	1,074,838	342,039	633,298	403,404	176,838	53,056

Table 1.12 *Continued*

		General government S.13	Central government S.1311	Local government S.1313	Households and non-profit institutions serving households S.14+S.15	Rest of the world S.2
F.A	**Net acquisition of financial assets**					
F.1	Monetary gold and SDRs	–956	–956			956
F.2	Currency and deposits					
F.21	Currency				1,707	65
F.22	Transferable deposits					
F.221	Deposits with UK MFIs	15,798	15,193	605	30,729	199,170
F.229	Deposits with ROW MFIs	–840	–840		3,589	
F.29	Other deposits	2,918	2,918	–	–197	527
F.2	Total currency and deposits	17,876	17,271	605	35,828	199,762
F.3	Securities other than shares					
F.331	Short-term: money market instruments					
F.3311	Issued by UK central government	–218		–218	7	–251
F.3312	Issued by UK local authorities	–	–		–	–
F.3315	Issued by UK MFIs	1,850	1,435	415	–418	38,277
F.3316	Issued by other UK residents	59	–	59	–	2,703
F.3319	Issued by ROW	244	244			
F.332	Medium- (1–5-year) and long-term (over 5-year) bonds					
F.3321	Issued by UK central government	–195		–195	–1,336	–663
F.3322	Issued by UK local authorities				–73	–
F.3325	Medium-term bonds issued by UK MFIs					2,705
F.3326	Other medium- and long-term bonds issued by UK residents	11	11		168	10,528
F.3329	Long-term bonds issued by ROW	5,418	5,418		256	
F.34	Financial derivatives	–84	–84	–	–	
F.3	Total securities other than shares	7,085	7,024	61	–1,396	53,299

F.4	Loans					
F.41	Short-term loans					
F.411	Loans by UK MFIs, excluding loans secured on dwellings and financial leasing					
F.419	Loans by ROW MFIs					30,817
F.42	Long-term loans					
F.421	Direct investment					47,666
F.422	Loans secured on dwellings	209	–1	210		
F.423	Finance leasing					
F.424	Other long-term loans	4,484	4,512	–28	183	
F.429	Other long-term loans by ROW					–293
F.4	Total loans	4,693	4,511	182	183	119,614
F.5	Shares and other equity					
F.51	Shares and other equity, excluding mutual funds' shares					
F.514	Quoted UK shares	54	–103	157	–16,713	121,583
F.515	Unquoted UK shares	–	–	–	–6,182	60,826
F.516	Other UK equity (including direct investment in property)	–	–		–24	1,629
F.519	Shares and other equity issued by ROW	53	53		–824	
F.52	Mutual funds' shares					
F.521	UK mutual funds' shares				6,780	43
F.529	ROW mutual funds' shares				–	
F.5	Total shares and other equity	107	–50	157	–16,963	184,081
F.6	Insurance technical reserves					
F.61	Net equity of households in life assurance and pension funds' reserves				43,681	–4
F.62	Prepayments of insurance premiums and reserves for outstanding claims	26		26	77	1,054
F.6	Total insurance technical reserves	26		26	43,758	1,050
F.7	Other accounts receivable	2,556	2,194	362	6,704	–90
F.A	**Total net acquisition of financial assets**	31,387	29,994	1,393	68,114	558,672

Table 1.12 *Continued*

		UK total economy S.1	Non-financial corporations S.11	Financial corporations S.12	Monetary financial institutions S.121+S.122	Other financial intermediaries and auxiliaries S.123+S.124	Insurance corporations and pension funds S.125
F.L	**Net acquisition of financial liabilities**						
F.2	Currency and deposits						
F.21	Currency	678		448	448		
F.22	Transferable deposits						
F.221	Deposits with UK MFIs	342,782		342,782	342,782		
F.229	Deposits with ROW MFIs						
F.29	Other deposits	6,253		2,918		2,918	
F.2	Total currency and deposits	349,713		346,148	343,230	2,918	
F.3	Securities other than shares						
F.331	Short-term: money market instruments						
F.3311	Issued by UK central government	–1,653					
F.3312	Issued by UK local authorities	–					
F.3315	Issued by UK MFIs	23,953		23,953	23,953		
F.3316	Issued by other UK residents	1,373	1,334	–16		–16	
F.3319	Issued by the ROW						
F.332	Medium- (1–5-year) and long-term (over 5-year) bonds						
F.3321	Issued by UK central government	–12,701					
F.3322	Issued by UK local authorities	–12					
F.3325	Medium-term bonds issued by UK MFIs	4,750		4,750	4,750		
F.3326	Other medium- and long-term bonds issued by UK residents	75,899	40,601	35,298	11,006	24,073	219
F.3329	Long-term bonds issued by ROW						
F.34	Financial derivatives	–113	–	–113	–113	–	–
F.3	Total securities other than shares	91,496	41,935	63,872	39,596	24,057	219
F.4	Loans						
F.41	Short-term loans						
F.411	Loans by UK MFIs, excluding loans secured on dwellings and financial leasing	97,112	25,592	56,067		54,566	1,501
F.419	Loans by ROW MFIs	72,241	12,368	58,177		59,480	–1,303

F.42	Long-term loans						
F.421	Direct investment	47,666	47,332	334	1	241	92
F.422	Loans secured on dwellings	42,405					
F.423	Finance leasing	–291	–199	–127	–61	–66	
F.424	Other long-term loans by UK residents	26,766	–573	17,508		17,631	–123
F.429	Other long-term loans by ROW	–293	–	–30		–30	
F.4	Total loans	285,606	84,520	131,929	–60	131,822	167
F.5	Shares and other equity						
F.51	Shares and other equity, excluding mutual funds' shares						
F.514	Quoted UK shares	227,164	209,418	17,746	2,410	6,750	8,586
F.515	Unquoted UK shares	41,030	12,729	28,301	10,907	17,350	44
F.516	Other UK equity (including direct investment in property)	1,605	1,605	–	–		
F.519	Shares and other equity issued by ROW						
F.52	Mutual funds' shares						
F.521	UK mutual funds' shares	14,012		14,012		14,012	
F.529	ROW mutual funds' shares						
F.5	Total shares and other equity	283,811	223,752	60,059	13,317	38,112	8,630
F.6	Insurance technical reserves						
F.61	Net equity of households in life assurance and pension funds' reserves	43,677		43,677			43,677
F.62	Prepayments of insurance premiums and reserves for outstanding claims	1,466		1,466			1,466
F.6	Total insurance technical reserves	45,143		45,143			45,143
F.7	Other accounts payable	33,062	1,520	7,803	1,499	33	6,271
F.L	**Total net acquisition of financial liabilities**	1,088,831	351,727	654,954	397,582	196,942	60,430
B.9	**Net lending/borrowing**						
F.A	Total net acquisition of financial assets	1,074,838	342,039	633,298	403,404	176,838	53,056
-F.L	*less* Total net acquisition of financial liabilities	–1,088,831	–351,727	–654,954	–397,582	–196,942	–60,430
B.9f	Net lending (+) / net borrowing (-), from financial account	–13,993	–9,688	–21,656	5,822	–20,104	–7,374
dB.9f	Statistical discrepancy between financial and non-financial accounts	–3,392	5,702	235	1,381	13,653	–14,799
B.9	**Net lending (+) / net borrowing (-), from capital account**	**–17,385**	**–3,986**	**–21,421**	**7,203**	**–6,451**	**–22,173**

Table 1.12 *Continued*

		General government	Central government	Local government	Households and non-profit institutions serving households	Rest of the world
		S.13	S.1311	S.1313	S.14+S.15	S.2
F.L	**Net acquisition of financial liabilities**					
F.2	Currency and deposits					
F.21	Currency	230	230			–11
F.22	Transferable deposits					
F.221	Deposits with UK MFIs					
F.229	Deposits with ROW MFIs					209,468
F.29	Other deposits	3,335	3,335			
F.2	Total currency and deposits	3,565	3,565			209,457
F.3	Securities other than shares					
F.331	Short-term: money market instruments					
F.3311	Issued by UK central government	–1,653	–1,653			
F.3312	Issued by UK local authorities	–		–		
F.3315	Issued by UK MFIs					
F.3316	Issued by other UK residents				55	
F.3319	Issued by the ROW					–2,508
F.332	Medium- (1–5-year) and long-term (over 5-year) bonds					
F.3321	Issued by UK central government	–12,701	–12,701			
F.3322	Issued by UK local authorities	–12		–12		
F.3325	Medium-term bonds issued by UK MFIs					
F.3326	Other medium- and long-term bonds issued by UK residents				–	
F.3329	Long-term bonds issued by ROW					54,868
F.34	Financial derivatives				–	
F.3	Total securities other than shares	–14,366	–14,354	–12	55	50,857
F.4	Loans					
F.41	Short-term loans					
F.411	Loans by UK MFIs, excluding loans secured on dwellings and financial leasing	–607	–325	–282	16,060	57,683
F.419	Loans by ROW MFIs	–39	–	–39	1,735	

F.42	Long-term loans					
F.421	Direct investment					22,579
F.422	Loans secured on dwellings				42,405	
F.423	Finance leasing	35	15	20		–
F.424	Other long-term loans by UK residents	1,418	–26	1,444	8,413	–1,910
F.429	Other long-term loans by ROW	–263	–114	–149		
F.4	Total loans	544	–450	994	68,613	78,352
F.5	Shares and other equity					
F.51	Shares and other equity, excluding mutual funds' shares					
F.514	Quoted UK shares					
F.515	Unquoted UK shares					
F.516	Other UK equity (including direct investment in property)					
F.519	Shares and other equity issued by ROW					205,730
F.52	Mutual funds' shares					
F.521	UK mutual funds' shares					
F.529	ROW mutual funds' shares					–
F.5	Total shares and other equity					205,730
F.6	Insurance technical reserves					
F.61	Net equity of households in life assurance and pension funds' reserves					
F.62	Prepayments of insurance premiums and reserves for outstanding claims					
F.6	Total insurance technical reserves					
F.7	Other accounts payable	25,164	25,037	127	–1,425	283
F.L	**Total net acquisition of financial liabilities**	14,907	13,798	1,109	67,243	544,679
B.9	**Net lending/borrowing**					
F.A	Total net acquisition of financial assets	31,387	29,994	1,393	68,114	558,672
-F.L	*less* Total net acquisition of financial liabilities	–14,907	–13,798	–1,109	–67,243	–544,679
B.9f	Net lending (+) / net borrowing (-), from financial account	16,480	16,196	284,871		13,993
dB.9f	Statistical discrepancy between financial and non-financial accounts	–851	42	–893	–8,478	–3,392
B.9	**Net lending (+) / net borrowing (-), from capital account**	**15,629**	**16,238**	**–609**	**–7,607**	**–17,385**

Chapter 2

Financial intermediation and recent developments in the UK financial system

2.1 Introduction

In this chapter our primary aim is to describe the process of financial intermediation and in doing so we examine the arguments as to why we need financial institutions such as banks. We also examine the evolution of financial systems and in particular distinguish between the more market-oriented systems of the UK and US, and the more bank-oriented systems of Germany and Japan. Finally we provide an overview of the tremendous changes that have taken place in the UK financial system over the last 20 years. This will provide a framework for the more specific discussion of events affecting financial institutions and markets which make up the remainder of this book.

2.2 The nature of financial intermediation

In developed economies, decisions to invest (in capital projects) are often taken separately from decisions to save. There are some exceptions to this: for example, firms which do not distribute all profits as dividends but retain some to finance investment are both saving and investing. However, even when saving and investment are carried out by the same economic agent, the timing of the decisions will often be different. Saving may precede the investment as sufficient funds are accumulated, or the saving may follow the investment as the debts used to finance it are paid off. However, it is a general feature of developed economies that a high proportion of saving is not used immediately by the saver but is made available to investors elsewhere. In chapter 1, one of the roles of a financial system was described as the channelling of funds from those economic agents with a financial surplus (lenders) to those economic agents with a financial deficit (borrowers). Whilst most borrowing is used to finance investment, this more precise statement acknowledges that there will be some economic agents

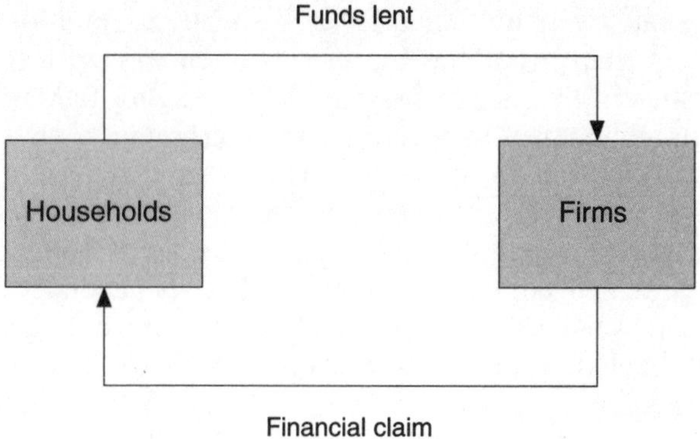

Figure 2.1 Direct financing.

who borrow to finance a deficit that has arisen not from investment but from an excess of consumption over income.

A financial system essentially consists of financial markets and financial institutions. In this section we examine the role of the financial system, in particular financial institutions, in the process of channelling funds from lenders to borrowers. To begin the analysis we return to our simple economy, introduced in section 1.2, which consists of households and firms. Assuming that households in aggregate are lenders and firms in aggregate are borrowers, then the only way in which funds can flow from lenders to borrowers is directly, as shown in figure 2.1.

In this simple economy, firms will finance some part of their investment by borrowing funds from households and in return households will hold the financial claims issued by firms. Investment, which takes the form of the purchase of physical assets such as buildings or machinery, will generally be long term in nature and the borrower is likely to want to repay the amount borrowed over a long period, in line with the flow of expected returns from the project. Further to this, investment returns are likely to be uncertain. The firm making the investment may have misjudged the market for the product, or the cost of producing the product may be higher than anticipated. Both these factors would cause returns to be less than expected. Furthermore, the purchased physical assets are generally highly specialised, making them difficult to sell, if problems occur, except at a loss. The claims that firms issue will have characteristics reflecting the nature of the investment project. They will seek to issue long-term claims to provide a reasonable prospect of the investment generating sufficient returns to repay the claim. The uncertainty of investment returns is likely to lead firms to seek to finance some part of the investment in the form of equity, so that the claim can be remunerated according to the profitability of the investment.

Whilst some (wealthy) lenders will be happy to hold long-term, risky claims, it is likely that the majority of lenders will seek different characteristics in the claims they hold. By lending funds, the lender is indicating a willingness to give up some consumption now in return for greater consumption in the future. However, there are a great many uncertainties in life and many lenders will wish to retain discretion as to when that future consumption takes place. It is clear from this discussion that the requirements of borrowers and lenders are generally different. The claims issued by borrowers are likely to be long term and high risk whereas lenders are likely to prefer to hold claims which are short term and more certain. In addition, borrowers are likely to be seeking to borrow a sum of money greater than the sum that an individual lender will typically lend. In the absence of organised financial markets or financial institutions, as presented in figure 2.1, lending/borrowing will occur as a result of direct negotiation between two parties. The claims produced as a result of direct negotiation will be highly illiquid since it will be difficult to sell them in the absence of an organised market. There are also various types of cost involved in direct lending, which are:

(i) search costs – the costs of searching out potential transactors, obtaining information about them and negotiating a contract;
(ii) verification costs – lenders will incur costs in evaluating borrowing proposals;
(iii) monitoring costs – lenders incur further costs, after the loan is made, from monitoring the actions of borrowers to ensure that the terms of the contract are met;
(iv) enforcement costs – further costs arise should the borrower be unable to meet the commitments as promised and a solution must be worked out between the lender and borrower or other aspects of the contract enforced.

In addition to these transaction costs, lenders are also faced with the problems arising out of asymmetric information. This refers to the situation where one party to a transaction has better information than the second party. In this case the borrower has more information than the lender about the potential returns and risks of the investment project for which funds are being lent. The existence of asymmetric information creates problems in the financial system both before a transaction is entered into, in evaluating borrowing proposals, and after, in monitoring and enforcing the loan contract.

2.2.1 *Asymmetric information: adverse selection and moral hazard*

The first problem created by the situation of asymmetric information is that of adverse selection. This is a problem at the search/verification stage

of the transaction, when the lender is selecting a potential borrower. Adverse selection occurs when the potential borrowers who are the most likely to produce an adverse outcome are the ones who most actively seek out a loan and hence are most likely to be selected. Because adverse selection makes it more likely that loans will be made to borrowers who are likely to default, lenders may decide not to lend at all, even though there are borrowers who are good credit risks in the market.

To understand why adverse selection occurs, suppose you have two friends to whom you might make a loan. Your first friend, Sally, is a cautious person who borrows only when she has an investment project she is sure will generate a return that will safely pay off the loan. By contrast, your second friend, Anna, loves taking risks and has a scheme which she is sure will make her a lot of money. Unfortunately, as with most risky investments, there is a high probability that Anna will lose money from the investment and be unable to pay off the loan. Which of your friends is most likely to ask you for a loan? The answer is, of course, Anna, as she has a lot to gain if the investment does well.

If information were not asymmetric, in other words if you knew the likely risks and returns of the investment projects suggested by your friends, then you would not make a loan to Anna as you would know there is a good chance that you would not be repaid. However, given the existence of asymmetric information, you are more likely to lend to Anna than Sally because Anna is the friend who is more likely to ask you for a loan. Given the possibility of adverse selection you may decide not to lend to either of your friends. This will mean that Sally, who is good credit risk, would be denied finance when she has a worthwhile investment project.

A second problem that arises out of asymmetric information is moral hazard. This can occur before or after the loan has been made. First, the intending borrower may wilfully misrepresent the circumstances surrounding the loan, such as the purpose of the loan or the likely profitably of the project for which money is borrowed. Moral hazard after the loan has been granted is associated with the monitoring and enforcement stages. Moral hazard, in financial markets, is the risk that the borrower will engage in activities that are undesirable (immoral) from the lender's point of view because they make it less likely that the loan is repaid. The existence of moral hazard may make lenders less likely to make loans.

As an example of moral hazard suppose you have made a loan of £1,000 to another friend, Joe, who has asked you for the loan so that he can purchase a computer and set himself up in business as a graphic designer. Once you have made the loan there is a risk that Joe will not use the money for what he claimed he was going to use it for, but instead use it to bet on the horses. If he bets on a 25–1 long shot and wins then he is able to repay the loan and keep £24,000 for himself. On the other hand, if he loses, which is likely as

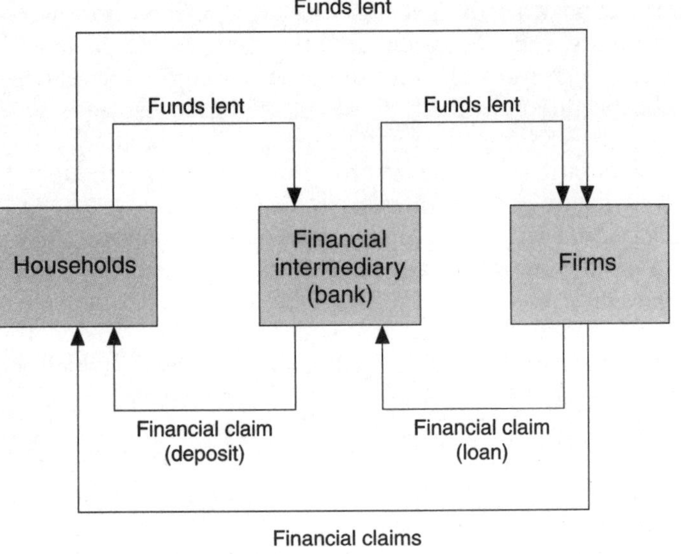

Figure 2.2 Intermediated financing.

long shots do not often win races, then you do not get paid and Joe loses his reputation as a reliable friend. If Joe believes the gains from correctly betting (£24,000) are of more value than the cost (his reputation) if he bets incorrectly then Joe is more likely to place the bet with the borrowed funds. If you knew that Joe was likely to make the bet then you would prevent him doing so. However, it is difficult for you to monitor the activities of Joe once you have made the loan because information is asymmetric. The potential for moral hazard may make you reluctant to lend money.

2.2.2 *Markets and intermediaries*

Transaction costs and information asymmetries are important impediments to well functioning financial transactions. One solution is the emergence of organised financial markets where tradable equity or debt (bond) financial instruments can be issued and acquired. Such markets are labelled capital markets as they allow firms to issue financial claims to enable them to raise finance to acquire capital (physical) assets. The existence of such markets overcomes some of the obstacles to lending/borrowing. In particular the ability to sell on claims in a market will enhance the liquidity of those claims to the lender and so encourage more lending to take place. A central feature of organised markets is the existence of specialised brokers who bring together buyers and sellers and so reduce search costs. However,

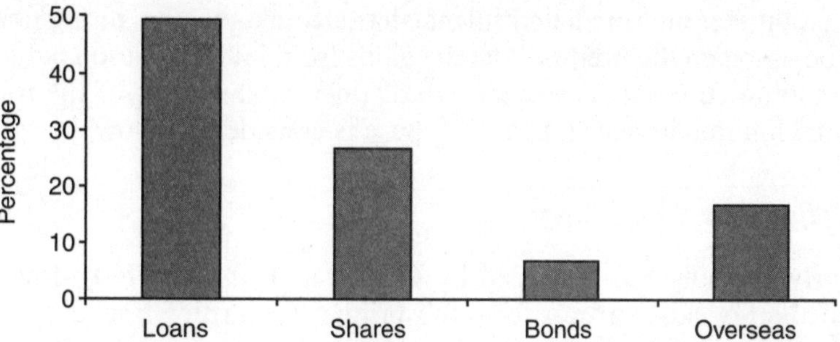

Figure 2.3 Sources of external funds for UK non-financial firms, 1970–2000. Loans are made up primarily of bank loans but include loans made by other financial institutions. Shares consist mainly of issued share capital. Bonds consist mainly of debentures. Overseas capital refers to capital funding originating outside the UK – mainly loans. Source: *Financial Statistics*. National Statistics online database (http://www.statistics.gov.uk/statbase/TSDTimeZone.asp).

there are still substantial transaction costs and high risks for the lender as well as the problems of adverse selection and moral hazard. As we will see in section 2.3.2 though, there are ways in which traded equity and debt contracts can be designed to minimise adverse selection and moral hazard, and financial intermediaries are able to reduce transaction costs and alleviate the problems of adverse selection and moral hazard. With the existence of financial intermediaries, small savers are able to lend money to them with lower transaction costs and in return hold the claims issued by those intermediaries; these claims will have characteristics such as high liquidity and low risk which are more attractive to savers. Financial intermediaries will use the funds to lend to borrowers and thus hold the higher-risk and longer-term claims issued by borrowers. This is illustrated in figure 2.2.

The success of financial intermediaries, such as banks, is evidenced by the fact that most external funds for non-financial businesses in the UK are provided by banks – see figure 2.3.

In the next section we examine the main reasons suggested to explain why financial intermediaries exist.

2.3 What do financial intermediaries do?

Before considering the advantages over direct finance of intermediated finance through organised markets, it is useful to observe that under intermediated finance the chain of transactions between the firm and ultimate lender is longer and this is likely to entail additional transaction costs. Any

proposition that intermediated finance has advantages over direct finance must be based on the premise that the gains from intermediation outweigh these additional costs. There are two distinct explanations of the role of financial intermediaries and each of these is considered below.

2.3.1 *Banks as transformers*

An early account was provided by Gurley and Shaw (1960): financial intermediaries exist to transform the primary securities issued by firms into the indirect securities desired by ultimate lenders. So an intermediary, such as a bank, will issue deposit claims which have the characteristics of small size, low risk and high liquidity, and use a proportion of the funds raised to acquire the larger, high-risk and illiquid claims issued by firms. The intermediary is undertaking three main transformations, involving the maturity, risk and size of the claims.

Maturity transformation

The liabilities of intermediaries such as banks are on average of a much shorter term than are their assets. In fact, approximately half of UK retail banks' deposits are repayable on demand. Banks are said to be mismatching their balance sheets, or borrowing 'short' and lending 'long'. Mismatching exposes the intermediary to liquidity risk, which is the risk that it will have insufficient liquid funds to meet its commitments. Under normal circumstances only a small fraction of depositors demand repayment of deposits at a particular time and other depositors will be placing new deposits. It is therefore possible for a bank to estimate its liquidity needs and to provide for them by holding some of its assets in liquid form. However, if a large number of depositors demand repayment (i.e. a 'run' develops on the bank), perhaps because of concerns about the bank's solvency, the bank's ability to meet deposit withdrawals breaks down. Some of the strategies that banks use to manage liquidity risk are discussed in chapter 3.

Risk transformation

Financial intermediaries such as banks hold in their asset portfolio mainly loans which carry a higher risk of default than the deposits they issue to finance these loans. Banks are able to transform risky assets into virtually riskless deposits by:

(i) minimising the risk of individual loans it takes on (i.e. by screening out bad risks);
(ii) diversifying risks (i.e. spreading risks by lending to different types of borrower – this brings about a greater independence of loan risks);

(iii) pooling risks (i.e. having a large number of loans so that, as a consequence of the law of large numbers, the variability of losses is reduced);
(iv) holding sufficient capital to meet any unexpected losses.

These techniques for managing this process of risk transformation are discussed in more detail in chapter 3.

Size transformation
It was noted above that lenders tend to want to lend smaller amounts of funds than the amounts which borrowers generally wish to borrow. Financial intermediaries are able to collect together the small amounts made available by lenders and parcel these into the larger amounts required by borrowers.

The reason why we need financial intermediaries to undertake this transformation process is that there exist indivisibilities and/or economies of scale in lending/borrowing. For example, if an individual wanted to make a loan, to protect his investment he would probably have a contract drawn up by a lawyer where the terms of the loan are specified. The cost to the individual of having the contract drawn up may make it uneconomic to make the loan. However, a financial institution like a bank will be able to use a standard loan contract for a wide range of loans, so the unit cost of the contract per loan is much smaller for the bank than for the individual. Thus financial institutions are able to take advantage of economies of scale to reduce transaction costs.

To illustrate more formally how financial intermediaries are able to reduce transaction costs, we denote the rate of interest as R, transaction costs as T and subscripts L and B as the lender and borrower, respectively (note that these costs are calculated as a percentage of the loan):

the net return for the lender $\qquad R_L = R - T_L$

the net cost for the borrower $\qquad R_B = R + T_B$

then $\qquad R_B - R_L = T_B + T_L$

The introduction of an intermediary introduces a new element of cost, C, which we, for convenience, assume is paid by the borrower and is again expressed in percentage terms. Thus now:

$$R_L = R - T_L'$$

$$R_B = R + T_B' + C$$

where the prime indicates transaction costs after the introduction of the intermediary. Hence:

$$R_B - R_L = T_B' + T_L' + C$$

The gap between lending and borrowing rates will be lower and benefit both parties provided:

$$(T_B + T_L) - (T_B' + T_L') > C$$

that is, provided the intermediary has lowered transaction costs by more than its charge.

2.3.2 *Banks reduce the problems arising out of asymmetric information*

The second approach to explaining the existence of financial intermediaries views intermediaries as institutions that reduce or eliminate problems relating to asymmetric information in the lending/borrowing process. As we saw in section 2.2.1, lenders typically have less information than borrowers and as a consequence are faced with the problems of adverse selection and moral hazard. The problem of adverse selection can be solved by the production of more information on the circumstances of the borrower. One way this can be done is for private companies to collect and produce information which distinguishes good firms from bad firms and sell this information to lenders. In the US, companies such as Standard and Poor's, and Moody's collect and publish information on firms' balance sheet positions and financial statements. This system of private production and sale of information does not completely solve the problem of adverse selection because of the free-rider problem. This problem occurs when people who do not pay for information take advantage of information that other people have paid for. So, if one person pays for information on a firm and then purchases directly the securities issued by that firm she may be observed by other investors who have not purchased the information but who also buy the same securities. If enough investors buy the securities the price will be bid up, thus negating the benefits to the original purchaser of the information. If this free-rider problem is known to investors then private firms will not be able to sell as much information, as the value of this information is limited by the free-rider problem.

However, financial intermediaries can help solve the adverse selection problem more fully. A financial institution, such as a bank, can develop an expertise in information production that enables it to select mainly good risks. One particular advantage that banks possess in this area is that they can gain information about potential borrowers from their transactions accounts held with the bank. If these potential borrowers route most transactions through their accounts, information is gained that enables the bank to build up a profile of a customer's suitability for credit and ability to repay loans. Such informational economies of scope provide one rationale

for the joint packaging of payments and loan services (discussed in chapter 3). Because the bank lends to mainly good risks then it is more able to make a profit on its lending. An important element in the bank's ability to profit from information it produces is that it avoids the free-rider problem by mainly making private loans. A private loan is one that is not traded and therefore other investors are not able to observe the bank and bid up the price of the bank's loan to the point where little or no profit is made. The fact that the majority of the loans made by banks are non-traded is very important in their success in reducing the adverse selection problem in financial markets.

A bank is also able to reduce the adverse selection problem by asking the borrower to provide security (collateral) for the loan. Security is property provided by the borrower to the lender which, if the borrower defaults on the loan, can be used by the lender to reduce its losses. For example, with a mortgage loan made to enable a borrower to purchase a house, the house will be pledged as security. If the borrower fails to repay the full amount of the loan the house can be sold and the proceeds used to pay off the loan. The provision of security therefore guarantees that most of the loan will be repaid, thus reducing the problem of adverse selection for the lender.

The problem of moral hazard in financial markets was described in section 2.2.1 as the borrower engaging in undesirable activities after the loan is made which make it more likely the loan will not be repaid. This can be reduced by banks through the use of restrictive covenants. A restrictive covenant is a provision written into a debt contract that restricts the borrower's activities. A restrictive covenant can be directed towards discouraging undesirable behaviour, for example by restricting the borrower to purchasing only particular items of equipment with the loaned funds. A restrictive covenant can also be used to encourage a borrower to undertake activities that make it more likely that a loan is repaid. For example, a mortgage loan may require a borrower to carry life assurance which pays off the loan in the event of the borrower dying. As a consequence of restrictive covenants, debt contracts are often complicated legal documents with various provisions which affect a borrower's behaviour.

For restrictive covenants to work they clearly need to be monitored and enforced by the lender. This involves a cost and where the debt contract is traded the free-rider problem, discussed above, exists. If an investor knows that other investors are monitoring and enforcing restrictive covenants in debt securities (bonds) then he or she can free ride on their actions. If most bond holders do likewise then the likelihood is that not enough resources are devoted to monitoring and enforcement. This clearly increases moral hazard. However, because banks, as we saw above, provide non-traded loans, they are able to avoid the free-rider problem. Therefore a bank will receive the full benefits of monitoring and enforcement and is thus more likely to devote enough resources to this to reduce the moral hazard problem.

The provision of security by the borrower will also enable the lender to exercise control over the borrower.

Lewis (1991) states that banks can therefore be viewed 'as "social accountants", specialising in the acquisition and dissemination of information, and "delegated monitors", who stay informed about developments inside borrowing enterprises and control their managers' behaviour'. Diamond (1984, 1996) also introduces the notion of banks as delegated monitors. He demonstrates that it is more efficient for lenders to delegate the monitoring of loans to banks. This is because, in general, many lenders are required to generate the funds required for one borrower and there are scale economies in monitoring, so it is more efficient to have one lender (the intermediary) monitor the borrower than many. This then prompts the question of who monitors the bank. Here Diamond shows that where the bank has a large number of loans and the loan portfolio is well diversified (thus making the individual loan risks more independent) then the costs to depositors in monitoring the bank (the delegation costs) are arbitrarily small. This is because where independent risks are pooled, that is, there are a large number of loans, you can rely upon the law of large numbers – as you increase the number of loans then the variability of losses reduces towards zero and actual defaults approach the expected level. If a bank can predict with greater certainty its actual loan losses then it can cover this by building a default premium into the interest rate charged to borrowers. So the bank is unlikely to become bankrupt and default on deposits if it has a large, diversified loan portfolio. From the depositor's point of view there is little or no cost involved in monitoring the bank as bank deposits are virtually default free. Diamond therefore shows that banks, as financial intermediaries, perform an additional transformation from monitored debt into unmonitored debt.

2.4 The implications of financial intermediation

We have seen that financial intermediaries increase the amount of lending/saving in an economy by reducing the frictions that impede this process, in particular transaction costs and asymmetric information. As a consequence more funds will flow from lenders into productive investment. We can also examine the implications of the existence of financial intermediaries for individual lenders and borrowers using the Hirshleifer model (see e.g. Hirshleifer 1958). This is a two-period investment/consumption model, the initial assumptions of which are:

(i) two-period analysis;
(ii) the existence of a perfect capital market, implying that:
  (a) the individual can borrow or lend what he or she wishes at the same ruling rate of interest,

(b) there is perfect knowledge of the investment and borrowing opportunities open to the individual;
(c) access to the capital market is costless;

(iii) there are no distorting taxes;
(iv) the individual allocates consumption expenditure over the two periods so as to maximise utility;
(v) investment opportunities are infinitely divisible.

The first important component of the analysis is the physical investment opportunities line (PIL) depicting the physical investment opportunities available to the firm/individual in period 0. These are ranked in descending order of profitability. This is shown in figure 2.4, where the vertical axis represents period 1 and the horizontal axis period 0. We assume for sake of ease of exposition that the individual has an initial endowment of goods equal to Y_0 and none in period 1. Hence any consumption in period 1 must be financed by saving goods in period 0 and investing them. Thus, point *A* represents a consumption of C_0, with $Y_0 - C_0$ being invested to produce consumption goods of C_1 for consumption in period 1. The slope of the PIL curve reflects diminishing returns to investment.

Consequently, given the amount of resources in period 0, Y_0, without a capital market or financial intermediaries the individual's consumption in period 1 is restricted to the proceeds from investment in period 0. Similarly any investment reduces the level of consumption in period 0. The optimum allocation of consumption between the two periods occurs at the familiar point of tangency between the PIL and the individual's indifference curve (i.e. point *A* in figure 2.5). At this point the marginal return on investment equals the individual's time preference as indicated by the slope of the

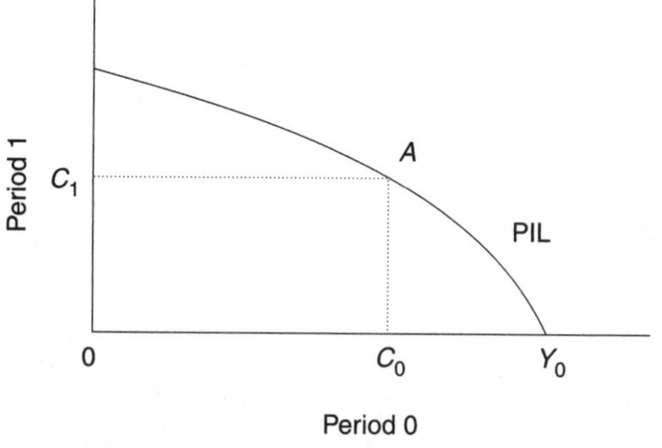

Figure 2.4 Hirschleifer model: physical investment opportunities line (PIL).

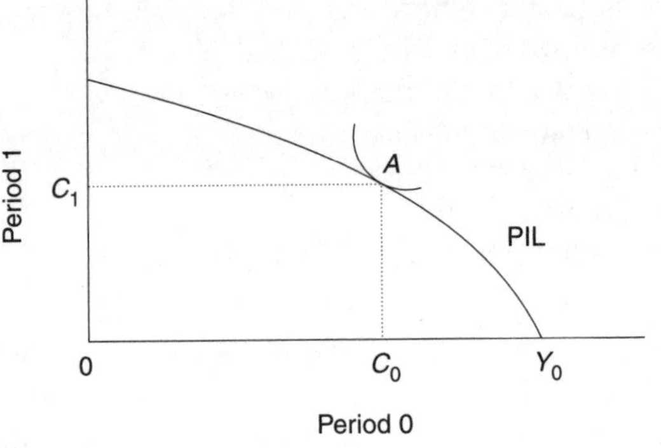

Figure 2.5 Hirschleifer model: optimal allocation of consumption between period 0 and period 1.

indifference curve. Note the return is given by C_1 and the cost of the investment by $Y_0 - C_0$.

The introduction of a capital market or financial intermediaries changes the situation since the individual can borrow or lend so as to rearrange her or his investment opportunities. The borrowing/lending opportunities can be represented diagrammatically using the financial investment opportunities line (FIL), as shown in figure 2.6. The straight line represents the perfect capital market assumption that borrowing and lending can be achieved at the same rate of interest. The slope of the FIL is given by $-(1 + r)$, where r is the market rate of interest. The individual can move up and down the FIL; for example, investment of $0A$ funds in the financial market in period 0 would produce $0B$ in period 1 $\{0A(1+r)\}$. Similarly investment

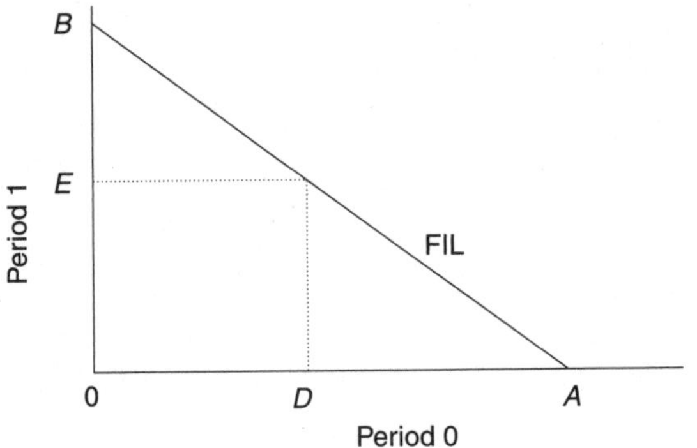

Figure 2.6 Hirschleifer model: financial investment opportunities line (FIL).

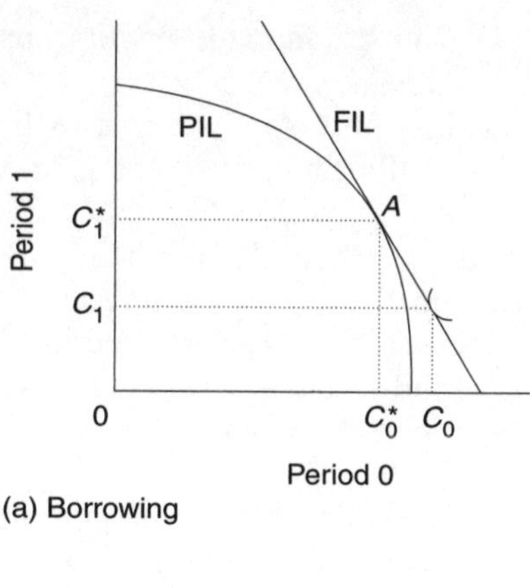

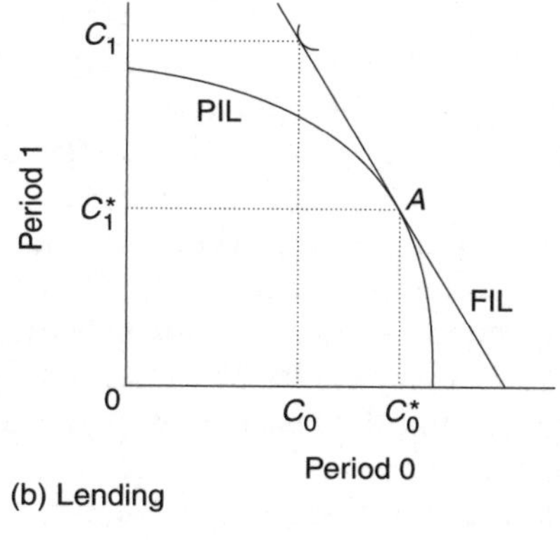

Figure 2.7 Hirschleifer model: borrowing (a) or lending (b) to increase utility.

of *DA* in the financial market in period 0 would produce 0*E* in period 1 $\{DA(1 + r)\}$.

The impact of the introduction of a capital market (financial intermediation) can be seen by combining the information given in figures 2.5 and 2.6 to arrive at figure 2.7. The individual can separate the two decisions (production and consumption) so that the following two conditions apply:

(i) The present value of production is maximised at point *A*, where the marginal return on investment equals the capital market rate of interest, that is, where the PIL is tangential to the FIL furthest from the origin. Optimal production in the two periods is then C^*_0 and C^*_1, respectively.

(ii) Utility is maximised where the individual's time preference equals the capital market rate of interest. This occurs where the individual's indifference curve is tangential to the FIL so that the market rate of

interest is also equal to the individual's time preference. This can occur by one of two means:

(a) Borrowing against further production to finance present consumption. This is illustrated in figure 2.7a, where $(C_0 - C^*_0)$ is borrowed in period 0, with consumption being C_0. In period 1 consumption is C_1, with $(C^*_1 - C_1)$ being the loan repayment.
(b) Lending to finance future consumption. This is illustrated in figure 2.7b, where $(C^*_0 - C_0)$ is lent in period 0, with consumption being C_0. In period 1 consumption is C_1, with $(C_1 - C^*_1)$ being the proceeds of loan repayment.

Consequently utility has been increased by the introduction of a financial intermediary since the individual would have remained at point *A* without the intermediary, with consumption equal to C^*_0 and C^*_1 in the two periods, respectively; that is, the individual is on a higher or the original indifference curve following the introduction of an intermediary.

This analysis is only as good as its underlying assumptions. It is apparent that these are very (perhaps overly) restrictive. A perfect capital market is unlikely to occur in the real world for three reasons. First, in all markets borrowers pay a higher rate of interest than that earned by lenders. Hence the slopes of the FIL will differ for lenders and borrowers. Second, operators do not have perfect foresight and financial markets are characterised by a degree of uncertainty. Third, access to the capital markets is not costless. Furthermore, taxes do exist and consequently distortions are introduced into the raising of finance. Also, the assumption of a two-period analysis may appear to be restrictive but, in fact, is merely used to simplify the exposition. Similar results could be obtained from multi-period analysis but would be more complicated to derive.

2.5 The future for financial intermediation

We have demonstrated that financial intermediaries have a role to play in financial markets because of the existence of frictions in markets or incompleteness of markets. It would appear that financial intermediaries have emerged as a response to transaction costs or asymmetric information. Some economists have argued (e.g. McCulloch 1981; Tobin 1984) that financial intermediaries are a transitory phase in an evolutionary process where the final phase is a complete set of markets embracing all commodities and all contingencies. Such markets are referred to as complete markets or Arrow–Debreu markets, following the Arrow–Debreu equilibrium model (for a theoretical exposition see Arrow and Hahn (1971) or for an introduction to the concepts of complete markets see Flood (1991)). Complete markets are characterised by negligible transaction costs. Complete markets

would embrace futures markets, which allow trade in all commodities for delivery in the future, and options markets, which provide insurance against particular contingencies. The nature of futures and options markets is discussed in chapter 13. The existence of complete markets covering all commodities and contingencies is, of course, a theoretical construct. The question that is posed here is whether developments that lower transaction costs and alleviate the problems of asymmetric information in markets will lead to a decline in financial intermediation. There is evidence that large companies are moving away from intermediated finance through banks towards raising funds directly from capital markets. This phenomenon is referred to as disintermediation or securitisation and is discussed in relation to international financing in chapter 12.

Diamond (1989, 1991) suggests that borrower reputation is important in the financing process. Where a borrower has no reputation then the problems of asymmetric information will mean that the borrower is likely to be dependent on banks for external finance. Once a borrower establishes a reputation (through, for example, a history of making good profits) the borrower is able to access the capital markets by issuing equity or debt claims. Reputation becomes a capital asset, so consequently firms are more likely to select safe rather than risky investments to protect that capital asset. The information provided by the firm's track record reduces the adverse selection and moral hazard problems for investors. It could also be argued that these companies are so large and well diversified that their debts may be considered to be of low risk.

Allen and Santomero (1998) provide an alternative view of the reasons why financial intermediaries exist. They argue that current explanations rely too much on market imperfections. They suggest that, while market imperfections were once important, they are increasingly less relevant. The evidence for this is that although transaction costs have reduced and information has become cheaper and more readily available, there has been no reduction in intermediation. To understand this we need to analyse a financial system from a functional perspective rather than an institutional perspective. A functional perspective is one based on the services provided by the financial system, such as origination, distribution, funding and so on. In contrast, an institutional perspective focuses on the activities of particular types of financial institution, such as banks or insurance companies. Merton and Bodie (1995) have suggested such an approach. Functional needs are more constant over time, whereas institutions change and adapt. Some commentators have pointed to the relative decline in bank assets compared with the assets of pension funds or mutual funds and have argued that this reflects a decline in banking. However, this analysis is based on an institutional perspective. Whilst there has been a relative reduction in bank assets, there has also been an increase in financial institutions' assets relative

to gross domestic product (GDP). The overall size of the assets of US financial institutions in relation to GDP increased from 100% in 1950 to 250% in 1995. Why has the relative importance of financial intermediaries as a whole increased? Allen and Santomero suggest one factor is the growing importance of risk management. By specialising in information production and processing, financial intermediaries are facilitators of risk transfer. This role has become more important in recent years as derivative markets and instruments have increased in size and scope. A second factor emphasised by Allen and Santomero is the cost of participating in financial markets. Although trading costs in equity and bond markets have reduced significantly since the early 1980s, there has been no relative increase in direct holdings of equities and bonds by individuals. This is because the cost of participating in such markets is high (e.g. monitoring costs). Financial intermediaries facilitate participation in such markets by creating financial products with stable returns and low participation costs, for example unit trusts. So the evidence appears to suggest that financial intermediation will continue to be important but the way in which this is provided may change. We return to this discussion in chapter 12, when we examine the decline of traditional intermediation in international financing.

2.6 The evolution of financial systems

The financial systems that have emerged in the major developed economies have some important differences in structure. The differences that exist, in particular the different relationships between the financial system and the corporate sector, have been suggested as one explanation for the different economic performances of countries since the Second World War. We will examine this debate in chapter 15; however, to provide some background to it we consider here the relationship between the evolution of a financial system and the different phases of economic growth (see Rybczynski (1988) for further discussion).

In the early stages of the growth of an economy, that is, when an economy transforms itself from agrarian to industrial, it is banks which act as the main intermediary providing the external finance for the investment required for this restructuring. During this bank-oriented phase of the financial system, ownership of the productive resources of the economy is concentrated in few hands and there is little separation of ownership and control of these resources. As industrialisation continues it is usual for firms to obtain a larger proportion of their externally raised funds through the capital markets. This inevitably leads to a separation of ownership from control of firms, with ownership (i.e. holders of the equity claims issued by firms through the capital market) held by households both directly and increasingly indirectly through non-bank financial companies. The control of firms

is delegated to professional managers subject to satisfactory performance of the company. In this market-oriented phase of the financial system the role of the banks in providing finance for firms is less important and generally passive. As industrialisation reaches a peak, there is greater restructuring of economic activity, that is, redirection of the resources in the economy through a change in the ownership and control of firms. This active restructuring takes place through the capital markets. As the economy moves into what has been termed the de-industrialisation phase, when the relative importance of the traditional manufacturing industries declines and the relative importance of service industries increases, there is a much greater level of economic restructuring. This places greater demands on the financial system, which, it is argued, moves into the securitised phase. The functions of the financial system expand under this phase so that enhanced capital and credit markets emerge along with markets for corporate control and venture capital. The financial system is more complete under the securitised phase and more importantly plays an active role in the restructuring of the economy. This restructuring takes place through the new markets in corporate control and venture capital. The market for corporate control is concerned with changing the ownership and control of existing firms and is increasingly carried out through the use of takeovers. Such takeovers are often hostile (i.e. the bid from the company proposing the takeover is opposed by the target company's management) but the takeover process may be seen as providing a discipline on companies, allowing control to be transferred from inefficient to efficient management – see chapter 15 for further discussion of this. The market for venture capital is concerned with the provision of finance to the new firms which emerge in this restructuring process.

The preceding description of the evolution of financial systems is very general and does not apply to all countries. The description is probably most applicable to the Anglo-Saxon economies of the US and the UK, with the transformation to a securitised financial system taking place earlier in the US. In contrast, countries such as Germany and Japan have continued to operate with a financial system which more closely represents the bank-oriented system.

2.6.1 *The Japanese and German financial systems*

An important feature of the Japanese economy is the *keiretsu*, which is a grouping of industrial firms with a core set of banks and other financial intermediaries. Many of the industrial firms will trade with each other. Linkages between the members of the group are enhanced by cross-shareholdings (i.e. each group member holds equity shares in the other members of the group). As banks in the group have equity ownership in the firms, this allows them to have representation on the firms' supervisory boards.

The banks therefore have a close relationship with the firms in the *keiretsu* and the banks will favour these firms when it comes to making loans.

German banks also have close ties with industry through the *Hausbank* system. Banks hold shares in firms and, in addition, bank customers keep equity shares 'on deposit' at banks and give the bank proxies to vote with these shares. As a consequence, German banks have a controlling interest in many of the large firms and bank representatives sit on the boards of directors of these firms.

In countries like Germany and Japan, banks can and do act in an active way in industrial restructuring, providing risk capital (equity) to companies and then working closely with those companies. This close relationship also involves performance monitoring of the management of the company and where necessary banks may initiate a change in the management or ownership of companies. Such changes, in contrast to the market-oriented or securitised systems, are generally carried out without hostile confrontation. A long-term relationship is established between a bank and company in Germany and Japan and this gives the bank a number of advantages. In particular, banks have timely access to information and this helps the bank to monitor the firm more effectively. This enables a bank to reduce the adverse selection and moral hazard problems discussed in section 2.2.1.

The foregoing discussion of the evolution of financial systems presents a clear-cut distinction between bank-oriented and market-oriented or securitised systems. In recent years certain developments have blurred this distinction. As countries loosely associated with bank-oriented systems have moved into the de-industrialisation phase, the accompanying increased level of restructuring has tended to encourage a transition to more market-oriented or securitised financial systems. Countries experiencing such a transition are France and Italy. Also, companies in both Germany and Japan are now increasingly making greater use of capital markets, with a greater proportion of risk capital being provided by non-bank institutions. In addition, countries more strongly associated with bank-oriented systems have recently experienced more hostile takeover activity, although the regulatory and institutional impediments to hostile takeovers in such countries suggest that such activity is unlikely to grow at a significant rate. Finally, although there are clearly advantages to a financial system where banks have a close relationship with the firms to which they provide capital, this does not imply that banks in these countries do not make mistakes. The recent experiences in Japan illustrate this: deregulation of the banking system in the 1980s led to a boom in bank lending, with banks lending aggressively in the property market. When property values collapsed in the early 1990s, many banks were left holding massive amounts of bad loans. This has led to a number of banks failing, including the tenth largest commercial bank in Japan, Hokkaido Takushoku, as well as Yamaichi Securities, in late 1997.

2.7 Recent developments in the UK financial system

There has been a tremendous change in the UK financial system since the early 1980s. The changes that have taken place can be analysed in a systematic way and in this section we provide a perspective on the main forces leading to change and the major changes that have taken place. This analysis, adapted from Llewellyn (1985, 1991), provides a framework for assessing and interpreting the more specific discussion of events in financial markets throughout the rest of this book.

Some of the main forces leading to the modification of any financial system are:

(i) changes in the market environment;
(ii) changes in the portfolio preferences of users of financial intermediation services;
(iii) changes in the preferences of and constraints on the providers of financial intermediation services.

The interaction of these forces produces financial innovation, which is essentially the development of new financial instruments and techniques of financial intermediation, and structural change in the financial system, with the appearance of new financial markets and changes in the organisation and behaviour of institutions. With this general framework in mind we can now examine the main changes in the UK financial system.

Over the postwar period up to the end of the 1960s the UK financial system was characterised by strict demarcation between the various types of financial institutions. So banks provided banking services and building societies provided housing finance services. As a consequence there was little competition between the different types of institution. There was also little competition within a particular financial market as, for example, banks and building societies operated cartels which set interest rates. Similarly within stock markets, restrictive practices, in particular the existence of minimum non-negotiable commissions, had the effect of reducing competition. Towards the end of the 1960s the first competitive pressures were felt by banks as the relaxed requirements for entry into the City of London saw penetration by foreign banks into the UK banking system. In 1971, reform of the banking system, through a package of measures known as competition and credit control, led to the removal of the banking cartel and greater competition within the industry. However, most of the deregulation of the financial system occurred after 1980, with the aim of introducing greater competition. Alongside this deregulation there was a parallel trend to tighten up the prudential regulation of the system, with the aim of protecting the user of financial intermediation services. In 1980 controls on bank lending were abandoned, leaving banks free to expand into new

areas and one area which was targeted was housing finance. Banks therefore entered into competition with building societies, which led to building societies abandoning their cartel arrangement, and, in 1986, to the Building Societies Act, which relaxed, to some extent, the constraints imposed on building societies. Also in 1986 the stock market underwent deregulation, with a set of changes in trading arrangements known as Big Bang. As a consequence of these developments, financial markets became much more competitive than they had been at the start of the 1980s. Developments to protect users of financial intermediation services included the Banking Act 1987, which tightened the prudential regulation of banks following the collapse of the Johnson Matthey Bank in 1984, the Basle convergence accord of 1988, which introduced a new measure of capital adequacy of banks, which relates the capital held by banks to the risks they undertake, and the Financial Services Act 1986, which introduced a new system of investor protection. Most of these regulatory measures have since been updated as regulators have attempted to keep up with the rapid pace of change in financial markets.

As described above, various forces in the financial system have led to both financial innovation and structural change. The main developments are now summarised.

2.7.1 *Financial conglomeration*

Deregulation and the greater competition it produced eroded the demarcation between the different types of financial institution. Financial institutions have sought to reduce their dependence upon their traditional core business and to diversify into a wider range of products and services. One consequence of this is that function and institution are no longer closely aligned. Banks now provide a wide range of financial services in addition to their core business of intermediation and payments services. In the 1980s banks began providing mortgages and more recently have moved into life assurance and insurance business.

2.7.2 *Entry barriers have declined*

In retail financial markets the combined impact of new technology and the process of deconstruction (see box 3.1, p. 60) reduced barriers to entry into these markets. These developments are discussed in more detail in chapters 3 and 5. The mortgage market from the late 1980s onwards and retail banking from the mid-1990s saw new entrants, which made them more competitive. Insurance institutions and non-financial firms (such as supermarkets) have also established a presence in retail banking.

2.7.3 *Growth of investment institutions*

Over the period 1980–2000, the investment institutions (pension funds, life assurance companies, unit and investment trusts) grew at a faster rate

than banks and building societies (see table 2.1). The banks partly reflects a trend towards larger companie proportion of external finance from capital markets and off-balance-sheet business and other fee-paying busi sought to diversify their income base (discussed furth faster growth in the assets of pension funds and life assura (as providers of personal pensions) partly reflects tax advantages for saving towards a pension. The growth in investment institutions' assets also reflects a move away from direct investment in equities and bonds by individuals towards indirect investment.

Table 2.1 Growth of assets of UK financial institutions for selected years, 1980–2000 (£billion)

	1980	1984	1988	1992	1996	2000	% growth, 1980–2000
Banks[a]	117.4	271.4	401.8	552.6	817.1	1,405.0	1,097
Building societies	54.3	103.3	189.9	266.6	301.0	159.0	202
Pension funds	52.6	130.3	214.5	382.0	543.9	765.2	1,355
Life assurance companies	53.7	114.2	198.3	327.6	549.7	932.7	1,637
Unit trusts, OEICs[b] and investment trusts	12.5	30.4	60.9	92.6	181.9	321.4	2,471

[a] UK-owned banks. Note that the growth in bank assets since 1996 mainly refers to the transfer of the larger building societies to the banking sector.
[b] OEICs are open-ended investment companies (on which see section 6.7). They are similar to unit trusts in that they are open-ended. A number of unit trusts have converted to the OEIC structure in recent years.
Source: *Financial Statistics*. Office for National Statistics online database (http://www.statistics.gov.uk/statbase/TSDTimeZone.asp).

2.7.4 *Financial innovation*

The 1980s in particular saw the development of new types of financial instruments, financial markets and techniques. One of the main innovations was the development of financial derivatives, initially exchange traded but now also traded 'over the counter'. These include financial futures, options and swaps. These instruments, discussed in detail in chapter 13, have emerged partly in response to volatility in financial markets and have widened the financial management and hedging techniques available to firms and financial institutions.

Another important development has been securitisation. A distinction needs to be made between primary and secondary securitisation. The former

lates to borrowers bypassing lending institutions and raising finance directly from capital markets. Secondary securitisation is the process whereby assets originally held on the balance sheet of a bank or building society are packaged and sold to a capital market institution, which funds this purchase by issuing securities. In effect, secondary securitisation is the conversion of cash flows from a portfolio of assets (normally loans) into negotiable instruments which are secured on the underlying assets. The instruments are sold to investors. It is an increasingly used and flexible technique that allows lending institutions to increase the liquidity of the balance sheet and release capital that would normally be held against the loan. In the US in 1996, over two-thirds of residential mortgages and about half the credit card receivables were funded via securitisation programmes. Secondary securitisation by banks and building societies in the UK is growing (see section 4.3 for further discussion of this phenomenon).

2.7.5 *Importance of the UK financial services industry*

The importance of financial services to the UK economy is illustrated in table 2.2, which shows the relative contribution to GDP and employment by the financial services sector since 1991.

Table 2.2 Gross domestic product (GDP) and employment accounted for by financial services, as a percentage of total

	1991	1993	1995	1997	1999	2001
GDP	5.7	6.9	7.1	6.1	5.8	5.3
Employment	4.1	4.0	4.0	3.9	3.9	3.7

Source: *Financial Statistics*. National Statistics online database (http://www.statistics.gov.uk/statbase/TSDTimeZone.asp).

2.8 Conclusion

In this chapter we have described the process of financial intermediation and discussed the reasons why we need financial intermediaries. We have also set out, in broad terms, some of the tremendous changes in market structure and innovations that have taken place in the UK financial system over the last two or three decades. In the rest of this book we examine in greater detail the changes to the various financial institutions and markets that make up the UK financial system, beginning with the banking industry.

Chapter 3

Retail banking

3.1 Introduction

In this chapter we examine the nature of retail banking as distinct from wholesale banking. Whilst such a distinction has in recent years become less relevant in practice, as most retail banks also undertake wholesale business, we feel there is still some advantage to be gained from retail banking being considered separately from wholesale banking. The best way to approach this is to distinguish between banks and the retail banking industry. In the retail banking industry certain processes take place in order to supply retail banking services/products. Firms which specialise in these processes, called banks, have traditionally been the suppliers of these services/products. However, owing to technological developments firms whose business is not predominantly banking are entering the retail banking industry. Banks have therefore lost their monopoly position in this industry but can use their core competencies to diversify through the provision of other services. As a consequence of these developments the retail banking industry is becoming increasingly characterised by a heterogeneous range of suppliers. In this chapter therefore we focus on retail banking, rather than retail banks, and begin by examining the nature of retail banking and recent developments in the industry. We then investigate the provision of payments services, one of the main types of service provided by the retail banking industry. Finally we discuss the risks inherent in retail banking and the strategies adopted by firms to manage these risks. Wholesale banking is discussed in chapter 4.

3.2 The nature of retail banking in the UK

The traditional business of banking involves taking in deposits, which are then packaged and on-lent as loans. Retail banking refers to the large-volume, low-value end of this business, where deposits are typically attracted

from individuals and small businesses and loans are made to the same groups. This is in contrast to wholesale banking, where transactions are typically small in volume but large in value and customers are mainly medium/large companies and large organisations. In practice it is difficult to distinguish between retail and wholesale banks in the UK as many of the banks operating in the retail markets also operate, to some degree, in the wholesale markets. To operate as a bank and to be able to accept deposits in the UK a firm must seek permission from the Financial Services Authority (FSA) (before June 1998, the Bank of England). Once the bank is authorised, its depositors are protected under the UK financial compensation scheme – see chapter 17 for a discussion of deposit insurance.

By examining the combined balance sheet for retail banks in the UK (table 3.1) we can discern their main activities.[1] Examining the liabilities side of retail banks' balance sheet, first we find the small item 'Notes outstanding', which refers to private bank notes issued by Scottish and Northern Ireland banks. The bulk of a bank's liabilities are deposits, accounting for 87 per cent of total retail bank liabilities, with 24 per cent of these deposits being in foreign currency. The majority of sterling deposits come from the UK private sector, that is, mainly individuals and firms. Of these sterling deposits, about 45 per cent are sight deposits, which are defined as repayable on demand. This illustrates the extent to which banks rely upon demand debt rather than fixed-term debt to finance their assets. The other main liabilities are items in suspense and transmission, which refer for example to cheques drawn and in the course of collection, and capital and other funds, which refer mainly to banks' issued share capital, long-term debt and reserves. These latter capital funds are important items when it comes to assessing a bank's capital adequacy in relation to the risks it faces.

Turning now to the assets side of the balance sheet, we find a small item referring to balances with the Bank of England. This is mainly accounted for by the compulsory 'cash ratio' requirement, whereby all authorised banks are required to hold 0.15 per cent of their eligible sterling liabilities, charged on those liabilities exceeding £400 million, in a non-interest-bearing account at the Bank of England. Note that no interest is paid on balances held at the Bank of England. The cash balances held outside the Bank of England (notes and coins) account for roughly 0.7 per cent of total assets, which is a very low cash base. Additional liquidity is provided by market loans, which refer to short-term loans made through the money markets. Traditionally banks' market loans were 'call' or overnight loans to the discount houses. These loans are used to even out cash positions within the banking system. However, the retail banks' involvement in the inter-bank markets since 1971 and the structural changes in the money markets discussed in chapter 10 have eliminated this function and inter-bank loans

now account for approximately 86 per cent of total market loans. Dealings between banks and the Bank of England, however, take place in order to smooth out shortages or surpluses of cash arising out of dealings between the banking system as a whole and non-banks as, clearly, the inter-bank market cannot perform this function. This is dealt with in more detail in chapter 10. Further liquidity is provided by the next item on the assets side, which is bills. These are mainly Treasury bills and bank bills eligible for rediscounting at the Bank of England via discount houses. The item investments refers to retail banks' holdings of marketable securities. These are mainly government bonds or government guaranteed stocks and therefore have the characteristics of low default risk and marketability. The main assets of retail banks are sterling advances, which, according to table 3.1, accounted for 48 per cent of total assets or 65 per cent of sterling assets (i.e. total assets less other currency and miscellaneous assets). Many of these advances are the traditional overdraft facility made to business borrowers. However, since the mid-1970s banks have increasingly made term loans to businesses, with an average original term to maturity of around seven years. In addition, since the 1980s, following the removal of controls on bank lending, the banks have increasingly targeted customers in the personal sector with both long-term mortgage lending and unsecured term loans. The next item on the assets side of the retail banks' balance sheet is other currency and miscellaneous assets. Of the other currency assets, around 20 per cent is accounted for by advances, with the remainder being mainly

Table 3.1 The combined balance sheet of UK retail banks at 31 December 1996

Liabilities	£billion	Assets	£billion
Notes outstanding	2.7	Notes and coins	4.8
Total sterling deposits	467.8	Balances with the Bank of England	1.7
(of which, sight deposits)	(210.1)		
Foreign currency deposits	148.6	Market loans	102.1
Items in suspense and transmission plus capital and other funds	92.0	Total bills	12.2
		Repo bills	13.6
		Investments	50.7
		Advances	338.5
		Other currency and miscellaneous assets	186.5
		Banking Department lending to central government	0.9
Total liabilities	711.0	Total assets	711.0

Source: *Bank of England Statistical Abstract*, 1997, table 3.4.

made up of market loans and investments. Miscellaneous assets include the banks' physical assets, mainly premises and equipment, which provide the infrastructure of the business. The item repo bills refers to sale and repurchase agreements, where banks acquire balances through the operation of the new system of monetary control discussed in chapter 10. The final item is Banking Department lending to central government, which refers to the Banking Department of the Bank of England, which is included in the retail banks classification owing to its involvement in the clearing system. We consider the function of the Banking Department and the other functions of the Bank of England in chapter 16.

3.3 Recent changes in retail banking in the UK

To operate in the retail markets, banks have traditionally required an extensive branch network. However, technological developments, in particular the growth in automated teller machine (ATM) networks, telephone/internet banking, mobile phones and interactive digital television, have enabled a new type of bank to emerge that does not need branches to conduct business. In the UK the pioneer was First Direct, which began as a telephone bank in 1989 and is an operation of HSBC, one of the large clearing banks. By 2002 First Direct had around 1 million customers and offered a full range of retail bank services, from cheque accounts to personal loans. Over half of the customers of First Direct regularly use the internet to access their account. Most of the other established banks in the UK have followed the lead of HSBC and started up a remote banking service that allows customers to access their account using the telephone, internet or mobile phone. The British Bankers' Association (2002) reported that, in 2001, one-third of all bank accounts were accessed through the telephone or internet. Of these remote transactions, it is the internet that now dominates, accounting for 167 million transactions in 2001 compared with 127 million telephone transactions.

The traditional business of banking has been the provision of intermediation and payments services. Intermediation services, as we saw in chapter 2, involve the bank in issuing money-certain deposits and holding money-uncertain and non-marketable loan assets. Payments services are provided, as cheques drawn on bank deposits are accepted as a form of money. We saw in chapter 2 that banks exist either because they possess certain monopoly powers, in that they have a particular expertise not possessed by other firms, or because they have a comparative advantage in the marketplace. In recent years banks have seen their monopoly position eroded as the kind of technological developments discussed above have lowered barriers to entry. The process of deconstruction, discussed below, has also allowed firms to enter the industry by supplying just part of a

banking service, and out-sourcing the other parts, again lowering entry costs. The consequence of these pressures is that banks now face greater competition in their traditional markets. Banks may also be losing some of their traditional comparative advantages in terms of information or cost. The consequence of this is that banks are losing their comparative advantage over capital markets and so large companies are increasingly raising capital directly from markets. These developments impinge more directly on the wholesale end of banking and are discussed in more detail in chapters 4 and 12.

Banks therefore are no longer monopoly suppliers of banking services. However, we need to be careful here to make the distinction between banks and banking. Banks are firms that are completely or predominantly in the business of supplying banking services, whereas banking is the industry supplying banking services. A good discussion of developments in the banking industry is provided by Llewellyn (1996) and we summarise some of his arguments here.

In recent years the UK banking industry has seen the emergence of a number of non-banking firms supplying retail banking services. These new entrants fall into two categories:

(i) *Supermarket banks*. For example, Sainsbury and Tesco, which are already in the retailing business, now offer retail bank services alongside other retail product lines and do so through an extensive branch network. At present the supermarket banks supply banking products in partnership with existing banks but in the future may decide to go it alone. Sainsbury's bank, for example, is authorised to collect deposits.

(ii) *Other non-bank firms*. These are offering retail banking services using remote banking delivery channels, that is without a branch network. Examples include insurance firms, such as Prudential and Scottish Widows, and Virgin, a retail conglomerate, which have diversified into banking.

For new entrants to retail banking, both entry and exit costs are relatively low. For those firms operating a telephone banking service the costs of setting up a call centre are lower than the costs of establishing a branch network. For supermarket banks, the supermarkets already have in place an extensive branch network used for delivering other retail products. Exit barriers are also low because for most of the new entrants banking is only a relatively small part of their overall business and because the fixed costs of setting up the operation are relatively low. Another development which is also leading to lower entry costs is the process of deconstruction, described in box 3.1. This allows new entrants to focus on that part of the process in

Box 3.1 Deconstruction of banking services

The process of deconstruction refers to the decomposition of services or products into their component parts, thereby allowing the individual parts to be provided by separate firms. A good example of this is the provision of a mortgage loan. Recent financial innovation allows the components of this provision to be broken down into:

(i) origination – the mortgage is brokered to a customer;
(ii) administration – the paperwork is processed;
(iii) risk assessment – the credit-worthiness of the borrower is assessed;
(iv) funding – finances are raised, assets are held on the balance sheet and capital is allocated to the risk.

One firm may have a comparative advantage in, say, risk assessment, whereas another firm may have a comparative advantage in origination. Also, a firm may originate the loan but may not be efficient in terms of funding the loan because of a capital constraint. It is becoming increasingly commonplace, in the US in particular, for banks to securitise their mortgage loans and issue subsequent securities into the capital market, thereby taking the loans off the balance sheet. The process of deconstruction lowers barriers to entry into the banking industry, as firms can now enter the market without undertaking the whole process. They need provide only that part of the process in which they have a comparative advantage. A firm that originates the loan but does not wish to undertake the other parts of the process can subcontract (or out-source) these to other firms. Another firm may develop an expertise in risk assessment and take on only this part of the process from other firms.

By subcontracting, a small firm is able to buy into economies of scale which it could not achieve on its own because of the limited scale of its operation. We are likely to see the development of *contract banking* over the next few years as firms supply some parts of the process of a banking service and subcontract others. Therefore in the near future we are likely to see a spectrum of providers of retail banking, ranging from, at one extreme, the very large banks providing most or all subcomponents of a wide range of services (i.e. both horizontally and vertically integrated) to, at the other extreme, the virtual bank, which has an interface with customers, supplies a wide range of banking services but which subcontracts all the subcomponents of these services to other firms and just manages the contracts with these suppliers. A virtual bank supplying a wide range of services/products would be highly horizontally integrated but have low vertical integration. A virtual bank may sound unrealistic but out-sourcing is now very common in most manufacturing industries. Toyota, for example, supplies finished cars to its customers but subcontracts the production of many of the subcomponents. An example of a virtual firm is the typical supplier of personal computers, which buys in all the subcomponents and assembles to order.

which they have a comparative advantage and to subcontract the other parts of the process to other firms which possess a comparative advantage there (probably established banks). By subcontracting in this way new entrants can effectively buy into economies of scale without incurring high fixed costs. This again lowers both entry and exit barriers. One consequence of low entry and exit barriers is that the market for retail banking services has become more contestable (see chapter 5, box 5.1, for further discussion of contestable markets). However, there are parts of retail banking in the UK where uncompetitive practices exist – see box 3.2. A further development affecting the UK banking sector has been the conversion of many of the larger building societies into banks (see chapter 5 for discussion). These newly created banks, such as Halifax and Abbey National, are focused on the retail end of banking, that is, supplying banking, insurance and other financial services to the personal sector. As a consequence of all these developments there is clearly excess capacity in the retail banking industry and further mergers are likely to bring about its consolidation.

What are the likely consequences of these developments? In terms of retail banking we are likely to see further differentiation between firms providing banking services. We will continue to see large financial conglomerates undertaking both retail and wholesale banking and undertaking most of the processes within the organisation. The banks that have converted from the building society sector and some of the new 'internet' banks will develop further as retail conglomerates. We are also likely to see more specialist institutions offering some banking services or parts of banking processes. In summary the industry will become more heterogeneous.

The main implication of these developments for the established banks is that as they lose their comparative advantage in banking they are having to diversify into new activities. At the retail end of the industry one clear trend that has emerged is for banks to provide insurance services. 'Bancassurance' firms, where deposit taking and insurance are combined, are commonplace in Europe. It is an open question as to whether banks will diversify into non-financial business. Banks have developed certain core competencies that could be applied to other types of business. These competencies or areas of comparative advantage include:

(i) information advantages – that is, the information they possess about the financial affairs or lending risks associated with their customers, information which comes partly from the provision of payments services (see next section) and hence which relates to the customer's credit-worthiness through the operation of their bank accounts;
(ii) risk analysis expertise;
(iii) expertise in monitoring and enforcement of loan contracts;
(iv) delivery capacity.

Box 3.2 Competition in UK banking – the Cruickshank report

In November 1998 Gordon Brown, the Chancellor of the Exchequer, set up an enquiry into competition in UK banking under the chairmanship of Don Cruickshank. The terms of reference for the enquiry were to examine innovation, competition and efficiency in the retail banking industry in the UK, to see how these compared with international standards and to consider options for change. The enquiry team reported in March 2000 (Cruickshank 2000).

The report identifies that banks are treated differently from other industries in many respects, including high regulatory barriers to entry and diluted exposure to competition law. This special treatment is likely to be the result of an informal contract between government and banks, designed to deliver confidence in the banking system. However, the report argues that this special treatment of the industry has allowed banks to escape the rigours of effective competition. This conclusion is supported by reference to the fact that the return on equity for UK banks is well in excess of their cost of capital. The three areas of retail banking investigated in depth were: the payments system; services to personal customers (current accounts, savings products, personal loans, mortgages and credit cards); and services to small and medium-sized businesses (current accounts and external finance).

Competition problems were found in each area. However, the report noted that, as a result of new entrants into the market for the supply of services to personal customers, competition is increasing and prices should fall in the future. The most severe competition problems were found in the area of payments services and, as the current account is one of the main products provided to retail and small business customers, restrictions in payments services have an impact on other retail banking markets. The UK payments system consists of a series of unregulated networks (such as the Bankers' Automated Clearing Services and ATM networks – see later in this chapter) mostly controlled by the main banks. Access to the systems is restricted to banks or similar institutions. This clearly creates barriers to entry and therefore stifles innovation and competition. The Cruickshank Committee recommended the establishment of a payments system regulator with powers to deliver competitive outcomes. The government has instead proposed that the Office of Fair Trading (OFT) be given new powers to promote competition in payments systems.

The Cruickshank review also concluded that the supply of banking services to small and medium-sized businesses was less competitive than the supply to personal customers. The market is more concentrated and has higher barriers to entry. As a consequence, the government referred the problem to the Competition Commission. The Competition Commission confirmed that a complex monopoly exists in the supply of banking services to small and medium-sized businesses (Competition Commission 2002). It recommended a number of measures to reduce restrictive practices, including allowing small business customers to switch accounts to other banks quickly and with minimum cost.

Therefore, although established banks are likely to see some decline in their share of retail banking services in the new competitive industry, they are likely to compensate for this through diversification.

In the next section we examine the nature of the payments system in the UK and consider why it is that banks have traditionally combined payments with intermediation services.

3.4 Payments services

Banks until quite recently were the sole providers of payments services. A payments service is merely an accounting procedure whereby transfers of ownership of certain assets are carried out in settlement of debts incurred. Payments facilities generate a desire for instruments which:

(i) serve as a medium of exchange that enables consumers to acquire goods;
(ii) serve as a medium of payment to effect payment for the good acquired;
(iii) act as a temporary store of purchasing power, since income receipts and payments are generally not synchronised.

As we saw in chapter 1, a commodity that takes on these three characteristics is termed money and any commodity can act in this role as long as it is generally accepted. In most developed economies the payments system that has evolved is based on government-issued paper money and cheques drawn on a bank deposit. The reasons for this are covered adequately in most texts on money and banking. What we propose to examine here are some recent developments in the UK payments system.

Financial innovation has made it possible to 'unbundle' the three functions of money so they can be separately carried out using different instruments. So, for example, a credit card may serve as the medium of exchange that enables goods to be purchased. A direct debit from a bank deposit account may then be used to effect payment at a later date, and between the purchase and payment the funds used for payment may be held in a high-yielding account.

Developments in technology, in particular in electronic funds transfer, are also bringing about changes in the payments system. The main types of trend in payments systems are shown in table 3.2. One clear trend is the decline in the use of paper cheques and an increase in the use of plastic cards (debit, credit and store cards) for payments. In 2001 the debit card was the main non-cash method of payment. The growth in regular electronic payments through direct debits, standing orders, direct credits and CHAPS sterling (see section 3.5.3) is also evident. Most employees now get their salaries credited to their account (direct credits) and direct debits have become the most popular way of paying bills, with more than half of regular

bills paid this way in 2001 (see Association for Payment Clearing Services 2002). However, cash is still the dominant payment method in volume terms, with over two-thirds of all personal payments made in cash. So the much talked about 'cashless society' is still some way off.

Table 3.2 Payment trends, 1991–2001: transaction volumes (millions)

	1991	1993	1995	1997	1999	2001
Plastic card purchases						
Debit card	359	659	1,004	1,503	2,062	2,696
Credit/charge card	699	748	908	1,128	1,344	1,558
Store card (estimated)	46	82	109	128	131	117
Total plastic card purchases	1,104	1,488	2,023	2,759	3,537	4,371
Plastic card withdrawals at ATMs/counters	1,112	1,277	1,512	1,809	2,025	2,269
Direct debits, standing orders, direct credits and CHAPS sterling	1,848	2,047	2,402	2,826	3,252	3,705
Cheques						
For payment	3,450	3,163	2,938	2,838	2,641	2,399
For cash acquisition	432	396	345	245	213	166
Total non-cash transactions	7,946	8,371	9,220	10,477	11,672	12,909
Cash payments (estimated)	28,022	27,273	26,270	25,540	25,596	27,860

Source: Association for Payment Clearing Services (2002) *Annual Clearing Statistics*, APACS.

Smart cards, or stored-value cards, are prepaid cards the size of a debit or credit card. They contain an electronic chip which allows a customer to transfer money from an account on to the card. This transfer could take place from an ATM or a specially equipped personal computer. The smart card can then be used for payment at a retailer's point-of-sale terminal. The retailer transfers accumulated balances to its account. Some UK banks have run local trials with smart cards but these have not been hugely successful and so no bank has immediate plans to introduce them on a national scale. However, when smart cards are introduced they will considerably reduce the amount of cash in use.

Internet accounts (e.g. those provided by PayPal) allow a customer to undertake transactions over the internet, for example to purchase a compact

disk. The internet retailer would electronically debit the customer's internet account. If, to realise its value, this 'internet cash' needs to be converted into traditional money, there is a role for banks. However, if internet cash becomes a form of money in its own right then banks' role in the payments system will start to decline.

As we have noted above, payments services are generally provided together with portfolio services by an institution. This is because there are certain advantages in combining the two. The funds which are held in bank accounts before being used to finance purchases – although customers will attempt to keep these at a minimum as they can most likely obtain a higher return by lending them elsewhere – can in aggregate be used to on-lend profitably. Thus intermediation emerges as a byproduct of payments services. The profits from the intermediation services have generally been used to subsidise the costs of providing the payments service, notably in relation to personal accounts. Various schemes have been adopted by banks to enable the profits earned from the use of the idle balances of a customer to reduce or eliminate charges for the use of the payments service. For example, customers who kept a positive minimum and average account balance were then exempt from charges for payments services. Another method used was the calculation of implicit interest on a customer's idle balances, which was used to offset charges. The policy of deregulation of the financial system over the 1980s affected these arrangements. In particular, deregulation of the building societies – covered in chapter 5 – allowed them to set up current accounts. These accounts generally paid interest on the idle funds in them whilst at the same time did not charge for the payments service. This additional competition for banks induced them to introduce current accounts which either pay interest or involve no bank charges. Deregulation and the increased competition it brings have so far not led to the removal of cross-subsidisation, whereby explicit rates of interest are paid on account balances but payments services are fully charged for, as suggested by Fama (1980), for example.

The providers of payments services, though, obtain certain advantages which enable them to be more efficient in their intermediation operations. In particular, they will obtain valuable information about the financial circumstances of the customer. This enables them to judge whether it is suitable to extend that customer credit and once the loan is extended the transactions account can be used as a source of information in the monitoring process. Such specialised information, as we saw in chapter 2, provides part of the explanation for the existence of financial intermediaries. Also, the access to transaction details enables an institution to target other financial services at customers. These advantages therefore partly explain why institutions such as building societies have sought to introduce payments services.

3.5 Risks in retail banking

Banks, like all financial intermediaries, as we saw in chapter 2, are involved in managing risk. The principal risks that are managed by retail banks in the intermediation process are:

(i) liquidity risk – this is a consequence of issuing liabilities which are largely payable on demand or at short notice whilst holding assets which have a longer term to maturity;
(ii) asset risk – the risk that assets held by the bank may not be redeemable at their book value owing to default, price risk or forced-sale risk.

Two additional sources of instability in the banking system stem first from the nature of the payments system and second from banks' increasing undertaking of business which involves contingent commitments. The payments system risk arises from the exposures created when funds are committed by a bank before final settlement. This is a feature of payments systems where settlement occurs at the end of the day. The second risk arises from transactions termed 'off balance sheet' as they do not appear on the balance sheet until the contingency arises. This is a feature of banking which relates more to the wholesale side, though it is relevant to retail banking to the extent that most retail banks also undertake wholesale business. We leave discussion of the nature of off-balance-sheet business and its implications for regulation until the next chapter.

In this section we examine first the nature of the two principal risks inherent in retail banking identified above, and briefly examine the methods used by banks in their management. We also consider the nature of payments risk and moves by the Bank of England to tackle this problem.

3.5.1 *Liquidity risk*

Bank deposits can be withdrawn at call or very short notice, whereas a large proportion of a bank's assets are illiquid (advances typically make up some 50 per cent of the assets of a retail bank). This practice of mismatching or maturity transformation, discussed in chapter 2, exposes the bank to liquidity risk and as a consequence it is important that banks manage the inflow and outflow of their funds. The inflows and outflows of much of the funds passing through a bank are uncertain. Deposit inflows and outflows are largely uncertain and, on the assets side of the balance sheet, overdraft commitments introduce another element of uncertainty. The inflow and outflow of funds through a bank will be predictable to some extent on the basis of what has happened in the past. However, there will be a stochastic element to these flows and banks will have to structure their balance sheet in such a way that they can manage this uncertainty. A fundamental element in a bank's management of this uncertainty comes from the large scale of its operation and more importantly from a diversified base of deposit

accounts. When a large number of uncertain net flows (mostly deposit accounts) are combined then a greater degree of predictability is achieved. The basic principle here is that it is better to have a large number of small accounts than a small number of large accounts. This reduces the uncertainty of the bank's cash flows but the remaining uncertainty still needs to be managed.

We will examine the requirements set out by the Financial Services Authority to ensure that banks adequately cover this liquidity risk in chapter 17. What we concentrate on here are the two main strategies that banks can adopt to manage this liquidity problem.

Reserve asset management

Figure 3.1 simply illustrates the reserve asset management approach to liquidity risk. Inflows in the form of new deposits and loan repayments are added to the holdings of cash and liquid assets. Loan repayments will clearly be a more predictable element of cash inflows, determined by the loans made in the past, though the bank will have to allow for potential default on repayment of the loan. The outflows, in the form of deposit withdrawals and new loans made, will deplete the holdings of cash and liquid assets. The illiquid loan portfolio is protected from an unexpectedly large net outflow of funds by the holding of a buffer stock of cash and liquid assets. That is, the bank will hold cash and liquid assets at a level above that which is required to meet the expected volatility of cash flows.

The assets held in liquid form do not have to comprise only cash with a zero rate of interest – a tiering or maturity ladder approach is generally adopted, whereby some of the reserve assets held are short term and

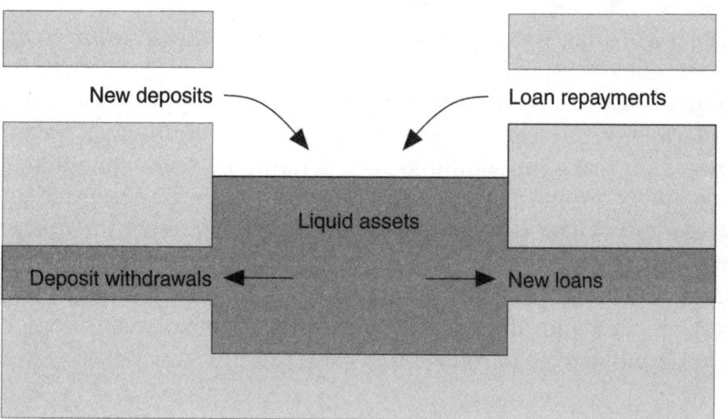

Figure 3.1 The reserve asset management approach to liquidity risk.

therefore easily realisable, such as callable or overnight deposits, and others are longer term and therefore less easy to realise but still liquid because of their marketability, such as bills, certificates of deposit, government securities and so on. By holding these liquid assets rather than just cash the bank is obtaining at least some return on its funds. However, the return is still less than that it would obtain on its main earning asset, which is advances.

Liability management

Liability management involves relying on instruments bearing market rates of interest to fund activity. At its most general it involves determining a desired quantity of assets and then adjusting interest rates to attract in the desired level of deposits to fund this. This is in contrast to reserve asset management, where interest rates are held constant, at least in the short term, and the scale of the asset portfolio is adjusted in line with the quantity of deposits attracted at that rate. The form that liability management takes depends on the market for funds where existing deposits are drawn. If a bank is reliant on retail deposits then, leaving aside its ability to vary other characteristics of the deposits such as term, in order to attract new deposits it generally has to increase the interest rate on a wide range of other deposits.[2] This makes the marginal cost of the additional funds raised high. The existence of a market for deposits where the bank is effectively a price taker, so its borrowing does not lead to a rise in the interest rate, means the marginal cost of the funds raised is reduced. As we describe in chapter 10, the inter-bank market is such a market in the UK. Banks can therefore use the inter-bank market as a marginal source of funds and for the marginal use of funds, so that at the end of a working day if the bank has a shortage of funds it can borrow short term from the inter-bank market, or if the bank has a surplus of funds it can lend short term. The existence of an inter-bank market means that banks can raise additional funds at a lower marginal cost than raising interest rates across the board and also more quickly than from retail sources. As a consequence, retail banks in the UK have largely moved away from reserve asset management to liability management as a technique for managing liquidity risk. It has to be noted though that inter-bank markets are not perfect and that banks are not pure price takers in these markets. There is therefore some uncertainty about the quantity and price of funds raised through these markets and hence banks still require some level of reserve assets as a backup. Note also that if there is a net shortage of funds in the banking system then banks have to look outside the inter-bank market to relieve this shortage.

3.5.2 *Asset risk*

The Bank of England (*Bank of England Quarterly Bulletin*, May 1980) has identified three ways in which a bank's assets are subject to the risk of a

fall in value below that recorded in the balance sheet (their 'book value'). First, and most important in terms of the structure of the bank's assets, is the risk of default on the part of borrowers on the advances made by the bank. In chapter 2 we summarised some of the ways in which a bank can reduce credit risk.

As a first step, a bank can minimise the risk of default on an individual advance by, for example, considering the use of the loaned funds and the financial circumstances of the borrower. Credit scoring plays an increasing role in selecting good risks in consumer lending. A potential borrower is asked a standard set of questions relating to factors such as age, assets held, financial commitments and so on, and on the basis of the answers a score is calculated reflecting the credit risk of the person. The use of credit scoring has largely replaced judgement in determining whether to grant a loan and can easily be automated, so reducing the costs of acquiring information to judge a borrower's suitability. Another method of reducing risk for the lender is to require the borrower to provide security. In the event of the borrower defaulting the bank can sell the secured assets and recover part or all of the loan. A well known type of secured lending is mortgage lending, where the property is used as security. Second, a bank can increase the predictability of default by spreading its loan portfolio over many borrowers. This is known as pooling risks and requires the bank to make a large number of small loans rather than a small number of large loans. The bank can then rely on the law of large numbers to achieve a smaller variation in loan loss experienced, so that the actual loan loss will be very close to the average loan loss for that type of business. This outcome depends critically on the default risks across the loan portfolio being independent. To achieve this the bank needs to diversify its loans over different types of borrower. If, for example, a bank lends only to firms involved in the commercial property construction industry and there is a recession in that industry then the bank will suffer a high number of defaults (i.e. the default risks are not independent). If, however, the bank spreads its loans across firms in different industries and consumers then it is not as badly affected by a recession in one sector. Of course, if the whole economy goes into recession then it will incur a higher number of defaults. International diversification of loans may help to reduce this problem.

A second asset risk considered by the Bank of England is investment risk, which relates to capital-uncertain assets and refers to the risk of a price fall, thus reducing the value of the asset. The main capital-uncertain assets held by banks are government securities and if the general level of interest rates increases then the value of the bank's government securities will decline.

The final risk considered by the Bank of England is forced-sale risk, which refers to the risk that the realisable value of the asset may fall below its book value if the asset has to be sold at short notice.

A bank's exposure to these risks is an important consideration in determining its solvency and we consider this in detail in chapter 17, which examines the regulation and prudential control of banks.

3.5.3 *Payments risk*

As we saw in section 3.4, a payments system provides for the transfer of funds between accounts at different institutions. In the UK, on an average day in 2001 the payments systems processed over 21 million transactions with a total value of some £350 billion (see table 3.3). We can separate payments systems into two types: wholesale and retail. Of the wholesale type, dealing with large-value, same-day sterling transfers, the main system is the Clearing House Automated Payments System (CHAPS). CHAPS regularly processed total daily payments of £200 billion through its member banks in 2001. CHAPS can be separated into CHAPS sterling and CHAPS euro, with CHAPS euro facilitating euro wholesale payments between parties in the UK and cross-border from and to the UK through its link with TARGET (a euro clearing system for Europe – see chapter 16 for a discussion of TARGET). Although CHAPS is mainly a wholesale payments system the fastest growing use of CHAPS is for payments initiated by retail customers. Solicitors, for example, use CHAPS sterling for the vast majority of housing completion payments. Of the retail payment systems, the cheque clearing and credit clearing systems deal with cheques and paper items, respectively. In addition, there is the Bankers' Automated Clearing Services (BACS), which is an electronic clearing house for items such as standing orders and direct debits. The relative sizes of these payments systems are shown in table 3.3.

Table 3.3 Major UK payments systems: average daily volume and values, 2001

	Volume (1,000s)	Value (£m)
CHAPS sterling	94.7	209,142
CHAPS euro	15.7	126,043
BACS	13,942	8,562
Cheque and credit clearing	7,470	5,545

Source: Association for Payment Clearing Services (2002) *Annual Clearing Statistics*, APACS.

CHAPS allows a bank to make guaranteed and irrevocable sterling credits to other banks in the system, either on its own account or on behalf of customers. Settlement is achieved through settlement accounts held at the Bank of England (see chapter 10 for further discussion). One kind of risk associated with this type of system is known as receiver risk. This arises

when a system member provides funds to its customers, having received a payment instruction from another member but before final settlement. The receiving bank which has offered irrevocable funds to its customers is exposed to the sending bank until final settlement occurs at the end of the day. Those customers receiving funds before settlement may then initiate further transfers, creating additional obligations for their settlement banks. This may be repeated several times during a day, building up large exposures. If one of the settlement banks were to fail before final settlement the other members would be deprived of the money needed to fund their own payments. Thus a failure at one bank may lead to settlement failures at other banks and create a systemic crisis.

The solution to this problem is real-time gross settlement (RTGS). This requires that all inter-bank transactions are recorded in the accounts of the central bank as they occur. It is then possible to structure the system so that a settlement bank receives an incoming payment instruction only after the payment has been settled by the central bank. Thus there is little scope for them to pass funds to their customers before final settlement. Such a system was implemented in the UK in 1996 for CHAPS sterling and in 1999 for CHAPS euro.

3.6 Conclusion

In this chapter we have considered the changing nature of retail banking. As in most other areas of the financial services industry, technological developments are dramatically changing the methods of supplying services. These developments have lowered barriers to entry to the industry and we are now beginning to see a wider range of firms supplying retail banking services. Technological developments are also changing the nature of payments services, again lowering barriers to entry to the industry. To complete our picture of banking we turn in the next chapter to consider the nature of wholesale and investment banking, where competition from overseas markets has been powerful since the 1980s.

Notes

1 Note that 1996 is the latest date for which a separate balance sheet for retail banks is available. Although this is somewhat out of date it is still indicative of the structure of a retail bank's balance sheet today.
2 Of course, it is possible for banks to introduce new accounts with better interest rates than those on existing accounts. However, such practices have been widely criticised and are now declining.

Chapter 4

Wholesale and investment banking

4.1 Introduction

In the last chapter we examined the nature of retail banking in the UK and noted that the distinction between this type of banking and wholesale banking has become increasingly blurred over recent years. To complete our discussion of banking we turn in this chapter to examine the nature of wholesale and investment banking. Wholesale banking is essentially the provision of traditional banking services, provided normally at negotiated rates, to large companies and institutions. The blurring of the boundaries between banking and capital markets and the trend of disintermediation have led many of the wholesale banks to engage in capital market activities, typically underwriting new security issues and merger and acquisition advice. These kinds of banks are termed investment banks. Some of the larger banks are involved in retail banking, wholesale commercial banking and investment banking. We begin by examining the general nature of wholesale and investment banking in section 4.2. This examination relates to activities which are captured on the balance sheet. Banks are increasingly using a technique known as asset-backed securitisation to remove assets from the balance sheet. We examine this process in section 4.3. An increasing amount of the business of banks does not appear on the balance sheet and is termed off-balance-sheet business. We discuss the nature, causes and consequences of this type of business in section 4.4. In section 4.5 we discuss the nature of eurocurrency banking, which is now the most dominant form of international banking. Finally, in section 4.6 we briefly consider the issue of sovereign lending, that is, lending by banks to sovereign countries. A boom in this type of lending over the 1970s had consequences which blighted the international banking system over the 1980s.

The international significance of British banks to investment banking has declined. Both Barclays and National Westminster withdrew from investment banking in the 1990s and this has left the field to the major US

banks and other European banks. Presumably this was because of their perception that size was to become more important in investment banking and these banks were unwilling to allocate sufficient resources to this activity. The search for size in banking can be ascertained from the announcement in April 1998 of the merger between the two US banks Citicorp and Travelers Group, which created the largest company in the world, financial, commercial or industrial. Other mergers have included Nations Bank and Bank America in April 1998, Union Bank of Switzerland and the Swiss Banking Corporation in June 1998, and J. P. Morgan and Chase Manhattan in 2000.

4.2 The nature of wholesale and investment banking

A large number of banks which operate in the UK do not come under the category of retail banks as defined in the last chapter. Until 1996, the Bank of England in its statistical analysis separated them on the basis of the country where the headquarters were located, and then for the non-retail UK banks further subdivided these to identify those operating as investment banks. In the analysis which follows we use the figures for 1996, which is the latest year for which a breakdown of UK retail and non-retail banks is available. As noted in chapter 3, although these figures are somewhat out of date they are still indicative of the balance sheet structure of wholesale and investment banks. The breakdown of non-retail banks operating in the UK is as follows:

(i) UK investment banks. These have traditionally financed commerce and trade by the 'accepting' of bills. Their activities are now much broader and include direct lending to industry, underwriting new issues and providing advice on mergers, acquisitions and portfolio management.
(ii) Other UK banks. This group captures all financial institutions registered as banks which are not included in the retail and investment bank categories. As a consequence the activities of these institutions are diverse, ranging from small regional banks to finance houses, leasing companies and other specialised institutions, some of which are the subsidiaries of retail banks.
(iii) US banks.
(iv) Japanese banks.
(v) Other overseas banks.

We now examine the balance sheets of these different categories of non-retail banks, so as to identify some of the aspects of wholesale banking and in particular those features which distinguish it from retail banking. The sterling and foreign currency breakdown of the deposits of the different categories of banks is provided in table 4.1.

Table 4.1 Sterling and foreign currency deposits of non-retail banks at end December 1996 (£million)

	UK investment banks	Other UK banks	US banks	Japanese banks	Overseas banks
Sterling	23,440	42,592	26,234	29,728	159,623
Foreign currency	13,317	8,832	121,450	149,465	533,958
Steling sight as a percentage oftotal sterling	21	14	26	7	14

Source: *Bank of England Statistical Abstract*, 1997, tables 3.5, 3.6, 3.7, 3.8, 3.10.

One salient feature of wholesale banking which contrasts with retail banking is the large size of the deposits and loans, and consequently the smaller number of depositors and borrowers. Minimum values for sterling deposits and loans are typically £250,000 and £500,000, respectively. The structure of the sterling deposits of these wholesale banks is also quite different from those of retail banks. For sterling deposits, the sight element is considerably lower for non-retail banks, with US banks showing the largest proportion at 26 per cent (see table 4.1), compared with 45 per cent for retail banks. This reflects the absence of these banks from retail banking. Approximately 22 per cent of sterling wholesale deposits are inter-bank (i.e. deposits of one UK bank placed with another bank – see chapter 10 for further discussion), the remainder being mainly time deposits from UK private companies and overseas companies and banks. For the foreign currency business a smaller proportion (approximately 10 per cent) originates from other UK banks, with by far the largest proportion originating from overseas customers and banks. One other feature of wholesale banking, indicated in table 4.1, is the greater extent of foreign currency business for both UK and overseas banks when compared with retail banks (where foreign currency deposits accounted for approximately 21 per cent of total liabilities). The overseas banks though, whilst engaging in a considerable amount of sterling wholesale business, are more heavily involved in foreign currency business. The reasons why overseas banks locate in the UK but deal mainly in foreign currencies are explored in section 4.5.

The assets held by non-retail banks are summarised in table 4.2, again broken down by type of bank. Non-retail banks, because the nature of their business is low volume, large value and hence unlikely to be conducted through cash transactions, require little in the way of cash balances. Much of the first item in table 4.2 is made up of the compulsory cash balance which the Bank of England requires of all banks. In terms of sterling assets, market loans are clearly important, with the main item here being inter-

bank loans – the counterpart to inter-bank deposits. Compared with retail banks, a larger proportion of the sterling assets of non-retail banks is accounted for by market loans. The item 'Claims under repo agreements' refers largely to balances acquired through the operation of the new system of monetary control discussed in chapter 10.

Table 4.2 Assets of non-retail banks operating in the UK at end December 1996 (£million)

	UK investment banks	Other UK banks	US banks	Japanese banks	Overseas banks
Sterling					
Notes and coins and balances at the Bank of England	57	114	96	78	369
Market loans	8,194	9,561	8,819	11,758	64,646
Bills	35	160	6	46	1,183
Claims under repo agreements	5,079	230	1,333	2	9,277
Advances	7,988	38,702	12,478	15,932	66,187
Investments	4,672	3,437	1,739	1,871	17,419
Total sterling assets	26,025	52,204	24,471	29,687	159,081
Foreign currency[a]					
Market loans	5,811	6,778	70,567	105,210	311,900
Advances	4,706	1,789	41,884	34,237	136,650
Bills, investments etc.	5,142	3,645	17,487	12,311	116,374
Total foreign currency assets	15,659	12,212	129,938	151,758	564,924

[a]Selecte d foreign currency assets – some miscellaneous assets excluded.
Source: *Bank of England Statistical Abstract*, 1997, tables 3.5, 3.6, 3.7, 3.8, 3.10.

The extent to which overseas banks based in the UK have become involved in domestic UK activity is also revealed in table 4.2. Taken together, in 1996 overseas banks accounted for 27 per cent of total sterling lending by way of advances to the UK private sector.[1] A significant part of this lending was directed towards large construction projects, including the Canary Wharf development in the London Docklands and the Channel Tunnel. As is also the case for the liabilities side of the balance sheet, foreign currency assets form a significant proportion of total assets. Reference back to table 4.1 illustrates a fair degree of currency matching, since foreign currency assets for each category of bank are similar in total to foreign currency liabilities.

A common hypothesis about wholesale banks is that they aim to 'match' the term to maturity of their liabilities and assets. So, for example, a £100,000 three-month certificate of deposit in its liability portfolio may be used to finance the purchase of a three-month commercial bill of value £100,000. Under this hypothesis wholesale banks are simply liquidity distributors or brokers of liquid assets and do not produce liquidity by undertaking maturity transformation. It is sometimes argued that wholesale banks cannot mismatch because, unlike retail banks, they typically have a small number of large-value deposits and therefore cannot rely on the law of large numbers effect which comes from having a large number of small-value deposits. This effect, as we saw in chapter 3, makes net withdrawals of deposits more predictable. Thus it is claimed that, in the face of uncertainty, wholesale banks will aim to match the maturity of their assets with those of their liabilities. If wholesale banks are simply distributing liquidity then the justification for the existence of such banks is dependent solely on their ability to reduce the costs of liquidity distribution to a lower level than would exist if borrowers and lenders sought out each other directly. As we saw in chapter 2, banks can reduce costs in credit markets through specialisation, which enables them to achieve economies of scale in their lending and borrowing operations. However, unlike the normal type of financial intermediation described in chapter 2, there will be no reflection of the liquidity generated by the bank in its interest rate margin, as no liquidity is being generated. Of course this does not preclude other types of transformation, such as risk transformation.

We now turn to examine whether there is any evidence to support the hypothesis of matching by wholesale banks. The Bank of England has published the findings of a survey of retail and non-retail banks operating in London, which show the maturity profiles of the aggregate asset and liability portfolios at the end of January 1987 (see Lewis and Davis 1987). The results are shown in table 4.3. It should be noted that the figures in table 4.3 refer to business with non-banks, that is, the inter-bank positions are netted out, as these positions will be matched positions in aggregate. Whilst it is recognised that these figures refer to 1987, it is not thought that the overall position will have changed greatly since that date. The figures for business with non-banks reveal considerable mismatching by wholesale banks, with the overwhelming majority of deposits having a maturity of under three months whilst a majority of assets have a maturity of over one year. The main features of this mismatching are:

(i) the similarity in the degree of maturity mismatching between sterling and foreign currency business;
(ii) wholesale banks, whilst significantly mismatching, appear do this to a lesser extent than retail banks – for example, for retail banks roughly 84 per cent of deposits fall in the category 0–7 days and 66 per cent

Table 4.3 Maturity analysis of sterling and foreign currency business with non-bank customers of retail and wholesale banks in the UK at end January 1987

	Sterling						Foreign currency			
	Retail banks (%)		British non-retail banks (%)		Overseas banks (%)		All banks banks (%)		British banks (%)	
	A	L	A	L	A	L	A	L	A	L
0–7 days	3.54	83.51	13.98	52.83	12.64	41.29	11.96	38.15	11.11	47.95
8 days–1 month	3.49	7.89	3.09	18.74	12.75	21.97	11.00	23.97	8.20	20.70
1–3 months	6.18	6.28	6.27	15.61	15.35	20.88	13.71	18.15	10.21	17.19
3–6 months	5.01	1.00	6.19	4.36	5.69	5.16	9.33	6.87	7.86	6.71
6 months–1 year	5.91	0.67	10.42	4.70	7.20	4.03	6.09	2.68	6.61	2.29
1–3 years	10.21	0.24	18.11	1.83	12.65	2.37	13.11	2.02	15.20	1.74
Over 3 years	65.68	0.41	41.94	1.93	33.72	4.30	34.80	8.16	40.81	3.42

A = Assets.
L = Liabilities.
Source: Bank of England, *Sterling Business Analysed by Maturity and Sector*, March 1987; Bank of England, *Maturity Analysis by Sector of Liabilities and Claims in Foreign Currencies*, March 1987.

of assets have a maturity of over three years, whereas for British wholesale banks the figures are 53 per cent and 42 per cent, respectively;

(iii) UK wholesale banks appear to mismatch to a greater extent than overseas banks – in their operations in London.

This evidence therefore does not support the view that wholesale banks are only liquidity distributors but rather that they transform the maturity characteristic of the funds flowing through the institution, albeit to a lesser extent than retail banks. This result begs the question of how they are able to engage in maturity transformation and hence liquidity production for their non-bank customers when they do not have the advantage of the retail banks of the law of large numbers effect. That is, how do wholesale banks manage their liquidity risks? A related problem is that, given the small number of advances on the assets side of the balance sheet, there is less scope for pooling and diversifying default risks than with retail banking. The solution to the problem of liquidity risk is provided first by the practice of liability management, which, as we discussed in chapter 3, involves banks having access to inter-bank borrowings and other market-based deposits as an immediate source of funds to replace any shortfall in the event of maturing or withdrawn deposits. A second strategy, which became more widely available to banks after the mid-1980s, is the securitisation of assets. This involves transforming previously illiquid assets such as mortgages into marketable instruments, which can then be sold on to a third party. This phenomenon is discussed in section 4.3 and is one aspect of the more general process of securitisation, which refers to the switch away from indirect, bank financing to direct financing through the capital markets observed since the mid-1980s (discussed in chapter 12). The solution to the problem of default risk has been for wholesale banks to form syndicates to spread the default risk of a large loan over a number of banks. This is examined further in section 4.5 in connection with eurocurrency lending.

The discussion of wholesale banking so far has focused on the activities which appear on the balance sheet. We now examine asset-backed securitisation, which is the process whereby banks remove illiquid assets from the balance sheet. We follow this up with a look at the business of banks which is not captured on the balance sheet, or off-balance-sheet business.

4.3 Asset-backed securitisation

Securitisation is a process in which some of the illiquid assets of a company or financial institution are pooled together, with their cash flows used to support payments on related securities. These securities, known as asset-backed securities (ABSs), are bonds that are sold on to investors. At first, ABSs were mainly based on a pool of residential mortgages. However, increasingly a wider range of assets have been securitised, including credit

card balances, consumer loans, student loans and car loans. Also, a growing number of entertainers have securitised cash flows in order to raise capital. One of the first to do this was David Bowie in January 1997, when he raised $55 million through the issue of ten-year bonds (Bowie bonds) backed by the royalties from his previously issued music albums. The bonds were bought by the Prudential Insurance Company. It can be seen from this that securitisation can be applied to virtually any asset that has a reasonably predictable future stream of revenues.

The first issue of an ABS was in the US during the 1970s. The first issue in the UK came in 1985 and the UK ABS market is now the second largest in the world. However, in the UK only a small proportion of lending has been securitised. In 2002, some $53 billion of ABSs were issued in the UK, accounting for 35 per cent of the issues in the European market (see European Securitisation Forum 2003). This compares with $420 billion of issues in the US.

The main advantage of ABSs for the lender is that by removing assets from the balance sheet (provided the relevant risks are transferred to the investors) the institution frees up capital for other, perhaps more profitable uses. It may also assist a bank in complying with the Basle capital requirement (see chapter 17), in that it may be less expensive to remove assets from the balance sheet than to raise additional capital. Securitisation also allows an institution to concentrate on those aspects of the lending business in which it has a comparative advantage. Thus, for example, a small building society may feel it is more efficient at originating loans and so once the loans are obtained it can securitise the assets and sell them to institutions that are more efficient at securing the necessary funding. Another advantage of securitisation to a lender is that when it feels overexposed to a particular sector or set of borrowers it can securitise part of its lending. The main attraction of ABSs to an investor is the margin they offer over other highly rated bonds. They also allow investors an opportunity to diversify their portfolios, increasing their exposure in areas to which they may not have direct access.

The common structure for an ABS issue in the UK is similar to the US 'pass through'. This is illustrated in figure 4.1. First, an originator separates suitable assets from its portfolio, normally assets of similar quality and repayment calendar. These assets are then sold to a special-purpose vehicle (SPV), thus providing a legal separation of the assets from the originator. The SPV then sells securities to investors to fund the purchase of the assets, which it holds in a trust on their behalf. The issued securities will normally have at least one credit rating in order to make them attractive to investors (see section 9.6). In addition, most issues have credit enhancement in order to boost the credit rating. A credit enhancement provides a degree of assurance to investors that the principal and coupon payments will be paid

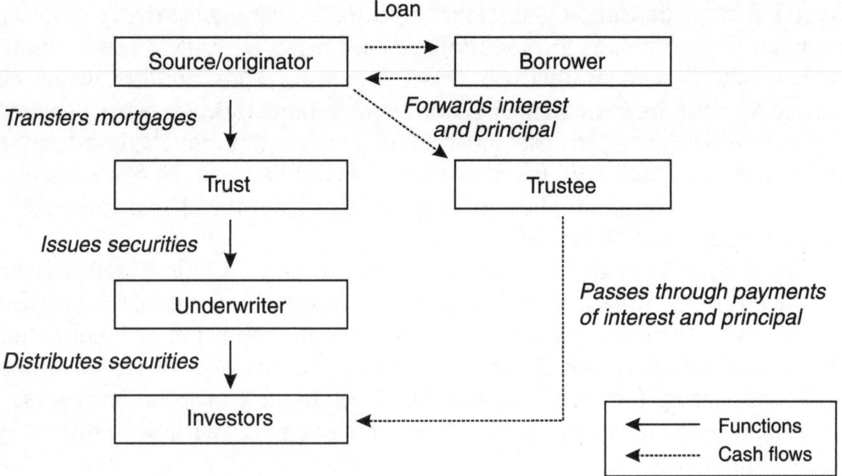

Figure 4.1 The securitisation process.

in a timely manner. Various methods of credit enhancement are used, with the most common, until recently, being an insurance contract. An ABS is normally issued as a floating-rate note (see chapter 12), paying the London inter-bank offer rate plus a margin.

4.4 Off-balance-sheet business

Off-balance-sheet business refers to business undertaken by a bank which generates a contingent commitment and generally an income to the bank without the business being captured on the balance sheet under conventional accounting procedures. This type of business has long been undertaken by banks but has grown rapidly in both volume and scope since the early 1980s on an international basis, although for UK banks it has fallen off in recent years, probably because they have been less involved in investment banking. In this section we examine the nature of off-balance-sheet business and the reasons for its growth. In order to consider the latter we broaden the picture to examine more generally the causes of financial innovation. Finally we examine some of the implications of off-balance-sheet business, in particular for the regulation of banks.

4.4.1 *Types of off-balance-sheet business*

If we consider first of all the narrow definition of off-balance-sheet business, that is, activities giving rise to contingent commitments, then four broad areas can be identified.

(i) *Loan commitments*. These cover any advance commitment by a bank to provide credit. Examples are: revolving lines of credit, where a bank provides a line of credit to which it is committed often for several years ahead; overdrafts, where a bank has agreed a facility but can withdraw it in certain circumstances; and note issuance facilities (see chapter 12), where the bank provides credit only in the event of others being unable to. Provision of these commitments generates a fee income for banks.

(ii) *Guarantees*. This involves a bank in underwriting the obligations of a third party, thus relieving the counterparty from having to assess the ability of the customer to meet the terms of the contract. Examples of such guarantees are acceptances, whereby the bank guarantees payment of a customer's liability to the holder of the debt, and performance bonds, which support the good name of a customer and its ability to perform under a particular contract. The bank receives a fee for providing such guarantees.

(iii) *Swap and hedging transactions*. These involve the bank in a transaction using a 'derivative' instrument such as a swap, forward contract, option, financial futures, interest cap or collar. Many of these instruments are discussed further in chapters 11, 13 and 14. The transaction can be hedged (to neutralise a position exposure) or unhedged (left open to exposure).

(iv) *Securities underwriting*. Investment banks are involved in underwriting issues of securities, whereby they agree to buy a set amount of the securities which are not taken up in an issue. This guarantees the issuer that the whole of the issue is taken up and a fee is paid to the banks providing the underwriting service.

All the above examples involve the bank in a commitment which may or may not lead to a balance sheet entry in the future. There are a wide range of other financial services provided by banks which generate fee income and where the business does not lead to a balance sheet entry. These include loan origination, trust and advice services, brokerage and agency services, and payments services, such as the provision of credit cards and cash management systems. The total income of a bank can be roughly split into net interest income, that is, the margin between its lending and borrowing rates, and fee or commission income. The relative growth in fee or commission income and other non-interest income (excluding capital gains from selling investments) since 1980 for Barclays Bank Group, shown in table 4.4, illustrates a general trend for the UK clearing banks. The growth in importance of such income to banks is illustrated by the fact that in 2000 it represented 65 per cent of the bank's net interest income, compared with only 29 per cent in 1980, although this has declined since

the mid-1990s, possibly because of Barclays' withdrawal from investment banking from that time.

Table 4.4 Fee or commission income as a percentage of net interest income for Barclays Bank Group, selected years, 1980–2000

1980	1984	1988	1990	1994	1996	1998	2000
29	41	52	64	84	80	70	65

Source: Barclays bank annual report and accounts.

The relative growth in fee or commission income reflects both a growth in contingent commitment business and attempts by banks to diversify into related financial services, such as selling insurance policies and securities trading. In the remainder of this section we concentrate on the nature of contingent commitment banking, which we call off-balance-sheet business whilst recognising that this term covers a wider range of activities.

4.4.2 *Nature of contingent commitment banking*

It is traditional to view a bank as a collection of assets and liabilities making up its balance sheet. We have already discussed in chapters 2 and 3 why banks engage in the traditional business of borrowing and lending, in terms of lenders delegating the collection and use of information to banks and sharing risks with banks, in return for a charge obtained from the interest rate spread. Banks are able to perform these services at a lower cost than ultimate lenders by specialising in collecting and skilfully using information about credit risks, thereby leading to a better selection of risks and, because of their size of operations, enabling them to pool and diversify risks more effectively. Lewis (1987) argues that banks perform similar information-gathering and risk-sharing roles when they undertake off-balance-sheet activities. For example, the establishment of a loan commitment, such as an overdraft, reduces the liquidity risk faced by the customer but exposes the bank to greater liquidity risk, which it is better able to bear through its size of operations and access to the wholesale markets. When a bank provides a guarantee of a customer's ability to meet her or his debts, as with a bill acceptance, then this leads to a lower interest rate being required by the market. When looked at from the lender's, or bill holder's, viewpoint the effect is akin to a depositor accepting a lower rate of interest from a bank because of the safety provided by the bank compared with holding a primary security. Other transformations of asset characteristics performed on the balance sheet have their equivalent off the balance sheet. Note issuance facilities provide an example of maturity transformation, where issues of short-term paper generate longer-term funding. When banks make

available a syndicated loan, the borrower can negotiate the terms of the loan, including the interest rate basis, the currency and the date at which the loan is to be drawn down. All these choices can be made off balance sheet as well by means of currency swaps, interest rate basis swaps and financial futures contracts to alter draw down dates.

4.4.3 *Factors determining the growth in off-balance-sheet business*

The motives for banks' involvement in off-balance-sheet business are many. One motive indicated in the above discussion is the desire for the fee income that this type of business brings, thus diversifying the bank's income base. More generally banks have looked to diversify their operations and the liberalisation of financial services in most countries has allowed banks to expand into new areas of business. Whilst some of the contingent commitments described above have long been a feature of commercial banking, for example loan commitments and guarantees, other parts of contingent commitment banking, such as swaps and options trading, represent more recent innovations; banks, rather than creating these, have encouraged their growth in use by being willing to run an unhedged position. Banks' involvement in financial innovation, and hence off-balance-sheet business, is related to the changing policy and economic environment and the changing preferences of users of the financial system. In order to examine these motives in more detail we now widen the discussion to consider the factors determining financial innovation.

As we saw in chapter 1, a financial instrument can be described by its underlying characteristics of liquidity, risk and so on. Financial innovation, as related to financial instruments, can be defined as the process of unbundling the characteristics and repackaging them to create new instruments. Indeed, recent developments have made it easier to unbundle and repackage the characteristics of an instrument even after it has been issued. For example, a ten-year, fixed-rate, dollar-denominated eurobond represents a particular package of characteristics. Any of these characteristics can be unpackaged and traded separately. The holder of the bond can swap the currency to yen or swap the fixed-interest stream to a floating rate. This example illustrates the fungibility of financial instruments compared with physical products.

Demand factors

The demand for financial innovation can be explained by reference to a number of factors, discussed below (see Bank for International Settlements (1986) for further discussion).

(i) *Changes in the financial environment.* Changes of policy regimes over the last 30 years have led to greater volatility of asset prices. In

particular, the general move to floating exchange rates in the early 1970s after the breakdown of the Bretton Woods agreement and the use of interest rates to control inflation have increased the scope for fluctuations in exchange rates and interest rates (see figures 14.1 and 14.2 for an illustration of this). The greater the volatility of asset prices and other prices, such as of commodities, the greater is the uncertainty about future prices and hence the greater is the demand for instruments for hedging exchange rate and interest rate risk. We examine hedging strategies in greater detail in chapter 14.

(ii) *Greater perception of credit risks*. There was a deterioration in the credit standing of banks which had large exposures to the debts of developing countries following the onset of the debt crisis in 1982 – discussed in section 4.6. One consequence of this was a desire by some banks to sell or swap some problem debts to diversify extreme exposures, and so a secondary market in sovereign debt emerged. A further consequence of the decline in the credit standing of many banks was that investors were more wary of lending to banks and therefore were more willing to hold the direct securities of ultimate borrowers. In addition, large borrowers with good credit standing found they could obtain better terms by issuing their own securities through the capital markets rather than borrowing directly from banks. One result of this was a shift away from bank intermediation and towards capital market instruments as a source of financing – a process known as securitisation, which is further discussed in chapter 12. Banks, however, sought to benefit from this trend by securitising packages of their own loans so they could be sold on and by expanding their role in guaranteeing and underwriting securities issues so as to increase their fee income.

(iii) *Arbitrage opportunities in capital markets*. The existence of barriers, such as exchange controls, interest rate controls and reserve ratios, separating banking markets in different countries led to the development of eurocurrency banking. This in turn put pressure on domestic markets to lessen controls, thus eventually creating a global short-term money market. A similar process is occurring in the capital markets. Barriers separating capital markets have led to the emergence of eurobond and euronote markets (see chapter 12). However, the process of globalisation of capital markets is still incomplete, leaving banks to exploit arbitrage opportunities. The use of the swap transaction (see chapter 13) has enabled a borrower to raise funds in the capital market in which it has a comparative advantage and then swap the principal and interest on those funds to the currency in which it wishes to borrow. For example, a UK company which has a comparative advantage with its issues of sterling bonds but wanting to

raise US dollars can issue a sterling eurobond and then swap with a US company wishing to raise sterling but with a comparative advantage in the issue of dollar bonds.

Supply factors

Two factors which have had a major influence on the supply of innovations have been increased regulatory pressures and developments in technology.

(i) *Increased regulatory pressures*. One consequence of the deterioration in banks' credit standing has been greater pressure from regulators for increased levels of capital in banking. The need to operate on higher capital ratios led some banks to pursue business that was not subject to capital adequacy controls, that is, off-balance-sheet business. Thus, banks actively contributed to the development and growth in use of instruments such as swaps, options, note issuance facilities and so on. Another consequence of increased capital pressures was, as noted above, the development of securitisation, whereby banks packaged up parts of their loan portfolio (e.g. mortgages) so that they could be sold on in markets.
(ii) *Technology*. Advances in computing, information processing and telecommunications technology have enabled more complex instruments to be designed and priced on a continuous basis. In particular, they have enabled the complex financial engineering of already issued financial products, as described above, to take place.

4.4.4 *Implications of the growth in off-balance-sheet business*

The growth in off-balance-sheet business has been largely the result of the interaction of the demand and supply factors described above. An important implication of this growth stems from one factor in particular, which is the desire of banks to escape capital adequacy controls. This has concerned the regulatory authorities, as banks have taken on risks which are not explicitly related to the bank's capital. These risks are similar to the risks faced by banks in their on-balance-sheet activities but are heightened by the greater uncertainty arising from the novelty of many of the instruments traded. Such risks include: first, liquidity risk, which is the risk of banks having insufficient funding to meet their obligations as they fall due; second, credit risk, which covers both the risk of default by a loan counterparty and the risk of a customer whose performance is guaranteed by the bank failing to deliver; third, position risk, which is concerned with exposure to adverse movements in interest rates and exchange rates (in relation to swap and hedging transactions, banks are exposed to position risk when they take up an unhedged position); and fourth, price risk. There was concern that banks

might be underpricing new services in the sense that the income derived might not be sufficient to cover costs, including profit, over the long term. This fear was heightened by both keen competition, which could force prices down to uneconomic levels, and lack of experience of sufficient duration on which an assessment of the risks could be made.

Regulators have addressed the credit risk of off-balance-sheet transactions in their construction of the risk–assets ratio (a capital ratio where the capital of a bank is related to the risk-adjusted value of its assets – see chapter 17). In the construction of this ratio, off-balance-sheet instruments are converted to a credit equivalent and then risk weighted along with the on-balance-sheet instruments. An illustration of banks' greater exposure to position risk as a consequence of the growth of off-balance-sheet business is provided by the case of Midland Montague, the investment banking arm of the Midland Bank Group at the time. Its operations in 1989 were positioned towards declining interest rates, which failed to materialise, and as a consequence the net interest income of the group was considerably reduced. A further risk of off-balance-sheet business is related to the novelty and complexity of the new variants of these types of instrument, which are continually being developed. This risk was highlighted in the swap market in 1989 when banks suffered sizeable losses following the ruling of the UK High Court that swap deals undertaken by local authorities, in excess of their underlying borrowing, were *ultra vires*. The banks which had entered into these swap arrangements had clearly not fully considered the risks arising from the special legal status of the local authorities. More recently, Union Bank of Switzerland confirmed losses of £80 million on its equity derivatives business in the first half of 1997 due, among other things, to an error in a computer model to price options. The collapse of Barings, discussed in section 13.9.2, provides another illustration of the problems with derivatives trading.

4.5 International banking

As we have indicated in section 4.2, much of the business of wholesale banks based in the UK is not concerned with domestic sterling borrowing and lending, but with borrowing and lending in foreign currencies. The Bank of England defines international banking as all banking transactions in foreign currency – both cross-border and with local residents – plus cross-border transactions in domestic currency. From this definition we can identify two distinct types of international banking. The first is traditional foreign banking, which, for UK-based banks, involves transactions in sterling with non-residents. The second type of international banking is termed eurocurrency banking, which, for UK-based banks, involves transactions in currencies other than sterling with both residents

and non-residents. Traditionally the location of a bank determined the currency in which it would make loans, so to obtain dollar loans you would go to a US-based bank. Whilst such traditional foreign banking still exists, it has been largely replaced by eurocurrency banking, where the location of the bank is unrelated to the currency of its transactions.

Another type of banking, identified by the Bank for International Settlements (BIS) (see McCauley *et al.* 2002), is global banking. The main difference between international and global banking is the way in which the bank obtains funds to finance its foreign assets. A global bank will raise funds locally in the foreign market to finance its lending in that market. An international bank will raise funds in a different market to that to which it lends. Few banks are either pure international banks or pure global banks. By examining the ratio of locally funded business to total foreign business (international plus local) we can identify which banks are most global in their operations. The figures for 2001 presented by McCauley *et al.* (2002) show that UK banks are very global, with a ratio of over 0.9. Other highly global banks are US, Swiss and Irish banks. On the other hand German, French and Italian banks tend to be more international than global. The main reasons for the shift from international to global banking are the debt crisis (discussed below in section 4.6) and liberalisation of the financial sector in many countries, which has led to the relaxation of restrictions on the ownership of banks.

4.5.1 *Eurocurrency banking*

In this section we first of all define the term 'eurocurrency' and then examine the reasons for the development and growth of eurocurrency markets, and their nature and operation. We then discuss eurocurrency lending before reaching a conclusion on the role of these markets in the international financial system.

Definition

A eurocurrency can be defined as a deposit or loan denominated in a currency other than that of the host country where the bank is physically located. Thus, for example, a deposit denominated in US dollars placed with a bank located in London is a eurocurrency. In a similar manner, a deposit denominated in sterling placed with a bank located in Paris is a eurocurrency. It should be noted that whilst eurocurrency banking began in Europe it now takes place in many financial centres around the world. Consequently the existence of eurocurrency markets permits the separation of location of the market and the currency and therefore political and currency risks. It is not surprising that the main currency employed in eurocurrency markets is the dollar (about 75 per cent of the total market),

given the importance of the dollar in the international payments mechanism. Because of this dominant role, much of the following exposition will be in terms of the eurodollar market, though it can easily be extended to other currencies.

Reasons for the development and growth of eurocurrency markets

The interesting question is why the market developed outside the US. A number of reasons have been put forward. One suggestion is that during the early stages of the Cold War the Eastern bloc countries wished to hold dollar deposits for international payment purposes but were reluctant to hold them in the US for fear that they could be 'blocked' in time of dispute. A second reason put forward is the existence of regulations in the US covering interest rates payable on deposits and capital flows.

Since their development in the early 1960s the markets have experienced a fast rate of growth. One of the main reasons for this is an advantage in terms of cost. As noted above, US banks were restricted in terms of interest rates that could be paid on bank deposits and this restraint became more onerous as interest rates rose worldwide. Furthermore, other regulations in the form of reserve requirements and deposit insurance raised the cost of banking in the US compared with a centre such as London, where prudential control was more relaxed. Banks' costs were also lower in the eurocurrency markets since they operated as wholesale banks with no branch network. The effect of these cost advantages was that eurobanks could offer rates on deposits and charges on loans that were marginally more attractive than on similar transactions with banks located in the US. This raised the attractiveness of the eurocurrency markets and stimulated a fast rate of growth.

A second factor was the growth in international banking itself. This was stimulated by, first, the growth in world trade, necessitating a corresponding growth in the international payments system, and, second, a growth of financial imbalances worldwide. In particular, the vast surpluses earned by members of the Organization of Petroleum Exporting Countries (OPEC) following oil price increases in the early 1970s were an important factor. OPEC members placed their surplus dollar revenues from the sale of oil with eurobanks. It is often claimed that the large US balance of payments deficits also aided the development of the market. The importance of this factor may be overestimated since, whilst it increased the total quantity of dollars, it does not explain why these dollar balances were held outside the US. The main reason for the continued growth of the market appears to be the cost advantage and it remains to be seen whether the market will continue to grow as quickly once the relative advantage of offshore centres is reduced following harmonisation of prudential regulation noted in chapter 17.

Nature of eurocurrency markets

We now briefly examine the general nature of the market. The first point to note is that it is a wholesale market with transactions typically of $1 million or more. There is also a significant volume of inter-bank lending, so that the gross size of the market is larger than the size obtained when the inter-bank transactions are netted out (see table 4.5). Interest rates are clearly related to those charged in domestic markets. Thus, the rate charged on dollar loans by banks situated in the US sets an upper limit to the rates charged for similar loans in the eurocurrency markets. Similarly, there is a relationship between the rates ruling in a particular location. Interest rate parity requires the following relationship to hold between rates on sterling in the domestic market and those on dollars in the London eurodollar market for transactions of similar maturity and risk, and so on:

Nominal rate of interest on sterling	=	Nominal rate of interest interest on eurodollars in London	+	Expected appreciation/ depreciation of the dollar versus sterling

Arbitrage will ensure that this relationship holds provided the market is efficient – see chapter 7 for a fuller discussion of this point.

The market is essentially a market for short-term deposits, with the average maturity of a deposit being in the region of three months. The main depositors and borrowers are governments, multinational corporations and banks from a wide range of countries, including the US. Lending appears on the other side of the bank's balance sheet. Eurocurrencies are the major vehicle for international lending, for the same reasons as discussed above for the growth of eurocurrency markets. The reasons for this dominance of eurocurrencies in international lending follow from those discussed above for the growth of the eurocurrency markets.

Eurocurrency lending

It is difficult to obtain separate figures for net eurocurrency lending, so the figures reported below refer to gross claims on international banks. The figures for the volume of new gross claims from the late 1980s to 2002 are presented in table 4.5.

The gross claims of international banks are split into claims on other banks and claims on non-banks. It can be seen from the table that much of international bank financing is of an inter-bank nature and the majority of this is through redepositing. In terms of financing the non-bank sector (companies, governments and government agencies) we can see that the majority of this is through banks purchasing securities.

Most eurocurrency lending is syndicated – that is, the loans are spread among many, sometimes over 100, banks – and, conversely, most syndicated

Table 4.5 External claims on international banks (figures in $billion adjusted to exclude estimated exchange rate effect)

	1988	1990	1992	1994	1996	1998	2000	2002
Gross claims	444	610	179	264	560	285	1,221	794
Claims on banks:	360	395	23	263	260	151	933	495
inter-bank loans					179	40	680	461
securities					81	111	253	34
Claims on non-banks:	84	215	156	1	300	134	288	299
loans					157	–4.8	58	79
securities					143	139	230	220

Note: The breakdown of claims for banks and non-banks into loans and securities is available only from 1996.
Source: Bank for International Settlements, *International Banking and Financial Market Developments* (various issues).

lending is in the form of eurocurrency loans. They are generally medium-term loans with maturities ranging from three to fifteen years, although the average maturity of new loans is around six to eight years. Interest rates on the loans are floating, with the interest rate related to a reference rate such as the London inter-bank offer rate (LIBOR), plus a margin representing risk and so on, and adjusted several times a year. Syndicated loans can be denominated in any currency, though the US dollar is the most popular. Given the large number of banks involved in syndicated lending, it is natural that one bank will act as a 'lead' in organising the arrangements of the loan. The lead bank will receive a fee for this service in addition to the normal interest rate charge. Figures for the total sums of signed syndicated loans from 1992 are provided in table 4.6.

Table 4.6 International syndicated lending, 1992–2002 ($billion)

1992	1994	1996	1998	2000	2002
194	501	839	905	1,470	1,318

Source: Bank for International Settlements, *International Banking and Financial Market Developments* (various issues).

Eurocurrency loans and syndicated loans in particular were the method of financing the international imbalances of the 1970s following the oil price rises of 1973/74. Sovereign borrowers from the least developed countries (LDCs) and the newly industrialising countries (NICs) in Latin

America became important borrowers in this market. When the debt crisis broke in 1982 (see section 4.6) this had two main effects on the syndicated loan market. First, banks became reluctant to lend new money to emerging markets unless they were forced to do so as part of a restructuring package of the International Monetary Fund (IMF) ('involuntary lending'). Second, those banks with a high ratio of sovereign debt to capital found their credit rating reduced, which made it more costly for them to raise funds in the capital markets and so led to higher lending charges. One consequence of this was that highly rated borrowers found they could raise funds at lower cost through the international capital markets than through borrowing from banks. This led to the phenomenon known as securitisation, which is further discussed in chapter 12. The overall effect of the debt crisis was to bring about a dramatic reduction in the volume of new syndicated lending, which continued until 1985. Since 1986 the market has grown again, with most of the growth of syndicated credits since the late 1980s coming from a greater use of this type of financing by industrial borrowers. By the early 1990s industrial borrowers accounted for over 80 per cent of total syndicated credits, compared with approximately 60 per cent in the early 1980s. The surge of corporate restructuring in the late 1980s and 1990s through mergers and acquisitions, particularly in the US and UK, has been one of the driving forces behind the growth of syndicated lending. An increasing proportion of the financing of such activity has been debt, partly marketable debt in the US ('junk bonds') but largely loans raised through the method of syndicated lending. The advantage of syndicated loans in this activity is again the speed with which funds can be raised and the ability to raise these funds more discreetly than through the capital markets. The scale of the growth in international syndicated lending is illustrated in table 4.6.

There are a number of advantages for borrowers in using the syndicated credits market compared with international capital markets. First, this type of loan typically provides a medium- to long-term source of funds, whereas the short-term underwritten instruments of the euronote markets (considered in chapter 12) would require more frequent renegotiation. Second, borrowers can generally raise larger sums of money than through the capital markets. For example, a $13.6 billion credit was raised for Kohlberg Kravis Roberts for the leveraged takeover of RJR Nabisco in 1989. Third, deals can be arranged quickly. For example, in 1987 BP sought to raise a syndicated loan to finance its offer to purchase the remainder of the stock of Standard Oil. A consortium of banks, led by Morgan Guaranty, took just five days to arrange $15 billion, which was $10 billion more than BP actually required. The syndication of a loan across many banks also brings advantages compared with a loan from one bank, in that an individual bank in the syndicate will be less affected by a default. The lower risk implies that the cost of a syndicated loan should be lower.

Consequences of eurocurrency markets

Finally in this section we consider the consequences of the development of the eurocurrency market. The market clearly carries out many of the facets of financial intermediation discussed in chapter 2. Maturity transformation is obviously present, with loans being of a longer term than deposits. Similarly, asset transformation is evidenced by the change of almost riskless deposits into more risky loans. This creates some dangers for the financial system, given the interdependence of the operators within the market due to the presence of inter-bank lending built on a relatively small base of deposits held in US banks. Failure of one bank may have a large knock-on effect, creating problems for national supervisors of the domestic monetary system. Furthermore, it is sometimes argued that the creation of such a large pool of acceptable currencies creates the potential for movement of funds in a manner that could lead to the destabilisation of exchange rates and the frustration of monetary policy.

A final concern has been expressed over the potential of the eurocurrency markets to propagate inflation. It is sometimes argued that the creation of these markets has led to an expansion of the world money supply, which in turn has led at times to higher inflation rates. However, a more correct analysis suggests that there has been no expansion in the quantity of US dollars held at US banks but secondary deposits were created in the manner of non-bank financial intermediaries building up credit on the base of bank deposits. This analogy suggests that the existence of the eurocurrency markets has permitted a growth of credit rather than the money supply per se, and as such may have increased the efficiency of the allocation of credit worldwide. This is also evidenced by the existence of syndicated lending, which permits the sharing of the risks of international lending amongst different banks from different locations.

In the next section we briefly examine one of the consequences of the growth of international lending over the 1970s.

4.6 The sovereign lending crisis

In the 1960s and early 1970s most lending to developing countries was carried out by official institutions such as the World Bank and the IMF. This position changed, largely as a result of oil price increases between October 1973 and January 1974, which saw oil prices rise by over 400 per cent. These price increases were initiated by OPEC, a cartel whose member countries as a consequence experienced a dramatic increase in their foreign currency receipts. Oil-importing countries, however, experienced balance of payments deficits. Some of the developed countries were supported by direct capital flows from OPEC members; for example, $6 billion was placed in investments in the UK in the years shortly after the oil price rises.

The oil-importing developing countries suffered the most problems, and those with access to the international financial markets generally chose to borrow to cover their balance of payments deficits in order to sustain growth. However, unlike the borrowing of the period prior to the oil price rises, developing countries turned increasingly to commercial banks. Developing countries were reluctant to borrow from the IMF because any funds provided were usually given as part of reconstruction packages which, because they were generally deflationary, were politically unpopular. The international agencies such as the IMF and the World Bank would in any event have been unable to support the scale of lending required, as the basis of their funding was the developed countries' governments, in particular the US, which were themselves experiencing problems. Since oil is priced in dollars, the commercial banks received a massive flow of liquid funds from the OPEC members in the form of eurodollar deposits and therefore had the ability to meet the developing countries' demands for funds. Much of this lending was to governments or was government guaranteed and was therefore termed sovereign lending. There was a widespread belief amongst the banking community that this lending was relatively safe, as countries could not go bankrupt. As a consequence any credit assessment was superficial and there was little monitoring by the banks as to the purpose to which the funds were put. Part of the blame for the crisis which came later can therefore be placed with the banks, which were imprudent in their lending. However, in mitigation, the banks were encouraged by Western governments to recycle the OPEC surpluses to offset the effects of higher oil prices on the world economy. Much of this lending was to the NICs of Latin America. The LDCs, particularly in the sub-Saharan region of Africa, generally did not have sufficient credit standing to gain access to loans from commercial banks.

To sum up this section, the developing countries borrowed heavily in dollars at floating rates of interest to finance balance of payments deficits (i.e. consumption) rather than investment. Consequently, adjustment to the higher oil prices was delayed and servicing the debt necessitated current-account balance of payment surpluses to earn the required dollars to meet the interest payments and repayment of principal.

There was little sign of problems resulting from this sovereign lending over the rest of the 1970s, partly because of negative real interest rates on the debt. Over the latter half of the 1970s though, the OPEC surpluses reduced as a result of dramatically increased imports.

In 1979, OPEC decided on a further sharp rise in the price of oil, which more than doubled the spot price, from $11 to $24 a barrel. Further increases also occurred in 1980. The response of the developed countries to this second round of oil price rises, however, was different. Around this time the governments elected in the UK, US and Germany adopted monetarist

policies and so attempted to control inflation arising from higher oil prices by monetary restraint. This time there was no attempt to borrow and spend a way out of the problem. The policy of monetary restraint, however, contributed to a world recession, which made it much more difficult for developing countries to expand exports to earn foreign currency. As part of the policy of monetary restraint, interest rates were increased, which led to a further deterioration in the debt-servicing capacity of the debtor countries. Thus, the combination of higher interest payments yet declining exports led to increased pressure on debtor countries. The first public sign of a crisis though did not occur until 1982, when Mexico, one of the leading borrowers and a country with proven reserves of oil which had achieved rapid economic growth in the previous four years, announced a moratorium on principal payments until the end of 1983. Pressure from the IMF on commercial banks with exposure to Mexico to provide new money prevented an actual default. However, the incident brought home to the international banking system the nature of the risks of sovereign debt.

The first initiative to alleviate the problem came in 1985, when James Baker, the US Treasury Secretary, announced a new package which was aimed at improving economic growth in the debtor countries. With this package, additional funds were to be provided to finance supply-side reforms, such as encouraging inward investment, tax reform and the encouragement of competition in their economies. The Baker plan was aimed at 15 heavily indebted countries, mostly in South America, with a total of $29 billion targeted over three years. Of this additional funding, $20 billion was to come from commercial banks and $9 billion from international agencies. However, as Sachs (1986) states, 'The Baker plan was significant not as a new policy, but rather an admission by the United States that the debt strategy up to 1985 had not generated adequate economic growth in the debtor countries'.

Over the latter half of the 1980s, a number of market-based solutions were used by the banks to reduce their exposure to LDC debt. Three of the main solutions are discussed below. The issue of third world debt is still a problem for the debtor countries but it no longer puts banks at risk of insolvency. The most recent attempt to solve the problem is the Heavily Indebted Poor Countries (HIPC) Initiative, launched in 1996 by the World Bank and IMF. The issue was publicised by the Jubilee 2000 campaign.

4.6.1 *Selling the debt in the secondary market in LDC debt*

A secondary market in LDC debt began in late 1983, and although much of the activity in this market is inter-bank trading (more recently particularly in Brady bonds – see below), with banks having the aim of adjusting their portfolio of risks, it has also been used as a basis for debt buy-backs by the debtor countries and as an intermediate stage for debt–equity swaps (see

below). The price of a country's debt in the market does provide some indication of the current and future performance of the debt and table 4.7 illustrates the generally deteriorating position for the three main Latin American debtors over the latter half of the 1980s, followed by an improvement in the early 1990s, the reasons for which are discussed below. Table 4.8 reports the total returns on 'Brady' debt (see below) for the same three countries and shows that the situation had continued to improve.

Table 4.7 Secondary market prices for selected LDC debt, 1986–92 (price in dollars of a $100 claim)

Country	August 1986	April 1987	October 1987	March 1989	May 1990	December 1992
Argentina	66	60	34	17	76	63
Brazil	76	63	38	34	25	30
Mexico	56	59	47	41	46	59

Source: Sachs and Huizinga (1987), *Barclays Bank Review*, August 1990, and Clark (1993).

Table 4.8 Total returns on Brady bonds, 1994–96 (1993 = 100)

	1994	1995	1996
Argentina	78.79	102.49	128.10
Brazil	89.85	108.93	146.59
Mexico	70.60	96.02	118.23

Source: J. P. Morgan.

The fact that a debtor's servicing record can influence the secondary market price of its debt introduces a moral hazard problem to the extent that any debt relief is tied to the secondary price of the debt and debtor countries can 'engineer' a reduction in the price to obtain greater relief.

4.6.2 *Debt–equity swap*

This involves a debt denominated in a foreign currency being paid by the debtor in local currency, at an agreed discount, to the debt's face value. The bank then uses the local currency to invest in the debtor country, thereby acquiring a claim on a real asset, with the potential of capital gain as well as income return. For example, Midland Bank in 1989 swapped $63 million of debt owed by Chile for a $53 million investment in a Chilean copper

mine. The discount in the swap was 16 per cent, which is better than the 35 per cent discount which would have resulted from selling through the secondary market.

4.6.3 *Debt–debt swap*

This involves a bank exchanging the debt for bonds issued by the debtor country's government, where the bonds are issued either at a discount on the par value but with a market rate of interest or at par value with a lower than market rate of interest.

It has been estimated that, by 1989, the 15 countries targeted in the Baker plan had reduced their bank debt by 13 per cent using these and other methods. Despite some success in reducing debt burdens it was accepted that the debt burdens of debtor countries remained too high. A further initiative came in March 1989 in the form of a set of proposals announced again by a US Treasury Secretary, this time Nicholas Brady. These proposals represented a shift from the earlier approaches to the debt problem in that they recognised the need for official backing of schemes designed to achieve voluntary reduction of market-based debt or debt service. However, the Brady arrangements also represent a continuation of the Baker approach in that participation is based on the pursuit of an IMF-approved economic adjustment programme and that new money is provided by the banks. Brady deals are still being struck with some eastern European and Asian countries. Under these proposals debt relief is provided by the three methods described above. Official money to back the initiative is provided primarily from the IMF and World Bank but also from the governments of developed countries such as Japan. Positive developments followed the Brady initiative, but significant problems still remain for the debtor countries. Despite the permanent improvements in debtor countries' positions, debt service obligations remain heavy and whilst re-entry to the private capital markets is helpful, the key to long-term recovery is improvement in the real economy, which occurs more slowly than improvement in the financial economy. The debtor countries were also helped after 1990 by significant reductions in US interest rates. The LIBOR for US deposits, to which most loan contracts were linked before the Brady deals, declined by about 500 basis points between 1990 and 1993, and increased only slightly after 1993. Those countries that agreed a deal early on obtained interest savings on that portion of their debt that was left at floating rates. Countries agreeing later will have obtained much larger interest savings. Indeed, the relationship between the decline in international interest rates and the improvement in secondary market prices has been found to be very strong (see Dooley *et al.* 1994) and thus a reversal of these interest rates may bring back debt servicing problems.

4.7 Conclusion

In this chapter we have examined the nature of wholesale and investment banking in general and its international dimension in particular. Attention has also been focused on two developments concerning the wholesale banking sector, namely off-balance-sheet business and the sovereign lending problem. As we have noted in this chapter, the former development has implications for the way banks are regulated and we consider this issue further in chapter 17. The latter, although no longer a threat to the banking system, can still provide lessons to students of banking, in particular the need for banks to properly assess risks before undertaking new types of business.

Note

1 The figure of 27 per cent is obtained from a breakdown of sterling advances which is not shown in table 4.2 but which is in the *Bank of England Statistical Abstract*, 1997.

Chapter 5

Building societies and finance houses

5.1 Introduction

In this chapter we examine two other deposit-taking institutions, namely building societies and finance houses. In view of their greater importance in the financial system and the recent significant changes affecting them, the major proportion of this chapter will be directed towards the building societies.

The building societies have traditionally been mutually owned, specialist financial institutions, borrowing from the personal sector and lending back to the personal sector in the form of a mortgage to finance house purchase. Up until the beginning of the 1980s the building societies enjoyed a virtual monopoly in the mortgage market. On the borrowing side, although experiencing some external competition for personal sector deposits from banks and National Savings, there was little internal competition between different building societies owing to a cartel arrangement on the setting of interest rates. Over the 1980s, however, building societies experienced a considerable degree of change as various liberalisation measures stimulated competition in the mortgage and personal savings markets. The Building Societies Act 1986 allowed for progressive deregulation of the products that building societies can offer on both sides of the balance sheet. The specialist institutions which began the decade are, as a consequence of these changes, more able to emulate banks as general providers of financial services. The 1986 Act also provided a procedure for a society to transfer from mutual to company (i.e. bank) status. The Abbey National was the first to follow this route, in 1989. A wave of conversions and bank takeovers of building societies then took place between 1995 and 2001, resulting in nine of the top ten building societies in 1995 losing their mutual status. A further Building Societies Act in 1997 aimed to stem this loss from the mutual sector by taking regulation of the remaining building societies in the direction of a more permissive regime and away from the prescriptive

framework of the 1986 Act. Prudential control of building societies is now the responsibility of Financial Services Authority (FSA) – see chapter 17.

In this chapter, after providing a brief history of building societies, we concentrate on an examination of the pressures for change and the actual changes that have taken place in building society activity over the 1980s and early 1990s. Finally, we provide a brief survey of finance houses.

5.2 History of the building society movement

The first building societies were founded in the late eighteenth century. They were set up by a group of around 20 to 30 people who contributed on a weekly basis to a fund which financed the purchase of land and the building of houses. These early societies were known as terminating societies, because when all the contributing members had been housed, the society terminated. The next stage came with the development of permanent societies, which increasingly borrowed from those who did not wish to buy a house and lent to those who both financed the construction of new homes and purchased existing homes. By 1912 approximately half the building societies were of this permanent type and no new terminating societies have been formed since 1953.

Another characteristic of a building society is that it is a mutual organisation. This means it is owned by its members, principally its depositors and borrowers. A key difference then between the mutual organisation and a public limited company (p.l.c.) is that for a mutual the customers are themselves the owners of the firm whereas for the p.l.c. there is a separation of the two.

Up until the early 1980s there was little change in the activities of building societies, which had a specialist role involving intermediation within the personal sector, borrowing in the form of deposits and lending in the form of a mortgage to finance house purchase. Since then the structure of the industry has significantly changed in two respects: first, the branch networks of the societies have expanded; and second, the concentration of building societies has increased. This is illustrated in table 5.1 but it should be remembered that the figures post-1989 also reflect the move of some building societies to p.l.c. status.

The 2,286 building societies in existence at the beginning of the twentieth century were in the main small in size and operated over a limited local area. The inter-war period saw the beginning of branching, as societies sought to expand their catchment area for personal savings. Expansion of the building societies' branch networks appears though to have come to an end over the last half of the 1980s. Concentration of the building society sector proceeded at a rapid pace after 1960, with the majority of mergers between societies taking the form of a smaller society transferring its

Table 5.1 Changes to the structure of the building society industry

Year	Number of societies	Number of branches
1900	2,286	n/a
1920	1,271	n/a
1940	952	640
1960	726	985
1980	273	5,684
1990	101	6,051
2000	67	2,361

Source: Building Societies Association and Housing Finance, 2001.

engagement to a larger society. These developments were accompanied by a large expansion of the business of building societies, as shown by the figures shown in table 5.2 for the level of personal sector deposits with the banking sector and total shares and deposits of building societies. As noted above, the figures after 1988 are not strictly comparable with the earlier statistics because of the transfer of a number of building societies to bank status.

Table 5.2 Stocks of personal sector savings held with banks and building societies, 1965–2000 (£billion)

Year	a: bank deposits	b: building society deposits	Ratio of a to b
1965	7.21	5.211	0.72
1970	10.036	10.194	1.02
1975	19.206	22.748	1.18
1980	36.598	50.002	1.37
1985	61.488	104.922	1.71
1990	156.600	158.200	1.01
1995	174.600	203.800	1.17
2000	390.100	119.000	0.31

Source: National Statistics (formerly CSO), *Financial Statistics*, various issues.

The figures in table 5.2 illustrate the success of building societies in the competition for personal sector deposits compared with banks. We consider this competition in more detail in the next section. What we are concerned with here is the controversy which has arisen as to whether the growth of building society deposits adversely affected the banks to any extent. The traditional argument followed the rationale that since building societies maintain their own deposits with the banking sector, the growth of building society deposits did not entail deposit losses for the banking sector, but

rather a change in ownership. A second argument put forward noted that the societies lent exclusively on mortgages whereas banks conducted little mortgage lending and hence there was little competition between these two classes of institution on the assets side of the balance sheet.

The first argument is of an extremely dubious nature. To the extent that building societies keep reserves in the form of public sector debt (see table 5.5 for further details), funds are lost to the banks in precisely the same manner as any other open market sale of government securities. The second argument is certainly no longer true. As we will discuss in the next section, banks have become extremely active lenders in the mortgage market since the early 1980s. Even more significant is the fact that the traditional argument ignores the effect of competition on the terms under which banks raise deposits. Increased competition for retail deposits must have raised to some extent the cost to banks of obtaining such deposits. These costs could arise, apart from the direct impact on interest rates, in a variety of ways, including reversion to Saturday opening, innovative time deposit schemes and a reduction of charges on the operation of current accounts. Building societies' entry into the wholesale money markets – discussed in the next section – has also increased the demand for wholesale funds, which must have again raised to some extent the cost of funds for banks in this market.

5.3 Competitive pressures on building societies

Building societies have experienced greater competition in both their funding and lending activities since the end of the 1970s. As noted above, the main competitors to building societies in the personal sector savings market have been banks in particular and, to a lesser extent, National Savings, although, in the mid-1980s in particular, building society deposits also came under competition from equity instruments following a number of privatisation issues, the growth of unit trusts and the growth in equity prices over much of this period. Figure 5.1 illustrates the competition for personal sector liquid assets over the period 1978–98. It shows the annual inflow into bank and building society deposits as well as into National Savings. The graphs represent the percentage of the total for each item. The strength of the competition can be judged by noting that the expansion/contraction of bank deposits is well matched by the opposite movement of building society deposits.

Over much of the 1970s the building societies faced little competition from other institutions for personal sector deposits. As we saw in chapter 3, the banks changed the balance of their funding from the retail market towards the wholesale market over the 1970s. Banks, however, did make an adjustment to this balance at the end of the 1970s and targeted personal savings for a few years. This was repeated in the late 1980s and mid-1990s,

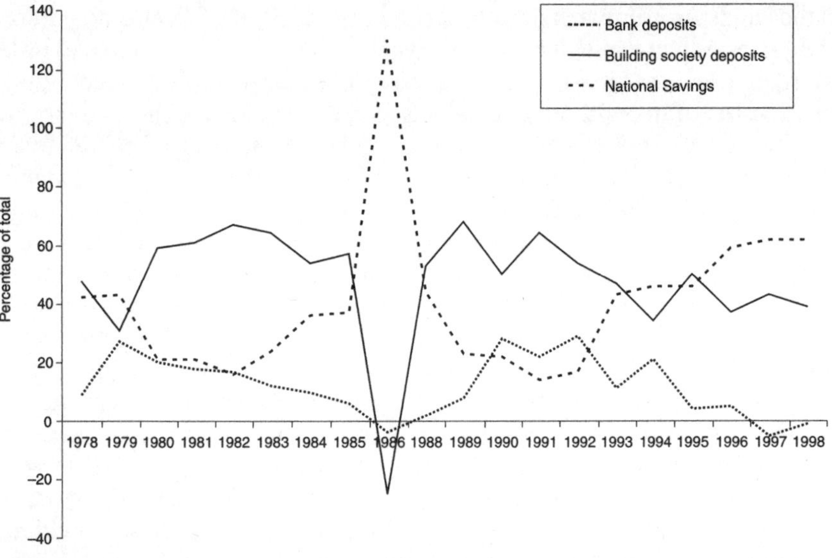

Figure 5.1 Competition for personal sector liquid assets, 1978–98. Source: National Statistics (formerly the CSO), *Financial Statistics*, various issues.

illustrating the ability of banks to move between the retail and wholesale markets for funding, according to relative availability and cost of funds. A further reason for banks targeting the personal savings market is that they view retail funding as a base for selling other retail financial services. In response to competitive pressures in the early 1980s, banks introduced high-interest deposit accounts similar to the building societies' short-notice and instant-access accounts. Later in the 1980s banks offered high-interest cheque accounts and more recently cheque accounts free of bank charges. As a consequence banks have regained some of the share of personal sector liquid asset holdings they had lost to building societies. Further competitive pressures on building societies' funding came from the government at times of high public borrowing in the early 1980s and 1990s, when greater emphasis was placed on funding the public sector borrowing requirement (PSBR) through National Savings.

Another major development in building society funding since the mid-1980s is the greater volume of funds raised from wholesale sources. A series of changes in the taxation position of building societies from 1983 allowed them to pay interest gross of tax on various wholesale instruments, thereby making the issue of such instruments more appealing to investors and hence making wholesale funding a more viable proposition for building societies. The Building Societies Act 1986 placed an upper limit on whole-

sale funding of 20 per cent, although this was raised to 40 per cent in 1988 and then 50 per cent in 1994 following representations from building societies. The percentage breakdown of retail and wholesale funding for building societies is shown in table 5.3. It is noticeable that since 1992 the percentage of wholesale funding has settled down to roughly 21 per cent of total external funding.

Table 5.3 Breakdown of building society funding, 1982–2000

Year	Retail funds	Wholesale funds
1982	100	0
1984	98	2
1986	96	4
1988	86	14
1990	81	19
1992	80	20
1994	79	21
1996	79	21
1998	79	21
2000	79	21

Source: National Statistics (formerly CSO), *Financial Statistics*, various issues.

A breakdown of the main wholesale instruments issued by building societies is provided in table 5.5 (see section 5.6). The largely floating-rate assets (mortgages) of societies means that they would prefer to hold floating-rate liabilities. Therefore the most attractive eurobond for societies (in cost terms as well) has been the floating-rate note (see chapter 12 for further discussion). These issues have largely been eurosterling floating-rate notes. Since March 1986, though, societies have been able to enter into interest rate swaps and so have started raising funds through the fixed-rate note market. The ability of societies to enter into currency swaps since the beginning of 1987 has added further flexibility, allowing societies to raise wholesale funds in a variety of currencies.

Access to the wholesale markets has allowed societies to practise liability management (see chapter 3). As with banks, which switched to liability management over the 1970s, societies have been able to reduce the level of liquid assets they hold – see section 5.6.

On the lending side, the building societies had a virtual monopoly on mortgage lending over the 1970s and accounted for some 82 per cent of the outstanding stock of mortgages at the end of 1979. Over the 1970s banks, although involved to a limited extent in mortgage lending, were restricted by direct controls on their lending which impinged on their lending

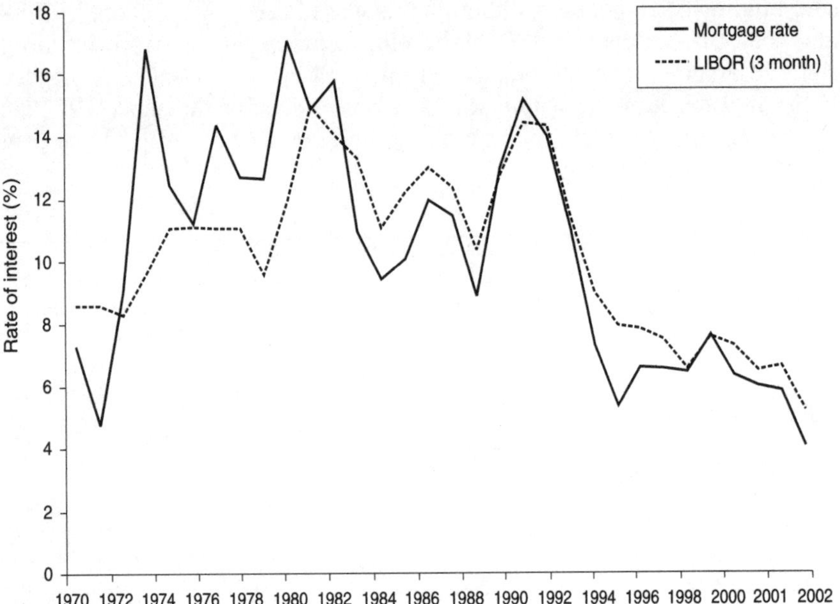

Figure 5.2 Average mortgage interest rates compared with the three-month London inter-bank offer rate (LIBOR), 1970–2002. Source: Building Societies Association, and National Statistics (formerly CSO), *Financial Statistics*, various issues.

to the personal sector. Building societies, as mutual organisations, were not profit maximisers but instead attempted to reconcile the conflicting demands of borrowers for low interest rates and savers for high interest rates by maintaining a relatively stable path for interest rates over time. This was made possible by the cartel arrangement which existed whereby the Building Societies Association (BSA) recommended rates of interest to be charged to borrowers and savers. Such an institutional structure minimised the role played by interest rates in equilibrating supply and demand for mortgages. The stickiness of rates offered by building societies on shares and deposits meant that at times the rates were uncompetitive, thus reducing inflows (see figure 5.2, which show periods when the average mortgage rate was significantly above or below the London inter-bank offer rate). The shortage of funds for lending that sometimes occurred as a result could be made up by the societies running down liquid asset stocks. However, this provided only a temporary solution and, given that societies would not raise interest rates to reduce the demand for mortgages, other means of rationing were pursued. These included queues and changes in lending

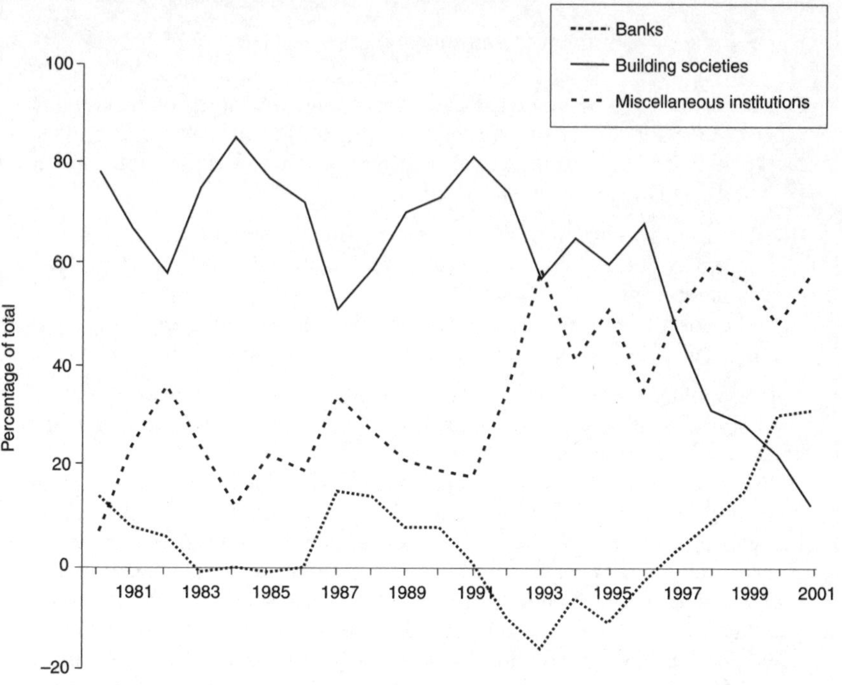

Figure 5.3 Share of net new mortgage lending, 1980–2001. A negative value indicates that repayments exceeded lending. Source: Building Societies Association.

arrangements. The latter generally took the form of lowering either the ratio of loan to borrower's income or the ratio of loan to the value of the associated property. Another criticism of the cartel arrangement was that the rates of interest set were designed to protect the smaller, less efficient societies. This had the effect of allowing the larger societies to operate on margins which would not occur in a competitive environment and therefore provided no incentive for them to cut costs, so that the industry as a whole operated at a higher cost. However, a defence of the cartel that was often made was that because the mortgage rate was frequently kept below market rates, the cartel kept the cost of borrowing low (although at the expense of savers).

The market structure just described began to break down shortly after the start of the 1980s. In mid-1980 direct controls on bank lending (known as the corset) were lifted and the banks immediately strove to develop new areas of business. In particular they entered the mortgage market (see figure 5.3) and by 1982 they had achieved a market share of new mortgage lending

Box 5.1 Contestability of the mortgage market

One consequence of the increase in competition in the mortgage market and process innovation (i.e. new ways of delivering products) is that the mortgage market now largely conforms to a contestable market. A contestable market (Baumol 1982) requires two conditions:

(i) The costs of entry into the market are low. In particular, a prospective entrant should be able to compete on the same (or lower) cost base than an incumbent.
(ii) The costs of exit from the market are low. This requires any fixed costs incurred to be recoverable or to be used to deliver other products/services.

If a market is contestable then new firms will enter it when there are supernormal profits and leave when these supernormal profits disappear. This strategy is sometimes referred to as 'hit and run'.

In the mortgage market, entry costs are now low because of the development of technology and the emergence of 'telephone banking'. Credit scoring has reduced the time it takes to assess risks and process a mortgage application. New entrants based on telephone delivery (with no branch networks to support) will be able to operate on fixed costs that are lower than those of incumbents. Exit costs are low because the fixed costs of establishing a telephone-based operation are low and because such an operation can be switched into delivering other financial products, such as car or home insurance. The banks have also been able to move into and out of the mortgage market at different times as their fixed costs (mainly branch networks) are used to deliver a wide range of financial products/services.

of 36 per cent. After this initial expansion bank mortgage lending slowed down, though picked up in the 1990s, when it reached peaks of 59 per cent in 1993 despite a depressed mortgage market and of 60 per cent in 1999 in association with an increased demand for mortgages. This illustrates that banks can enter and leave the mortgage market freely as factors such as demand and relative profitability change (box 5.1).

5.4 Consequences of the competitive pressures

Greater competition in the mortgage market and retail deposit markets had a number of consequences. First of all it made societies more sensitive to interest rate changes, which in turn led to the breakdown in the cartel arrangement between societies, precipitated by the decision of Abbey National to leave it in September 1983. The BSA recommendation of rates came to an end in October 1983, although it continued to advise rates until

November 1984. The greater competition in the mortgage market and the breakdown of the cartel led to both a greater availability of mortgage funds and price clearing in the market, and therefore to an end to non-price rationing. Mortgage rates now move more in line with money-market interest rates (see figure 5.2). When mortgage rates could be below money market rates, as was often the case when the BSA recommended rates, institutions which relied heavily on money market borrowing could not compete with the building societies. However, the removal of this restriction induced entry into the market by specialist mortgage lenders, which are funded completely from wholesale sources (the miscellaneous institutions in figure 5.3). These include mortgage lenders which are neither banks nor building societies, such as Britannic Mortgage p.l.c and UCB Home Loans. A rapid expansion in mortgage lending therefore occurred over the 1980s and this is reflected in the growth of home ownership, as illustrated in table 5.4. Although expansion also occurred in home ownership in the 1990s, the rate of expansion was considerably slower than in the earlier period.

Table 5.4 The stock of dwellings in the UK: distribution by tenure (as a percentage of total), 1960–2000

	1960	1970	1980	1990	2000
Owner-occupied	42.0	50.0	56.1	65.8	68.8
Rented from local authority or new town corporation	26.6	30.4	31.1	21.9	21.4
Rented from private owners	31.4	19.6	12.7	12.3	9.9

Source: Building Societies Association.

Whilst the main explanation of the growth in home ownership, particularly over the 1980s, is likely to be the greater availability of mortgage funding, other factors include the policy of tax relief on mortgage interest payments (which was ended in April 2000), the sale of council houses and the decline of the private rented housing stock.

The buoyancy in the mortgage market has also led to lending institutions, particularly building societies, extending the type of lending. Traditionally, mortgages have been predominantly in the form of first advances for the purchase of a house. In the latter part of the 1980s, second mortgages and further advances not necessarily directly connected with home improvements have been available. It is now relatively easy for owner-occupiers to withdraw cash from the equity built up in their property, without moving house, simply by increasing the debt on the property. Equity withdrawal is defined as the difference between the net increase in the stock of loans for house purchase and the private sector's net expenditure on additions to the

stock of owner-occupied housing, including improvements. There was a leakage of funds from housing into consumption, through equity withdrawal, over the 1980s, which contributed to the consumption boom in the latter half of that decade. The fall in house prices in the early to mid-1990s with the consequent fall in equity built up in houses led to equity withdrawal becoming negative over much of the 1990s. The more recent rise in house prices and low interest rates has once again caused a surge in mortgage equity withdrawal, which has helped to finance the recent consumption boom (Davey 2001).

The greater competition faced by building societies led the government to recognise that new legislation was required to enable them to compete with other financial institutions on a more equal basis. In 1981 the BSA established the Nature of a Building Society Working Group, under the chairmanship of John Spalding, who was the chief general manager of the Halifax Building Society. This led to a report in 1983 entitled *The Future Constitution and Powers of Building Societies.* The two key proposals of this report were:

(i) that the mutual status of building societies should continue but that a procedure should be established whereby a society could convert to p.l.c. status;
(ii) that societies should be permitted to undertake a wider range of business, but which should be related to the mainstream business.

After a period of consultation the BSA published its final proposals in February 1984, in a report entitled *New Legislation for Building Societies.* In July 1984, the government published its proposals in a green paper, *Building Societies: A New Framework.* This largely followed the proposals put forward by the BSA. This finally led to the publication of the Building Societies Bill, which received royal assent in 1986, with most of its provisions taking effect from 1 January 1987.

Under the Building Societies Act and subsequent revisions, societies are permitted to offer additional services, which fall into the categories of retail financial or land related. Examples of additional services under the former category are listed in box 5.2.

Under the category of land-related services are services relating to the acquisition, development, management or disposal of land primarily for residential purposes, in particular the provision of estate agency services, conveyancing and estates management.

A further provision of the Act allows a society to convert from mutual status to p.l.c. status. A society following this route ceases to be a building society and effectively becomes a bank. Therefore as part of the conversion procedure the society would have to obtain approval from the Bank of England. A building society that converts is afforded protection from

Box 5.2 Categories of additional retail financial services permitted under the 1986 Building Societies Act

(i) Banking services –
- money transmission (including providing chequebook accounts)
- credit cards
- unsecured lending (up to a maximum – see text)
- foreign currency services

(ii) Investment services –
- manage investments
- establish personal equity plans
- operate a stockbroking service
- provide investment advice

(iii) Insurance services –
- underwrite insurance
- provide insurance

Note that the Building Societies Act 1997 further relaxed the restrictions on building societies.

takeover for five years (though the 1997 Act added a caveat in this respect). The Act also allows societies to operate in the other member states of the European Union (EU). The Act introduced a new supervisory body for building societies, namely the Building Societies Commission, but in 1998 the role of supervising building societies passed to the new super-regulator, the FSA (see chapter 17).

5.5 After the 1986 Act

The services which societies most actively took up were in the category of banking services. In general, though, it is only the larger societies which had the capital and the size of operations to enter into competition with banks. The Nationwide Anglia was the first society to offer, in the spring of 1987, an interest-bearing current account with chequing facilities, called the FlexAccount. The other large building societies now also offer similar current account services. Most of the larger societies have also introduced a credit card, although the credit card market has been saturated since the end of the 1980s. A further development in 1990 was the expansion into banking services by the National and Provincial Building Society through the acquisition of Girobank. Most societies offer an automated teller machine (ATM) service through the Link network. In 1997 the Link network

comprised approximately 14,000 machines, compared with approximately 16,000 operated by the banks (though some of the smaller banks' machines were also part of the Link network); all the major banks have since become part of the LINK network, which in 2003 had over 47,000 ATMs connected, making it the largest ATM network in the world.

A second, and less successful, area of expansion by the larger building societies was into estate agency operations. These societies saw estate agencies as an additional channel for the distribution of their mortgages. However, this expansion occurred in the final stages of a housing boom, so that when the market went into depression in the early 1990s an excess capacity in estate agency operations was revealed and most agency chains made substantial losses. This prompted a number of societies to sell their estate agency businesses, generally at a significant loss.

The smaller societies, not having sufficient capital to diversify into banking services, have in the main concentrated on their traditional business of savings and mortgages. Merger activity continues as some societies have attempted to achieve a size which allows them to take advantage of more of the diversification possibilities provided by the Act. Some smaller societies have diversified into specialist services allowed under the Act that do not require such a large amount of capital. For example, some have set up a subsidiary to handle mortgage administration for other new lenders, such as foreign banks.

For one building society, the Abbey National, the Building Societies Act 1986 was perceived as not going far enough in removing restrictions. In July 1989 it became the first building society to take advantage of the relevant provision in the Act and convert to p.l.c. status. There are two main advantages to converting to p.l.c. status. First, it provides an escape from restrictions imposed on building societies. For example, building societies are not permitted to undertake corporate banking and there are limits on the extent of unsecured lending they can carry out (see below). International operations for building societies are still limited to the UK and other EU countries. Second, it is argued that societies need to convert in order to obtain additional capital, which they may use to diversify more quickly. The act of conversion itself leads to an injection of capital from the new shareholders and, by increasing the primary capital of the company, enables other forms of capital to be increased commensurately.

After the incorporation of Abbey National there was a gap of five years before the next major development, which was the transfer of business of the Cheltenham and Gloucester Building Society to Lloyds Bank (effectively a bank takeover of a building society). This was followed by a wave of conversions and takeovers, resulting in most of the top ten building societies at the start of 1995 losing their mutual status. Building societies that converted between 1995 and 2001 are the Halifax (after a merger with the Leeds),

Alliance and Leicester, Northern Rock, Woolwich, and Bradford and Bingley. Building societies that have been acquired by banks are the Bristol and West (1997) and Birmingham Midshires (in 1999). In 1997 the Nationwide Building Society, the largest one remaining, came under pressure at its annual general meeting to introduce a proposal for members to vote on conversion. This was defeated but pressure remains on the remaining larger building societies to convert to p.l.c. status. These pressures are accentuated by:

(i) The fact that, upon conversion, members obtain a share of the capital of the building society. Taking the Halifax conversion as an example, capital was paid out in the form of shares, with some basic payout to all members plus a variable payout to depositors relating to the size of the deposit. The capital of the society will have been built up over a long period of time, so the current generation of owners is effectively receiving a subsidy from all previous generations of owners.
(ii) The easy manner in which a person can become a member of a building society. To qualify as a depositing member in order to receive a share of the capital of the Halifax, the minimum deposit required was £100.

The wave of conversions has prompted a debate on whether the mutual organisation is no longer appropriate to the more competitive retail financial services sector. The arguments for and against the mutual organisation are presented in box 5.3.

The government in 1994 addressed some of the concerns of building societies about the restrictive nature of their regulatory framework by:

(i) increasing the limit on wholesale funding from 40 per cent to 50 per cent;
(ii) allowing societies to establish subsidiaries to make unsecured loans to businesses;
(iii) giving societies the right to wholly own general insurance companies which offer housing-related products such as building and contents insurance.

Further reform has come with the Building Societies Act 1997. This changed the regulatory regime for building societies away from the prescriptive framework introduced by the 1986 Act, where everything is prevented unless powers are granted to allow an activity, to a permissive regime where everything is allowed unless specifically prohibited. This should make it easier for a building society to diversify more easily within the retail financial sector. A second major change introduced by the 1997 Act is that it removes the five-year protection from takeover for building societies that have converted to p.l.c. status if they launch a hostile bid for

Box 5.3 Advantages and disadvantages of the mutual organisation

Mutual organisations, like building societies, have a fundamental advantage over p.l.c.s, which is the absence of external capital that needs to be serviced; thus a society does not have to pay dividends to equity shareholders. This may result in a lower cost base for building societies, so enabling them to follow one of two strategies: maintain a wider interest margin than is necessary and build up reserves through high profits; maintain a low (but sustainable) interest margin and increase market share. During the 1980s building societies chose to adopt the first strategy, probably to obtain advantages that come with large reserves such as security and a better credit rating. As reserves were built up, the implicit value to owners also built up, yet owners were unable to release this value. In the absence of a secondary market in mutual ownership stakes, the only feasible way a member of a building society is able to release such value is to vote for conversion.

A building society could adopt the second strategy and provide benefits to members through a higher interest rate to depositors and a lower interest rate paid by borrowers (compared with p.l.c. retail financial firms). Some building societies that have chosen to remain mutual have explicitly adopted such a strategy. In order to convince members of the benefits of mutuality a building society needs to demonstrate its margin advantage and, in addition, find ways, other than conversion to p.l.c. status, to release some of the accumulated reserves to members (one possibility is for a society to operate on a margin that generates a loss for a period of time).

However, there are a number of weaknesses with the mutual organisation:

(i) There are potential agency costs deriving from weak member control. Agency costs arise in any form of organisation where there is a separation of decision making and ownership. Potential conflicts of interest arise between managers and owners because of incomplete contracts. It is impossible to devise contracts for managers that specify courses of action for all future circumstances. Managers must inevitably have discretion, which, of course, may be abused. It is argued that these agency costs are more severe for a mutual than for a p.l.c., because owners have less influence on managers. This is a result of:
- a very diverse shareholding, that is, a large number of small shareholders;
- an absence of large shareholders who have an incentive to monitor and control;
- the absence of performance-related shareholdings for managers.

(ii) The absence of tradable ownership rights means that managers are not subject to capital market discipline through the effect of dissatisfied owners selling shares and so forcing down the share price. In addition, there is no takeover threat.

Although there are clear agency costs for the mutual, in practice there is no evidence that they have adversely affected the efficiency and performance of building societies. In fact, it can be claimed that the existence of building societies provides a spur to competition in financial markets, which in turn results in greater efficiency within the financial system as a whole.

any other company. This provision is designed to protect the remaining smaller mutual building societies from takeover. The third significant change was to make the societies more accountable to their members:

(i) borrowers were given the right to vote on general issues affecting the society;
(ii) polls were required for the election of directors;
(iii) significant diversification by a society requires approval by the membership. However, the problems regarding diverse membership noted in box 5.3 still apply.

5.6 The balance sheet of building societies

We now turn to examine some of the effects of the changes previously described, as revealed by the aggregate balance sheet position of building societies at the end of 2001 (table 5.5).

Table 5.5 Building societies' balance sheet at end 2001

Liabilities	£million	Assets	£million
Retail shares and deposits	126,061	Cash	461
Wholesale funds		Sterling and foreign currency bank deposits	14,105
Certificates of deposit	5,328		
Term deposits and commercial paper	18,955	Building society certificates of deposit	1,733
Bank borrowing	1,250	UK government stocks	850
Bonds	7,847	Other public sector debt	141
		Other liquid assets	20,726
Total wholesale funds	33,380	Total liquid assets	38,016
Other liabilities and reserves	14,245	Commercial assets:	
		Class 1	109,433
		Class 2	11,528
		Class 3	12,503
		Other assets	2,206
Total liabilities	173,686	Total assets	173,686

Note that:
(i) Liquid assets represent 22 per cent of total assets.
(ii) Foreign currency liquid assets represent 22 per cent (£7,004 million) of total liquid assets.
(iii) Class 1 commercial assets represent 82 per cent of total commercial assets.
(iv) Class 2 commercial assets represent 9 per cent of total commercial assets.
(v) Class 3 commercial assets represent 9 per cent of total commercial assets.

Source: National Statistics, *Financial Statistics*, 2002.

The balance between wholesale and retail funding for building societies has been discussed in section 5.3. The other part of liabilities is made up of the societies' capital, which is mainly reserves. As building societies are mutual organisations, owned by their depositors and borrowers, they do not make profits on their operations in the sense of an amount available for distribution to shareholders. Any surplus that is made on their operations is added to reserves. Specific capital adequacy requirements for building societies were introduced by the Building Societies Commission. These requirements set down a separate capital ratio for each category of asset as well as for off-balance-sheet items (see chapter 4 for further discussion). The capital ratios for each category held by a society are then aggregated and the desired capital ratio is this aggregate plus a margin of at least 0.5 per cent.

On the assets side of the balance sheet the first six items make up the societies' liquid assets. Up until the 1986 Building Societies Act, societies were required to operate with a minimum of 7 per cent of their assets in liquid form. The Act abolished this minimum requirement and instead stated that societies should keep sufficient assets in a form which enables them to meet liabilities as they fall due. However, a maximum level of liquid assets was set by the Act at $33^1/_3$ per cent. With the ability to raise up to 50 per cent of deposits from wholesale sources, building societies are now more able to practise liability management – see chapter 3 for a discussion of this concept – and as a consequence there is less need to hold a large cushion of liquid assets. In 2001 building societies' liquid assets amounted to approximately 22 per cent of total assets. The composition of building societies' liquid assets portfolio has changed since the 1980s; in particular, there has been a decline in holdings of government securities and an increase in holdings of short-term deposits and certificates of deposit.

Building societies' commercial assets are divided into three classes by the 1986 Act. Broadly speaking, class 1 assets are first mortgage loans to owner-occupiers of residential property, class 2 are other loans secured on property and class 3 are unsecured loans, investment in residential property and investments in subsidiaries and associates. Initially the limits for these three classes of commercial assets were set so that not less than 90 per cent of assets had to be in class 1 and not more than 5 per cent in class 3. In addition, smaller societies were prohibited from owning certain class 3 assets. Following representations from societies these limits were reviewed and are now set at a 25 per cent maximum for class 2 and class 3 assets combined, with a maximum of 15 per cent in class 3.

The introduction of class 3 unsecured lending allowed societies to offer credit cards and cheque accounts with overdraft facilities. At the end of 2001 building societies in aggregate were well below the prescribed limits, with class 2 lending at about 9 per cent and class 3 lending also at around 9 per cent.

5.7 The finance houses

Finance houses (or non-bank credit companies) comprise a rather heterogeneous group of financial institutions which include subsidiaries of UK banks and overseas financial institutions and several independent institutions. Their activities are specialised and they account for a very small proportion of total lending by financial institutions. At the end of 2001 they had total assets of £35.4 billion, compared with £173.7 billion for building societies. The combined balance sheet for finance houses at the end of 2001 is shown in table 5.6.

Table 5.6 Non-bank credit companies' balance sheet at end 2001

Liabilities	£million	Assets	£million
Commercial bills	1,002	Cash and balances with	
Bank loans	9,208	banks	1,399
Loans from other financial		Certificates of deposit	7
institutions	2,463	Other current assets	291
Other UK loans	233	Finance leases	1,205
Overseas loans	21	Loans and advances to:	
Other current liabilities	764	UK companies	3,990
Capital	21,700	persons	28,465
		Other financial assets	3
		Physical assets	31
Total liabilities	35,391	Total assets	35,391

Source: National Statistics, *Financial Statistics*, 2002.

Table 5.6 reveals the nature of the business of these institutions. The majority of their funding is by way of loans from banks and other financial institutions. On the asset side, their main business is the provision of instalment credit, with the majority of this going to the personal sector. Finance companies also provide a significant amount of finance to companies in terms of instalment loans as well as through leasing and factoring. Leasing involves the finance company (the lessor) purchasing a physical asset which is subsequently leased out to a firm (the lessee) in return for a series of rental payments over a term which usually approximates its economic life. As the lessee is in the same position as if the asset had been purchased outright then finance leases are equivalent to raising a loan. Factoring involves a finance company taking over all or some of the debts owed to a company. The purchase price represents less than the book value of the debts and the gap represents the potential profit, with a risk element, for the finance company. As far as the company whose debts have been taken over is concerned, the gap is equivalent to the interest on a similar loan,

with the benefit being an immediate acquisition of funds as compared with the delay before debts are normally paid.

This brief survey illustrates the nature of finance houses acting as financial intermediaries by obtaining funds mainly from banks, and therefore ultimately individuals and companies, and lending to individuals and companies. These institutions undertake a transformation of the characteristics of the funds as they pass through the institution. The transformation of risk is evident from the risky nature of their main lending activity, that is, consumer credit, as compared with the perceived nature of their liabilities. This transformation is of course reflected in the relatively high interest charges on their instalment loans.

5.8 **Conclusion**

In this chapter we have concentrated our attention on the significant changes that have taken place in building society activity since 1980. These changes were brought about largely by deregulation of the banking sector in 1980, which led to greater competition between banks and building societies on both sides of the balance sheet. This led to the breakdown in the building society cartel on interest rate setting and a virtual end to non-price rationing in the mortgage market. In fact the mortgage market now largely conforms to the proposition of a contestable market. The 1986 Building Societies Act enabled building societies to diversify their activities and so compete more effectively in the new environment. However, they were still largely confined to the provision of retail services and housing finance in particular. Further reforms of building society regulations in the 1990s have allowed societies even more scope for diversification. However, a number of large societies chose to escape the restrictions still imposed on building societies and convert to bank status. Others were the subject of a bank takeover. As some life assurance companies have sought to convert from mutual to p.l.c. status and several of the larger remaining building societies are under pressure to convert by some members, it would appear that the future of the mutual organisation in the UK financial services sector is under threat. We show in this chapter that the mutual organisation does have an advantage over the p.l.c. and if used appropriately this may serve to ensure its survival.

As restrictions on societies have been relaxed the demarcation between banks and the larger building societies has become blurred and the distinctive nature of building societies has, to some extent, been lost. Whether a role remains in the medium term for a distinct specialist institution providing housing finance is therefore an open question. A related issue commented upon in this chapter is that building societies are facing a significant degree of competition in their traditional business of mortgage lending. Furthermore, there has been some doubt expressed as to whether the rate of home

ownership, illustrated in table 5.4, will continue to grow as rapidly as it has done over the past two decades, with the consequence that the demand for mortgages may not grow as rapidly. The long-run outlook for home ownership and hence mortgage demand may not, however, be as gloomy as some have predicted. Support for this view is provided by the figures shown in table 5.7, which indicate that the proportion of home ownership was, in 2000, lower in the UK than in a number of other industrialised countries. This suggests that owner-occupation may not have reached saturation point.

Table 5.7 Owner occupation, 2000 (percentage of households)

Country	Percentage of all households
Germany	42
Denmark	51
Netherlands	52
France	56
Austria	57
Finland	58
Sweden	60
Portugal	64
US	67
Italy	68
UK	69
Luxembourg	70
Belgium	74
Norway	77
Greece	78
Ireland	78
Spain	81

Chapter 6

Investment institutions

6.1 Introduction

The investment institutions are a class of financial intermediary which enable small investors to participate in collective investment funds. These institutions pool together a large number of small-value contributions into a fund which is used to finance the acquisition of a diversified portfolio of assets. The small investor thus obtains the benefit of the lower risks that come from a large, diversified portfolio at a lower outlay than would be required if investing directly. Such indirect investment in capital market instruments has long since replaced direct investment by all but relatively few individuals, so that investment institutions now dominate the capital markets. This is illustrated in table 6.1, which shows the sectoral holdings of UK gilts and equities for 1996 and 2001, whence it can be seen that in 2001 pension funds and insurance companies held roughly 69 per cent of gilts and 36 per cent of equities. This type of financial institution contrasts with deposit-taking institutions such as banks and building societies principally in the nature of its liabilities. Investment institutions, unlike deposit-taking institutions, have long-term liabilities and this is reflected in the nature of their asset portfolios. In the next section we examine the different types of investment institution and their growth in recent years. The remainder of this chapter is concerned with the nature of the activities of the different types of investment institution.

6.2 Types of investment institution

There are four main types of investment institution:

(i) pension funds;
(ii) life assurance companies;
(iii) investment trusts;
(iv) unit trusts and open-ended investment companies (OEICs).

Table 6.1 Investment institutions' holdings of UK equities and gilts, 1996 and 2001: percentage of total holdings at market value

	Equities		Gilts	
	1996	2001	1996	2001
Persons	19.4	14.8	4.2	7.4
Pension funds and insurance companies	54.5	36.1	54.3	68.8
Other financial companies	7.3	15.2	21.7	3.9
Overseas investors	16.6	31.9	18.5	15.8
Other	2.2	2.0	1.3	4.1

Source: *Financial Statistics*, Office for National Statistics online database and *Bank of England Statistical Abstract.*

We do not include the category of general insurance companies in the class of investment institutions for reasons which we outline in the next section.

At the end of 2000 the combined assets of these four types of institution were £2,019.3 billion. This compares with total assets for building societies of £159 billion and £1,405 billion for banks owned by UK companies. Investment institutions have shown rapid growth over the last 20 years and this is illustrated in table 6.2.

Of the investment institutions, unit trusts have shown the most rapid growth over the period covered by table 6.2, albeit from a low base. The two largest investment institutions, namely pension funds and life assurance companies, have achieved roughly similar rates of growth over this period. One explanation for the growth of investment institutions relative to deposit-taking institutions is provided by the functional approach to financial intermediation (see chapter 2). Allen and Santomero (1998) argue that to understand developments in financial intermediation we should focus on the functions provided by intermediaries rather than on the institutions. It has been argued (see Davis 2001) that the reason for the faster growth of investment institutions (Davis concentrates on pension funds but the arguments are generally applicable to other types of investment institution) compared with that of banks is that, in some functional areas, investment institutions are more efficient than banks at direct financing. Some of these areas are:

(i) *Pooling and diversification*. Investment institutions are able to undertake large transactions at lower cost than individual investors, which means they can deliver a diversified portfolio more cheaply than direct investors, thus reducing risk.
(ii) *Overcoming incentive problems*. Investment institutions have a comparative advantage over individual investors in dealing with issues of corporate governance, given their size and hence voting weight at annual general meetings. The incentive problems referred to are the

Table 6.2 Assets of investment institutions for selected years (£billion)

	1982	1984	1986	1988	1990	1992	1994	1996	1998	2000	% growth 1982–2000
Pension funds	83.6	130.3	190.5	214.5	302.7	382.0	443.5	543.9	699.2	765.2	815.3
Life assurance companies	79.9	114.2	158.6	198.3	232.3	327.6	403.7	549.7	778.0	932.7	1,067.3
Investment trusts	10.1	15.3	20.7	19.3	19.1	28.7	39.6	50.0	47.0	60.5	499.0
Unit trusts/OEICs	7.8	15.1	32.1	41.6	46.3	63.9	91.8	131.9	182.8	260.9	3,244.9

Source: *Financial Statistics*, Office for National Statistics online database.

principal agent problems that arise in modern corporations given the separation of ownership and control. This applies to equity finance. Although banks specialise in debt finance, pension funds now hold a wide range of debt, as a result of the development of credit rating agencies, junk bonds and the expanding range of securitised debt.

So investment institutions tend to complement capital markets and so act as substitutes for banks. That said, there are limits to the involvement of investment institutions, especially in relation to debt finance, where (as we saw in chapter 2) private information is important. This leaves a continuing role for banks. In addition, it should be noted that there are demand-side and regulatory factors which have driven the growth in investment institutions and these are examined below. First of all we discuss the nature of general insurance and in particular the reasons why we do not consider it to be an investment intermediary.

6.3 General insurance

The 1982 Insurance Companies Act separated the business of insurance companies into two categories: general insurance and long-term business. The latter category essentially comprises life assurance, and this is considered in the next section. The former category encompasses a wide variety of business, all of which is concerned with providing insurance against specific contingencies, for example fire, accident and theft. Such insurance is provided over a fixed period of time, usually one year. The general insurance companies hold funds, or reserves, to enable them to meet claims on the insurance policies they have issued. As most of these policies are effective for one year and claims are usually made very soon after the event giving rise to the claim, general insurance companies' liabilities are mostly short term. Even where claims take a number of years to settle, a reserve is maintained to cover possible payments. The short-term nature of their liabilities is partly reflected in the assets making up the funds of general insurance companies – see table 6.3.

The majority of the long-term assets of general insurance companies are marketable and so can be called on at short notice, but they also provide a return to compensate for any underwriting loss – a common situation in the competitive general insurance industry, where premium income is less than claims and the shortfall has to be found out of earnings on investments. However, we are concerned in this chapter (and this book) with financial intermediaries, which, as we described in chapter 2, channel funds from savers through to investors. The premium income which flows into general insurance companies is essentially a payment for a consumption service (indemnity against loss) and therefore cannot really be classified as savings.

Table 6.3 Assets of general insurance companies at end 2001

Asset	£million
Short-term assets (net)	–802
UK government securities	15,064
Local authority securities	6
UK ordinary shares	10,140
Other UK company securities	5,575
Overseas securities	13,546
Unit trusts	1,186
Loans and mortgages	785
Property	860
Other	35,440
Total	81,800

Source: *Financial Statistics*, Office for National Statistics online database.

Also, whilst general insurance companies hold financial assets, these are more a byproduct than a central feature of their business. We therefore conclude that general insurance companies are not strictly financial intermediaries and we do not consider them further.

6.4 The nature of the liabilities of pension funds and life assurance companies

6.4.1 *Life assurance companies*

The long-term, or life assurance, business of insurance companies can be separated into four broad categories.

(i) term assurance;
(ii) whole-of-life policies and endowment policies;
(iii) annuities;
(iv) personal pensions.

Term assurance

A term assurance policy provides insurance cover, for a specified period, against the risk of death. If the insured survives the specified period then no payment is made. These term policies, which can be characterised as pure insurance policies, do not provide large sums for investment.

Whole-of-life policies and endowment policies

With a whole-of-life type of policy the insurance company pays a capital sum on the death of the person assured, whenever that event occurs. With

an endowment policy a capital sum is paid out at the end of some specified term or earlier if the assured dies within the term. Both types of policy provide cover against premature death and provide a vehicle for savings. The premiums for both will be higher than for term assurance because the company is committed to paying out a capital sum at some point in time. As a consequence the life insurance company has to accumulate a substantial fund out of which payments can be made as they fall due. Both types of policy may be 'without profits', in which case the money value of the benefit is fixed in advance, or 'with profits', where a minimum sum assured may be augmented by bonuses declared by the company. These bonuses will be related to the performance of the fund over the life of the policy and so the with-profits policies have the effect of transferring some of the risk of building up sufficient benefits to the policyholder when compared with without-profits policies. In some cases a policy may be 'unit linked', where the premiums paid are used to purchase units in a chosen unit trust and the final payment is then dependent on the performance of that trust.

The role of endowment policies has been recently subject to criticism on two counts. First, there is the level of commission paid to the insurance sales person at the time of initial sale of the policy. These initial costs incurred by the insurance company have caused such policies to have a low 'surrender' value, that is, the price the insurance company will pay the policyholder on cancellation of the policy in respect of payments already made on it. This problem is mainly in respect of the early years of a policy, when such commission charges are large relative to payments on the policy. Companies are required to be more open now and commission payments have to be disclosed to the potential policy purchaser.

The second criticism concerns the use of endowment policies with respect to house purchase, whereby the capital sum is paid directly to the mortgage company on maturity of the policy. As indicated earlier in this section, such policies can be with or without profits. Originally the policy value was fixed so as to be equal to the mortgage debt on maturity, so that any profits connected with the policy provided a windfall gain to the policyholder. However, the practice arose of assuming profit levels and taking out a policy that matched the mortgage debt only if the assumed profits were actually achieved. Consequently if the profits attached to the policy were less than the assumed level when the mortgage expired, the policyholder was left with a shortfall that had to be met from her or his own pocket. This problem was compounded by the decision of the Financial Services Authority (the financial services regulator – see chapter 17), in July 1999, to impose new (lower) projected return assumptions for endowments. These lower projected return assumptions reflect the lower expected returns on equities as a result of lower inflation and interest rates. Insurance companies were obliged to inform endowment policyholders of potential

Box 6.1 The case of Equitable Life

The Equitable Life Assurance Society (ELAS) was a mutual insurance company formed in 1762. Between 1957 and 1988 ELAS sold with-profits pension annuities with guaranteed annuity rates (GARs) fixed by reference to assumptions about interest rates and life expectancy. The GARs were fixed at a rate well below annuity rates available at the time. After 1988 only non-GAR policies were sold. In June 2001, 25 per cent of the with-profit policies had GARs and 75 per cent did not. In late 1993 open market current annuity rates (CARs) fell below the GAR annuity rates promised by ELAS. The CARs have remained below the GARs for most of the time since. In addition, life expectancy rates increased above those assumed when the GARs were set. Both factors raised the cost to ELAS of providing GAR pensions. Other life offices at the time chose to reinsure these risks, or bought out GAR rights or capped them. ELAS chose to recognise these risks by awarding a lower final bonus to GAR policyholders than to non-GAR policyholders. ELAS believed it had discretion to do this through its Memorandum and Articles of Association. Some policyholders complained that the differential bonus policy made the GAR policies valueless and a House of Lords ruling on 20 July 2000 accepted this argument and obliged ELAS to honour its guaranteed returns. The total cost to ELAS was estimated to be £1.5 billion and this had to be taken from the with-profits fund. As 75 per cent of the with-profits fund was represented by non-GAR policyholders the ruling implied a transfer of claims from non-GAR to GAR policyholders equal to 75 per cent of £1.5 billion (or £1.1 billion). In effect the non-GAR policyholders became the unwitting providers of insurance to the GAR policyholders. One of the problems with the way ELAS conducted business was that it offered a not-with-profits product (the GAR) from within a with-profits fund. The two should have been separated from the start, as they entailed different risks and should therefore have had different investment policies, with the GAR fund invested mainly in bonds. During the autumn of 2000, the management board offered to sell ELAS as a going concern but could not find a

Box continues opposite

shortfalls in meeting mortgage debt as a result of the reduction in projected rates of return. Most endowments were projected to return less than the mortgage debt, based on the assumption of the most likely projected annual growth rate, of 6 per cent. Endowment holders were advised to make other arrangements to meet the shortfall and were given the option of complaining and seeking compensation if they felt the policy had been mis-sold.

Box 6.1 Continued

buyer willing to inject the necessary capital. In December 2000, ELAS was closed to new business and the board offered their resignations.

In February 2001 most of the non-with-profits business of ELAS, along with its infrastructure, assets and workforce, was transferred to Halifax p.l.c. for £500 million. Other assets were also sold to Liverpool Victoria for £250 million. The Halifax also offered to pay an additional £250 million if ELAS, by 1 March 2002, was able to cap its GAR liabilities in a way that was fair and reasonable to the different classes of policyholders and preserved the solvency of the fund. The problems at ELAS were not helped by the falling stock markets around the world from early 2001, which reduced the value of its equity assets. As a result of this the ELAS board, in July 2001, took the decision to reduce all policy values by 16 per cent of their value as at the end of 2000. In December 2001 the board announced a compromise scheme which, if accepted, would lead to GAR policyholders having their GAR rights 'bought out' in return for an immediate uplift in policy values. The board calculated the value of the GAR rights as equivalent to an average uplift in policy values of 17.5 per cent. In return for this uplift, GAR policyholders had to relinquish their GAR rights and waive their right to sue for loss arising from mis-selling claims. In addition, non-GAR policyholders were compensated by an uplift of 2.5 per cent in return for waiving their right to sue for mis-selling. The proposal was accepted by the majority of policyholders in January 2002. This entitled ELAS to the Halifax payment of £250 million. The effect of the compromise scheme was to increase the financial strength of the fund by £1 billion. This was possible because the GAR reserves were calculated on a conservative basis and therefore included margins. Compensation for loss of GAR rights, though, was calculated on a realistic basis and the margins were released to the fund when the compromise scheme was implemented. Currently ELAS is solvent and the risks to solvency have reduced. It does, however, continue to face the risk that members who have withdrawn from the fund may still sue the Equitable for mis-selling.

Annuities

Annuities generally involve a policyholder paying an initial lump sum which is used by the insurance company to provide an agreed income until death. The insurance company then immediately creates a fund which is run down as payments are made to the policyholder. A recent interesting case is that of Equitable Life, which sold with-profits pension annuities with guaranteed annuity rates. The case outlined in box 6.1 illustrates the risks for insurance companies of offering guaranteed rates of return on policies.

Personal pensions

These are schemes provided mainly by insurance companies, for contributors who have contracted out of the State Second Pension Scheme (see section 6.4.3). They are defined contribution schemes such that, on the retirement date, up to 25 per cent of the accumulated fund may be taken as a tax-free lump sum with the remainder used either to buy an annuity or to provide pension income by way of a draw-down facility until the age of 75, when an annuity must be purchased with the remaining assets.

Stakeholder pensions were introduced in 2001. These are low-cost personal pensions, aimed at middle-income earners, that have to meet certain standards laid down by the government. These standards, known as CAT (charges, access, terms) standards, include a stipulation that charges can be no more than 1 per cent of the fund. Personal pensions and the reason for their growth are discussed in more detail in section 6.4.3.

6.4.2 *Pension fund liabilities*

Pension provision in the UK comes from three basic sources: the state scheme, an occupational scheme and a personal pension. The state scheme consists of a first component, a flat-rate pension, paid since 1925, and a second component, which is earnings related. We examine recent developments in the provision of state pensions later in this section. Occupational pensions are provided by employers in both the public and private sector. It is these pension schemes which involve the build-up of an investment fund and which form the pension funds we refer to in this chapter. Personal pensions are pensions tailored to an individual's requirements and until recently were provided only by life assurance companies. As a consequence such pensions are counted as part of life assurance business. Recent reforms, outlined later in this section, have, however, widened the range of institutions which can provide personal pensions.

There are two basic types of occupational pension scheme: the unfunded or pay-as-you-go scheme and the funded scheme. Many of the public sector schemes are unfunded schemes, whereby the costs of providing benefits are met out of current contributions. In such schemes, therefore, there is no build-up of an investment fund, and they have little impact on the capital markets. All the state pensions are run on an unfunded basis, with benefits provided out of the general revenue of the government. The occupational schemes of the Civil Service, the National Health Service, teachers, police and other parts of the public sector are also unfunded, although in some instances a notional fund is maintained. The public sector industries and local authorities, however, run funded schemes. The disadvantage of unfunded schemes is that if the number of contributing members declines or the number of people receiving benefits increases relative to contributors (owing, for example, to medical advances leading to longevity, a decline in

the birth rate, early retirement, etc.) then the burden on contributors can become excessive. The burden of unfunded schemes is likely to become extremely onerous in the near future. This is often referred to as the 'demographic time bomb'. This danger is particularly important since most unfunded schemes refer to government employees and therefore the cost will be borne by the taxpayer.

However, the UK is recognised to be one of the few major economies which does not face a serious long-term problem with pension payments. The present value of net public pension liabilities is estimated at 5 per cent of gross domestic product (GDP) compared with over 100 per cent in Japan, Germany and France. There are two principal reasons for this:

(i) the basic state pension has been held constant in real terms since 1980 (it is currently about 15 per cent of average earnings),
(ii) there is a second-tier State Earnings-Related Pension Scheme (SERPS) but only 17 per cent of employees belong to it – most employees belong to funded private occupational schemes.

There is also a risk with occupational unfunded schemes that the company may be wound up, thus making the pensions provided by the company insecure. In the private sector it is therefore the funded pension scheme which is the norm. There are two types of funded occupational pension schemes: defined benefit and defined contribution. Both types of scheme involve the contributions of working members, along with in most cases the contributions of employers, being paid into a fund which is invested to yield income and capital gain, out of which benefits are paid. With the defined benefit scheme the benefits paid are determined by the contributing member's length of service and final salary before retirement. A typical scheme is a 1/80th scheme, where for each year of contributing, the member will receive 1/80th of final salary as annual benefit upon retiring and also 3/80ths of the final salary for each year's service as a lump sum free of tax. So, after 40 years of contributions, the member would receive half final salary as annual benefit in retirement together with a lump sum of 1½ times the final salary on retirement. In contrast, the benefits paid under a defined contribution scheme are based on the size of the fund accumulated and the annuity rates available when the fund is used to buy an annuity. It is clear that the defined benefit scheme involves more risk for the sponsoring employer. The risk of defined benefit schemes has been increased by the decline in equity prices after 2000 (see chapter 8), which has caused many occupational schemes to show substantial deficits, which the firms must correct. The *Financial Times* reported (7 March 2003) that the Morgan Stanley bank had estimated a gap of £85 billion between the value of UK pension funds' assets and liabilities. This has led a number of firms to wind down their defined benefit schemes, usually by closing the scheme to new

members, who can join only defined contribution schemes. Amongst companies closing defined benefit schemes to new members were Sainsbury, ICI, Barclays, Marks and Spencer. This list is not exhaustive but does indicate the scale of the problem

6.4.3 *Growth of pension funds and life assurance companies*

We noted in section 6.2 that the assets of pension funds and life assurance companies increased in value at a rapid rate over the 1980s and 1990s. In this section we examine the reasons for this growth.

The contractual nature of premiums for life policies and contributions for pension schemes provides stability for the funds. Most life policies and pension schemes are paid into over a period of many years and, as we have noted above, there are penalties involved in cashing in life policies in the first few years after commencement. Life policies as a vehicle for long-term savings were encouraged up to 1984 by the existence of tax relief on premiums, at 15 per cent. Building societies were active in selling endowment mortgages, in order to earn commissions, and the strong marketing of endowment mortgages continued after 1984 when the ending of tax relief increased the costs of this type of mortgage relative to the straight repayment mortgage. A further development was the introduction of mortgage interest relief at source (MIRAS) in 1982 (ended in 2000), which gave a boost to the housing market in general and therefore also to the sale of endowment policies. We have already indicated in section 6.4.1 the problems with the use of endowment policies as a vehicle for house purchase.

A boost for assurance companies has come from changes in the state pension system (described below) that have made personal pensions more attractive. Assurance companies are the main providers of personal pensions. A recent development in the area of personal pensions is the introduction of stakeholder pensions in 2001, discussed above.

The important factors explaining the growth of pension funds over the last 20 years are related to government policies. The first of these is the taxation treatment of 'approved' occupational pension schemes. The contributions of both employers and employees are deductible from taxable income. In the 1997 July budget, the advance corporation tax credit was abolished for most tax-exempt investors. This was a credit representing the tax paid by companies on the dividends they distributed. Up until July 1997, pension funds were able to claim this tax back from the Exchequer. It is estimated that the removal of this source of tax benefit for pension funds has reduced their income by about £5 billion per annum. Finally, the benefits payable by a fund are subject to the pensioners' rate of personal income tax, except for any lump sum paid, up to a set limit, which is tax exempt. The fiscal privilege given to pension funds at various times undoubtedly had a positive impact on their growth.

Government policies with regard to the state pension have also had an effect on occupational and private pension schemes. In 1978 the government introduced the SERPS, which provided greater benefits than the second-tier state earnings-related scheme it replaced. At the same time tougher minimum requirements on benefits paid out by occupational schemes were laid down if employers were to contract out of the state scheme. Most schemes in fact chose to contract out, which in many cases meant that benefits had to be raised. In 1988, approximately 13 million people were contracted into SERPS and were not in an occupational scheme. After a review of social policy in the mid-1980s, the government argued that, with increasing longevity and a declining birth rate, the burden on the working population in supporting pensioners when SERPS matured early in the twenty-first century would become intolerable. As a consequence SERPS was reformed and the central feature of the new pension arrangements, which came into force in April 1988, was to transfer the responsibility for pension provision from the state to the private sector. To achieve such a transfer, first, benefits available from SERPS were curtailed in order to provide an incentive to take out a private pension or join an occupational scheme and, second, the procedures for contracting out of SERPS were made easier and financial incentives were provided to individuals to take up a personal pension and to employers to start up occupational schemes. The monopoly on the provision of personal pensions held by assurance companies was also removed to allow other financial institutions such as banks and building societies to become providers. The aim here was to encourage competition in provision. Such developments led to an expansion of personal pensions. However, one consequence of the competition in selling personal pensions was that, in some cases, customers were sold pensions that were not appropriate. This led to compensation payments, by assurance companies, to quite a large number of the purchasers of personal pension schemes. SERPS was replaced by the more generous State Second Pension Scheme in 2002. This has made the advantage of opting out into a personal pension less clear for many low- and middle-income workers. The introduction of low-cost stakeholder pensions in 2001 has not led to a big increase in the take-up of personal pensions. This is partly because the government decided not to make second-tier pension saving compulsory. So the problem of myopia continues to lead to a large proportion of workers not making provision for a retirement income beyond the basic state pension.

6.5 Portfolio investment of pension funds and life assurance companies

The portfolio investment of both life assurance companies and pension funds is determined by the nature of their liabilities and the return and

availability of the various types of financial asset. In the previous section we noted that the liabilities of both life assurance companies and pension funds are long term. In evidence to the Wilson committee in 1977, the life assurance companies stated the objectives of their investment strategy as being to maximise return, subject to risk, within an asset structure that takes the term structure of their liabilities into account. A particular risk faced by life assurance companies is that when a contract is written, certain sums are guaranteed to be paid in the future and these sums exceed the value of the premiums over the life of the contract. For example, in the case of an endowment policy, a guaranteed sum is assured at the outset. This sum will have been determined by reference to actuarial calculations about mortality and a prediction of likely returns on investment of the premiums. There is therefore a risk that outcomes of mortality, investment returns and so on may prove worse than the life assurance company's assumptions. In order to protect itself against such a risk the company can 'match' the term structure of its assets and liabilities. In this situation the assets should have a given yield which should be at least equal to the investment returns assumed in the calculation of the sum assured. The ideal type of asset for matching purposes is the UK government (gilt-edged) security. As we saw in chapter 1, this asset possesses the characteristics of safety, known term to maturity, fixed interest rate and known redemption value if held to maturity. By carefully selecting gilts with terms to maturity which match the term to maturity of its liabilities, a life assurance company can protect itself against changes in investment returns and so be in a position to meet its contractual requirements. However, there are several disadvantages with this strategy of matching. First, life assurance companies also write with-profits policies and the holders of these policies will expect bonuses to be paid. To achieve the returns necessary to pay bonuses, life assurance companies will need to hold some proportion of their asset portfolio in assets which yield higher returns than gilts. Indeed, competition between life assurance companies will encourage them to hold high-yielding assets such as equities. Second, there is a practical constraint to life assurance companies holding portfolios constructed only of gilts, which is that there are insufficient quantities of gilts across the range of maturities required for matching. However, the matching strategy provides a benchmark for life assurance companies in that the further away the fund is from a fully matched position, the greater will be the risk for the company of not meeting its contractual requirements.

The liabilities of pension funds, whilst being long term, are also different in nature to those of life assurance companies, as in most cases benefits to be paid out are not known with certainty. As we noted in the last section, the benefits of most occupational pension schemes are related to the final salary of the contributor, which is not known in advance. Wage inflation

complicates matters further as it increases the benefits to be paid by the fund, which has been accumulated from lower contributions over past periods. Index linking of final benefits, which occurs with some schemes, provides an additional uncertainty. As a consequence, the concept of matching is less relevant to pension funds. A greater consideration is to achieve returns in excess of the rate of inflation. Hence pension funds will look to hold assets which, over the long term, yield positive real returns. Examples of such assets are equities and property. Index-linked gilts, introduced in the early 1980s, provide a benchmark in this regard.

We now turn to examine the actual investments made by life assurance companies and pension funds. We consider first the holdings of the main categories of assets for the two types of institution at the end of 2001. We then examine the investment strategies of the institutions over the recent past as revealed by net investment of cash flows, which represent the conscious investment decisions of the institutions.

The figures in table 6.4 reveal that life assurance companies held a greater proportion of their portfolio as UK government securities than did pension funds. This follows from the discussion above where we noted that the principle of matching is more relevant to life assurance companies. (Holdings of other UK company securities, mainly fixed-interest debt with characteristics similar to gilts, are greater for life assurance companies for the same reasons.) The difference between pension funds and life assurance holdings of gilts is not quite as pronounced as in the past, for a number of reasons, including that pension funds' holdings have risen slightly over the last few years as a consequence of the minimum funding requirement, discussed below. Pension funds have placed greater emphasis on index-linked gilts, which make up a larger proportion of their total holdings of gilts compared with life assurance companies. Index-linked gilts are perhaps more relevant to pension funds, as we noted above. Whilst equities are the main asset held by both life assurance companies and pension funds, they make up a greater proportion of the portfolio of pension funds. This reflects the greater requirement on the part of pension funds to achieve positive real returns. When we take into account overseas securities, which are mainly ordinary shares of overseas listed companies, the proportion of equities held by pension funds is approaching 60 per cent of the portfolio. This proportion of equity funding together with the heavy fall in equity prices has led to the occupational fund deficits discussed earlier. Another asset which generally yields positive real returns over the long term is property. Surprisingly, life assurance companies have been more active investors in property than pension funds, with the latter concentrating their investment attentions mainly on equities in recent years. We can observe this more clearly by examination of cash flow investment for each type of institution over the period 1988 to 2002, which is summarised in table 6.5.

Table 6.4 Asset portfolios of life assurance and pension funds at end 2001 (percentage of total)

	Life assurance companies	Pension funds
Short-term assets	6.9	3.0
UK government securities	13.0	11.8
(of which index linked)	(16.1)	(55.3)
UK ordinary shares	33.9	36.9
Other UK company securities	13.4	3.2
Overseas securities	16.1	21.9
Unit trusts	7.8	6.1
Property	5.8	4.3
Other assets	3.1	12.8

Source: *Financial Statistics*, Office for National Statistics online database.

Table 6.5 Investment of life assurance companies' and pension funds' net receipts, 1988–2002 (percentage of total)

	1988	1990	1992	1994	1996	1998	2000	2002
Life assurance companies								
Short-term assets	8.0	35.7	11.3	–3.1	16.3	7.9	14.8	2.6
UK government securities	9.4	–4.6	46.6	30.5	32.3	4.4	–18.2	18.0
UK ordinary shares	36.9	32.5	14.1	35.2	21.8	17.5	33.8	–21.5
Other UK company securities	16.4	8.5	13.4	12.6	7.6	31.1	52.3	63.6
Unit trusts	–	0.5	–0.3	3.8	1.7	0.1	5.8	–1.4
Overseas securities	8.5	17.3	5.8	13.6	11.8	30.0	2.0	32.7
Property	10.8	6.0	3.1	10.7	1.9	6.8	8.3	6.8
Other	1.1	2.3	2.8	–0.1	12.3	1.5	1.4	–0.1
Pension funds								
Short-term assets	14.6	17.0	0.4	34.0	37.3	34.8	45.9	14.5
UK government securities	–13.7	–19.9	35.6	146.9	104.8	35.9	39.1	–29.9
UK ordinary shares	50.5	59.0	7.3	6.5	–60.5	–44.6	–57.6	0
Other UK company securities	5.9	3.7	0.0	–2.2	–1.0	6.2	28.3	17.5
Unit trusts	–	–0.2	0.0	0.2	0.0	13.9	21.0	12.2
Overseas securities	28.7	48.5	7.6	–78.0	33.6	12.2	–35.9	61.8
Property	2.8	–3.6	13.8	–2.0	–3.2	6.0	8.9	2.6
Other	11.4	5.7	31.0	–12.5	9.4	9.7	50.3	21.7

Source: *Financial Statistics*, Office for National Statistics online database.

The figures in table 6.5 reveal the importance of UK equity investment for both types of institution for much of this period, as they took advantage of the rising equity market in the 1980s and 1990s (see figure 8.2). For life assurance companies the figures portray a picture of allocation of funds to UK ordinary shares over practically the whole period, with net sales only in 2002, as stock market falls from 2001 led to a withdrawal from the market. The position for pension funds is more variable, with a particularly large proportion of funds being allocated to UK ordinary shares in 1988 and 1990 with a slowdown in the proportion invested up to 1994 and then net sales thereafter. The popularity of equities for institutions over the 1980s is mainly explained by the fact that the real return (i.e. nominal return less the rate of inflation) on UK equities averaged approximately 13 per cent per year over the 1980s (compared with 1 per cent over the 1970s). The dis-investment in UK equities by pension funds since the early 1990s is partly explained by a switch back into UK government securities as the supply of these increased following a return to budget deficit (after a period of gilt buy-backs in 1986–88) and a decline in the rate of inflation which made fixed-interest securities more attractive. As the supply of UK gilts again slowed down at the end of the 1990s both pension funds and, to a greater degree, assurance companies sought alternative fixed-interest investments through corporate bonds. Another factor behind the net sales of UK equities was the switch to overseas equities (except for 1994, when there was a downturn in global equity markets) as investment institutions continued to diversify geographically. A final comment on investment strategies concerns the variable inflows into short-term assets. Investment institutions have relatively low liquidity requirements and although short-term assets provide some return, this is generally lower than that from the main assets held by these institutions. Short-term assets therefore represent a depository for funds awaiting investment in the main earning assets. High investment in short-term assets generally implies uncertainty about the future returns on the main earning assets. Thus, for example, we note high investment in short-term assets in 1990, particularly by assurance companies, reflecting an increase in receipts following the buy-back of gilts by the authorities. What is more striking is the high investment in short-term assets by pension funds from 1994 to the end of the decade. This is more difficult to explain but is probably related to the concerns about the solvency of pension funds following the Maxwell pension scandal – discussed below.

6.6 Regulation of pension funds

We now turn to an examination of the future investment behaviour of pension funds. During the early 1990s two major scandals hit the pension fund industry. In 1991, the directors of Belling, the UK cooker manufacturer,

Box 6.2 The Myners review of institutional investment

In March 2001 the Treasury-sponsored review of institutional investment, chaired by Paul Myners, chief executive of Gartmore, was published (see Myners 2001). Its recommendations were accepted in full by the government. The report identified several problems with institutional investment and suggested the introduction of a statement of principles of institutional investment along the lines of the Code of Good Practice for Corporate Governance introduced by Cadbury (and others). The main problems identified were:

(i) Pension fund trustees, who make some of the most important investment decisions, often lack expertise or support.
(ii) Fund managers are often set objectives which do not relate to the ultimate objective of the pension fund, which is to meet its pension obligations.
(iii) The timescales over which fund managers are judged is a real cause of short termism in fund managers' approach to investment (see chapter 15).
(iv) Fund managers remain reluctant to take an activist stance in relation to corporate underperformance, in companies of which they own substantial shareholdings.
(v) The main costs to pension funds, namely broking costs, are not sufficiently scrutinised.

Box continues opposite

acting in their capacity as trustees of the company pension scheme, purchased a Belling subsidiary for the scheme using £5.5 million of pension assets. In addition, they borrowed £2.1 million from the company pension fund. These cash injections were designed to salvage the ailing Belling company. However, Belling went into liquidation in 1992 and the liquidators valued the subsidiary at £2.5 million. As a consequence, Belling pension scheme members suffered a considerable loss of money from their fund. This, however, pales into insignificance when compared with the disappearance of £440 million from pension funds controlled by the late Robert Maxwell. As a result of the Maxwell deficit, the government set up the Goode committee to review the legal and general environment of pension funds. Following receipt of the report, the 1995 Pensions Act went on to the statute books, becoming law in 1997. This Act introduced many new provisions for the governance of pension funds, including setting out the composition and responsibilities of the trustees. A pensions regulator, termed the Occupational Pensions Regulatory Authority, was also established.

Two key areas of the Act concerning investment are the statement of investment principle (SIP) and the minimum funding requirement (MFR). All fund trustees must produce an SIP, which lays out the rationale and

Box 6.2 *Continued*

The proposed statement of the principles of institutional investment would be a voluntary code. However, where a pension fund chose not to comply with them, it would have to explain to its members why not. The main principles are:

(i) Trustees should be paid and have sufficient in-house resources to support them in their investment responsibilities.
(ii) Trustees should set out an overall investment objective for the fund that both represents their best judgement of what is necessary to meet the fund's liabilities and takes account of attitudes to risk. Objectives should be expressed in terms which bear a relationship to the fund's liabilities.
(iii) More attention should be given to asset allocation (i.e. allocation to different asset classes, such as UK ordinary shares, etc.).
(iv) Fund managers should have a duty to intervene in companies where it is in the shareholders' interest.

Furthermore, a strengthened statement of investment principles should set out:

(i) who is taking which decisions and why this structure has been selected;
(ii) the fund's investment objective;
(iii) the fund's planned asset allocation strategy;
(iv) the mandates given to all advisers and managers;
(v) the nature of the fee structures in place for all advisers and managers.

The review also proposed other changes, including changes to the MFR regime (see text). The interested reader should see the Myners report for more detail.

assumptions underlying the investment strategy to be followed by the fund. This statement must be reviewed annually. The introduction of the MFR was designed to increase the security of the benefits of members of specified schemes where members receive a pension based on the individual's final salary level. The sponsors of the pension scheme are required to publish, annually, the level of funding against the scheme's liabilities. Remedial measures must be taken if the ratio drops below 100 per cent. However, a number of problems with the MFR have emerged:

(i) It did not guarantee that pensions to all contributing members would be paid in full if the sponsoring company became insolvent. This is because claims of retired members are met first.
(ii) It has encouraged funds to switch out of 'volatile' equities into bonds, which may have led to a less than optimal mix of assets.

As a result of these criticisms the Myners review of institutional investment – see box 6.2 – recommended that the MFR be replaced by a scheme-specific regime, based on transparency and disclosure. Under such a regime every defined benefit pension scheme is required to publish information, including its asset classes and the current value of assets, the assumptions used to determine liabilities, its planned asset allocation in the next few years, and assumed returns and volatilities of those returns for each asset class. This recommendation has been accepted by the government and is expected to be implemented in 2005.

Changes to the accounting framework for defined benefit occupational pension schemes have also had an impact on investment decisions. In November 2000, the Accounting Standards Board (ASB) issued Financial Reporting Standard (FRS) 17 with the objective of replacing SSAP24, the existing standard for reporting pension costs in company accounts. The main changes are:

(i) actuarial gains and losses will be recognised fully and immediately (instead of being spread over periods of up to 15 years);
(ii) scheme assets and liabilities will be valued using current market valuations.

The main consequences of this are that where stock market values or interest rates fluctuate during an accounting period this can have a large effect on the firm's balance sheet. FRS17 therefore makes explicit the financial risks, to a sponsoring company, of operating a defined benefit scheme. The dramatic falls in equity values after 2000 led many companies to move their pension provision to a defined contribution scheme.

6.7 Unit trusts, open-ended investment companies and investment trusts

Unit trusts, OEICs and investment trusts are all institutions which allow individuals or companies to purchase a stake in a larger and more diversified portfolio than they would normally be able to hold directly and at the same time to obtain the benefits of a sophisticated portfolio management service.

A unit trust is a fund to which individuals and companies may contribute in order to obtain a share in the returns generated by the fund. The institution is legally constituted as a trust, where a trustee acts as guardian of the assets on behalf of the beneficial owners and a separate management company is responsible for investment decisions. The terms and conditions governing these investment decisions are specified in the trust deed under which the institution operates. The management company is generally a bank or insurance company. The industry of fund management underwent diversification over the 1980s and many institutions, including retail banks,

merchant banks, stockbrokers and insurance companies, have become more involved. At the end of the decade insurance companies accounted for the largest share of ownership of unit trust management companies.

A contributor to a unit trust purchases 'units' at a price which reflects the aggregate value of the trust's net assets divided by the number of units outstanding. The funds are termed 'open ended', which means that they can expand by issuing new units at the same value as existing units at that point in time, or it may contract, through unit holders selling back their units to the fund at the prevailing price. There is no secondary market in units, as all sales and purchases of units are made with the trust managers, although another intermediary may act as an agent to the transaction. Unit trusts typically have a dual pricing structure, with a separate buy and sell price. It is now possible for unit trusts to adopt a single pricing structure but few had done so at the time of writing. With the dual pricing structure the price at which an investor purchases units is known as the offer price and the price at which he or she sells them back to the trust is known as the bid price. To determine these prices the trustee will request the investment manager to value the assets held at bid or offer price. The price of units is then calculated by adding to the offer price stamp duty, stockbroker's commission and managers' charges (including VAT). With managers' charges typically in the region of 5 per cent and a dealing spread (the difference between the bid and offer prices on the underlying assets) of 2 per cent then the difference between unit offer and bid prices can be around 9 per cent. The prices of most units are calculated daily and the changing prices therefore reflect the changing prices of the underlying assets. The calculation of bid and offer prices just described represents a maximum spread. The quoted spread is normally much lower, as fund managers do not always have to buy or sell the underlying securities when they are buying and selling units but match a certain proportion of buying and selling orders. The quoted price will therefore lie within the maximum calculated spread so that during periods of net sales of units the quoted offer price will be at the calculated offer price, with the quoted bid price at a higher price than the calculated bid price. Conversely, during periods of net redemption of units, the quoted bid price will be equal to the calculated bid price, with the quoted offer price lower than the calculated offer price.

Traditionally the price at which the unit trust managers have transacted with investors has been the price related to the last valuation – known as historical or backward pricing. An alternative method, known as forward pricing, means that units are sold at prices that prevail at the valuation (a few hours after the order is processed). Unit trust managers may now choose to price on a forward or backward basis, with the investor being informed of the chosen method. The advantage of forward pricing is that investors are sold units at (almost) current rather than historical prices.

The disadvantage is that investors do not know the transaction price when the order is made.

In 1997 a new type of fund was introduced, termed an 'open-ended investment company' (OEIC). This fund operates in a manner similar to that of a unit trust since it can expand or contract as investors pay money into the fund – hence the term 'open-ended'. They can invest in the same kinds of assets as unit trusts and are subject to the same regulatory regime through the FSA. However, an OEIC has a company structure and can be listed on the Stock Exchange. One salient difference from unit and investment trusts is the fact that the shares will reflect the value of the fund and will therefore not trade at a discount or premium. Furthermore, the shares will have a single price rather than the separate buying and selling prices typically indicated for unit trusts. The OEIC structure has proved very popular, with many unit trust providers converting existing unit trusts to OEICs. By March 2003, 48 per cent of open-ended funds were OEICs, compared with 35 per cent in March 2002.

We noted in section 6.2 that open-ended investment schemes (unit trusts and OEICs) grew rapidly over the 1980s and at the end of 2000 had assets of just over £260 billion. They can invest in a wide variety of assets, including bank deposits, UK and overseas company shares and government securities. As we can observe from table 6.6, the main asset held is company shares, both UK and overseas.

Table 6.6 Investments held by unit trusts and OEICs at end 2000

	Percentage of total
Short-term securities	3.6
UK government securities	2.1
UK company securities	56.8
Other sterling assets	0.1
Overseas company securities	35.8
Other overseas securities	0.1

Source: *Financial Statistics*, Office for National Statistics online database.

In contrast to unit trusts, investment trusts are companies whose business is the investment of funds in financial assets. Investment trusts raise their finance like any other company, through the issue of shares and debentures, by retaining income and so on. Therefore if an investor wishes to acquire an interest in an investment trust he or she must acquire its shares either by subscribing to a new issue or by purchasing the shares on the stock market. These shares can be sold on to a third party through the stock market.

The investments held by the investment trust industry are summarised in table 6.7. As with open-ended investment schemes, ordinary shares make up the overwhelming majority of securities held.

Table 6.7 Investments held by investment trusts at end 2000

	Percentage of total
Short-term securities	0.1
UK government securities	1.4
UK company securities	58.6
Other sterling assets	1.7
Overseas company securities	37.9
Other overseas securities	0.2

Source: *Financial Statistics*, Office for National Statistics online database.

The existence of borrowed funds, as opposed to equity, in the capital structure of an investment trust means that if the value of the underlying securities fluctuates there is a 'gearing' effect on the value of the shares issued by the trust. To illustrate this effect we will consider a simple example of an investment trust which has a capital structure comprising £8 million in shareholders' equity claims, attributable to 4 million issued shares, and £2 million of outstanding debt. The total value of funds invested by the trust is therefore £10 million, which we assume is invested only in ordinary shares. The net asset value (NAV) per share (the value of assets less debt divided by the number of issued shares) is thus £2. Now, if the value of the investment trust asset portfolio were to double to £20 million then the NAV per share would increase to £4.50. Therefore a 100 per cent increase in the value of assets held has led to an increase in the NAV per share of 125 per cent. The gearing effect of course can work to the detriment of shareholders when the assets of the investment trust fall in value. There is also a gearing effect on the income to be distributed to shareholders resulting from a change in the net income (before interest) derived from the investment trust's asset portfolio. Whilst the gearing effect is always of benefit to shareholders, in terms of NAV of their shares, in a rising stock market, the effect from income generation will be of benefit only if the return from utilising the borrowed funds is greater than the interest cost. The actual gearing of investment trusts in aggregate in recent years has been relatively modest, averaging around 8 per cent.

A particular curiosity of investment trusts is that the share price of most of them is at a significant discount to the NAV per share. The price of shares is of course determined by demand and so the existence of a discount would imply that demand for the investment trust's shares is lower than the

demand for its portfolio of shares bought independently. We noted in section 6.2 that investment trusts have not grown as rapidly as unit trusts over the last 20 years. One factor which discourages investors may be the greater risk of the investment, which comes from the gearing effect. The existence of a discount makes investment trusts vulnerable to takeover, especially when a trust owns an appreciable stake in a target company. The potential bidder can acquire up to 30 per cent of the trust and therefore the shares owned by it at a discount. The full bid for the remainder will have to reflect the NAV. An example of such a process includes, in 1979, Lonhro's agreed acquisition of the Scottish and Universal Trust, which held 10.29 per cent of the shares in House of Fraser, which Lonhro went on to bid for.

6.8 The performance of institutional investors

Rising equity markets around the world over most of the 1980s and 1990s resulted in historically high performances, with regard to returns, by UK fund managers. The downturn in global equity markets from early 2001 reversed this trend and led to reductions in the value of many funds of up to 50 per cent. The move to a low-inflation and low-interest-rate environment will mean that a repeat of the exceptional returns of the 1980s and 1990s is very unlikely. The discussion that follows focuses on the nature of this performance over the 1980s and 1990s.

Average annual returns on pension fund investments over the 1980s were 19.5 per cent, which compares favourably with average inflation and wage inflation, over the same period, of 6.9 per cent and 9.5 per cent, respectively. The figure for wage inflation represents a form of target return for those pension funds where benefits are linked to final salary. This performance over the 1980s contrasts strongly with performance over the 1970s, where pension fund investment returns underperformed wage inflation by, on average, approximately 6 per cent per year. The consequence of this was that pension fund actuarial deficits had to be met by higher contributions from employers. The considerably higher investment income over the 1980s and 1990s resulted in actuarial surpluses for many funds, which allowed companies to take 'contribution holidays'.

The investment performance by pension funds over the 1980s and 1990s was largely a consequence of rising equity markets, which, as we noted in section 6.5, were tapped by funds which invested most of their cash flows into equities. The diversification into overseas equities, where growth has at times been stronger in particular markets than in the UK, has also been a contributory factor. However, the diversification into overseas equities has not been as successful as it could have been, as evidenced by a failure of funds to match closely the index in overseas equity markets. The return on UK equities achieved by institutional investors was on average 23.2 per

cent per year over the 1980s, compared with a 23.6 per cent return on the Financial Times Stock Exchange Index of 100 leading shares (FTSE 100) – a close match after taking costs into account. In contrast there was underperformance relative to the indexes in the US by, on average, 3.6 per cent and in Japan by, on average, 2.5 per cent. The underperformance has continued to occur and performance measurers WM reported that, over the period 1986–96, managed funds achieved an annual return of 13.9 per cent against 14.2 cent for the FTSE 100 (*Financial Times*, 8 October 1997). This underperformance has led some funds to move to passive management, by investing in index-tracking funds. These are funds which are constructed according to a chosen index, with the shares making up that index included in the fund according to the weightings in the index. Such a management strategy has the advantage of low transaction costs, as shares are bought and sold only to keep the fund in line with the index. Depending on how well the index has been tracked (measured by tracking error), this type of passive management yields returns in line with returns on the index. Index funds were first established in the US and have become increasingly popular in the UK in recent times. It has been estimated that about 60 per cent of assets under management in the UK have an index-tracking mandate (Investment Management Association 2002).

6.9 Conclusion

In chapter 2 we noted the significant growth of assets held by investment institutions in recent years when compared with the growth of assets held by the deposit-taking institutions. In this chapter we have shown that one reason for this is that the main assets held by investment institutions are equities, which achieved substantial returns, in terms of both income and capital gain, over the 1980s and 1990s. Another suggested reason is that investment institutions are displacing banks in carrying out an intermediation function. Other reasons suggested to explain the growth of investment institutions relate to government policy and include tax-privileged contributions to pension funds and changes in the state pension scheme, which have encouraged private provision.

We have now completed our discussion of financial institutions and so in the next section of this book we turn our attention to financial markets.

Chapter 7

Financial markets: introduction

7.1 Introduction

With this chapter we begin our look at the main financial markets making up the UK financial system. All the markets we consider in subsequent chapters are located in London and, although they serve the domestic economy, a substantial amount of transactions through these markets are international. In the case of markets such as foreign exchange (see chapter 11) and eurosecurities (chapter 12) the majority of transactions conducted through London are for non-UK residents. We therefore begin this chapter by considering the importance of London as an international financial centre and some of the reasons for this. We then turn to consider in sections 7.3 and 7.4 some general issues relating to the nature of financial markets, including types of trading systems and types of trading activity. Section 7.5 considers the efficient markets hypothesis, which is one of the main propositions of finance theory. However, this proposition has come under attack in recent years and in section 7.6 we examine some alternative views of financial markets, collectively known as behavioural finance.

7.2 London as an international financial centre

Three international centres dominate the financial scene. These are New York, London and Tokyo. The main exception to the dominance of the so-called golden triangle which these three centres make up lies within the sphere of exchange-traded futures and options, for which Chicago is an important centre. We now outline the position of London in the various international financial markets.

7.2.1 *Derivatives*

During 1989 the major markets in Chicago (the Chicago Board of Trade and the Chicago Mercantile Exchange) accounted for 65 per cent of total

world trade in derivatives (as measured by number of contracts traded in these increasingly used instruments) (see chapter 13 for a general discussion of derivatives). At this time London and the rest of Europe attracted 6.25 per cent and 7.14 per cent, respectively. It is, however, pertinent to note that the US share is decreasing and by 2002 the US exchanges together accounted for just 30 per cent of total world trade (by volume of contracts). This compares with around 6 per cent through UK exchanges and 21.3 per cent for the rest of Europe. The largest derivative exchange in the UK, the London International Financial Futures and Options Exchange (LIFFE), has been taken over by Euronext to form Euronext.liffe (incorporating the derivatives exchanges of Paris, Amsterdam, Brussels and Lisbon, as well as LIFFE). In terms of value of turnover, Euronext.liffe is the second largest exchange after the Chicago Mercantile Exchange (with nominal values of turnover in 2002 of $1302 billion and $761 billion, respectively).

London is also the world's leading centre for over-the-counter (OTC) derivatives activity. A survey in 2001 found that London accounted for 33.7 per cent of activity, with New York, the second largest centre, accounting for 15.3 per cent. Paris and Frankfurt accounted for 5.7 per cent and 8.5 per cent of global OTC derivatives business, respectively (Bank for International Settlements 2002).

7.2.2 *Banking*

London has long been a major international banking centre and has developed since the 1960s as a eurocurrency banking centre. At the beginning of the 1980s, London was by far the largest international banking centre in the world, accounting for 27 per cent of total international lending. Table 7.1 shows that by the end of the 1980s the figure had declined to just over 19 per cent and London had lost its dominance to Japan, which accounted for 21.5 per cent. However, in the early 1990s Japanese banks began withdrawing from international banking following a decline in Japanese stock markets, which reduced their capital, and a decline in Japanese property prices, which reduced their profits. Thus, by the end of 2001 the positions of London and Japan in the ranking of international banking had reversed again, with London having a share of 20.9 per cent and Japan taking only about 5 per cent. The US was in third place with 11.5 per cent. The UK accounted for over 30 per cent of such lending in European countries. In fact, the UK is responsible for more cross-border lending than Germany and France combined.

The 1980s saw a marked increase in Japanese international banking conducted through both Tokyo and its overseas establishments in London, the US and elsewhere. This growth largely reflected the growth in Japanese international trade and investment. London, in fact, is the most important

Table 7.1 International banking: analysis by centre, 1980–2001 (percentage of total external liabilities outstanding)

	December 1980	December 1985	December 1989	December 1993	December 2001
Belgium	4.2	3.8	3.2	4.2	2.7
France	10.8	7.1	6.4	10.3	6.8
Germany	5.5	3.2	3.7	8.9	8.8
Luxembourg	6.6	4.1	4.0	6.6	3.6
Switzerland	4.5	6.4	5.5	7.2	5.7
UK	27.0	25.4	19.3	21.1	20.9
Japan	5.0	10.8	21.5	18.4	4.7
US	13.4	13.3	9.4	10.9	11.5

Sources: *Bank of England Quarterly Bulletin* (various issues) and *BIS Quarterly Review*, June 2002, table 2A.

Table 7.2 International banks in London: share of foreign currency lending to non-UK residents through London, April 2002

	Percentage of total
US	17
Japan	9
UK	20
Other European Union countries	35
Other overseas countries	19

Sources: *Bank of England Monetary Statistics*, August 2002, table B1.2.1.

centre for Japanese banks outside of Japan. The decline in Japanese banks' international lending, referred to above, is therefore reflected in the decline in Japanese bank lending through London (see table 7.2).

The US banks were the dominant international banks in London over the 1960s and 1970s. However, over the 1980s and early 1990s they experienced a decline in their share of total international lending, both generally and through London. This partly reflects a retrenchment by US banks, to concentrate on domestic business, following the sovereign debt crisis, which broke in 1982. However, whilst the on-balance-sheet business of US banks operating in London has declined, these banks continue to be the main players in international off-balance-sheet activities, such as foreign exchange dealing and swaps. The other main source of growth of international banks based in London is other European banks.

The dominance of London in international banking is reflected in the fact that, at the end of 1993, 521 foreign banks were established in London. This compared with 340 in New York, 170 in France and 150 in Germany. By the end of 2001 the number of foreign banks in London had increased to 570, making the total number of authorised banks in the UK 664. This included 98 banks from the European Economic Area.

7.2.3 *Foreign exchange*

The London foreign exchange market is the largest in the world. This was confirmed in the 2001 survey by the Bank for International Settlements (2002). London accounted for 31 per cent of global foreign exchange business, with New York, the next largest centre, accounting for 16 per cent of business. More than half of foreign exchange business done in European countries is done in London. Average net daily turnover in London is 6 times greater than that in Frankfurt and 11 times that in Paris.

7.2.4 *Equities*

Whilst it is only the third largest equity market (after New York and Tokyo), London's importance as an international centre for equity dealing is shown by the fact that there are more foreign companies listed on the London Stock Exchange (LSE) and turnover in foreign company equities is larger than on any other world equity market. In 2002, 48 per cent of all cross-border equity trading carried out on national exchanges was done through the LSE.

7.2.5 *International bonds*

Given its importance in international banking business and foreign exchange dealing, it is not surprising that London is one of the major centres for dealing in eurocurrencies and eurobonds (discussed in chapter 12). An indication of London's dominance of the secondary trading of eurobonds is given by the fact that estimates for 2001 suggest that London accounts for 60 per cent of primary eurobond syndication and 75 per cent of secondary market trading.

7.2.6 *Fund management*

In 1999 London managed the largest volume of funds in terms of institutional equity holdings ($2,461 billion). This compares with figures of $2,363 billion and $2,058 billion for New York and Tokyo, respectively. The next largest European centre was Paris, with $458 billion in equities under management. Edinburgh was ranked as the fifteenth largest fund management centre, with institutional equity holdings of $253 billion (International Financial Services 2002).

7.2.7 *Commodity markets*

A number of commodity markets operate in London. These include various metals at the London Metal Exchange, the London gold bullion market and various energy commodities at the International Petroleum Exchange. Although these markets operate for spot transactions, they are similar to financial markets in as much as they engage in derivative transactions such as futures and options (see chapter 13 for a discussion of the financial derivatives markets).

7.2.8 *Insurance markets*

The UK insurance industry ranks third in the world after the US and Japan, with gross insurance premiums in 2000 estimated at $237 billion, $865 billion and $504 billion, respectively. The London market itself consists of insurance and reinsurance companies, Lloyds, and protection and indemnity clubs and brokers, and is, in fact, the main international centre for reinsurance business. Gross premiums on the London market were conservatively estimated at around £18 billion (International Financial Services 2002). The sources of the premium income were roughly 48 per cent each for insurance companies and Lloyds and 4 per cent for protection and indemnity concerns.

7.2.9 *Reasons for London's importance*

The emergence of London as an international financial centre can be explained with reference to a number of factors. The first is the time zone factor: London occupies a position mid-way between the western and eastern time zones, which allows financial trading to take place 24 hours a day, with business switching between the three major financial centres of New York, Tokyo and London. However, this does not explain why London rather than another European centre developed.

London has a long tradition of international business, arising from the development of the Empire and the accompanying international trade. International financial institutions have been attracted to London because of the existence of a number of features. These include a suitable pool of experienced and skilled labour, relatively light restrictions on access to financial markets, a tax regime which is not hostile to financial innovation, the absence of exchange controls since 1979, relatively light reserve requirements, a stable political regime and the English language. This last factor is an important consideration for US institutions setting up a European base. A more detailed discussion is provided by Davis and Latter (1989) and Davis (1990), with the latter paper examining the development of international financial centres from a more theoretical perspective.

The growing concentration of financial firms in London due to these factors will have attracted to London new firms, which are likely to have

been the more innovative financial institutions, at the forefront of the development of new instruments and techniques. This in turn will have reinforced the importance of London as a financial centre. In addition the concentration of a large number of firms in one area will have led to economies of scale and also greater liquidity, as well as the development of specialised and skilled support services such as accounting, legal and information technology services. These will, in turn, reinforce London's position as an international financial centre.

The importance of financial services to the UK economy was noted in chapter 2 (table 2.2). The UK's finance, banking, insurance and financial auxiliary services accounted for 5.3 per cent of gross domestic product (GDP) and roughly 4 per cent of employment in 2001. Using a wider definition, which includes financial, business and professional services, such as accountancy, consultancy, computing and legal services, the contribution is 26 per cent of GDP and 17 per cent of total employment. In 2001, the UK financial sector was the largest net contributor to the UK's balance of payments current account, with net overseas earnings exceeding £14 billion.

All the markets mentioned above are both global and 'wholesale' markets and deal only in large-value transactions between both domestic and foreign institutions. The retail markets are linked to these markets via banks and other financial institutions. Thus, for example, a private individual buying foreign currency for a holiday would go along to a high street bank, which would have obtained the currency originally on the London foreign exchange market. The markets are also organised, in the sense that trading there requires operators to conform to rules specified within a 'rule book' and/or those imposed by the supervisory authority. These markets, together with the financial institutions which use the markets, are known colloquially as 'the City'. In the next section we examine in more detail the nature of markets.

7.3 The nature of markets

In the past, it was easy to define a market according to the geographical location where deals were made; for example, a stock exchange was a building where interested traders could meet and strike bargains. In many cases the growth of screen-based information systems has changed all this. This has removed the need to meet fellow traders and deals can be made over the telephone or on the screen itself. Up to now this has not been true of all markets since, for example, the largest financial futures exchanges have tended to maintain the 'open outcry' system of trading, although this is now changing, as discussed below. This raises the question of how to define an organised market, since asset prices are now publicly available via the payment of a subscription to an information system (the pricing function is said to be 'transparent'). Three core functions can be identified:

(i) There is the price discovery system, whereby demand for and supply of the particular asset are brought together to determine the equilibrium price. The trading rules of the market determine how this function is to be carried out.
(ii) There is the surveillance function, through which the public can be guaranteed as far as possible that any deal is fair. The market is, in effect, giving its stamp of approval. This latter function is also ensured through the trading rules by such means as regulations concerning disclosure, settlement and so on.
(iii) An organised market provides either a meeting place where, or a network through which, interested parties can be brought into contact with each other.

The problem for the organised market is that these functions are in the nature of public goods. Consequently there is little to stop individuals extracting the information and dealing on their own account (i.e. 'piggy-backing').

Markets can be characterised in a number of ways. First, a distinction can be drawn between continuous and batch markets. In a continuous market, as the name suggests, buyers and sellers are in continuous contact with each other throughout the period the market is open and deals can be concluded at any time. On the other hand, in a batch market, orders for purchases and sales are accumulated and are executed together at particular times.

A second distinction can be made between auction and dealers' markets (sometimes these two market types are called 'order-driven' and 'quote-driven' markets, respectively). Futures markets are examples of auction markets, where either an 'open outcry' or electronic trading system is used for dealers to strike individual bargains between each other. Open outcry is characterised by the presence of traders in close physical proximity, in a trading pit, who must verbally or otherwise publicly announce their bids and offers. To execute a trade, a trader must establish eye contact with the trader bidding or offering and say 'sold'. At any given time only the best bid and offer price are valid for execution. Another feature of the open outcry system is the presence of a type of trader known as a local. Local traders are members of the exchange but have limited capital compared with the institutional members. Locals will trade primarily for their own personal account and generally trade by taking small, short-horizon (e.g. seconds or minutes) positions. The role of locals is important in this type of market and this is reflected in the fact that they generally account for more than 50 per cent of total trading volume in the market. The existence of locals means that customer orders arriving in a trading pit usually find a two-sided market that can accommodate their trades immediately. Thus, locals provide liquidity in the market.

In the case of the dealers' markets, market makers exist and they guarantee to operate throughout the time the market is open. They publicise two prices for an asset throughout the market. The first is known as the 'bid' price and refers to the price at which the market maker is prepared to buy the asset. The second and higher price is termed the 'ask' price and is the price at which the market maker is prepared to sell the relevant asset. The gap between the two prices is known as the 'bid–ask spread' (or more simply the 'spread') and provides funds to meet the market maker's operating costs and the provision of profits. Normally there is some slight variation between quotes by different market makers and the spread between the highest bid price and the lowest ask price is termed the 'market touch'. This provides an indication of the liquidity of the market. A market is said to be 'tight' if prices are close to the true market value for small transactions and 'deep' if this applies to large transactions. Thus, for example, a market for which the bid–ask spread is small for large and medium transactions but widens substantially for small transactions would be said to be deep but not tight.

A final attribute of a market is termed 'immediacy', which is the speed with which a proposed transaction can be completed. In the case of continuous dealers' markets, immediacy is present provided the dealers do not suspend trading for any reason.

7.3.1 *Electronic trading*

A growing number of stock and futures exchanges use electronic trading systems. In this section we compare the main features of electronic trading with more traditional trading systems and identify some of the reasons for the trend towards adopting electronic trading.

The LSE in October 1997 introduced an electronic order book system (the Stock Exchange Automatic Trading System, SETS – see section 8.4.5) for trading in shares making up the FTSE 100. The 'old' quote-driven trading system of deals struck with market makers over the telephone has continued alongside electronic trading, but during 2002 the average SETS order book market share was 61.6 per cent and the highest daily share was 72 per cent (on 23 September 2002) (London Stock Exchange 2002). There are currently over 200 stocks traded on SETS.

Most exchanges have moved from the open outcry system to electronic trading. In the futures markets this includes Euronext.liffe. The daily level of electronic trading at the Chicago Mercantile Exchange doubled over the period September 2001 to June 2002 (*Financial Times*, 17 June 2002). On the foreign exchange market electronic trading now accounts for between 50 and 70 per cent of trades between major currency pairs (*BIS Quarterly Review*, December 2001). Similarly, electronic brokerage transactions as a percentage of total transactions for the major developed nations ranged

from 22 per cent for Australia to 56 per cent for the US (Bank for International Settlements 2001). So the question posed by these developments is, what is motivating this move by exchanges to adopt electronic trading platforms?

An electronic matching system is made up of a set of computer terminals connected via high-speed communication links to a central host computer. Bids and offers are entered into a remote terminal and sent to the host computer, which queues them according to price and for bids/offers at the same price, according to time received by the host. Only the host computer has complete information on the market. A trader will see only the best bid or offer. All trades take place through the host, which automatically executes an order.

Open outcry systems used to be popular in some derivatives trading markets although, as noted above, most exchanges are now automated, and the few open outcry markets remaining provide for automated trading outside normal trading hours.

A number of studies, for example those by Massimb and Phelps (1993) and Sarkar and Tozzi (1998), have examined the relative merits of open outcry and electronic matching systems. There are two important measures of a trading system's effectiveness: liquidity and cost. The general result from these studies is that electronic matching improves the operational efficiency of the market in terms of customer order delivery, accurate record keeping and so on, and operates at a lower cost, as evidenced by a narrower spread between bid and offer rates. As an example, the German Futures Exchange (Deutsche Terminbörse, DTB – now part of Eurex) and LIFFE both traded the Bund futures contract (a contract on the German government bond) but the DTB used an electronic trading system and LIFFE at the time was open outcry. In 1997 the cost of a round trip for the Bund (i.e. the buying and selling of one contract) on the DTB was $0.66 compared with $1.50 on LIFFE. However, the open outcry market has a number of advantages; in particular, it offers greater liquidity. High liquidity is important when executing large or complex orders, where it is important that the trade has minimal impact on the price. As noted above, locals supply liquidity on open outcry markets. The existence of locals is partly dependent on their ability to observe other traders in the marketplace. This allows a trader to identify when another trader has a large buy or sell position and thus infer the future trading behaviour of that trader. This is not possible using electronic trading systems. However, a further advantage of electronic trading is the ability to have remote trading. It is possible for a trader with an appropriate connection to the host computer to be located anywhere, even in another country. The DTB was particularly successful in promoting remote trading and by November 1997, 65 of its 171 members were remote traders.

So there are advantages with both electronic trading and floor trading. As noted above, the trend is towards electronic trading, which suggests that cost advantages and the ability to have remote trading outweigh the disadvantages of this type of system. As electronic trading systems become more sophisticated it is likely that some of the disadvantages of current systems can be overcome. Nevertheless, dangers with electronic trading arise from human error. Once a trade is entered into the system, it is not possible to cancel it. It is rumoured that there was such an error during 2002 when one trader erroneously entered a large trade twice (or even three times) into the bank's dealing system, which gave the bank concerned a loss of £100 million in two minutes (*Guardian*, 21 September 2002).

Financial markets provide opportunities for many different types of activity and we now consider three specialist activities, namely hedging, speculation and arbitrage.

7.4 **Hedging, speculation and arbitrage**

These techniques originally developed in the commodity markets and we shall use a hypothetical example of the sale/purchase of grain in the following discussion to illustrate their role.

The term 'hedging' refers to the purchase of a financial instrument or portfolio of instruments in order to insure against a possible reduction in wealth caused by unforeseen economic fluctuations. For example, a producer of grain may wish to hedge against a fall in the price of grain over some future period. One method of achieving such a hedge is to find a party who wishes to hedge against the opposite risk, that of a price rise. One example of such a person would be a bread producer who wishes to avoid a rise in price of future purchases of grain. The two parties can then agree on the price of grain for future delivery and this removes the risk of adverse price changes for both parties. This type of transaction would take place in a futures market, where trade is highly organised. Such markets exist for all major commodities traded and for many financial assets, including foreign currency, short-term deposits, bonds and equities. At this stage it is worth emphasising that both traders have gained certainty of price rather than made a profit. For example, if the price of grain does fall the purchaser has foregone profits which would have been obtained if he or she had deferred purchasing grain until later. The converse would apply in the case of a price rise.

A second hedging possibility for the grain producer is to transfer the risk to a party who is less risk averse than the hedger. Such a party is a speculator who would purchase (or sell goods) for later resale (or purchase) in the hope of profiting from any intervening price changes. In this example, the speculator would purchase the grain at a set price for delivery in the

future (the 'futures' price) in the expectation that the market price at that time (the future 'spot' price) would have risen above the purchase price. If speculators make accurate forecasts they improve the efficiency of markets. They buy when prices are perceived to be low and sell when prices are perceived to be high, thus evening out price fluctuations. However, inexpert speculators (and in some instances rational speculators) can destabilise markets – for further discussion see Newberry (1989). Speculative activity is prevalent in all the major commodity and financial markets.

An arbitrage opportunity is an investment strategy that, in a particular situation, guarantees a positive pay-off with no possibility of a negative pay-off occurring. Thus, arbitrage takes advantage of price or yield differentials in different markets (geographically or over time) in a riskless transaction. A simple example of an arbitrage transaction would be to borrow at one rate and lend at a higher fixed rate of interest when there was virtually no risk of default. Given the growth of information technology such differentials would not be expected to exist for any significant period of time, since the action of arbitrageurs serves to eliminate them.

7.5 **The efficient markets hypothesis**

At this stage it is also useful to examine in general terms the nature of the term 'efficiency' as applied to markets. Efficiency can take three meanings: operational efficiency, allocative efficiency and informational efficiency. The first type of efficiency is concerned with whether the market operates at the lowest level of cost or whether excessive resources are allocated to the operation of the market. In this connection it is likely that absence of price competition and the presence of cartels will lead to economic inefficiency. This was one of the motives behind the drive to liberalise financial markets. The second facet refers to the role of the market in the allocation of resources. The third aspect deals with the question of whether market prices reflect all available information. The 'efficient markets hypothesis' is restricted to this narrow and technical meaning of the term efficiency but it is worth noting that it would be difficult to conceive how allocative efficiency is possible if informational efficiency is not present.

If market efficiency is present anywhere, it is likely to be in the context of some financial markets. This is so for a number of reasons. First, financial assets are akin to durable assets in the sense that they are not purchased for immediate consumption. In fact, as we noted in chapter 1, they are purchased because of both the running yield or return they offer and, probably what is more important, the expectation of a capital gain, which may occur due to price change. Second, continuous trading is a feature of financial markets and in many cases this is international rather than just national continuous trading. Consequently prices are free to move to eliminate any imbalance

between demand and supply. It may be expected that, given these two features, dealing between sophisticated traders would force financial asset prices to reflect all available information. There will be clearly some dispersion in the interpretation of information but, on average, the market will arrive at the 'correct' view.

The idea of market efficiency embodies two components: first, the belief that an equilibrium market price exists; second, the actual observed market price of the asset will adjust to this equilibrium price quickly. Two predictions follow from these observations:

(i) prices will alter only if new information is received on the market – this is technically known as 'news';
(ii) since all information within the designated information set is reflected in the price, all knowable above-normal profits will have been eliminated by trading, or 'arbitrage' in the technical jargon.

The second prediction carries with it the belief that trying to outperform the market by forecasting is not worthwhile because the market price will contain an accurate prediction in the light of current conditions. The qualification concerning above-normal profits is particularly important. Trading on financial markets is risky and, unless it is assumed that operators are risk neutral or indifferent to the degree of risk, it is natural to assume that a relatively high level of profit is necessary to induce them to enter the market. However, it is very difficult to quantify a precise numerical value for this element of profit necessary to compensate for the high degree of risk (or 'risk premium' as it is called in the literature), so that the 'efficiency' of the financial markets is still a controversial issue.

A formal definition of the 'efficient markets hypothesis' is that a specific market may be termed efficient if the prices of the assets traded on that market instantaneously reflect all available information. Fama (1970) neatly defines three types of empirical test of market efficiency defined according to the extent of the information set available:

(i) *Weak efficiency*. In this category the asset price is tested to see whether it reflects fully the information concerned in the history of both the price and volume of trading of that asset.
(ii) *Semi-strong efficiency*. In this instance the asset price is required to reflect fully all publicly available information; the information set here would include all reports and statistics available in the media.
(iii) *Strong efficiency*. This embodies the requirement that the asset price should reflect all information, whether publicly available or not; this category would include all privileged (inside) information.

In a further article, Fama (1991) modified the categories of efficiency tests. Instead of tests of weak efficiency, he used the title 'test for return

predictability'. This would include not only tests based on the past performance of the variable but also tests based on any form of forecasting and as such includes some tests previously included under the heading of semi-strong tests. For the second category, Fama proposes the title 'event studies' and for the third category 'tests for private information'. This categorisation seems more suitable for some markets (e.g. stock exchanges) than others (e.g. foreign exchanges) because of the extensive use in studies of those markets of both pricing models to forecast stock prices and dividends and the effect of events such as stock splits, dividends and exchange listing on the value of a firm. Clearly, these categories are interdependent. Thus, a market which is strongly efficient must also satisfy the semi-strong and weak tests. Similarly, a market which satisfies the semi-strong test must also satisfy the weak test. It is unlikely that any market will fully satisfy the requirements of efficiency on all occasions but, conversely, it is difficult to conceive of a market which is perfectly inefficient – that is, a market in which asset prices never reflect any available information! Consequently the important question is whether markets approximate efficiency for all practical purposes.

Empirical testing of the efficient markets hypothesis is fraught with problems. Normally at least two hypotheses coexist in any such test: first, that expectations are formed in the manner prescribed in the particular test and are used to arrive at the information set; and second, that the market uses these expectations in an efficient way in the price-setting process. Thus, failure to find support for the efficient markets hypothesis may be due to failure of either (or both) of the sub-hypotheses. This is referred to as the dual hypothesis problem. A further difficulty arises because we observe price data at discrete periods, generally at the end of the day, which is the trading price reported most often in the media. The assumption underlying most empirical work is that the process of arbitrage has been completed during the trading period, so that the end-of-trading price reflects all the information in the prescribed test.

7.6 **Behavioural finance**

One of the main predictions of the efficient markets hypothesis is that security prices reflect their fundamental value (i.e. the equilibrium value reflects all available information). An alternative view of financial markets has emerged in recent years known as behavioural finance. This view is not represented by a single theory but is a collection of insights or concepts, drawn from the findings of psychological studies. Proponents of behavioural finance – see Shleifer (2001) or Barberis and Thaler (2001) for surveys – argue that investors can make systematic errors in forecasts and these errors can move security prices away from their fundamental value for extended

periods of time. The very rapid rise in US equity prices in the late 1990s (discussed in chapter 8) has led many observers to question whether people behave rationally and whether markets are efficient.

For example, it is argued that many investors are overconfident and attribute successes to their own insights but errors are put down to bad luck. Overconfident investors will tend to attribute successes in rising markets to their own abilities and therefore trade more, thus reinforcing the upward trend. When markets fall this reduces confidence and hence investment, thus reinforcing the fall. This is consistent with the argument that markets exhibit overreaction. Conservatism can lead to the reluctance on the part of investors to change an opinion when new information comes along. This can lead to long delays in security prices adjusting to a new equilibrium. 'Representativeness' leads investors to detect patterns in financial data that are in fact random. If prices have been rising in the past then this will be extrapolated into a prediction of rising prices in the future. However, those prices may have been random events and will not be repeated. 'Narrow framing' refers to the tendency of investors to focus too narrowly. For example, investors saving for retirement, with a long investment horizon, may tend to focus on short-term gains or losses in the assets they hold. A consequence of narrow focusing is for investors to overestimate risk. This is especially true if investors place more weight on losses than on gains (prospect theory suggests that investors weigh prospective losses about twice as heavily as prospective gains). This is because narrow focusing leads to greater focus on losses, as these occur more frequently over shorter periods than longer periods. This overestimation of risk leads investors to allocate less of their investment funds to equities and may partly explain the so-called 'equity-premium puzzle'. This refers to the question of why excess returns to equities over less risky assets such as bonds have been so high historically. Now, investors in equities do require additional returns to compensate them for extra risk but it is thought that the extra return earned has been greater than that justified by the extra risk. However, if investors are narrowly focused then they will require very high excess returns to make investment in equities acceptable.

Returning to prospect theory, this was first proposed by Kahneman and Tversky (e.g. Kahneman and Tversky 1979) and Kahneman received the Nobel prize in economics in 2002 for his work in this area. They argued that people are risk averse when it comes to gains but risk seeking when it comes to losses. For example, when given a choice between getting £1,000 with certainty or having a 50 per cent chance of getting £2,500 they may well choose the certain £1,000 in preference to the uncertain chance of getting £2,500, even though the mathematical expectation of the uncertain option is £1250. This is a perfectly reasonable attitude that is described as *risk aversion*. But Kahneman and Tversky found that the same people when

confronted with a certain loss of £1,000 versus a 50 per cent chance of no loss or a £2,500 loss do often choose the risky alternative. This is called *risk-seeking* behaviour. One of the main tenets of prospect theory is the endowment effect, which is that people place more value on things they already own. Various experiments have lent support to the endowment effect. In one famous experiment, university students were given either a coffee mug or a chocolate bar, each with the same market value. Before the experiment it was found that roughly half the students preferred each good. After the goods were randomly handed out the students could then trade to obtain their preferred good. However, barely 10 per cent of students traded (when you would expect 50 per cent to trade, given the random allocation of goods). This suggests that ownership had overwhelmed the students' prior tastes and supports the endowment effect. One implication of the endowment effect is that trading in financial markets may be lower than it otherwise might be and this may lead prices away from their equilibrium (as prices adjust to new information through trading).

These are just some of the biases which the behavioural finance literature suggests lead prices in financial markets to be inefficient. However, Fama (1998) cautions against a rejection of the efficient markets hypothesis, arguing that many of the anomalies found in empirical studies which challenge it, with careful measurement, can be shown to be chance results.

The plan for the following chapters on financial markets is as follows. In chapters 8 and 9 we discuss the equity and bond markets before proceeding in chapter 10 to examine the sterling money markets. In chapters 11 to 13 we examine the foreign exchange market, the international financial markets based in London and the traded options and financial futures market, respectively. In chapter 14 we finish this part of the book with a discussion of how these markets may be used to manage risk. Generally in each chapter we describe not only the institutional detail but also the extent to which the market concerned conforms to the efficient markets hypothesis.

Chapter 8

The market for equities

8.1 Introduction

The market for equities is part of the capital market, which refers to the market for long-term finance, as distinct from the money markets, which are markets for short-term funds. Clearly, this distinction is difficult to draw at the margin but the normal convention is to treat funds raised with an original maturity of greater than one year as capital funds. In principle the capital market can be divided into two segments: the primary market, where new capital is raised, and the secondary market, where existing securities are sold and bought. Again, this distinction is blurred since new capital can be raised via a stock exchange and existing securities can be sold on the same market. Furthermore, the existence of a secondary market is necessary to support the primary market since an essential prop to the market for long-term capital is the existence of a market where these long-term claims can be sold if the holder needs to obtain liquidity. A further distinction can be made between private sector finance and public sector finance. We can also distinguish between fixed-interest securities and equities. In this chapter we discuss the equity market and in chapter 9 the market for fixed-interest securities.

We begin by examining in section 8.2 some general issues relating to the raising of long-term finance by private firms. In section 8.3 we focus on the primary market for equity issues followed in section 8.4 by the secondary market, where equity securities are traded. We then examine in section 8.5 the nature of and causes of the global stock market crash of October 1987 and the more recent 'technology bubble' that led to global stock market falls from 2000. In section 8.6 we consider the degree to which stock markets conform to the efficient markets hypothesis. Our conclusions are presented in section 8.7.

8.2 The primary capital market

At the outset of this section it is worth examining the ways in which private firms can raise long-term finance. The main methods in recent years have been the following:

(i) internal funds;
(ii) long-term bank loans;
(iii) issues of equities;
(iv) issues of fixed-interest securities;
(v) finance from official sources.

An important source of finance for firms is the profits they have attained from trading but have not distributed to shareholders in the form of dividends. This is referred to as internal funds. All the other sources of capital in the list above are referred to as external sources of finance. We have discussed the nature of bank loans in chapters 1 and 2, so no further comment will be made in this section other than to draw the reader's attention to the importance of this source of finance. Equities are discussed below. Fixed-interest securities are referred to as bonds and the nature of the corporate bond market is discussed in chapter 9. Finally it is possible for firms to obtain government assistance, for example the award of investment grants in connection with the regional selective assistance policy of the UK government.

8.2.1 *Financing patterns of UK firms*

Figure 8.1 shows the pattern of finance raised by UK non-financial firms over the period 1970–2001. A few explanatory remarks concerning figure 8.1 are necessary. First, for some of the statistics, the categories pre-1987 are slightly different from those post-1987. However, this does not alter the overall trends. Second, the figures for the 1990s are averaged over the period 1990–2001. Internal funds are made up of income that has not been distributed to shareholders. UK loans are principally bank loans. Corporate bonds are mainly debentures. Overseas funds are mainly loans from overseas banks and other types of inward investment.

Figure 8.1 illustrates the changes in the relative importance of the various components over time. Over the whole period the importance of internal funds as opposed to external funds is patently obvious, with approximately 50 per cent of total funds raised being generated from within companies. It is interesting to note though that the proportion of internal funds has shown a steady decline since the 1970s. Of the external funds raised, bank loans were the most important component over the 1970s and 1980s. However, in the early 1990s bank loans to companies declined as a proportion of total external funds as, for this period, the UK economy was in recession

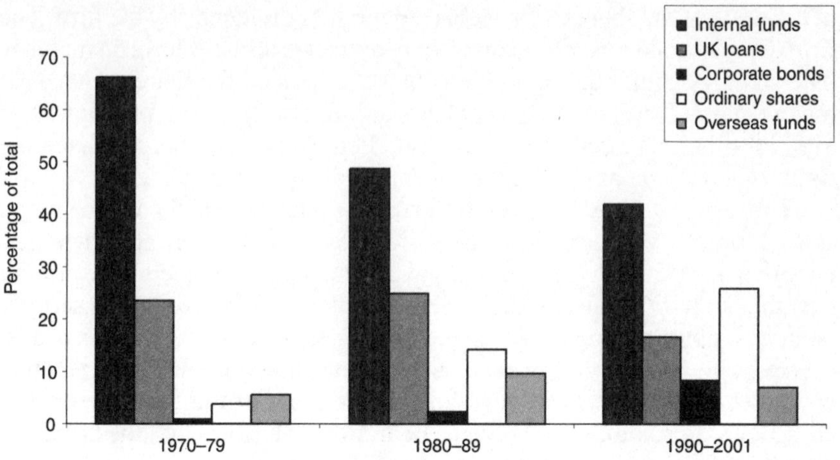

Figure 8.1 Sources of funds for private non-financial corporations, 1970–2001.

or just emerging from recession and companies were net repayers of bank loans. In the second half of the 1990s company borrowing increased again, which brought the overall share of bank loans, as a proportion of total capital raised over the 1990s, back to around 14 per cent.

Issues of ordinary shares as a proportion of total capital raised have shown a dramatic increase over the period, from around 4 per cent over the 1970s to 26 per cent over the 1990s as firms took advantage of rising equity markets (see figure 8.2). However, this figure includes shares issued to finance takeovers, so the additional or new corporate finance raised by firms through equity issues during this period was considerably smaller and was, in fact, negative during the period 1970 to 1985 (Mayer and Alexander 1990).

Capital raised through issues of bonds accounted for a very small proportion of externally raised capital until the end of the 1980s, owing no doubt to the high level of the rate of interest. As interest rates fell over the 1990s issues of bonds have shown a large increase. The overall trend, therefore, revealed by figure 8.1 is a greater use of external finance by firms since the 1970s, with greater use made of share and bond issues, particularly in the 1990s.

8.2.2 *Nature and valuation of equities*

An equity security refers, in the UK, to a share issued by a company (in the US an equity security is referred to as a stock). A share represents ownership in the firm that issued the security. A shareholder owns a percentage interest in the issuing firm. A shareholder can earn a return either through an increase

in the price of the share or through a payment of dividends by the firm. The firm though is under no obligation to pay dividends. Shares have no maturity date and they confer the right of residual claimant on the shareholder. That means that a shareholder has a claim on all assets and income left over after all other claimants have been satisfied. Most shareholders have the right to vote at the annual general meeting of the company.

There are two types of shares, ordinary or preference (in the US, common stock and preferred stock). The main differences between them are that preference shares receive a fixed dividend and preference shareholders have priority over the claims of ordinary shareholders, but after that of fixed-interest security holders. Finally, ordinary share issues far exceed issues of preference shares.

The value of an ordinary share can be determined in the same way that any asset is valued, that is, it is the present value of the future stream of cash flows received by the holder. The future cash flows that the holder of an ordinary share might receive are future dividends and the price the share will eventually sell for. The future price of the share, however, is itself the present value of the dividends that follow and a share price even further into the future. Taken to an extreme, the current price of a share is the simply the present value of the future dividend payments to infinity. Hence:

$$P_0 = \frac{D_1}{(1+i)} + \frac{D_2}{(1+i)^2} + \frac{D_3}{(1+i)^3} + \dots + \frac{D_\infty}{(1+i)^\infty} \tag{8.1}$$

where P_0 = price of share at time 0 (present); D_n = dividend paid at time n; i = discount rate.

Equation 8.1 provides us with an accurate measure of the price of an ordinary share; however, it is not a very useful method for computing the price as we do not know the future dividend payments. If we assume that dividends increase at a constant rate then equation 8.1 can be rewritten as:

$$P_0 = \frac{D_1}{(i-g)} \tag{8.2}$$

where P_0, i and D_1 are as before and g is the expected constant dividend growth rate. Equation 8.2 is known as the Gordon growth model and it is appropriate to use this for valuing an ordinary share when dividends are expected to follow a constant growth pattern in the future.

For example, suppose that you want to estimate the price of a share where the next dividend payment is expected to be £0.50 per share, the discount rate is estimated to be 10 per cent and dividends are expected to grow at a rate of 5 per cent per year. Applying the Gordon growth model, we find:

$$P_0 = £0.50 / (0.10 - 0.05) = £10.00$$

Thus the share should sell for £10.

8.3 The primary market for private sector securities

New issues of private sector securities, which include ordinary shares, preference shares and debentures, can be made by firms whose securities are already quoted on the London Stock Exchange (LSE) or by those companies seeking a listing on it. In this latter case companies must meet a list of requirements concerning financial status and past trading record. The main requirements are that companies must have a three-year trading record, the expected value of the shares after issue must exceed £700,000 and 25 per cent of the share capital must be held by the public. In March 2003 there were 2,367 UK companies listed on the LSE and the average capitalisation for a listed UK company was £451 million. The UK Listing Authority (UKLA) (part of the Financial Services Authority, FSA – see chapter 17) is the competent authority for listing in the UK and has the responsibility for overseeing the listing process and ensuring that the Listing Rules are met. In parallel to the UKLA's listing process, a firm must also apply to the LSE to have its securities admitted to trading on its markets. After admission to the LSE, a company must comply with the continuing obligations. These set out rules regarding the conduct of listed firms, in particular rules relating to the disclosure of information to the market.

Companies that want access to the stock market but do not meet the requirements for an official listing can join the Alternative Investment Market (AIM), which opened on 19 June 1995. AIM replaced the Unlisted Stock Market and there are no restrictions on entry relating to length of trading period or size of company. A nominated adviser, who is approved by the LSE, is responsible for deciding whether a company is suitable for the market. A nominated adviser is usually a bank or stockbroker. The adviser is also responsible for ensuring that the firm's affairs are in order and that its documentation has been adequately prepared. The applicant will also be required to find a minimum of one market maker prepared to deal in its shares. Similar to the requirements for inclusion in the official list, the applicant will be required to provide price-sensitive information to the market (including unaudited interim accounts), which will be disseminated in the normal manner. The purpose of the new market is to facilitate the raising of finance by small companies whilst still maintaining a satisfactory degree of investor protection. The number of companies listed on AIM in June 2003 was 651 UK companies and 51 international companies. Since the launch of AIM around $9 billion of new equity finance has been raised for smaller companies.

Every new issue will involve a sponsor, whose main role is to assess the company's suitability for a listing and prepare the company for it. The sponsor may be an investment bank or stockbroker. Where an investment bank is appointed as sponsor the firm may need to appoint a stockbroker as

well, which, in these days of financial conglomerates, may be part of the same company. The broker's responsibility is to advise on the timing and pricing of the issue. The investment bank/broker may act as a principal by buying the shares from the company and then disposing of them on its own account, or it may act as an agent. Even in the latter case, some risk is involved since the bank/broker normally provides a guarantee that a specified sum will be raised. In order to spread this risk of a failure to sell the whole issue to the public, the bank/broker will normally arrange for the issue to be 'underwritten'. This involves an institution guaranteeing that the whole issue will be sold at the price indicated. If the issue is taken up by the public the underwriter has no further liability. If, on the other hand, only part of the issue is sold to the public (i.e. is 'partly subscribed'), the underwriter will purchase the remainder of the issue itself. In return for this service the underwriter will obtain a commission on the issue in the region of 1 to 2 per cent of the capital raised. In the case of rights issues (i.e. of further shares in a listed company – see below), the new shares are generally offered to existing shareholders at a discount of around 15 per cent of the market price and the charge for underwriting appears, for the last 30 years or so, to have been fixed at 2 per cent irrespective of the quality of the issuer and has, therefore, attracted the attention of the Office of Fair Trading (OFT). The OFT investigated the underwriting of equity issues on two occasions, in 1995 and 1996, and found little evidence of competition in underwriting or a willingness of companies to use deep discounted issues to avoid underwriting fees altogether. As a consequence the OFT referred the matter to the Monopolies and Mergers Commission (now the Competition Commission) in November 1997. The Commission found a complex monopoly existed and recommended that this was counteracted by greater disclosure and explanation by companies of methods used. The main underwriters of new issues are the long-term investment institutions, that is, the insurance companies, the pension funds and investment trusts.

The main methods for new issues are the following:

(i) *Placings*. The issuing house purchases the securities from the issuer and places the shares with investors. Normal prudence dictates that the major proportion of these placings will be re-placed with further investors, who are generally the long-term investment institutions.
(ii) *Offers for sale by tender.* In this case the public is invited to purchase shares at any price over a publicised minimum. A single so-called 'striking price' is established at which it is believed the issue will be fully subscribed and all tenders at that or a higher price will receive an allotment at this striking price irrespective of whether the tender was at a higher price or not. This system of allocation is called a 'common price tender'.

(iii) *Offers for sale.* Here the issuing house purchases the whole issue at a specified price and then offers the issue for sale to the general public.
(iv) *Offers for sale by subscription.* This method is a variation of (iii), whereby the company rather than the issuing house offers the shares to the public.

For companies whose shares are already quoted on the LSE, further issues of equity are made by means of a 'rights issue' (i.e. a secondary issue). Existing shareholders have the right to purchase additional shares in proportion to their existing holdings at a fixed price. The price is normally at a discount to that currently quoted on the LSE so that the issuing price is unlikely to be higher than the price quoted on the LSE at the time of the issue due to price fluctuations. The shareholder does not have to take up the rights issue and may, in fact, sell the right. If it so wishes, the issuing company may avoid the need for the issue to be underwritten by making the rights at a large discount compared with the current market price (at a 'deep' discount) so as to make the offer attractive. Such rights issues must be approved by the shareholders and protection for existing shareholders against dilution of their holdings is afforded by the Companies Act 1985 and LSE rules. These are termed pre-emption requirements. A company can put forward a special resolution not to apply pre-emption rights, called a 'disapplication of pre-emption rights'. Shareholders must vote in favour for this to take effect. Other methods of raising equity finance, in particular a placing, are now more common for secondary issues, as funds are more speedily obtained than for rights issues. However, shareholders must give approval for this at the company's annual general meeting. The LSE followed this path mainly because it wished to reduce the possibility that new member firms would bypass the London market and issue securities through other world capital markets.

The method of issue adopted by an individual firm will depend on the costs involved relative to the total funds being raised. These costs include administrative expenses, advertising and, in the case of an issue by a company new to the LSE, any discount on the nominal price of the share. Placing is generally the cheapest method as there is no need for widespread advertising. As a consequence the placing is the most frequently used method of obtaining a listing. The main disadvantage with a placing is that the resulting shareholder spread is more limited.

8.4 The secondary market for private securities

The LSE, as well as being the market for primary private sector capital issues, is also the market for secondary trading of both private sector securities and public sector debt (gilt-edged securities – discussed in more

detail in chapter 9). In terms of turnover, trading in gilt-edged securities is the main component, although this declined over the 1980s and early 1990s. However, whilst the percentage of turnover attributable to gilt trading is higher than that for equities and debentures, the number of trades (bargains) is lower for gilts. This implies that the average size of order is much larger for gilts than equities.

In chapter 7 we saw that London is an international financial centre and the LSE reflects this. Table 8.1 shows that London is the fourth largest stock market in the world in terms of the market value of domestic equity and third largest in terms of domestic turnover. It is the largest exchange in Europe by market value. It is also, by far, the largest stock market in the world in terms of total turnover (net profit) of the foreign companies listed on it.

Table 8.1 Comparison of major world stock exchanges at end 2002

Exchange	Market value of domestic equity ($billion)	Number of companies		Turnover in 2002 ($billion)	
		Domestic	Foreign	Domestic	Foreign
New York	9,015	1,894	472	9,410	702
NASDAQ[a]	1,994	3,268	381	7,000	252
Tokyo	2,095	2,119	34	1,551	0.5
London	1,801	2,405	419	1,881	2,100
Euronext[b]	1,539	1,114	371	1,956	18
Duetsche Borse	686	715	219	1,110	101
Toronto	570	1,252	35	397	0.2
Switzerland	547	258	140	584	9.8

[a] National Association of Securities Dealers' automated quotation system.
[b] Formed on 22 September 2000 when the exchanges of Amsterdam, Brussels and Paris merged. The Euronext group expanded at the beginning of 2002 with the acquisition of LIFFE (London International Financial Futures and Options Exchange) and the merger with the Portuguese exchange BVLP (Bolsa de Valores de Lisboa e Porto).

Source: World Federation of Exchanges.

8.4.1 *Changes in trading arrangements: Big Bang*

The arrangements at the LSE were subject to a fundamental change on 27 October 1986, the so-called 'Big Bang'. Prior to this date the LSE was subject to a number of restrictive practices. Three in particular were important. First, there was single capacity, since the market makers in shares, termed jobbers, were able to deal only on their own account. All contact with the jobbers was to be conducted via stockbrokers, who, in turn, were unable to deal in shares. In other words, stockbrokers were purely agents

acting as intermediaries between the ultimate customer and the jobber. Second, a cartel arrangement applied whereby minimum commissions were fixed for all trades, irrespective of size. Third, ownership of brokers and jobbers was restricted to private partnerships until 1969. In that year brokers and jobbers were permitted to form public limited companies and further relaxation occurred in 1971 when corporate members could be owned by organisations that were not part of the stock exchange (termed 'outside members'), albeit subject to the severe restraint that no one shareholder could hold more than 10 per cent of the capital of a single firm. Economic theory predicts that cartels have the effect of raising members' income and consequently it is certain that the minimum commission arrangement raised dealing costs. On the other hand, it was suggested that it protected the interest of the public since there was no conflict of interest because the market makers could not deal directly with the public and brokers could not deal in shares. Thus, each party had no motive to act against the interests of the public.

There were two separate motives for change. First, after 1979, the Conservative government was interested in increasing the degree of competition throughout the economy. This resulted in a referral of the LSE rule book to the Restrictive Trade Practices Court in 1979. Second, the LSE was losing business following the abolition of controls on movements of capital for UK residents in 1979. Share dealings have become dominated to an increasing extent by the institutions. These are the agents most likely to suffer from minimum prices since their deals would be of a large size. A significant development at this time was the growth of American deposit receipts (ADRs). US financial institutions purchased blocks of shares in UK companies and then issued titles to the underlying shares which were traded on the New York Stock Exchange. Costs of trading were lower in New York, which had experienced its equivalent to Big Bang ('May Day') in 1975. Consequently, large dealings in UK shares tended to move to New York at the expense of London.

Agreement was reached in 1983 between the LSE and the government which led to the dropping of the referral to the Court. Three important components of the agreement were:

(i) the abolition of minimum commissions;
(ii) the permission of dual capacity;
(iii) relaxation of the rules of outside ownership.

With regard to point (ii), there is now a single form of institution called a broker-dealer, which can operate either on its own account or as an agent for another institution or person. Within this category there is a subset that are registered to act as market makers or dealers. These market makers may specialise in a particular group of shares. Restraints operate where

broker-dealers that are not market makers are acting as an agent, inasmuch as they can deal on their own account or match an order with another client only if they can show that they can execute the order at a superior price than by going to a market maker. Similarly, market makers can act as an agent only if they can deal at a price at least as good as that which could be obtained from another market maker.

The three components of the agreement were closely interconnected. Abolition of minimum commissions would place the income of brokers under great pressure, so that they would be likely to seek alternative sources of income. One such source would be market making. Second, dealing is a high-risk industry and new sources of capital would be needed in view of the likely fall in incomes. Thus, outside interests were permitted to own 100 per cent of the share capital of single-member firms as from 1 March 1986. This led to a scramble to buy up firms and to form financial conglomerates.

Along with changes brought about by 'Big Bang', a screen information system, SEAQ, described below, was introduced, so that the old 'face-to-face' discussions between LSE members were quickly eliminated.

The most important effect of Big Bang was a reduction in the level of commissions (particularly for large orders). In February 1987 the *Bank of England Quarterly Bulletin* suggested that, for an equity deal in the region of £10,000 to £1 million, commission rates fell from 0.4 per cent to 0.2 per cent. Larger falls were reported for larger deals, with the largest fall being obtained in deals carried out by the institutions, which now conduct a large part of their business net of commission.

8.4.2 *Pre- and post-trade transparency*

Price information on equities is distributed through the Stock Exchange Automated Quotations System (SEAQ), which supports two market segments, domestic and international. Quoted prices are indicated to the market via an information service provider such as Reuters. Shares are allocated to bands according to their 'normal market size' (NMS), based on market turnover. A well informed equity market requires public disclosure of information relevant to the pricing of shares. This information includes such items as price quotations, prices at which deals are made, and trade volumes, in addition to general macroeconomic information and specific information relating to individual companies. The technical term for the presence of such information in the market is 'transparency'. Transparency can be subdivided into two categories, pre-trade and post-trade. Pre-trade transparency is provided by SEAQ price quotations and the requirement for companies to provide the market with relevant information. The requirement for post-trade transparency is met through the publication of details of the prices at which deals have been made. Deals for all shares with a NMS greater than 2,000 shares must be reported to the system within

three minutes of the trade taking place, provided the transaction is less than six times the NMS of that share. A delay of 60 minutes is allowed before reporting in the case of deals greater than six times the NMS of that share. A third reporting class occurs in the case of 'block deals' between market makers. These are defined as trades greater than 75 times the NMS of that share. In this case notification must be carried out after five days or after the market maker has offset 90 per cent of the trade (whichever is the earlier). Note that the LSE monitors closely the unwinding of the block trade. All 'agency crosses' (in-house deals) must be reported, irrespective of the NMS of the equity concerned. A further example of the lack of transparency concerns the permission granted to market makers to avoid disclosure of the quantity of any given stock owned by them. Normally, disclosure is required by an investor who owns more than 3 per cent of the total shares in one company.

The justification of the delay in reporting large trades is based on the view that details concerning the large trades provide competitors with information on which to base their strategies. Thus, for example, knowledge that there was a large seller in the market following a block trade may lead to a fall in prices and hence losses for the market maker.

The LSE also operates a screen-based market for shares which is restricted to market makers; this is termed the inter-dealer broker (IDB) market. Transactions for this market executed on IDB screens are also disclosed.

The analogous system for leading international stocks which are traded by international market makers operating in London is the SEAQ International. Reporting of transactions are less onerous in this market, which, given the degree of international competition, seems reasonable.

Illiquid stocks have presented a problem to the LSE since the fall in trading volume consequent upon the 1987 stock market crash. 'The bottom 50% of listed stocks (about 1200 issues) represent just 1.2% of LSE turnover' (Securities and Investments Board 1994). This makes it difficult to devise a trading structure which meets the needs of both the market makers and potential buyers and sellers, and in particular the LSE's requirement for the existence of at least two market makers. The LSE has attempted to deal with this problem through the creation of the Stock Exchange Alternative Trading Service Plus (SEATS Plus). This is a combination of an order-driven system (see section 8.4.5 below) with competing quotes. The service therefore offers the execution advantages of an electronic order book with guaranteed liquidity supplied by market makers.

8.4.3 *Settlement*

Each day's transactions are settled three business days after the transactions take place (a so-called 'T + 3' rule). In addition a new settlement system,

CREST, was introduced in July 1996, replacing Talisman. This system was designed by the Bank of England following a failed attempt by the LSE to develop a paperless share transfer system, named Taurus. Ownership of CREST has been handed over to an independent company, Crestco. Under CREST, share transfers are carried out using an electronic book-entry system. This eliminates from share trading the need for paper certificates and should lead to a reduction in costs and an improvement in settlement arrangements. However, whilst the bulk of trades will not involve share certificates, some investors who rarely trade are permitted to retain the use of certificates.

8.4.4 *Competition*

Stock exchanges are subject to ever-increasing competition. There is a considerable degree of actual and potential competition with the LSE in dealing in both UK and foreign equities from such channels as:

(i) ADRs traded on US exchanges. US financial institutions purchase blocks of shares in UK companies and then issue titles to the underlying shares which are traded on the New York Stock Exchange and the National Association of Securities Dealers' Automated Quotations System (NASDAQ), an electronic securities exchange. Large investment institutions may choose to trade UK shares this way if there are cost advantages.

(ii) Over-the-counter (OTC) dealing in equities between institutions.

(iii) Equity and equity derivative indexes (both exchange traded and OTC). Futures and options contracts on LSE indexes, as well as options on individual shares, can be traded on Euronext.liffe (see chapter 13 for a full description of these instruments) as well as OTC. Trading equity derivatives allows investors to gain exposure to the equity market without actually trading on the LSE.

(iv) virt-x (formerly Tradepoint). This is an electronic order-matching exchange that permits both dealers and professional investors with an electronic link to trade the shares making up the FTSE 100 (as well as shares in many other large European companies). Virt-x is commercially operated and is a recognised investment exchange regulated by the FSA. Its turnover is a small percentage of the volume of the LSE and it is not a serious competitor at present.

(v) Other European exchanges. The LSE has been successful in attracting listings of foreign shares and for many years was able to attract business that would normally be transacted through overseas exchanges. Other European exchanges, in particular the French (now part of Euronext) and German bourses, have competed intensely with London since the 1990s to win back business.

8.4.5 *Change to electronic trading*

As discussed in section 8.4.1, the LSE, following Big Bang, was a continuous dealers' market that used screens to display prices but not for actual trading. Such a market is termed 'quote-driven' since market makers registered with the LSE indicate firm quotes for buying and selling specific securities up to a specific size. As we saw in chapter 7, the main alternative to a quote-driven market is an 'order-driven auction market'. The rules applying to auction markets are quite different from those applying to quote-driven markets. There is the complete absence of market makers indicating firm prices at which they are prepared to deal. In the case of order-driven markets, orders are executed on the basis of price and time. Consequently, orders at the best price will be executed first. The price is kept near the equilibrium price by a steady flow of orders. Deviations from the perceived equilibrium price will stimulate offsetting intervention by speculators. In recent years most of the major stock markets in Europe have moved over to electronic order-driven systems. To maintain its competitive position, the LSE moved to an order-driven system in October 1997 for the trading of shares making up the FTSE 100 index. The order-driven system is known as the Stock Exchange Automatic Trading System (SETS).

A broker will normally route an order to SETS and the order will be matched automatically by the system. Two types of order are possible: 'limit' and 'market fill' (or 'at best') orders. In the former case the deal takes place only at a price indicated as the limit. So, if there is a suitable matching order on the order book then the order is executed immediately. Otherwise the order will wait until suitable matching orders come along. In the latter (market fill) case the deal takes place at the best price displayed in the market at that time. So, a 'sell' order will be matched with the highest available buying price. Likewise, a 'buy' order would be matched with the lowest available selling price.

Not all orders for FTSE 100 shares will be executed through the order book. Large trades, which are defined as eight times the NMS, can be executed through a worked principal agreement, which occurs off the order book. Also, where an order is relatively small or will not be settled within the standard settlement period then it will not be channelled through the order book. Instead a broker will conduct the trade through a retail service provider (playing a similar role to a market maker). Retail service providers will still be required to execute the trade at the best price that would have been available had the trade been conducted through the order book.

So the LSE now operates a hybrid trading system. A large number of trades of FTSE 100 shares are routed through an electronic order book while trades in less liquid securities take place through a market maker system. The LSE plans to extend SETS trading to shares in the mid-250

index (shares in the 250 companies after the FTSE 100 index companies) although this will be backed by market maker quotes to provide liquidity.

8.5 **Recent global stock market corrections**

8.5.1 *The global stock market crash of October 1987*

There is no consensus concerning the reasons for the dramatic fall in stock market prices which began on Monday 19 October 1987 ('Black Monday') when the New York Stock Exchange suffered a drop of 22.6 per cent (its largest ever in a single day), which quickly spread to most exchanges around the world, including London. Four possible causes have been suggested.

First, there was uncertainty over the international payments situation. Recent years had seen persistent balance of payments disequilibria. The US and the UK had experienced large deficits, which had been matched by large surpluses obtained by Japan and Germany. At the same time corrective measures for the US federal budget deficit seemed to be proving inadequate. Perhaps the perception of the serious nature of these problems was enhanced by the continued problem of sovereign debt (see chapter 4). It could be argued therefore that bad US trade figures on the Thursday before the crash provided the trigger for the fall in stock prices. Two problems remain with this approach. First, the worldwide nature of the crash across a wide number of exchanges in different countries seems to be out of keeping with the weight of news. On the other hand, a look at the fundamentals suggests that share prices should be sensitive to changes in expectations. We have seen in section 8.2 that the value of a share can be calculated using the Gordon growth model – equation 8.2 is reproduced here, but note that we do not know the next dividend payment, so this is represented by the investor's expectation of the next dividend, E_tD_t, where E_t is the expectations operator:

$$\text{Current price} = \frac{E_tD_t}{(i-g)} \tag{8.2}$$

Note that equation 8.2 requires the discount rate (i) to be larger than the expected growth rate of dividends (g). If values of £0.30 for forecast of dividends and 8 per cent and 6 per cent for the discount rate and dividend growth rate, respectively, are assumed, then the share value will be £15. If the expected growth rate of dividends falls to 5 per cent, the price of each share falls to £10. This explanation would, therefore, require investors to revise downwards their expected rate of growth of dividends (or equivalently the forecast of dividends) or to revise upwards the required rate of discount in the light of uncertainty about future events due to the international financial problems. A difficulty with this approach is that survey evidence

in the US suggested that investors regarded the equity market as being overvalued before the crash. This evidence was, however, collected after the crash and may be tainted with wisdom after the event.

The second potential cause for the crash has been identified with 'speculative bubbles'. The basis of the belief in the existence of speculative bubbles is that rises in share prices induce expectations that the price will rise even further. This has been dubbed 'the greater fool theory', in the sense that each purchaser believes that he or she will find an even bigger fool who will buy the equity at a higher price, which, by definition, is not related to the fundamentals. This cause implies market failure in the sense that shares become increasingly overvalued until the bubble bursts at a particular point in time for what may seem a trivial reason. Examination of the time pattern of the share price index in figure 8.2 shows the index increasing at a fast rate throughout the early months of 1987 and this might be taken as casual support for the 'speculative bubble' hypothesis. However, existence of speculative bubbles would require that sequences of price changes are related but Santoni (1987) presents evidence that this requirement was absent from daily data for the US for the period 2 January 1986 to 25 August 1987. Two tests were applied to the Dow–Jones index for this period, one based on an examination of the autocorrelation coefficients and one based on runs of positive and negative changes. Neither of these tests supported the rejection of the hypothesis that the data conformed to a random walk.

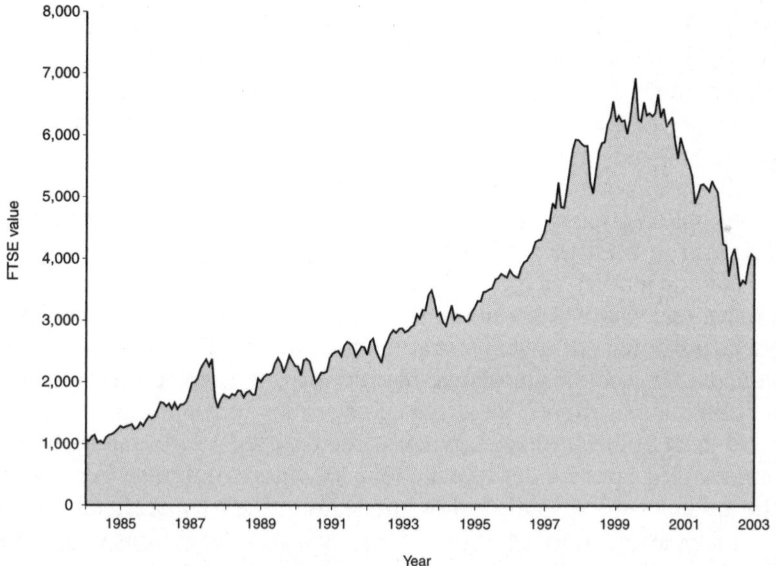

Figure 8.2 Changes in the value of the FTSE 100 index, 1984–2003.

The third possible cause was a temporary market failure triggered by an initial price decline. Suggested causes of this failure include:

(i) value-insensitive trading due to automatic computer trading;
(ii) false price signals resulting from the abnormally heavy trading observed;
(iii) the absence of countervailing price-sensitive market traders acting from a viewpoint of the fundamentals.

It could be argued that the heavy price falls themselves induced a change in market expectations which then validated the new, lower prices. It may also be argued that the growth of high-speed communications and trading mechanisms increased the possibility of such crises and this led to a demand for the introduction of circuit breakers in markets. These would have the effect of suspending trading when prices fall (or rise) beyond a specific amount during the day. For example, in October 1997 the New York Stock Exchange introduced circuit breakers, so that if the Dow–Jones Industrial Average stock index declines by 250 points below the previous day's closing price, the Exchange prohibits trading for one hour. The idea is that a 'cooling off' period may restore calmer conditions during the subsequent trading period. Two problems arise with such proposals. First, if traders wish to trade, they may well do so off the market. Second, is it appropriate to suspend trading just at the time when the public has a strong desire to trade?

A fourth reason for the crash, suggested by the Brady Commission (1988), concerns the use of the futures market to obtain portfolio insurance. Discussion of the futures market takes place in chapter 13 but it is possible to outline here the main thread of the argument. If it were possible to enter into a series of put options (i.e. the right to sell all the securities in a portfolio at predetermined prices) then the risks of adverse price changes would be reduced. Portfolio insurance replicates this position by taking a simultaneous position in a risky portfolio and a synthetic put option by shifting funds from the risky portfolio into a safe liquid asset on the basis of the Black/Scholes option pricing model. This involves selling shares when prices are falling and, if used by sufficient operators, will increase the volatility of prices on the market. In the US, portfolio insurers bought and sold futures contracts on a share index rather than the shares themselves. This has the obvious advantage of lower cost since it would be difficult, and therefore costly, to carry out the alternative of entering into contracts to purchase or sell shares across the whole range of securities in a share price index. A second facet of the argument concerns the practice of arbitraging between shares making up the index and the relevant futures contract. For example, if the futures contract falls below the share price by a sufficient amount then it is possible to make a profit by purchasing the futures contract and selling the shares making up the index. Clearly, the futures price discount must be sufficiently large to offset the transactions costs. During the week

preceding the crash, portfolio insurers were selling futures heavily and this induced index arbitrage purchasing futures and selling shares. It appears that at certain critical times the volume of this trading accounted for up to 66 per cent of transactions. In addition, the underlying techniques of portfolio insurance are well known on the market so that other operators could identify when insurers were likely to sell securities. This would lead them to try to sell in advance of the insurers in the hope of buying stock back later, at the lower price induced by the sales of the insurers.

It is claimed that the volume of sales on the futures market was so large on the Monday and Tuesday of the crash that index arbitrageurs were unable to absorb the pressure by purchasing futures, but the falling futures price still provided a guide as to the likely price of the shares making up the market, thus inducing more sales and price falls.

The causes of the crash are still controversial and we are unable to come to any firm conclusion. We now move on to consider the next major price correction in the stock market in recent years.

8.5.2 *The 'technology bubble' of the late 1990s*

A further downturn in global stock markets occurred in 2000 after a bull market that lasted most of the 1990s. Unlike the crash of 1987 this fall was not sudden but lasted two or three years (see figure 8.2). From a peak of around 7,000 in early 2000 the FTSE-100 had fallen by almost 50 per cent by the end of 2002. This fall occurred in all of the major stock markets around the world.

One of the main suggested explanations for this dramatic fall was a speculative bubble (see section 8.5.1). The evidence for this comes from an examination of price/earnings (P/E) ratios. The P/E ratio is simple a ratio of a firm's stock price relative to its recently reported earnings per share. The P/E ratio therefore provides an indicator of an investor's potential return from owning a share in that firm. For example, consider two shares that have the same current earnings but different expected future earnings. The share expected to yield higher future earnings will clearly cost more, as investors will be willing to pay more to obtain higher earnings in the future. So, the faster earnings are expected to grow, the higher the share price relative to current earnings will be, and hence the higher the P/E ratio. When looking at the P/E ratio of the US Standard and Poor (S&P) stock market index, this had averaged, historically, around 14 (based on monthly data from 1871 to 1999 – see Shiller 2000). By 2000 the P/E ratio for shares making up the S&P 500 index had reached around 34. The earnings growth of these shares implied by such a P/E ratio was considerably out of line with even the rapid growth in earnings experienced over the latter part of the 1990s. In other words, prices had become disconnected from fundamentals. With a fall in consumer confidence and rising energy

prices in the US in 2000, many firms cut back their earnings forecasts and the market fell back. At the time of writing (July 2003) the S&P index P/E ratio (at 25) is still higher than its historical average. This suggests either a further period of stock price falls or earnings have to rise more quickly. In the UK stocks were fairly priced, on a historical P/E basis, by 2003.

The speculative bubble was even more evident in NASDAQ stocks. Over the 1990s many of the larger firms trading on NASDAQ were technology companies such as Microsoft. In the late 1990s many of these technology stocks had P/E ratios in excess of 100. There was a belief at the time that the economy of the US had moved into a new era of high productivity gains generated by new technology. However, in hindsight, it now seems clear that P/E ratios in excess of 100, and in some cases 200, were not justified by realistic earnings projections. So when the correction to stock prices occurred, the prices of technology stocks fell even further than the prices of 'old economy' stocks.

At the time of writing it is too early to say when stock markets around the world will recover. There have been some sustained rises in stock prices over the first half of 2003. The evidence does seem to suggest that we have witnessed another speculative bubble.

We now move on to consider the empirical evidence concerning the efficiency of the stock market.

8.6 The stock markets and the efficient markets hypothesis

In this section we briefly survey the literature on the informational efficiency of the stock market. As the literature on this topic is extensive, some degree of selection is inevitable. We therefore concentrate on representative studies. At this stage we would, however, like to stress the practical importance of the efficient markets hypothesis. If the stock market conforms to it, then forecasting future movements in share prices is not likely to be worth the effort involved because the market price reflects all available information. Thus, on average it will not be possible to outperform the market consistently. The caveat applying to this statement is that of risk aversion and it may be that the operator's degree of risk aversion is less than that ruling in the market.

Most early studies tended to support the hypothesis that the LSE was efficient. Using Fama's (1991) categorisation we discuss the efficiency of the LSE under the headings of return predictability, event studies and private information (see section 7.5).

8.6.1 *Return predictability*

One interesting approach to considering the predictability of stock returns is to examine the role of filter rules. Basically a filter rule is an automatic

instruction to buy a stock after it rises x per cent above a recent trough and sell again after it falls y per cent below a recent peak. The object of the rule is to identify cycles from which it is hoped to make profits. The size of x and y (which may be the same) is determined empirically from past data. If the two filters are small a large number of transactions will be undertaken. This increases cost but at the same time, hopefully, identifies profitable trading opportunities. Thus, there is a trade-off between costs and the identification of potential for profit. An early study by Alexander (1954) suggested that filter rules did offer scope for obtaining profits above those realised from a buy and hold strategy. These conclusions were modified in the light of biases in the original study. A subsequent study, by Fama and Blume (1966), investigated the profitability of a wide range of filters for the 30 individual securities in the Dow–Jones index. The period involved was between 1957 and 1962 and the total number of observations ranged between 1,200 and 1,700 per share. After taking commissions into account, filter rules failed to provide as profitable a strategy as that obtained from buying and holding the securities.

If profits can be made by studying past behaviour it would be expected that daily share prices would exhibit a degree of serial correlation. Serial correlation would be positively signed if a change one day were followed by a change in the same direction the following day. Filter rules should pick up such changes. However, it may be that changes in one direction are followed by changes in the opposite direction the following day – that is, price reversal takes place. Filter rules would not pick up such changes but an examination of the degree of serial correlation would detect such price movements. In fact, most studies of serial correlation of daily changes in security prices have failed to reveal many significant coefficients (e.g. Fama 1965).

8.6.2 *Event studies*

Event studies examine the behaviour of share prices following an announcement of an event such as a merger or profits warning (or for that matter an announcement of increased profits). One problem with such studies is the dual hypothesis problem mentioned in chapter 7 (section 7.5). Generally, event studies require a model to explain the share price and ascertain whether the actual price diverges from the theoretical price. Two examples of event studies are free from this restraint. These are 'stock splits' and 'stock dividends'. In the former case the shares are split into smaller units – say shares of £5 nominal value instead of £10 each. The resulting nominal value of capital remains unchanged but it is represented by a larger number of shares denominated in proportionately smaller value (50 per cent in the example quoted above). Stock dividends occur where dividends are paid in shares instead of cash. In both cases the underlying value of the company remains unchanged. Consequently the aggregate value of the firm should remain

unchanged. In fact the empirical evidence supports this view (e.g. Fama *et al.* 1969). This perhaps represents the 'cleanest' information concerning the efficiency of stock markets.

8.6.3 *Private information*

On the other hand, there is evidence of some forecasters being able to 'beat' the market. First, regarding predictive evidence, Dimson and Marsh (1984) describe a study covering 3,364 one-year horizon share forecasts by a number of brokers for a large UK investment institution during the calendar years 1981 and 1982. They found that acting on these forecasts produced profitable trading. Similarly Bjerring *et al.* (1983) examined the profitability of the recommendations of a Canadian brokerage house for forecasts involving both US and Canadian stocks. After allowing for transaction costs Bjerring *et al.* calculated that an investor who followed the recommended list would make 9.3 per cent more than those who bought and held the market. Finally, Value Line in the US categorises stocks according to the expected performance over the next 12 months. The prediction of Value Line is good – see for example Stickel (1985) – enabling above-market returns to be obtained. These forecasts suggest either that the analysts have information not fully incorporated into the share price (insider information) or confirm that they are good forecasters compared with other market forecasters.

Other evidence against the efficient markets hypothesis as applied to the stock market comes from two different sources: the volatility of the prices of stocks; and the so-called anomaly literature.

The first attack on the efficient markets hypothesis came from the observed volatility of share price changes. This work is particularly associated with Shiller (e.g. 1981). Shiller studied the aggregate dividends and earnings of the S&P index from 1871 to 1979. This information was used to calculate what the price of the index should be if investors possessed perfect foresight. The actual value of the index was more volatile and this led Shiller to conclude that the market was excessively volatile, which could be explained only by irrational behaviour of the operators. The method involved may be illustrated quite easily with reference to a single share. Define the perfect foresight market value (V^*) as:

$$V^*_t = \Sigma \delta^{t+k} D_{t+k} \tag{8.3}$$

where $\delta = 1 / (1 + R)$, which is the discount factor. D represents dividends and R is the constant real rate of return.

The rational expected value of V^*_t is equal to the observed value V_t plus a random uncorrelated error term e_t, that is:

$$V^*_t = V_t + e_t$$

This leads to the variance bound:

$$\mathrm{Var}(V^*) > \mathrm{Var}(V) \tag{8.4}$$

However, it has been argued (see Kleidon 1986) that it is inappropriate to use time series data from one economy to construct variance bounds and that the correct method would be to derive cross-section statistics for expectations and realisations from identical economies.

The second criticism involves the anomaly literature discovering that prices vary according to an unusual pattern. Typical examples are the fact that returns measured from the close of Friday to the close of Monday are typically negative over a wide range of securities (see e.g. Gibbons and Hess 1980). However, more recent studies, for example Mehdian and Perry (2001) for the US and Holden and Thompson (2003) for Europe, have indicated that this effect has disappeared in recent years. Blume and Friend (1974) showed that there were large differences between the returns on large firms and those on small firms and these differences were not explainable by models of security pricing. It was also noticed that the majority of these differences occurred in January (Keim 1986). These anomalies are difficult to explain within the context of acceptance of the efficient markets hypothesis.

The efficiency of the stock market is still an open question but a growing volume of evidence may point to a refutation of this hypothesis in its extreme form. In particular, the two stock exchange crashes of 1987 (see section 8.5.1) and the late 1990s (see section 8.5.2) raise the question as to how far stock exchange efficiency is compatible with such bubbles. Whether this evidence is sufficient to claim that the LSE does not approximate an efficient market remains a matter of judgement.

8.7 Conclusion

In this chapter we have focused on the market in London for equities. We have shown that a relatively small, but growing, proportion of new finance is raised by way of new issues of equities. The main source of finance for UK firms is internally generated finance from the ploughing back of profits. We have also discussed the competitive pressures on the LSE that led to a fundamental change in trading arrangements for the secondary market in 1986. This introduced the system of market makers providing firm quotes on a continuous basis. This system served the LSE well for a number of years. However, competitive pressures from European exchanges forced it to re-examine its trading arrangements and as a consequence a hybrid trading

system has emerged whereby most trades in FTSE 100 shares are through an electronic order book, whilst the remaining trading in shares takes place through market makers. As we observed in chapter 7, the trend in financial markets throughout the world is towards electronic order matching. Finally, the extent to which the equities market conforms to the efficient markets hypothesis was examined and we were unable to reach a definite conclusion in one direction or the other.

Chapter 9

Interest rates and the bond market

9.1 Introduction

In this chapter the main foci of discussion are the bond market (in particular the market for gilt-edged securities) and the term structure of interest rates. We have linked these two topics together because the discussion of the term structure of interest rates is mainly conducted in the context of government securities. First, in section 9.2 we briefly discuss the reasons why different securities have different interest rates. In section 9.3 we survey the differing theories of the level of interest rates. In section 9.4 we examine the general nature of bonds and this is followed in section 9.5 by a look at the market for UK government securities (gilt-edged market) in terms of new issues, secondary market trading and the recent innovation of gilt strips. In section 9.6 we briefly examine the nature of corporate bonds and credit ratings. In the final section we examine the term structure of interest rates or why interest rates on securities vary according their term to maturity. In particular we discuss the three main theories which explain the term structure and review some of the evidence relating to these theories.

9.2 The structure of interest rates

Two interest rates are quoted in the press. The lower figure represents the rate at which funds are accepted on deposit (the 'bid' rate) and the higher figure the rate at which the institution is prepared to lend out funds (the 'offer' rate). At the outset of the discussion it is necessary to emphasise that interest rates on different securities differ for a number of reasons, in particular:

(i) the risk of default;
(ii) the cost of administering the security;
(iii) tax arrangements;
(iv) the term of the security.

The relationship between interest rates and the term of a security is discussed in section 9.7. Clearly, the risk of default is an important determinant of the difference between interest rates charged to different borrowers. Market arbitrage should equalise the risk-adjusted rate of return rather than the actual rate itself. The role of risk can be illustrated with reference to the structure of rates for one-month securities on the London money markets at close of trading on 31 August 2002, shown in table 9.1. It can be seen that these short rates rise slightly as the risk of default (almost non-existent on Treasury bills) increases. Because interest rates were very low at this time, the gap between the rates is also small.

Table 9.1 Selected one-month market rates (offer rates)

Treasury bills	Bank bills	Sterling certificates of deposit
$3^{7}/_{8}$	$3^{29}/_{32}$	$3^{31}/_{32}$

Source: *Financial Times*, 'London money market rates', 31 August/1 September 2002.

Later in this chapter we investigate the market for bonds, both government-issued and corporate-issued bonds. The default risk associated with government bonds is virtually non-existent (as with Treasury bills in table 9.1) as the government can always increase taxes or print money to pay off its obligations. The return on these bonds is therefore termed the risk-free return. The return on corporate bonds will generally be higher than on UK government-issued bonds as investors perceive a greater risk of default. The difference between the risk-free return and the rate of interest on securities with default risk is termed the risk premium, and this indicates how much additional interest must be paid so that an investor is willing to hold the risky security.

The other factors are fairly easily dealt with. Very small loans at, say, pawnbrokers incur not only a high risk but are also costly to administer, with the result that the interest rate charges involved are also high. Tax arrangements differ between financial securities, with some being tax exempt and others bearing taxes at the normal rates. Clearly, it would be anticipated that the rates charged would differ in such circumstances.

A final distinction must be made between nominal and real rates of interest. The nominal rate is the rate paid on the loan or security whereas the real rate is the rate paid after making allowance for inflation. The relation between these two rates is shown below:

$$(1 + R) = (1 + i)(1 + E\Delta p) \qquad (9.1)$$

where R is the nominal rate and i is the real rate (both rates applying to a single period) and $E\Delta p$ is the rate of inflation expected during the period to maturity.

Simplifying equation 9.1 produces:

$$R = i + E\Delta p + iE\Delta p \qquad (9.2)$$

Since the last term on the right-hand side is the product of two decimals, which are both likely to be quite small, the relationship may be approximated by:

$$R = i + E\Delta p \qquad (9.2a)$$

Equation 9.2a is the normal formula used to link the real rate of interest and the nominal rate (often called the Fisher equation). Market efficiency suggests that short-term, nominal rates of interest for differing maturities should therefore be a function of both the real rate for the relevant maturity and the level of inflation expected during the maturity of the security. We return to this topic in the next chapter, in section 10.7.

9.3 The level of interest rates

The level of interest rates can be considered to be an index or some average value around which individual interest rates vary according to the factors discussed above. This is the approach taken in basic macroeconomic textbooks which discuss the determination of 'the' rate of interest via IS and LM curves. In this connection two distinct theories can be discerned: the monetary approach, and loanable funds theory.

The monetary (not monetarist) approach explains the level of interest rates in terms of the demand for and supply of money. Typically, money demand equations depend on factors such as real income, rate(s) of interest on money (this may be implicit or a convenience yield) and alternative assets, and possibly inflation, and incorporate some form of dynamic adjustment to the desired long-run equilibrium. Money supply is normally specified to depend on a variety of rates of interest, such as those paid on deposits and earned on bank loans, and the monetary base. Non-domestic factors can be allowed for by the inclusion of foreign rates of interest in both the demand and supply functions. The equilibrium rate of interest then follows from the equality of the demand for and the supply of money. In terms of the economy as a whole these are of course only the proximate determinants of the level of interest rates, because the levels of real income and other explanatory variables will themselves be determined within the context of a simultaneous model, at the same time as the interest rate. Notice that this explanation is in terms of *stocks*. Increases in the rate of interest can be due to either an increased demand for money or a reduction in the supply of money.

In contrast, the loanable funds approach emphasises *flows*, in the form of the demand for and supply of credit by the various sectors, including the

overseas sector. In turn, savings come from the financial surpluses of the various sectors in the form of excess of income over expenditure. The main sources of savings are personal savings and retained profits by firms. At times, however, the overseas sector provides credit by way of balance of payments capital inflows. Borrowings are required to finance either consumption or investment expenditure. For ease of exposition in the following narrative we shall assume that borrowing to finance consumption expenditure can be considered as negative saving and that all borrowings are made for the purpose of financing investment. Links to the monetary sector are introduced via increases in the money supply being representative of an additional source of credit but provided by the banks. Similarly, increases in the demand for money (technically known as hoarding) are akin to a demand for loanable funds. Hence the supply of loanable funds can be defined as the sum of saving (S) plus increases in the money supply (ΔM), whereas the demand for loanable funds is specified as investment (I) plus increased demand for money (ΔH). Thus, the equilibrium rate of interest is determined by the equality of the demand and supply schedules for loanable funds, that is, where:

$$I + \Delta H = S + \Delta M \qquad (9.3)$$

It is argued that both investment and saving are functions of the rate of interest, with savings increasing and investment declining as the domestic rate of interest rises. The allocation of savings to and borrowings from overseas as opposed to domestic sources will depend on the relative levels of domestic and foreign rates after taking into consideration the prospects of exchange rate changes during the period of the loan. The other two components may in the main reflect changes in taste (hoarding) and government policy and so can be considered as an addition to the interest rate components. However, this is not a vital assumption since, if anything, the money supply is likely to increase and hoarding to decrease as domestic interest rates rise, in the same manner as savings and investment.

Equilibrium in the credit market is demonstrated in figure 9.1. Increases in the rate of interest can, according to this approach, be caused by an increase in the demand (i.e. a shift in the demand curve to the right) for loanable funds attributable to increased investment or hoarding, or a reduction in the supply (i.e. a shift in the supply curve to the left) due to reduced saving or a reduction in the money supply. A rise in the foreign rate of interest (given expectations of future interest rate changes) would also cause a rise in domestic rates through a reduction in the supply of, and an increase in the demand for, domestic loanable funds. It should be noted that this explanation of the level of interest rates emphasises real factors, such as productivity determining investment opportunities and saving as a function of thrift, so that the rate of interest is the real rate.

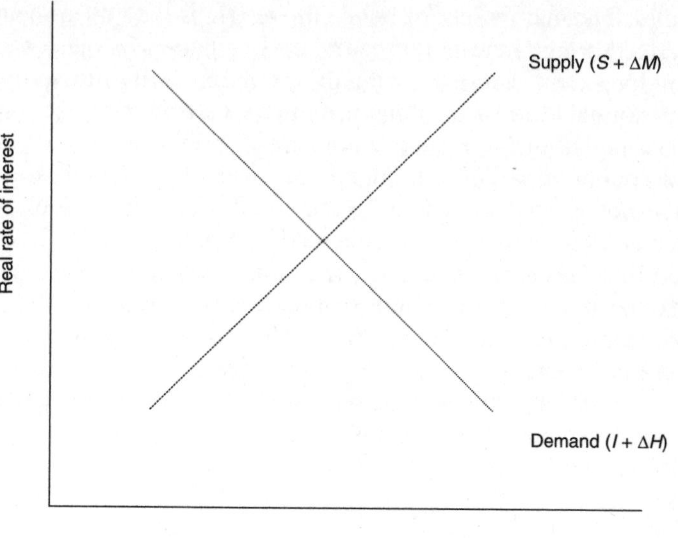

Figure 9.1 Real rate of interest as a function of the supply of loanable funds.

Although the two theories have a different rationale, they are consistent with each other to a considerable degree. First, long-run equilibrium requires that both:

(i) savings equal investment (using the broad definitions adopted in this section);
(ii) changes in the money supply equal changes in the demand for money.

Second, the predictions of the two theories are the same following, for example, an increase in the quantity of money. Similarly, an increase in investment will raise the rate of interest directly in the case of the loanable funds theory and indirectly in the case of the liquidity preference (i.e. monetary) theory via the resulting increase in income (from the invested funds) raising the demand for money. A possible reconciliation is that the liquidity preference theory applies mainly to the short run, where for example factors in the money market are predominant, whereas the loanable funds theory is more relevant to the long run, where agents have sufficient time to adjust their expenditure and financing plans.

9.4 The nature and valuation of bonds

In the UK, fixed-interest securities, or bonds as they are more commonly referred to, are issued by the government (gilt-edged securities) and by

companies. The main issuer of bonds in the UK is the government. What we briefly examine here is the nature and valuation of these securities. They are long-term securities, with an original maturity of over one year, although normally the original maturity is well above one year and can be over 20 years. They pay a fixed rate of interest, at set intervals until maturity, called a coupon. For UK gilt-edged securities the interval is every six months. Another characteristic of a bond is its par value, which refers to the price at which the bond is redeemed at maturity. In the UK the par value is £100. This is not necessarily the price at which the bond is issued – they may be issued at a discount or premium to the par value. As with equity securities, discussed in chapter 8, the value of a bond is calculated as the present value of the stream of future cash flows generated by the security. These cash flows are the regular (known) coupon payments plus the (known) redemption value payable on the maturity date. Thus the value of a bond can be found using the following expression:

$$P_0 = \frac{C_1}{(1+i)} + \frac{C_2}{(1+i)^2} + \frac{C_3}{(1+i)^3} + \dots \frac{C_n}{(1+i)^n} + \frac{M_n}{(1+i)^n} \qquad (9.4)$$

where P_0 is the price of the fixed-interest security at time 0 (the present); C_n is the fixed-interest (coupon) payment at time n; M is the redemption value of the security; and i is the discount rate.

To take an example, Treasury 7.5 per cent 2006 is a UK government-issued bond which pays £7.5 per annum to its holder and has a maturity date of 2006, at which time the holder of the bond will be paid the redemption value, which is £100. If we assume that there are three years left to maturity and the interest is paid annually (in fact UK gilts pay interest semi-annually but we ignore this to simplify the analysis[1]), then, given a discount rate of 10 per cent and using expression 9.4, the value of the bond is:

$$P = \frac{7.5}{(1.10)} + \frac{7.5}{(1.10)^2} + \frac{7.5}{(1.10)^3} + \frac{100}{(1.10)^3}$$

$$P = £93.78$$

Thus a fair price to pay for the bond is £93.78. This does not mean the price in the market will be £93.78, as other factors affecting supply and demand for the bond may lead the price to diverge from its calculated price.

9.5 The market for UK government bonds (gilt-edged securities)

In this section we examine the reasons why the UK government issues bonds, the methods of issue of these bonds and the market for trading the bonds after they have been issued.

9.5.1 *The public sector's net cash requirement (PSNCR)*

The central government requires finance to meet the surplus of its expenditure over revenue and to meet the cost of refinancing debt as it matures. Further funds may be necessary to cover the cost of intervention in the foreign exchange markets. If the government intervenes to push the exchange rate down, this entails the selling of sterling on the foreign exchange markets in return for convertible currency reserves. Thus, finance has to be raised over and above that required for purely domestic purposes. In contrast, intervention to push the exchange rate up involves the loss of convertible currency reserves and a gain of sterling finance, thus reducing the amount of finance that needs to be raised for purely domestic purposes. Consequently, even if the central government is in fiscal balance during any one year, new issues of debt may be necessary to refinance maturing existing debt and to finance intervention in the foreign exchange market, though of course this last component may be negative. Any finance that may be necessary is obtained through the issue of new securities of a variety of types and maturities including:

(i) bonds, termed gilt-edged securities;
(ii) non-marketable debt (e.g. National Savings and tax reserve certificates);
(iii) Treasury bills.

Most government debt issues, by value, are in the form of gilt-edged securities.

Figure 9.2 shows the PSNCR over the period 1983 to 2001 expressed as a percentage of nominal gross domestic product (GDP) at market prices. This ratio therefore shows the financial deficit of the public sector in relation to the output of the economy. Note that the Stability and Growth Pact, which applies to all countries in the euro-region, restricts the financial deficit of a government to no more than 3 per cent of GDP. The UK (at the time of writing) had not joined the euro-region and therefore was not constrained by this restriction.[2]

One feature of figure 9.2 is the move into budget surplus in the period 1987–90 and again after 1998, although more recently the budget has moved again into deficit. Some of this surplus was due to the revenue achieved from the sale of assets through the policy of privatisation but the remainder is due to a positive fiscal balance. The surplus meant that the markets tended to be short of funds, causing upward pressure on interest rates. As we discuss in chapter 10, this forced the Bank of England to intervene in the money market originally by purchasing commercial bills of exchange, thus providing extra funds for the money market. The other side of this coin was of course the bill mountain, that is, the stock of commercial bills held by the Bank of England as a result of purchases in the market.

The early 1990s saw the UK economy in recession, with a consequent rise in the PSNCR as tax revenues fell and welfare spending increased. As

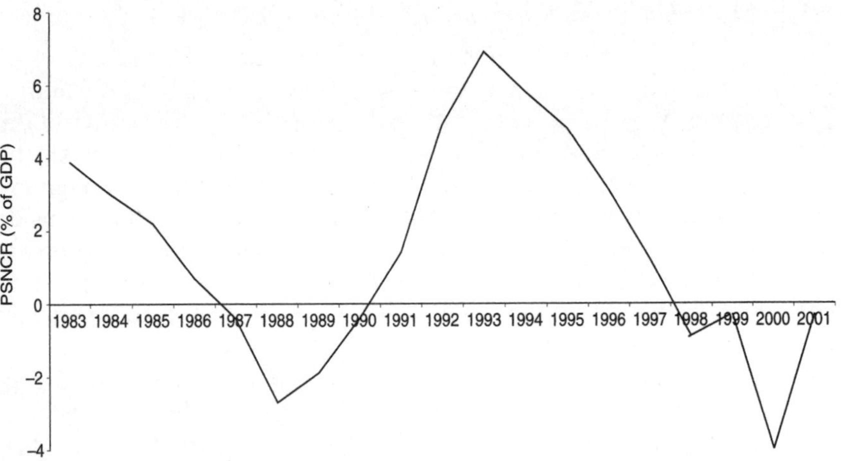

Figure 9.2 UK public sector's net cash requirement (PSNCR) as a percentage of nominal GDP (at market prices), 1983–2001. Source: DMO and *Economic Trends Annual Supplement*, 2001, table 1.2.

the economy has grown again since 1993 the PSNCR as a percentage of GDP has fallen to the extent that, by the end of 1997, the ratio was 1.6 per cent, which is below that required for entry into the European single currency. Ironically though the UK government announced in late 1997 that it would not enter the single currency at its starting date of January 1999.

Turning now to the various methods of raising finance, we have already discussed the nature of Treasury bills in chapter 1. These are money market instruments, normally with a three-month maturity, issued by the government. They are an instrument traditionally used by the Bank of England for managing its operations in the money markets and do not contribute in a significant way to financing the government's deficit. Sales of non-marketable debt are achieved by varying the returns on National Savings from time to time, according to prevailing interest rate conditions. In addition, major innovations are made, though very infrequently. Such innovations include the introduction of premium bonds and index-linked National Savings. In the next section we consider the issue of gilt-edged securities, which are the main instrument for funding the government's debt.

9.5.2 *Gilt-edged securities market: new issues*

The management of government debt was traditionally undertaken by the Bank of England. However, from April 1998 this role was transferred to

the Debt Management Office (DMO), an agency of the Treasury. This transfer coincided with the government's decision to give the responsibility for setting short-term interest rates to the Bank of England. The reasons given by the government to explain this transfer of debt management responsibility were twofold:

(i) inside information – the gilts market might have charged a premium if debt management were believed to be open to influence from inside information on interest rate decisions to the detriment of private investors;
(ii) possible conflict of interest – monetary policy considerations might have had an influence on debt management policy.

Despite a change in responsibility for debt management there has been no significant change in policy arising out of the change, since the stated aim is 'to minimize over the long term the cost of meeting the government's financing needs, taking into account risk, whilst ensuring that debt management policy is consistent with the objectives of monetary policy' (Debt Management Office 2001).

Gilt-edge securities can be separated into two main categories: conventional and index-linked. Conventional issues are standard issues of gilts paying a fixed-rate coupon. Index-linked gilts are securities whose coupon and redemption value are adjusted (i.e. uplifted in official terminology) to account for movement in the retail price index, with a time lag of eight months. They therefore provide a hedge against inflation. The cost, to investors, of providing this hedge is a lower nominal coupon payment compared with conventional gilts.

The main method for the issue of both conventional and index-linked gilts is through regular auctions, which during 2002 varied in quantity between £400 million and £3,000 million. With this method for conventional stock issues, all stock is sold to the highest bidders[3] at the price bid (i.e. a competitive price basis) and the issue is not underwritten. In the case of index-linked stock the auctions are conducted on a 'uniform' price basis, which means that all successful bidders will receive the stock at the same price. For conventional stocks the auction is open to all bidders, but in the case of index-linked stocks bidding is restricted to gilt-edged market makers (GEMMS – see section 9.5.3 for a fuller discussion). All dealings between GEMMS and the DMO are in large quantities. For example, the minimum quantity for a competitive bid at an auction for conventional stocks is £1 million.

9.5.3 *Gilt-edged securities: the secondary market*

Major changes in the market for gilts occurred in October 1986 at the same time as changes to the market for UK equities (Big Bang), discussed in

chapter 8. Prior to Big Bang there were eight gilt-edged jobbers, of which two accounted for 75 per cent of the turnover. The new system of trading created an institution known as a GEMM, which acts in a dual capacity as market maker and broker. GEMMs have an obligation to communicate, on demand, to other market participants continuous and effective bid–ask prices for a wide range of gilts in any trading conditions. GEMMs have a direct dealing arrangement with the DMO in gilts such that the DMO will bid to buy gilts from the GEMMs at prices of its own choosing and will respond to bids for gilts from the GEMMs at its discretion. GEMMs are expected to participate actively in the gilts issue process, in particular by bidding competitively at auctions. In return for these obligations GEMMs are given special facilities not available to other gilt market participants. One such facility is that the GEMMs have sole access to the inter-dealer broker mechanism. The essential purpose of the inter-dealer brokers is to enable the market makers to unwind their stock positions as and when required without trading directly with each other whenever they wish this dealing to be anonymous. A further important support to the market-making function is provided by Stock Exchange money brokers, which both lend stock to the GEMMs and also money generated from their equity lending operations at rates which are competitive with those in the money market. From March 1997 GEMMs are no longer required to be separately capitalised and most GEMMs have assimilated their businesses into group-wide securities trading operations, enabling them to benefit from lower regulatory capital requirements. At the end of 2001 there were 16 GEMMs.

The total nominal value of gilt-edged stock outstanding at the end of 2001 was £281 billion in nominal terms (including uplift on index-linked stock). The market holdings of gilts were made up of approximately 33 per cent 0–7 years of outstanding maturity, 18 per cent 7–15 years, 21 per cent 15 years and above, 27 per cent index-linked stock and 1 per cent undated stock. The estimated sectoral holdings of gilts for 2001 are given in table 9.2. This shows that the main holders of gilts are the investment institutions, in particular life assurance funds. The reasons for this are discussed in chapter 6.

The DMO is involved with the gilt secondary market in a number of other ways:

(i) Reverse auctions, whereby the DMO invites offers to resell stocks to itself. The bidding is on a competitive bid basis.
(ii) Switch auctions, which allow the holders to switch from one type of gilt to another. The DMO indicates the price of the source stock and invites bids for quantities and prices for the destination stock. The auction is conducted on a competitive bid basis for conventional stocks and a uniform price basis for index-linked stocks.

Table 9.2 Sectoral holdings of gilts, 31 March 2001

	Holdings (£million)	Percentage
UK residents		
Public sector[a]	3,664	1.3
Financial companies and institutions		
Banks	5,862	2.1
Building societies	963	0.3
Insurance companies	106,953	37.9
Pension funds	87,009	30.9
Investment and unit trusts	4,266	1.5
Individuals and private trusts	20,889	7.4
Other	397	0.1
Total UK residents		81.6
Non-UK residents	44,608	15.8
Official holding	7,266	2.6
Total holdings of gilts	281,877	100

[a] Comprises public corporations and local government.
Source: *Bank of England Annual Abstract*, 2002, table 15.4.

(iii) Conversions, whereby the DMO will indicate prices for conversions from one stock (the source stock) to another (the destination stock).
(iv) 'Tap' and 'reverse tap' transactions, in which the DMO will invite offers from GEMMS for quantities of specific stocks. The auction may indicate a minimum price (tap) or a maximum price (reverse tap). Allocations are on a uniform price basis.
(v) The DMO will bid for near-maturity stocks and 'rump stocks' (i.e. the remnants of an issue) when requested to do so by a GEMM.
(vi) Sales via the 'shop window', where the DMO will indicate on its screen list the amounts of each stock available for purchase. GEMMS can bid for these stocks.

It should be noted that methods (i) to (v) above are used to manage the gilt market by initiating changes in the structure of gilts on the secondary market rather than to raise finance directly to meet the PSNCR.

9.5.4 *The gilt strips market*

Another innovation occurred in December 1997 when a facility for 'stripping' gilt-edged securities was introduced. Stripping is the process of separating a conventional coupon-bearing gilt into its constituent interest and principal payments, so they can be separately held or traded as zero-coupon bonds. For example, a two-year gilt (which consists of four semi-

annually paid coupons and one payment of principal at the maturity date) could be separated into five zero-coupon bonds. So, after stripping, the coupon payment payable after six months would become a six-month maturity zero-coupon bond, the coupon payment payable after 12 months would become a 12-month maturity zero-coupon bond, and so on. Note that a zero-coupon bond is a bond that pays no coupon payment and its only cash payment is the one paid on maturity of the bond.

Gilt strips, created through the official gilt strips facility, remain direct obligations of the UK government. The advantage to investors of zero-coupon bonds is that they provide a much simpler cash flow structure, which can be used to match liability cash flows more precisely. Not all gilts are strippable and at the end of 2001 ten strippable stocks existed, with the amount held in stripped form totalling 1 per cent of total conventional stocks in issue. It is also possible to reconstitute a coupon-bearing gilt from the constituent strips. Both stripping and reconstitution take place through GEMMs.

This completes our discussion of the gilt-edged market and we now turn to examine briefly the corporate bond market and the importance of credit ratings in this market.

9.6 The corporate bond market and credit ratings

Gilt-edged securities are perceived by investors as having virtually zero risk of default, as the UK government is the guarantor. Bonds issued by the governments of developing countries are likely to have a higher associated risk of default, as are issues of bonds by companies. The main domestic issuers of sterling bonds other than gilts are UK companies and local authorities. The volume of issues has been variable over the last 20 years and reference to figure 8.1 (p. 159) will give some idea of the magnitude of recent issues.

A wide variety of bonds exist. The typical bond offers a fixed return each year (i.e. the coupon) and has a fixed date for redemption. The bond indenture is a contract that states the lender's rights and privileges and the borrower's obligations. Most UK-issued bonds are secured either by specific assets of the issuer or by a floating charge against the issuer's assets, so that in the case of bankruptcy the proceeds from the sale of those assets accrue to the bond holders. Secured bonds in the UK are termed debentures and a mortgage debenture would be a bond secured on specific land or buildings. Bonds that are not secured are termed unsecured loan stock. Other bonds carry what is termed a negative pledge, which commits the company to refrain from subsequently issuing bonds which carry greater security or preference in the event of default by the company. Some bonds also carry the right to convert into equity of the company at specific dates and terms. These are called convertibles.

The risk of default clearly differs for different borrowers and so the returns demanded by investors to induce them to hold bonds will also vary. Investors can obtain information on the likelihood of default or delayed payment of a security from the rating assigned by a credit ratings agency. Originally these ratings were applied solely to corporate bond issues but over recent years coverage has extended to a wide variety of debt instruments: local authority bonds, asset-backed securities, medium-term note programmes (see chapter 12), commercial paper programmes and bank certificates of deposit. The main rating agencies are the US-based Moody's Investors Service and Standard and Poor's (S&P), although many smaller, more specialised agencies have emerged in recent years. Most agencies use their own system of symbols to rank securities according to risk of default. For example, for S&P the highest-quality ranking is AAA and the lowest is D, with a further 19 grades between these two extremes. A distinction is usually made between investment-grade ratings and speculative-grade ratings, with bonds graded BBB or above under the S&P system designated as investment grade. Generally the rating agency charges a fee to the issuer related to the size and type of the issue. Increasingly regulators, particularly in the US, have used the ratings applied to bonds and other debt instruments to simplify their prudential control of financial institutions. For example, the Basel Committee on Bank Supervision proposed in its 1993 market risk guidelines that internationally active commercial banks dealing in securities should hold extra capital against their non-investment-grade bonds.

Given the growth in the credit ratings industry and the increasing reliance being placed on the ratings they produce, it is important to consider their reliability. One study of the reliability of credit ratings, by Cantor and Packer (1994), found that the two main agencies referred to above do a reasonable job of assessing relative credit risks, so that lower-rated bonds were found to default more frequently than higher-rated bonds. However, they also found that assessments of absolute credit risks have been less reliable, as default probabilities associated with specific rankings have drifted over time. This latter result suggests that the use of a specific grade as a cut-off to determine which securities are investment-grade securities, and therefore should be assigned less capital for prudential purposes, is suspect. Cantor and Packer also report the fact that for US corporate bonds the yields are closely related to the rating grade. Table 4 from their article is reproduced as table 9.3 to illustrate this point. Clearly, the yield increases as the credit rating falls and this helps explain why companies are prepared to pay fees to credit rating agencies for this service. However, an important caveat is necessary. The figures in the table do not prove that there is any causal relationship between credit ratings and yields; in other words, the credit ratings may not provide any information in addition to that contained in market prices. It may be that the market had assimilated the available

information and produced results similar to those derived by the credit rating agencies.

Table 9.3 Spreads between corporate bonds and US Treasury bonds, 1973–87 (averages)

Rating	Basis points
AAA	43
AA	73
A	99
BBB	166
BB	299
B	404
CCC	724

Source: Cantor and Packer (1994).

A recent development in the market concerns 'cross-over' debt. This is debt which was originally of investment status but, because of the problems for the issuer, has been downgraded to junk bond (high-yield) status (the so-called fallen angels include such companies as Worldcom and Ericsson). Cross-over debt differs from both investment-grade and high-yield bonds. Obviously the difference from investment-grade bonds is that the issuing company's future is problematic. The cross-over bonds also differ from high-yield bonds in two respects:

(i) the issuing company may be restored to full health and may therefore regain investment status for its bonds;
(ii) most high-yield bonds are subordinated so that bondholders receive their money after banks in the case of bankruptcy, whereas most cross-over bonds which were originally issued as unsubordinated debt.

The amount of cross-over debt is quite large – Morgan Stanley has estimated that fallen angels made up about 30 per cent of all outstanding European high-yield debt in 2002. Similarly it also estimates that cross-over debt arising from downgrades of companies to junk bond status amounted to more than $100 billion during the first half of 2002 (*Financial Times*, 17 September 2002). This new category of debt is quite difficult to value given the variety of possible outcomes for the issuing company.

9.7 The term structure of interest rates

We have seen, in section 9.2, how risk can influence interest rates. Another factor that influences the interest rate on a security is its term to maturity. Securities with identical risk characteristics may have different interest

rates because the time remaining to maturity is different. A plot of the yields on securities with differing terms to maturity but the same risk and other characteristics is called a yield curve. First of all we need to define the term 'yield to maturity' as the return on a security which is held to maturity. Thus, if we take as an example a three-year bond, redeemable at par (£100) and returning a coupon of £X paid once a year and with a current market price of £V, then solving equation 9.4 for R provides the yield to maturity on that bond:

$$V = \frac{X}{(1+R)} + \frac{X}{(1+R)^2} + \frac{X}{(1+R)^3} + \frac{100}{(1+R)^3}$$

Notice that in this example we are assuming the interest received is immediately reinvested in the security. The term structure then refers to the differences in yields to maturity on securities, which are identical except for the outstanding (not initial) maturity. The yield curve itself is a representation of the term structure in a graphical form.

It is difficult to find examples of securities identical in all respects save for the outstanding term to maturity, with one major exception. This is for government securities, where the risk of default is virtually zero but more crucially is the same on all issues. For example, the UK government had approximately 80 different issues of gilt-edged securities at the end of 1997 with similar terms, although there were differences (e.g. index-linked, undated stock, etc.). Thus, the quantity of different stocks issued is sufficient to derive yield curves. This contrasts with issue of bonds by companies although, in principle, their debt issues would be subject to the same term structure plus a risk premium, which might vary over time, and between different companies. Figure 9.3 depicts some of the patterns of yield curves which have been observed over time. However, it should be noted that yield curves almost always slope upwards.

Consequently, any credible theory of the term structure must be able to explain a variety of patterns of yield curves but also explain why the usual pattern is upward sloping. Three theories have been put forward to explain the term structure of interest rates: the expectations theory; the preferred market habitat theory; and the market segmentation theory. We now consider each of these theories in turn.

9.7.1 *The expectations theory of the term structure*

The expectations theory explains the term structure of interest rates as being a function of rates of interest expected to exist in the future. Thus, for example, if short-term interest rates were expected to rise, it would be reasonable to assume that long-term rates encompassing the period of those future short-term rates would be higher than current short-term rates. According to this theory, arbitrage ensures that the return for holding

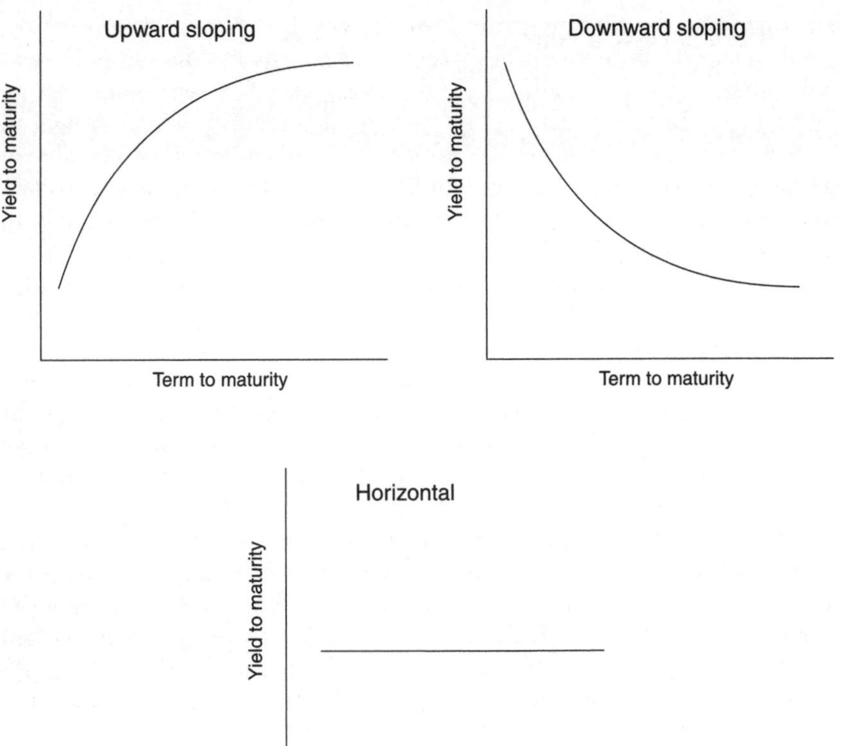

Figure 9.3 Observed shapes of yield curves.

different securities for a specific period will be the same irrespective of their outstanding maturity. This is the basis of the expectations theory and in the following paragraphs we critically examine this theory. We make the following preliminary assumptions:

(i) agents possess perfect foresight, so they know all current and future interest rates;
(ii) a perfect capital market exists;
(iii) interest is paid once a year and is immediately reinvested in the same bonds;
(iv) two classes of bonds only are available –
    (a) a one-year bond,

(b) a three-year bond,
both of which are issued at par;

(v) the investor has a holding period of three years, that is, he or she wishes to invest funds for three years.

Assumptions (iii) to (v) are merely simplifying assumptions to facilitate the exposition. Assumption (i) is clearly unrealistic and is made as a temporary aid to the explanation and will be relaxed later in this section. The second assumption is one normally made in the analysis and implies the absence of transaction costs, a spread between buying and selling prices and so on. It is a useful approximation to the truth as long as it is realised that the resulting predictions are likely to be less precise in practice.

Investors then have a choice of investment strategies. They can either buy a three-year bond or alternatively buy a sequence of one-year bonds, reinvesting the proceeds as the first two bonds mature. The choice of which strategy to follow will depend on which offers the higher return. Consequently arbitrage and market clearing will force the yields on the two strategies to be equal. For example, if the yield on the three-year bond is higher then agents will buy three-year bonds at the expense of one-year bonds. This raises the yield on one-year bonds (lowers the price) and lowers the yield (raises the price) on three-year bonds. The converse would apply if the yield on one-year bonds was higher than that on three-year bonds. Thus, given the assumptions made, market clearing ensures that:

$$(1 + {}_{t}R_{3})^{3} = (1 + {}_{t}R_{1})(1 + {}_{t+1}R_{1})(1 + {}_{t+2}R_{1}) \tag{9.5a}$$

where the first subscript applied to R refers to the time to which the interest rate pertains (i.e. t represents year 1, $t + 1$ represents year 2, etc.) and the second subscript the time period of the rate (e.g. 1 is the one-year rate and 3 the three-year rate). The term on the left-hand side represents the return from purchasing a three-year bond at time t and that on the right-hand side the return from investing in a succession of one-year bonds for three years. Consequently the three-year rate can be expressed as the geometric average of the current and subsequent one-year rates. Note also that we have ignored the redemption of the bonds at the end of year 3 because the sum obtained would be the same in both cases.

Patently, the assumption of perfect foresight is absurd if applied to the real world and must therefore be relaxed. This entails replacing the known future rates with their expected values, denoted as $E_{t\ t+1}R_1$ and so on. The first subscript (t) refers to the time period at which expectations are formed and the second subscript the time period over which the rate is to hold, so that $E_{t\ t+2}$ refers to an expectation formed at time t of the rate ruling in period $t + 2$. At this stage we introduce another assumption at the same time as relaxing that of perfect foresight. This is the assumption that the

agents are risk neutral, that is, they are indifferent to risk due to the uncertainty of the future interest rate (not default) and motivated solely by the return on the security. In this case market equilibrium would for all practical purposes be the same as that given perfect certainty but with the expected values replacing the perfect foresight variables, and would therefore be represented by:

$$(1 + {}_tR_3)^3 = (1 + {}_tR_1)(1 + E_{t\ t+1}R_1)(1 + E_{t\ t+2}R_1) \tag{9.5b}$$

So now the three-year rate is the geometric average of the known one-year rate and the expected future one-year rates. More generally, any long-term rate can be decomposed into a series of short-term rates and for the one-period rates (R) the equilibrium condition can be shown as:

$$(1 + {}_tR_n)^n = (1 + {}_tR_1)(1 + E_{t\ t+1}R_1)(1 + E_{t\ t+2}R_1) \ldots (1 + E_{t\ t+n-1}R_1) \tag{9.6}$$

Solving for R_n gives:

$$R_n = \{(1 + {}_tR_1)(1 + E_{t\ t+1}R_1)(1 + E_{t\ t+2}R_1) \ldots (1 + E_{t\ t+n-1}R_1)\}^{1/n} - 1 \tag{9.7}$$

showing that the long-term rate will be the geometric average of the current known and future expected short-term rates into which it can be decomposed. This result is perfectly general and is not restricted to the one-period rates used for the above demonstration.

We now look at the predictions of the expectations theory. First, the shape of the yield curve reflects expectations of future interest rates. Thus, if interest rates are expected to rise in the future the yield curve will slope upwards, whereas if they are expected to fall a downward-sloping yield curve will be observed. The second prediction follows from this dependence on expectations of future interest rate movements: the relative supply of securities with different maturities will not affect the yield curve. This has implications for government policy. If the expectations theory is correct, it is irrelevant, in terms of the impact on the economy, whether the authorities intervene at the short or long end of the market. Arbitrage will cause the shape of the yield curve to remain the same in either case, since the long rates will retain the same relationship to short-term rates given by expectations. Arbitrage will also ensure that inflation expectations are incorporated into the term structure via their impact on current and expected short-term rates. Finally, external effects would also be included via the interest rate parity condition applying to the various term rates.

The expectations theory is open to a number of objections. First, over long periods of time upward-sloping yield curves are more commonly

observed in the markets than other shapes. Whilst it is certainly true that interest rates have tended to rise since the 1950s, this is unlikely to be sufficient to account for the general preponderance of upward-sloping yield curves. It is likely that some other factor has also been at work. The second source of criticism is that the degree of forecasting ability credited to market operators is to say the least excessive. Is it really credible to assume the existence of agents able to forecast future movements of interest rates for a large number of years ahead? The third objection arises in connection with forecasting difficulties. The existence of uncertainty regarding future movements in interest rates casts doubts on the appropriateness of the assumption of risk neutrality. Casual observation of portfolios suggests diversification, rather than concentration of asset holdings in areas where the highest expected mean returns exist, as would be suggested by the dominance of risk-neutral operators. Similar to the third objection is the problem of the potential existence of diverse expectations which, according to the expectations theory, would suggest an infinite amount of dealing between operators. The problem of the existence of diverse expectations can be accommodated by appealing to pragmatic considerations such as transaction costs or limitations on borrowing, which, in practice, prevent unlimited dealing between operators.

We now turn to an examination of the preferred market habitat theory, which meets these objections to some extent.

9.7.2 *The preferred market habitat theory of the term structure*

The preferred market habitat theory assumes that market operators are in fact risk averse, that is, they are unwilling to incur extra risk without some extra reward in the form of a premium. Given that the risks on long-term securities are greater than those on short-term securities, it would be expected that long-term rates would be higher than short-term rates; that is, the yield curve would normally slope upwards. This does not imply that expectations of future rates are irrelevant and, as we shall see in the following explanation, these expectations will be incorporated into the yield curve.

It is believed that there is a difference between the preferences of lenders and borrowers. Lenders will prefer to hold short-term securities so that they can liquidate their loans more easily in the event of cash shortages. In contrast borrowers prefer to borrow long term so as to obtain greater security of funding. This is another illustration of the conflicting requirements of lenders and borrowers encountered generally in direct financing (see chapter 2). This divergence of preferences is reinforced as far as the lenders are concerned since long-term lending involves a greater degree of risk, as the future is uncertain and the market prices of long-term securities fluctuate more than those of short-term securities. Note the risk that we are considering is not one of default since the securities are identical in this

respect by assumption. The logical consequence of these points is that lenders demand, and borrowers are prepared to pay, a risk premium for long-term lending over the rates for short-term lending. The risk premium is also likely to rise as the term of lending increases and may vary over time according to the degree of uncertainty present. The important point is that the risk premium is unlikely to be constant. Hence a risk premium (L) is introduced into the market clearing equilibrium discussed earlier, so that agents will enter arbitrage arrangements only if the gain is greater than the risk premium. This means that the long-term rate will be greater than the geometric average of the current actual and future expected short-term rates. More formally the equilibrium condition described by equation 9.6 has to be replaced by:

$$(1 + {}_tR_n)^n = (1 + {}_tR_1 + L_1)(1 + E_{t\,t+1}R_1 + L_2)(1 + E_{t\,t+2}R_1 + L_3) \ldots (1 + E_{t\,t+n-1}R_1 + L_n) \quad (9.8)$$

where $L_n > L_{n-1} > \ldots L_1$.

Similarly, solving for R_n, it is necessary to replace equation 9.7 with:

$$R_n = \{(1 + {}_tR_1 + L_1)(1 + E_{t\,t+1}R_1 + L_2)(1 + E_{t\,t+2}R_1 + L_3) \ldots (1 + E_{t\,t+n-1}R_1 + L_n)\}^{1/n} - 1 \quad (9.9)$$

Note that in this theory expectations still play an important role but their impact is modified by the existence of a risk premium. This leads to the prediction that the normal shape of the yield curve will be upward sloping owing to the existence of the risk premium but that downward-sloping yield curves will be observed in instances when the expected fall in interest rates is sufficient to offset the risk premium. Debts of the various maturities are no longer perfect substitutes for each other, so that changing the relative supply of debt with different maturities will, according to this theory, alter the term structure and the shape of the yield curve.

Moving from postulating that debts with different maturities are imperfect substitutes to the belief that no substitution at all is possible leads to the market segmentation theory.

9.7.3 *Market segmentation theory of the term structure*

The essence of this approach to the explanation of the term structure is that there are completely separate markets for debts of different maturities. Substitution between these markets is not possible, which explains the title of market segmentation. This leads to the prediction that the shape of the yield curve reflects the differing demand and supply conditions in the various markets. It is quite plausible to see the bond market as segmented, with investment institutions such as pension funds and the life assurance companies preferring to operate at the long-term end, and with banks and

building societies, for which liquidity is more critical, preferring to operate at the short-term end.

In this extreme form it is easy to be critical of the view that no substitution is possible. For example, if it is felt that long-term rates are more attractive than short-term returns, it is not necessary for, say, five-year bonds to be substituted for three-month Treasury bills. All that is necessary is that portfolios go longer so that, say, five-year debt is substituted for four-year bonds in one portfolio and, say, two-year bonds for one-year bonds in another. Substitution over small but overlapping segments of the maturity spectrum means substitution over the whole spectrum. A ripple effect will occur so that in the end the more attractive (in terms of yield) longer-term debt has been substituted for shorter-term debt across portfolios in total until equilibrium is restored.

We have completed our review of the theory of the term structure and now move on to examine briefly the relevant empirical evidence.

9.7.4 *Empirical evidence on the term structure*

Early empirical studies tended to favour the expectations theory. For example, Modigliani and Shiller (1973), building on earlier work by Modigliani and Sutch (1966), approached the problem of testing the role of expectations in the term structure by obtaining forecasts of short-term rates and then examining how well these forecasts explained the term structure in conjunction with a risk premium. Forecasts of future rates were based on averages of past observed nominal rates and inflation, on the grounds that the expected nominal rate could be considered to be the sum of the expected real rate and the expected rate of inflation. The estimating equations were quite satisfactory, with a high degree of explanatory power and well determined coefficients. Further support for the role of expectations was obtained by Meiselman (1962), who, using an error correction model, found firm evidence of correlation between forecasting errors and the changes in the expected one-year rates implied by the expectations hypothesis. The way these are derived can easily be seen by assuming a two-year holding period and the existence of only one-year and two-year bonds. In this case, according to the expectations hypothesis, market clearing would require that:

$$(1 + {}_tR_2)^2 = (1 + {}_tR_1)(1 + E_{t\,t+1}R_1) \tag{9.10}$$

The expected short rate implied by the expectations theory can then be obtained by solving for $E_{t\,t+1}R_1$ from equation 9.10 to obtain:

$$1 + E_{t\,t+1}R_1 = \frac{(1 + {}_tR_2)^2}{(1 + {}_tR_1)} \tag{9.11}$$

$E_{t\,t+1}R_1$ can also be defined as the expected forward rate, that is the one-period rate expected to run from $t + 1$ for one period. This can be compared

with the subsequently observed one-period rate in $t + 1$. Thus a regression of the following form:

$$ {}_{t+1}R_1 = \alpha + \beta\, E_{t\; t+1}R_1 \tag{9.12} $$

should produce estimated coefficients such that $\alpha = 0$ and $\beta = 1$ if the expectations hypothesis is to be substantiated. Similarly, equation 9.12 can be amended by subtracting ${}_tR_1$ from both sides of the equation so as to obtain:

$$ {}_{t+1}R_1 - {}_tR_1 = \alpha + \beta\, E_{t\; t+1}R_1 - {}_tR_1 \tag{9.13} $$

The left-hand side of equation 9.13 represents the actual change in the one-period interest rate and the right-hand side the expected change in the one-period rate. If the expectations hypothesis is correct, again we should find estimated coefficients such that $\alpha = 0$ and $\beta = 1$.

Numerous studies have been carried out using this methodology – see for example Shiller (1990) for a summary of such studies in the 1980s and Dahlquist and Jonsson (1995), Hurn *et al.* (1995) and Cuthbertson (1996) amongst others for later studies. The evidence, to say the least, is mixed but it is fair to state that expectations do seem to play a role in forecasting with short horizons as far as securities with a short term to maturity are concerned.

Further evidence supporting the role of expectations in the determination of the term structure came indirectly from the difficulty in identifying any role for supply-side effects in the form of alterations in the available quantities of securities with differing maturities – see for example Malkiel (1966) for the US and Goodhart and Gowland (1977) for the UK but Taylor (1992) for a contrary conclusion also using UK data. Possibly the apparent absence of these effects can be attributed to the authorities supplying debt with maturities which compensate for any changes in relative yields.

However, the role of expectations in the determination of the term structure has come under attack from two sources. First, similar to our discussion of excess volatility in chapter 8, section 8.4, with reference to the stock market, the volatility of long rates seems excessive (see for example Shiller 1979). The second line of attack concerns the behaviour of short-term rates. Sargent (1972) noted that short rates exhibit a high degree of first-order correlation, so that equations of the form

$$ R_t = b + R_{t-1} \tag{9.14} $$

produce estimates of b greater than 0.8 and often not significantly different from unity, thus implying a random walk. This information should be incorporated into expectations of future short-term interest rates but evidence by Sargent (1972) for the US and Goodhart and Gowland (1977) for the

UK suggests that the revision of expected rates is less than that im[illegible] the observed historical autoregressive properties. This characteri[illegible] more destructive implications for the expectations theory of the term struc-ture. Since long rates under-predict changes in short rates, any movement in short rates would alter the slope of the yield curve. Thus, for example, an increase in short-term rates would produce less than appropriate changes in long rates, so that the slope of the yield curve would tend to decrease (assuming that it was upward sloping for purposes of exposition) or even become negative if the change in short rates was sufficiently large. Goodhart (1989) points out that, on balance, the long rate has tended to fall when the yield curve is upward sloping and rise when it is downward sloping. In the case of a major fall in short rates this also has the implication that operators could profit from selling long-term bonds since it is likely that long rates will rise (i.e. bond prices fall) in the future. Evidence by Mankiw and Summers (1984) suggests this directional failure is also matched by an inability of the term structure to predict future short-term rates of interest.

This survey of the empirical evidence has of necessity been brief and we have merely tried to identify the important strands of the literature. For further detail the reader is referred to Goodhart (1989) and the original studies. Nevertheless, we have covered sufficient ground to indicate the main areas of controversy and to draw the conclusion yet again that the efficiency of yet another financial market, in this case the bond market, is an open question.

Notes

1 The formula for bonds paid more frequently is:

$$P_0 = \frac{(C_1/f)}{(1 + i/f)} + \frac{(C_2/f)}{(1 + i/f)^2} + \frac{(C_3/f)}{(1 + i/f)^3} + \ldots \frac{(C_n/f)}{(1 + i/f)^{nf}} + \frac{M_n}{(1 + i/f)^{nf}}$$

where the symbols are as defined before, with the exception of f, which is the frequency of payment. Thus for the example quoted above with the coupon paid half-yearly ($f = 2$), the value of the bond is:

$$P_0 = \frac{3.75}{(1.05)} + \frac{3.75}{(1.05)^2} + \frac{3.75}{(1.05)^3} + \frac{3.75}{(1.05)^4} + \frac{3.75}{(1.05)^5} + \frac{3.75}{(1.05)^6} + \frac{100}{(1.05)^6}$$

= £93.66, or approximately the annual compounding in this case.

2 It has been suggested that the Stability and Growth Pact is too rigid and would be an obstacle to UK entry to the euro. It has also come under criticism from the President of the European Commission and the EU Trade Commissioner, which suggests that it may be reformed. The system of fiscal rules currently operating in the UK are principally (i) the golden rule – over the economic cycle the government will borrow only to invest – and (ii) the sustainable investment rule –

public net debt as a proportion of GDP will be held at a prudent level over the economic cycle (40 per cent is suggested as desirable).

3 Each GEMM is also permitted to submit one 'non-competitive' bid (i.e. one that is not part of the competitive procedure). In this case the stock is allocated at a price equal to the weighted average of the successful competitive bids. Other bodies can bid 'non-competitively' but with a more complicated procedure. A non-competitive bidder presumably wishes to have the stock irrespective of the precise price.

Chapter 10

The sterling money markets

10.1 **Introduction**

The sterling money markets located in London are markets for short-term funds and consequently provide facilities for economic units to adjust their cash position quickly. The rationale for their existence is that receipts of and payments in cash are not generally synchronised. Quite large cash balances are needed if these variations in payments made and received are to be accommodated. The problem here is that cash holdings provide either no or a very low return, so that the opportunity cost of holding large working balances is quite high. If on the other hand markets exist which can, at short notice and with low transaction costs, absorb surplus cash and also provide facilities for borrowing, then agents can economise on cash holdings and earn a higher rate of return on the deposits made in the money markets. Thus, cash positions can be adjusted by placing funds on deposit in the money markets when cash balances are temporarily too high and withdrawing or borrowing funds when the balance is too low. The success of this strategy depends on the existence of well functioning markets which can offer facilities for such transactions by catering for short-term deposits or lending without large fluctuations in rates of interest. This is particularly true of the banks themselves, which keep their working balances at the Bank of England and no interest is paid on these balances. Therefore the banks have a clear incentive to reduce these balances to the absolute minimum.

Sections 10.2 and 10.3 of this chapter review the assets traded in the money markets and their valuation. In section 10.4 we examine the supply of central bank money and the Bank of England's and Debt Management Office's operation in the money markets are reviewed in sections 10.5 and 10.6.[1]

A brief review of the extent to which short-term rates of interest incorporate inflation expectations is presented in section 10.7. The institutional

detail covering the banks is discussed in chapters 3 and 4 and the reader may find it necessary to refer to these chapters in order to appreciate the following analysis.

10.2 The London money markets

The size of the various money markets and their growth since 1990 are shown in table 10.1.

Table 10.1 London sterling money markets: stock outstanding (£billions)

Year end	Inter-bank	Certificates of deposit	Gilt repo	Stock lending	Eligible bills	Commer-cial paper	Other	Total
1990	89	53	n.a.	n.a.	23	5	14	184
1995	93	66	n.a.	n.a.	20	6	11	196
2000	151	130	128	62	11	18	9	509
2002[a]	229	130	144	46	11	26	20	606

[a] Refers to end of the second quarter.
Source: *Bank of England Quarterly Bulletin*, spring 2001, 'Sterling wholesale markets: developments in 2000', and autumn 2002, 'Markets and operations'.

It should be noted that the three most important markets are the inter-bank, certificates of deposit (CDs) and gilt repos, which account for 83% of the total market size. It is also noticeable that the fastest rate of growth over 2000–02 was in the inter-bank money market.

We now turn to discuss the actual markets.

10.2.1 *The inter-bank market*

The inter-bank market, as its name suggests, is a market for unsecured lending between banks. The market grew rapidly during the 1960s when the international banks, newly located in London, extended their inter-bank lending practice from foreign currencies to sterling deposits. In fact the market now is considerably broader than just between banks (both retail and wholesale) as depositors include large industrial and commercial companies, international institutions and other financial institutions. Borrowing in the inter-bank market provides an indication to the banks of the marginal cost of raising new funds, so that one rate in particular, the London inter-bank offer rate (LIBOR), is widely used as a basis for calculating charges on loans with variable interest rates. In addition, their own lending rates are sensitive to movements in this rate.

This market provides a means for banks to balance their inflow of deposits with the demand for loans (see discussion of liability management in section 3.5.1). Thus, for example, a bank with a new deposit and no foreseeable

immediate demand for a loan can make a deposit in the inter-bank market and earn a rate of interest. Similarly, a bank with a demand for a loan from a customer and no new deposit to hand can raise the necessary deposit in the market. In this way the market serves a smoothing function. A second function of the market is the provision of facilities for non-banks to make deposits for short periods as part of their cash management techniques. The third function of the market is to enable less well known banks to raise finance by borrowing in the inter-bank market rather than direct from customers. As a final comment it should be noted that the existence of inter-bank lending increases the connecting links between banks and raises the potential risk of systemic failure following the collapse of one institution.

10.2.2 *The CD market*

A CD is a negotiable certificate confirming that a deposit has been made with a UK office of a UK or foreign bank or, since 1983, with certain large building societies. Issues in London can be denominated in either dollars or sterling, with the latter market being the larger. They are issued in multiples of £10,000 from a minimum of £50,000 and are usually for a maturity of between three months and five years. The key advantage of a CD as distinct from a straight deposit for the holder is that it is negotiable, that is, the holder can liquidate the loan should a need for the funds arise.

10.2.3 *The gilt repo market*

A major new innovation occurred in the gilts market in January 1996 when a gilts repo market was introduced. A repo is a sale and repurchase agreement, where one party sells securities to another party for cash, with an agreement to repurchase those securities at an agreed future date and price. In effect it is a way of borrowing securities (here specifically gilts), with the sellers (or borrowers) obtaining better terms than would normally be obtained if they simply borrowed cash. The opposite side of the transaction involves the purchase of a security and its subsequent resale and is termed a reverse repo. The buyer of the repo (i.e. the lender of money) should be less concerned about the possibility of default by the borrower since, if default does occur, the lender has the security. Where the gilts surrendered as security are not specified, the repo is known as a GC (general collateral) repo. A specific repo occurs when a particular gilt is required and in this case the repo rate of interest will reflect the relative scarcity in the market of that gilt. Repos, then, are a form of secured borrowing or lending.

The introduction of a repo market has allowed repo activity to be widened beyond the existing gilt-edged market makers (GEMMs) (see chapter 9 for a discussion of GEMMs). This has allowed all market operators to adopt a wider range of trading strategies. A common use of the gilt repo is to finance long positions in gilts. By undertaking a purchase of gilts and at the same

time repoing that stock (usually repoing it to the seller) an investor can simultaneously take on and finance a long position in the market. Investors can therefore obtain exposure to the market with minimal financing costs. Another strategy made possible by repos is to 'short' the market – selling stock that is not owned (see section 10.2.4 for a brief description of this market). By making trading more flexible it is hoped that the liquidity of the gilt market is enhanced, so increasing the attractiveness of gilts to investors. There is some evidence to suggest that liquidity in the gilt market has improved, with firms able to transact larger deals than previously without moving market rates or spreads against them. The resulting increased demand for gilts should lead to the additional benefit of lower funding costs for the government by several basis points. It is estimated that a reduction in yields of one basis point will eventually lead to an annual reduction in public spending of £25 million.

There are no formal market makers in gilt repos although GEMMs and a number of other financial institutions are active in the market and quote repo rates on request. The repo rate is the rate of interest on the cash extended under the agreement. In the early stages of the market's development the activity was concentrated (and largely still is) at the very short end of the maturity spectrum, with around 90 per cent of trading at overnight to one week's maturity. However, trades of up to three months are now common and some trading at six months' maturity is taking place. The gilt repo market has developed alongside the existing unsecured money markets in offering an alternative liquid form of funds. By November 2001 the amount of gilt repo outstanding was £130 billion, representing some 21 per cent of the total money market. It is estimated that about half of all overnight transactions in the sterling money markets is accounted for by gilt repos. Since March 1997 gilt repos have been used in the Bank of England's daily money market operations. This is considered in more detail in section 10.5.

10.2.4 *Stock lending*

Before January 1996 eligibility to borrow stock was restricted to GEMMs, to facilitate their operations. For example, if a GEMM was required to sell a stock it did not hold, the facility to borrow allowed a GEMM to meet its obligations. The situation changed from January 1996, when restrictions on who could borrow or lend stock were removed. Collateral is required and very often this will take the form of CDs and eligible bills.

10.2.5 *Eligible bills*

Eligible bills are those that are accepted by the Bank of England in its money market operations – see section 10.5. They are bills drawn by an industrial or commercial company and accepted by an eligible bank. This market has remained fairly steady since 2000.

10.2.6 *Commercial paper*

In 1986 the powers conferred on the Treasury by the Banking Act of the same year to remove specified transactions from the definition of deposit taking were exercised. This relaxation permitted the issue of short-term sterling debt. Further relaxations occurred in 1987 and more fundamentally in 1990. This last revision permitted an extension to five years of the maximum permissible maturity of the paper issued under this facility. Paper issued with an original maturity of up to and including one year is termed 'commercial paper', whereas issues with an original maturity exceeding one year but less than five years are called 'medium-term notes'. It is only the first category which really forms part of the money markets. Thus commercial paper is a short-term financial instrument, similar to a promissory note. It is a general unsecured financial instrument with a maturity typically between seven days and three months. Commercial paper contrasts with bills of exchange since it is the liability of the issuer only, whereas bills are obligations of the drawer and the accepting house, except when issued by the Treasury, banks and building societies.

Issues can be in sterling or other currencies. Sterling issues can be made by companies with net assets valued in excess of £25 million. In addition, they must have shares and debt listed on the LSE or on the unlisted securities market. In the case of issues by non-resident companies, the qualification is that similar criteria have to be met on an 'authorised' stock exchange in the country where the company is located. Authorisation in this case entails recognition and approval by the LSE. Issues can also be made by financial institutions. Although not a legal requirement, issues are normally restricted to investment-grade ratings (see chapter 9 for a discussion of credit rating).

10.2.7 *Other instruments traded on the money markets*

This category comprises Treasury bills (see section 10.6.2 for a description of Treasury bills), sell/buy-backs and local authority bills. Sell/buy-backs occur when a spot sale and forward purchase are undertaken as a linked transaction. The requirement of local authorities to raise short-term finance arises from the different timing of their receipts and payment. Finance can be raised in a variety of ways. The first method is through the issue of bonds, normally for maturities of one to five years. The second method is through the issue of bills. Normally these are offered for tender and possess maturities of up to six months. The third method of interest in this discussion is by way of what is called temporary money. These are deposits with local authorities for varying periods up to one year but, in fact, the average maturity is for a much shorter time, with the greater proportion of deposits being for less than seven days. The minimum size of deposit is £100,000 and the deposits are non-negotiable. The sources of the deposits are

monetary institutions (roughly 50 per cent), large industrial and commercial companies and overseas institutions.

10.2.8 *Links between the markets*

Although in the above classification we have distinguished between different markets, we would like to emphasise that these are all closely interrelated, with the same institutions operating in many of the markets. Interest rates will vary only slightly between the various markets because of the slightly differing intrinsic characteristics of the instruments involved. For example, inter-bank deposits will command a small premium over CD interest rates for comparable maturity terms because the latter have a greater degree of liquidity. Similarly, deposits with differing terms will also attract differing rates of interest, as will deposits with institutions of varying degrees of credit worthiness. Nevertheless, these differences are likely to be fairly minor so that arbitrage will ensure that the interest rates in the various markets will tend to move together, as they reflect a similar trading environment. The basic similarity between these markets is that they all cater for short-term funds.

Having discussed the various markets we now move on to consider the valuation of the securities in these markets.

10.3 **The valuation of securities in the money markets**

10.3.1 *Securities quoted at par*

The first category includes inter-bank deposits and negotiable CDs. The return on an inter-bank deposit is straightforward to calculate and is given by the following formula:[2]

$$r = P \times i(n/365) \tag{10.1}$$

where r = the rate of return, P = the par value of the deposit, i = the annualised rate of interest on the deposit and n = number of days to maturity.

For example, a deposit of £1,000,000 bearing an annual rate of interest of 6 per cent and a maturity of 91 days would provide the following return to the holder:

$$r = 1{,}000{,}000 \times 0.06(91/365) = £14{,}958.90$$

Clearly, the end value of the deposit is $P + r = 1{,}014{,}958.90$.

The formula for the calculation of the return on a CD is more complicated because allowance must be made for the fact that the security can be traded on the secondary market. The relevant formula is:

$$r = \{(P/MP) \times [1 + i(nim/365)] - 1\}(365/nrm) \tag{10.2}$$

where r is the annualised rate of return on the CD, MP is the current market price of the CD, nim is the number of days for which the CD was issued,

nrm is the number of days remaining to maturity and *P* and *i* are as defined for equation 10.1.

For example, a £50,000 91-day CD with a fixed rate of interest of 7 per cent per annum purchased in the market for £50,500 with 61 days remaining to maturity would provide the following return:

$$r = \{(50{,}000/50{,}500) \times [1 + 0.07(91/365)] - 1\}(365/61)$$
$$= 0.044 \text{ or } 4.4 \text{ per cent}$$

Solving formula 10.2 for *MP* gives the market price of the CD:

$$MP = \frac{P \times \{1 + i(nim/365)\}}{1 + r(nrm/365)} \qquad (10.3)$$

In this case *r* measures the rate of return required on the security. Using the same example given above but solving for *MP* gives:

$$MP = \frac{£50{,}000 \times \{1 + 0.7(91/365)\}}{1 + 0.044(61/365)}$$

$$= \text{approximately } £50{,}500$$

10.3.2 *Valuation of securities quoted on a discount basis*

The valuation of securities quoted on a discount basis is obtained using the valuation formula for bonds quoted as equation 9.4 (see p. 184). In this case there is a single pay-off for a portion of a year, so that the formula becomes:

$$MP = \frac{P}{1 + r(nrm/365)} \qquad (10.4)$$

with *MP*, *P*, *r* and *nrm* as defined earlier.

For example, a £50,000 Treasury bill due in 40 days' time with a rate of interest on comparable securities equal to 4 per cent per annum is valued at:

$$MP = \frac{£50{,}000}{1 + 0.04(40/365)} = £49{,}781.78$$

Alternatively, given the market price the return could be calculated by the following formula:

$$r = \frac{(P - MP)}{MP} \times \frac{365}{nrm} \qquad (10.5)$$

or in the above example:

$$r = \{(50{,}000 - 49{,}781.78) / 49{,}781.78\}(365/40)$$
$$= 0.04 \text{ or } 4 \text{ per cent per annum.}$$

Securities quoted on a discount basis include bills of exchange and commercial paper.

10.3.3 *Repos*

The nature of the repo was discussed in section 10.2.3, so here we will restrict the discussion to the valuation of a repo. It should be noted that most repos are of a short-term nature so that they are instruments used primarily in the money market, rather than capital market instruments. Note that the security being repo'd can be a long-term security, such as a gilt, whilst the repo itself is a short-term instrument. Quotes are usually made on a yield basis using the formula appropriate to the market concerned. For example, consider a Treasury bill repo. The Bank of England agrees to buy a £100,000 bill with an outstanding maturity of 60 days for £99,346.76 and resell the bill to the purchaser in ten days' time for £99,455.04. The repo rate on this transaction is then:

$$r = \{(99{,}455.04 - 99{,}346.76) / 99{,}346.76\}(365/10)$$
$$= 0.03978 \text{ or } 3.98 \text{ per cent per annum.}$$

10.4 The supply of central bank money

Central bank money can be defined as money which is a direct liability of the central bank (i.e. Bank of England bank notes and deposits) and is the fulcrum on which control of interest rates rest. Hence it is necessary to discuss how central bank money is created or destroyed. We start the discussion by presenting in table 10.2 a stylised version of the Bank of England's balance sheet, incorporating only the items of interest to the supply of central bank money.

Table 10.2 The Bank of England's balance sheet as it pertains to the supply of central bank money

Liabilities	Assets
Bank note issues	Stock of refinancing assets
Bank deposits	
Government deposits	

Banks which hold settlement balances (i.e. balances used for settling transactions with other banks) with the Bank of England (denoted the Bank hereafter) are called settlement banks. The majority of banks hold settlement balances with settlement banks rather than the Bank. These balances (i.e. bank deposits) are kept to a minimum to settle inter-bank indebtedness but they are not allowed to move into deficit. When payments are made between customers of different banks, or between settlement and non-settlement banks, or between the Bank and the rest of the system, settlement ultimately

occurs over the accounts that settlement banks keep at the Bank. The stock of refinancing assets represents assets purchased by the Bank in its money market operations (see section 10.5). They are termed refinancing assets because the money market operators will be required to repurchase these assets if they are acquired by the Bank through repo operations. Any payment or receipt to the Bank will lead to a corresponding change in banks' deposits. For example, an increase in the public's holdings of notes and coins will cause them to be demanded from the Bank by the settlement banks and give a consequent decrease in banks' deposits. Movements in banks' deposits can occur through the following:

(i) *Increases in the volume of notes and coins in circulation.* As noted above, increased holdings of notes and coins ultimately are supplied by the Bank and therefore involve a payment to the Bank for them. In recent years the stock of bank notes has been growing by around £2 billion a year, thus draining liquidity from the banking system.

(ii) *Intervention by the Bank in the money markets.* When securities are purchased by the Bank, bank deposits rise as the funds are paid into the settlement banks' account at the Bank. Thus acquisition of assets by the Bank (stock of refinancing assets in the Bank's balance sheet shown in table 10.2) provides the banking system with liquidity, so relieving the shortage arising from the increase in the stock of notes and coins noted above. Conversely, when repos reach their maturity, the counterparties have to pay for securities under the repo agreement, causing bank deposits to fall.[3]

(iii) *Payments and receipts from and to central government.* For example, payments to the government decrease banks' deposits, and receipts from the government increase banks' deposits. For instance, a tax payment will involve the individual writing a cheque in favour of the government. Hence the individual's bank account will be debited with the amount of the tax payment. The final leg of the payment involves a transfer between the individual's bank deposit and deposits of the government at the Bank, so that the funds reach the government. The converse effect arises from payments by the government.

It is important to understand the effect of these transactions, as they form the basis of the interventions in the money markets of the Bank – items (i) and (ii) above – and of the Debt Management Office – item (iii) above. These are discussed in sections 10.5 and 10.6 below.

10.5 The Bank of England's sterling money market operations

As from 3 April 2000 the Debt Management Office (DMO) took over the responsibility for government cash management from the Bank of England.

However, the Bank of England retained responsibility for the operation of monetary policy. In this section we consider intervention in the money markets by the Bank of England and in section 10.6 the operations of the DMO in the money markets. In this process the Bank is the price setter in the money markets and, as we shall see in section 10.6, the DMO is a price taker.

Table 10.3 Average daily money market shortages

Year	Period	Shortage (£billions)
1998	Year	1.4
1999	Year	1.2
2000	Year	2.0
2001	Year	2.5
2002	January	2.1
2002	February	2.8
2002	March	2.6
2002	April	2.2

Source: *Bank of England Quarterly Bulletin*, summer 2002, table 1, p. 145.

The general effect of the increase in the general public's holdings of bank notes is, as we have seen, to drain funds from the banking system. In fact the very short-term nature of the Bank's assistance (see below) ensures that the banking system is short of funds on most days, enabling the Bank to enforce its interest rate policy. Table 10.3 shows the average daily market shortages over a number of years. It can be seen that these shortages are in fact very large. Any shortage would ultimately have its impact on settlement banks' balances at the Bank – see section 10.4 – causing them to move into deficit, but the shortage is relieved by the Bank. Consequently the Bank will deal, that is, undertake open market operations, with authorised counterparties. Counterparty status is open to banks, building societies and securities firms that are subject to adequate prudential control (see chapter 17) and are considered to meet the Bank's criteria. In May 2002 there were 17 counterparties. Dealings are mainly conducted through repo transactions in gilts,[4] marketable government foreign currency debt, sterling and euro-denominated securities issued by the European Economic Area and eligible bills (Treasury, eligible local authority and eligible bank bills), causing an increase in the stock of refinancing assets. The term 'eligible' refers to bills that are of sufficient quality for the Bank to accept them in its daily market operations. The Bank will also purchase Treasury bills and eligible bank bills and local authority bills outright.

In this way the Bank is the marginal supplier of liquidity to the banking system and can therefore influence short-term interest rates through the

price at which it relieves liquidity shortages. Other interest rates will tend to follow the official repo rate but not necessarily exactly. The correlation will be closest for other short-term rates and lowest for the very long rates. In the following sections we move on to consider the mechanics of the Bank's intervention in the money markets.

Each morning at 9.45 a.m. the Bank indicates its forecast of the daily shortage via financial news screens such as Reuters and Telerate. This prediction will be amended in the light of new information received by the Bank. The Bank conducts two main daily open market operations, at 9.45 a.m. and 2.30 p.m. At the 9.45 round, the Bank states the interest rate (i.e. the repo rate) at which it is prepared to operate and indicates the dates for which the repo is to be implemented (normally with a two-week maturity). The counterparties then bid for funds at these rates. At the 9.45 round the Bank does not relieve the total shortage forecast so the whole process is repeated at 2.30 p.m.

A special late repo facility is available for the settlement banks. At 3.30 p.m. the Bank publishes a forecast of residual shortage and invites bids for overnight repos. The rate applicable to these repos is normally set at 100 basis points above the official repo rate so as to encourage full participation in the earlier rounds. If after the conclusion of the 9.45, 2.30 and 3.30 rounds there is still a shortage in the market, the settlement banks are invited to apply for further funds. If this further shortage is caused by a late revision to the day's forecast, then funds are provided at the official repo rate. Otherwise a further penalty is imposed on such borrowings and the rate is set at 150 basis points above the base rate. Over the period February 2002 to April 2002, 81 per cent of the daily money market shortages were financed at the two main rounds (9.45 and 2.30) and 19 per cent in the late rounds of operation.

Also at 3.30 p.m. the Bank offers a special deposit scheme whereby counterparties can make overnight deposits so as to mop up excess liquidity, thus avoiding excessive downward pressure on overnight interest rates. However, to try to ensure that this facility does not impinge on normal trading activities the deposit rate is set normally at 100 basis points below the official repo rate. The deposits made under this facility are collateralised by gilts.

10.6 Operations by the DMO in the sterling money markets

10.6.1 *DMO cash-smoothing operations*

Government cash flows are centralised around two main accounts: the 'consolidated fund', for government revenue and expenditure; and the national loans fund (NLF), which represents money borrowed to finance expenditure. The accounts are organised so as to minimise the government's

cash borrowing requirements. Any surpluses remaining in government accounts at the end of the day are channelled into the main government account. If the consolidated fund has a surplus this is then transferred to the NLF to reduce the government's borrowing requirements. Similarly a deficit on the consolidated fund is financed by a transfer from the NLF. This arrangement of accounting is called the 'Exchequer pyramid'.

The DMO's market objective is to offset the cash imbalances on every business day so as to avoid any disturbance in the supply of central bank money and, therefore, pressure on interest rates, that is, point (iii) in section 10.4. There are two sources of imbalance. First, there is the seasonal pattern. Over the year the government's cash flow has a fairly regular pattern due to the pattern of tax receipts and expenditure. The net cash receipts tend to be positive in the summer and negative in the winter. Second, net cash receipts vary on a daily basis.

With respect to the seasonal pattern, the DMO has used the size of the Treasury bill issue (particularly one-month bills) to achieve intra-year cash-flow smoothing. Treasury bill issues are discussed in section 10.6.2. With regard to the second source of imbalances between government receipts and payments, the DMO has traded on a daily basis with a number of counterparties in the following wide range of assets: repos and reverse repos, outright purchase of bills (Treasury bills, eligible bills and bank bills), commercial paper and gilts within six months to maturity. Also included in the assets in which the DMO is prepared to trade are CDs and high-quality debt issued by foreign governments and supranationals. Finally, the DMO is prepared to undertake unsecured lending to and borrowing from its counterparties.

Other special arrangements are available to meet unforeseen circumstances. First, the DMO holds a special balance at the Bank of £200 million. Second, if there is an unexpected surplus at 4.05 p.m., this will be taken up into the Bank's late repo facility with the settlement banks but without imposition of the penal rate of interest being applied.

By these means the DMO will offset any imbalance so as to ensure that government finances will not impact on money market shortages/surpluses and therefore will not affect the Bank's short-term monetary policy operations. This is what we mean by saying that the DMO is a price taker in its market operations.

10.6.2 *Treasury bill issues*

The DMO is empowered to issue Treasury bills for maturities of one month, three months, six months and 12 months. At the time of writing only Treasury bills with an original maturity of one or three months have been issued. Issues are made by a weekly tender with bids to be received by 11.00 a.m. on the day of tender. Bids are to be made on a money market

yield basis (i.e. equation 10.4) for a minimum of £500,000. The bills are issued in denominations of £25,000 after the minimum of £500,000.

A group of nine banks act as primary participants and bid on behalf of other investors at the weekly tender. They have also agreed to provide secondary dealing for their customers. Other eligible bidders are DMO cash management counterparties and a number of wholesale market participants.

Bills are allocated to those bids which are at or below the yield considered by the DMO to be the highest acceptable yield. The DMO also reserves the right not to allot the total amount of bills or to scale down bids.

10.7 Short-term interest rates and inflation

It may be considered difficult to apply tests of market efficiency to markets for short-term deposits given the degree of intervention by the authorities. However, one interesting question was raised by Fama (1975) concerning the role of inflationary expectations in the setting of short-term rates of interest. Equation 9.2a is reproduced below for the sake of convenience:

$$R_t = i_{t\,+} E\Delta p_{t+1} \quad (9.2a)$$

where R is the nominal rate of interest, i is the real rate and $E\Delta p$ refers to the expected rate of inflation. Equation 9.2a (the 'Fisher' hypothesis) has often been tested by running a regression of the general form:

$$R_t = \alpha + \beta\, E_t\Delta p_{t+1} \quad (10.6)$$

Comparing equation 10.6 with equation 9.2a reveals the explicit assumption made that the real rate, i, is a constant. An estimated value for β of unity supports the existence of complete adjustment of the nominal rate to inflation expectations – often called the strong Fisher hypothesis. A value between zero and unity supports the weak Fisher hypothesis, that inflation expectations have some role to play in the determination of short-term rates of interest but are not completely anticipated. Early evidence failed to support the view that the markets were incorporating efficient forecasts of inflation in the setting of interest rates. Various reasons were suggested, including poor price data and faulty representation of the inflation series – normally carried out by a distributed lag of past price changes.

Using US data, Fama (1975) tested whether the nominal interest rate acted as a good predictor of inflation by transforming equation 10.6 to obtain:

$$\Delta p_t = \beta' R_t - \alpha' \quad (10.7)$$

where $\alpha' = \alpha/\beta$ and $\beta' = 1/\beta$.

Fama found support for the strong Fisher hypothesis since the estimate of β' was not significantly different from unity. This result was criticised

by a number of investigators. The first criticism was that it was possible to obtain alternative estimators of the future rate of inflation using time series analysis and, when compared with the predictions from the rate of interest, it was found that these provided additional information. This suggested that the market's setting of short-term rates of interest failed to take into account all available information concerning future rates of inflation. The second approach followed the inclusion of additional variables on the right-hand side of equation 10.7, and it was found that these improved the fit of the equation, thus implying an improvement in the forecasts of future inflation. Fama (1977) conceded that these criticisms were correct but argued that the improvements were very small quantitatively, so that his initial result was largely intact.

Demery and Duck (1978) carried out a similar analysis based on UK data and also found support for the Fisher hypothesis but, in this case, the weak version. They concluded that nominal rates of interest rise as expectations of inflation rise but that, even in the long run, they probably fail to adjust fully for the increase in expectations of future inflation.

10.8 Conclusion

In this chapter we have reviewed the nature of the London money markets. We have also explained the pricing of securities on these markets. We have drawn the important distinction between the operations of the Bank of England and the DMO in the operation of the money markets. The Bank of England is a price setter since it controls the important repo rate in these markets. In contrast the DMO intervenes to smooth out government receipts and payments to ensure that they do not have any impact on the repo rate. In other words the DMO is a price taker. Finally we briefly reviewed the impact that the expected rate of inflation has on short-term rates of interest. The conclusion here is that the expected inflation rate does affect short-term interest rates but they do not rise by the full extent of the expected rate.

We now move on in chapter 11 to consider another important London financial market, namely the foreign exchange market.

Notes

1 The division between monetary policy and debt management is a major new development in the financial structure of the UK and the interested reader is referred to two publications on this topic: Bank of England (2002) 'The Bank of England's operations in the sterling money markets', *Bank of England Quarterly Bulletin*, summer 2002, 153–61; and Debt Management Office (2002) *Exchequer Cash Management: A DMO Handbook*, DMO.

2 Note that in the UK the financial year is assumed to consist of 365 days. This is not always the case and in some countries (e.g. in the US) it is assumed to consist of 360 days.

3 On average around £2 to £2.5 billion of refinancing matures each day (*Bank of England Quarterly Bulletin*, summer 2002, p. 155).

4 During the period May–July 2002, gilts accounted for 62 per cent of the stock of collateral taken up by the Bank in its money market operations.

Chapter 11

The foreign exchange market

11.1 Introduction

In this chapter we first examine, in section 11.2, the nature of exchange rates and this is followed by a discussion of the determination of exchange rates in section 11.3. In sections 11.4 and 11.5 we explore the nature of the foreign exchange market (the 'forex') and the types of business carried out on the market. We briefly summarise the empirical evidence concerning the efficiency of the forex in section 11.6 before presenting our conclusions.

11.2 The nature of exchange rates

The first step in our analysis is to clarify certain concepts with respect to the exchange rate. There are two ways in which exchange rates can be quoted. First, it is possible to define the exchange rate in terms of units of foreign currency per unit of domestic currency, for example \$1.5 per £1 – this is known as the 'indirect' quotation. Equivalently we could say the price of \$1 is £0.67, that is, in terms of units of domestic currency per unit of foreign currency – this method is known as the 'direct' quotation. It is the custom in the UK to use the first method (i.e. the indirect quotation of exchange rates) of defining the exchange rate whereas in the rest of the world it is more usual to use the second method (i.e. direct quotation). We shall use the normal UK method. In fact the rate we have been discussing, that is, the rate quoted in the financial media and determined in the foreign exchange markets, is termed the 'nominal' exchange rate. In practice many commercial decisions are made with respect to the 'real' exchange rate, that is, the nominal exchange rate adjusted for the relative prices of the countries concerned. This can be specified algebraically as:

$$S^{R}_{t} = S_{t}(P/P^{F})_{t} \tag{11.1}$$

where S^{R} is the real exchange rate at time t, S is the nominal exchange rate (units of foreign currency per unit of domestic currency) and P and P^{F} are

indices of domestic and foreign prices, respectively. One further clarification of exchange rate definitions is appropriate. We have so far discussed exchange rates in terms of two countries and these are called 'bilateral' rates. If it is desired to measure the average level of the exchange rate against a range of representative currencies, it is necessary to construct an index of the exchange rate valued against a representative basket of currencies with weights attached to the relevant bilateral rates based on their importance in trade with the country concerned. The International Monetary Fund has developed a model for calculating effective exchange rates termed the 'multilateral exchange rate model'.

11.3 The determination of exchange rates

It is also useful as a prelude to the consideration of the foreign exchange markets to summarise current theories concerning the determination of exchange rates. It is an area of great controversy and it will not therefore be a great surprise to the reader to learn that there is no single theory which commands a wide degree of acceptance. All agree that, in the absence of intervention by the authorities, the exchange rate is determined by the demand and supply of currencies on the market, but there is little agreement on the factors underlying the forces of demand and supply. There are basically four main models, which differ from each other to a greater or lesser degree. A good, detailed account of exchange rate determination is given in Copeland (1994).

The first, the simple monetary model, assumes flexible prices and combines the purchasing power parity (PPP – see below) view of exchange rates with a simple quantity theory. Consequently changes in the exchange rate in the case of flexible exchange rates or in the balance of payments given fixed rates are attributable to differences in the rate of monetary expansion in the two countries involved.

In contrast, the second model, commonly designated the Mundell–Flemming model, assumes fixed prices. In a regime of floating exchange rates, balance of payments equilibrium is obtained through the sum of the current and capital accounts being zero. A zero balance on the current account is not required even in the long run and the offsetting balance on the capital account is achieved via the equilibrium rate of interest which clears the domestic goods and money markets. In the case of the fixed exchange rate regime, balance of payments equilibrium is achieved through changes in official reserves caused by intervention by the authorities in the foreign exchange markets.

The third model, the Dornbusch model, is an amalgam of the previous two models. Financial markets are supposed to clear instantaneously, that is, prices are perfectly flexible. This contrasts with the goods markets, where

prices are sticky. This results in the well known prediction that the exchange rate overshoots the long-run equilibrium level following a shock. The long-run equilibrium level is, however, consistent with the predictions of the simple monetary theory discussed earlier.

The fourth model is the portfolio balance model, which widens the choice of assets available rather than concentrating simply on money. Consequently the exchange rate arises from the determination of equilibrium portfolios and any shock will change the desired composition of the portfolio and therefore the equilibrium returns, including that on foreign assets, which includes expected exchange rate changes.

Foreign exchange markets are about arbitrage and this process is likely to establish certain relationships between bilateral rates. First, it would be expected that prices in domestic or foreign currency of traded commodities would be the same whether priced in domestic or foreign currency. This is PPP. Second, it would also be expected that returns on financial investment in different international centres would be the same after allowing for potential exchange rate changes. This is called 'interest rate parity' (IRP). Third is the relationship which may be expected to exist between interest rate differentials between two countries and the respective real rates of interest and expected inflation (i.e. the international Fisher relation). We now discuss these three propositions in more detail.

11.3.1 *Purchasing power parity*

The modern doctrine of PPP is due to the work of the Swedish economist Gustav Cassel, though in fact it can be traced back to David Ricardo. The basis for the analysis is the 'law of one price'. Suppose a car sold in the UK for £10,000 and the identical model sold in the US for $15,000. Clearly, abstracting from transport costs, the equilibrium exchange rate is $1.5 per £1. At any other exchange rate arbitrage is possible. Thus, for example, if the exchange rate was $1 = £1, then the car could be purchased for £10,000 in the UK and transported to the US and sold for $15,000, earning a nice profit. Because cars were being purchased in the UK and sold to the US, this would set up an increased demand for pounds on the market (or equivalently an increased supply of dollars) thus causing the pound to appreciate (or equivalently the dollar to depreciate). This arbitrage would be possible until the exchange rate equalled $1.5 per £1. The converse process would occur if the dollar/sterling exchange rate exceeded $1.5 per £1. PPP extends this relationship (i.e. the law of one price) from a single identical good to bundles of internationally traded goods. PPP also comes in two forms, absolute PPP and relative PPP. Absolute PPP contends that the bilateral exchange rate will depend on the relative prices in domestic currency of goods in the two countries. More formally:

$$S^{PPP} = P^{F} / P \qquad (11.2)$$

where S^{PPP} is the PPP exchange rate (units of foreign currency per unit of domestic currency) and P and P^F are domestic and foreign price indices, as before. Relative PPP is a weaker concept and portrays the bilateral exchange rate changing in line with the difference between the inflation rates of the two countries concerned. More formally:

$$\Delta S^{PPP} = \Delta P^F - \Delta P \tag{11.3}$$

where ΔP^F and ΔP refer to the percentage rates of inflation in the two countries. Thus, for example, if inflation in the UK is expected to be 5 per cent and in the US 2 per cent (both per annum) the exchange rate would be expected to depreciate at the rate of 3 per cent per annum. Given that arbitrage in goods takes time, it would be expected that an efficient market would cause the market exchange rate to tend to PPP over time rather than at each instant. We review the evidence concerning PPP in section 11.6.1.

11.3.2 *Interest rate parity*

The second relationship, IRP, concerns movements of capital between financial centres. It would be expected that the total expected return in each centre would be the same or otherwise opportunities for profitable arbitrage would exist. To illustrate this point, let us suppose that the arbitrageur starts by holding sterling; the one-period return from assets in sterling ($P^£$) is simply $(1 + R^£)$ where $R^£$ is the relevant interest rate on sterling securities. In contrast, the one-period return from assets denoted in foreign currency (say dollars for illustrative purposes) may be defined as:

$$P^\$ = \frac{S_t(1 + R^\$)}{(E_t S_{t+1})} \tag{11.4}$$

where the time periods are consistent and $R^\$$ represents the one-period nominal rate of interest on dollar securities and $E_t S_{t+1}$ is the spot rate ($ per £1) expected to exist at the end of the single period. Thus, the equation represents a spot purchase of dollars at the rate of S_t, the subsequent purchase of a dollar security yielding a rate of interest equal to $R^\$$ during the period t to $t + 1$ and the subsequent repurchase of sterling at period $t + 1$ expected to be at the spot rate $E_t S_{t+1}$. Arbitrage would be expected to ensure that $P^£ = P^\$$, otherwise opportunities for profitable arbitrage would exist and capital flows would remove the incentive for arbitrage. For example, if the return in New York was higher than that in London, funds would flow from London to New York, thus causing the sterling spot rate (S_t) to depreciate (or equivalently the dollar to appreciate) and the rate of interest in New York to depreciate. Both phenomena would reduce the return in New York, so eliminating the differences in return between the two centres.

Equation 11.4 can be modified by substituting the forward rate (F_t) for the expected spot rate so that all rates (both interest and exchange rates)

are known with certainty at time t. Hence equation 11.4 is rewritten as:

$$P^{\$} = \frac{S_t(1 + R^{\$})}{F_t} \tag{11.5}$$

where F is the forward rate (\$ per £1).

To illustrate this calculation, consider the following constellation of closing rates on 16 April 1998 as reported in the *Financial Times* currencies and money report dated 17 April.[1] $S_t = 1.6924$; F_t (for 12 months) = 1.6668 and the eurodollar rate of interest for 12 months = 5.75 per cent per annum. Hence the return from the eurodollar investment would be:

$$1.6924(1 + 0.0575)/1.6668 = 1.0737$$

making a return of 7.4 per cent. Again, arbitrage should ensure that $P^{£} = P^{\$}$. In fact on the day the 12-month rate of interest on eurosterling was 7.4 per cent.

In this case IRP is termed covered interest rate parity because forward cover has been taken out against future movements in the exchange rate (see section 11.5 for a full discussion of forward and spot rates). The previous type of IRP, when no forward cover is taken out, is termed uncovered interest rate parity. The efficient markets hypothesis implies that the returns in the two centres should be equal, so that both types of IRP should exist in the foreign exchange market. The evidence for the existence of this type of efficiency will also be examined in section 11.6.

11.3.3 *The international Fisher relation*

The domestic Fisher equation was summarised in equation 9.1, which is reproduced below for convenience:

$$(1 + R) = (1 + i)(1 + E\Delta p) \tag{9.1}$$

where R is the nominal rate and i is the real rate (both rates applying to a single period) and $E\Delta p$ is the rate of inflation expected during the period to maturity. A similar relationship could be applied to a foreign country, say the US, such that:

$$(1 + R^{\$}) = (1 + i^{\$})(1 + E\Delta p^{\$}) \tag{9.1a}$$

where \$ indicates the corresponding US variable.

Dividing (9.1a) by (9.1) produces:

$$\frac{(1 + R^{\$})}{(1 + R)} = \frac{(1 + i^{\$})(1 + E\Delta p^{\$})}{(1 + i)(1 + E\Delta p)} \tag{11.6}$$

Equation 11.6 may be approximated by:

$$R^{\$} - R = (i^{\$} - i) + (E\Delta p^{\$} - E\Delta p) \tag{11.6a}$$

In other words the nominal interest rate differential between two countries will equal the sum of the gaps between the respective real rates and the expected inflation differentials.

11.4 The nature of the forex

In this section we review the nature of the London foreign exchange (forex) market. Much of the quantitative detail concerning the institutional framework about the forex is derived from Bank of England surveys of the operators within the market carried out every three years from March 1986 onwards. The most recent survey at the time of writing was in April 2001. This was carried out at the same time as other central banks' surveys and the results were reported in the *Bank of England Quarterly Bulletin* (winter 2001). As a result of the information derived from the 2001 surveys, the Bank for International Settlements estimated that the total global foreign exchange turnover (net of all double counting) amounted to a staggering US$1,210 billion per day (although this represented a fall of 19 per cent compared with 1998).[2]

The UK forex is located in London and there is no significant market for foreign exchange elsewhere in the UK. Retail transactions are of course carried out by local financial institutions but these institutions ultimately obtain their currency mainly from transactions on the London forex.[3] London continues to be the largest centre worldwide for foreign exchange dealing and the average dealing turnover was estimated by the Bank of England to be about $504 billion per day in 2001. This represents 31.1 per cent of global turnover (after adjustment for double counting) and compares with global turnover shares in the next three largest centres of 16 per cent in New York, 9 per cent in Tokyo and 6 per cent in Singapore. The magnitude of these flows indicates that the trading in currency in London is far greater than that warranted by trade flows[4] into and from the UK, thus demonstrating the importance of London as a world financial market. A second feature revealed by the surveys is the very fast rate of growth in the volume of transactions. This far outweighs the growth of physical trade and no doubt is a reflection of the liberalisation of capital markets and, in particular, a general relaxation of capital controls.

The US dollar is the main currency in the London market, being used on one side of a transaction in 92 per cent of deals. The euro is the second most heavily traded currency in London, accounting for 41 per cent of deals, followed by sterling at 24 per cent of deals. The most actively traded currency pair was the dollar–euro, accounting for 34 per cent of business.

The market is a continuous dealers' market and there are four types of operators within it:

(i) *Market makers*. These are mainly the major banks, which agree to buy and sell currencies on a continuous basis. Although the detail

may be finalised using other means, such as the telephone, trading is carried out via quotes on screens, so there is no building serving as a market meeting place. The gap between the bid and ask prices reflects the market maker's margin to cover costs and make a profit. Profits will also accrue from taking a view of the future course of exchange rates, that is, speculation. The market maker carries a stock of currencies and is the operator who incurs the risk of unanticipated changes in exchange rates. Business in the market is quite concentrated, with the combined market share of the top ten principals equal to 58 per cent in 2001 (up from 50 per cent in 1998). This is partly explained by several mergers of large market players.

(ii) *Brokers*. These are institutions which act as intermediaries. They act as agents seeking out bargains and do not trade on their own account. The total share of business passing through brokers amounted to 34 per cent of the total in 1998. This has declined since then as more business passes through electronic broking systems such as Reuters (rather than traditional telephone broking). It has been estimated than around two-thirds of inter-dealer business is now conducted through electronic broking.

(iii) *The Bank of England*. Apart from its role of supervising the market, the Bank will, as is true of other central banks, intervene in the foreign exchange markets to influence the exchange rate. Intervention is normally carried out via a broker, with the identity of the Bank being kept secret.

(iv) *Customers*. Customers for foreign exchange transactions on the forex are large companies and other financial institutions. The proportion of turnover reported to have been accounted for between market makers and their customers has seen a steady increase since surveys began, from 9 per cent in 1986 to 32 per cent in 2001. This reflects increased sophistication and activity on the part of asset managers.

11.5 The nature of forex business

Two types of cash market transactions can be distinguished:

(i) spot transactions;
(ii) forward transactions.

Discussion of derivative transactions is reserved until chapter 13.

Spot transactions are required to be settled within two working days of the agreement. These have fallen as a proportion of total turnover from 1986 to 2001 (73 per cent to 30 per cent) whereas the proportion of forward transactions has increased from 27 to 70 per cent over the same period. In the following discussion we will use the dollar/sterling rate for illustrative

purposes. Market makers quote two rates. The lower rate represents the rate or price at which they are prepared to buy sterling in exchange for US dollars (or equivalently sell dollars in return for sterling). The higher rate is the rate at which they are prepared to sell sterling in return for US dollars (or buy dollars in exchange for sterling). For example, the *Financial Times* in the currency market report section on 9 July 1998 gave, amongst other information, the following for the US 'pound spot – forward against the pound' for 8 July:

(i) closing midpoint, 1.6372;
(ii) bid–offer spread, 368–376.

The spot quotation shows the best closing sterling midpoint rate, that is, the average of the buying and selling. On this day the spread was given by 1.6368 to 1.6376 so that market makers would buy pounds from the seller at the rate of $1.6368 for each pound. Conversely they would be prepared to sell sterling at the rate of $1.6376 per £1. The bid–offer spread quoted above indicates this range in shortened form, by omitting the 1.6 from the full quote.

Forward transactions represent an agreement to purchase the currency at a later date but at a price agreed now. An outright forward transaction occurs where there is an agreement to purchase/sell a currency forward without any corresponding agreement to resell/repurchase that currency at a later date. A margin may be required by the seller of the forward contract but some market makers merely require the purchaser to hold cash in a deposit account with them. As evidenced by the Bank of England 2001 survey, the bulk of such forward contracts were for maturities of up to seven days (69 per cent of total forward transactions). Thirty per cent of total forward business represented maturities greater than seven days but up to one year, with the remaining 1 per cent being for maturities of more than one year. In some instances the trader will not be certain when the precise payment is required and he or she can, in such circumstances, arrange for an option forward contract, which enables the trader to purchase (or sell) the currency at an agreed rate within a specified time period rather than on a particular date. A further type of forward contract is a 'swap', either a spot purchase against a forward sale (or vice versa) or a purchase and sale of currencies forward for different dates. This type of contract formed the major component of the forward transactions (60 percentage points out of the total of 70 per cent).

The forward rates at the end of trading on 8 July 1998 were shown in the same *Financial Times* currency market report as $1.6345 for delivery in one month's time, $1.6286 in three months' time and $1.6405 in one year's time. Also quoted was the percentage gap between the spot and forward rates (i.e. [spot rate – forward rate]/spot rate) at an annualised rate; for

example, for the three-month forward rate 2.1 per cent, calculated as 4[100{(1.6372 – 1.6286)/1.6372}].[5]

11.6 The efficiency of the foreign exchange market

The question of whether the foreign exchange market is efficient (in the informational sense) is one of considerable importance for the end customer of the market. If arbitrage between sophisticated traders produces prices which do reflect instantaneously all available information, then forecasting by end customers is not a worthwhile exercise since the market has already processed the available information. In this section we provide a brief survey of the current literature on market efficiency with respect to the foreign exchange markets. This research is ongoing and the interested reader is recommended to examine the original literature. A particularly good survey is by Taylor (1995).

11.6.1 *Purchasing power parity*

We first consider the evidence concerning the existence or otherwise of PPP. Efficiency with respect to PPP is different from the types of efficiency so far examined because it involves a time element. Arbitrage in goods is not instantaneous as is the case in arbitrage in financial instruments. Hence PPP would be expected to apply in the long run (unspecified period) but not in the short run. The empirical literature on this subject is, to say the least, voluminous. It is therefore possible to present here only the main themes of the various studies – see Copeland (1994), Pilbeam (1992) and Taylor (1995) for further discussion and references. The main conclusions from the literature are as follows:

(i) The evidence concerning the existence of PPP is ambiguous: some studies find support whilst others do not. Evidence is more supportive of the existence of PPP in the long run rather than the short run. It is also true that more recent studies find quite strong support for PPP in the long run.
(ii) Evidence is more supportive of PPP for traded than non-traded goods.
(iii) The exchange rate is more volatile than national price levels. This is contrary to PPP.
(iv) Graphical presentation of bilateral exchange rates demonstrates periods of prolonged departure from PPP but also a tendency to fluctuate around the PPP level.

11.6.2 *Weak and strong market tests*

Reverting back to Fama's (1970) classification of types of efficiency (see chapter 7), we first deal with the weak tests. One type of study concerning

the weak efficiency of the foreign exchange markets relates to filter rules. As noted in chapter 7, the nature of a filter rule is to buy the currency if the price rises x per cent above a recent trough and sell the currency if it falls y per cent below a recent peak. The object of the rule is to identify upturns and downturns other than small fluctuations and the values of x and y are set by the speculator in the light of previous experience of the series. Clearly, the smaller are x and y the greater will be the number of profitable opportunities identified but also the greater the cost of the transactions, which will offset and perhaps eliminate the profits obtained. On the other hand, large values for x and y will reduce the transaction costs but miss some profitable opportunities. Two major studies of the profitability of filter rules were carried out by Dooley and Shafer (1976) and Logue and Sweeney (1977). Both these studies identified profits above those obtainable with a 'buy and hold' strategy but losses were incurred in some periods. This raises the question whether these profits were the reward for incurring risk of exchange rate losses. Also, there is a fundamental problem with this type of study concerning whether the profitable filter rules derived in such studies are genuinely *ex ante*, that is, represent trading opportunities open to traders. In any case one can argue that if a profitable filter rule were identified traders would use the rule and the resulting arbitrage would eliminate the profits. Taylor (1986) examined time series analysis methods of forecasting the sterling/dollar exchange rate using daily observations for the period 1974 to 1982. He again found some improvement of the forecasts over predictions by market prices but the improvement was quite small.

One type of semi-strong test of market efficiency arises from covered interest arbitrage establishing IRP (see equation 11.5 and related discussion). This hypothesis has been tested by a number of researchers, including Frenkel and Levich (1975, 1977) and Taylor (1987). In general, Frenkel and Levich, using end-of-day data, found that profits were not available from covered interest arbitrage in the eurocurrency markets after taking into consideration transaction costs. In the case of domestic centres some profits were available but these could perhaps be accounted for by the greater risks involved, such as actual or potential controls on capital movements. Taylor, using high-frequency data (i.e. observations of actual rates during the day), found some departures from IRP during times of turbulence on the foreign exchange markets but that in general IRP held. Further casual evidence arises from the fact that many banks define the forward rate by solving equation 11.5 for F_t given the spot rate and appropriate rates of interest. The quotation indicated above from the *Financial Times* is derived in this manner.

A second type of semi-strong test involves testing for 'speculative' efficiency. Given the existence of risk-neutral speculators, the expected (*ex ante*) return in different centres should be the same if the market is

efficient. The linchpin for testing speculative efficiency is the uncovered IRP condition, which states that:

$$\Delta E_t s_{t+k} = R^*_t - R_t \quad (11.7)$$

where $\Delta E_t s_{t+k}$ is the expected change in the spot rate between time t and $t + k$ with the expectation formed at time t (s represents price of foreign currency per unit of domestic currency in logarithms) and R represents the interest rate appropriate for period t to $t + k$. The asterisk denotes the foreign rate of interest.

To illustrate this condition, consider what would happen if this equality did not hold, taking, as an example, the UK as the domestic country and the US as the foreign country. Hence the exchange rate is quoted in the form of dollars per pound. If $R^£_t > R^\$_t$, with the superscripts £ and \$ representing the domestic (UK) and foreign (US) rates of interest, then the pound is expected to depreciate (i.e. $\Delta E_t s_{t+k} < 0$) by the same amount so that the return in the two countries is the same. If $\Delta E_t s_{t+k} < R^\$_t - R^£_t$ then the return in the UK will be greater than that in the US so that the resulting arbitrage (i.e. funds flowing to the UK) should eliminate this gap. The converse would occur if $\Delta E_t s_{t+k} > R^\$_t - R^£_t$. Note that this condition critically depends on the existence of risk-neutral speculators and would be vitiated if a risk premium was necessary to compensate speculators for taking risky positions in the forex. Equating the return in the overseas centre with that in the domestic centre using equation 11.5 we obtain:

$$(1 + R^£_t) = \frac{S_t(1 + R^\$_t)}{F_t} \quad (11.8)$$

Taking logarithms and noting that the logarithm of (1 + a small decimal) is approximately equal to the original number and rearranging gives:

$$s_t - f_t = R^£_t - R^\$_t$$

or equivalently:

$$f_t - s_t = R^\$_t - R^£_t \quad (11.9)$$

where the lower-case letters denote logarithms.

Substituting equation 11.9 into equation 11.7 and noting that, with rational expectations, the gap between the expected change and actual change will differ only by a random forecast error term with a mean of zero:

$$\Delta s_{t+k} = f_t - s_t + e_t \quad (11.10)$$

This can be estimated by the regression equation:

$$\Delta s_{t+k} = \alpha + \beta(f_t - s_t) + e_t \quad (11.11)$$

Equation 11.11 will be equivalent to equation 11.10 only if $\alpha = 0$ and $\beta = 1$. Empirical studies over a number of currencies with differing time periods have failed to validate this requirement (see e.g. Fama 1984). In fact most studies derive an estimate of β nearer -1. Thus the joint hypothesis of risk neutrality and speculative efficiency is decisively rejected.

11.6.3 *Forecasting*

In a similar manner we can evaluate the forecasting ability of the forward exchange rate. If we assume again that speculators are risk neutral, then their sole motivation will be to attain profits. If the forward rate for the dollar against the pound is below the level they expect at the end of the period in question, then they will buy sterling forward and sell the sterling spot on the maturity of the agreement. If their expectations are correct they will obtain a profit denominated in dollars. Conversely, if the risk-neutral speculators expect a lower spot rate as compared with the relevant forward rate, then they will sell sterling forward and buy spot later to cover the forward contract. Obviously if the exchange rate moves in the reverse direction to that expected, then the speculators will make a loss but the assumption of risk neutrality implies that they are not deterred from their attempt to take advantage of potential profits by the chance of a loss. Hence, given the existence of risk-neutral speculators, the forward rate should provide a good prediction of the spot rate in the future. More formally:

$$F_t = E_t S_{t+k} \tag{11.12}$$

where F_t is the forward rate observed at time t for the delivery of currency at time $t + k$ and $E_t S_{t+k}$ is the expected spot rate at time $t + k$ with the expectation formed at time t.

It is possible to test equation 11.12 by running regressions of the form:

$$S_{t+k} = \alpha + \beta F_t \tag{11.13}$$

If the forward rate is an unbiased predictor of the spot rate, it is necessary that the estimates of α and β are not statistically different from 0 and 1, respectively. It appears conclusively that this relationship is rejected by the data – for example see Baillie *et al.* (1983) using data for the US dollar, sterling, the Deutschmark, lira and the French franc (1973–80) and the Canadian dollar (1977–80). There is, however, a technical econometric problem with the estimation of equations of the form given by equation 11.13 since the series are not stationary. An alternative approach is to examine the forward premium (i.e.$\{F_t - S_t\}/S_t$) as a predictor of the future movement in the exchange rate. This can be tested by running regressions of the form:

$$\Delta S_{t+k} = \alpha + \beta FP_t \tag{11.14}$$

where ΔS_{t+k} is the change in the spot exchange rate between time t and $t + k$, and FP_t refers to the forward premium at time t for delivery of currency at time $t + k$. Again, if the forward premium is an unbiased predictor of future movements in the spot rate, it is necessary that the estimates of α and β are not statistically different from 0 and 1, respectively. It appears conclusively that this relationship is also rejected by the data – see for example Fama (1984), amongst many others.

Finally in this respect, it is possible to look at the forecasting errors, e_t (defined as $S_{t+k} - F_t$), to see if they were correlated with information available to agents at time t. This can be checked by running a regression of the following form:

$$e_t = \Gamma X_t \tag{11.15}$$

where X_t is a vector of variables known at time t. If the Γ coefficients are not all zero, then the market is not processing all available information. This requirement is known more technically as a requirement that the errors should be orthogonal to any information available to the agents.

The types of variable in X can be divided into two categories: lagged values of e, and information additional to lagged e (i.e. weak and semi-strong tests). Tests of both types again conclusively reject the error orthogonality – see for example, amongst many others, Macdonald and Taylor (1989).

Two explanations are possible for this rejection of the hypothesis that the forward rate is an unbiased predictor. First, the market is inefficient and is not processing all available information correctly. Second, speculators are not risk neutral but are, in fact, risk averse, so that they require a risk premium (which may vary over time) to compensate them for the risk of a loss following an adverse movement in the exchange rate, such that:

$$\Delta E_t s_{t+k} + \rho_t = R^*_t - R_t \tag{11.16}$$

where ρ_t is a time-varying risk premium correlated with the interest differential or forward premium. So far little progress has been made in identifying such a premium. Whatever the reason, it is apparent that the dual hypothesis of risk neutrality and market efficiency is decisively rejected by the data. Survey data on expected exchange rates have been used to try to disentangle the two effects in the dual hypothesis (see e.g. Froot and Frankel 1989). The general conclusion from this literature seems to be that both risk aversion and failure of the rational expectations hypothesis are responsible for the rejection of the hypothesis of speculative efficiency.

Finally in this section we look at the performance of professional forecasting agencies. The test examines whether forecasting agencies can consistently outperform the market, that is, a strong test in the Fama terminology. It is of course difficult to obtain information on forecasts sold to clients. However, a limited number of tests have been carried out by

researchers, including Goodman (1979), Levich (1979), Bilson (1983) and Blake *et al.* (1986). The studies by Goodman, Levich and Blake *et al.* suggested that the forward rate was at least as good a predictor as that provided by the forecasting agency. Bilson found that the gain from combining forecasts (including those of a forecasting agency) with a portfolio approach involving more than just one currency offered the prospect of gaining substantial profits.

11.6.4 *Conclusion*

The question of whether the foreign exchange market conforms to the efficient markets hypothesis remains open. One salient factor which supports the view that the forex significantly departs from it is the degree of intervention by the authorities. Neely (2000) reports intervention by the US authorities (mainly in the Deutschmark and yen markets) from the third quarter of 1973 to 1998 and gives the following summary statistics:

(i) average absolute monthly intervention, $355 million;
(ii) maximum monthly intervention, $6,735 million (purchases of foreign currency);
(iii) minimum monthly intervention, –$3,413 million (sales of foreign currency)

It is not apparent that such large intervention by the authorities is compatible with the efficient markets hypothesis. It also seems that the evidence clearly points to the rejection of the dual hypothesis of risk neutrality and efficiency.

11.7 **Conclusion**

In this chapter we first considered the ambiguity concerning the determination of exchange rates. Whilst there is broad agreement that the exchange rate is determined by demand and supply, there is little, if any, agreement as to what factors influence the demand for and supply of currency in the foreign exchange markets. Three principal relationships were discussed, namely PPP, covered IRP and the international Fisher relation. This was followed up by a discussion of the nature of the foreign exchange market and the extent to which it conforms to the efficient markets hypothesis. Apart from the tests of this hypothesis, the level of government intervention casts doubts on the efficiency of this market. In the next chapter we proceed to discuss another type of international financial market, namely eurosecurities markets.

Notes

1 Note we are working from midpoints (see section 11.5 for an explanation of this term) and the period is for one year to simplify the mathematics. Also note

that the forward rate is for delivery in 12 months' time and the interest rates are quoted on an annual basis. This is what is meant by the statement 'where time periods are consistent'. The same calculations would apply for different time periods but would require the interest rates to be adjusted from an annual basis, for example, for three months, to be divided by four.

2 This reduction in global foreign exchange turnover is partly due to the creation of the euro, in 1999, which eliminated dealing between the European currencies that disappeared.

3 One example of retail business is money conversion for tourists. Compared with the rates quoted in the wholesale market, the tourist rates quoted in the press and at points of sale are generally both higher and command a wider spread between the bid and offer rate (see section 11.5 for a discussion of the bid–offer spread). This is partly due to the smaller denomination of the transaction. A second possible reason is that the retail market comprises operators who are likely to have a lower level of knowledge of rates charged elsewhere than the wholesale market operators.

4 This is true of the market in general. The average daily turnover of $1,210 billion per day far exceeds the average daily level of trade payments. This indicates the important role of capital movements in the forex.

5 The multiplication by 4 is to convert the figure to an annual basis.

Chapter 12

Eurosecurities markets

12.1 **Introduction**

In chapter 7 we established that London is one of the main international financial centres in the world. Three main areas of international financial activity can be distinguished: banking, bonds and similar types of securities, and equities. We have already discussed the nature and extent of international (mainly eurocurrency) banking in chapter 4 and the extent of international equities trading through London in chapter 8. In this chapter we examine the eurosecurities markets which have developed out of the eurocurrency markets and then discuss some of the wider developments in international financing. The eurosecurities markets we consider, in sections 12.2 to 12.4, are those of eurobonds, money market instruments and euro-equities. We consider the use of swaps in eurosecurities markets in section 12.5. These markets have been the subject of a great deal of financial innovation over the past 20 years and the new financial instruments which have emerged have tended to blur the distinction between traditional international banking and securities trading. We finish this chapter therefore with a discussion of disintermediation. This process describes how changes in the financial environment and the changing preferences of borrowers and international banks have led to a move away from international financial intermediation through banks to direct financing through greater use of the international capital markets.

12.2 **Eurobonds**

In this section we examine the nature of eurobonds, the reasons for the growth in the issue of such bonds and the variety of types of eurobond issued, and the methods of issuing them.

12.2.1 *Nature of eurobonds*

A large borrower wishing to raise long-term funds through bond issues can turn to either the domestic bond market, as we saw in chapter 9, or to the international bond markets. We can distinguish between two types of international bond. A traditional foreign bond is one issued by a non-resident borrower on the market of a single country and denominated in that country's currency. For example, foreign bonds issued in New York in dollars, London in sterling or Tokyo in yen are known respectively as yankee, bulldog and samurai issues. The other type of international bond is the eurobond, which is a bond issued in markets other than that of the currency of issue and sold internationally. Thus, a German company which issues a US dollar bond in New York is issuing a foreign (yankee) bond, whereas if the company issues the bond in a number of national markets, other than the US, then it is classed as a eurobond. Table 12.1 illustrates the difference between domestic, foreign and eurobond issues.

Table 12.1 Classification of international bonds

	Bond issues	
	By residents	By non-residents
In domestic currency	Domestic bonds	Traditional foreign bonds
In foreign currency	Eurobonds	Eurobonds

Traditional foreign bonds and eurobonds together comprise all international bonds.

Eurobonds are generally issued 'offshore', which means that the issue of such bonds is not subject to the rules and regulations which govern the issue of foreign bonds in that currency, such as obligations to issue detailed prospectuses and any interest-withholding taxes, that is, taxes deducted at source before interest is paid for non-resident holders of bonds. This is not to say that there are no restrictions on eurobond issues and trading, since the International Securities Markets Association (ISMA), which is a self-regulatory body, has introduced trading rules and standardised procedures in the eurobond market.

12.2.2 *Growth of the eurobond market*

The first eurobond was issued in 1963; the use of eurobonds grew only slowly throughout the 1960s and 1970s but then explosively over the early 1980s. Table 12.2 illustrates the growth of international securities issues since 1988 and identifies the main currencies of the issues. Note that the figures available do not separate eurobonds and euronotes. Euronotes are essentially short-term eurobonds with an initial maturity of between one and five years. We discuss the nature of euronotes in section 12.2.4.

Table 12.2 Growth of international securities issues, 1988–2002

	1988	1990	1992	1994	1996	1998	2000	2002
Net international bond and note issues ($billion)	159	165	159	224	499	669	1,091	1,022
Currency of issue (%)[a]								
US dollar				31	48	60	46	43
Euro[b]				33	28	32	38	48
Yen				36	16	–5	1	–1
Sterling				6	6	8	6	5

[a] The percentage totals do not add up to 100 because of the issues of international debt in currencies other than those listed, the net issues of some of which were negative.
[b] The euro figures for dates prior to its introduction in 1999 represent international securities issues in currencies that subsequently converted to the euro.
Source: BIS, *Quarterly Review: International Banking and Financial Market Developments*, various issues.

There are a number of reasons for the rapid growth of eurobond activity from the early 1980s. Over this period international interest rates fell steadily, making the issue of both equities and fixed-interest bonds more attractive to borrowers. Banks have generally been reluctant to lend at fixed rates of interest over the long term. In addition, the problems of banks over the 1980s and the greater cost of borrowing through banks, described in section 12.6, led borrowers to look more to the international capital markets as a source of funds. Whilst international bond issues grew rapidly from the 1980s, the proportion made up of eurobonds (as opposed to traditional foreign bonds) has grown over time so that eurobonds now account for over 80 per cent of issues. One reason for this is the lower cost of eurobond issues compared with domestic or foreign bond issues. The ability of buyers of bonds to escape withholding tax and income tax on interest receipts enables borrowers to issue at lower yields. Eurobonds are generally issued in bearer form, eliminating the need for registration of ownership, as ownership is vested in the holder. The anonymity this brings allows owners to avoid tax on interest. The repeal of withholding tax on interest paid to foreign purchasers of domestic bonds in the US in 1984 together with changes to allow US residents to issue bearer bonds to non-resident borrowers may have been expected to make eurobonds less attractive. However, there are other advantages to issuing eurobonds, which account for the continued growth. The lack of restrictions on eurobond trading makes it easier and therefore speedier to make issues and thus take advantage of a favourable 'window' in interest rate movements or other economic changes. Also, the liberalisation of domestic capital markets in the US, the UK,

Germany and Japan and the general globalisation of capital markets that took place over the 1980s encouraged borrowers and investors to look more to international capital markets.

The rapid growth in eurosecurity issues in the latter part of the 1990s reflects the strong surge in corporate restructuring and the growth in 2000 in particular was partly due to European telecommunication companies issuing securities to finance the purchase of third-generation mobile phone licences.

International bond issues are denominated in currencies which are important for international trade. This explains the importance of dollar-denominated eurobonds. However, the dollar-denominated dominance of the eurobond market is not quite as great as the dollar dominance of the eurocurrency loans market and in fact dollar issues were more than matched by euro issues in 2002 (see table 12.2). This is because borrowers have also tended to issue bonds to tap the savings of countries which have a high savings ratio, in particular the economies of the euro zone. Furthermore, investors look for securities denominated in strong currencies. As we shall see in section 12.5, the use of swap contracts allows the currency denomination of the funds raised to be swapped into a different currency if required.

12.2.3 *Types of eurobonds*

The eurobond market has been the subject of a great deal of financial innovation since the early 1980s and many different types of eurobond have been created. It is possible though to classify eurobonds as belonging to one of three basic types:

(i) *Straight fixed-rate bonds*. These are the traditional type of bond with a fixed coupon payment.

(ii) *Floating-rate notes (FRNs)*. These are bonds issued with coupon payments made on a floating-rate basis. The coupon, which usually consists of a margin over a reference rate such as the London inter-bank offer rate (LIBOR), is paid at the end of each interest period, usually six months, and then reset in line with the reference rate for the next interest period. FRNs are generally medium-term bonds, that is, with maturities from 5 to 15 years.

(iii) *Equity-related bonds*. There are two types of equity-related bonds:

  (a) *Convertibles*. These give the holder the right to convert the bond into ordinary shares, with the terms and conditions of the conversion set at the time of issue.

  (b) *Bonds with equity warrants attached*. Warrants are options which give the holder the right to buy shares in a company at a given price in the future. Warrants are attached to the bonds but are securities in their own right and so can be stripped from the bond

and sold separately. This distinguishes them from convertibles, where the conversion rights are an integral part of the issue.

A breakdown of issue volumes by type is shown in table 12.3.

Table 12.3 Eurobond issues classified by type, 1980–2002 (percentages)

	1980	1982	1984	1986	1988	1990	1992	1994	1996	1998	2000	2002
Straight	68	70	52	65	72	69	80	70	68	71	66	66
Floating-rate note	22	22	39	25	11	18	13	21	25	25	30	32
Equity-related	9	9	8	8	17	14	7	9	7	4	4	2

Source: Bank for International Settlements, *Quarterly Review: International Banking and Financial Market Developments*, various issues.

Floating-rate notes were the fastest-growing section of the eurobond markets in the early 1980s. There were various innovations on the standard FRN, and issues by UK building societies and other UK financial institutions pushed sterling into the second largest currency for FRNs. The FRN market is dominated by financial institutions, banks in particular, which both issue and invest. A particular form of FRN, the perpetual FRN, so called because it is never redeemed, was popular with banks as it qualified as primary capital. All these developments receded with the virtual collapse of the FRN market at the end of 1986. This was for a variety of reasons, including excess competition in the issue side of the market, which drove down yields on some issues to unattractive levels, and concern from central bankers that perpetual FRNs both issued and held by banks did not properly spread risk outside the banking system. A further contributing factor to the decline of the FRN market at that time, namely growing interest in the euro-commercial paper market, is discussed below.

The FRN market appears to have recovered since 1992 as investors looked to longer-term issues of bonds and away from short-term notes such as commercial paper. One of the reasons for this is that investors are attracted to long-term floating-rate debt when interest rates are expected to rise and there was an expectation in the market in 1992 that US interest rates in particular had reached a trough. More recently, as interest rates have fallen since the late 1990s, FRNs have become increasingly attractive to investors.

Another factor behind the renewed interest in FRNs by borrowers is the increased use of structured FRNs. These are designed to respond to investors' views of future interest rate trends but do not expose the issuer to associated interest rate risk. There are three principal types of structured FRNs.

(i) Reverse FRNs are structured to produce rising coupons as a floating reference rate falls. The notes contain an implicit interest rate cap, with a strike price equal to the fixed-rate element, as well as non-negativity clauses to prevent rates falling below zero.
(ii) Collared FRNs contain caps and floors, thereby generating maximum and minimum returns. They contain two embedded options and in effect the issuer purchases a cap from the investor and at the same time sells the investor a floor.
(iii) Step-up recovery FRNs (SURFs) pay coupons linked to yields on comparable longer-maturity bonds. With a rising yield curve they therefore pay the higher yield available at the longer maturity.

So, in 1993, with investors' expectations that US interest rates were reaching a trough, there was a high demand for collared dollar FRNs. Investors with views on the shape of the US yield curve could have alternatively purchased SURFs. However, in Europe in 1993 investors expected interest rates to fall further in many countries and thus were keen to invest in reverse FRNs. These swap-related derivative strategies (caps and floors) are discussed further in chapter 13.

The equity-related issues of international bonds saw rapid growth over the latter part of the 1980s. These issues have been predominantly of bonds with attached warrants issued mainly by Japanese investors denominated in US dollars. This was related to the strength of the Japanese stock market in the late 1980s, which made the issues attractive to investors. As the Japanese equity indices fell in the late 1990s, issues of equity-related bonds, which are related to these indices, have fallen.

12.2.4 *Euro medium-term notes*

These are borrowing facilities backed by issues of paper where the paper generally has a maturity of over one year. The maturity of the paper can in theory be any length of time up to infinity but in practice is limited to around five years. The market has shown steady growth since its emergence on a significant scale in 1986, with an acceleration in growth since 1993. One factor behind the recent growth has been the relaxation of issuing constraints in several countries. Japanese companies have been permitted to tap the euro medium-term note (EMTN) market directly since July 1993 and in a number of European countries deregulation measures have been taken to facilitate the use of the national currency in EMTN programmes. Another feature of the market in recent years has been that more than half the issues have been linked to derivative instruments (termed 'structured'). The recent growth in the EMTN market has taken business away from the international bond markets. EMTNs accounted for 45 per cent of international securities issues in 2002 compared with 20 per cent in 1990. There

are three key reasons for this. First, medium-term notes (MTNs) are more flexible instruments than bonds: the maturity of the note issues together with the characteristics of the drawings under a MTN facility can be varied to meet the needs of investor and borrower. Second, the liquidity of a bond issue is to a large extent determined by its size and investors may require some minimum issue size in order to attract them to hold the bond. In contrast, the liquidity of MTNs is provided by the guarantee of dealers to buy and sell the security. Finally, recent developments in the US domestic market, where corporate borrowing appears to have shifted from bonds to MTNs, suggest that this may carry over to the international capital markets.

12.2.5 *Methods of issue of eurobonds*

Since the 1980s the standard method of issuing eurobonds is by way of a bought deal. This involves a lead manager buying the entire issue at an agreed price before the announcement of the issue. The issue is then resold (i.e. syndicated) after the announcement.

Since the late 1980s, members of the syndicate enter into a contractual agreement not to resell at a lower price until the full issue has been completed. In US terminology this is termed a 'fixed priced reoffer' technique.

The secondary market in eurobonds is mainly over the counter, with settlement being achieved via one of the international clearing systems (i.e. Euroclear or Clearstream).

12.3 **Money market instruments issued through the eurosecurities markets**

In contrast to the longer-term eurobonds, the money market instruments encompass the various types of short-term securities issued to tap the eurocurrency markets. There are two basic types of money market instruments, although there are many variations on these. The original instruments were note-issuance facilities (NIFs), which first appeared in 1978. The other type is eurocommercial paper (ECP), which is based on the NIFs and made a significant appearance in the mid-1980s. The amounts outstanding of the money market instruments issued through the eurosecurities market over the period 1990–2002 are shown in table 12.4.

12.3.1 *Note-issuance facilities*

These are formalised, syndicated, underwritten medium-term loans which enable borrowers to issue a stream of short-term bearer notes, usually of one, three or six months' maturity, on a rollover basis. These are generally issued through a tender panel and if the borrowers are unable to sell the notes at a given spread over LIBOR to investors in the market, then the underwriting banks guarantee to purchase the notes themselves. Thus,

Table 12.4 Money market instruments issued through the eurosecurities markets: amounts outstanding at year end, 1990–2002 ($billion)

	1990	1992	1994	1996	1998	2000	2002
Money market instruments total	89.3	114.8	125.5	176.6	233.0	493.8	438.5
Eurocommercial paper (ECP)	70.3	78.7	81.5	103.0	132.7	223.3	292.2
Other short-term instruments	19.0	36.1	44.0	73.6	100.3	270.5	146.3

Source: Bank for International Settlements, *Quarterly Review: International Banking and Financial Market Developments*, various issues.

borrowers obtain medium-term funds, generally for seven to ten years, financed by successive issues of short-term notes. NIFs therefore transform short-term funds into long-term funds, a transformation which is normally carried out through banks in their role as financial intermediaries. In this situation banks are, however, simply earning fee income for arranging and underwriting the facility and, as long as the notes are placed at the maturity dates without problems, then the business is off the balance sheet.

Note-issuance facilities were developed as an alternative to syndicated loans and partly performed that role in 1984 and 1985 as issues of these facilities increased at a rapid rate. Issues have declined relative to other types of short-term notes since the late 1980s, largely because of the action of central banks, which sought to ensure that banks increase their capital when underwriting NIFs for borrowers with low credit standing. This led to banks limiting NIFs to borrowers with high credit standing and, partly in response to this, new types of short-term credits have emerged, in particular ECP.

12.3.2 *Eurocommercial paper*

The issue of ECP is a more recent development in the euromarkets, making a significant appearance in late 1984, although the issuance of commercial paper dates from the mid-nineteenth century in the US (see chapter 10, section 10.2.6, for a description of commercial paper). ECP programmes differ from NIFs in two important respects: first, they are not underwritten; and second, borrowers use a small group of appointed banks and dealers to distribute the notes on a 'best efforts' basis. In addition, the paper generally has more flexible maturities than NIFs, and so can be tailored to investors' preferences. Dealers impart marketability to the paper by agreeing to repurchase them from holders before maturity. An important difference between US commercial paper and ECP is that the former is always credit rated. When ECP first appeared, very few of the issues were credit rated, although in recent years the majority of new issues have had a credit rating. This trend towards a fully credit-rated market appears to have been

accelerated by defaults by some ECP issuers in 1988 and 1989. As shown in table 12.4, the greater emphasis on credit ratings appears to have had a slowing effect on the market for ECP as the proportion of ECP of total money market instruments declined from 79 per cent in 1990 to 67 per cent in 2002. One reason is that lesser-rated borrowers who were originally attracted to the market in 1986–88 found it difficult to establish facilities. Another factor behind the slowdown in the growth of issues in the ECP market is competition from the newly developing domestic commercial paper markets in Europe and the more mature US market. Also, in recent years ECP has faced competition from the more flexible EMTNs, discussed in the previous section.

12.4 **Euro-equities**

Euro-equities or international equities are equities issued for sale outside the issuer's domestic market. The term 'international equity issues' is used to refer to both primary issues of shares and secondary placements of existing shares. The equity instrument is the same as that issued in domestic markets, so the only difference between domestic and international issues of equities is the method of distribution. One method of international equity issue is to obtain a simultaneous listing on more than one national exchange. This method has become less popular as it can be costly, owing to widely different listing procedures across the various exchanges. A method that is increasingly used is the two-tranche issue, where all the issue is listed on a domestic exchange but one tranche is targeted at foreign investors. The distribution of the foreign tranche is increasingly organised through a syndicate made up of one financial institution in each country where the issue is targeted.

Table 12.5 shows the volume of international equity issues since the mid-1980s. Up until 1987 growth of international equity issues was rapid owing to rising world stock markets and an increasing tendency towards international portfolio diversification following both liberalisation of financial markets and the abolition of capital controls in many countries. This growth was reversed following the world stock markets crash of 1987. Growth resumed in the 1990s as world stock market indices grew. This growth was interrupted again by the fall in equity prices in 2000–02, although the trend growth appears likely to continue, fuelled by the continuing trend towards international portfolio diversification.

There are a number of advantages to a company from an international issue of its equity. First, it has the effect of widening the ownership of the company beyond that of the domestic market. Second, it may be possible to issue at lower cost in foreign markets. Finally, it provides an escape from the size constraint of the domestic market. This is particularly the

Table 12.5 Volume of international equity issues, 1986–2002 ($billion)

	1986	1988	1990	1992	1994	1996	1998	2000	2002
International equity issues	14	11	15	26	62	83	126	318	102

Source: Bank for International Settlements, *Quarterly Review: International Banking and Financial Market Developments*, various issues.

case for companies in some European countries with small stock markets. At present the management of international equity issues can be more profitable for a bank than an international bond issue. Greater competition in the future, however, is likely to reduce margins and therefore issue costs.

12.5 The use of swaps in eurosecurities markets

The nature of swaps is discussed in chapter 13, on derivative instruments. Swaps are widely used in international capital market transactions and were one of the forces behind the rapid growth of the eurobond markets over the 1980s and 1990s. Swaps enable a borrower to raise funds in the market in which it has a comparative advantage and then swap into a liability with preferred characteristics. For example, a borrower, X, may have a competitive advantage in the fixed-interest bond market but a preference for floating-rate funds to match its floating-rate assets. Thus, the borrower can raise funds at a competitive cost through the issue of a fixed-rate bond but swap for a floating-rate obligation with borrower Y, which has a competitive advantage in the floating-rate market but is looking for low-cost fixed-rate funds. Such swaps will normally be facilitated by a bank. As long as the interest rates swapped into by the two parties are lower than the interest rates obtainable from direct borrowing through the markets where they do not have a competitive advantage then the swap is worthwhile. This fixed/floating-rate swap is a classic type of interest rate swap and, if the floating rate is one linked to LIBOR, is known as a ‘plain vanilla’.

A second type of swap transaction used in the international capital markets is the currency swap. Here the swap involves an exchange of interest payments and principal denominated in one currency for payments in another. Again, borrowers will borrow in the currency in which they have a comparative advantage and then swap into the preferred currency. There are two main types of currency swap in the capital markets: fixed/fixed currency swaps, and fixed/floating currency swaps. The latter, referred to as cross-currency interest rate swaps, involve both a currency and interest rate swap.

Table 12.6 Over-the-counter derivative markets, 1988–2002: notional principal outstanding

	1988	1990	1992	1994	1996	1998	2000	2002
Interest rate swaps	1,011	2,311	3,851	8,816	19,171	56,015	64,668	101,699
Currency swaps	320	578	860	915	1,160	18,011	15,616	18,469

Source: Bank for International Settlements, *Quarterly Review: International Banking and Financial Market Developments*, various issues.

Table 12.6 indicates the size of the interest rate and currency swap markets in recent years. There has been a dramatic increase in the use of swap contracts, and interest rate swap contracts in particular. This growth partly reflects the growth in international bond issues, where a large proportion of fixed-rate bonds involve an interest rate or currency swap. Another factor behind this growth is the continuing volatility in interest rates and currency markets. The growth in other swap-related derivatives reflects the growing use of derivatives such as collars and caps with issues of FRNs and MTNs (see discussion above). The US dollar market accounts for approximately 70 per cent of the interest rate swap market and 85 per cent of activity in the currency swap market involves the US dollar on one side of the transaction.

12.6 **Disintermediation**

Major borrowers can raise funds in the international markets in three ways: they can borrow from the banking system, issue equities, or issue debt securities such as bonds or notes.

As we established in chapter 2, one of the reasons for banks' existence as financial intermediaries is that of transaction and information costs. This applies as much to international financing as it does to domestic financing. Over the 1980s international banks were beset by problems such as bank failures in the US and the sovereign debt crisis, which reduced the credit standing of many banks and thus the competitiveness of their lending rates. It was suggested (see for example Bank for International Settlements 1986) that banks had lost their comparative advantage in international financing. In addition, information costs fell because of the emergence of a large number of credit rating agencies over the 1980s. As a consequence, many of the larger borrowers with good credit ratings found they could raise funds more cheaply through the international capital markets. That is, there has been a greater preference, during some periods since 1980, for direct financing rather than indirect financing through a bank intermediary. This can be seen in table 12.7, which shows the relative volumes of the various forms of international finance since the late 1980s.

Table 12.7 Breakdown of international financing, 1988–2002 ($billion)

	1988	1990	1992	1994	1996	1998	2000	2002
Change in net international bank claims[a]	152	278	110	–24	356	125	432	308
Net international bond and note financing	159	165	159	285	499	669	1,091	1,022
Total international financing	311	443	269	261	855	794	1,523	1,330
Minus double counting[b]	69	80	75	60	143	139	230	220
Total net international financing	242	363	194	201	712	655	1,293	1,110
Bank financing as a proportion of total net financing	63	77	57	–12	50	19	33	28

[a] Changes in bank holdings of international non-bank claims. These claims include bonds purchased by banks as well as loans. The figures exclude inter-bank lending but include banks' own use of external funds for domestic lending.
[b] Purchases of bonds by banks where those bonds are issued by non-banks and therefore included in the figures for both the first and second lines of this table.
Source: Bank for International Settlements, *Quarterly Review: International Banking and Financial Market Developments*, various issues (authors' calculations).

Net international bank lending, which is made up of syndicated credits as well as short-term lending, was a declining proportion of total net international financing from the early 1980s. This is because of a switch from bank financing to indirect financing through the capital markets, a process known as disintermediation, for the reasons outlined above. Eurobonds were the main alternative long-term funding security to bank intermediation in the early 1980s. From the late 1980s, short- to medium-term direct financing through the issue of euronotes also emerged to compete with syndicated bank lending. However, this process of disintermediation (i.e. a switch from bank lending to securities issues) was halted in the latter half of the 1980s. The reason for this was principally the renewed growth in bank lending, which can be explained by the ambitious expansion of the Japanese banks over this period (discussed in chapter 7) and the increase in corporate restructuring in the US and UK financed largely by debt. In addition, issues of international securities are subject to considerable volatility owing to linkages with stock markets. The global stock market crash in 1987 halted the growth in international securities issues, with bond issues reaching pre-crash levels again only in 1989. In the early 1990s bank lending slowed down considerably as a consequence of a slowdown

in growth in many developed countries, and related to this was banks' poor performance on the domestic front (particularly in Japan), which constrained their international lending as a result of having to set aside high loan loss provisions. The recent expansion of bank lending is partly accounted for by a growth in syndicated lending to borrowers with low credit ratings in emerging markets. These borrowers do not generally have access to the international securities markets.

Looking to the future, the factors which led to the expansion of bank lending in the late 1980s look unlikely to be repeated, whilst the spread of disintermediation habits to Europe and the growth in the credit rating industry suggest that disintermediation may be a long-run trend.

It is a mistake, however, to equate disintermediation with a decline in the role of banks. Banks are actively involved in the securities markets in arranging the issue of securities and underwriting or providing guarantees of liquidity in the euronote markets. Banks are also the important players in the derivatives markets (chapter 13), such as swaps, futures and options, which underlie many security market transactions. Banks often act as counterparts in swap transactions or perform a transformation of characteristics as they construct tailor-made options and futures retail contracts from the wholesale standardised contracts traded on the exchanges. It can be argued, then, that disintermediation has not excluded banks from the international financing process but that banks have transferred their intermediation business, which appeared on the balance sheet, to fee-earning business, which is conducted off the balance sheet. Banks can be seen to have adapted, and more importantly innovated, in response to the changing preferences of international borrowers. The innovation that has taken place has tended to blur the boundaries between traditional intermediation and securities transacting.

12.7 **Conclusion**

In this chapter we have looked at the development of eurosecurities markets, which are the international equivalents of the domestic securities markets discussed in chapters 8, 9 and 10. These have grown rapidly since the 1980s and represent one facet of the internationalisation of finance.

Chapter 13

Financial derivatives

13.1 Introduction

Financial derivatives can be defined as instruments whose price is derived from an underlying financial security. The price of the derivative is linked to the price of the underlying asset and arbitrage maintains this link. This makes it possible to construct hedges using derivative contracts so that losses (gains) on the underlying asset are matched by gains (losses) on the derivative contract. In this chapter we will examine the main derivative contracts used in financial markets: financial futures, options, swaps and forward contracts. Derivatives can be categorised according to the type of trade. First, there is the category of exchange-traded instruments and in this case the instruments are purchased or sold on an organised financial exchange or market. This category includes financial futures and traded options. The second category refers to those instruments bought directly from a bank or other financial institution and these are called over-the-counter (OTC) derivatives. OTC derivatives include swaps, forward contracts and options.

The organisation of this chapter is as follows. In the next section we consider reasons for the development and growth of trading of financial derivatives over the past 20 or so years. In section 13.3 we examine the organisation of trading on Euronext.liffe, the second largest derivatives exchange in the world and the largest in Europe. In the remaining sections we examine the nature of financial futures (section 13.4), options (section 13.5), swaps (section 13.6), forward rate agreements (section 13.7) and credit derivatives (section 13.8). In section 13.9 we include a number of case studies illustrating possible dangers from derivatives trading and in section 13.10 we summarise a selection of the studies that have examined the efficiency of derivatives markets, before concluding in section 13.11. However, a word of caution is appropriate here. Derivatives markets are dynamic and new products are continuously evolving. Hence our discussion of this topic is not likely to remain comprehensive for many years.

13.2 The development and growth of financial derivatives

Exchange-traded financial derivatives were first developed in the US, by the Chicago Board of Trade (CBOT) in 1975. This was followed in September 1982 with the establishment in London of LIFFE, which became the first financial futures market in Europe. Traded options were a later development, appearing in the early 1980s. The first recognisable swap contracts also appeared in the early 1980s. So financial derivative contracts are a fairly recent development. The exception to this is the forward currency contract, which has a much longer history. In addition, derivative contracts on commodities, such as gold, other metals and agricultural products have existed for centuries.

Before we move on to consider the growth and volume of derivative trading, a word of caution is appropriate here. The volume of trade can be measured in two ways: by the notional value of contracts (i.e. the unit of trading) and the number of contracts. These two measures can give very different pictures because the notional value of contracts differs significantly. For example, the short sterling contract at Euronext.liffe has a nominal value of £500,000 whereas the nominal value of the long gilt contract is only £100,000. Thus comparisons between the value and contract number measures are inappropriate unless the pattern of trading is the same for the two exchanges being compared. As shown in figure 13.1, financial derivative

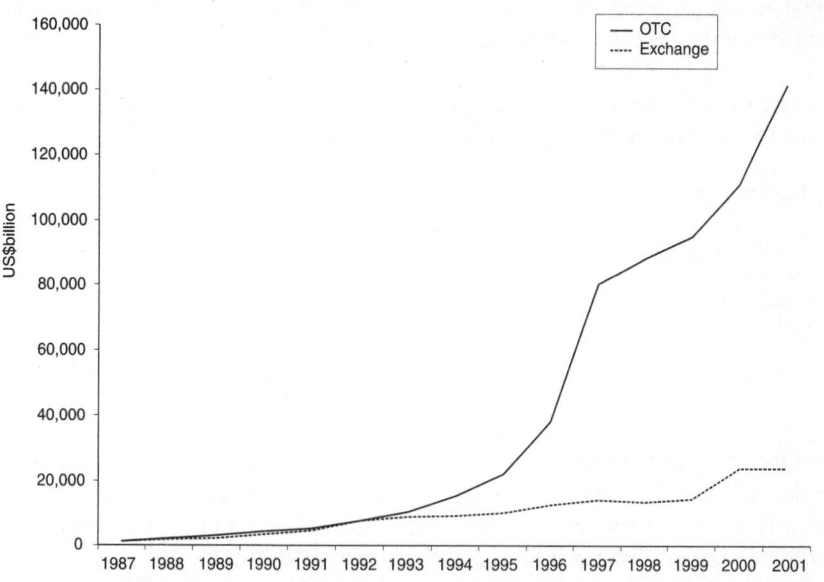

Figure 13.1 Derivatives contracts: notional amounts outstanding as at year end, 1987–2002. Source: Bank for International Settlements, *Quarterly Review: International Banking and Financial Market Developments*, various issues.

contracts have seen a very rapid rate of growth over recent years, with a truly spectacular rate of growth in the OTC sector.

One of the reasons for this spectacular growth is the high degree of volatility experienced in interest rates, inflation and exchange rates since the collapse in 1971 of the regime of fixed exchange rates established by the Bretton Woods agreement (see chapter 14, figures 14.1 and 14.2 for more details). In particular, the growth in the quantity of primary securities issued has led automatically to a higher volume of secondary market transactions and therefore a greater demand for hedging instruments and hence financial derivatives. The rapid growth of information technology and consequent reduction in transaction costs have also played a role by stimulating the development of new trading strategies which enable agents to use financial derivatives as a means of reducing risk. This aspect of the role of financial derivatives is considered in greater detail in chapter 14.

Table 13.1 shows the relative importance of various geographical regions in derivatives trading. Because US exchanges were the first to develop financial futures contracts, they dominated the trading of derivatives until recently. The North American markets still accounted for about 57 per cent, by value of outstanding contracts, of total exchange-traded financial derivatives in 2002 but that share had diminished from 95 per cent in the mid-1980s because the other markets had experienced a faster rate of growth. In particular, the European markets now account for approximately 37 per cent of total amounts outstanding.

Table 13.1 Regional pattern of derivatives exchange trading: percentage of total amounts outstanding at December 2002

Region	Percentage of total
North America	57.3
Europe	37.1
Asia and Pacific	5.1
Other	0.5

Source: Bank for International Settlements, *Quarterly Review: International Banking and Financial Market Developments*, March 2003, table 23A.

Table 13.2 shows the relative importance of the various types of contracts traded worldwide (again, the statistics refer to outstanding values). It can be seen by this measure that financial futures dominate trading and that within financial futures interest rate derivatives dominate.

The structure of derivatives exchanges, throughout the world but particularly in Europe, is changing. A number of mergers between derivatives exchanges have taken place and more are planned. In addition, cross-border cooperation between exchanges is taking new forms. In the UK, the London

Table 13.2 World derivatives contracts: notional amounts outstanding, analysed by type of contract at December 2002

Type of contract	$billion	Percentage of total
Forex	18,543	11.2
Interest rate	123,410	74.4
Equity linked	4,398	2.7
Commodity	923	0.6
Other[a]	18,337	11.1
Total	165,611	100

[a] 'Other' includes reporting positions of non-regular reporting institutions.
Source: Bank for International Settlements, *Quarterly Review: International Banking and Financial Market Developments*, March 2003.

Traded Options Market merged with LIFFE in 1992 and then in 1996 LIFFE and the London Commodities Exchange merged. LIFFE also introduced cross-listing of some of its contracts with other exchanges. Another important development was the agreement between the German and Swiss derivatives exchanges, DTB and the Swiss Options and Financial Futures Exchange, to establish a common trading and clearing platform for their products, in late 1998, called Eurex. In 2001 Euronext purchased LIFFE to form a major international derivatives market comprising the Amsterdam, Brussels, LIFFE, Lisbon and Paris derivatives exchanges. The fast rate of growth of trading at this new exchange is illustrated in figure 13.2, where the trades of the individual exchanges have been amalgamated.

In the next section we outline the general organisation of Euronext.liffe, which, given its relative importance as indicated in table 13.1, will provide an indication of how futures markets typically operate.

13.3 The organisation of Euronext.liffe

A range of financial and commodity futures and options are traded on Euronext.liffe. In this book we are interested only in the financial derivatives. We consider the nature of financial futures and options in more detail in sections 13.4 and 13.5, but we begin here with a brief definition of these two types of contract. A financial futures contract can be defined as an agreement to sell or buy a financial instrument (or quantity of instruments) on an organised market or exchange at a future date and at a price specified at the time of making the contract. In contrast, an option confers the right, but not the obligation, to the purchaser to buy (a 'call' option) or the right to sell (a 'put' option) an underlying financial instrument at a specified

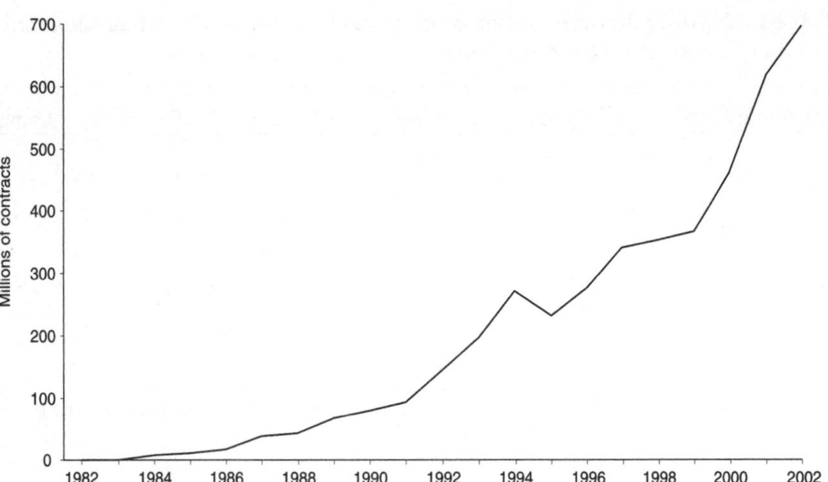

Figure 13.2 Derivatives trading at the exchanges comprising Euronext.liffe, 1982–2002. Source: LIFFE.

price and time in the future. The practical distinction between traded and OTC options is that the former can be bought from and sold to parties other than the original writer (i.e. seller) of the option. The market in the underlying or actual financial instrument is called the cash market and the options or futures market the derivative market. One characteristic of traded derivative contracts is that certain features are standardised. This of course enables them to be traded, unlike OTC derivatives, for which the terms of the contract are negotiated. On Euronext.liffe the standard unit of trading is £500,000 for three-month sterling futures, $1,000,000 for three-month eurodollar futures and £100,000 for long gilt futures. The minimum unit of trading decreases as the maturity of the underlying cash market security increases, owing to the increase in its price volatility – this is evidenced by the difference in the notional principal of the short sterling and gilt contracts. Delivery of the security is also made on specific dates according to a fixed sequence of months, March, June, September and December being the most common. The contract usually extends up to two years in advance but can be up to four years. These standard features reduce the flexibility of the contracts available compared with, say, the provision of tailor-made forward foreign exchange contracts provided by the banks, as was discussed in chapter 11 (section 11.5). On the other hand, the provision of standardised contracts enables trading to be carried out at a low cost since the buyers and sellers know precisely what they are trading.

The second general point to note is that although the transactions are originally made between two parties on the exchange, the two resulting contracts are then transferred to the London Clearing House,[1] which clears and guarantees all transactions carried out on Euronext.liffe and a number of other London exchanges. Consequently the Clearing House has a zero net position since it has acquired both sides of the trade. This system has a number of advantages. First, the risk of default is eliminated for both parties to the transaction since it is borne by the Clearing House. In order to protect itself against default, the Clearing House requires both parties to deposit cash against the transaction (the 'initial margin') and this margin is revalued daily to take account of movements in the price of the underlying security (the 'variation margin'). Further protection is gained by restriction of dealing facilities to 'members' of Euronext.liffe, who themselves are representatives of a wide range of financial institutions. Second, it enables transactions to be 'closed out' before the maturity date since the party wishing to terminate the agreement merely takes out an exactly opposite liability. In fact over 90 per cent of agreements are closed out before the maturity date and we discuss the reasons for this in section 13.4.

A wide range of contracts are available on Euronext.liffe, including short-term and long-term interest rate contracts, government bond contracts, swap contracts and equity contracts (on both indices and individual company shares). In addition a number of commodity contracts are available on, for example, cocoa, coffee, sugar and wheat. A recently developed contract covers weather futures.

The relative importance of the various contracts traded at Euronext.liffe for 2002 is indicated in table 13.3. Note that this table is framed in terms of the total number of outstanding contracts rather than their notional value. Hence these statistics are not strictly comparable with those in tables 13.1 and 13.2. The statistics also demonstrate the relative importance of individual equity (chiefly in options contracts) and equity index contracts. Notable is the absence of significant dealings in currencies. The probable reason for this is that the OTC market (i.e. the forward market discussed in section 11.5) offers comparable products which are perceived by traders to be more advantageous. As far as currency futures are concerned, the forward market provides a similar and flexible opportunity to hedge against future exchange rate changes through either fix-dated or option-dated forward contracts. This eliminates the need to sell the instrument in the market. Nevertheless currency options and futures are available, for example on both the Chicago Mercantile Exchange and the Philadelphia Stock Exchange.

Dealing on Euronext.liffe is now carried out on an electronic trading platform called LIFFECONNECT. This is an electronic order matching system and the advantages of such a system are discussed further in chapter 7 (section 7.3).

Table 13.3 Numbers of contracts (in millions) outstanding at Euronext.liffe at end 2002

Product	Futures	Options	Total
Individual equity	0.2	63.1	63.3
Equity index	1.0	14.0	15.0
Short-term interest	3.0	5.0	8.0
Long-term interest	0.3	0	0.3
Commodity	0.4	0.1	0.5
Other	0	0.2	0.2
Total	4.9	82.4	87.3

Source: Euronext.liffe.

13.4 **The nature of financial futures**

In order to demonstrate the nature of financial futures it is necessary to describe their function. As is the case for all traded financial instruments (see chapter 7, section 7.4), three uses of financial futures are traditionally identified. These are hedging, trading (or perhaps more appropriately speculation) and arbitrage. In practice, however, it may be difficult to make this a clear-cut and unambiguous distinction since financial institutions are making greater use of derivatives markets for the purpose of asset/liability management.

13.4.1 *Hedging with financial futures*

Hedging can be considered a defensive operation by risk-averse operators to insure themselves against adverse movements in, for example, interest or exchange rates. As an outline of this function prior to consideration of particular hedging operations in detail, consider the position of an operator who buys a three-month sterling interest rate financial future. If current actual interest rates fall then the value of the future will increase since it is offering higher rates than can be obtained in the marketplace. Conversely, if current actual interest rates rise then the value of the financial future will fall since actual deposits will earn higher rates of interest. Consequently, the price of the financial future will move in the opposite direction to the movement of interest rates. Thus, it is possible for an agent to offset – at least partially – the effects of movements in interest rates by profits or losses on the value of the financial future by selling the futures contract back to the market. The basic trading rule is that if the trader's cash position will be adversely affected by higher than anticipated interest rates, then a futures contract should be sold. Conversely, if it is the prospect of lower rates that worry the trader, then a futures contract should be bought.

We now illustrate the procedure more precisely using as an example the three-month sterling interest rate futures contract. A company has obtained a loan of £1,000,000 at a rate of 12 per cent from the money markets which is due to be rolled over on 1 June. The company is concerned that interest rates will change, with a probability that the loan will be rolled over at a higher rate. In order to protect itself the company sells two three-month sterling interest rate financial futures (each valued £500,000) which are due for delivery after 1 June – it is of critical importance that the delivery date of the futures contract is later than the date when the risk to be hedged disappears, otherwise there will be a period of time when potential changes in prices of the cash instrument are not hedged. Assuming the current interest rate is 12 per cent, the price of each contract is (100 – the annual rate of interest), that is, 88 in this example. The price of the contract will move up or down in minimum amounts of 0.01 per cent, which are known as a 'ticks' or basis points. The value of a tick varies for each type of financial future but may, in this case, be derived by applying the 0.01 per cent rate of interest to the face value of a £500,000 contract for one-quarter of a year and is therefore £12.50. On 1 June the company will buy the two contracts back from the exchange. We can now examine the effect of this transaction if interest rates had risen to 14 per cent per annum on 1 June. The first point to note is that the company will bear extra borrowing costs of £5,000 for the next quarter due to the rise in interest rates of 2 per cent per annum. We next look at the futures market transaction and we initially assume that the futures price has also moved in line with the cash market rate. The company:

(i) sells two contracts at 88 (rate of interest 12 per cent);
(ii) buys back two futures at 86 (rate of interest 14 per cent) on 1 June;
(iii) gains 200 ticks per contract (i.e. 400) at £12.50 = £5,000.

In this case the higher cost of interest is exactly matched by the profit on the two futures transactions. If, on the other hand, interest rates had fallen, then the company's borrowing cost would have fallen but this would have been offset by the loss on buying back the futures contract. This clarifies what the company has gained from its financial futures operation, namely that the uncertainty surrounding the future interest rate on its borrowing cost has been removed. It is important to realise that the company has not necessarily made a gain on its futures transactions. In fact in the case of an interest rate fall it would have incurred a loss on the futures, but it would have reduced the uncertainty of future costs. This example also illustrates the reason why most contracts are 'closed out' (i.e. reversed) before the time for delivery of the futures contract, since the offsetting gain/loss on the futures contract is realised when the futures contract is closed out.

Basis risk

The precision of the hedge in the above example is due to the fact that we assumed that the price of the futures contract has moved exactly in line with the cash market rate. This degree of precision is unlikely to occur in practice and, to understand why, we need to consider a concept known as basis. This may be defined as:

basis = cash price – futures price.

In the example quoted above the basis is zero at the start and the finish of the hedging operation. It is quite common, however, for a non-zero basis to exist, since the cash and futures prices are subject to different influences. In particular, the futures price will reflect the market's view of the level of the interest rate in the future. If we return to the above example, consider the case where the futures price at the time the hedger sells the contracts is not 88 but rather 87.50: the existence of a futures price of 87.50 and a cash price of 88.00 implies that the market expects interest rates to rise in the period up to the date of the futures contract. The basis at the start of the hedge is therefore (88.0 – 87.5) or 0.5. If the basis is different at the time the hedger 'closes out', then the hedge will not be perfect. To illustrate this point, consider the position if the futures price had been 86.00 on 1 June (i.e. a zero basis given an interest rate of 14 per cent) then the gain on the hedge would have been 150 (8,750 – 8,600) ticks per contract, or £3,750 in total. In this case a partial hedge has been achieved since the gain on the futures contract does not cover the additional interest charges on the rolled over loan.

It is also quite possible that the change in basis could work in favour of the hedger. For example, again starting from an original price of 87.5, if the futures price was 85.00 on 1 June (i.e. a basis of 1.0) then the gain would have been 250 ticks per contract, or £6,250 in total. A further point worth noting is that, if the futures contract purchased by the hedger had been for delivery in June, then it is quite likely that the basis on 1 June would have been close to zero. This is because as the delivery date on the futures contract approaches, then the cash price and the futures price tend to equality because the influences on the two contracts are identical on the delivery date. As is shown below, any difference between the two prices would lead to arbitrage.

A non-zero basis can occur for a number of reasons. Thus, if the basis is close to zero when the contract is being taken out then it is sensible to choose futures contracts that mature soon after the disappearance of the risk to be hedged. In general, however, cash and futures prices of similar instruments do exhibit a fairly high degree of correlation, so that basis risk (the risk of movements in basis) is less than outright risk (the risk of an

unhedged position) as long as the characteristics of the instrument being hedged are not very different from those of relevant futures instrument.

13.4.2 *Speculation with financial futures*

We now turn to examine the role of trading or speculation in the operation of financial futures markets. Providers of a hedge can protect themselves by negotiating an offsetting contract. In the example of the company quoted above, the purchaser of the futures may at that time be able to identify a customer who wishes to buy two similar contracts. In this instance the financial institution providing the hedge has incurred no risk since it has two offsetting contracts with windfall gains on one contract matching windfall losses on the other. In practice it is highly unlikely that the quantity of hedging demanded for a change in one direction will exactly match that required in the opposite direction, so traders fill the gap by making the market and therefore provide a useful economic function.

Trading is basically a non-defensive activity undertaken by those agents willing to bear the risk of price changes. Their income comes from two sources, which in practice may be difficult to distinguish: first, there is the reward for undertaking risk, and second the potential profits to be earned from taking a correct view of the future course of the prices of the underlying cash market securities. Financial futures are a particularly useful vehicle for speculation since transaction costs are low and there is no need to purchase or sell the underlying instrument and the cash outlay is restricted to the initial margin (typically varying between 0.1 per cent and 6 per cent of the face value of the contract) and the variation margin, thus offering potential for high degrees of leverage. If the price of the underlying security is expected to rise, speculators will go long, that is, buy financial futures, or if the price is expected to fall they will go short, that is, sell financial futures. Clearly, this is a risky operation and losses will be incurred if the prices move in the opposite direction to those anticipated by the trader. We use the long gilt futures contract as an illustration of the potential for trading contracts. Again we would like to emphasise that this is just one particular example of a wide range of potential trading activities available.

As was pointed out in chapter 9, prices of gilts are sensitive to interest rate changes and the degree of sensitivity increases directly with the outstanding maturity of the stock in question. Assume that a trader feels that the next round of publications of the various official statistics will be more favourable than has hitherto been the case. He also feels that this is likely to lead to a reduction in interest rates which has not fully been reflected in the current prices of gilt-edged stock. He therefore purchases one unit of gilt futures of £100,000 nominal value for the next delivery date after the publication of the last in the round of the official statistics he considers relevant. If he is correct and the statistics on balance are sufficiently favourable

to permit a fall in interest rates then gilt prices will rise and so consequently will the gilt futures contract, so that the trader will make the expected profit. It should be emphasised that the profit is entirely dependent on the accuracy of the trader's forecast as against that implicit in market prices.

13.4.3 *Arbitrage in financial futures markets*

The third activity in futures markets is arbitrage – to take advantage of price anomalies between either the underlying cash market instruments and the different futures contracts. Such price anomalies are likely to be quite small and short lived since other traders will quickly perceive the opportunity of making a profit with minimal risk. As one example we consider the position of the long gilt futures contract. This contract can be carried out by delivery of gilts from a list of deliverable gilts. For example, for the September 1998 long gilt futures contract, the list refers to any stock maturing between the years 2008 and 2012 inclusive but excludes convertible and index-linked stocks. Thus, if the prices of the futures and underlying stocks are misaligned it may be possible to borrow funds, purchase the misaligned deliverable stock and sell an appropriate futures contract. This is called cash and carry arbitrage. Little risk is attached to such an operation provided all the contracts are undertaken simultaneously. Anomalies between the prices of futures contracts may occur between different types of contracts such as between the various three-month interest rate futures noted in section 13.3 or between different delivery dates of the same futures contract. This latter arbitrage is known as spreading. We now demonstrate the process of cash and carry arbitrage more formally.

Assuming continuous discounting, then the following condition must hold if no arbitrage possibilities exist:

$$F = Se^{r(T-t)} \tag{13.1}$$

where F is the forward price, S the price of the underlying security, r the risk-free rate of interest, T the time when the contract matures and t current time. If, for example, $F > Se^{r(T-t)}$ then profits can be made by borrowing S for the period $T - t$, buying the asset and selling (taking a short position) the forward contract. At time $T - t$, a profit equal to $F - Se^{r(T-t)}$ has been obtained. The converse would apply if $F < Se^{r(T-t)}$, that is, the forward contract would be purchased and the asset sold, with the proceeds from the asset being invested at the risk-free interest rate until the forward contract matures. To illustrate this point consider a share for which the market price is £40, the risk-free rate of interest is 4 per cent per annum and, for sake of ease of exposition, the time period involved ($T - t$) is one year (note if the futures matured in three months' time, then $T - t = 0.25$). Given this information, the equilibrium futures price is given by equation 13.1 as (£40 × $e^{0.04}$), or £41.63. If the actual market price of the forward contract is

£40, then sale of the stock would produce £40 and the proceeds would be invested to obtain £40 × $e^{0.04}$, or £41.63, as compared with the £40 required to purchase the forward contract in one year's time. Conversely if the forward price is £42, then £40 is borrowed for the year at the risk-free rate of 4 per cent, and the asset purchased for £40. In one year's time the asset would be sold for £42 in accordance with the forward contract as against the cost of borrowed funds of £41.63. This analysis applies strictly to forward contracts but would also apply to futures if either the risk-free interest rate is constant and the same for all maturities or is a known function of time. The intuitive reason for differences between forward and future prices is that the latter involve margin payments whereas the former do not. Also, equation 13.1 ignores costs involved in carrying the instrument. In the case of financial assets this is likely to be very near zero, so equation 13.1 can be regarded as depicting what is known as the 'cost of carry' relationship between the spot and the futures price. This cost would be reduced if the futures instrument yielded some known dividend or return and can be described by:

$$F = Se^{(r-i)(T-t)} \tag{13.2}$$

where i is the return on the futures instrument. In the case where the dividend is not known, i will represent the average dividend.

13.4.4 *Portfolio management using futures contracts*

In addition to the three traditional uses discussed above, futures markets can be used to vary a portfolio's overall maturity structure by altering the maturity of individual securities. For example, the average maturity of a portfolio can be 'synthetically' reduced by the sale of, say, a long gilt futures contract in five months' time and using a 'deliverable' gilt from the portfolio to complete the transaction. Thus, the maturity on the security has been changed from its previous term to five months and the new redemption value is the price implied by the futures contract. Similarly, the average length of a portfolio of short-term securities can be lengthened by purchasing a series of short-term contracts.

13.4.5 *Nature of currency futures*

Before turning to a discussion of the nature of options in section 13.5, it is worthwhile examining, albeit briefly, the nature of foreign currency futures on the International Money Market (IMM) at CME. The four major currencies traded are the euro, Swiss franc, Japanese yen and sterling. The largest of these four types of contract concerns the euro and the market report for this contract in the *Financial Times* (25 July 2003) quoted a latest price of \$1.1468 (the equivalent of a closing price) for delivery in September. We use this quotation to demonstrate the principles of this

market. As is the case for other futures contracts, settlement is made on a specific date and can be by way of cash settlement or delivery of the currency. IMM quotes the rate as dollars per euro and the size of the contract is €125,000, so the buyer of the contract has agreed to pay $143,350 for €125,000 for delivery in September (125,000 × 1.1468). If the price of the euro rises to 1.1500, the value of the contract rises to $143,750 and the buyer has made a profit of $400. As in the case of Euronext.liffe and other futures contracts, the seller of the contract would have to pay and the buyer receive additional margins.

Clearly, on the expiry date the underlying (i.e. the spot) rate and the futures price would coincide. Before this date there will be a gap between the current spot rate and the futures price and this is called the 'swap'. The level of the swap reflects the interest differentials and can be calculated according to the following formula (assuming interest is paid at discrete intervals):

$$\text{swap} = (\text{spot exchange rate}) \times (\text{eurodollar rate} - \text{euro rate}) \times (\text{days to delivery}/360)$$

(We have assumed 360 days per year, as is the custom in many derivatives markets.)

Thus, for example, suppose at the close of trade on a particular day, the eurodollar and euro three-month deposit rates were 6.5 per cent per annum and 5.5 per cent, respectively, and the spot exchange rate was $1.1500 per euro. On a contract which has, say, 90 days to delivery, the swap is:

$$1.1500 \times (0.065 - 0.055) \times (90/360) = 0.002875$$

The trader could then add the swap to the current spot rate to arrive at a theoretical futures price of 1.1529. If the actual futures price were less than 1.1529, a trader could make a profit by selling euros spot and buying futures. Similarly, if the futures price were above 1.1529 the trader could buy euros spot and sell futures. Of course in practice the differential would have to exceed transaction costs, which in any case are likely to be low.

13.5 The nature of options

Options give the purchaser, in return for a premium, the right to buy (a 'call' option) or the right to sell (a 'put' option) a financial instrument at an agreed exchange rate (the 'striking' price) at a specified date or dates. No obligation is imposed on buyers to carry out the obligation so they will choose to do so only if it is profitable for them. Two classes or types of options can be distinguished. As was discussed in section 13.3, an option can be either an OTC option or a traded option. OTC options have to be either exercised or allowed to lapse. Traded options offer the additional

choice to the holder of reselling them on the market. In fact, as we shall see later, it is more likely that a traded option will be resold rather than exercised. Trading on organised options markets can be for the purposes of both speculation and hedging, and it is the presence of speculators which provides liquidity for the market. Options can be further categorised into American and European options. An American type of option can be exercised at any date up to its expiry, whereas the European type can be exercised only on a specified date. The options traded on Euronext.liffe are generally of the American type. Premiums for traded options are quoted in market statistics and we show in table 13.4 the relevant details at the close of trading for just two of the share options (BP and ICI) which were traded at Euronext.liffe as reported in the *Financial Times*. Whilst this example is framed in terms of options on individual shares, it is illustrative of the whole genre of options, as they are all priced in the same manner.

Table 13.4 Examples of LIFFE equity options

	Strike/exercise price	Calls			Puts		
		January	April	June	January	April	June
BP	420	13	23	31½	10½	17½	24
(421[a])	460	1½	8	16	39½	43	48
ICI	700	53	66½	75½	3½	20	25½
(746[a])	750	19	35½	47	20	43½	49

[a] Underlying security price.
Source: *Financial Times,* market report dated 17 December 1994.

The detail contained in table 13.4 can be interpreted in the following way. A trader can purchase a call option (i.e. the right to buy BP shares) expiring in January at a strike/exercise price of 420p per share for a premium (i.e. price) of 13p per share. For April expiry and the same strike price the premium is 23p per share. Similarly, the purchase of a put option (the right to sell) with a strike price of 460p per share and June expiry would require a premium of 48p per share. A similar interpretation is easily derived for ICI shares. Shares have to be purchased in quantities of 1,000.

We use the quotation for April calls and puts at a strike price of 420p per share to derive the diagrams used to illustrate the profit and loss situation for the purchaser and the writer of the option.

In the first example the purchaser of a call option will exercise it to purchase BP shares only if the market price rises above 420p per share. At market prices lower than this it is more profitable for the trader to purchase BP equity in the market so that the loss is restricted to the 23p premium

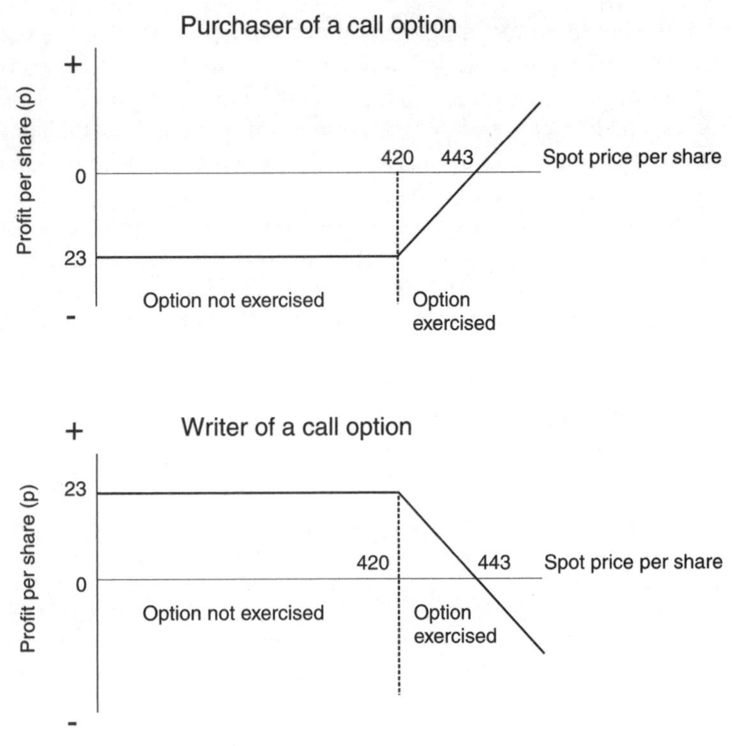

Figure 13.3 Profit/loss profile of a call option.

paid on taking out the option. The break-even point occurs when the actual market price is 443p per share so that the premium just matches the gain on the option contract of 23p. In effect, therefore, the purchase of the call option has fixed the maximum price to be paid for BP shares at 443p per share. As the market price rises above 443p per share the purchaser obtains profits which in theory are unlimited but in practice are limited to the likely range of market fluctuations. The position for the seller (i.e. the 'writer') of the option is the mirror image of that of the purchaser. Figure 13.3 illustrates the above situation.

The position in the case of the purchase of a put option is the reverse of that in the case of a call option and is illustrated in figure 13.4. For an exercise price of 420p per share the option will be exercised only when the market price for BP equity falls below 420p per share. At prices above 420p it is more profitable to sell the shares in the market. Consequently, the break-even price for the purchaser is 402½p per share, when the profit on the sale of shares just matches the premium paid (i.e. 17½p per share). As

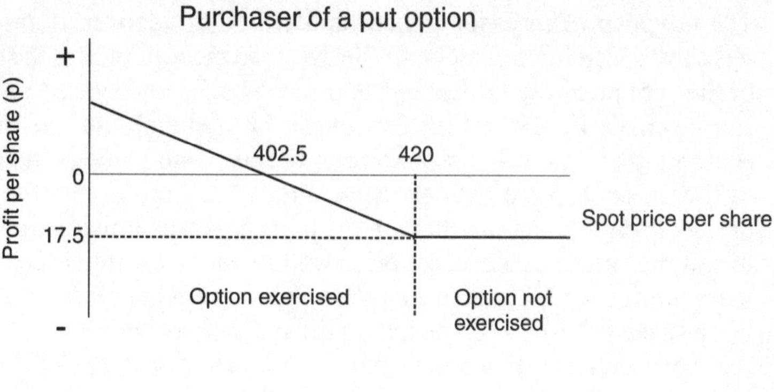

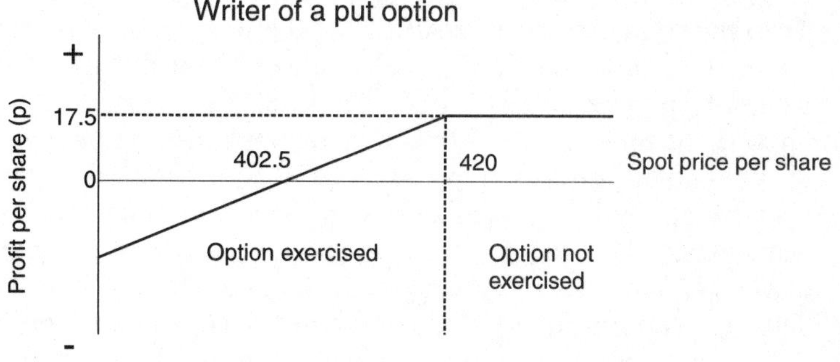

Figure 13.4 Profit/loss profile of a put option.

the actual market price falls below 402½p per share the purchaser makes gains which in theory are limited only by a market price of zero but, in practice, are again limited by the likely range of fluctuations. As for the case of a call option, the position of the writer is the mirror image of that of the purchaser.

Remember, the exercise of an option lies entirely in the hands of the purchaser. The writer has no control over whether the option is exercised or not. It is in the nature of a contingent liability which may or may not be incurred. As far as the purchaser is concerned, an option contract is analogous to an insurance policy with the premium for the option representing the premium paid for the policy and the risk insured is the downside risk of an adverse movement in the share price, with the purchaser taking all the benefits of a favourable movement.

13.5.1 *Pricing of options*

The price of an option contract can be divided into two components:

(i) The *intrinsic value* is the gain which would be realised if an option were exercised immediately. In the case of a call option it is the excess of the spot price over the exercise price. This represents the gain that can be made by exercising the option immediately and selling the share in the market. For a put option the intrinsic value is the excess of the exercise price over the spot rate, which represents the profit derived from buying the share in the market and exercising the option to sell the shares at the strike price. In the above example the current market price for BP shares was 421p per share at the close of trading. For a strike price of 420p per share the intrinsic value for a call option for April delivery is 1p per share. Similarly, for a put option at a strike price of 460p per share for April delivery the intrinsic value is 39p (460 – 421). The intrinsic value is always positive or zero.

(ii) The *time value* represents that part of the premium not represented by the intrinsic value. For the call example given above, an intrinsic value of 1p per share and a premium of 23p per share (April call option), the time value is 22p per share; similarly, the time value for the put quoted above is 4p per share (43 – 39). Time value cannot be negative and will approach zero at an increasing rate as the option nears expiry. This can be seen from table 13.4, where the time value of a call option at a strike price for ICI shares of 700p is 7p for January delivery (current price = 746p, hence intrinsic value = 46p, which with a premium of 53p gives a time value of 7p), 20½p for April delivery and 29½p for June delivery.

When a non-zero intrinsic value of an option exists the option is said to be 'in the money'. For a put option, if the strike price is less than the current spot rate, then the option is said to be 'out of the money'. A call option is said to be 'out of the money' if the strike price is more than the current price. If the exercise (strike) price is equal to the spot price then the option is 'at the money'. Time value is at its maximum for a given expiry date when an option is at the money and tends to zero for options deeply out of the money or deeply in the money. This can be rationalised intuitively by considering the position of an option deeply out of the money. The further the option is away from the strike price the more unlikely it becomes that it will ever be exercised. Hence both the value to the holder and the risk to the writer are reduced, thus lowering the premiums required for taking on the risk. For an option in the money, intrinsic value exists so that the holder incurs the risk of this value being eroded by adverse movements in the spot price. As far as the writer of the option is concerned, the adverse movement to the holder would be a gain. The larger the intrinsic value the greater is the risk of erosion of the intrinsic value. Thus, the premium will compensate the buyer of the option with a reduced time value in the premium

and the writer will be willing to grant the lower premium owing to the lower risk involved.

The presence of the time component in the price of an option means that it is likely that the holder will sell the option in the market rather than exercise it. To illustrate this point consider again the case of the call option expiring in April with a strike price of 420p per share. The premium is 23p per share, which exceeds the intrinsic value of 1p, so that sale of the option in the market would permit the holder to extract the time value for herself or himself.

The price of an option mainly depends on the factors listed below:

(i) the strike or exercise price;
(ii) the current market price of the underlying asset, in the case of BP or ICI shares 421p and 746p, respectively (see table 13.4);
(iii) time to the expiry of the option;
(iv) the volatility of the price of the underlying asset;
(v) the risk-free interest rate.

The precise relationship between these factors is derived by various mathematical formulae, of which perhaps the most well known is the Black–Scholes formula. Discussion of the mathematical methods necessary to derive such relationships is beyond the scope of this text but it is possible to identify intuitively how these factors influence the price of an option.

In the case of a call option, the lower the exercise or strike price the more likely it is to be exercised and therefore the higher the price (i.e. the premium). The second factor is the current spot price. In this case the higher the spot price the more likely the option is to be exercised. Two other factors are the volatility of the price of the underlying cash asset and the maturity of the option. The option is more likely to be exercised if the price of the cash instrument is volatile and/or the greater is the length of time before the option expires. Anything which increases the probability of the option being exercised raises the price of the option, that is, the premium. In the case of a put option the premium would be raised if the direction of the first two factors is reversed; that is, the option will be more valuable the lower the price of the underlying cash instrument and/or the higher the strike or exercise price. Finally, a rise in the risk-free rate of interest is likely to be accompanied by expectations of increased growth rate of the price of the share. However, the increased interest rate will reduce the present value of any future cash flows associated with the holding of the option. Both these effects will reduce the value of a put option. In the case of a call option, following a rise in the risk-free interest rate, the first effect discussed above raises its value but the second effect lowers it. However, the first effect dominates so that a rise in the risk-free rate of interest always increases the price of call options.

The effect of changes in the strike/exercise price and time can easily be seen from the detail contained in table 13.4. The effect of changes in the exercise price can be observed by looking down the columns and in time by looking along the rows.

13.5.2 *Exotic options*

In addition to the standard American-type and European-type options so far discussed, a number of options with non-standard or more complicated pay-offs exist. These are termed 'exotic options'. They are generally OTC options and are designed by banks to meet the specific needs of their customers. A large number of such options exist and we mention only a few to illustrate their nature. One such option is called a 'Bermudan' option, which, like American-type options, can be exercised up to and including the maturity date but, unlike American-type options, such early exercise is restricted to specific dates. Another type is 'forward start options', for which payment is made now but the option does not start until a later date. Similarly, options can be made up of a package of options in the manner discussed in chapter 14, where pay-offs of a combination of options are illustrated. One further example is provided by 'compound options', which are in fact options on options. As noted earlier, the types of exotic options are exceedingly numerous and our examples are designed merely to point out how departures from the standard European and American types of options can be engineered. We now turn to a discussion of swaps.

13.6 **Swaps**

A swap is an agreement between two parties to exchange future cash flows in accordance with a previously agreed formula. Normally such arrangements involve a bank acting as an intermediary rather than being directly between two companies. In this case the bank has entered into two contracts, one with each party. This causes the bank (or other financial intermediary) to incur the additional risk that one party may default, leaving the bank with an open contract. It is often the case that only one customer has approached a bank to arrange a specific swap. In this case the bank may assume the position of the counterparty until such time as the second part of the swap can be arranged. In this case the bank is said to 'warehouse' the swap. Again, additional risk is incurred by the bank until the offsetting transaction is arranged. Swaps are OTC derivatives and arise in a variety of forms. We begin our discussion with the simplest and most common form of a swap, between fixed and floating interest rate payments in the same currency. This is called a 'plain vanilla' interest rate swap.

Table 13.5 Hypothetical example of borrowing costs of two companies

	Fixed rate	Floating rate
Company A	8%	0.5% above LIBOR
Company B	9%	1.0% above LIBOR

13.6.1 *Example of a plain vanilla interest rate swap*

Consider the matrix of borrowing costs for two companies, A and B, shown in table 13.5. Suppose also that B wishes to borrow at fixed rates and A at floating rates. It may appear that since A can borrow more cheaply at both fixed and floating rates that no profitable swap is possible. This is not so, since the gap between the two fixed rates is different from that for the two floating rates. Company A pays 1 per cent less than B for fixed-rate loans but only 0.5 per cent less in the case of floating-rate loans. Thus, company A has a comparative advantage in the fixed-rate loan market and company B in the floating-rate loan market. The two companies profitably exploit this situation through:

(i) A borrowing at fixed rates and lending to B at, say, 8.2 per cent;
(ii) B borrowing at floating rates and lending to A at, say, the London inter-bank offer rate (LIBOR) + 0.5 per cent.

For ease of exposition we shall assume that the loan period is one year. The two companies' cash position is as follows.

Company A:
borrows at 8 per cent,
lends to B at 8.2 per cent,
pays B LIBOR + 0.5 per cent.

Hence net cost of a floating-rate loan to A is LIBOR + 0.3 per cent.

Company B:
borrows at LIBOR + 1 per cent,
lends to A at LIBOR + 0.5 per cent,
borrows from A at 8.2 per cent.

Hence net cost of fixed-rate loan to B is 8.7 per cent.

Note that the cost of the preferred type of borrowing is lower for both companies after the swap. This is the case even though company A has cheaper access to finance than company B in both markets. It is the existence of comparative advantage that matters.

In practice, as we have already noted, the swap would be arranged via a financial intermediary and the margins of lower cost in our hypothetical example show that the financial intermediary could easily exploit the situation to obtain a profit for itself. Also, it is important to realise that the principals themselves would not be exchanged, merely the net difference between the two streams of interest payments at periodic intervals as set out in the agreement.

It is interesting to speculate why such differences would occur. One reason put forward, as illustrated in the above example, is the existence of comparative advantage. However, this view does come up against the problem of why such differences are not eliminated by arbitrage in the manner indicated above. One possible explanation centres around the term of a loan and the possibility of default. If during the period of the loan contract the default risk of a company which had borrowed at floating rates increased, the desired margin over LIBOR would also increase. Normally the lender has the option of reviewing the margin during the period of the loan. The providers of fixed-rate loans do not have this option so the comparative advantage of A in the fixed-rate loan market may reflect differing probabilities of default in the future. Thus, B has secured a fixed rate of interest lower than would otherwise be the case.

13.6.2 *Other types of swaps*

A second type of swap is a 'plain deal currency' swap. Suppose company D wished to borrow in dollars and company C in sterling but the comparative advantages favoured dollar borrowing for C and sterling for D. In this case company C would borrow in dollars and company D in sterling. They would exchange the two sums borrowed and agree to pay the interest rates associated with the swapped sums (C in dollars and D in sterling). At the end of the period of the loan, they would again exchange the original principal sums so that no risk would arise from exchange rate changes. Again, the reason for this type of swap is probably differences in comparative advantage. As was the case for plain vanilla swaps, such a contract would normally be arranged via a financial intermediary, which is likely to 'warehouse' the swap if a counterparty is not immediately available.

A number of variations on the simple swaps discussed above exist. It is possible for example to combine a plain vanilla swap with a plain deal currency swap so that fixed-rate borrowing in one currency is swapped for floating-rate borrowing in another currency. Another alternative is an amortising swap, whereby the notional principal is reduced in a similar manner to a scheduled amortisation on a loan. Deferred or forward swaps are available and in this case the swap is negotiated now but comes into operation at a later date. Similarly, swaps can be 'extendable' (i.e. one party has the right to extend the life of the swap) or 'puttable' (i.e. one party has

the right to terminate the swap). Finally, options are available on swaps and these are called 'swaptions'.

13.7 **Forward rate agreements**

A forward rate agreement (FRA) is very similar to the interest rate futures discussed in section 13.4. It is an agreement in which two parties agree on the level of an interest rate to be paid on a notional deposit for a specific maturity at some specified time in the future. For example, a contract could be arranged for an agreed interest rate to be applied to, say, a six-month deposit commencing in three months' time. This particular contract would be quoted as 'three against nine months'. As in the case of interest rate futures, the deposit itself cannot be exchanged, so cash settlement is practised. Settlement takes place at the commencement of the contract, after three months in our example. The actual settlement is the difference between the interest rate agreed in the contract and a reference rate, which is normally LIBOR. If LIBOR is higher on the settlement date than the agreed rate then the buyer of the FRA receives from the seller the gap between the two rates (assuming of course that LIBOR is the reference rate). Conversely if the agreed rate is lower than LIBOR, the buyer pays the seller the gap between LIBOR and the agreed rate. In effect, then, a FRA is an OTC interest rate futures contract.

We now discuss briefly the nature of the FRA market. FRAs are usually traded for standard periods such as three, six, nine or twelve months. The market is primarily an inter-bank market although banks do conclude a number of agreements with their customers. FRAs are predominantly a US dollar market although contracts are specified in other currencies. Individual contracts are quite large, with agreements for $20 million being quite common by late 1985 and some contracts amounting to $50 million (Cross report – Bank for International Settlements 1986). London is one of the main centres of the market and the Cross report estimated that about 40 per cent of total FRA market activity occurred in London in 1985.

Forward rate agreements are popular as a means of managing interest rate risk. Thus, in the example quoted above, the buyer of the FRA has protected itself against a rise in interest rates as represented by the reference rate. Whatever happens to market rates of interest in three months' time, the buyer is locked into the agreed rate. The position for the seller is the converse. The seller has been assured of receiving the agreed rate, again irrespective of what happens to the reference rate. Both parties have purchased interest rate certainty and have given up the chance of random gains or losses. In other words it is a risk-averse strategy. For the policy to work the reference rate must be chosen to be representative of interest

rates in general, hence the choice of LIBOR. Clearly, FRAs also offer the opportunity of speculating against future interest rate movements.

13.7.1 *Example of the use of an FRA for hedging*

We now demonstrate the calculation of payments on FRAs. The standard formula is:

$$\pi = \frac{P \times (S - R) \times (m/\text{year})}{1 + S(m/\text{year})} \qquad (13.3)$$

where π is the payment to be made to the buyer by the seller if $S > R$, or to the seller if $S < R$, S is the reference rate at the settlement date and R the agreed rate; m is the number of days in the FRA. For the purpose of calculation, a year can consist of either 365 days (UK or Australia) or 360 days (e.g. US). Note that the payment is discounted by the market rate of interest (S) for the length of the FRA because the payment is made at the commencement of the contract.

To illustrate this formula consider the example quoted at the beginning of this section ('three against nine months') and assume that the agreed rate was 7 per cent and LIBOR 8 per cent on the settlement day and the agreement was for \$1,000,000. The buyer would receive from the seller of the FRA the following amount:

$$\pi = \frac{1{,}000{,}000 \times (0.08 - 0.07) \times (182/360)}{1 + 0.08(182/360)}$$

$$= \$4859.03$$

The buyer of the FRA has successfully been locked into a rate of 7 per cent at the end of the FRA period. This can easily be seen from the following calculations:

Borrowing at LIBOR:
\$1,000,000 @ 8 per cent for 182 days = 40,444.44
less receipt on FRA invested until end of agreement:
$4{,}859.03 \times \{1 + 0.08(182/360)\} = 5{,}055.55$
net payment = 35,388.89

Borrowing at 7 per cent:
$1{,}000{,}000 \times 0.07(182/360) = 35{,}388.89$

This numerical example demonstrates that the buyer of the FRA has, in effect, a fixed-rate loan at 7 per cent. Similarly, the seller has supplied a loan at a fixed rate of 7 per cent. In this example, the buyer has gained and the seller lost compared with transactions at LIBOR in three months' time. If interest rates had fallen, the loss would have been borne by the buyer of

the FRA. The significant point is that both parties have guaranteed themselves the fixed rate of 7 per cent for their respective transactions.

13.8 **Credit derivatives**

As we noted in chapters 3 and 4, credit risk (i.e. the risk that the borrower will default on either the interest payments due or the advance itself) is important to banks and, for that matter, other financial intermediaries. A fairly new instrument for managing this risk is a 'credit derivative'. The market for credit derivatives is fast growing but, at the moment, details of the volume of trading are not recorded in the statistics from the Bank for International Settlements (BIS) reported in table 13.2. However, it is estimated that the amount outstanding at the end of 2002 was in the region of $2,000 billion, with a forecast to grow to roughly $5,000 billion by the end of 2004. Nevertheless this total is quite small when compared with the figures contained in table 13.2.

We now move on to discuss the nature of credit derivatives. Credit derivatives are financial instruments designed to protect institutions from risk arising from defaults. Three of the most popular types of credit derivatives are:

(i) credit swaps;
(ii) credit options;
(iii) credit-linked notes.

Perhaps the most used credit swap is the 'total return swap', whereby two intuitions swap total loan payments. This is illustrated in figure 13.5. Bank A transfers a loan portfolio of value, say, £100 million to bank B so that bank B receives all payments (i.e. interest and debt repayment) on this loan portfolio. The converse transaction is made from bank B so that it transfers a £100 million loan portfolio to bank A, so that bank receives all payments associated with that portfolio. This transaction would be arranged through a financial institution acting as the intermediary. The gain for both

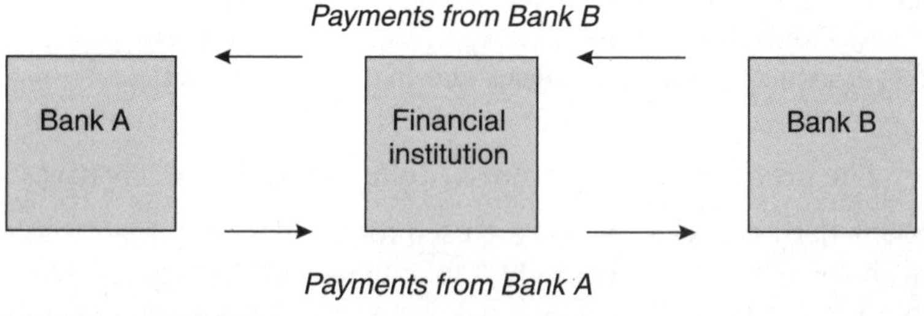

Figure 13.5 Total loan swap.

banks would come in the form of greater diversification of their loan portfolios. For example, if bank A's lending was excessively concentrated in a particular industry or region and bank B was similarly exposed but in a different industry or region, the swap would achieve greater diversification for both banks and therefore greater protection against default risk.

The second type of credit derivative is credit options. These operate in the same manner as other options, discussed in section 13.5. One example is the purchase of a call option to hedge against a rise in the risk premium as reflected in the interest rate. Suppose a firm proposes to issue bonds in the near future and wishes to ensure that it does not pay more than the current premium over LIBOR, which is, say, 2 per cent per annum. The firm can purchase a call option fixed on the current risk premium of 2 per cent. If at the time of issue the credit risk premium has risen to 2.5 per cent, then the firm will exercise the option and receive payment of the gap between the current risk premium and 2 per cent. If, on the other hand, the risk premium falls the firm will issue the bonds without exercising the option. Clearly the transaction costs will reduce the benefit to the firm.

Similarly bond investors can purchase an option which has a pay-off in the event of the downgrading of the company's debt. If the debt is downgraded the investment loss will be partially or wholly offset by the option receipts. A variation of this type of option is one called a 'credit default swap'. In this case the owner of the swap receives a payment if more than a specified number of bonds in the portfolio default. This is, in effect, a put option on part of the portfolio.

Finally the third type mentioned above is credit-linked notes. This type of security is a combination of a normal debt instrument together with a clause typically allowing the issuer to reduce the instrument's interest rate payments if a key financial variable specified in the instrument deteriorates. One example would be the issue of debt against credit card debt. If defaults are normal, the full interest would be paid but, if the default rate rose above a specified level, the interest payments would be reduced. Thus the debt issuer would lose by the increased credit card defaults but gain by the reduced interest payments on the debt issued.

Consequently credit derivatives can be used by a number of institutions to protect themselves against downside risk. The main participants in this market are banks, securities houses and insurance companies.

13.9 **The problems arising from hedging or trading derivatives**

Although derivatives can be and are used for a variety of purposes as indicated above, they are not themselves inherently riskless. This is evidenced by the detail in table 13.6, which lists some well publicised examples of companies incurring losses through derivative products. With the exception

of Barings (where the loss was due to fraud and inappropriate internal control procedures) and Long-Term Capital Management (LTCM), all the other companies are users of derivatives rather than suppliers. This suggests that there is a relatively high degree of ignorance on the part of users.

Table 13.6 Examples of companies incurring losses through the use of derivatives products

Company	Estimated loss reported in the media
Allied Lyons	£150 million
Ashanti Goldfields Company Ltd	$100 million
Atlantic Richfield	$22 million
Barings	£860 million
Codelco	$200 million
Gibson Greetings	$73 million
Long-Term Capital Management	Over $4 billion
Maryland County Administration[a]	$1.3 million
Metallgesellschaft	$1.3 billion
Orange County[a]	$1.7 billion
Proctor and Gamble	$100 million

[a] US local authorities.

The first point for any user to note is that hedging an exposure by writing (or selling) options incurs a considerable risk, since writing an option involves the seller incurring potentially unlimited losses. Reference to figures 13.3 and 13.4 demonstrates this point in the case of a simple (single) transaction. In the case of both call and put options the writer faces potentially very large losses if the price moves against the writer so that it is profitable to exercise the option. This contrasts with the position of the purchase of options, where the maximum loss is limited to the premium paid for the option. Consequently hedging using options should be carried out by purchase of rather than by writing options. Similarly, when using the futures market, it is essential that the price of the instrument of hedging moves in parallel with the instrument hedged. A hedger is always trading a greater price risk for the (hopefully) smaller basis risk. In other words hedgers are speculating on 'basis'. However, other problems exist and we will use the cases of Metalgesellschaft (MG), Barings and LTCM to illustrate these.

13.9.1 *Case study of Metalgesellschaft*

This section draws heavily on work by Franklin Edwards (see Edwards and Cantor 1995). Briefly, MG Refining and Marketing (MGRM), a subsidiary of MG, wished to establish long-term relationships with customers

and so entered into contracts to supply approximately 160 million barrels of gasoline and heating oil to end users over the next ten years. Mark-ups of \$3–\$5 over current prices were established. This marketing strategy carries a massive risk of price rises. There are three ways of minimising this risk, but each has problems:

(i) buy the quantity of fuel necessary to meet the contract at the outset – this has the major problem that it involves massive warehousing costs and these would make the deal unprofitable;
(ii) buy futures contracts to purchase the oil with a time profile that matches the delivery contracts – but no exchange-traded contracts exist for ten years' maturity and the cost of negotiating OTC contracts for such a maturity would be enormous;
(iii) buy exchange-traded contracts within the existing maturity trading arrangements and roll them over (renew them) periodically.

Strategy (iii) was used by MGRM. It purchased the contract with near maturities and rolled them over periodically – that is, it followed a short-term stacking policy – reducing the derivative commitment in respect of any oil delivered. Even without the benefit of hindsight this strategy involved considerable risk, since any price changes would involve MGRM in margin payments/receipts in the opposite direction to spot price changes *before* the receipt of cash from the relevant oil deliveries (see section 13.3 for an explanation of margin payments). In fact the price of oil fell consistently during 1993 so MGRM was continually making margin payments, leading to it having to post nearly \$900 million to maintain its hedge. Note, however, that if the price of oil had risen then MGRM would have received substantial inflows of margin payments. The danger of having to make large margin payments on a hedging contract is known as 'funding risk'. This type of risk is endemic in any hedging contract using futures.

An additional risk occurs at the time of the renewal of the contracts in the case of hedging risks with a longer maturity than that of the relevant financial instruments which are readily available in the markets. This necessitates purchasing a sequence of short-term securities, that is, 'rolling over' the contracts. If the price of the new contract is above the price of the old contract additional losses are incurred in the hedge on the roll-over date – if nearby prices are below deferred prices the market is said to be in 'contango'; the converse is referred to as 'backwardation'. In fact, throughout 1993, the market was in contango virtually every month, thus adding to the losses on the strategy. In part this was not foreseeable since over the period 1983–92 the market was, on average, in backwardation. Critics have also pointed out that the strategy was prone to credit risk through the possibility of default by the counterparties. This did not arise.

The strategy MRGM adopted was probably defective in construction in other respects as well. The company appears to have hedged the contract on a one-for-one basis; that is, each delivery of one barrel of oil was hedged by a futures contract for one barrel. This is not necessarily the correct strategy. If the price of the futures contract fluctuates more than (but in the same direction as) the price of the underlying commodity, then a one-for-one strategy is inappropriate as a defensive mechanism and a ratio of less than one for one would be appropriate. In fact the formula for the minimum variance hedge (h) is:

$$h = \rho(\sigma_S / \sigma_F)$$

where ρ is the correlation coefficient between the price of the futures and that of the underlying commodity, σ is the standard deviation and S and F represent spot and futures. Edwards and Cantor (1995) report h as less than one. If fewer future contracts had been entered into then the margin payments would have been smaller.

One of the problems with regard to the use of derivative instruments occurs if such instruments are 'marked to market'. As noted above, users of such instruments may incur a significant negative cash flow if the price of the instrument moves against them because margin payments have to be made. Such payments have to be made before maturity of the futures contract and hence before any profit/loss on the derivatives contracts have been offset by those on the underlying cash market transaction. The case of MG illustrates this point only too well. The scale of the margin payments led the company to wind up the contracts and incur substantial cash losses, as indicated in table 13.6.

13.9.2 *Case study of Barings Bank*

Barings is one of the more recent and spectacular instances of financial disaster for a well established bank. This section draws on the official report into the collapse of Barings (Board of Banking Supervision 1995). In outline, Barings succeeded in losing an equivalent of £860 million through futures trading via the now notorious fraudulent rogue trader Nick Leeson, who engaged in unauthorised trading. All such losses were transferred to a hidden account denominated '88888', which was opened in July 1992 shortly after Leeson arrived in Singapore as a trader for Barings Futures (Singapore). The trading losses were incurred mainly through two types of activity. First, Leeson rapidly built up a long position of futures contracts on the Nikkei 225 stock index and a short position on Japanese government bonds. In both cases the market moved against him. Second, he also engaged in volatility trading on the options market by writing (selling) a 'call' and a 'put' at the same exercise price (i.e. 'straddle', described in section 14.4.4) on the Nikkei index. This strategy is used by a trader who does not believe

that the market will move outside its existing trading profile. As soon as the index of the underlying moves outside the range as defined by the break-even points such as those illustrated in figure 14.4 then losses are incurred. Note the position of the writer is far more risky than that of the purchaser since the latter has no further obligations after payment of the premiums. In fact, the index moved outside the range of his straddle contracts, no doubt due in part to the Kobe earthquake on 17 January 1995. His overall position on 24 February 1995 was short a total of 37,925 call options and 32,967 put options. All but one of the put options were in the money, leading to substantial margin payments from Barings to the exchange.

One salient feature of the debacle is the speed with which the losses built up. From 1 January to 27 February, Leeson's trading activities resulted in losses of £619 million. In fact, on Thursday 23 February, his trading activities succeeded in losing £144 million in that one day and, to quote the succinct comment of the report, 'it was at this point that he left BFS [Barings Futures (Singapore) PTE Ltd], never to return'. The interesting question is why Leeson engaged in these activities to such an extent and built up such a long position after a period of long decline in the index. Two possible reasons can be put forward: first, the desperate gambler trying to recoup his losses in the hope that the index would appreciate later; and second, an attempt to move the market in his favour.

Who was culpable? We would argue that it was not the existence of derivative securities per se but rather incompetent management. The report is littered with examples of what many would consider to be evidence of gross incompetence. A few examples are appended below:

(i) Leeson was both the senior trader and manager responsible for the back office (administration), an arrangement singularly prone to fraud. Separation of the two functions was recommended in an internal audit report in August 1994. Action then would have prevented the collapse.
(ii) No organisation chart existed, with the consequence that various executives seemed to be confused as to who reported to whom.
(iii) 'At that point in time [early 1994] I never really thought much about why it is so profitable' (Ron Baker, head of Barings' Financial Products Group, quoted in Board of Banking Supervision 1995: p. 28, para. 2.47).
(iv) One executive felt that his inexperience contributed to the fiasco: 'There is no doubt that if I had ten years' experience in exchange traded equity derivatives, this would not happen. The fact is that I did not' (Ron Baker, p. 49, para. 3.61).
(v) The massive quantity of funds was transferred for margin payments without any real query by raised by Barings' Treasury Group for the reasons behind the transfers.

Queries raised by outsiders regarding the trading activities in Asia were not checked out. The queries arose from a number of sources, including the BIS on 27 January 1995, Schroders on 16 February 1995 and an employee on the Japanese market in general on 17 February 1995. It is perhaps surprising that Barings' apparently sole response to the query from the BIS was, according to a tape of a telephone conversation: 'For the BIS to ring us was a bit embarrassing'.

13.9.3 *Case study of Long-Term Capital Management*

Long-Term Capital Management was a hedge fund which failed dramatically in 1998. The term 'hedge fund' is misleading as hedging is not used in its normal sense. Hedge funds often take counterbalancing positions, for example in different securities by going long in under-valued securities and going short in over-valued securities. Thus they are immunised (i.e. hedged) against general movements in the security prices but hope to profit from relative movements in the prices. They are therefore *speculating* on these movements and will gain if their view is correct and lose if they are wrong.

They are largely free from supervision as they are formed under US legislation, which permits exemption from regulation if the fund is restricted to wealthy and sophisticated investors (those with over $5 million). Generally there are also restrictions on the withdrawal of funds by the investors. Fees for the management are higher than those for normal mutual funds.

In 1994 LTCM was formed with equity of just over $100 million. Minimum investment was $10 million and no withdrawals were permitted for three years. Fees were 2 per cent of assets and 25 per cent of new profits. The fund returned to investors (after fees) 19.9 per cent, 42.8 per cent, 40.8 per cent and 17.1 per cent in the years 1994 to 1997. Capital rose to over $7 billion at the end of 1997 and $2.7 billion was returned to investors in December 1997 because of lower-return investment opportunities. At the beginning of 1998 leverage was very high – capital was $5 billion and borrowing from banks $125 billion, a ratio of 25 to 1. This high degree of leverage increased the potential both for profits and losses.

LTCM entered into derivative contracts, buying high-yielding, less liquid securities and selling low-risk, more liquid bonds. Thus it was protected from general movements but would gain if the spread narrowed. Conversely it would lose if the spread widened. The margins were small but the volume of trading was immense – at the start of 1998 the notional value of LTCM's derivative contracts was over $1 trillion ($1,000 billion). Consequently this large volume of trading meant that total profits would be high if the spread narrowed but conversely losses would also be large if margins widened.

A number of factors caused LTCM problems:

(i) The trading strategy could easily be replicated by other institutions, so the 'money-making' machines would become less profitable – hence the return of capital.
(ii) The Asian crisis led to a movement towards quality. Institutions started to unload low-quality (high-risk, high-return) securities so that the markets became illiquid and spreads widened.
(iii) LTCM took large losses in April and May 1998. Value-at-Risk (VAR) suggested that such events were extremely unlikely and LTCM took little action save to sell some of its more liquid assets.
(iv) The Russian repudiation of debt (August 1998) caused severe problems for LTCM. The direct loss from Russian operations was quite small (estimated at $400 million including other emerging markets) but it enhanced the flight to quality. Given the nature of LTCM's assets, liquidation would entail large price reductions and losses – selling on a falling market is disastrous.
(v) The spreads widened even further and higher margin payments were necessary.
(vi) This widening of spreads was exactly opposite to what LTCM had speculated on, so heavy losses were incurred and by mid-September 1998 LTCM's equity dropped to $600 million – a loss of more than $4 billion.

In early September 1998 LTCM advised the Federal Reserve Bank of its difficulties and a rescue operation was arranged whereby a 16-member consortium of major creditors to LTCM agreed to put in additional capital of $3.625 billion in exchange for 90 per cent of the equity. It was reported that at the end of September 1999 the stakes of the LTCM partners had fallen from $1.6 billion a year earlier to $30 million. By the end of 1999 LTCM had repaid $2.6 billion to the consortium and had been reduced in size and leverage.

There are two reasons why the Federal Reserve Bank intervened, even if indirectly:

(i) There was a fear of a systemic risk, given the fragility of the financial system at that time.
(ii) There was a fear of formal bankruptcy, which would have led all LTCM's counterparties to cancel their contracts – derivative contracts normally contain a clause permitting cancellation of contracts in the event of any default by a counterparty. This would have led them to liquidate any assets under their control. Prevention of a bankruptcy order would permit an orderly winding up of LTCM's operations.

Was the failure due to incompetent management or inherent risks in derivatives? In other words, do we need more regulation or will all institutions

have tightened up their risk management positions so that market forces will operate? Has the rescue increased moral hazard? The interested reader is referred to Edwards (1999) for a full discussion of these issues.

13.10 **The efficiency of derivatives markets**

Futures and options are derivatives markets, so their prices are a function of the anticipated movements in the price of the underlying cash market asset. It is therefore possible to impute equilibrium prices from the prices of options and futures. Efficiency requires that these imputed prices should provide accurate forecasts. The literature on the efficiency of these markets is more limited than that for the cash markets and so our survey of the evidence is more restricted. We describe studies of the role of options prices in the stock market and foreign currency markets, and futures in relation to the foreign currency markets and interest rate markets.

The method adopted by Manaster and Rendleman (1982) in respect of the stock market was to use option prices to calculate the market's implied equilibrium stock price using the Black–Scholes formula for close-of-market option prices on all listed options exchanges for the period 26 April 1973 to 30 June 1976 (approximately 37,000 observations). This price was compared with another estimate of the equilibrium price given by the actual observed stock price and the divergence between these two estimates of the unobservable equilibrium price calculated. If this divergence is related to future movements in stock price then there is a suggestion that options prices contain some information not contained in the observed price. Manaster and Rendleman found that a relationship does exist between these two variables but simulation of an *ex ante* trading rule suggested that this information was not sufficient to generate significant economic profits.

The method used by Manaster and Rendleman was adopted by Tucker (1987) for a study of the foreign exchange market using the implied exchange rates in comparison with the forward rate to derive a profitable trading strategy. The database consisted of 608 observations of options for sterling, the Deutschmark, the Swiss franc and the Japanese yen over the period November 1983 to August 1984. The assumption of interest rate parity and the observed forward rate were incorporated into the calculation of the implied equilibrium exchange rate. This resulted in a trading rule which suggested that when the implied spot rate is greater than the observed spot rate, then the currency options market assessment is that the forward rate is underpriced, so the currency should be bought forward. In a result similar to that obtained by Manaster and Rendleman, Tucker also found that whilst the deviation between the observed and implied spot rates was a statistically significant determinant of future returns, this information was insufficient to generate significant economic profits.

Cavanaugh (1987) looked at the potential to use futures contract prices to generate profits. The data represented daily changes in the logarithm of futures prices for delivery of currency on specific days. Fifteen series for the Canadian dollar and sterling were examined by Cavanaugh and he found evidence of serial correlation. Tests of simulated trading strategies suggested that this dependence could have been exploited by members of the exchange to generate profits in excess of those obtained by a policy of buy and hold. Because of the higher costs of trading involved, it was also suggested that these opportunities for profit could not have been exploited by non-members.

Elton *et al.* (1984) based their study on intra-day quotations for Treasury bills (cash and futures) for the period 6 January 1976 through to 22 December 1982. Elton *et al.* note that an investor can purchase an N-day Treasury bill in either of two ways using the futures market:

(i) purchase an N-day Treasury bill in the cash market;
(ii) purchase a $(91 + N)$-day Treasury bill in the cash market and sell a Treasury bill in the futures market for delivery in N days, then deliver the $(91 + N)$-day bill against the futures contract.

An efficient market implies that the returns on the two strategies should be the same after allowance for transaction costs. Three strategies were examined. First, there was the simple strategy of purchasing the lower-priced instrument. Second, an arbitrage strategy could be followed whereby the lower-priced instrument was purchased and this was financed by shorting the higher-priced instrument. The third strategy examined was a swap, whereby holders of the higher-priced instrument liquefied their holdings and used the proceeds to purchase the lower-priced instrument. Elton *et al.* found that profits could be made from all three strategies, which suggests that the US Treasury bill futures market is not perfectly efficient. Since the study did not depend on any assumptions concerning an equilibrium model, these are direct tests of efficiency rather than joint tests of efficiency and a particular equilibrium model as was the case for the earlier tests discussed.

An alternative procedure is to examine the forecasting ability of futures markets as predictors of the subsequently observed spot prices. It is well known that the forward rate is a poor predictor of the subsequently observed spot rate in the forex, but what about other markets? Laws and Thompson (2003) examined prediction tests for two interest rates, the short sterling and eurodollar three-month interest rate contracts. The authors found that the futures contracts provided reasonable forecasts. It was also found that both profits and losses would be made by simulating trading rules and betting against the forecast provided by the futures markets. This suggests that these two markets at least approximate efficiency.

Finally we mention assessment of market efficiency through an examination of the volatility of options prices. It is possible to derive an estimate of the expected volatility of option prices through use of the Black–Scholes model. All the other variables in the model are known so it is relatively easy to calculate the implied volatility and compare this figure with the actual volatility observed in the market. A number of studies have been carried out using this method and the general conclusion is that the implied measure of volatility is biased (e.g. Beckers 1981; Gemmill 1986; Gwylim and Buckle 1994). While this does not prove the market is inefficient, it does tend towards the rejection of the combined hypotheses that the Black–Scholes model is appropriate for the valuation of option prices and that the market is efficient. Unfortunately it does not suggest which (or perhaps both) is irrelevant.

13.11 **Conclusion**

We have surveyed the development of the financial futures markets in London and found that they have grown rapidly. The conditions for this rapid growth, that is, the observed volatility of asset prices in the related cash markets, are likely to continue and use of these markets is therefore likely to grow both in volume and in number of securities traded in the future as they offer traders some opportunity to hedge against adverse price movements. The question of the efficiency of these markets is, like that of the other markets surveyed, an open question. In this connection it is relevant that many of these markets are relatively new and that the operators may still be on a learning curve.

Finally, the development of derivatives markets has increased the risk attached to the operations of banks. The existence of losses on the scale noted in table 13.6 has led to discussion of whether these markets should be more tightly regulated. It is a salient feature of the losses noted in table 13.6 that, with the exceptions of Barings and LTCM, all were in respect of non-financial companies. It would seem reasonable to assume that companies would operate in such markets only if they possessed the necessary financial expertise to comprehend the risks involved.[2] Customers who feel they have been misled or ill advised in any way have recourse to legal action. In fact, it was reported in the media that such action was undertaken by Procter and Gamble and Atlantic Richfield. It has also been reported that a bank, CS First Boston, has made repayments to three customers totalling $40 million in respect of derivatives advice it provided. Consequently no further prudential control would seem to be necessary to protect customers. The case of regulating banks' operations in derivatives markets raises different issues, which are considered in chapter 17.

Notes

1 Note that at the time of writing (September 2003) Clearnet and the London Clearing House were proposing to merge, in which case they will become the dominant central counterparty in the European Union. Creation of a large clearing house should lower costs of clearing transactions and benefit the European capital market as a whole. However, opponents of this particular merger claim that because Euronext (an exchange, not customer) will have a strong say in the management of the new clearing house, it is not clear that benefits will accrue to the users of the new clearing house.

2 This expertise may well be absent, given the comments made in relation to a Price Waterhouse (1995) survey (see p. 303).

Chapter 14

Managing risk via the financial markets

14.1 **Introduction**

In this chapter we survey the various methods that are open to firms to manage risk. The risks we are concerned with arise in connection with unforeseen changes in exchange rates and interest rates. Quite obviously a rise in interest rates raises both costs to borrowers and also returns to lenders. Similarly, changes in exchange rates alter the domestic currency equivalent of foreign currency. This is easily demonstrated by reference to the sterling equivalent of $500,000 at exchange rates of $1.95 per £1 and $2.0 per £1. At the former rate the sterling equivalent is £256,410 but only £250,000 at the latter rate. Thus, a person making a payment denominated in dollars benefits as sterling appreciates from $1.95 to $2.0 per £1 but the recipient of a payment denominated in dollars loses out. This causes problems for traders. In a similar way changes in interest rates can cause problems for the borrower and lender when these are made at floating rates of interest.

In this chapter we discuss how firms may attempt to manage this risk. This type of risk has increased in severity since the beginning of the 1970s owing to the increasing volatility of prices on security markets, although recent years have seen a decline in such volatility. This is demonstrated in figures 14.1 and 14.2, which show changes in volatility in representative exchange and interest rates since 1960.

In the case of figure 14.1, the volatility of the pound/dollar exchange rate is represented by the moving 12-month standard deviation of percentage monthly changes. The picture shown before 1970 is one of relative stability with the exception of the one-off change in volatility due to the 1967 devaluation of the pound from £1= $2.80 to £1 = $2.40. With the change from fixed to floating exchange rates at the beginning of the 1970s a steep increase in volatility can be observed and this increase persisted until 1992, after which time the volatility decreased substantially. Interest rate volatility is also measured by the moving 12-month standard deviation of percentage

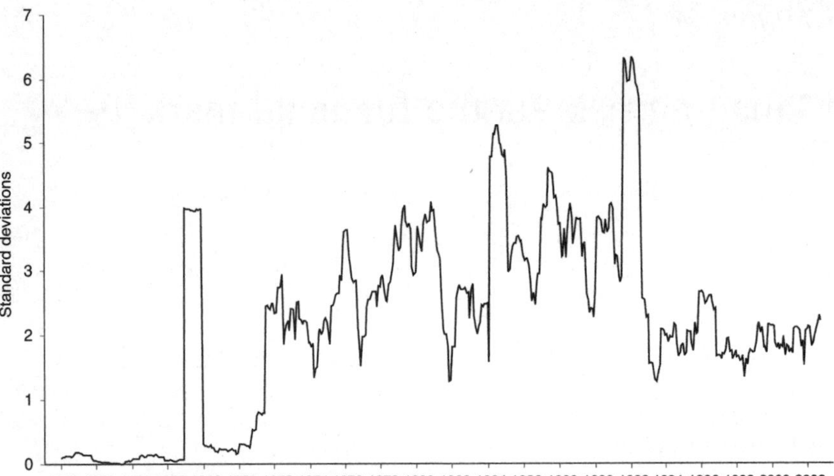

Figure 14.1 Exchange rate volatility: moving 12-month standard deviation of monthly percentage changes (sterling/dollar rate, 1960–2003). Source: DataStream.

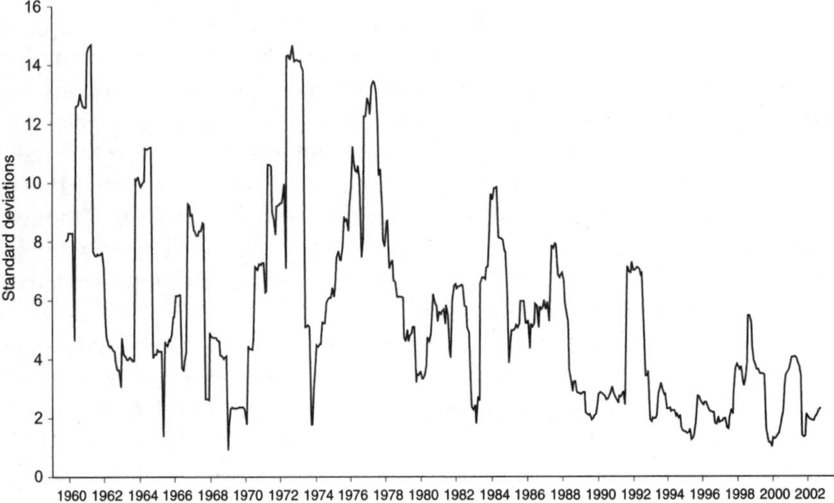

Figure 14.2 Interest rate volatility: moving 12-month standard deviation of monthly percentage changes (LIBOR, 1960–2003). Source: DataStream.

monthly changes but in the London inter-bank offer rate (LIBOR) in this case. The changes depicted in figure 14.2 are more volatile than those for exchange rates shown in figure 14.1 but generally interest rate volatility was more pronounced in the 1970s and 1980s than during the 1960s. This is particularly true of the late 1970s and early 1980s. The general picture revealed by these two figures is, then, one of increasing volatility of exchange and interest rates from the early 1970s to the early 1990s, which in turn enhanced the uncertainties faced by firms. The reduction in volatility since 1992, particularly in interest rates, is partly explained by the reduction in inflation since that time and the relative stability this has created in the economic environment.

In section 14.2 we discuss in more detail the precise nature of exchange and interest rate risk before proceeding in section 14.3 to discuss how firms can use internal methods of managing exchange rate risk. In section 14.4 we discuss external methods of managing exchange rate risk and in section 14.5 the management of interest rate risk. Finally in section 14.6 we present our conclusions.

14.2 The nature of exchange and interest rate risk

Exchange rate risk can arise in a number of different ways. First, there is transaction risk, which arises because the exchange rate has changed between the date of the commitment and the date the payment is made or received. For the exporter uncertainty is increased by the possibility of exchange rate changes if the commodity is invoiced in foreign currency and costs are primarily in domestic currency. A similar problem arises for importers, who find the domestic currency costs of their inputs denominated in foreign currency rising and falling in an unpredictable manner. This raises the possibility of unforeseen windfall losses or profits, making foreign trade considerably more risky than domestic trade. It also makes it difficult for firms engaged in foreign trade to quote prices, for fear of exchange rate changes altering costs. It is important to define when this risk is incurred. It arises from the date the commitment is entered into. In the case of exports, this dates from the time the price quotation has been communicated to the purchaser. This may be a special quotation or it may date from the time a price list is circulated to actual or prospective customers. In a similar manner for importers, the risk dates from the time they have communicated their acceptance of the purchase of the goods from the foreign company. It is also important to realise that, when the trade is priced in one currency and payments are to be made in another, it is the currency in which the payment is priced that is subject to exchange rate risk.

The second type of exposure to exchange rate changes is defined as translation risk. This arises when it is necessary to value overseas assets

and liabilities for their incorporation into a consolidated balance sheet. If a company has a net surplus or deficit of assets defined in non-domestic currencies, then the balance sheet valuation will change as the relevant exchange rate alters. This particular exposure would not pose serious difficulties if the changes in the exchange rates were purely random around a relatively constant value. In fact, since the abandonment by the UK of fixed exchange rates in 1972, long swings in exchange rates have been observed. Again, the nature of the commitment of the asset or liability is relevant. The translation exposure on a short-term liability or asset which is likely to be realised in the fairly near future (say one to five years) is similar to transaction exposure since their renewal might occur at the time of an unfavourable exchange rate. Therefore potential serious translation risk exists for the firm unless these risks are hedged. In contrast, permanent investment in subsidiaries can be treated as non-renewable and therefore impose a much lower incidence of exposure, though this could be serious if the currency in which the asset/liability is priced has shown a long-trend movement against the domestic currency.

The third type of exposure is economic exposure. In this case changes in exchange rates alter the relative prices of exports and imports. Over time this can adversely affect the position of firms where exchange rates have moved against them or alternatively help those firms whose products are made cheaper by the exchange rate change. This type of exposure is of a long-term nature and is brought about by changes in the volume of sales following a change in the exchange rate. One example of this type of exposure is the pricing of oil in dollars. Thus, if the domestic currency depreciates against the dollar, the price of oil rises, adversely affecting those companies whose products have a large oil component. It should be emphasised that the exchange rate which matters for international trade is the real exchange rate, which may be defined as the nominal rate corrected for price changes. Thus, if nominal rates always moved to correct differing rates of inflation in the countries concerned then the dangers arising from economic exposure would be considerably reduced. In fact there is a considerable volume of evidence suggesting that purchasing power parity (PPP) does not exist in the short run so that changes in real exchange rates do occur. There is little a company can do to protect itself against this type of risk except to diversify its products and production centres.

The final type of risk can be termed hidden exposure. A firm may not be directly affected by exchange rate changes since its products may be sold entirely to domestic customers and its raw materials bought from domestic producers. Despite this concentration on the domestic market, the firm would be exposed to indirect transaction and economic risk via one of its suppliers. Similarly, exchange rate change may beneficially affect potential competitors from abroad. An alternative form of indirect exposure can arise

from the operation of a subsidiary which is itself affected by exchange rate changes in a third market even if the currencies of the principal and its subsidiary are linked together by fixed exchange rates.

So far we have concentrated on exchange rate exposure, but interest rate exposure may be analysed in the same way. Transaction exposure occurs through changing interest payments or receipts following a change in the interest rate structure. Translation exposure can occur through changes in the value of financial assets held originating from changes in interest rates. This is particularly applicable to the position of investment institutions, which hold large volumes of long-term financial securities. Economic exposure arises because changes in interest rates affect the general business environment as well as having an impact on firms according to the degree of leverage, that is, the proportion of capital raised by way of loans as distinct from equity finance. Thus, a rise in interest rates will reduce consumer demand, generally raise the cost of investment and impose costs on particular firms which have undertaken to raise finance by way of loans subject to interest rate adjustment.

In the following section we discuss how firms may reduce exchange rate exposure by methods internal to the firm and in section 14.4 the role of methods external to the firm.

14.3 **Managing exchange rate risk: internal methods**

A number of methods exist to manage exchange rate risk which are internal to the firm. These include:

(i) doing nothing;
(ii) forecasting exchange rate movements;
(iii) invoicing or accepting invoices denominated only in domestic currency;
(iv) operating a foreign currency bank account.

In summary, the individual firm has a choice of doing nothing (i) or hedging (ii–iv). The first option offers the lowest cost but the least protection against exchange rate exposure whereas hedging offers the highest degree of protection but also the highest cost because of the number of transactions involved.

The first method of managing exchange rate risk is simply to accept the spot rate at the time the payment is made or received. Appeal to the efficient markets hypothesis suggests that the current spot rate may well be the best available forecast of the future spot rate. In this case the most profitable policy for the firm would be to rely on the future spot rate for conversion of the foreign currency. Two problems arise with this approach. First, there is a distinct possibility that the foreign exchange market does not conform to

the efficient markets hypothesis (see chapter 11, sections 11.6 and 11.7) and that therefore the current spot rate is not the 'best' forecast of future exchange rates. Second, the firm may value certainty or near certainty of the domestic currency equivalent of the foreign currency receipt or payment, or in other words it may be risk averse in this respect. To illustrate this point, a firm is able to plan its pricing policy if it knows in advance the sterling value of future imports and exports. This may well be preferable even to a trading system that lowers the average domestic currency cost of imports and raises the average domestic currency receipts for exports if this policy involves relatively large gains and losses around the average. It is quite possible that the firm, in these circumstances, may place a higher value on certainty than profitability in areas where it lacks expertise.

The policy of relying on the future spot rate to convert foreign currency into domestic currency is really nested in the second option, that of forecasting. In reality, doing nothing is equivalent to using the current spot rate as the optimal forecast of future spot exchange rates. It may, however, be the view of the firm that it can improve on the current spot rate as a predictor so that it forecasts the future pattern of spot exchange rates itself. The policy for the firm to manage exchange rate risk would then be to forecast and to choose between the use of internal and external methods of managing the risk in the light of a comparison of its internal forecasts and the constellation of market spot rates, forward rates and options prices. In a similar manner the firm could speed up payments in foreign currency (or purchase of the foreign currency) when the domestic currency was expected to depreciate and retard conversion of foreign currency receipts into domestic currency. The converse behaviour would occur when the domestic currency was expected to appreciate. This overall strategy of forecasting would be consistent with the view that the foreign exchange market does not conform to the efficient markets hypothesis. Apart from the comments made above with respect to risk aversion, the strategy of forecasting the future pattern of exchange rates also suffers from the defect that it requires resources to develop the expertise necessary to provide accurate forecasts. The firm may feel that its available resources are more profitably directed towards its primary functions.

The third internal method is to require invoices to be denominated in domestic currency. In this case there is no exchange rate exposure as far as the transaction component is concerned. However, this exposure has not been eliminated but rather transferred to the foreign purchaser or supplier of the goods. It is also more than likely that the foreign purchaser of goods would not be willing to accept invoices denominated in the domestic currency of the supplier and, given the existence of competition, this would be likely to cause loss of orders. In effect, transaction exposure has been changed into economic exposure.

The final internal method of managing exchange rate risk is to operate foreign currency bank accounts. Thus, as long as receipts and payments are in balance over a reasonable period of time, the exposure on receipts would match and offset the exposure on payments in a specific foreign currency. This type of account could also be allowed to run into deficit by way of an overdraft for a short period of time provided this overdraft was eliminated by future receipts of that currency. This type of risk management has only a limited application since it does require receipts and payments of that currency to cancel each other out over a reasonably short period of time. A persistent balance, particularly a persistently growing balance (either in deficit or in surplus), leaves the firm open to exchange rate exposure on both a transaction and a translation basis.

It was seen that internal methods offer the firm only limited scope to manage exchange rate risk, so we now turn to discussing the external methods open to the firm.

14.4 Managing exchange rate risk: external methods

In this section we discuss how a firm might manage exchange rate risk by having recourse to the financial institutions and markets. A number of such methods exist and these are the use of:

(i) the forward exchange market;
(ii) temporary foreign currency deposits and loans;
(iii) forfaiting;
(iv) options;
(v) back-to-back loans.

Currency futures offer another method, but we do not consider these in this section because they seem to play a less important role in the management of exchange rate risk than in the case of other financial risks. However, a brief discussion of the nature of currency futures is provided in chapter 13 (section 13.4.5).

14.4.1 *Forward contracts*

We discussed the forward exchange market in chapter 11, where it was seen that it is possible to purchase or sell foreign currency for delivery at a future date at a rate agreed at the time of the transaction. For example, if a firm was due to receive \$500,000 in three months' time, it could sell the \$500,000 forward for sterling, thus fixing the rate for conversion into sterling in three months' time. Clearly, this method of managing risk provides the firm with certainty of the domestic currency equivalent of the foreign currency receipts or payments. For example, if the relevant forward rate is

$1.9398 per £1, then the sterling value of the $500,000 is £257,758.53. Again, it is worth emphasising that the firm does not necessarily make a profit by trading in the forward exchange market. At the time of the conversion out of or into foreign currency the spot rate may be higher or lower than the agreed forward rate of $1.9398 per £1. In fact our survey of the empirical evidence on the efficiency of the forward rate as a predictor of the future spot rate (chapter 11, section 11.6.3) suggests that the forward rate will deviate from the future spot rate because of the existence of a risk premium. In other words, the firm will on balance pay a premium to the provider of the forward exchange as a compensation for the transfer of risk. Thus, the firm's gains arise purely from knowing what the rate will be, that is, it has purchased certainty, which, in the case of the above example, means it is sure that it can convert the $500,000 into £257,758.53. Even here a caveat must be raised. The certainty is obtained only provided the second party (i.e. the body buying or selling the goods) does not default. If it fails to complete its part of the transaction, the original firm is left with a forward contract not matched by a future spot receipt or payment so that it then has a foreign exchange rate exposure.

A further restriction on a straight forward contract is that it applies to a fixed date whereas in many commercial transactions the precise date of receipt of or payment in foreign currency is uncertain. One way around this is to choose an option date forward contract. This provides the right to buy or sell foreign currency, typically from a bank, up to a particular date. The disadvantage with this type of purchase is that the bank will offer the contract at the rate most favourable to itself. Thus, for an option contract for three months forward to sell sterling, the bank would select the highest rate out of the spot and individual outright forward rates up to three months. Conversely, in the case of an option date forward contract for the bank to purchase sterling, it would apply the lowest of the relevant rates. The firm can mitigate the impact of the adverse (from the firm's point of view) selection of rates by entering into overlapping option date forward contracts so that, for example, receipts of foreign currency expected in instalments over the next three months might be covered by an option forward contract for one month for a proportion of the total receipts and the balance by way of an option forward contract for two to three months.

Another restriction may occur because the forward market for the desired currency is very thin or, in the extreme, non-existent. This may be overcome by exercising two forward contracts. In the case of a future receipt of a thinly traded currency, for example, it may be possible, given the importance of the dollar in international financial transactions, to sell dollars forward for domestic currency and simultaneously to buy dollars forward for the thinly traded currency. By this method the firm has achieved an indirect forward sale of the currency concerned.

14.4.2 *Temporary foreign currency deposits and loans*

A firm can use temporary foreign deposits and loans to achieve the same degree of protection against transaction exposure as is afforded by forward transactions. Reverting to the example of the future receipt of $500,000, the firm can achieve protection in the following manner:

(i) borrow $500,000 from a bank for three months at the time of entering into the contract leading to the receipt of dollars;
(ii) convert the dollars into sterling at the current spot exchange rate;
(iii) deposit the sterling received in a three-month interest-bearing sterling deposit.

The dollar loan is then paid off by the $500,000 receipt in three months' time. The sterling equivalent of the $500,000 depends on the two interest rates (the dollar borrowing and the sterling deposit) and the spot exchange rate. Since all these rates are known, this strategy fixes the sterling equivalent of the future receipt of dollars. In the case of a payment of $500,000 by a firm, steps (i) to (iii) above are reversed, that is:

(i) borrow the sterling equivalent of the quantity of dollars which will increase to $500,000 when invested; alternatively the firm could use any spare cash holdings to finance step (ii);
(ii) convert the sterling into dollars at the current spot rate;
(iii) invest the dollar receipts from (ii) above into a three-month interest-bearing dollar deposit.

On maturity of the deposit, the dollars are used to make the dollar payment.

In principle the cost of using this type of strategy should be the same as using the forward exchange market since it is in effect equivalent to covered interest rate arbitrage discussed in chapter 11 and interest rate parity (IRP) would imply that no profits could be made through moving funds between various centres.

14.4.3 *Forfaiting*

The third method of avoiding transaction exposure is to use a technique known as forfaiting. This involves transferring the risk to a bank by obtaining domestic currency from the bank in return for the transfer of the foreign currency debt to the bank. The most common types of debt instruments transferred are promissory notes and bills of exchange, and the usual currencies are euros and US dollars. The base interest rate for the transaction would be the relevant eurocurrency rate and, in addition, the bank would charge a commitment fee representing the delay between the agreement and the delivery of the instrument and the risk of exchange rate changes.

14.4.4 *Options*

Options also offer a method of managing exchange rate risk. As noted in chapter 13, options give the purchaser, in return for a premium, the right to buy (a 'call' option) or the right to sell (a 'put' option) at an agreed exchange rate (the 'striking' price) at a specified date or dates. No obligation is imposed on buyers to exercise the option so they will choose to do so only if it is profitable for them. Remember, the exercise of an option lies entirely in the hands of the purchaser. The writer has no control over whether the option is exercised or not. As was demonstrated in chapter 13, an option contract is analogous to an insurance policy, with the premium for the option representing the premium paid for the policy and the risk insured is the risk of an adverse exchange rate movement, with the purchaser taking all the benefits of a favourable movement.

Options are also particularly useful in the case of contingent exposures, for example in the case of a tender in foreign currency. If the firm does not win the contract, there is no need for the foreign currency and the option will be exercised only if it offers the chance of immediate profit because it is 'in the money'. Similarly, the firm may wish to take out options because the precise quantity of foreign exposure is not known, for example in the case of an uncertain volume of sales of goods abroad or in the case of domestic sales requiring imported raw materials. In such cases the firm can use options to provide a hedge against foreign currency exposure.

Over-the-counter (OTC) options would be arranged as a private contract with a bank and offer the advantage that the conditions attached to the contract exactly match those required by the purchaser. In contrast traded options are standardised and therefore may not match the precise quantity requirements of the purchaser. For example, the sterling options quoted on the Philadelphia Stock Exchange are denominated in units of £31,250. On the other hand they offer the additional benefit of being able to be sold on the market rather than just being exercised or allowed to lapse. The fact that options are not currently traded by Euronext.liffe suggests that the disadvantage of standardised contracts at present outweighs the advantage of tradability.

Various option strategies are possible and we use the quotations for December delivery on the Philadelphia Stock Exchange listed in table 14.1[1] to illustrate them – note in the following examples the spot rate is assumed to be $1.9750 per £1 for illustrative purposes.

In the case of options, the firm has a choice of exercise rates. If it purchases, for example, a call option for December delivery with a strike price of $1.875 per £1 the premium is 9.33 cents, implying a maximum price for the purchase of pounds of $1.9683 per £1 (1.875 + 0.0933). Thus, the firm is sure that the minimum quantity of sterling obtained for a future receipt of $500,000 is £254,026.31. If the spot rate at the time of receipt of

Table 14.1 Philadelphia Stock Exchange sterling/dollar options (£31,250) (cents per £1)

Strike	Calls				Puts			
price	Oct.	Nov.	Dec.	March	Oct.	Nov.	Dec.	March
1.875	9.10	9.20	9.33	9.79	–	0.70	1.41	3.56
1.900	6.60	7.04	7.31	8.02	0.04	1.22	2.01	4.56
1.925	4.11	5.17	5.57	6.49	0.07	2.02	2.91	5.71
1.950	1.97	3.61	4.11	5.20	0.29	2.88	4.05	7.06
1.975	0.53	2.43	3.00	4.12	1.37	4.24	5.47	8.55
2.000	0.07	1.65	2.08	–	3.29	5.89	7.11	–
2.025	0.01	1.08	1.56	–	5.67	7.77	8.94	–

the dollars is less than $1.875, then the option will not be exercised and the trader will purchase the sterling in the market at the lower price but lose the option premium. Similarly, at strike prices of $1.975 and $2.025 per £1, the maximum prices rise to $2.005 and $2.0406, respectively.

In a similar manner buying put options for December delivery with strike prices of $1.875, $1.975 and $2.025 per £1 fixes the minimum prices obtained by the sale of sterling at $1.8609, $1.9203 and $1.9356, respectively. It can be seen that the analogy to insurance is very close. The higher the premium paid the greater is the degree of protection against the downside risk of adverse changes in the spot exchange rate. This leaves the firm a choice of strategies with which there is a trade-off between protection and cost. More complex strategies are discussed below.

Vertical spread

One such strategy goes by the name of a vertical spread, which involves the simultaneous purchase and sale of options with different exercise prices. In the case of a vertical bull call spread (so called because of the expectation of rises in the exchange rate) the firm would buy a call option for December delivery with a strike price of, say, $1.975 per £1 at a premium of 3.00 cents and write (sell) a call with a higher strike price, say $2.025 per £1 at a premium of 1.56 cents. Thus, the premium income incurs a loss of 1.44 cents (3.00 – 1.56) or equivalently $0.0144. At a spot rate below $1.975 per £1 neither option is exercised and the trader's loss is 1.44 cents. At spot rates between $1.975 and $2.025 only the purchased call option is exercised, so the firm benefits from the increasing profitability of this option. At the rate of $2.025 per £1 the firm's profit (compared with the spot rate) is at a maximum since thereafter any profit on the purchase of the call option is matched on a one-for-one basis by the loss on the option sold. At a spot rate of $2.025 per £1, the firm's profit (as compared with the spot rate) is

given by the profit on the option purchased minus the loss on the premium, that is:

$$\$(2.025 - 1.975) - \$0.0144 = \$0.0356 \text{ or } 3.56 \text{ cents.}$$

In this case the firm has given up the potentially unlimited gain above a spot rate of $2.005 per £1 offered by a simple call option purchase with a strike price of $1.975 per £1 in return for a lower premium, that is, 1.44 cents as against 3.0 cents. In terms of hedging the firm has ensured a minimum sterling equivalent for the $500,000, due in December, of £251,332.06 {500,000/(1.975 + 0.0144)} provided the spot exchange rate remains below $2.025 per £1. As the rate rises above $2.025 per £1 the firm (as a hedger) is fully exposed to potential losses on the combined spot and option positions as the profit on the options is limited to 3.56 cents per £1. Firms would use this strategy when they thought that the exchange rate was likely to rise above the current spot rate but not by any great amount.

In an analogous manner a firm which believed that the spot rate was likely to fall from the current level but not to any great extent would buy a put, again say with a strike price of $1.975 per £1 (premium 5.47 cents) and sell a put with a lower strike price, say $1.950 per £1 (premium 4.05 cents). At an exchange rate greater than $1.975 per £1 neither option would be exercised and the trader's loss would be limited to the premium deficiency of 1.42 cents per £1. At rates below $1.975 per £1 but above $1.950 per £1 only the put option purchased would be exercised and below $1.950 per £1 both options would be exercised. Thus, the firm's maximum profit at $1.950

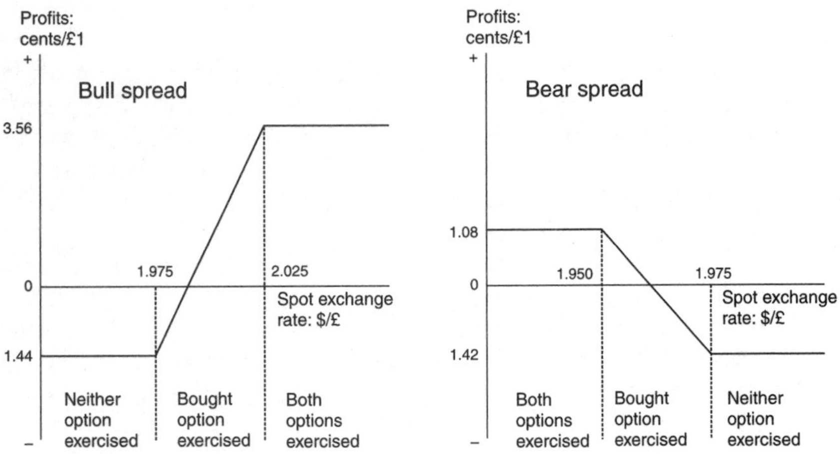

Figure 14.3 Profit and loss for vertical spreads, for the option position.

per £1 would be $0.0108 or 1.08 cents per £1 ($1.975 – $1.950 – $0.0142). Again, the firm has given up the opportunity of obtaining an unlimited profit at rates below $1.950 per £1 in return for the lower premium of 1.08 cents per £1. In terms of hedging, the firm, which has to make a payment of $500,000, has ensured a maximum sterling cost of £254,556.56 provided the spot rate remains above $1.950 per £1 {500,000/(1.975 – 0.0108)}. As the spot rate falls below $1.950 per £1, the firm (as a hedger) is fully exposed to potential losses on the spot position. This type of strategy is called a vertical bear spread.

The vertical spread strategy is also called a 'collar' because of the restricted range of protection as compared with a traditional option. Note that this restricted range of protection is obtained through payment of a reduced premium. This type of trade can be gainfully used by either a hedger or a speculator. In the case of a hedger, it is no longer a pure hedge since the firm has taken a view on the likely direction and magnitude of future exchange rate movements. A diagrammatic presentation of profit/loss situations for the option positions alone is shown in figure 14.3.

Volatility trading with options

The concluding types of option trading strategies examined are concerned with volatility trading. These are straddles, strangles and butterflies. In each case the operator takes a view on the likely course of movements in exchange rate volatility and backs this view by entering into an appropriate option strategy. For this reason these strategies are more likely to be adopted by speculators and writers of options than firms using the market as a facility to hedge.

(i) *Straddle*. A straddle involves writing or purchasing a call and put option at the same strike price. In the case of a sale of a straddle (sometimes called a short straddle) the writer could, for example, write (sell) a December call and a December put each with a strike price of $1.975 per £1. The combined premium received from the sale would be 8.47 cents per £1 (5.47 + 3.00). At the strike price (i.e. $1.975 per £1) neither option would be exercised. At spot exchange rates below $1.975 per £1, only the put option would be exercised and the break-even point for the writer of the option occurs where the loss on this option is just matched by the combined premium receipts. This occurs at a spot exchange rate of $1.8903 per £1. In a similar way, as the spot exchange rate rises above $1.975 per £1, only the call option is exercised and the break-even rate is $2.0597 per £1 (i.e. $1.975 + $0.0847). Whilst the rate remains within the two bounds ($1.8903 and $2.0597) the speculator will profit but otherwise faces unlimited loss. This type of trade is likely to be used by a speculator who believes that volatility is not likely to increase to any great extent and it is often therefore called a bear straddle.

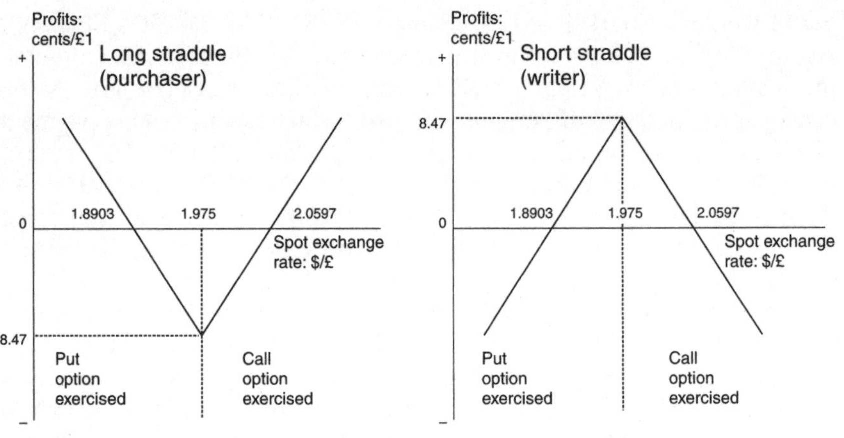

Figure 14.4 Profit and loss for a straddle.

In contrast, a speculator who believes that volatility is likely to increase will buy a straddle (a 'long' or 'bull' straddle). In this case he or she would purchase a call and put option for the same delivery date and strike price. Using the above example as an illustration the speculator could purchase a December call and put, each with a strike price of $1.975 per £1. In this case he or she pays out the combined premium of 8.47 cents per £1 and this is the maximum loss. The profit is potentially unlimited as the spot exchange rate rises above $2.0597 per £1 or falls below $1.8903 per £1.

In both cases of long and short straddles, the speculator is not forming a view as to the direction of the exchange rate movement but rather its volatility or the likelihood of it moving beyond specified limits. The profit and loss situations for both types of straddle are shown in figure 14.4.

(ii) *Strangle.* The second type of volatility strategy is a strangle. It is similar to a straddle and has the same underlying rationale but two different strike prices are involved and this lengthens the area of maximum profitability in the case of a short strangle or maximum loss in the case of a long straddle. In the case of a short strangle, the speculator could write a December call with a strike price of $2.000 per £1 (premium 2.08 cents) and a December put with a strike price of $1.950 per £1 (premium 4.05 cents). The combined premium income is 6.13 cents per £1 (2.08 + 4.05). At spot rates below $1.950 per £1 only the put option is exercised so that the break-even point is $1.8887 per £1 ($1.950 – $0.0613). Between rates of $1.950 and $2.000 per £1, neither option is exercised so the speculator earns a profit of 6.13 cents per £1. At rates above $2.000 per £1, only the call option is exercised and the break-even point is $2.0613 per £1 ($2.000 + $0.0613). The case

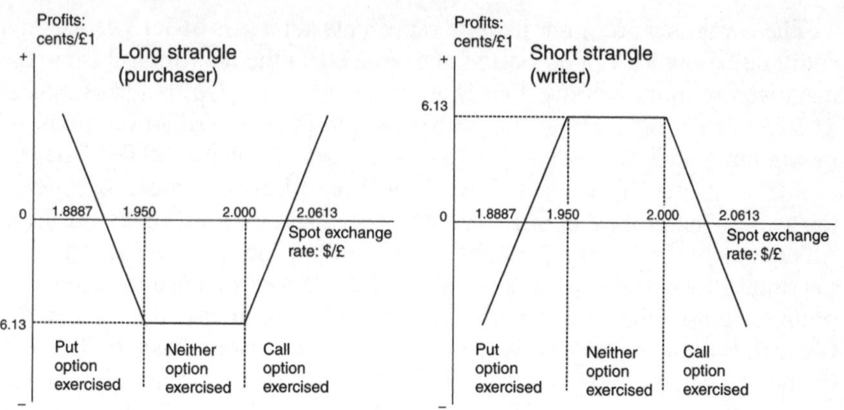

Figure 14.5 Profit and loss for a strangle.

of a long strangle can be illustrated by the same example but in this case the speculator purchases the two options. Consequently her or his maximum loss is given by the combined premium income and positions of profit are given when the spot exchange rate either falls below \$1.8887 per £1 or rises above \$2.0613 per £1. Diagrammatic representations of the profit and loss situations for strangles are shown in figure 14.5.

(iii) *Butterfly*. The final option strategy considered is a butterfly. A butterfly strategy is also similar to a straddle and has the same underlying rationale of trading against movements in the volatility of exchange rates. In this strategy, however, a floor is provided for the maximum loss or a ceiling to the maximum gain. Purchase of a butterfly (a long butterfly) entails buying an out-of-the-money call, writing two at-the-money calls and buying an in-the-money call. As an illustration of this strategy the calls purchased could be as shown in table 14.2.

Table 14.2 Illustration of a butterfly

	Strike price ($ per £1)	Premium (cents per £1)	Spot rate when exercised ($ per £1)
In the money (purchased)	1.925	5.57	>1.925
At the money (sold)	1.975	3.00	>1.975
Out of the money (purchased)	2.025	1.56	2.025

The combined premium income represents a net loss of 1.13 cents. At a spot rate below \$1.925 no option is exercised so the maximum loss is the negative premium income, that is, 1.13 cents per £1. Up to a spot rate of \$1.975 per £1, only the in-the-money option is exercised so the point of maximum gain is \$(1.975 – 1.925 – 0.0113) per £1, that is, \$0.0387 per £1 or 3.87 cents per £1. At rates above \$1.975 per £1 but below \$2.025 per £1 the two at-the-money options (written) are exercised so losses on these offset the profits gained on the in-the-money option purchased. The maximum loss occurs at a spot rate of \$2.025 per £1 because after this point the out-of-the-money call is exercised. Consequently the gain on the two call options purchased is matched on a one-for-one basis by the loss on the two call options sold. The maximum loss is therefore the gain on the option with a strike price of \$1.1925 per £1 less the loss on the two options written with a strike price of \$2.000 less the net premium deficiency: \${(2.025 – 1.925) – 2(2.025 – 1.975) – 0.0113} per £1, which is \$0.0113 per £1 or 1.13 cents per £1.

Selling a butterfly (a short butterfly) would entail the reverse procedure, that is, writing an in-the-money call, buying two at-the-money calls and writing an out-of-the-money call. The profit and loss situation would be precisely opposite to that illustrated for the above example, that is, a maximum loss of 3.87 cents per £1 and a maximum profit of 1.13 cents per £1. The profits and losses for this situation are illustrated in figure 14.6.

As noted above, figures 14.5 and 14.6 illustrate the essential difference between a butterfly and a straddle, that is, the maximum loss or gain is restricted to a fixed amount.

A variant of a 'butterfly' is a strategy known as a 'condor'. The general principle is the same but, in the case of a purchase, the two options sold are at different prices. An example is given in table 14.3 and interested readers are advised to derive for themselves the graph of the profit/loss situation arising from this transaction. As in the case of a butterfly, for writing a condor the transactions are reversed.

Table 14.3 Illustration of a condor

	Strike price (\$ per £1)	Premium (cents per £1)	Spot rate when exercised (\$ per £1)
In the money (purchased)	1.925	5.57	> 1.925
Option (i) (sold)	1.950	4.11	> 1.950
Option (ii) (sold)	1.975	3.00	> 1.975
Out of the money (purchased)	2.000	2.08	> 2.000

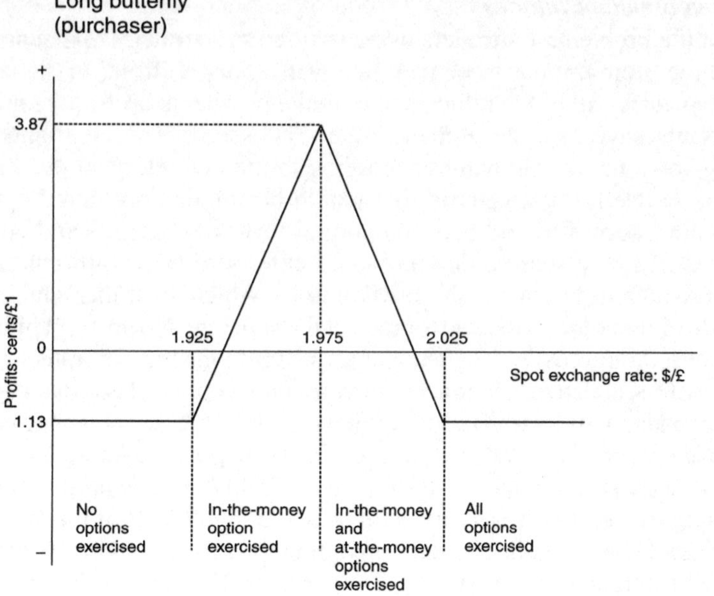

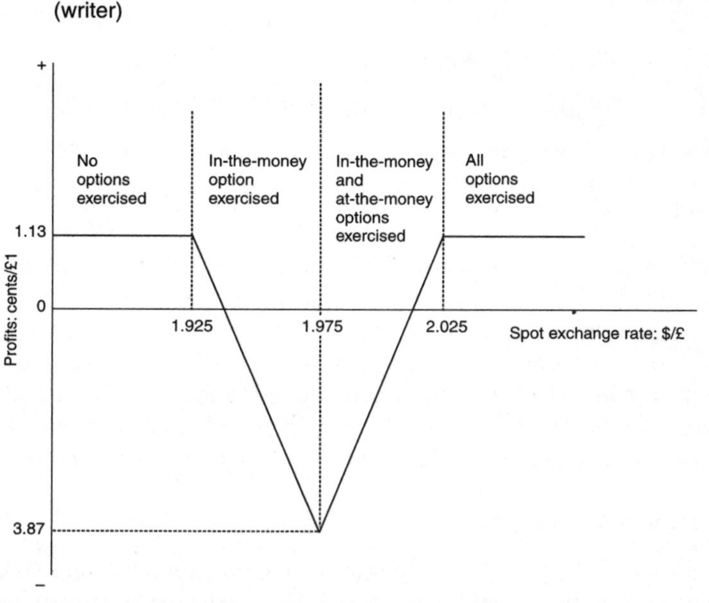

Figure 14.6 Profit and loss for a butterfly.

'Hidden premium' options

One of the problems for traders using options as a strategy to manage risk is that the premium has to be paid in advance, or 'up front' in the jargon. Partly in response to the reluctance to make payments up front, a number of variants have been developed in the OTC sector. These variants have been given a number of names according to the marketing strategy of the institution itself, but a generic title would be 'hidden premium' options. These are a sort of hybrid between normal forward contracts and options. The trader due to receive dollars would enter into a forward contract to purchase pounds but one with a break point at which the trader could break out of the forward position and transact at the spot rate. No up-front premium is involved as the cost would be incorporated into the forward rate. Clearly, in view of the added protection, the forward rate would be less advantageous than for a standard forward contract; it would be a higher rate in the case of purchases of, or a lower rate in the case of sales of, pounds. As an illustration, consider again the situation of the receipt of $500,000. The normal forward rate discussed earlier was assumed to be $1.9398 per £1. For illustration of the principle behind hidden premium options, we assume that the rate for a forward contract with a break at $1.90 per £1 is $1.9980 per £1. This gives the trader the right to break the contract if the spot rate at the maturity of the contract is less than $1.90 per £1. If on maturity the spot rate was $1.80 per £1 the following transactions are implied, leaving the trader with net receipts of £264,870.14:

sale of $500,000 at the forward rate (1.9980)	£250,250.25
purchase of $500,000 at the break rate (1.90)	–£263,157.89
sale of $500,000 at the spot rate (1.80)	£277,777.78
net receipts	£264,870.14

Note that, by this strategy, the trader is protected against loss from falls in the spot rate against the forward rate below the break rate. At the same time the trader is protected against rises in the spot rate above the agreed forward rate. The protection strategy in the case of sale of sterling would be the mirror image of that discussed above for the purchase of sterling. The trader would enter into a contract with an enhanced forward rate but one which provided a break if the spot rate rose above a specified rate.

14.4.5 *Back-to-back loans*

The final method of using the market to hedge exchange rate risk is to arrange a back-to-back loan. Back-to-back loans can take two forms: parallel loans or swaps. Multinational corporations use these types of loans for

subsidiaries wishing to raise finance in foreign currencies. Assume there are two parent companies, one in the UK and one in the US, each with a subsidiary in the country of the other parent company. Thus, the UK parent company lends in sterling to the subsidiary of the US company located in the UK and the US parent company lends in dollars to the subsidiary of the UK company located in the US. Each subsidiary company has a loan and cash denominated in the currency where it operates and has, therefore, avoided exchange rate exposure. If each parent company had borrowed in its domestic currency it would then have to transform the loan into foreign currency for the use of its subsidiary and it would therefore be exposed to exchange rate risk. Swap loans involve the exchange of debts denominated in different currencies. Thus, a firm with easy access to the UK capital market may wish to finance an investment in the US. If it is possible for that firm to find a corresponding US firm which has easy access to the US capital market but wishes to finance a sterling investment, then it is possible for both firms to gain by swapping their respective liabilities for repayment of the debt principal and interest payments. Such parallel and swap loans may be arranged through banks.

Finally, we look at currency exchange agreements, which are in essence similar to swap loans. Returning to the example used to illustrate the parallel loan, the two parent companies would agree to lend to each other, the US company to the UK company in dollars and the UK company to the US company in sterling. These loans would then be passed on to their subsidiaries, and hence each subsidiary has a loan denominated in the desired currency. Swaps are discussed in more detail in chapter 13 (section 13.6). The repayment terms, including any interest differentials, would be agreed at the time of the original loan, thus removing any exposure to subsequent exchange rate movements.

We now turn to examine strategies to manage interest rate risk.

14.5 Managing interest rate risk

We shall spend rather less time discussing interest rate risk, not because we regard this type of risk as being of less importance than exchange rate risk but rather because many of the strategies have already been discussed in the previous section. Internal methods of managing interest rate exposure take the form of doing nothing or forecasting, with all the inherent problems examined at the beginning of section 14.3. External methods of managing risk include use of the futures market, of options and of interest rate swaps. In chapter 13 (section 13.4.1) we illustrated the position of a company which wished to hedge against a rise in rates of interest by selling a financial futures short-term deposit. We also noted that the hedge may be less than perfect due to a change in basis. We also emphasised that the hedger should

sell futures if the company would be harmed by rising interest rates but buy futures if its position would be adversely affected by falls in interest rates.

14.5.1 *Interest rate futures*

Euronext.liffe offers a range of interest rate futures contracts, including futures on the three-month sterling interest rate, the three-month EURIBOR and three-month euroyen. This provides a number of possible strategies to manage interest rate exposure. However, a single interest rate contract is likely to involve more than one instance of exposure. Thus, a loan which is to be rolled over every three months for one year involves four instances of, rather than a single, risk. This can be covered by utilising a strip hedge, that is, taking out sales of four futures contracts, one for each time the loan is to be rolled over. This may prove to be difficult if the market for distant futures is illiquid. An alternative strategy is to employ a rolling hedge. Successive hedges are obtained on the earliest interest rate revisions only. An alternative strategy is to take out a 'piled up' hedge, in which futures amounting to a multiple of the loan would be taken out. Thus, if the interest rate on the loan is to be reassessed four times, futures contracts equal to four times the loan would be sold. These contracts would be closed out and renewed at each of the reassessment dates. The advantage of piled up hedges is that they avoid distant futures but on the other hand they incur a large number of contracts and therefore commission charges.

14.5.2 *Interest rate options*

Over-the-counter options are provided by some banks and Euronext.liffe also offers options on interest rate futures on some of the most important contracts. This provides hedging opportunities, in the same way as was discussed for exchange rate exposure in the previous section, for fixing maximum and minimum rates of interest. An interest rate cap gives a borrower an opportunity to purchase an agreement that will compensate the borrower if interest rates rise above a specific level. Similarly, an interest rate floor gives an investor the opportunity to purchase an agreement that will compensate the investor if interest rates fall below a certain level. In return for these facilities the borrower or investor will pay a premium to the seller and this cost can be seen as an insurance against adverse interest rate movements. As an example, consider the case of a company borrowing $10 million from a bank on a floating-rate basis linked to three-month LIBOR. The treasurer is concerned that interest rates may rise over the next three years and so purchases an interest cap at 8 per cent based on three-month LIBOR for a period of three years. If three-month LIBOR rises to 10 per cent on the first settlement date the company would be paid an amount by the seller to compensate for the 2 per cent difference between

the cap rate and the LIBOR rate. The cap rate will continue to be checked against LIBOR at each settlement date (every three months) until the end of the three-year period. If interest rates were to fall to say 6 per cent, then the company would receive no benefit under the cap facility but would be able to take advantage of the lower rate on the underlying loan. Thus, the advantages of the cap facility are that the borrower can quantify maximum borrowing costs over the term of the facility and that, unlike futures or fixed-rate funding, the borrower is protected from rising interest rates but is able to benefit from any downturn in rates.

An interest rate floor is an option contract which compensates investors for falls in interest rates but allows them to take advantage of interest rate rises. A collar, as discussed in section 14.4, on exchange rate hedging, is effectively a combination of an interest rate cap and floor. One party to the agreement will sell the cap and the other party will sell the floor. A borrower therefore will buy the cap to establish a maximum borrowing cost and simultaneously sell a floor, which will set a minimum borrowing cost. The value of the floor will be used either partially or fully to offset the cost of the cap. In practice the value of the floor agreement is usually less than the value of the cap agreement and so a net payment is required. The advantage of the collar agreement over the cap is the reduction (or elimination) of charges. However, this saving is achieved by giving up some part of the gain that could be achieved if rates fall. A collar can also be used by an investor. An investor would buy a floor and sell a cap, which would give protection against rates falling below the floor level but by sacrificing some of the potential gain available when rates rise above the cap level.

The preceding discussion of caps, floors and collars related to OTC option contracts. Traded options on interest rate futures can also be used to provide the same sort of protection. With a traded option, instead of the seller of the option compensating the buyer for adverse changes in interest rates, the protection is obtained by first buying an option and then selling before maturity with the net gain providing compensation. For example, a lending floor can be obtained by buying call options that will increase in value if interest rates decline. Assume the option selected is a December 89.00 call with a premium of 0.61. This option achieves a minimum effective lending rate of 10.39 per cent:

interest rate implied by exercise price =	11.00 per cent (100 – 89)
less call premium	–0.61 per cent
= minimum effective lending rate	10.39 per cent

If the interest rate underlying the option falls before the option expires then the value (premium) of the option will rise. If, say, interest rates fall from 11 per cent to 10 per cent and the call option value increases to 1.00,

then the option can be sold and a gain of 1.00 – 0.61 = 0.39 is made. This gain compensates the investor for a fall in the underlying interest rate. The effective lending rate has thus been fixed at 10.39 per cent:

lending rate	10.00 per cent
plus gain on option	0.39 per cent
= effective lending rate	10.39 per cent

14.5.3 *Interest rate swaps*

Finally in this section we discuss the nature of interest rate swaps. An interest rate swap entails the exchange by two parties of interest rate payments of a different character based on a notional principal amount. Three types of swap are probably the most important. These are coupon swaps, basis swaps and cross-currency interest rate swaps. In chapter 12 (section 12.5) we described the dramatic growth in the interest rate swap market in recent years, partly reflecting the growth in fixed-rate eurobond issues. In chapter 13 (section 13.6) we discussed the nature of the interest rate (coupon) swap. The classic example of this type of swap is to exchange a floating-rate loan for a fixed-rate one. This may be carried out to eliminate the risk of changes in interest rates. Note again that the benefit of this strategy is the substitution of certainty for uncertainty. This swap may be carried out directly by the two liability holders or through a bank acting as an intermediary. In the latter case anonymity is preserved. The second type of interest rate swap is a basis swap, where a loan with interest rates based on one key rate is swapped for another loan based on an alternative key rate (e.g. a LIBOR rate for a local authority rate). In both cases it may be possible for a borrower with a low credit rating to obtain a lower charge than would otherwise be the case. Finally, we have examined the nature of the cross-currency interest rate swap in section 13.6.2.

14.6 **Conclusion**

We have examined a wide range of strategies for firms to manage exposure to risk. Since these risks have increased since the early 1960s it is not surprising that the number of instruments available to hedge risk has also increased. This is just one further example of financial innovation.

We would like to emphasise that hedging is not an ephemeral concept. In a survey carried out by the Bank of England on behalf of the Bank for International Settlements, of the 396 firms surveyed, 43 per cent said they used derivatives for both trading and hedging, 32 per cent for hedging alone and 14 per cent for trading and hedging and market making (*Bank of England Quarterly Bulletin*, spring 1996). These figures give some indication

of the importance of the hedging function. Further corroboration of the importance of derivative contracts is provided by a survey of 386 major international corporations (Price Waterhouse 1995). This found that:

(i) 73 per cent of the respondents used derivatives to manage their interest rate risk on their borrowings;
(ii) 96 per cent of the respondents partially or fully hedged their foreign exchange transactions exposure. The main vehicle used was the forward exchange market, with only 4 per cent using futures. Option-based products, swaps and foreign currency balances were also used by 50 per cent of the respondents.

The findings by Price Waterhouse (1995) also drew attention to concern over the control standards applied by the companies. This concern was more pronounced in the case of foreign exchange transactions – for example only 36 per cent of respondents imposed limits on dealer trading. It should also be noted that financial risk is just one of the risks facing a company. In some cases insuring against financial risk may increase the total risk incurred by a firm. To illustrate this point, consider the example of a firm which sells a product in an overseas market with the price denominated in the overseas currency. Before delivery of the product the firm's costs rise due to a higher relative rate of inflation. In a floating exchange rate regime, the exchange rate will depreciate so that the domestic currency receipts will rise compared with the level anticipated at the time of making the contract. This will offset the rise in costs. The extent of the offset will depend on the extent of the depreciation, which itself depends on the efficiency of the foreign exchange market. In contrast, if the firm hedges the exchange rate risk, no offset to the relative rise in domestic costs will have occurred.

Note

1 Note the rates quoted in this table are illustrative and should not be taken as the rates ruling at the time of reading the text. The interested reader can find such rates quoted daily in the *Financial Times* and other commercially oriented media.

Chapter 15

The efficiency of the UK financial system

15.1 Introduction

The criticisms of the UK financial system are generally based on the following rationale. Growth of UK gross national product since 1945 has been less than that of many other countries. Over this period gross domestic capital formation has been lower in the UK than in other countries and this has caused the lower rate of growth of gross national product. In turn this lower level of investment has been caused by deficiencies in the UK financial system. Complaints have focused on the excessive amount of resources devoted to speculation on secondary markets, inadequate provision of funds for investment, excessive cost of capital, and 'short termism', that is, excessive concentration on the short term as opposed to the long term. Such criticisms have come from a wide range of sources, not just the left in political terms. For example, a Conservative Chancellor referred to market operators as 'teenaged scribblers'. Nevertheless, these arguments appear to be rather tenuous in the absence of other confirmatory evidence.

It is factual to note that both the rate of growth and also the level of investment have been lower than those observed in many Continental countries. This, as any student of statistics knows, does not of necessity indicate a causal relationship flowing from the lower level of investment to the lower rate of growth. It could be plausible to argue that the lower rate of growth in the UK has led to ('caused'?) the lower level of investment or that they were both caused by a third variable. Similarly, it is a large step to assume that, in the absence of other confirmatory evidence, the lower level of investment has been caused by deficiencies in the financial system. Equally it is true to add that additional evidence may well support these criticisms.

It is as well at this stage to remind the reader of the functions of the financial system discussed in chapter 1. These are the provision of:

(i) a payments mechanism;

(ii) a mechanism for financial intermediation between surplus and deficit units;
(iii) primary and secondary markets so that portfolio holders can adjust their portfolios;
(iv) various financial services, such as foreign exchange, pension provision and insurance.

As can be seen from the opening remarks, most of the complaints have centred on functions (ii) to (iv) rather than on the provision of the payments mechanism. Consequently we concentrate on these aspects of the financial system in the following assessment though, in view of the large volume of literature on this topic, we are able only to indicate the main themes of the various arguments. In section 15.2 we examine the efficiency of the various markets and in section 15.3 discuss the nature of short termism, which is perhaps the most consistent criticism raised. In section 15.4 we present our remedies for short termism.

15.2 **The efficiency of the financial system**

In chapter 7 we reviewed the various meanings of the word efficiency as applied to financial markets. These were: allocative efficiency, operational efficiency and informational efficiency.

15.2.1 *Allocative efficiency*

Allocative efficiency is a broad concept and is likely to be achieved provided that the market is giving out correct signals (i.e. that informational efficiency is achieved) and that incentives exist to follow the direction of these signals. There is just one proviso to this statement and this concerns the possibility that certain types of undertaking may not be able to obtain finance owing to gaps in the market.

The proposition that it is difficult for entrepreneurs to obtain small amounts of capital to finance the start-up of a company or to expand it in its early years is of long standing. In 1931 the Macmillan Committee on Finance and Industry brought attention to such a gap in the provision of finance (the 'Macmillan gap') and as a consequence the forerunner of the 3i Group (previously Investors In Industry – owned by the clearing banks and the Bank of England) was established in 1945. In 1971, the Bolton Committee in its report highlighted both an 'equity gap' in terms of raising long-term finance below £250,000 (£1 million in current prices) and an information gap, where small firms were unaware of sources of finance or could not present a reasoned request for finance. The Wilson Committee reported on the financial problems of small companies in 1979 and highlighted the information gap and commented on the difficulties for small

firms in obtaining venture capital (i.e. for high-risk ventures with little track record).

Since the 1980s there have been a number of developments which have gone some way to closing the finance and information gaps identified. What follows is a brief summary of these developments. Detailed surveys of the earlier initiatives can be found in the *Bank of England Quarterly Bulletin* (autumn 1990) and Boocock (1990).

With regard to the information gap, the Department of Trade and Industry set up a number of small-firm information centres, which provide free information and advice. In addition, a number of regional development agencies and other specialised agencies have been established, which also provide advice. There was also a growth in venture capital providers which provide equity and other forms of long-term capital to small/medium-sized firms at both the early stages of development (e.g. seed capital) and later stages (e.g. expansion, management buyouts/ins). Institutions offering this type of financing can be divided into two broad groups. First, captive funds are subsidiaries of the major UK pension funds, insurance companies and banks. These captive funds obtain their finance from the parent company. Second, independent funds raise capital for investment from a wide variety of sources, including private investors and some financial institutions. In 1988 the independents accounted for approximately 66 per cent of the amount invested by venture capital funds, with captive funds accounting for most of the rest. The distinction between captive and independent is not so clear-cut though, with most independent funds having some links with financial institutions and captive funds having some degree of independence.

The finance provided by the venture capital industry substantially increased over the 1980s so that in 1988 over £1 billion was invested. During the 1990s the sum invested further increased and in 1997 UK venture capital investment reached a figure of approximately £3 billion. However, there has been a change in the nature of the finance provided over this period, illustrated in table 15.1. There was an increasing emphasis on financing buyouts, buyins and acquisitions at the expense of start-up and other early-stage financing. UK corporate restructuring over the latter half of the 1980s led to the sale of non-core businesses by many diversified companies as they reverted back to core activities. These sales were often to incumbent management (management buyout) and financed by venture capital funds. This type of financing was attractive to venture capital funds as it was less risky than the traditional investment and usually offered a quicker exit route (i.e. realisation of the fund's investment) through a trade sale or flotation.

Two government initiatives in the early 1980s also addressed the funding gap for small companies. The first was the Loan Guarantee Scheme, which was introduced in 1981 following a recommendation of the Wilson

Table 15.1 UK venture capital financing by financing stage, 1984–2001 (percentage of total invested)

	1984	1985	1986	1987	1988	1997	2001
Start-up	17	13	16	8	5	2	3
Other early stage	10	6	7	4	2	3	7
Expansion	39	36	27	22	27	22	37
Buyout/in and acquisition[a]	28	38	44	63	62	65	46
Secondary purchase[b]	5	6	5	3	4	6	7
Other	1	1	1	–	–	–	–
Total (£million)	228	279	396	795	1,006	3,066	1,412

[a] Purchase of an existing company as a going concern.
[b] Acquisition of existing shares in a company from another venture capital firm or other shareholders.
Source: British Venture Capital Association.

Committee. The scheme was extended indefinitely following a review by the government in 1989 and is still operating today. The aim of this initiative is to encourage banks and some other credit institutions to supply medium-term loan finance (for two to ten years), up to a maximum of £100,000, where the risks involved would normally mean the loan request is rejected. The government guarantees 75 per cent of any loan approved and the borrower pays a premium on top of the normal interest rate. This suggests that the government perceives there is a funding gap requiring a scheme of this sort. The scheme has been criticised though, as it provides loan finance whereas equity risk capital is considered more appropriate for small but growing companies.

A further government initiative was the Business Expansion Scheme, introduced in the 1983 Finance Act. This was designed to persuade investors to provide equity finance to non-quoted companies, by giving tax relief to investors at the marginal rate paid for amounts up to £40,000 per annum. This tax relief was to compensate investors for the extra risks involved. Most finance of this sort was obtained by companies making a direct issue of shares to the public. The advantage to the company was that investors could not sell shares purchased under the scheme before five years had elapsed without losing the tax relief. The Business Expansion Scheme ended in December 1993 and was regarded as having had only limited success.

Despite the developments in funding for small business over the 1980s and in particular the growth in venture capital providers, it is still widely believed that there exists an equity gap for amounts below £1,000,000. Further new developments have occurred, with a number of funds being established to lend to small and medium-sized companies. One such fund

is the Merseyside Special Investment Fund, which was established with £16 million of European Union money and a further £9 million derived from private sources. The aim of the fund is to assist firms which are too small to utilise traditional venture capital equity finance. Similar schemes based on private and public funding have sprung up elsewhere across the UK (e.g. Finance Cornwall) to try to meet the gaps mentioned above.

Overall, the importance of external finance to small and medium-sized firms fell during the 1990s. The Bank of England (2003) reported that over the period 1987 to 1990 external finance amounted to 65 per cent of total finance for small and medium-sized firms but that over the period 1997 to 2000 this had fallen to 40 per cent. Similarly, over these periods the importance of bank finance had risen from 48 per cent to 61 per cent of external finance. The Bank further reported that during its discussions with trade associations, any problems concerning the availability of bank finance were not raised. This evidence is supportive of the view that the system is operating reasonably efficiently for small and medium-sized firms.

15.2.2 *Operational efficiency*

It is difficult to obtain hard evidence concerning operational efficiency but what we can obtain is indirect evidence from the structure of the financial system and also the cost of capital. In a competitive system we would expect to see inefficiencies competed away and, in the long run, profits to be 'normal', reflecting the degree of risk involved in the industry. As we have seen in earlier chapters, the UK financial system has certainly been subject to a large degree of liberalisation in areas of pricing and range of business conducted.

To take just a few examples, the era of liberalisation saw the relaxation of controls over the banking industry, and the death of some cartels, such as 'Big Bang' on the London Stock Exchange (LSE) removing fixed commissions and opening it up to a greater degree of competition. The building societies' interest rate cartel also ended and, as a consequence, the mortgage market is now a 'competitive price-driven' market. The incidence of competition has increased not only in the domestic context but also on an international scale. The abolition of exchange controls allows residents to invest overseas without restraint. As we have seen in chapter 4, a large number of foreign banks now operate in London. Consequently it would be reasonable to expect that the increased competitive environment would have led to a greater degree of efficiency. We certainly have seen a fairly high degree of financial innovation, that is, the development of new markets and financial instruments. In chapter 13 we discussed the development in London of a major new financial market, LIFFE (now Euronext.liffe). The increased volume of trading on this market noted in chapter 13 indicates a successful development. New instruments have been developed and extended,

such as in the commercial paper market, together with all those available to manage risk as indicated in chapter 14.

Nevertheless, critics have pointed to the volume of trading carried out on the major markets and in particular the LSE and the foreign exchange market. With reference to the LSE, we noted in chapter 8, figure 8.1, the importance of internally generated funds as a source of business finance. In connection with the foreign exchange market, the average figure for daily trades of US$1,210 billion per day quoted in chapter 11 (section 11.4) dwarfs the daily volume of international trade requiring currency exchange.

One other aspect of the operational efficiency of markets concerns the cost of capital. A number of commentators have argued that the cost of capital is higher in countries such as the UK and the US compared with other countries such as Germany and in particular Japan. Perhaps one of the most widely quoted studies was that carried out by McCauley and Zimmer (1989), who claimed that the real cost of funds after tax was some 3 per cent higher in the UK than in Germany and Japan. The main reasons given for this difference were higher savings ratios and lower risk premiums. These reasons are not unambiguous with respect to their theoretical underpinning. If real returns on savings are lower in some countries then, given the current level of globalisation of finance, it would be expected that international arbitrage would lead to funds moving out of countries with a lower rate of return in favour of centres with higher real rates of return. This would tend to lead to real rates of return being equalised across international centres. Supportive evidence for this role of the international capital market is provided by the statistics contained in the Myners report (2001). Over the decade 1989 to 1999, the UK investment institutions' ownership share of UK-quoted equity fell from 58.5 per cent to 51.9 per cent, whereas that of non-residents (mainly overseas investment institutions) rose from 12.8 per cent to 29.3 per cent. Similar trends were observed in the private equity market, where US pension funds invest more than their UK counterparts.

The second reason put forward by McCauley and Zimmer for their findings suggests that high levels of inflation lead to volatility of nominal returns and a higher risk premium. Marsh (1990) suggests that examination of the gap between the risk-free return and the return on equities shows that risk premiums were higher in Japan than in the UK. This is supported also by the fact that the standard deviations on stock market returns were higher in Japan than in other countries. Marsh also argued that McCauley and Zimmer used an inappropriate measure of the cost of equity capital in their study, that is, the inverse of the price/earnings ratio. This is inappropriate because it makes no allowance for future growth potential; the correct measure is the risk-free real rate of interest plus a premium for investing in equities. However, a contrary argument must also be raised at

this juncture. High nominal rates of interest can cause cash flow problems, particularly for firms with high gearing. It could be claimed that nominal interest rate stability permits firms to utilise a more highly geared capital structure with its cost advantage without the danger of a financial crisis due to restrictive monetary policy. Clearly, this has not been the case for UK firms during periods of high nominal interest rates. All in all it seems that the cost of capital may well have been higher in the UK than in other countries but that the extent of the margin has been exaggerated. Furthermore, any higher cost due to higher nominal rates of interest must have been the responsibility of the government for permitting higher and more volatile rates of inflation rather than that of the financial system.

One final criticism of the operational efficiency concerns the response of the financial system to firms in difficulty. It is often claimed that the financial institutions are too keen to foreclose on debt rather than allow sufficient time for a firm to recover its former position of financial strength. This is of course the classic dilemma for banks. Do they force the firm into bankruptcy and accept the loss without a chance to recoup their losses, or do they lend additional funds, thus incurring additional risk, in the hope of obtaining repayment of all lending eventually? The criticism suggests that the banks and other lenders too often follow the first course of action. There appears to be some force in this argument and the Bank of England has negotiated with the commercial banks to produce an agreed procedure to deal with companies with a liquidity crisis. This is termed the 'London approach' and full details are provided in the *Bank of England Quarterly Bulletin* of spring 1996. Basically the approach is to provide funds for the company to keep it afloat until such time as a considered judgement can be made about its long-term future. The funds are to be provided by the lending banks in proportion to their existing exposure. A lead bank is to be identified to keep the other creditors informed. This is necessary because of the large number of banks often lending to a single firm. For example, in the case of the troubled Goodman International empire in Ireland, it was reported that 33 different banks were involved in lending the equivalent of £500 million. The lead bank is likely to be the bank with the largest exposure. Finally, in this interval all other lending to the company should be suspended.

15.2.3 *Informational efficiency*

It has been argued that excessive resources have been devoted to speculation as distinct from the raising of capital. A similar objection could be raised against the operation of the foreign exchange market, where the daily volume of trading dwarfs any requirement to finance UK overseas trade. The counterargument is that the speculators are necessary to ensure that prices of the various securities reflect all available information. The aim of speculators is to make a profit. They do this by identifying securities which

are incorrectly priced in the market, purchasing those which are identified as underpriced and selling those identified as overpriced. In this manner the speculator contributes to market efficiency in the informational sense. Correct decision making will reward the speculator and, in the same way, the inefficient speculator, who makes wrong decisions, will be penalised. A 'Darwinian' process will ensure the survival of efficient speculators at the expense of the inefficient ones. Speculation will, therefore, be stabilising. However, it is of course perfectly possible to argue that the process is not as efficient as that described above. Whilst persistently inefficient speculators must leave the market through shortages of finance, it is quite possible (though improbable over a long period) that successive waves of inefficient speculators will appear on the market, leading to the existence of destabilising speculation.

A second criticism arising from the relative volume of speculative activity on financial markets points to the likelihood of increased volatility of market prices. It is quite probable that this increased volatility may have detracted from the efficiency of the market mechanism by obscuring the price signals given out by the market. Some casual empirical support for an adverse effect of market volatility on business operation is given by the rapid growth of hedging instruments such as financial futures since 1980. However, the real test of these criticisms must be whether the market conforms to the efficient markets hypothesis or not. Clearly, no market can be absolutely efficient in the sense that market prices always fully reflect all available information. The acid test is more sensibly one of examining whether market prices usually reflect all available information, so that the market approximates to the efficient markets hypothesis. In this connection we examined the efficiency of the stock market (chapter 8), the bond market (chapter 9), the foreign exchange market (chapter 11) and the financial derivatives market (chapter 12). Our conclusions were not decisive in either direction but it is certainly true to say that no conclusive evidence was presented against market efficiency in the informational sense.

A second aspect of informational efficiency concerns the advice given by City analysts about the advisability of purchasing equity in a company. In this connection the *Observer* (28 October 1990) provided an interesting commentary on analysts' reports on Polly Peck, which foundered in the autumn of 1990. Throughout 1990 a considerable number of analysts were recommending the purchase of Polly Peck shares on the ground that the shares were undervalued. At least ten analysts were quoted as recommending the purchase and some with a repetition of a buy and hold strategy even as late as September. It is patently obvious that the advice was ill-founded and this may raise doubts over this aspect of the City's work. This, incidentally, adds support to the efficient markets hypothesis since, at least in this case, market experts failed to beat the market.

We now turn to discuss short termism, which is perhaps the main thrust of common criticism of the UK financial system.

15.3 Short termism

In general terms, short termism can be defined as a climate in which companies concentrate on short-term profits rather than long-term investment. Associated with the concept of short termism is the view that the UK financial system suffers from myopia. One aspect of this view on short termism is the belief that the takeover mechanism contributes to companies concentrating on short-term issues because of the necessity of having to look continually over their shoulders, as it were, to identify possible predators. This is particularly true when a company's share price falls. This is largely a consequence of the type of financial system that exists in the UK. As we saw in chapter 2, the financial systems in the UK and the US can be broadly categorised as market based. Thus, financial markets play an important role in terms of both raising long-term capital and changing corporate control. In contrast, in bank-based financial systems, such as those of Germany and Japan, the banks play a greater role in providing external finance. The finance provided by banks consists of loans and equity so that the banks often take a more active role in the running of the companies they finance. In particular they will often initiate changes in management and sometimes ownership. However, such changes are carried out without hostile confrontation.

Certainly it is true that expenditure on takeovers increased in the 1990s compared with the 1980s, but the question remains as to whether this would have encouraged the growth of short termism. The role of the financial system in mergers and acquisitions is highlighted by the advisory fees earned from both the predators and the victims. The fact that such fees add to a bank's profitability without incurring any of the balance sheet restraints imposed through prudential control provides an additional stimulus for banks to engage in this type of business. A counterargument would suggest that takeovers are part of the discipline of the market and are necessary to provide a spur for the stimulation of efficiency and the removal of inefficient managements. However, the discipline is rather a blunt instrument which may threaten efficient as well as inefficient companies.

Proponents of the view that the financial system is responsible for short termism suggest that the equity of a company is subject to a dual valuation situation. First, there is what may be called the normal valuation, when the price of equity reflects the marginal trading in company shares between portfolio investors. There is, however, a second valuation, which occurs when a potential bidder is attempting to acquire control of a business and so is bidding for the whole of the company's equity. In this case the share

price will rise above the normal price and the difference between the two prices is the bid premium. This provides an incentive for shareholders, particularly the institutions, to accept the bid because it is unlikely that the share price will continue to remain at that level in the absence of the predator. The source of the bid premium can be construed to be the increased efficiency with which the firm taken over is managed or alternatively increased economies of scale attributable to the integration of the firm into the predator's operations. An alternative view of the source of the bid premium is, however, that it represents the anticipated profit through asset stripping, including sale of assets and perhaps the acquisition of pension fund surpluses. In this case the bid premium represents a transfer from the other stakeholders in the firm, such as employees, to the predator company without conferring any benefit to the economy as a whole.

In the UK the investment institutions dominate holdings of equities in companies so it is their decisions which matter as far as the success of takeovers is concerned. In this connection it is also important to note that the institutions have incentives to accept takeover offers for reasons other than that described above. Fund managers prepare statistics every quarter and have therefore an additional incentive to accept bids for companies whose shares are held in their portfolios to boost the quarterly performance of the fund that they manage. This also raises the question of their commitment to the companies whose securities are held in their portfolios. In general they seem quite reluctant to become involved in the management of these firms, possibly owing to a lack of expertise. A second possible reason for this is that the possession of detailed knowledge of any firms would make it more difficult for them to deal in their securities for fear of falling foul of legislation on insider trading. A further reason for a 'hands-off' approach to the management of the companies is the number of different funds which are likely to hold the equity of any one individual company. This general situation is contrasted with the position of countries where the banks provide a major source of funds for industrial and commercial companies. It appears that these banks are more firmly committed to their clients and are represented in top management and have, therefore, a voice in the firm's policy-making process.

However, there is evidence to suggest that fund managers in the UK are taking an increasingly active role. Gartmore, the fund management arm of National Westminster Bank, and the fifth largest fund manager in the UK, in 1997 created the new post of head of corporate governance. Standard Life has circulated lists of its corporate governance proposals to the chairs and chief executives of the main quoted companies. Prudential, one of the UK's largest life assurance companies, has set up a mechanism to enable companies to discuss strategic issues in confidence with the chair of its fund management arm. All these developments suggest that institutional

fund managers are beginning to stimulate strategic change in companies. The successful campaign by fund managers in 2003 to prevent Michael Green, the chairman of Carlton, becoming the chairman of ITV (the company resulting from the merger of Carlton and Granada) is a recent example of this. Despite this evidence the Myner report (2001) criticised the reluctance of the institutions to take a proactive role in addressing management failure.

The general tenor of the argument above depends on the hypothesis that share prices do not reflect the long-run profit potential of the company concerned, or in other words that the efficient markets hypothesis is breached since some facets of information are not fully reflected in the price of equity. Marsh (1990) disputes this with the aid of an illustration derived from the valuation of ICI shares according to a standard valuation model. The then current share price and price of capital for ICI implied:

> that the market is expecting ICI's dividends to grow at the rate of 13% per annum. In turn this implies that of ICI's current market capitalization, only 8% is attributable to the current year's dividend, only 29% can be explained by the present value of dividends expected over the next five years and only 50% by the value of the dividends expected over the next 10 years. (Marsh 1990)

Marsh admits that analysts' judgements on the cost of capital are tentative but nevertheless the figures are not suggestive of short termism in share valuation. This point seems to us to be critical, since if the price of equity is representing, albeit as an approximation, the long-term profit potential of firms then the search for short-term profits by fund managers will not provoke short-term profit decisions by firms. A fund manager will seek to identify shares which are incorrectly valued and then buy any undervalued shares or sell any shares which are considered to be overvalued. Consequently, even though the manager's actions are motivated by short-term gains, he or she is in fact moving share prices towards their correct price. Clearly, if the market is not efficient in an informational sense then the foregoing argument is not correct and the manager's actions will be stimulating short-term behaviour.

A further consideration concerns the influence of investment on the price of a company's shares. There is a not inconsiderable volume of evidence derived from the US to suggest that the announcement of long-term investment often enhances the value of a company's shares – see for example McConnell and Muscerella (1985). This implies that investment is not of necessity an activity to be avoided for fear of inducing takeover bids through lower share prices. In this connection it may also be argued that the perception that investment and dividend payments are necessarily alternative sources of demand for a company's resources is incorrect. Successful

investment projects will enhance a company's profit-making potential and therefore dividends in the long run.

An alternative explanation of short termism is provided by Marsh (1990). This is based on the view that it is the management itself which is subject to myopia, or 'managerial short termism'. Marsh presents a number of arguments to support this hypothesis. The first point concerns the system of remunerating top managers, in that only a small proportion of managers' remuneration is directly linked to the performance of the corporation. Furthermore, the majority of executive schemes are based on short-term indicators, such as accounting profit. The underlying argument is that such schemes may provide an incentive for executives to pursue short-term objectives at the expense of a long-term strategy. Marsh's second point concerns the role of investment appraisal. It is often argued that current profitability influences the divisional allocation of capital budgets. The problem arises because profitability is assessed via accounting profits and this may provide incorrect signals for investment appraisal, which should be based on discounting methods. The third broad strand of the argument for managers suffering from myopia relates to a perceived lack of investment opportunities, for example because of poor industrial relations potentially diluting the benefits from innovation and investment.

In the following section, we discuss possible remedies for short termism.

15.4 **Remedies for short termism**

Assuming that short termism is a problem for the UK economy, the proposal of adequate remedies requires identification of its causes. One reform, which has been widely adopted, is a change in the method of remuneration of managers by providing incentive schemes which link their salaries to the medium-term (say in the region of five years) market value of their companies.

A similar proposal is to extend the appointment of non-executive directors and the separation of the duties of managing director and chairperson of a company. Advocates of this strategy claim that this would provide a more independent element on the board of directors and remove an element of passivity and self-selection. It would also facilitate a more objective assessment of past policies and remedies where appropriate. A basic requirement for this strategy to be successful is that the non-executive directors must be genuinely independent and not just 'old cronies' of the existing directors.

The above two proposals are promoted by the voluntary Principles of Good Governance and Code of Best Practice, which apply to all UK listed companies.

It is also advocated that banks should become more like banks in Germany and Japan by being closely identified with their borrowers. This would

include lending by way of equity and becoming involved in management decisions.

Further remedies suggested depend on the view that short termism is attributable to the deficiencies of the financial system – for such a view see for example Cosh *et al.* (1990). They argue that remedies such as those indicated above will require a fairly long time to implement. It is therefore suggested that some 'grit' should be introduced into the takeover mechanism. First, terms of reference to the Competition Commission should be broadened so as to enable a better distinction between takeovers which result in economies of scale and greater efficiency of operation and those which are designed to gain profits by asset stripping. Currently criteria are restricted to the effect on competition, which provides a reasonably clear framework for decisions. Extension of the criteria to incorporate public interest would permit the authorities to filter out, albeit judgementally, takeovers which were not designed to increase efficiency of operation. Further restraints could be introduced by requiring all contested bids to be submitted to the Competition Commission.

Another suggestion on a similar line takes the form of restricting the voting rights from newly acquired shares for a specific period of time after the acquisition, such as 12 months. Similarly, it is also suggested that the threshold at which a predator is obliged to make an offer to all shareholders is reduced from the current 29.9 per cent to a lower figure, such as 14.9 per cent (Plender 1990). Both these measures would increase the cost and difficulty of making predatory bids, especially where they are contested.

A further proposal along these lines advocates the imposition of tax penalties on share transactions to encourage the institutions to take a longer view in their portfolio decisions. This seems to us to be a step in the wrong direction, for three reasons. First, the existence of a secondary market provides liquidity, so that existing individuals as well as institutions can change the composition of their portfolios. Restriction on this important function may well reduce the willingness of individuals to hold equity in their overall portfolio of wealth. Second, as we have noted earlier, dealings by institutions is a mechanism which pushes equity prices towards their true value. Third, imposition of taxes on share dealings on the LSE would force business away to other international stock exchanges. It is quite likely that attempts to tax dealings on other exchanges would create massive scope for evasion. It would therefore in all probability be ineffective and costly to operate.

15.5 **Conclusion**

Certain facets of the debate appear to be clear. Short termism is generally perceived to be a problem for the UK economy. Investment has been lower

in the UK economy and this is presumably owing to short termism, at least in part. Certain of the proposed remedies command fairly widespread support. These include the proposals for the introduction of long-term incentives for managers and increased representation of genuinely independent non-executive directors. Beyond this, little agreement on either the causes or the remedies exists. Those who believe that the volume of takeovers is excessive advocate legal or quasilegal restraints on the takeover process. Believers in the efficient markets hypothesis argue that such restraints would do more harm than good. In this connection, it is interesting to note that a report by the McKinsey Global Institute (1996), entitled *Capital Productivity*, suggested that short-termism actually brings productivity gains for the US. Capital productivity was significantly higher in the US than in either Germany or Japan. In the period 1990–93 Germany's and Japan's capital per head were 13 and 22 per cent higher than in the US. Yet capital productivity in the two countries was 35 and 37 per cent lower than in the US. This higher capital productivity creates higher financial returns and it is argued that concentration on financial returns stimulates managerial efficiency.

The arguments have continued. For example, Will Hutton (*Guardian*, 3 January 1995) argued strongly that the 'City' has failed UK industry over a long period of time. The main criticism, due to Professor C. Mayer, is based on the alleged failure of the City to provide either 'a stable long-term ownership base' or cheap long-term debt. Similarly, arguments continue to be made that the cost of capital is higher in the UK than elsewhere because of the alleged requirement of the City for high rates of return. The problem with these arguments is that they do not provide irrefutable evidence of the failure of the financial system. As noted earlier, arbitrage, given the current freedom of international movement of capital, should stimulate movement towards equality of risk-adjusted rates of return across national boundaries. The higher rates that have been required by UK financial institutions could therefore have reflected higher risk in the UK arising from more volatile conditions partly (or perhaps wholly) due to inappropriate government macroeconomic policy. The lack of availability to private firms of cheap long-term debt may be attributable to the size of the public sector borrowing requirement over the postwar period. It can be argued that excessive borrowing by the government 'crowded out' private sector borrowing. Finally, we have discussed the problem of short termism at some length in the previous section.

On the other hand, we would not argue that the financial system is perfect. Financial scandals such as occurred in the Lloyd's insurance market and the Maxwell raid on pension funds are pertinent in this respect. Similarly, problems have occurred in the life assurance industry, with salespersons selling inappropriate pensions, and in the mortgage market, with the sale of inappropriate endowment-linked mortgages. Regulation has appeared

to be questionable from time to time, both in the examples quoted above and with respect to the supervision of banking – the example of the Bank of Credit and Commerce International is relevant here (see chapter 17).

As in most cases discussed in this text, there is no clear-cut objective answer. It is a question of judgement and, as we have stated above, the arguments are likely to continue for some time.

Chapter 16

Central banking

16.1 **Introduction**

In this chapter we begin by examining the role of central banks in the financial system and whether, in fact, this role is necessary for the smooth running of financial systems. We then discuss, in section 16.3, the current position of the Bank of England following the important changes made in the autumn of 1997. In 16.4 we move on to consider the role of the European Central Bank and in section 16.5 we look at the arguments for granting central banks independence in their operation of monetary policy. Our conclusions are presented in section 16.6.

16.2 **The role of central banks**

Central banks generally provide both microeconomic and macroeconomic services. The macroeconomic services arise from their participation in monetary policy and their microeconomic services from their support and control of the institutions and markets comprising the financial system. In this section we are interested in the question of why it should be necessary for a financial system to have, in effect, a 'super bank' responsible for the operation of the financial system. Other industries may form trade associations but these are rarely endowed with legal powers to control the industry in question. Some examples do occur in the professions, where bodies such as the Chartered Accountants for England and Wales, the Law Society and the British Medical Association are at least in part responsible for the regulation of the conduct of their members. There is of course the counter-argument put forward by the 'free banking' school, who argue that regulation would be best left to the market. This argument is examined in chapter 17; in this chapter we content ourselves with an examination of why central banks may be necessary.

Fama (1980) notes that banks provide two services: operation of the payments mechanism, and portfolio services such as the acceptance of

deposits and lending. Many have argued that this dual function necessitates the presence of a central bank to avoid the risk of systemic failure (i.e. failure within one institution leading to failure in others) within the financial system due to bank inter-indebtedness arising from their participation in the payments mechanism. A number of suggestions have been made regarding how to avoid such a risk. These include 'narrow' banking, daily revaluation of bank assets and mutual fund banking. The first suggestion has been endorsed by two winners of the Nobel prize for economics, namely Milton Friedman and James Tobin. Briefly, the idea is that banks engaged in the payments mechanism should be required to hold highly liquid government securities to back chequable deposits and that these securities should be specifically allocated to these deposits. This would remove any risk of failure. One problem with such a plan is that the profitability of such bank operations would be severely restricted, leading to rises in charges for payments. On the other hand, if payments services attract the full cost, this could provide incentives for economic use of the services, leading to a better allocation of resources. Nevertheless, as Goodhart (1989, p. 182) has pointed out, narrow banking is the 'reverse of the evolution of banking', which has traditionally been based on fractional reserves.

The second suggestion, put forward by some US economists (e.g. Benston *et al.* 1986), is that banks should be required to revalue all assets at market prices at the end of the day. If the revalued assets fell such that their net capital was approaching zero (i.e. before bankruptcy occurred) the bank would be closed as a separate entity and either merged with another bank or taken over by the regulatory authorities. The advantage claimed for this system is that a financial cost would not be involved since the bank would be approaching bankruptcy but not yet be bankrupt. The disadvantages spring from three sources. First, the revaluation sets up costs for all banks. Second, there is the creation of an incentive for fraudulent revaluation as the bank approaches bankruptcy, which would necessitate increased monitoring costs borne by the authorities. Third, revaluation would be difficult in the case of some assets, such as loans, for which there are limited markets. To some extent the force of this objection is being reduced due to the creation of asset-backed securities markets (see chapter 4 for discussion of asset-backed securities).

The third suggestion, put forward by Goodhart (1989, ch. 8), is that the liabilities (i.e. deposits) of the banks used for transaction purposes be revalued. Currently, chequable deposits are guaranteed in nominal terms with complete convertibility as and when required. This idea of the mutual fund intermediary is that such deposits would be revalued according to the assets of the fund, again on a daily basis, although the cheques would be defined in terms of a constant 'numeraire'. In order to provide for unforeseen fluctuations in the value of the fund (and therefore the value of individual

deposits) between the time of writing and the presentation of the cheque, the fund could impose minimum balance requirements on deposit holders and also set up emergency overdraft facilities. This latter provision would eliminate the problems for customers should the value of the fund decline for a significant period of time even though the fall in value was likely to be reversed at a later date. Apart from the question of revaluing assets, the problem for this latter suggestion is customer acceptance. It may appear to be unlikely that the general public would wish to hold transaction balances in a form in which the value is uncertain.

The suggestions examined above would provide for a change in the role of the central bank as far as monitoring or supporting the financial system is concerned rather than elimination of the central bank itself. Further arguments can be made for unsupervised banking, that is, 'free banking', and their adoption would render central banks redundant. The question of free banking is examined in chapter 17.

16.3 **The Bank of England**

In the autumn of 1997 important changes were made to the role of the Bank of England (hereafter 'the Bank'). Briefly, these were:

(i) the Bank was granted independence in the sense that it was given freedom to set interest rates;
(ii) prudential control of banks was transferred from the Bank to the new Financial Services Authority (FSA), which became responsible for prudential control of the whole of the financial services industry;
(iii) management of the government's debt was transferred to the Debt Management Office (DMO).

These developments are examined in more detail below. Under these arrangements, the Bank is managed on a day-to-day basis by the governor and two deputy governors. One deputy governor supports the governor on monetary stability and the other on financial stability. The Bank is accountable to a court that consists of the governor and deputy governors plus up to 16 non-executive members appointed from a wide range of interests. It is hoped that this will increase the transparency of the operations of the Bank.

The Bank was formally recognised as a central bank by the 1946 Bank of England Act, which effectively nationalised it. Prior to this Act, from its establishment in 1694, the Bank had carried out the functions of a central bank but operated as a private concern. Under the Act the subordinate status of the Bank to the Treasury was statutorily established and this was changed only in 1997. We now describe the structure of the Bank and then outline its main functions.

The Bank is separated into two departments for accounting purposes: the Issue Department, which is treated as being part of the government, and the Banking Department, which is a public corporation. The Issue Department has as liabilities notes in circulation or held by the Banking Department. Whilst it was possible to call upon the Bank to redeem these notes for gold up until 1931, since that date the note issue has been a fiduciary one backed by securities. These securities, held as assets by the Issue Department, include government securities as well as privately issued securities such as commercial bills.

The Banking Department obtains its deposits from two main sources. First, acting as banker to central government, it has the item referred to as 'public deposits', which represents the consolidated accounts of the various revenue collecting and spending departments of the government. Second, it has 'bankers' deposits', which include the mandatory deposits of UK banks and building societies, set at 0.15 per cent of eligible deposits. The remainder of the Banking Department's liabilities are made up of accounts held by other bodies such as overseas governments and central banks, capital and reserves. The assets of the Banking Department include: first, government securities, which comprise government bonds, Treasury bills and ways-and-means advances to the government; second, advances and other accounts and holdings of commercial bills; and third, notes and coins, which represent the reserve held by the Bank to meet any deposit withdrawals. Details are shown in table 16.1.

Table 16.1 Bank of England balance sheet as at 31 December 2002

Liabilities	£million	Assets	£million
Issue Department			
Notes in circulation	33,897	Government securities	14,011
Notes in Banking Department	3	Other securities	19,889
Banking Department			
Public deposits	690	Government securities	1,510
Bankers' deposits	1,828	Advances and other accounts	7,302
Reserves and other accounts	12,222	Premises, equipment and other securities	5,939
Capital	15	Notes and coin	4

Source: *Bankstats*, January 2003, table B1.

By holding balances at the Bank, banks are able to settle any inter-bank indebtedness in a convenient way. This works through the operation of a clearing house, so that at the end of a working day the net debts between

any two banks are settled by means of an ar
between the two banks' accounts at the B
move to 'real-time' settlement, that is, almo
payments for all wholesale transactions so that
they arise rather than waiting for the end of the day.
gross settlement is to avoid settlement risk through the
the failure of a counterparty. One example of this risk is
Bankhaus Herstatt failure in 1974 when, because of time zone
customers with some foreign exchange contracts were left unpaid
they had completed their own side of the transaction.

A further role played by the Bank is that of note issuing. If the gen
public increase their demand for notes then this will show up as a decrease in notes held by the banks. The banks can then replenish their stocks by exchanging for notes their balances held at the Bank. The Banking Department in turn can replenish its stock of notes, if required, by authorising a change in the fiduciary issue from the Issue Department. The resulting transfer of notes from the Issue Department to the Banking Department will generate a corresponding balancing transfer of securities in the opposite direction (see also section 10.4 for a discussion of the impact of increases in the general public's demand for notes on bank liquidity).

Although no longer responsible for supervision as far as protection of depositors is concerned the Bank is still responsible for the stability of the financial system, which involves the collection of regional and sectoral information. It is not clear how this split of responsibility for supervision between depositor protection and stability will work in practice. For example, where does the dividing line lie between rescue of a bank and its prudential supervision? Presumably the Bank will retain its role in the future development of markets so as to maintain the position of London as an international financial centre. Support to the banking sector is also provided on a day-to-day basis through the Bank's operations in the money markets, which were examined in chapter 10. When the banking system as a whole runs short of cash, then it is ultimately the Bank which restores the cash position of the banks. The Bank also operates as lender of last resort to any bank or group of banks experiencing liquidity problems. The Bank's aim here is to maintain the stability of the banking system. As the banking system is based on confidence then the failure of one or more banks can rapidly lead to a collapse in confidence in the banking system generally. A classic example of the Bank acting in this role was the operation of the 'lifeboat' to help a number of secondary banks in 1974/75. We examine the 'lifeboat' operation in more detail in chapter 17.

The main role of the Bank in the financial system is that of operational decision making with regard to the determination of interest rates to achieve price stability as defined by the government's inflation target. Decisions

e level of interest rates are taken by the Monetary Policy Committee C), which has nine members. Five of the members are Bank staff cluding the governor and two deputy governors) and the other four are cognised experts, who will be permitted to engage in other activities which do not 'give rise to a conflict of interest' (Chancellor's letter to the governor). Decisions on the level of the 'repo' rate (see chapter 10 for a discussion of money market intervention by the Bank) are made on the basis of a majority vote with the governor having the casting vote in the event of a tie. A representative of the Treasury is entitled to attend the meetings of the MPC but in a non-voting capacity. It can be seen therefore that the Bank has been given limited independence in that it is responsible for setting the repo rate but only so far as to achieve the inflation target set by the government (i.e. instrument but not goal independency). The case for independence and the degree of 'democratic' control is examined in section 16.5.

16.4 Monetary policy in the euro zone

In chapter 10 (section 10.4) we examined the Bank of England's money market operations in pursuit of its policy objectives. For the sake of comparison we now review the operation of monetary policy in the euro zone. At the outset it should be remembered that Eurosystem was created from the amalgamation of a number of independent central banks and institutions, which had different systems of operation. Hence the introduction of the euro zone necessitated a new allocation of responsibilities between the European Central Bank (ECB) and the member national central banks. This has taken the form of the ECB assuming responsibility for the direction of policy, with the national central banks taking on the practical aspects of the operation of monetary policy, in a decentralised manner.

As a first step to examining the operating methods within the Eurosystem, it is useful to look at a stylised Eurosystem balance sheet. This is shown in table 16.2. Autonomous factors are balances that are outside the control of the ECB. The balances of monetary policy instruments are the result of ECB-initiated operations, so that the current account holdings can be taken to be the balancing item. Consequently the initial impact of changes in the autonomous balances is on the item 'current account holdings'. For example any increase in autonomous liquid assets will increase liquidity in the system, which will be matched by a rise in current account holdings. Conversely a decrease in autonomous liquid liabilities will decrease liquidity in the system and this will be reflected by a decrease in current account balances. Monetary policy can therefore be taken either to offset such changes or to initiate a change in interest rates.

Table 16.2 Stylised balance sheet of the Eurosyster

Assets	Liabilities
Autonomous liquidity factors	
Net foreign assets	Bank notes in circulat
	Government deposits
	Other autonomous factors
	Current account holdings (including minimum reserve sys
Monetary policy instruments	
Main refinancing operations	Deposit facility
Longer-term refinancing operations	
Marginal lending facility	

of th
rol
li

Before moving on to discuss policy operations, we provide a brief description[1] of the individual items in the stylised balance sheet as this will be helpful in understanding the tactics used within the system. The first point to note is that the sum of autonomous liquid liabilities is larger than the corresponding figure for assets so that the banking system incurs a liquidity deficit against the Eurosystem. Consequently there is a continual need for liquidity by the banking system. This is satisfied through the use of the monetary policy instruments, thus providing the pivot for the determination of the short-term rate of interest which is, in itself, the centre-piece of the operation of monetary policy. The current account holdings include the minimum reserves imposed on credit institutions within the system. Currently the minimum reserve ratio is set at 2 per cent of specified short-term liabilities of the institutions and this requirement has to be met on average over a one-month maintenance period. The fact that the reserve basis is calculated on an average rather than on a daily basis removes some of the pressure from banks in their day-to-day operations. Reserve surpluses on some days can be offset by deficits on others and conversely. The institutions receive interest on these compulsory balances at a rate equal to the average rate of the weekly tenders (see below) over the maintenance period. Excess reserves receive no such interest.

The most important policy instrument is main refinancing operations (MROs). MROs have provided roughly 75 per cent of the liquidity needs of the institutions since the system started. They are implemented through weekly tenders and have a maturity of 14 days – see below for further details of the tender. A further 25 per cent of liquidity needs have been provided through the longer-term refinancing operations (LTROs). LTROs are instituted once a month and have a maturity of three months. The level

ese balances is set in advance by the ECB so that they play no active e in the management of liquidity. The last two instruments for relieving quidity[2] shortages or absorbing surpluses are the two remaining items in he balance sheet, that is, the marginal lending and the deposit facilities. Each accounted for around 0.3 per cent of liquidity needs so that the net provision of liquidity through these two facilities was zero.

We now move on to discuss the actual operation of monetary policy. The first step in the procedure is for the ECB to obtain a forecast of the total amount of liquidity necessary at the forthcoming tender. This requires a forecast of the autonomous items on the stylised balance sheet together with an assessment of average reserve requirements. The ECB calculates the forecasting error for autonomous items (the main components) as being in the order of 25 per cent to 30 per cent, depending on the length of the forecast horizon. This then provides the benchmark for liquidity allocation, though it is often amended on the day of allocation. It is a matter of historical fact that the actual allocation very closely follows the benchmark allocation.

As noted above, the main policy instrument is the MRO. Since June 2000, the weekly tender for MROs has been conducted at variable rates of interest but the ECB publishes a minimum rate for a tender,[3] below which no bids will be accepted. Bids at the highest rate are accepted first and bids with successively lower rates are accepted in turn until the total liquidity to be allotted has been exhausted. Tenders can be received from eligible counterparties, of which there were roughly 3,600 in May 1999. Not all of these counterparties take part in tenders – between January and May 2003 the average number of participants per tender varied between 124 and 350. The main instrument used in MRO operations is the repo (see chapters 9 and 10 for a discussion of repos). From the stylised balance sheet in table 16.2, it can be easily seen that an increase in the purchase of repos by the Eurosystem induces a corresponding increase in its current account holdings and therefore of liquidity for the banks.

At the time of writing (June 2003), the minimum bid rate is 2 per cent and the lending and deposit facility rates 1 per cent and 3 per cent, respectively. These two rates provide upper and lower bounds for overnight interest rates in the Eurosystem. As noted above, the minimum reserve is applied on an average basis and this provides the potential for arbitrage. For example, if the overnight interest rate is considered to be too high the banks could run down reserves and invest in the overnight market. In the converse position the banks could borrow in the overnight market and place money on deposit in the Eurosystem deposit facility. Consequently we should see overnight interest rates close to the minimum bid rate. This is exactly what has been observed. The representative overnight euro rate is an average derived from a panel of banks and is termed the euro overnight index average (EONIA). For the period January 1999 to December 2001

EONIA always lay well within the bounds indi[illegible] average absolute spread between EONIA and [illegible] basis points within this period.

The introduction of an integrated monetary policy [illegible] payments mechanism within the Eurosystem. Given tha[illegible] was a number of separate national financial systems, it w[illegible] devise a new area-wide payments system. This resulted in th[illegible] the Trans-European Automated Real-time Gross Settlemen[illegible] Transfer, which is normally referred to by the acronym TARGE[illegible] system links the national real-time gross settlement systems together [illegible] the ECB payments mechanism. This enables quick and easy transfer [illegible] large-value cross-border payments. Its main objective is to facilitate inter-bank payments and settlement of payments caused by monetary policy operations. However, it can also handle payments for other customers.

It is useful to summarise at this stage the differences and similarities between the methods of operating monetary policy in the UK and in the euro zone:

(i) A target rate of inflation is set for the Bank of England. It is the responsibility of the Bank to achieve this target. Significant deviations from the target (either below or above, so that undershooting is just as bad as overshooting) have to be explained to the Chancellor of the Exchequer. The ECB's target is framed in more general terms of price stability.
(ii) Monetary policy is effected through interest rate determination in the money markets by both institutions.
(iii) The Bank of England intervenes in the money markets on a daily basis whereas the ECB operates on a weekly basis.
(iv) In the UK, banks and building societies are required to maintain only minimal non-operational balances at the Bank. No interest is paid on bankers' deposits held at the Bank. In contrast the Eurosystem requires banks to maintain with it, on average over a month, 2 per cent of specified assets. These balances earn a representative rate of interest. Excess reserves earn no interest.
(v) Intervention by both banks is mainly conducted via repos.
(vi) The number of potential counterparties is much larger in the case of the ECB than for the Bank of England.

It is too early to pass a judgement on the Eurosystem but the stability of the overnight interest rate noted above indicates a fair degree of success achieved so far.

Finally in this section we review the powers of the two central banks. Details of the various central banking duties conducted by the Bank of England and ECB are shown in table 16.3, which draws heavily on table 1

ollard (2003). In interpreting this table it should be remembered that e national central banks of the Eurosystem still retain operational esponsibilities, so that not all these banks have the same powers. Clearly, here are similarities between the duties of the two institutions but there are also differences. Also it should be remembered that, as we have noted above, the operational tactics adopted by the two institutions differ widely.

Table 16.3 The Bank of England and the European Central Bank: operational duties

	Bank of England	European Central Bank
Specify policy target	No	Yes
Implementation of monetary policy	Yes	Yes
Issue bank notes	Yes	Yes
Conduct foreign exchange operations	Yes	Yes
Hold and manage official reserves	Yes	Yes
Act as fiscal agent for the government	Yes	NCBs
Promote stability of the financial system	Yes	Yes
Supervise and regulate banks	No	Some NCBs
Implement consumer protection laws	No	Some NCBs
Promote smooth operation of the payments system	Yes	Yes
Collect statistical information	Yes	Yes
Participate in international monetary institutions	Yes	Yes

NCB, national central bank.

16.5 The independence of central banks

As we have noted above, before 1997 the politically controlled Treasury had the ultimate say on the monetary policy objectives pursued by the Bank. In such a situation there was a temptation for a government to finance its current borrowing requirement and to reduce its real burden of accumulated debt through increasing the money supply and thereby inflation. There are also some suggestions that over the period 1950–79 the government relaxed monetary policy at politically convenient times, for example in the period leading up to a general election, rather than pursue the monetary policy most appropriate for reducing or controlling inflationary pressures.

The two most notable examples of independent central banks are the US Federal Reserve System ('the Fed'), established in 1913, and the ECB, created in May 1998. The legislation governing these central banks stipulates that they pursue price stability. The legislation does assign a great deal of power over economic and monetary policy to these unelected bodies, which may inevitably bring them into conflict with the elected governments.

Indeed, the lack of accountability of an indepen cited as a counterargument to independence. How to take into account the fact that the independence o permanently guaranteed, as the government could introdu to remove its independence. Central banks must maintain by being accepted as legitimate. For example, the Bundesbank legitimacy through the widespread popular support it enjoyed in which came from its achievement of low and stable inflation, a assisted the economic success of the country. The legitimacy of the has been achieved largely as a result of successive Fed chairmen exploitin the conflict between President and Congress built into the US constitution. It is too early to judge whether the same degree of credibility and accountability has been achieved by the ECB.

'Credibility' of the central bank becomes the main theoretical argument supporting the granting of independence to central banks. The argument proceeds along the lines that democratically elected governments have an incentive to boost the economy prior to an election so as to achieve re-election (as noted above in the case of UK governments during the postwar period). The proposition was put forward by Barro and Gordon (e.g. Barro and Gordon 1983a, 1983b) that there is a strong incentive for governments to 'cheat' in their conduct of monetary policy. Having both adopted declared policies of a specified inflation target and convinced the general public of its serious intent (i.e. having attained credibility), the government has an incentive to cheat and renege on its commitment to the specified rate of inflation in order to achieve a lower rate of unemployment. In the long term such policy changes are ineffective if the long-run Phillips curve is vertical at the natural rate of unemployment. Furthermore, after episodes of reneging on commitments, the government loses credibility and its policy announcements will not be believed. One solution is to delegate price stability to a central bank unfettered by the political consideration of re-election and which, it can be argued, would then pursue the desired price policy with greater determination than elected governments.

Beyond the euro zone there has been a trend to the removal of government control of central banks. For example, between 1989 and 1991 the central banks of New Zealand, Chile and Canada were made independent. In view of these developments it is therefore helpful to examine the empirical evidence on the relationship between central bank independence and economic performance.

One of the first empirical studies of this kind was that of Bade and Parkin (1988), who examined the relationship between the degree of central bank independence and inflation for 12 countries of the Organization for Economic Cooperation and Development (OECD) in the post-Bretton Woods era. Central bank independence was split into two types: financial

dependence, as measured by the government's ability to set salary levels or members of the governing board of the central bank, to control the central bank's budget and to allocate its profits; and policy independence, as indicated by the government's role in appointing members of the governing board of the bank, government representation on the board and whether the government was the final policy authority. Bade and Parkin found that financial independence was not a significant determinant of inflation outcome, but policy independence had a role to play. Alesina (1989) extended the Bade and Parkin study by adding four more countries to the analysis and also found an inverse relationship between the degree of central bank independence and inflation outcome. Grilli *et al.* (1991) found a negative relationship between inflation and central bank independence over the full sample period (1985–88) and over the post-Bretton Woods sub-sample. A more extensive study was undertaken by Cukierman (1992) for the period 1950–89. He extended the work of the previous studies by using not only legal or *de jure* measures of independence but also practical measures which attempted to capture the actual or *de facto* independence of the central bank. The measures of *de facto* independence included the frequency of turnover of central bank governors and the response to a questionnaire from qualified individuals from central banks. In addition, Cukierman extended the study to 70 countries by including less developed countries in addition to the developed countries examined in the previous work. Cukierman also found the degree of central bank independence affected the rate of inflation in the expected (negative) direction, with the relationship being stronger for developed countries.

Most of the empirical evidence therefore suggests that creating an independent central bank will improve a country's inflation performance. Furthermore, a recent review of the research on central bank independence came to the conclusion that the negative relationship between central bank independence and inflation is robust (Berger *et al.* 2001). There are, however, a number of weaknesses with studies of this kind, as highlighted by Pollard (1993). Most of the studies created indexes of independence by identifying a relevant set of factors and then looking for compliance with the factors in the central bank charters, with each factor being given an equal weight in constructing the index. Thus, in the study by Grilli *et al.*, the factor that the governor's term of office must exceed that of the political term of office is given the same weighting as the factor that no government approval is required for the central bank in setting monetary policy. Clearly, the latter factor has more bearing on the central bank's actions. The only study that attempted a weighting of the criteria was that of Cukierman, but there, per force, the weights were subjective. Another problem with the analysis is that most of the studies use a legal or *de jure* measure of independence, which may not reflect the actual or *de facto* experience of

central banks. Cukierman, in fact, examined the legal index of independence and a measure of *de facto* on his questionnaire results. A correlation of 0.33 between suggested that the legal measure could give misleading re concern with these studies is that most of them consider only independence as a determinant of inflation. When other deter inflation are included in the analysis, it is possible that central b dependence may have no role to play. As a final point, a negative corre between central bank independence and inflation does not imply causal Countries averse to inflation may formalise this aversion through the creation of an independent central bank. Thus, it is inflation aversion in a country which may be the causal factor in explaining low inflation so that the policy of making a central bank independent, where there is insufficient aversion to inflation, may not yield the desired outcome in the long run.

The UK government has granted the Bank of England operational or instrumental independence. This means it is free to select the level of interest rates it considers appropriate to the state of economy so as to achieve the target rate of inflation set by the government. Democratic control is retained through the government setting the target rate of inflation. This contrasts with the situation in other countries where the central bank also determines the rate of inflation consistent with the general aim of price stability. Additional controls have been built into the system to meet the criticism of a ‘democracy’ deficit. First, the Bank reports to the House of Commons Treasury Committee. The second control arises from the broadening of the composition of the court to represent broad sectors of the economy. Third, each time inflation is 1 per cent below or above the target, the governor and the MPC will be required to write an open letter to the Chancellor explaining why the target has been missed. The letter will also have to contain a statement of the remedial measures to be undertaken by the Bank and a prediction as to when inflation will return to the target level. Note that a level of inflation below the target is also considered a failure of policy. This latter measure is directed to ensuring that the Bank pursues the government target rather than one of its own.

How successful have the new UK arrangements been? Six years is quite a short time over which to assess their efficacy, particularly as inflation targeting itself was introduced five years earlier by Chancellor Norman Lamont. Consequently changes in inflation rates can or may be viewed as resulting from the combination of inflation targeting and central bank independence. Nevertheless the Bank has not so far (i.e. up to September 2003) been required to write a letter to the Chancellor explaining why inflation has deviated from the target by more than 1 per cent. Moreover, since inflation targeting was introduced the real average growth rate of the UK economy has exceeded the rate of inflation. This had not been the

xperience of the UK since the early 1960s. On the other hand some criticism has been made that the effect on industry tends to be ignored owing to the overriding inflation target. On balance it would seem that so far the new arrangements have worked satisfactorily.

16.6 Conclusion

There has been a radical change in the position of the Bank of England. It has been granted operational independence in the conduct of monetary policy but, unlike many of its counterparts, is subject to the constraint of the government determining the policy target. In the operation of monetary policy, the Bank is assisted by the MPC. On the other hand, powers of prudential control and management of the national debt have been transferred to the FSA and to the DMO, respectively. The Bank retains responsibility for the financial system and it will be interesting to see how the division of responsibility between the Bank and the FSA works out in practice. Removal of supervisory powers from central banks is a topic of discussion at the present time and the experience of the Bank of England in this respect will become relevant for a larger number of countries.

Notes

1 Further detail may be obtained from articles contained in the ECB's monthly bulletins for May 1999, July 2000 and May 2002, on which this section of the text is based.

2 In fact a further facility exists for fine-tuning operations but, since these accounted for only approximately 0.1 per cent of liquidity needs, we have not discussed these. It is sufficient to note that this facility is related to exceptional events such as 11 September 2001.

3 The linchpin of monetary policy is the minimum bid rate for MROs and monetary policy changes are implemented by changing this rate.

Chapter 17

Regulation of the financial system

17.1 **Introduction**

The type of regulation we discuss in this chapter is termed prudential regulation since it is designed to ensure prudent behaviour by financial institutions. In contrast to the rest of the financial sector, prudential regulation of banks has been the subject of analysis over quite a long period of time. Consequently the major part of the discussion in this chapter is directed to prudential control of banks. However, the UK has recently moved to an integrated system of regulation with a single regulator responsible for regulating the whole of the financial services sector. We examine the arguments for integrated regulation and the approach adopted in the UK in section 17.4. We then focus on supervision of liquidity and capital adequacy in relation to banks in section 17.5 before presenting our conclusions in section 17.6. We begin with a brief survey of recent bank failures and an examination of the type of risks faced by the banking industry.

17.2 **History of bank failures**

Regulation of banks must be examined against the background of bank failures. Any major problem results in changes to the regulatory environment as the regulators try to block any loophole in the rules. Concentrating on events this century, the greatest incidence of bank failure occurred in the US between the years 1929, when there were 25,000 banking firms, and 1934, when the number had been reduced to 14,000. These failures led to the introduction of fairly restrictive bank legislation, such as single-state operations, which have remained characteristic of the US banking scene until recently. Broadly speaking, there were no further major problems until 1973, which saw the start of the fringe banking crisis in the UK.

17.2.1 *The fringe banking crisis, 1973/4*

Over the early 1970s, following rapid credit expansion, which was a consequence of the introduction of the policy of competition and credit control, many secondary or 'fringe' banks increased their deposits rapidly and lent a large proportion of these funds to property-related companies. Following a slump in property values in 1973 the secondary banks began to experience difficulties. As a consequence the inter-bank market, upon which the secondary banks were heavily dependent for deposits, dried up for all but banks of good standing and in addition deposits were withdrawn from the secondary banks. At the end of 1973 the Bank of England, seeing the problem as one of illiquidity, stepped in and organised a rescue of the secondary banks which has come to be known as the 'lifeboat'. Under this operation the Bank of England sought the help of the clearing banks in recycling the deposits they had gained following the withdrawal of deposits from the secondary banks. However, the problems in the property market, which had caused the loss of confidence in the secondary banks, deteriorated further over 1974 and several of the banks receiving support under the 'lifeboat' moved into a position of insolvency. Whilst a few banks were allowed to fail the majority were kept going. The Bank of England's intervention was justified in the following way (*Bank of England Quarterly Bulletin*, summer 1978):

> The Bank thus found themselves confronted with the imminent collapse of several deposit-taking institutions and with the clear danger of a rapidly escalating crisis of confidence. This threatened other deposit-taking institutions and if left unchecked, would have quickly passed into parts of the banking system proper. While the UK clearing banks still appeared secure from the domestic effects of any run … their international exposure was such that the risk to external confidence was a matter of concern for themselves as well as for the Bank. The problem was to avoid a widening circle of collapse through the contagion of fear.

At the height of the rescue operations total lending amounted to over £1,000 million. This crisis led to a rethink of banking supervision and subsequently to the introduction of the 1979 Banking Act, which provided the first legal codification of the Bank of England's regulatory powers. This Act required the licensing of banks and deposit-taking institutions and also transferred the duty of supervision entirely to the Bank of England.

Further major failures occurred in 1974, namely Bankhaus Herstatt (Germany) and the Franklin National Bank (US). The latter was the twelfth largest bank in the US. Also in the US, 1984 saw the failure of Continental Illinois Bank, which was the eighth largest bank in the US. In the same year the Johnson Matthey Bank failed in the UK – this failure is discussed

in detail below. Other bank failures occurred over a range of countries, including Denmark, Canada and Ireland.

17.2.2 *Johnson Matthey Bank, 1984*

The Johnson Matthey Bank (JMB) faced financial difficulties in 1984, which resulted in the Bank of England purchasing JMB for £1 on 1 October from its parent company, Johnson Matthey p.l.c., and subsequently reselling it. This was the first rescue of an ailing bank by the Bank of England since the lifeboat operation of 1974. The Bank of England sought to justify the rescue of JMB with arguments similar to those used to justify the lifeboat operation, in particular the fear of contagion if JMB were to collapse. There were also reasons put forward which were specific to the JMB case. JMB was one of a group of five gold bullion dealers which jointly fixed the price of gold on a twice-daily basis in London. It was feared that the other gold bullion price fixers might have encountered liquidity problems if JMB were allowed to collapse, which would have put in jeopardy London's position in the international bullion market.

The rescue of JMB, like the lifeboat operation of 1974, involved the participation of other banks and the clearing banks in particular. These banks were persuaded by the Bank of England to provide indemnities against potential loan losses by JMB in order to keep JMB's credit lines open. This time, however, the clearing banks publicly objected to being forced into a rescue. As Goodhart (1988) argued: 'In today's more competitive conditions, the banks at the centre of the system frequently see the failing bank as being a relatively imprudent competitor. Why then, they feel, should they penalise their own shareholders for the sake of such a competitor?' Goodhart went on to argue that the clearing banks' reaction in the JMB affair 'is a clear warning now that the Bank of England, and other central banks, may find it increasingly hard, if not impossible, to persuade other commercial banks to assist them in future rescue packages'. Goodhart suggested this should lead to a consideration of alternative strategies to deal with a future illiquidity/insolvency problem, and we consider one such alternative (namely deposit insurance) in section 17.5.4.

There are other issues highlighted by the JMB affair – see Hall (1987) for further discussion – which merit comment. It can be argued that the act of rescuing JMB introduced moral hazard into the banking system; that is, other banks may now act less prudently in the belief that the Bank of England will not allow them to fail. The Bank of England, however, stated that the rescue of JMB was a special case and did not imply that all banks in difficulties would be rescued but, as Hall (1987) argues, 'no amount of exhortation is likely to persuade market operators to ignore the Bank's actual deeds in the market place'. The JMB affair also opened to question the adequacy of the supervisory arrangements and authorisation procedures

at that time. The supervisors of JMB did not chase up late quarterly returns and allowed JMB to postpone meetings with Bank of England staff. Also, the escalating problems of JMB were not seen by the supervisors, despite the breaches of the Bank's guideline on loan exposure. The Bank expects to be notified of any single non-bank exposure of over 10 per cent of the bank's capital. In its 1985 annual report the Bank of England stated that two large exposures at the end of June 1983 were reported by JMB to be 15 per cent and 12 per cent of capital (in fact these were understated and the true figures were 26 per cent and 17 per cent, respectively) and at the end of June 1984 were reported to be 38 per cent and 34 per cent (true figures being 76 per cent and 39 per cent, respectively). Leaving aside the understatement, the Bank's guidelines on loan exposure were known to be breached, with the problem getting worse, well before JMB had to be rescued. The Bank, however, stated that breaches of this guideline were commonplace and that complete observance of this rule would have been too restrictive. The catalogue of incompetence by JMB management, related in the Bank of England's annual report for 1985, also calls into question the adequacy of the vetting arrangements undertaken by the Bank. One final issue raised by the JMB affair was the role of auditors in the supervision process. The auditors of JMB, Arthur Young, were criticised and successfully sued by the Bank of England. However, at the time the auditors of a bank were not allowed to express fears to supervisors without the client's permission. Therefore the only action the auditors could take was resign or qualify the accounts, both of which risked a run on the bank, thereby complicating any future rescue.

17.2.3 *Bank of Credit and Commerce International, 1991*

The next significant bank failure in the UK was the collapse of BCCI, which was forced to close its operations in July 1991. BCCI was first registered in Luxembourg in 1972 and opened its first UK branch a year later. By 1977 it had 45 branches in the UK and planned to increase the number to 150 but the Bank of England refused this expansion because of concerns regarding its Middle Eastern connections. In 1980 the Bank refused BCCI full banking status but allowed it to act as a second-tier licensed deposit taker. Over the 1980s a number of incidents occurred which cast doubt on the competency of management at BCCI and revealed criminal activity in its operation. For example, in 1985 BCCI reported large losses on its futures and options trading. After this BCCI moved its treasury operations out of London to the Gulf region. In 1990 BCCI was found guilty in a Florida court of conspiring to launder money for a Colombian drug cartel. Later on that year the bank's auditors revealed the use of false accounting practices and fictitious loans. In 1990 BCCI moved its operations to Abu Dhabi, making it less accessible to its regulators. Also in that year

the auditors of BCCI produced a report to the Bank of England estimating that £1.5 billion was required to cover potential losses. Early in 1991, after a tip-off to the auditors revealing fraudulent activity on a massive scale, the Bank of England initiated a further study from the auditors. This found that accounts had been falsified for a number of years, that transactions had been disguised and that BCCI was insolvent. The Bank of England shut down BCCI in July 1991. It later emerged that BCCI had worldwide debts of $10 billion (in the UK £400 million). UK depositors were entitled to receive only 75 per cent of their deposits, up to a maximum of £20,000, under the deposit insurance scheme (see below).

The main criticism of the Bank of England in this case was why it failed to close down BCCI during the 1980s, when there was evidence of fraudulent activity. Indeed, the Bank attempted to restructure BCCI in 1990 to save it from closure. In order to investigate this and other aspects of the supervision of BCCI, the government and the Bank of England set up the Bingham inquiry, which reported in October 1992. The inquiry cleared the Bank of England of any negligence in its supervisory activities. However, it did comment on the slack supervisory regime, which took too long to investigate reports of fraud and close BCCI down. The report can be summarised in the following points.

(i) The auditors of BCCI may not have pursued evidence aggressively enough, nor did they pass on their concerns to the Bank of England as fully as they might have done.
(ii) The Bank of England failed to understand BCCI's legal status, wrongly leading it to rely on the Luxembourg authorities' judgement.
(iii) Although fraud was brought to light by other parties, the Bank of England did not investigate; the Bank did not see itself in an investigatory role.
(iv) When BCCI faced closure, the Bank of England tried to restructure it and did not take enough notice of reports of lack of fitness and properness.

Among the recommendations of the Bingham inquiry was the establishment of the Special Investigations Unit in the Bank of England to examine any warning signs received by the Bank. One of the main lessons to come out of the BCCI affair though was that banking group structures which deny supervisors a clear view of how business is conducted should be outlawed. This has since been addressed by the Basel Committee, discussed in section 17.5.2.

17.2.4 *Barings Bank, 1995*

The most recent major bank failure was that of Barings in February 1995. Barings was placed in administration following a failed attempt by the Bank of England to secure a buyer. Barings group operations were then

taken over by the Dutch financial services group ING. A case study outlining the details of the collapse of Barings Bank is provided in chapter 13 (section 13.9.2). Here we examine the regulatory implications.

The failure of Barings was brought on by losses incurred on unauthorised transactions in derivatives undertaken by a single trader operating in a Singapore subsidiary of the group. The size of the losses (which turned out to be £860 million) exceeded the bank's capital. The cause of failure in this case appears to be inadequate internal controls within the Barings group. However, the Bank of England, in its role as lead regulator, was also criticised for its failure to heed earlier warnings of problems in the Barings Singapore subsidiary and its failure to ensure that the group had adequate internal controls. As with BCCI, when the Barings group was faced with closure the Bank of England's preferred solution was a rescue by a bank or syndicate of banks. Justification for such a rescue was weak, as the systemic risks associated with failure were relatively low. Although Barings was allowed to fail in the end, thus sending signals to the marketplace that banks in difficulty would not automatically be bailed out, the signal was not as clear as it could have been.

17.3 **Reasons for prudential control of banks**

As indicated above, the occurrence of bank failure provides the trigger for further regulation but, before looking at the detail of the system of control in the UK, we examine why financial institutions are subject to a degree of prudential regulation and supervision. This contrasts with the position of industry and commerce in general, where imprudent behaviour (other than illegal activities such as fraud) likely to lead to bankruptcy is the concern of the owners rather than any supervisory authority. In discussion of the reasons for prudential control of the financial system, we follow the direction of most of the early literature on this topic, which was focused on prudential control of the banks rather than the financial system as a whole.

17.3.1 *The risks faced by banks*

First of all we need to examine the nature of the risks faced by banks. These can be categorised as:

(i) systemic failure arising from liquidity risk;
(ii) market risk;
(iii) default (credit) risk;
(iv) operational risk;
(v) regulatory risk.

Systemic risk arises from the fact that banks' assets and liabilities have a particular feature which may render them liable to financial difficulties

even when they are basically sound. Their liabilities are very liquid, often withdrawable on demand, whereas a large proportion of their assets are in the form of loans and advances which are illiquid owing to both the difficulty of securing repayment at short notice and the absence of a wide secondary market in bank debt. Consequently exercise of the right to withdraw by a large number of depositors (i.e. a run on the bank) may cause failure of a bank which is perfectly viable in the sense that the discounted value of its assets exceeds that of its liabilities. This problem is enhanced by the procedure followed by banks in the event of a run occurring. Until insolvency is declared the bank is obliged to pay out the full amount of any deposit withdrawn. Once insolvency is declared the depositors must await realisation of the bank's assets in the company of other creditors and have their claims assessed by the courts. Thus, in the event of a rumour of difficulties being faced by a bank, there is likely to be a run on that institution since it is in the interest of each depositor to be at the head of the queue. In fact the risk is wider than that so far discussed since, for similar reasons, the 'run mentality' can spread to other banks even though those banks may not be in difficulties. This is because depositors have only imperfect information about a bank's safety. If they see one bank in difficulty they do not have the information to assess whether the problems are specific to that bank or affect all banks. In such circumstances it is rational for depositors to withdraw funds from sound banks in order fully to guarantee safety for their deposits. Thus, the run can spread through the banking system. This danger is reinforced because the individual banks are linked together through both the payments system (see section 3.5.3 for a discussion of payments risk) and the inter-bank markets. Hence failure of one bank will adversely affect the financial position of other banks. An unregulated banking system is therefore susceptible to swings in public confidence and this provides one of the main reasons why the banking system is regulated. This danger is termed 'systemic risk', or contagion.

Market risk refers to the possibility of asset prices changing in a manner which will have adverse effects on the bank's financial position. A good illustration of this was provided by the position of the savings and loans associations in the US in the 1980s. If assets are held with a longer maturity duration than liabilities, then unanticipated rises in interest rates will cause losses unless the lending is at floating rates of interest. It is estimated (see for example Benston and Kaufman 1988) that at least 500 savings and loans associations were merged or failed in the 1980s because of this type of risk. Open currency positions also incur market risk since unanticipated changes in the relevant exchange rate will result in windfall gains or losses to the bank concerned. Involvement of a bank in futures or options also leaves it exposed to the risk of price changes. The final type of market risk occurs when an institution is forced to sell an asset to obtain funds quickly.

The necessity of a speedy sale may prevent the bank from seeking out the most advantageous deal, and so incur some form of loss. This is in effect a liquidity risk. Market risk in general has increased because of the rising volatility of asset prices, illustrated in figures 14.1 and 14.2.

The risk of default (or credit risk) is endemic in bank lending and arises for example from changes in economic climate, which will induce the failure of some firms. The impact of monetary restraint, with its accompanying high interest rates, on firms with a large percentage of capital in the form of debt provides a good illustration of increased risk of default due to a changing economic climate. Another potential source of debt failure arises from country risk, which refers to the failure of foreign governments and other borrowers to repay loans. The problem of sovereign lending was examined in chapter 4. As was discussed in chapters 3 and 4, a bank can reduce the incidence of default risk by spreading its lending activities (i.e. portfolio diversification) over a wide number of customers, so that failure of any one customer imposes only a light burden on the bank, and over different categories of borrowers (geographical or type of industry/person), so as to reduce the risk of failure. Banks can also further reduce the incidence of this type of risk by applying an adequate system of scrutiny to loan applications. A more recently developed technique for managing credit risk is the use of credit derivatives, discussed in chapter 13. Nevertheless default risk is always present for banks.

Operational risk, which refers to the risk arising from inadequate or failed internal processes, people or systems, is a risk that has been given increased attention by regulators in recent years. In the UK the closure of BCCI in 1991 – discussed above – was a direct consequence of fraud on a massive scale on the part of the management. In the US it seems that fraud was the reason for the failure of some savings and loan associations. Yang (1987) reported that fraud and misconduct were the principal reasons for the failure of some 30 associations in California between 1983 and 1986. Operational risk was probably one of the main reasons for the 1984 failure of JMB in the UK and was clearly a reason for the failure of Barings Bank in 1995.

The final type of risk faced by a bank is the potential impact of the regulatory environment, which may impair the safe and efficient operation of a bank. One example of this type of risk in the UK was that, in the past, banks were subject to imposed lending restraints as part of the government's monetary policy. Similar restraints were not imposed on lending by the building societies.

For the sake of ease of exposition, we have examined these risks as though they were independent of each other. In fact they are interdependent in a number of ways. Thus, for example, inefficient management is likely to lead to inadequate scrutiny of loan applications and hence greater default risk. Market risk can be reduced by appropriate interest-rate pricing and

taking a balanced currency position. Liquidity risks can be avoided by holding a sufficient level of highly liquid assets. Fraud can be prevented by good internal supervision as well as the supervision provided by auditors.

17.3.2 *Reasons for regulating banks*

We now turn to the justification for external regulation of banks in the light of the risks examined above. The first reason offered concerns systemic risk. It is argued that the financial system is subject to waves of confidence and so external regulation is necessary to prevent financial panics.

A second reason offered for the control of banks is that the social costs of a major bank failure are far more wide reaching than the failure of a single firm. Failure of any firm affects shareholders. The difference is that the customers (i.e. the depositors) of a bank are likely to be much larger in number and wider in geographical distribution than with a comparable commercial undertaking. In addition, there is the adverse impact on the function of channelling savings to prospective investors, which is likely to lower the aggregate level of investment within an economy.

A third reason offered is the possible lack of sophistication of the general public. It is argued that they lack the expertise to differentiate between safe and risky investments. One consequence of this is that the public would be likely to accept a higher return offered for investment in one direction without analysing any extra risk which may be involved. This problem is reinforced by the difficulty of obtaining adequate statistics to assess the risk or safety of an individual institution. Balance sheets tend to conceal the type of lending and the risks involved. In addition, as we saw in chapter 2, banks' existence is partly based on asymmetric information since banks have access to information not available to depositors. Adequate risk assessment requires information supplementary to that contained in the financial reports. The justification for regulation under this heading may be conveniently summed up as depositor protection.

As we have seen in chapters 3 and 4, banks often find themselves under considerable pressure for a variety of reasons, such as the sovereign debt overhang, bad debts arising from company failure due to high interest rates and falling property values and keen competition. These facets provide a fourth reason for supervising banks, which is to prevent banks undertaking excessively risky operations in an effort to restore their financial position. There is also the feeling that excessive competition may lead to underpricing of services, which in turn has an adverse effect on long-run profitability and therefore the viability of banks. This fear is compounded by the fact that the 'correct' price for a new service may be difficult to determine without adequate experience.

The final reason offered for prudential control of banks is the prevention of the entrance of undesirable firms or individuals into an industry in which

the preservation of confidence is so vital. A supporting argument is that the industry offers considerable scope for fraud and that, therefore, this restraint is essential.

It should be noted that the arguments so far presented favour regulation of banks. Nevertheless, certain caveats can be entered against the exercise of excessive prudential control over banks. The first consideration is the incontrovertible fact that regulation imposes costs in the form of real resources on both the regulators and the regulated. The central bank has to employ the expertise necessary to carry out the prudential control and the banks have to employ resources to complete the returns required by the controller. These costs can be relatively high and it is therefore a question of cost–benefit analysis to determine whether the benefits gained by prudential regulation outweigh the costs incurred. The budget for the operation of the Financial Services Authority (FSA) for the financial year 1998/9 9 was set at £153.9 million. This represents the cost to the taxpayer in real resources and does not include costs imposed on the banks to complete the necessary returns and so on. The sum is significant and lends support to the argument that the burden of proof rests on the advocates of prudential control rather than those who favour a free-market approach.

Second, there is the danger of the regulation becoming so excessive as to reduce competition, raising costs and lowering the pace of financial innovation. A similar argument is often presented in terms of the institutions 'capturing' the regulator by the introduction of practices favourable to themselves, for example the introduction of a cartel restraining competition and raising profits. A further argument against regulation is that the form of the regulations will distort the market mechanism by diverting resources to fields of activity favoured by the regulators.

Finally by way of arguments opposed to regulation is the danger that onerous regulations imposed in one centre will merely lead to the movement of the activity to centres where regulation is more relaxed. This is of course one of the main reasons for the development of offshore banking and is perhaps the main incentive for a common regulation system across banks operating in different countries, often termed a 'level playing field'. This aspect of prudential control is discussed in section 17.5.5.

In summing up the arguments for and against prudential regulation of banks, perhaps the most telling argument is the lack of expertise and knowledge possessed by the individual depositor to assess the quality of the bank. It can therefore be argued that retail banking should be subject to fairly rigorous control (some options are examined in section 17.5) whereas wholesale banking should be subject to a much lighter measure of prudential control. The reason for the suggested difference between the degree of regulation imposed on the two types of banking lies in the perceived expertise of their customers. Wholesale customers are (or should be)

financially aware whereas it is arguable that at least some of the customers of retail banks will be financially illiterate.

17.3.3 *Free banking*

In recent years a small but growing group of economists have argued that banking markets are no different to any other markets and so the principle of laissez-faire should also apply. These 'free bankers' believe that banks should be allowed to operate in a truly competitive market environment, with no restrictions on the types of assets they hold or the liabilities they issue and in addition no protective restrictions, such as restrictions on entry to banking, deposit insurance (see later) or lender of last resort. In such a competitive banking system depositors would be aware that they would lose their funds if the bank failed. Depositors would want reassurance that their funds were safe. Bank managers would want to keep depositors' confidence because if depositors had any doubts about the safety of the bank they would start to withdraw deposits. Bank managers would therefore want to reassure depositors that they were not taking excessive risks and would expose their policies to outside scrutiny. Bank managers would also want to maintain adequate capital, again to reassure depositors. Competition would ensure that bankers struck the right balance between return to investors and depositor protection. According to Dowd (1993), history shows us that banks in relatively unregulated systems maintained strong capital. Dowd also argued that bank runs were usually constructive events that weeded out the weaker banks.

One interesting suggestion put forward by Benston (see e.g. Benston and Kaufman 1988) is for a bank's assets and liabilities to be revalued at market prices and that when economic capital becomes negative (or perhaps positive but only by a small margin) the bank should be reorganised or taken over. One of the main advantages claimed for this system is that the cost of any bank rescue would be quite small. Second, it is argued that depositors would have increased confidence in the banking system, so that runs on banks would become less frequent. Third, the requirement for much of the system of prudential control would be removed. Implementation of such a system would require periodic revaluation of assets and this would cause major difficulty given the high proportion of UK bank assets in the form of loans, which, as we have already seen, are difficult to recall or sell on a secondary market. Nevertheless, this option may become more viable in the future if and when the secondary market in loans further develops.

Since 1996 New Zealand has had essentially a free banking approach to regulation of the banking system. Its system is based on disclosure requirements and uses the market to police the behaviour of banks. Every bank must provide a comprehensive quarterly assessment that provides information on its assets, its capital adequacy measure (risk/assets ratio), its

lending activities and its ratings from private credit rating agencies. These financial statements must be audited twice a year and must be made public. The disclosure statements are in two main forms: a comprehensive 'general disclosure statement' for readers with greater knowledge of financial affairs and a two-page 'key information summary' for the non-expert investor. The general disclosure statement is aimed at financial professionals who would monitor the bank in their capacity as agents for the non-expert investor. The key information summary must be displayed prominently in every bank branch. In addition, bank directors are required to validate these statements. These directors face unlimited liability (that is, they can lose all their personal assets as well as their shareholding in the bank) if they are found to have made false or misleading statements.

The rationale for this approach is in line with the free banking approach in that the market will provide the necessary discipline to prevent bankers from taking excessive risks that would put depositors' funds in danger. The market now has the necessary information to undertake the monitoring and has the incentive as there is no deposit insurance system in New Zealand. The banks benefit from lower costs of compliance with regulation and fewer rules stifling competition and innovation. Critics of the New Zealand approach argue that:

(i) The bank may be less willing to admit to problems if the information is to be made public.
(ii) Depositors may not have the expertise to understand the information disclosed.
(iii) Unlimited liability for directors may discourage the best people from taking these positions, thus weakening the management of banks.

17.4 The UK system of regulation and supervision of the financial services industry

The argument in favour of prudential regulation of the financial industry was framed above in terms of banks but most of the arguments can easily be extended to incorporate prudential regulation of financial institutions in general. The system of regulation now in place in the UK applies essentially the same approach to authorising and supervising financial firms whether they are banks, building societies or insurance companies. We examine the nature of that system in this section before moving on to some aspects of regulation that are specific to banks, in particular liquidity and capital adequacy.

The FSA is the single regulator for the financial services sector in the UK. The FSA was formed in 1997, when it took over responsibilities from the Securities and Investments Board (SIB). However, the SIB was

responsible for overseeing only the investment industry. The FSA has gradually assumed responsibility for regulating banking, building societies, insurance and the investment industry. It is now responsible for regulating over 10,000 firms. In addition the FSA regulates financial exchanges such as the Stock Exchange and Euronext.liffe as well as clearing houses. It is also responsible for regulating the admission of firms to the Official List, through the UK Listing Authority (see chapter 8).

The first stage in the further development of the FSA came in 1998, when responsibility for banking regulation and supervision was transferred from the Bank of England to the FSA (see chapter 16 for further discussion). The next main stage came with the passing of the Financial Services and Markets Act (FSMA) 2000, which came into force in December 2001. This is when the FSA took on its full powers as the single regulator. Under the FSMA 2000, the FSA is required to pursue four statutory objectives:

(i) to maintain market confidence in the UK financial system;
(ii) to promote public awareness and understanding of the financial system;
(iii) to secure an appropriate degree of protection for consumers whilst recognising consumers' own responsibilities;
(iv) to reduce the scope for financial crime.

The Regulated Activities Order 2001 sets out all the activities that are regulated by the FSA. These include accepting deposits, effecting or carrying out contracts of insurance as principal, dealing in investments, advising on investments and managing investments. The FSA is responsible for both authorising and supervising firms carrying out regulated activities. The integrated structure of the FSA means that any firm wishing to carry on a regulated activity must apply to a single authorisation department. The authorisation provided is like a driving licence, with a list of permissions on it. These permissions are the activities the FSA will allow the firm to do. Thus a bank will apply for permission to be a deposit taker. However, if it wishes to provide financial advice it will also need to seek permission to do so. Supervision by the FSA is also operated in an integrated way, so there is no banking supervision department. Instead there is a Major Financial Groups Division, which looks after the 50 largest financial groups operating in the UK, from Barclays through to Prudential Insurance to Goldman Sachs and Deutsche Bank. There is also a Deposit Takers Division that handles smaller banks, building societies and credit unions.

It should be noted that various European Union Directives designed to create a single market in financial services throughout Europe (including the Second Banking Coordination Directive and the Investment Services Directive) permit banks and securities firms that are incorporated in a member state (now extended to cover the countries of the European

Economic Area) to set up branches throughout the European Union on the basis of authorisation by their home supervisor. So for example a bank incorporated in Germany that wishes to set up a branch in the UK will be permitted to do so on the basis of its German authorisation.

There are several arguments in favour of adopting an integrated system of financial services regulation. First, the increase in the number of financial conglomerates and the blurring of the boundaries between financial products makes sectoral regulation less feasible. There have been an increasing number of cross-sectoral acquisitions in the financial sector in recent years. For example, Lloyds–TSB bought the insurance company Scottish Widows and the Prudential Insurance Company bought M&G, a large fund manager, and has opened an internet bank named Egg. Second, a single regulator should be able to achieve economies of scale and scope. It is probably in the area of economies of scope that the main advantages of a single regulator are evident. For example it is easier and more cost-effective for a single regulator to examine and manage the impact of an industry-wide development on the financial sector. Incidents such as the collapse of Enron or the effects of the terrorists attacks of 11 September 2001 can be managed better by an integrated regulator. In addition, where risks are increasingly transferred between different sectors of the financial system an integrated regulator is better able to monitor the effects of this. One example is the transfer of credit risk, through credit derivatives, between the banks and insurance companies.

There are also arguments against a single regulator. First, such a regulator may be a very powerful institution inclined to act in a high-handed manner. This is a particular risk with the UK model, where the FSA is responsible for both regulating and disciplining. Another criticism of a single regulator is that a broad regulator with extensive reach may lack expertise relating to the problems of individual sectors.

17.4.1 *The FSA's approach to supervision*

The FSA's approach to supervision is risk based. The first stage is to identify the risks to the four statutory objectives identified above. To achieve this the FSA draws upon a wide range of sources, including intelligence gathered in the course of supervision of firms and direct contacts with consumers. These risks arise from the external environment, within specific firms and across product markets or industries. The next stage is to prioritise the risks. This involves scoring the risk against a number of probability and impact factors. The probability factors relate to the likelihood of the event occurring and the impact factors refer to the scale and significance of the problem if it were to occur. The impact factors are similar for all types of risk, irrespective of the source. They include considerations such as the number of retail customers affected and the systemic nature of the risk. For

firm-specific risks there is a common set of probability factors under three headings: business risk (capital adequacy, volatility of balance sheet, volatility and growth of earnings and strategy), control risk (internal systems and controls, management skills, controls culture) and consumer relationship risk (nature of customers and products, marketing and advice practices). The nature and intensity of the FSA's supervisory relationship with a firm will depend upon its assessment of the impact of the firm on consumers and on market participants. High-impact firms therefore have more intensive supervision. Supervisors of firms in this category maintain regular working relationships with the firm's senior managers in order to understand the firm's systems and controls. However, well managed firms whose own assessment of risk is sophisticated and effective require less supervisory attention. At the other end of the spectrum, low-impact firms (mainly small firms with local customers) are supervised less intensively through remote monitoring of returns and occasional visits.

Once the risks have been assessed and prioritised, the next stage is to decide how to respond. This will involve the FSA utilising a wide range of tools. These can be divided into two categories:

(i) those designed to influence the behaviour of consumers, groups of firms or the industry as a whole;
(ii) those designed to influence the behaviour of individual institutions.

Included in the first group are disclosure of information, consumer education, the compensation scheme and product approval. The second group includes authorisation of firms and individuals, visits to firms, discipline and restitution of loss.

17.5 **Key elements of bank regulation and supervision**

17.5.1 *Liquidity risk*

One of the consequences of financial intermediation (discussed in chapter 2) is a mismatching of the asset and liability structure of banks owing to the liquid nature of their liabilities and the illiquid nature of their assets. A bank can fail through an inability to meet deposit withdrawals through lack of liquidity even though it is viable in the long run. Liquidity can be provided in a number of ways, including:

(i) holding sufficient cash or assets which are easily liquefied;
(ii) holding an appropriately matching portfolio of cash flows from maturing assets;
(iii) maintaining an adequately diversified deposit base in terms of maturities and mix of depositors.

The supervisors have the duty to ensure that banks maintain an appropriate mix of all three. With specific reference to the liquidity position, no minimum overall liquidity ratio is applied to all banks because it is felt that the allocation of specific assets to a liquidity category is bound to be arbitrary. Banks engage in maturity transformation, so that the term structure of their assets is longer than that of their liabilities. Hence assessment of the liquidity risk of a bank can be achieved by preparing a maturity ladder, showing the accumulated mismatch of short-term assets and liabilities over a variety of time periods up to one year. In this ladder marketable assets are shown as maturing immediately but are subject to a discount for valuation in the liquidity ladder so as to reflect potential variations in market price; for example, certificates of deposit with less than six months remaining to maturity are subject to a 5 per cent discount and those up to five years a 10 per cent discount. The time periods of this maturity ladder are: sight to eight days; eight days to one month; one to three months; three to six months; and six to twelve months. It would be expected that the maximum point of excess of liabilities over assets will occur in the first six months. Each bank will be given its own mismatch ratios for control purposes for the various periods of the analysis by the supervisor. The bank is expected to monitor its mismatch positions and report breaches of the control ratios to the supervisor. A recent revision to this approach has been to switch to an analysis of mismatch positions on the basis of cash flows rather than maturities. This cash flow approach captures interest payments and receipts, other income and expenses and off-balance-sheet cash flows and therefore provides a more detailed picture of the liquidity risk of the bank.

17.5.2 *Capital adequacy*

As we have noted in the last section, liquidity is essentially a short-term concept referring to the ability of an institution to meet day-to-day cash outflows, whereas solvency is a longer-term concept referring to the prospective ability of a bank to meet all its liabilities as they fall due. The distinction between liquidity and solvency is not as clear-cut as these definitions imply. There is a view that if a financial institution is confidently believed to be solvent then it should be able to borrow through the markets to meet any short-term liquidity difficulties. It follows therefore that the existence of liquidity problems that cannot be resolved through the markets implies that other market participants believe the risk of insolvency for that institution to be high. The reverse is generally not the case as it is possible to face insolvency problems without any illiquidity problems first showing up, as was the case with JMB. The view that 'banks with liquidity problems that cannot be solved through the markets implies the bank is likely to be insolvent' was seen by Quinn, then the Executive Director of the Bank of England with responsibility for banking supervision, to be one

which is 'absolutist and neglects the vital role that time plays in assessing the quality of a bank's assets, quite apart from being a high risk strategy' (*Bank of England Quarterly Bulletin*, spring 1988). Quinn argued that there are great difficulties in establishing the value of a bank's assets and that it is possible for assets to gain or lose value very quickly, thus creating liquidity problems. A bank's management may be able to turn round the problem over time or the problem may disappear through an improvement in external circumstances. However, if a bank is denied short-term funding, its capacity to recover claims is put in doubt and other debtors may then stop paying, believing that the institution is likely to become insolvent, thus compounding the problem. Thus, the Bank of England and subsequently the FSA placed emphasis on banks managing their liquidity as part of the overall policy of minimising the risk of insolvency. However, the most important aspect of policy in this regard relates to the monitoring of each bank's capital adequacy.

The capital of a bank is seen as financing the infrastructure of the business and providing a cushion to absorb any losses on its assets. As we saw in chapter 2, a bank can minimise credit risk with regard to its loans by:

(i) limiting the risk of default on individual loans through appropriate selection of borrowers;
(ii) reducing the overall risk of its loan portfolio by diversifying;
(iii) pooling its risk so as to make the overall risk of default more predictable.

The last point enables the bank to cover its expected losses by incorporating a premium in its loan rate of interest. Unexpected loan losses are then covered by the bank's profits in the first instance and ultimately by its capital. Thus, the level of a bank's capital is important in assessing its solvency in adverse circumstances. The underlying principle is that it is the shareholders rather than the depositors who should bear the risks of the business undertaking.

The question of capital adequacy was first addressed by a working party set up by the Bank of England in 1974, which reported in 1975 (see *Bank of England Quarterly Bulletin*, autumn 1975). This working party recommended the use of two ratios: the free resources (gearing) ratio and the risk/assets ratio. These ratios were further revised in 1979 and the system of assessing capital adequacy that operated throughout most of the 1980s was set out in the *Bank of England Quarterly Bulletin* of autumn 1980. The gearing ratio is a very simple measure, essentially relating the value of a bank's capital to the value of its deposits. Thus, it takes no account of the riskiness of the bank's assets and as a consequence is rarely referred to nowadays for supervisory purposes. The risk/assets ratio has become the key to monitoring capital adequacy and this relates the value of a bank's

capital to the value of its assets weighted according to their inherent riskiness. However, it does so only to the extent that these activities appear on the balance sheet. As we have discussed in chapter 4, since the early 1980s banks have increasingly undertaken activities which do not result in a balance sheet entry under normal accounting procedures ('off-balance-sheet' business). Thus, in order to measure the adequacy of a bank's capital to all, or at least most, of the default risks it is exposed to, the risk/assets ratio has been modified to incorporate 'off-balance-sheet' business.

Basel Capital Accord, 1988

The system of risk weightings and capital definitions underlying the risk/assets ratio was proposed in an agreement reached by the Basel Committee on Banking Supervision (1988). This accord, which provides for a common system of prudential control for banks operating in the major industrial countries, came into effect at the beginning of 1993. Under this approach banks' assets are divided into various categories and each category is given a weighting according to its perceived relative riskiness. Each asset is multiplied by this risk factor and the total of the risk-adjusted assets are then related to the bank's capital. For example, cash has a risk weight of 0 per cent, loans to money market institutions 10 per cent and commercial loans 100 per cent. A two-step process is involved for off-balance-sheet items. First, they are transformed into an on-balance-sheet item using standard conversion ratios. Second, the risk weightings are then applied to the converted values. The capital base itself consists of two components: core capital, or tier 1, and supplementary capital, or tier 2. The first component broadly comprises shareholders' equity and published accumulated profits, and the second consists of medium- and long-term subordinated debt instruments (i.e. debt ranking after all other debt for winding up purposes), general provisions and unpublished profits. Three restrictions are imposed. First, the total of tier 2 components should not exceed a maximum of 100 per cent of the total of tier 1 items. Second, subordinated debt should not exceed a maximum of 50 per cent of the total of tier 1 items. Third, general provisions should not exceed 1.25 per cent of weighted risk assets. A minimum level for the risk/assets ratio of 8 per cent is prescribed but it is not expected that all banks will work to this figure and capital adequacy is considered for each bank against the background of its operations; for example, a higher ratio is set for a bank with inexperienced management or a high concentration of risks.

To illustrate the calculation of the risk/asset ratio, consider tables 17.1 and 17.2. From the former, the capital base (tier 1 capital + tier 2 capital) is £83 million, and from the latter, the total risk-weighted assets are £718.7 million. The risk/assets ratio is therefore 11.6 per cent (83/718.7). This illustration is not meant to represent a typical bank but is used to show how

Table 17.1 Example calculation of a bank's capital base, categorised into two tiers, for an assessment of the risk/assets ratio

Tier 1 items	Value (£million)	Tier 2 items	Value (£million)
Equity	40	Current year's unpublished profit	4
Accumulated profits	8	General provisions	7
		Subordinated term debt	27
Total tier 1	48	Total tier 2	35[a]

Capital base = tier 1 capital + tier 2 capital = £48 million + £35 million = £83 million.
[a] In calculating tier 2 capital, only £24 million of subordinated debt is permitted as subordinated debt cannot exceed 50 per cent of tier 1 capital.

Table 17.2 Example calculation of a bank's risk-weighted assets, for an assessment of the risk/assets ratio

Assets	Value (£million)	Weight (%)	Weighted value (£million)
Cash	30	0	0
Treasury bills	7	10	0.7
Secured loans to discount market	80	10	8
Other eligible bills	40	20	8
UK government stocks	60	20	12
Commercial loans	350	100	350
Personal loans	200	100	200
Mortgage loans	100	50	50
Total on-balance-sheet assets	867		628.7
Off-balance-sheet risks:			
guarantees of commercial loans	50	100	50
standby letters of credit	80	50	40
Total risk-weighted assets			718.7

the ratio is constructed. However, the weights shown in table 17.2 are the actual weights used by regulators.

The theoretical basis of the risk/asset ratio is perhaps suspect since it is based on the assumption that the risks are independent, otherwise it would not be possible to add the risk-adjusted assets together. Portfolio theory suggests that risks may be interdependent in some instances; for example, a general recession will induce failures of a number of companies. On the other hand, portfolio theory suggests that diversification should make the

risk of the whole portfolio less than the aggregation of the risks of the individual securities. It is difficult, however, to design a scheme which would take this factor into consideration. A second problem arises if the risk factors do not accurately measure the relative degree of risk in each asset. This problem is made worse because the effect of the risk weightings is likely to induce lending favourable to the arbitrarily imposed risk factors and may therefore distort the market mechanism.

Another serious concern with the system relates to the 100 per cent risk weighting applicable to commercial loans to the private sector. The implication is that the capital requirement for a loan to an AAA-rated multinational company (see chapter 9, section 9.6, on credit ratings) is precisely the same for a loan of the same size to a small company with a lower credit rating. As banks' main assets are loans it is not clear why the designers of the system did not allow for differential risk weightings in this area. One consequence may be that aggressively managed banks may be tempted to shift their lending towards high-risk (high-return) borrowers, thus increasing their exposure to the risk of default, while cautiously managed banks are not rewarded for their prudence.

Partly as a consequence of some of the failings of the risk/assets ratio, a new Basel Capital Accord, termed Basel II, has been proposed. We examine this in the next section.

Basel Capital Accord II

A new approach to assessing the capital adequacy of banks has been proposed by the Basel Committee on Banking Supervision. At the time of writing this is intended to be implemented by the end of 2006. The new accord consists of three pillars:

(i) minimum capital requirements;
(ii) supervisory review of capital adequacy;
(iii) public disclosure.

Whilst the new accord differs from the 1988 accord in a number of respects it is important first to state what is not changing. The numerator, or the definition of regulatory capital, remains unchanged. Also the minimum required ratio of 8 per cent remains unchanged. What is changing are the methods used to measure the risks faced by banks and hence the calculation of the denominator. The Basel II accord explicitly covers credit risk and market risk (discussed below). The pillar 1 proposals introduce changes to the treatment of credit risk and explicit treatment of operational risk. The treatment of market risk remains unchanged.

The new accord introduces three approaches for the treatment of both credit risk and operational risk (see section 17.3.1 above for definitions). The selection of approach, in each case, will be made by the bank and its

supervisor. For credit risk the simplest approach is the standardised approach. This is similar to the 1988 accord in that exposures are put into specified categories, such as residential mortgages or corporate loans. What is different is that the risk weights for sovereign, inter-bank and corporate exposures are determined by external credit ratings. The credit ratings may be supplied by private rating agencies such as Moody's, and Standard and Poor's. This allows more sensitivity in the treatment of risk compared with the 1988 accord. So an exposure to a company with a credit rating of AAA to AA– will be given a risk weight of 20 per cent; for a company with a credit rating of A+ to A– the risk weight is 50 per cent; and for a company with a credit rating of BBB+ to BB– the risk weight is 100 per cent. For a credit rating below BB– the risk weight assigned is 150 per cent. Where no external rating is available then a risk weight of 100 per cent should be used (as with the 1988 accord).The other two approaches to assessing risk are known as internal ratings based (IRB) approaches. The IRB approaches allow a bank to use its own internal assessment of risk of an exposure as an input to the calculation of capital requirement. This does not mean the bank is able to determine all the elements used to determine its capital requirement. Instead the bank's inputs are turned into risk weights through formulas (or risk weight functions) specified by the Basel Committee. The two IRB approaches are the foundation IRB and the advanced IRB. They differ in terms of the degree to which the bank provides inputs to the calculation of risk weights, with banks operating under the advanced IRB approach providing more inputs.

As indicated above, the treatment of operational risk is also split into three approaches, with the more sophisticated internationally active banks likely to use an advanced measurement approach. The simpler approaches, the basic indicator and the standardised approach, are aimed at banks with less significant operational risk exposures. These simpler approaches require banks to hold capital for operational risk equal to a fixed percentage of a specified risk measure. For example, for the basic indicator approach the measure is the bank's average annual gross income over the previous three years. This average is multiplied by a factor of 0.15 (set by the Basel Committee) to determine the capital requirement.

The second pillar of the new Basel accord is supervisory review. This is particularly relevant to banks adopting the IRB approach to credit risk. Supervisors are expected to monitor and evaluate how well banks are assessing their capital needs in relation to their risk exposures and to intervene where appropriate.

The third pillar, market discipline, is there to complement the other two pillars. The Basel Committee has devised a set of disclosure requirements that allow market participants to assess key information about a bank's risk profile and level of capital. The interested reader should look at the

website of the Bank for International Settlements (www.bis.org), where the Basel Committee capital accord documents are located, for further developments.

Serious criticisms can be laid against the Basel II agreement. First, it is overly complicated, with 200 pages of complex regulations. Rarely is complexity an aid to good supervision. Second, many commentators have queried the role given to internal or market assessment of risk. Past experience of financial crises raises doubt about the ability of financial institutions to assess risk adequately. Third, the accord does not seem to have any regard for the degree of danger posed to the financial system at large. Failure of a badly managed bank which has little danger to the financial system as a whole is of less importance than the potential failure of a large bank which is highly interconnected with the rest of the financial system.

At the time of writing, it is not at all clear that there will be international agreement on implementing Basel II in 2006. In addition, some countries have announced serious reservations over Basel II – for example, the US and China have announced that they will pursue alternative regulation for most of their banking systems. India has also rejected Basel II. This makes it extremely doubtful whether the target implementation date for 2006 will be achieved.

17.5.3 *Market risks*

The increased amount of trading activities by large banks has focused attention on a bank's exposure to market risk, defined as the risk of loss from adverse movements in financial market rates and prices. The risk/asset ratio introduced by the Basel Capital Accord of 1988, discussed above, addressed a bank's exposure to credit risk. An amendment to the Basel accord set new minimum capital requirements for a bank's market risk exposure (Basel Committee on Banking Supervision 1996). These requirements were introduced into the system of UK bank supervision in 1998. Under these requirements a bank must separate its long-term investments in securities from its trading book. Trading refers to positions taken with a view to resale or short-term profit, rather than to holding the securities until maturity. Thus trading book exposures are treated as short term and valued on a mark-to-market basis (i.e. at the current price at which they could be sold in the market). The long-term investments (mainly its loan book) would be subject to the original credit risk capital requirements under the 1988 accord. The bank's trading book positions in debt, equity and derivative securities are then subject to the market risk capital requirements. In addition, commodity and foreign exchange positions held by the bank (both inside and outside the trading book) are subject to the market risk capital requirements.

An innovative feature of the market risk requirements is that they provide for the use of banks' own internal value-at-risk models for measuring market risks. Briefly, a value-at-risk model estimates the maximum amount a bank

can lose on a particular portfolio over a given holding period with an associated degree of statistical confidence. These estimates are normally derived from the recent behaviour of underlying risk factors, such as interest rates and exchange rates. The estimate is then multiplied by a scaling factor to produce a capital charge that the bank is required to hold. The advantage of using a bank's own internal models for calculating the minimum capital requirement is that the resulting requirement should more accurately match a bank's true risk exposure. Of course, the supervisor will require a bank to perform testing exercises and provide other information to check the validity of these models. Those firms that do not have a comprehensive internal model apply a standardised measurement framework. The market risk capital requirements introduce a new element of bank capital, tier 3 capital, which comprises short-term subordinated debt. This should have an original maturity of at least two years and will be limited to 250 per cent of a bank's tier 1 capital that is allocated to support market risks. Tier 3 capital is eligible to cover only market risks.

In addition, the Basel Committee on Banking Supervision (1997) has published a set of principles for the assessment and management of banks' interest rate risks. Interest rate risk refers to the difference between the interest rate structure of loans and deposits. These principles apply to interest rate risk arising from both trading and non-trading activities. There are no explicit capital requirements in these principles but emphasis is placed on banks having appropriate measurement, monitoring and other control systems to deal with these risks and, of course, prudent behaviour would require a bank to hold capital to cover such risks. Appropriate action on dealing with excessive risk taking in this area is left to the discretion of the supervisory authority.

17.5.4 *Deposit insurance*

The final component of the UK system of prudential control is the existence of insurance of deposits. This is now covered by the industry-wide compensation scheme introduced by the Financial Services and Markets Act 2000. In the event of failure, depositors would be eligible to receive a maximum payout of £31,700 (100 per cent of deposits up to £2,000 and 90 per cent of the next £33,000). The scheme is financed by a flat-rate contribution by banks in proportion to their deposits. The advantages claimed for deposit insurance are threefold. First, such schemes are designed to provide for speedy compensation for depositors, who then have no need to wait for the completion of the winding up of the institution. Second, systemic risk should be reduced since the incentive to be first in the queue to withdraw deposits is reduced. This point is critically dependent on the public being aware that deposits are insured in this manner. This is far from evident. As an interesting exercise the reader should try asking friends

or a class of students if they know that their deposits are insured! Third, perhaps the hidden rationale for the scheme is that it provides the finance for compensation of depositors without recourse to the government.

Deposit insurance is not without its critics and is open to a number of objections. It can be argued that the existence of deposit insurance increases the problem of moral hazard. As far as the banks are concerned the wrath of the depositors may be averted because of the knowledge that they will obtain compensation for any deposit loss. This could act as an incentive to bank managers to take excessive risks since any profits gained will be theirs but any loss will be borne by the insurer. For similar reasons the depositors may be less careful in their monitoring of banks and may select institutions which offer the highest rate of interest on deposits regardless of the risks involved because they know any loss will be reimbursed by the insurer. Presumably the restriction of reimbursement to a maximum payout of £31,700 is an attempt to overcome the moral hazard problem and a recognition that large deposits are likely to be made by persons or institutions with an awareness of the financial risks involved.

Apart from the question of moral hazard, there is doubt over the precise form of insurance charge levied in the UK and most other countries. The charge is levied on the quantity of deposits at a flat rate. Many argue that the charge should be linked to the risk involved, in the manner of car insurance. The problem with this suggestion is who is going to make the risk assessment? It is likely that a central bank would baulk at that type of decision for fear of complaints of discrimination. It also remains a moot point whether ratings provided by private agencies would be satisfactory for the purpose of fixing deposit insurance rates. Nevertheless, the Federal Deposit Insurance Corporation in the US has introduced a system of risk-based insurance premiums whereby premiums for banks rated as well capitalised and well managed, by the supervisory authority, are set at 4 cents per $100 of deposits. In contrast, banks regarded as risky have to pay the much higher premium of 31 cents. This provides a rough and ready approximation to a risk-related premium.

The last point to be made about deposit insurance is that it is not likely to be an adequate substitute for prudential control unless regulators are prepared to permit banks to become bankrupt so that insurance would be seen as protection rather than compensation. In particular, there is a belief that the regulator would not permit a large bank to fail because of the effect on confidence in the banking sector. The evidence is mixed as far as the Bank of England is concerned, as the JMB was rescued whilst BCCI and Barings were allowed to fail.

In the 1980s the US system of banks saw a dramatic increase in the number of institutions failing, particularly thrift institutions, which put the Federal Deposit Insurance Scheme under a tremendous strain. The Federal

Savings and Loan Insurance Fund was overwhelmed and federal taxpayers had to bail the Fund out to the tune of several hundred billion dollars. This prompted a lively debate in the US about reform of the deposit insurance system and the interested reader is referred to a series of essays which examine reform from a variety of angles (Russell 1993).

17.5.5 *International cooperation in banking supervision*

Banking is an international function, with many banks operating outside the country where their head office is located. Types of foreign banking establishments comprise branches, subsidiaries and joint ventures or consortia. Thus, some difficulties could occur for effective prudential control because of ambiguities as to the precise division of the responsibility for supervision. In 1975 the Basel concordat set out guidelines defining the responsibilities of the parent and the host country for supervision. This was reformulated again in 1983. The main principle of these guidelines was that no foreign banking establishment should escape adequate supervision. It was agreed that supervision of consortia should be exercised by the authorities in the country of incorporation. With respect to the remaining two categories, host authorities are primarily responsible for supervision of their liquidity and foreign currency positions. Capital adequacy is the responsibility of the parent country. As described above (section 17.5.2), in July 1988 the Basel Committee launched a major regulatory initiative with an agreement by the Group of 10 industrial countries to establish minimum capital adequacy standards for international banks. A reassessment of the Basel approach to banking regulation was prompted by the supervisory weaknesses revealed by the collapse of BCCI in the summer of 1991. In particular, the BCCI collapse demonstrated the ease with which a fraudulent bank could exploit weakly regulated offshore centres. This led in July 1992 to the Basel Committee issuing a new set of minimum standards for the supervision of international banks. The main requirement is that all international banks should be supervised by a home-country authority 'that capably performs consolidated supervision' (Basel Committee on Banking Supervision 1992). That is, the authority concerned should:

(i) monitor banks' global operations on the basis of verifiable consolidated data;
(ii) be able to prohibit the creation of corporate structures that impede consolidated supervision;
(iii) be able to prevent banks from establishing a presence in a suspect jurisdiction.

In 1996, the Basel Committee issued new proposals to extend the 1988 accord to cover market risks (the 1988 accord was principally concerned with credit risk).

Finally in this section, regulatory agencies around the world have become increasingly concerned about the rapid growth in derivatives trading by banks (see chapters 13 and 14 for discussion) and the potential risks arising out of this. The main concerns are that the complexity of these instruments may impede effective risk control by bank management and supervisors, and that the market linkages created by derivatives increases the potential for financial contagion. This latter concern is another form of the systemic risk problem discussed in section 17.3.1. A number of regulatory authorities, including the US Federal Reserve, the Bank of England and the Bank for International Settlements, undertook reviews of the derivatives situation and each expressed concern. These concerns were heightened by the collapse of Barings in February 1995 following losses sustained in derivatives trading (discussed in sections 17.2.4 and 13.9.2). The capital adequacy regime arising out of the 1988 Basel capital accord covers the credit risk side of derivatives and the new market risk proposals cover derivatives market risks. Differences may exist between exchange-traded derivatives, which are transparent, and over-the-counter derivatives, which are more opaque. Hence further developments in this area are likely to focus on encouraging institutions to disclose more information about their risk positions and risk control systems. This control refers to banks, not customers. The latter may be assumed to have expertise in assessing risks though examples of losses made by companies through misuse of derivatives (e.g. MG, and Procter and Gamble) may suggest otherwise (see chapter 13, section 13.9).

17.6 Conclusion

We have surveyed the UK system of prudential control of financial institutions. The main thrust of our argument has been concerned with the banks. Because of the central position of financial institutions as intermediaries between lenders and borrowers, it is generally (but not always) agreed that some form of external control should be exercised over their behaviour to ensure that they act in a prudent manner. However, all financial behaviour involves risk and prudential control should not be too excessive otherwise competition may be restrained in a manner which leads to excessive operating costs and a lack of financial innovation.

Chapter 18

Conclusions

In this chapter we provide a brief summary of the nature of the UK financial system as presented in this book. In chapter 2, we defined the financial system as a set of markets and institutions which provide the means of raising finance, and which supply various financial services. The institutions we have considered in this book can be usefully subdivided as follows:

(i) the banking sector – retail and wholesale banks (chapters 3 and 4, respectively);
(ii) other deposit-taking institutions – building societies and finance houses (chapter 5);
(iii) long-term investment institutions – pension funds, life assurance companies, investment and unit trusts (chapter 6).

In a similar manner, discussion of markets proceeded as follows:

(i) introduction to financial markets (chapter 7);
(ii) equity markets (chapter 8);
(iii) the bond market, including the term structure of interest rates (chapter 9);
(iv) the sterling money markets (chapter 10);
(v) the foreign exchange markets (chapter 11);
(vi) the eurosecurities markets (chapter 12);
(vii) the newer derivatives markets, that is, financial futures, options and swaps markets (chapter 13).

This was followed by a discussion of the role of these markets in the management of risk (chapter 14). The nature of central banks was discussed in chapter 16. This section also included a discussion of the new arrangements underpinning the European Central Bank.

The operation of the financial system raises a number of issues. The first concerns how far prudential control should be exercised over the

institutions/markets. This was considered in chapter 17. Efficiency of the system was examined in two ways. First, consideration of the application of the efficient markets hypothesis took place against the background of each of the markets. An agnostic conclusion was reached for all markets, implying that the hypothesis was still an open question. Second, the broader aspect of the efficiency of the UK financial system was discussed in chapter 15, and here again our conclusions were not firm but tended to point towards efficiency.

By any standard, the UK financial system described is a sophisticated one. It is also an open financial system, without restriction of flows of funds into or out of the country for either residents or non-residents. It has seen a considerable degree of change in recent years in the development of new markets (e.g. financial futures) and new instruments (e.g. commercial paper), the introduction of central bank instrumental independence and liberalisation in the sense of the removal of controls restricting competition between institutions. At the same time, prudential control has increased.

The pace of change has continued to be fast. Since the third edition of this book, major changes have taken place in the nature and role of the Bank of England. Similarly, the operation of the gilt-edged, equity and money markets has changed dramatically. Similar changes will continue to take place in the future and the interested reader is recommended to keep abreast of future changes by reading the financial reports of the quality press and other media.

References

Alesina, A. (1989) 'Politics and business cycles in industrial democracies', *Economic Policy*, 8, 55–98.

Alexander, S. S. (1954) 'Price movements in speculative markets: trends or random walks', *Industrial Management Review*, 5, 25–46.

Allen, F. and Santomero, A. M. (1998) 'The theory of financial intermediation', *Journal of Banking and Finance*, 21, 1461–85.

Arrow, K. J. and Hahn, F. H. (1971) *General Equilibrium Analysis*, Holden Day.

Association for Payment Clearing Services (2002) *Annual Clearing Statistics*, APACS.

Bade, R. and Parkin, M. (1988) *Central Bank Laws and Monetary Policy*, mimeograph, University of Western Ontario.

Baillie, R. T., Lippens, R. E. and McMahon, P. C. (1983) 'Testing rational expectations and efficiency in the foreign exchange market', *Econometrica*, 51, 553–64.

Bank for International Settlements (1986) *Recent Innovations in International Banking* (the Cross report), BIS.

Bank for International Settlements (1996) *Central Bank Survey of Foreign Exchange and Derivative Market Activity*, BIS.

Bank for International Settlements (2001) *Electronic Finance: A New Perspective and Challenges*, BIS Paper no. 7, BIS.

Bank for International Settlements (2002) *Triennial Central Bank Survey: Foreign Exchange and Derivatives Market Activity*, BIS.

Bank of England (2002) 'The Bank of England's operations in the sterling money markets', *Bank of England Quarterly Bulletin*, summer 2002, 153–61.

Bank of England (2003) *Finance For Small Firms – A Tenth Report*, Bank of England.

Barberis, N. and Thaler, R. (2001) *A Survey of Behavioral Finance*, Graduate School of Business Working Paper, University of Chicago.

Barro, R. J. and Gordon, D. B. (1983a) 'Rules, discretion and reputation in a model of monetary policy', *Journal of Monetary Economics*, 12, 101–21.

Barro, R. J. and Gordon, D. B. (1983b) 'A positive theory of monetary policy in a natural rate model', *Journal of Political Economy*, 91, 589–610.

Basel Committee on Banking Supervision (1988) *International Convergence of Capital Measurement and Capital Standards*, Basel Committee.

Basel Committee on Banking Supervision (1992) *Minimum Standards for the Supervision of International Banking Groups and Their Cross-border Establishments*, Basel Committee.

Basel Committee on Banking Supervision (1996) *Amendment to the Capital Accord to Incorporate Market Risks*, Basel Committee.

Basel Committee on Banking Supervision (1997) *Principles for the Management of Interest Rate Risk*, Basel Committee.

Baumol, W. (1982) *Contestable Markets and the Theory of Industrial Structure*, Harcourt Brace.

Beckers, S. (1981) 'Standard deviations implied in option prices as predictors of future stock price variability', *Journal of Banking and Finance*, 5, 363–81.

Benston, G. J., Eisenbeis, R. A., Horvitz, P. M., Kane, E. J. and Kaufman, G. G. (1986) *Perspectives on Safe and Sound Banking: Past, Present and Future*, MIT Press.

Benston, G. J. and Kaufman, G. G. (1988) *Risk and Solvency Regulation of Depository Institutions: Past Policies and Current Options*, Monograph 1 in Finance and Economics, Saloman Brothers Centre for the Study of Financial Institutions.

Berger, H., de Haan, J. and Eijffinger, S. C. W. (2001) 'Central bank independence: an update of theory and evidence', *Journal of Economic Surveys*, 15, 3–40.

Bilson, J. F. O. (1983) 'The evaluation and use of foreign exchange rate forecasting services', in R. J. Herring (ed.), *Managing Foreign Exchange Risk*, Cambridge University Press.

Bjerring, J. H., Lakonishok, J. and Vermaelen, T. (1983) 'Stock prices and financial analysts' recommendations', *Journal of Finance*, 38, 187–204.

Blake, D., Beenstock, M. and Brasse, V. (1986) 'The performance of UK exchange rate forecasters', *Economic Journal*, 96, 986–99.

Blume, M. E. and Friend, I. (1974) 'Risk, investment strategies and the long-run rates of return', *Review of Economics and Statistics*, 56, 259–69.

Board of Banking Supervision (1995) *Report of the Inquiry into the Circumstances of the Collapse of Barings*, HMSO.

Boocock, J. G. (1990) 'An examination of non-bank funding for small and medium sized enterprises in the UK', *Service Industries Journal*, 10, 124–45.

Brady Commission (1988) *Report of the Presidential Task Force on Market Mechanisms*, US Government Printing Office.

British Bankers' Association (2002) *Banking Business: The Annual Abstract of Banking Statistics, Volume 19*, BBA.

Cantor, R. and Packer, F. (1994) 'The credit rating industry', *Federal Reserve Bank of New York Review*, 19, no. 2, 1–26.

Cavanaugh, K. L. (1987) 'Price dynamics in the foreign currency futures market', *Journal of International Money and Finance*, 6, 295–314.

Clark, J. (1993) 'Debt reduction and market reentry under the Brady Plan', *Federal Reserve Bank of New York Quarterly Review*, 18, no. 4, 38–62.

Competition Commission (2002) *The Supply of Banking Services by Clearing Banks to Small and Medium-Sized Enterprises*, CM 5319, HMSO.

Copeland, L. (1994) *Exchange Rates and International Finance*, 2nd edition, Addison-Wesley.

Cosh, A., Carty, J., Hughes, A., Plender, J. and Singh, A. (1990) *Take-overs and Short-termism in the UK*, Industrial Policy Paper no. 3, Institute of Public Policy Research.

Cruickshank, D. (2000) *Competition in UK Banking: A Report to the Chancellor of the Exchequer*, HMSO.

Cukierman, A. (1992) *Central Bank Strategy, Credibility and Independence*, MIT Press.

Cuthbertson, K. (1996) 'The expectations hypothesis of the term structure: the UK interbank market', *Economic Journal*, 106, 578–92.

Dahlquist, M. and Jonsson, G. (1995) 'The information in Swedish short-maturity forward rates', *European Economic Review*, 39, 1115–31.

Davey, M. (2001) 'Mortgage equity withdrawal and consumption', *Bank of England Quarterly Bulletin*, spring, 100–3.

Davis, E. P. (1990) *International Financial Centres – An Industrial Analysis*, Discussion Paper no. 51, Bank of England.

Davis, E. P. (2001) *Pension Funds, Financial Intermediation and the New Financial Landscape*, Discussion Paper PI-0010, Pensions Institute.

Davis, E. P. and Latter, A. R. (1989) 'London as an international financial centre', *Bank of England Quarterly Bulletin*, autumn, 516–28.

Debt Management Office (2001) *Official Operations in the Gilt-Edged Market*, Operational Notice by the UK Debt Management Management Office.

Debt Management Office (2002) *Exchequer Cash Management: A DMO Handbook*, DMO.

Demery, D. and Duck, N. W. (1978) 'The behaviour of nominal interest rates in the United Kingdom 1961–1973', *Economica*, 45, 23–37.

Diamond, D. (1984) 'Financial intermediation and delegated monitoring', *Review of Economic Studies*, 51, 393–414.

Diamond, D. (1989) 'Reputation acquisition in debt markets', *Journal of Political Economy*, 97, 728–62.

Diamond, D. (1991) 'Monitoring and reputation: the choice between bank loans and directly placed debt', *Journal of Political Economy*, 99, 689–721.

Diamond, D. (1996) 'Financial intermediation as delegated monitoring: a simple example', *Federal Reserve Bank of Richmond Economic Quarterly*, summer, 51–66.

Dimson, E. and Marsh, P. (1984) 'Unpublished forecasts of UK stock returns', *Journal of Finance*, 39, 1257–92.

Dooley, M. P., Fernandez-Arias, E. and Kletzer, K. M. (1994) *Recent Private Capital Inflows to Developing Countries: Is the Debt Crisis History?*, Working Paper no. 4792, National Bureau of Economic Research.

Dooley, M. P. and Shafer, J. R. (1976) *Analysis of Short-Run Exchange Rate Behavior: March 1973 to September 1975*, International Finance Discussion Paper no. 76, Federal Reserve System.

Dowd, K. (1993) 'Deposit insurance: a skeptical view', *Federal Reserve Bank of St Louis Review*, 75, no. 1, 14–17.

Edwards, F. R. (1999) 'Hedge funds and the collapse of Long-Term Capital Management', *Journal of Economic Perspectives*, 13, 189–210.

Edwards, F. R. and Cantor, M. S. (1995) 'The collapse of Metallgesellschaft: unhedgeable risks, poor hedging strategy or just bad luck?', *Journal of Futures Markets*, 15, 211–64.

Elton, E. J., Gruber, M. J. and Rentzler, J. (1984) 'Intra-day tests of the efficiency of the treasury bills futures market', *Review of Economics and Statistics*, 66, 129–37.

European Securitisation Forum (2003) *ESF Securitisation Data Report*, winter, ESF.

Fama, E. F. (1965) 'The behaviour of stock prices', *Journal of Business*, 38, 33–105.

Fama, E. F. (1970) 'Efficient capital markets: a review of theory and empirical evidence', *Journal of Finance*, 84, 499–522.

Fama, E. F. (1975) 'Short term interest rates as predictors of inflation', *American Economic Review*, 65, 269–82.

Fama, E. F. (1977) 'Interest rates and inflation: the lessons in the entrails', *American Economic Review*, 67, 487–96.

Fama, E. F. (1980) 'Banking in the theory of finance', *Journal of Monetary Economics*, 6, 7–28.

Fama, E. F. (1984) 'Forward and spot exchange rates', *Journal of Monetary Economics*, 14, 319–39.

Fama, E. (1991) 'Efficient capital markets II', *Journal of Finance*, 46, 1575–617.

Fama, E. F. (1998) 'Market efficiency, long term returns and behavioural finance', *Journal of Financial Economics*, 49, 283–306.

Fama, E. F. and Blume, M. E. (1966) 'Filter rules and stock market trading', *Journal of Business*, 39, 226–41.

Fama, E., Fisher, L., Jensen, N. and Roll, R. (1969) 'The adjustment of stock prices to new information', *International Economic Review*, 10, 1–21.

Flood, M. D. (1991) 'An introduction to complete markets', *Federal Reserve Bank of St Louis Review*, 73, no. 2, 32–57.

Frenkel, J. A. and Levich, R. M. (1975) 'Covered interest arbitrage: unexploited profits?', *Journal of Political Economy*, 83, 325–38.

Frenkel, J. A. and Levich, R. M. (1977) 'Transactions costs and interest arbitrage: tranquil versus turbulent periods', *Journal of Political Economy*, 85, 1209–24.

Froot, K. and Frankel, J. A. (1989) 'Forward discount bias: is it an exchange rate premium?', *Quarterly Journal of Economics*, 104, 139–61.

Gemmill, G. (1986) 'The forecasting performance of stock options on the London traded options market', *Journal of Business, Finance and Accounting*, 13, 535–46.

Gibbons, M. and Hess, P. (1980) 'Day of the week effects and asset returns', *Journal of Business*, 54, 579–96.

Goodhart, C. A. E. (1988) 'Bank insolvency and deposit insurance: a proposal', in P. Arestis (ed.), *Contemporary Issues in Money and Banking*, Macmillan.

Goodhart, C. A. E. (1989) *Money, Information and Uncertainty*, 2nd edition, Macmillan.

Goodhart, C. A. E. and Gowland, D. (1977) 'The relationship between yields on short and long-dated gilt-edged stock', *Bulletin of Economic Research*, 29, 96–111.

Goodman, S. J. (1979) 'Foreign exchange forecasting techniques: implications for business and policy', *Journal of Finance*, 34, 415–27.

Grilli, V., Masciandaro, D. and Tabellini, G. (1991) 'Political and monetary institutions and public financial policies in the industrial countries', *Economic Policy*, 13, 341–92.

Gurley, J. and Shaw, E. (1960) *Money in a Theory of Finance*, Brookings Institute.

Gwylim, O. and Buckle, M. (1994) *Volatility Forecasting in the Framework of the Option Expiry Cycle*, European Business Management School Discussion Paper, University of Wales.

Hall, M. (1987) 'UK banking supervision and the Johnson Matthey affair', in C. Goodhart, D. Currie and D. Llewellyn (eds), *The Operation and Regulation of Financial Markets*, Macmillan.

Hirshleifer, J. (1958) 'On the theory of optimal investment analysis', *Journal of Political Economy*, August, 329–52.

Holden, K. and Thompson, J. L. (2003) *Changes in the Monday Effect in Financial Markets: Evidence from Europe,* mimeograph, School of Accounting, Finance and Economics, Liverpool John Moores University.

Hurn, S., Moody, T. and Muscatelli, V. A. (1995) 'The term structure of interest rates in the London interbank market', *Oxford Economic Papers*, 47, 418–36.

International Financial Services (2002) *International Financial Markets in the UK*, IFS.

Investment Management Association (2002) *Fund Management Survey*, IMA.

Kahneman, D. & Tversky, A. (1979) 'Prospect theory: an analysis of decision under risk', *Econometrica*, 47, 263–91.

Keim, D. B. (1986) 'The CAPM and equity return regularities', *Financial Analyst Journal*, 42, 19–34.

Kleidon, A. W. (1986) 'Variance bounds tests and stock price valuation models', *Journal of Political Economy*, 74, 639–55.

Lancaster, K. (1966) 'A new approach to consumer theory', *Journal of Political Economy*, 74, 132–57.

Laws, J. & Thompson, J. L. (2003) 'The efficiency of financial futures markets: tests of prediction accuracy', *European Journal of Operational Research*, 155, 284–98.

Levich, R. M. (1979) 'On the efficiency of markets for foreign exchange', in R. Dornbusch and J. A. Frenkel (eds), *International Economic Policy*, Johns Hopkins University Press.

Lewis, M. K. (1987) 'Off-balance sheet activities and financial innovation in banking', *Banca Nationale del Lavoro Quarterly Review*, 167, 387–410.

Lewis, M. K. (1991) 'Theory and practice of the banking firm', in C. J. Green and D. T. Llewellyn (eds), *Surveys in Monetary Economics, vol. 2, Financial Markets and Institutions*, Blackwell.

Lewis, M. K. and Davis, K. T. (1987) *Domestic and International Banking*, Philip Allan.

Llewellyn, D. T. (1985) *The Evolution of the British Financial System*, Gilbart Lectures on Banking, Institute of Bankers.

Llewellyn, D. T. (1991) 'Structural change in the British financial system', in C. J. Green and D. T. Llewellyn (eds), *Surveys in Monetary Economics, vol. 2, Financial Markets and Institutions*, Blackwell.

Llewellyn, D. T. (1996) *Banking in the 21st Century: The Transformation of an Industry*, Research Paper no. 105/96, Loughborough University Banking Centre.

Logue, D. E. and Sweeney, R. J. (1977) 'White noise in imperfect markets: the case of the franc/dollar exchange rate', *Journal of Finance*, 32, 761–8.

London Stock Exchange (2002) *SETS: 5 Years On*, LSE.

Macdonald, R. and Taylor, M. P. (1989) 'Economic analysis of foreign exchange markets: an expository survey', in R. Macdonald and M. P. Taylor (eds), *Innovations in Open Economy Macroeconomics*, Blackwell.

Malkiel, B. G. (1966) *The Term Structure of Interest Rates*, Princeton University Press.

Manaster, S. and Rendleman, R. J. (1982) 'Options prices as predictors of equilibrium stock prices', *Journal of Finance*, 37, 1043–57.

Mankiw, G. and Summers, L. H. (1984) 'Do long-term interest rates overreact to short-term interest rates?', *Brookings Papers on Economic Activity*, 1, 223–42.

Marsh, P. (1990) *Short Termism on Trial*, Institutional Fund Managers' Association.

Massimb, M. and Phelps, B. (1993) 'Electronic trading, market structure and liquidity', *Financial Analysts Journal*, 50, no. 1, 39–50.

Mayer, C. and Alexander, I. (1990) *Bank and Securities Markets: Corporate Financing in Germany and the UK*, Discussion Paper no. 433, Centre for Economic Policy Research.

McCauley, R., Ruud, J. and Wooldridge, P. (2002) 'Globalising international banking', *BIS Quarterly Review*, March, 41–51.

McCauley, R. N. and Zimmer, S. A. (1989) 'Explaining international differences in the cost of capital', *Federal Reserve Bank of New York Quarterly Review*, summer, 7–28.

McConnell, J. J. and Muscerella, C. S. (1985) 'Corporate capital expenditure decisions and the market value of the firm', *Journal of Financial Economics*, 14, 399–422.

McCulloch, J. H. (1981) 'Misintermediation and macroeconomic fluctuations', *Journal of Monetary Economics*, 8, 103–15.

McKinsey Global Institute (1996) *Capital Productivity*, McKinsey Global Institute.

Mehdian, S. and Perry, M. J. (2001) 'The reversal of the Monday effect: new evidence from the US equity markets', *Journal of Business, Finance and Accounting*, 28, 1043–65.

Meiselman, D. (1962) *The Term Structure of Interest Rates*, Prentice-Hall.

Merton, R. C. and Bodie, Z. (1995) *A Conceptual Framework for Analysing the Financial Environment: The Global Financial System – A Functional Perspective*, Harvard Business School.

Modigliani, F. and Shiller, R. J. (1973) 'Inflation, rational expectations and the term structure of interest rates', *Economica*, 40, 12–43.

Modigliani, F. and Sutch, R. C. (1966) 'Innovations in interest rate policy', *American Economic Review*, 56, 178–97.

Myners, P. (2001) *Review of Institutional Investment: Final Report*, HMSO.

Neely, C. J. (2000) 'Are changes in foreign exchange reserves well correlated with official intervention?', *Federal Reserve Bank of St Louis Review*, 82, no. 5, 17–31.

Newberry, D. J. (1989) 'Futures markets, hedging and speculation', in J. Eatwell, M. Milgate and P. Newman (eds), *The New Palgrave Dictionary of Finance*, Macmillan.

Pilbeam, K. (1992) *International Finance*, Macmillan.

Plender, J. (1990) 'Throw sand in the take over machine', *Financial Times*, 24 July.

Pollard, P. S. (1993) 'Central bank independence and economic performance', *Federal Reserve Bank of St Louis Review*, 75, no. 4, 21–36.

Pollard, P. S. (2003) 'A look inside two central banks: the European Central Bank and the Federal Reserve', *Federal Reserve Bank of St Louis Review*, 85, no. 2, 11–30.

Price Waterhouse (1995) *Corporate Treasury Control and Performance Standards*, Price Waterhouse.

Russell, S. (1993) 'The government's role in deposit insurance', *Federal Reserve Bank of St Louis Review*, 75, no. 1, 3–9.

Rybczynski, T. (1988) 'Financial systems and industrial restructuring', *National Westminster Bank Quarterly Review*, November, 3–13.

Sachs, J. (1986) 'Managing the LDC debt crisis', *Brookings Papers on Economic Activity*, 2, 397–440.

Sachs, J. and Huizinga, H. (1987) 'U.S. commercial banks and the developing-country debt crisis', *Brookings Papers on Economic Activity*, 2, 555–606.

Santoni, G. J. (1987) 'The great bull markets 1924–1929 and 1982–1987: speculative bubbles or economic fundamentals?', *Federal Reserve Bank of St Louis Review,* November, 16–30.

Sargent, T. (1972) 'Rational expectations and the term structure of interest rates', *Journal of Money Credit and Banking*, 4, 74–97.

Sarkar, A. and Tozzi, M. (1998) 'Electronic trading on futures exchanges', in *Current Issues in Economics and Finance*, Federal Reserve Bank of New York.

Securities and Investments Board (1994) *Regulation of the United Kingdom Equity Markets*, Discussion Paper, Securities and Investments Board.

Shiller, R. J. (1979) 'The volatility of long-term interest rates and expectations models of the term structure', *Journal of Political Economy*, 87, 1190–2119.

Shiller, R. J. (1981) 'Do stock prices move too much to be justified by subsequent changes in dividends?', *American Economic Review*, 71, 421–36.

Shiller, R. J. (1990) 'The term structure of interest rates', in B. M. Friedman and F. H. Hahn, eds, *Handbook of Monetary Economics, vol. 1*, North Holland.

Shiller, R. J. (2000) *Irrational Exuberance*, Princeton University Press.

Shleifer, A. (2001) *Inefficient Markets: An Introduction to Behavioral Finance*, Oxford University Press.

Stickel, S. E. (1985) 'The effect of Value Line investment survey rank changes on common stock prices', *Journal of Financial Economics*, 14, 121–43.

Taylor, M. P. (1987) 'Covered interest parity: a high-frequency, high-quality data study', *Economica*, 54, 429–38.

Taylor, M. P. (1992) 'Modelling the yield curve', *Economic Journal*, 102, 524–37.

Taylor, M. P. (1995) 'The economics of exchange rates', *Journal of Economic Literature*, 33, 13–47.

Taylor, S. (1986) *Modelling Financial Time Series*, John Wiley.

Tobin, J. (1984) 'On the efficiency of the financial system', *Lloyds Bank Review*, 153, 1–15.

Tucker, A. L. (1987) 'Foreign exchange option prices as predictors of equilibrium forward exchange rates', *Journal of International Money and Finance*, 6, 283–94.

Yang, J. E. (1987) 'Fraud is the main cause of failure at S&Ls in California, Congress says', *Wall Street Journal*, 15 June, 6.

Index

OUT NOVEMBER 2019

The second gripping thriller in
the FBI **Special Agent Atlee Pine** series,
following the bestselling *Long Road to Mercy*.